'... this novel with its shape and its economy, told with humour, intelligence, and a generous and fairminded spirit, is a tribute and a triumph.'

Globe & Mail

'This novel, so vast and so amiably peopled, is a long, sweet, sleepless pilgrimage to life. ... Such writing reminds us that there are secrets beyond technique, beyond even style, which have to do with a quality of soul on the part of the writer, a giving of oneself. ... His novel deserves thousands of long marriages and suitable readers.'

JAMES WOOD *Guardian*

'A phenomenon, a prodigy, a marvel of 19th century-style storytelling in the language of today. ... It is hard to believe that Seth is only one man. ... This is quite a novel.'

PATRICK SKENE CATLING *Evening Standard*

'*A Suitable Boy* modulates unawkwardly from moments of delicate emotional and psychological accuracy to scenes of panoramic drama ... it lines up with its eminent 19th-century predecessors in combining depth of imagination with breadth of appeal.'

PE___ ___MP *Sunday Times*

'No-one, surely, could w___ ___ ___orter. ... the greatness of the novel___ ___ulness, owes less to research th___ ___ive knowledge of the hu___

___ LAIRD *Observer*

'A big book ___ A Suitable Boy will win readers for dec___

Macleans

'... vastly entertaining.'

Ottawa Citizen

'. . . a wide-ranging, eminently readable epic work.'

Toronto Star

'If you study a map of India you will not find the city of Brahmpur, but if you travel to India you will find it almost everywhere. . . . This is . . . fiction on the grand scale. . . . By the time you reach the 1349th and last page you will have absorbed a splendid story, full of the tangle and perfume of India.'

TREVOR FISHLOCK *Sunday Telegraph*

'Vivid, evocative and beautifully written, *A Suitable Boy* casts its net far and wide across the country. . . . Seth has a wonderful sense of place and the (fictional) city of Brahmpur is almost a character in its own right. . . . The cast of *A Suitable Boy* is as vast and various as that of any 19th-century novel.'

SUSAN ALICE WATKINS *Literary Review*

'*A Suitable Boy* is not merely one of the longest novels in English: it may also prove to be the most fecund as well as the most prodigious work of the latter half of this century – perhaps even the book to restore the serious reading public's faith in the contemporary novel. . . . Vikram Seth is already the best writer of his generation. . . . You should make time for it. It will keep you company for the rest of your life.'

DANIEL JOHNSON *The Times*

'This mammoth novel takes to its heart the maxim that literature must delight and instruct.'

Montreal Gazette

'When I think of *A Suitable Boy*, a smile of sheer pleasure rises to my face. I do not expect to read another novel this lovely in my lifetime, so I will read *A Suitable Boy* again and again and again.'

Toronto Sun

ABOUT THE AUTHOR

Vikram Seth was born in 1952. He trained as an economist and has lived for several years each in the UK, California, China and India. He is the author of *The Golden Gate: A Novel in Verse*, described by Gore Vidal as 'The Great Californian Novel', *From Heaven Lake: Travels through Sinkiang and Tibet*, and four volumes of poetry.

A Suitable Boy

Volume Two

VIKRAM SETH

Little, Brown & Company (Canada) Limited

Boston   London   Toronto

Canadian Cataloguing in Publication Data

Seth, Vikram, 1952–
A suitable boy: a novel

ISBN 0–316–78152–5
I. Title

PR9499.3.S39S95   1993   823   C93–093137–8

Printed in England by Clays Ltd, St Ives plc

Little, Brown & Company (Canada) Limited
148 Yorkville Avenue, Toronto, Ontario, Canada

This Canadian edition dedicated to
Christine Cooke MacGregor
1950–1992
A very suitable girl

To
Papa and Mama
and
the memory of Amma

A WORD OF THANKS

To these I owe a debt past telling:
My several muses, harsh and kind;
My folks, who stood my sulks and yelling,
And (in the long run) did not mind;
Dead legislators, whose orations
I've filched to mix my own potations;
Indeed, all those whose brains I've pressed,
Unmerciful, because obsessed;
My own dumb soul, which on a pittance
Survived to weave this fictive spell;
And, gentle reader, you as well,
The fountainhead of all remittance.
Buy me before good sense insists
You'll strain your purse and sprain your wrists.

CONTENTS

ACKNOWLEDGEMENTS

The author and publishers would like to thank the following for permission to quote copyright material:

The Ministry of Human Resources Development, Govt. of India for extracts from *Letters to Chief Ministers*, Vol. 2, 1950–1952 by Jawaharlal Nehru, general editor G. Parthasarathi (Jawaharlal Nehru Memorial Fund, distributed by Oxford University Press, 1986)

HarperCollins Publishers Ltd. for extracts from *The Koran Interpreted* by A.J. Arberry (George Allen & Unwin Ltd.; and Oxford University Press, 1964)

Oxford University Press for an extract from *The Select Nonsense of Sukumar Ray* translated by Sukanta Chaudhuri (Oxford University Press, 1987)

Faber & Faber for an extract from the poem 'Law, Say the Gardeners' published in *W.H. Auden: Collected Poems* edited by Edward Mendelson (Faber & Faber)

Penguin Books Ltd. for extracts from *Selected Poems* by Rabindranath Tagore, translated by William Radice (Penguin Books, 1985)

Bantam Books Inc. for extracts from *The Bhagavad-Gita* translated by Barbara Stoler Miller (Bantam Books, 1986)

The Sahitya Akademi for extracts from *Mir Anis* by Ali Jawad Zaidi published in the series 'Makers of Indian Literature' (Sahitya Akademi, 1986)

The Gita Press, Gorakhpur for extracts from *Sri Ramacharitamanasa* translated into English (Gita Press, 1968)

While every effort has been made to trace copyright holders and obtain permission, this has not been possible in all cases; any omissions brought to our attention will be remedied in future editions.

MEHRAS

DR KISHEN CHAND SETH *m* FIRST WIFE (d) *remarried* PARVATI

CHILDREN including ... RUPA *m* RAGHUBIR MEHRA (d)

ARUN MEHRA *m* MEENAKSHI (*née* Chatterji) — APARNA

SAVITA *m* PRAN KAPOOR

VARUN MEHRA

LATA MEHRA

KAPOORS

MR TANDON (d) *m* OLD MRS TANDON

MAHESH KAPOOR *m* MRS MAHESH KAPOOR

CHILDREN including ... KEDARNATH TANDON *m* VEENA — BHASKAR

PRAN KAPOOR *m* SAVITA (*née* Mehra)

MAAN KAPOOR

KHANS

OLD NAWAB SAHIB OF BAITAR (d) *m* WIFE (d)

NAWAB SAHIB *m* WIFE (d)   BROTHER *m* BEGUM   BROTHER (d)
OF BAITAR   (in Pakistan) ABIDA KHAN

ZAINAB *m* HUSBAND   IMTIAZ KHAN   FIROZ KHAN

HASSAN   ABBAS

CHATTERJIS

OLD MR CHATTERJI *m* WIFE (d)

MR JUSTICE CHATTERJI *m* MRS CHATTERJI

AMIT   MEENAKSHI *m* ARUN   DIPANKAR   KAKOLI   TAPAN
CHATTERJI   MEHRA   CHATTERJI   CHATTERJI   CHATTERJI

APARNA

(d)=deceased

The superfluous, that very necessary thing . . .
VOLTAIRE

The secret of being a bore is to say everything.
VOLTAIRE

Part Eight

8.1

NO ONE saw off Maan and his Urdu teacher Abdur Rasheed at the Brahmpur Railway Station. It was noon. Maan was in such unhappy spirits in fact that even the presence of Pran or Firoz or his more disreputable student companions would not have soothed him much. He felt that he was being exiled, and he was quite right: that was exactly how both his father and Saeeda Bai saw matters. His father's ultimatum to get out of town had been direct, Saeeda Bai's solution had been more artful. One had coerced him and one had cajoled him. Both liked Maan, and both wanted him out of the way.

Maan did not blame Saeeda Bai, or not much; he felt that his absence would be very hard on her, and that by suggesting that he go to Rudhia instead of back to Banaras, she was keeping him as close to herself as, under the circumstances, she could hope to. He was furious with his father, though, who had thrown him out of Brahmpur for hardly any reason at all, had refused to listen to his side of things, and had grunted in a satisfied way when told that he would be going off to his Urdu teacher's village.

'Visit our farm while you're there – I'd like to hear how things are getting on,' was what his father had said. Then, after a pause, he had added, needlessly: 'That is, if you can make the time to travel a few miles. I know what an industrious student you will turn out to be.'

Mrs Mahesh Kapoor had merely hugged her son and told him to come back soon. Sometimes, thought Maan, bridling and frustrated, even his mother's affection was unbearable. It was she who was unshakably set against Saeeda Bai.

'Not before a month is over,' countered Mahesh Kapoor. He was relieved that Maan, despite his chafing, was not going to defy him by remaining in Brahmpur, but annoyed that he himself would have to 'deal with Banaras' in both senses: with the parents of Maan's fiancée, and with Maan's assistant in the cloth business who – and he thanked heaven for medium-sized mercies – was tolerably competent. He had enough on his plate, and Maan was a drain on his time and patience.

The platform was as crowded as ever with passengers and their friends and families and servants, hawkers, railway staff, coolies, vagrants and beggars. Babies wailed and whistles blew. Stray dogs slunk about with punished eyes, monkeys bared aggressive teeth. There was a pervasive railway platform stench. It was a hot day, and the fans were not working in the bogeys. The train sat at the narrow-gauge platform for half an hour after it was due to depart. Maan was stifled by the heat in the second-class compartment, but did not complain. He kept looking up glumly towards his luggage: a deep blue leather suitcase and several smaller bags.

Rasheed, who, Maan decided, looked rather wolf-like in feature, had loped off to talk to some boys in another carriage. They were students at the Brahmpur madrasa – or Muslim school – who were going back to their districts for a few days.

Maan began to feel very sleepy. The fans were still not working, and the train showed no sign of starting. He touched the upper part of his ear, where he had placed a small piece of cotton-wool containing a drop of Saeeda Bai's rose perfume, and passed his hand slowly across his face. It was wet with perspiration.

To minimize the uncomfortable sensation of sweat trickling down his face, Maan tried to remain as still as he could. The man opposite him was fanning himself with a Hindi newspaper.

The train at last began to move. It passed through the city for a while, then moved into the open countryside. Villages and fields went by, some parched and dusty and fallow, others yellow with wheat or green with other crops. The fans began to whirr and everyone looked relieved.

In some of the fields along the railway track, the wheat harvest was going on. In others it had just taken place, and the dry stubble was glinting in the sun.

Every fifteen minutes or so the train stopped at a small railway station, sometimes in the middle of nowhere, sometimes in a village. Very occasionally it would halt in a small town, the headquarters of a subdivision of the district they were travelling through. A mosque or a temple, a few neem or pipal or banyan trees, a boy driving goats along a dusty dirt track, the sudden turquoise flash of a kingfisher – Maan vaguely registered these. After a while he closed his eyes again, and was overwhelmed by his feeling of separation from the one person whose company he desired. He wanted to see nothing and hear nothing, just to recall the sights and sounds of the house in Pasand Bagh: the delicious perfumes of Saeeda Bai's room, the evening cool, the sound of her voice, the pressure of her hand on his. He began to think even of her parakeet and her watchman with affection.

But even when he closed his eyes to cut out the dry brightness of the afternoon light and the monotonous fields stretching out to the huge visible quadrant of dusty sky, the sounds of the train bore in on him with amplified volume. The jolting and clicking of the train as it rocked sideways and slightly upwards, the sound of it going over a small bridge or the whooshing of a train rushing past in the opposite direction, the sound of a woman coughing or the crying of a child, even the dropping of a coin or the rustle of a newspaper, all took on an unbearable intensity. He rested his head on his hands, and stayed still.

'Are you all right? Are you feeling all right?' It was Rasheed who was speaking to him.

Maan nodded, and opened his eyes.

He looked at his fellow passengers, then again at Rasheed. He decided that Rasheed looked too gaunt for someone who was only his own age. He also had a few white hairs.

Well, thought Maan, if I can begin to go bald at twenty-five, why shouldn't he begin to go white?

After a while he asked: 'How's the water at your place?'

'What do you mean?'

'It's fine, isn't it?' said Maan anxiously. He was beginning to wonder what life would be like in the village.

'Oh yes, we pump it up by hand.'

'Don't you have any electricity?'

Rasheed smiled a little sardonically and shook his head.

5

Maan was silent. The serious practical implications of his exile were beginning to seep in.

They had stopped just beyond a small station. The train tanks were being filled with water from above, and, as the engine steamed out, the sound of water dropping on the roof of the compartment reminded Maan of rain. There would be weeks of unbearable heat until the monsoons.

'Flies!'

It was the man sitting next to Rasheed who had spoken. He looked like a dried-out farmer, about forty years of age. He was rolling some tobacco in his palm with the thumb of his other hand. He rubbed it, then tamped it down, threw off the excess, examined the residue with care, selected out the impurities, took a pinch, licked the inside of his lower lip, and spat out a bit sideways onto the floor.

'Do you speak English?' he said after a while in the local dialect of Hindi. He had noticed Maan's luggage tag.

'Yes,' said Maan.

'Without English you can't do anything,' said the farmer sagely.

Maan wondered what possible use English could be to the farmer.

'What use is English?' said Maan.

'People love English!' said the farmer, with a strange sort of deep-voiced giggle. 'If you talk in English, you are a king. The more people you can mystify, the more people will respect you.' He turned back to his tobacco.

Maan felt a sudden urge to explain himself. As he tried to think of what he should say, he heard the droning of flies getting louder and louder around him. It was too hot to think, and he felt overcome with sleepiness. His head sank on his chest. In a minute he was asleep.

8.2

'RUDHIA JUNCTION. It's Rudhia Junction.' Maan woke up to see several passengers getting their luggage out of the train, and several others clambering in. Rudhia, the district town, was the largest town in the district, but not a railway junction in the sense that Brahmpur was, and certainly not in the sense of a great junction like Mughalsarai. Two narrow-gauge lines intersected at Rudhia, that was all. But those who lived there thought that it was the most important centre in Purva Pradesh next to Brahmpur, and the words *Rudhia Jn* on the signs and on the six white-tiled spittoons at the station added to the dignity of the town as much as did the District Court, the Collectorate and other administrative offices, and the steam power house, which was run on coal.

The train stopped at Rudhia a full three minutes before panting on through the afternoon. A sign in front of the station master's office announced: *Our Goal: Security, Safety and Punctuality*. In fact, the train was already an hour-and-a-half late. This was nothing unusual, and most of the passengers, if inconvenienced, did not make things worse by distressing themselves. One-and-a-half hours was nothing.

The train turned a bend, and smoke began to enter the compartment in great gusts. The farmer started struggling with the windows, and Maan and Rasheed gave him a hand.

A large, red-leafed tree in a field caught Maan's attention. 'What's that tree?' he asked, pointing out of the window. 'It looks a bit like a mango with its red leaves, but it isn't a mango.'

'That's a mahua,' said the farmer, before Rasheed could reply. He looked amused, as if he'd had to explain what a cat was.

'Very handsome tree,' said Maan.

'Oh yes. Useful too,' said the farmer.

'In what way?'

'It gets you drunk,' said the farmer with a brown-toothed smile.

'Really?' said Maan, interested. 'Is it the sap?'

But the farmer, delighted with his ignorance, started giggling in his strange, deep way, and volunteered nothing else beyond the word: 'Sap!'

Rasheed leaned forward towards Maan intently and, tapping the steel trunk that rested between them, said:

'It's the flowers. They are very light and fragrant. They would have fallen about a month ago. If you dry them, they last for a year. Ferment them, and they'll give you a liquor.' He sounded slightly disapproving.

'Oh yes?' said Maan, livening up.

But Rasheed continued: 'Cook them, and they'll act as a vegetable. Boil them with milk, and they'll make the milk red and the person who drinks it strong. Mix them with the flour you use to make your rotis with in winter, and you won't feel the cold.'

Maan was impressed.

'Feed them to your cattle,' added the farmer. 'It'll double their energy.'

Maan looked towards Rasheed for verification, not trusting anything that the mocking farmer said.

'Yes, that's true,' said Rasheed.

'What a wonderful tree!' said Maan, delighted. He suddenly became less torpid, and began asking lots of questions. The countryside, which so far had looked entirely monotonous to him, became interesting.

They had just crossed a broad, brown river and entered a jungle. Maan immediately wanted to know if there was any game to be had there, and was pleased to hear that there was fox, jackal, nilgai, wild boar and even the occasional bear. And in the ravines and rocky outcrops not far from here there were wolves, who were sometimes a menace to the local population.

'Actually,' said Rasheed, 'this jungle is part of the Baitar Estate.'

'Ah!' said Maan, delighted. Although he and Pran had been friends with Firoz and Imtiaz from childhood, they had only known them in Brahmpur, and had never visited Baitar Fort or the estate.

'But this is wonderful!' said Maan. 'I know the family well. We must go hunting together.'

Rasheed smiled rather ruefully and said nothing. Perhaps, thought Maan, he was thinking that at this rate he would learn very little Urdu during his stay in the village. But what does that matter? he felt like saying. Instead he said:

'They must have horses at the fort.'

'They do,' said the farmer, with sudden enthusiasm and new respect. 'Many horses. A whole stable. And two jeeps also. And for Moharram they have a tremendous procession and lots of ceremonies. You really know the Nawab Sahib?'

'Well, it's his sons I know,' said Maan.

Rasheed, who was rather tired with the farmer, said quietly: 'This is Mahesh Kapoor's son.'

The farmer's mouth dropped open. This statement was so improbable as to be almost certainly true. But what was he – the son of the great Minister – doing, travelling for all the world like an ordinary citizen in a second-class carriage, and wearing a crumpled kurta-pyjama?

'And I have been joking with you,' he said, shocked by his own temerity.

Maan, whose discomfort he had enjoyed, now enjoyed his discomfort.

'I won't tell my father,' he said.

'He'll take my land away if he hears of it,' said the farmer – who either believed in the exaggerated powers of the Minister of Revenue, or else thought it politic to exaggerate his fear.

'He'll do nothing of the kind,' said Maan. Thinking of his father he felt a sudden spasm of outrage.

'When zamindari is abolished, all these lands will be taken by him,' said the farmer. 'Even the Nawab Sahib's estates. What can a small landowner like me do?'

'I'll tell you what,' said Maan. 'Don't tell me your name. Then you'll be safe.'

The farmer seemed amused by this idea, and repeated it to himself a couple of times.

Suddenly the train started jolting, as if the brake had been applied, and in a short while came to a halt in open countryside.

'This always happens,' said Rasheed with a flicker of irritation.

9

'What does?' said Maan.

'These schoolboys pulling the chain and stopping the train when it gets close to their village. It's just the boys of this particular locality. By the time the guards get to their carriage, they've disappeared into the sugarcane fields.'

'Can't they do something about it?' said Maan.

'There's no way of controlling them. Either they should simply halt the train here and admit defeat. Or else they should catch one of them somehow, and make an example of him.'

'How?'

'Oh, beat him up soundly,' said Rasheed calmly. 'And lock him up for a few days.'

'But that's very harsh,' said Maan, trying to imagine what it would be like to be locked up for a few days in a cell.

'It's quite effective. We were equally unruly at that age,' continued Rasheed with a brief smile. 'My father beat me up regularly. Once my grandfather – whom you will meet – beat my brother to within an inch of his life – and that was a turning-point in his life. He became a wrestler!'

'Your grandfather beat him, not your father?' said Maan.

'My grandfather. He was the one we were most terrified of,' said Rasheed.

'Still?'

'Less so now. He's over seventy. But well into his sixties he was the terror of ten villages. Haven't I mentioned him to you before?'

'You mean he terrorized them?' said Maan, trying to picture this strange patriarch.

'I mean, they all respected him, and came to him to solve their disputes. He's a landowner, a medium-sized landowner, so he has some standing in our community. He is a religious and just man, so that people look up to him. And he himself was a wrestler in his youth, so they're afraid of his arm. He used it to beat up any ruffians he could lay his hands on.'

'I suppose I shouldn't gamble or drink while I'm in your village,' said Maan cheerfully.

Rasheed looked very serious. 'No, really, Kapoor Sahib,' he said, quite formally, Maan thought. 'You are my guest, and my family does not know you are coming. For the month you are with me, your behaviour will reflect on me.'

'Oh, don't worry,' Maan said impulsively, 'I won't do anything that will cause you any trouble. I promise.'

Rasheed looked relieved, and Maan realized the rashness of his promise. He had never so far in his life succeeded in behaving himself for a whole month.

8.3

AT the small subdivisional town of Salimpur, they dismounted, loaded their bags on the flimsy back of a cycle-rickshaw, and got unbalancedly on.

The rickshaw jolted and swerved along the pitted road that led from Salimpur to Rasheed's native village of Debaria. It was evening, and everywhere birds were chattering in the trees. The neem trees rustled in the warm evening breeze. Underneath a small stand of straight, broad-leafed teak trees a donkey, two of its legs tied together, was hobbling painfully forward. On every culvert sat a crowd of children, who shouted at the rickshaw as it went along. There was very little traffic other than the many bullock-carts making their way village-wards from the harvest or a few boys driving cattle down the road.

Since Maan had changed into an orange kurta before getting off the train – the one he had been wearing earlier was drenched with sweat – he presented a colourful spectacle, even in the waning light. As for Rasheed, several people on foot or on bullock-carts greeted him along the way.

'How are you?'

'Very well. And you? Everything all right?'

'Everything all right.'

'How is the harvest?'

'Well – not too good. Back from Brahmpur?'

'Yes.'

'How long will you be staying?'

'A month.'

Throughout the conversation, they would stare not at Rasheed but at Maan, looking him up and down.

The sunset was pink, smoky, and still. The fields stretched out to the dark horizon on either side. There was not a cloud in the sky. Maan began to think once again of Saeeda Bai, and he felt in his bones that it would be impossible for him to live for a whole month without her.

What was he doing anyway in this doltish place so far away from all civilization – among suspicious peasants, illiterate and unelectrified, who knew nothing better than to stare at strangers?

There was a sudden lurch, and Maan, Rasheed, and their luggage were nearly pitched out of the rickshaw.

'What did you do that for?' said Rasheed sharply to the rickshaw-wallah.

'Aré, bhai, there was a hole in the road. I'm not a panther that I can see in the dark,' said the rickshaw-wallah abruptly.

After a while they turned off the road onto an even more inadequate mud track that led to the village, a mile away. This track would clearly become impassable in the rainy season, and the village would virtually be cut off from the world. At the moment it was all the rickshaw-wallah could do to keep his balance. After a while he gave up and asked his passengers to get off.

'I should charge you three rupees for this, not two,' he said.

'One rupee eight annas,' was Rasheed's quiet reply. 'Now get on with it.'

It was completely dark by the time they got to Rasheed's house – or, as he usually called it, his father's house. It appeared to be a moderately large single-storey building made of whitewashed brick. A kerosene lamp was burning on the roof. Rasheed's father was up on the roof, and called out when he heard the sound of the rickshaw – which was bumping along the village lane, guided by the light of Maan's torch.

'Who's that?'

'It's Rasheed, Abba-jaan.'

'Good. We were expecting you.'

'Is everything well here?'

'As well as can be. The harvest is not much good. I'm coming down. Is that someone with you?'

It struck Maan that the voice from the roof sounded like that of a toothless man, more like the voice that he imagined Rasheed's grandfather, not his father, would have.

By the time he came downstairs the man had two kerosene lamps in his hands and a couple of paans in his mouth. He greeted his son with very mild affection. Then the three of them sat on a charpoy out in front of the house under a great neem tree.

'This is Maan Kapoor, Abba-jaan,' said Rasheed.

His father nodded, then said to Maan: 'Are you here on a visit or are you an officer of some kind?'

Maan smiled. 'I'm here on a visit. Your son has been teaching me Urdu in Brahmpur. Now I hope he will continue to teach me in Debaria.'

Maan noticed, by the light of the lamp, that Rasheed's father had large gaps in his teeth. This explained his peculiar voice and the absence of certain consonants. But it made him look sinister even when he was attempting to be welcoming.

Meanwhile another figure emerged out of the dark from across the way to greet Rasheed. He was introduced to Maan, and sat down on another stringed bedstead, which had been laid out in front of the house. He was a man of about twenty, and, therefore, younger than Rasheed, though he was his uncle – his father's younger brother in fact. He was talkative – indeed, very full of himself.

A servant brought out some sherbet in a glass for each of them.

'You've had a long journey,' said Rasheed's father.

'Wash your hands, rinse out your mouth, and drink your sherbet.'

Maan said: 'Is there anywhere...'

'Oh, yes,' said Rasheed's father, 'go behind the cowshed if you want to piss. Is that it?'

'Yes,' said Maan, and went, gripping his torch tightly and stepping into cowdung as he made his way to the other side of the shed. One of the bullocks started lowing at his approach.

When he came back Rasheed poured some water over his hands from a brass pot. In the warm evening the water was wonderfully cool.

So was the sherbet. This was followed quickly by dinner, eaten again by the light of kerosene lamps. Dinner consisted of meat dishes and fairly thick wheat rotis. All four men ate together under the stars and among the insects that whirred all around. They concentrated on eating; conversation was desultory.

'What's this? Pigeon?' asked Maan.

'Yes. We have a pigeon-house up there – or, rather, my grandfather does.' Rasheed pointed into the dark. 'Where is Baba, by the way?' he asked his father.

'He's gone off on one of his tours of inspection of the village,' was the reply. 'Probably also to talk to Vilayat Sahib – to try to convert him back to Islam.'

Everyone laughed except Maan, who did not know the two people involved. He bit into a shami kabab, and began to feel somewhat forlorn.

'He should be back in time for the night prayer,' said Rasheed, who wanted Maan to meet his grandfather.

When someone mentioned Rasheed's wife, Maan sat up. He hadn't known or imagined that Rasheed had a wife. A little later someone mentioned Rasheed's two small daughters and Maan was further astonished.

'Now, we'll lay out some bedding for you,' said Rasheed's father in his brisk but toothless way. 'I sleep on the roof there. In this season, it's good to get what breeze you can.'

'What a good idea,' said Maan. 'I'll do the same.'

There was an awkward silence, then Rasheed said:

'Actually, we should try sleeping under the stars here — outside the house. Our bedding can be laid out here.'

Maan frowned, and was about to ask a question, when Rasheed's father said: 'Good, then, that's settled. I'll send the servant out with the stuff. It's too hot for a mattress. Spread a rug on the charpoy and a sheet or two on top of that. All right, I'll see you tomorrow.'

Later, lying on his bed, looking up at the clear night sky, Maan's thoughts turned towards home. Luckily he was quite sleepy, so thoughts of Saeeda Bai were not likely to keep him up the whole night. Frogs were croaking in a pond somewhere at the edge of the village. A cat yowled. A buffalo snorted in the cattle-shed. A few crickets cried, and the grey-white flash of an owl settled on the branch of a neem tree. Maan took this as a good sign.

'An owl,' he announced to Rasheed, who was lying on the charpoy next to him.

'Oh, yes,' said Rasheed. 'And there's another one.'

Another grey shape flew down onto the branch.

'I'm very fond of owls,' said Maan sleepily.

'Inauspicious birds,' said Rasheed.

'Well, they know they have a friend in me,' said Maan. 'That is why they are watching over my sleep. They will make sure I dream about pleasant things. About beautiful women and so on. Rasheed, you must teach me some ghazals tomorrow. Incidentally, why are you sleeping out here? Shouldn't you be with your wife?'

'My wife is at her father's village,' said Rasheed.

'Ah,' said Maan.

For a while Rasheed said nothing. Then he said, 'Do you know the story of Mahmud of Ghazni and his peaceful Prime Minister?'

'No.' What that great conqueror and despoiler of cities had to do with what had gone before Maan could not see. But in that twilight state that precedes sleep, it was not necessary to see.

Rasheed began his story: 'Mahmud of Ghazni said to his vazir: "What are those two owls?"'

'Oh yes?' said Maan. 'Mahmud of Ghazni was lying on a charpoy staring at these owls?'

'Probably not,' said Rasheed. 'Different owls, and probably not on a charpoy. So he, the vazir, said: "One owl has a young boy owl, and one has a young girl owl. They are well-matched in every way, and the marriage plans are going ahead. The two owls – fathers-in-law-to-be – are sitting on a branch discussing their children's marriage, especially the all-important question of the dowry." The vazir pauses here. So Mahmud of Ghazni says, "What are they saying?" The vazir replies: "The owl on the boy's side is demanding a thousand deserted villages as a dowry." "Yes? Yes?" says Mahmud of Ghazni, "and what is the other owl saying?" The vazir replies: "The owl on the girl's side is saying: After the latest campaign of Mahmud of Ghazni he can offer five thousand. ..." Good night. Sleep well.'

'Good night,' said Maan, pleased with the story. However, he remained awake for a minute or two thinking about it. The owls were still on the branch when he fell off to sleep.

The next morning he woke up to the sound of someone saying, with great affection and severity: 'Wake up! Wake up! Won't you say your morning prayers? Oh, Rasheed, go and get some water, your friend has to wash his hands before his prayers.'

An old man, powerful in build and looking like a prophet with his beard, bare-chested and wearing a loosely folded green cotton lungi, was standing over him. Maan guessed that this must be Rasheed's grandfather, or 'Baba' as Rasheed called him. So affectionate and determined was the old man in enforcing piety that Maan hardly had the courage to refuse.

'Well?' said Baba. 'Get up, get up. As it says in the call, prayer is better than sleep.'

'Actually,' – Maan found his voice at last – 'I don't go to prayer.'

'You don't read the namaaz?' Baba looked more than injured; he looked shocked. What kind of people was

Rasheed bringing home to his village? He felt like pulling the impious young lout out of bed.

'Baba – he's a Hindu,' explained Rasheed, intervening to prevent further embarrassment. 'His name is Maan Kapoor.' He emphasized Maan's surname.

The old man looked at Maan in astonishment. The thought had not occurred to him at all. Then he looked at his grandson and opened his mouth as if to ask him something. But he obviously thought better of it, because the question remained unasked.

There was a pause for a few seconds. Then the old man spoke.

'Oh, he's a Hindu!' he said at last, and turned away from Maan.

8.4

RASHEED explained to Maan a little later where they would have to go for their morning toilet – out in the fields with a brass lota to carry water in. It was the only time of day when it was somewhat cool and when there was a bit of privacy. Maan, feeling quite uncomfortable, rubbed his eyes, filled his lota with water, and followed Rasheed out into the fields.

It was a fine, clear morning. They passed a pond close to the village. A few ducks were swimming among the reeds and a glossy black water-buffalo was bathing in it, as deep as its nostrils. A young girl in a pink and green salwaar-kameez appeared from a house at the outskirts, saw Maan, gave a shy gasp, and quickly disappeared.

Rasheed was lost in his thoughts. 'It's such a waste,' he said.

'What is?'

'All this.' He pointed in a wide sweep to the countryside around him, taking in the fields, the pond, the village, and another village visible in the distance. Then, since Maan did not ask him why, he continued: 'It is my dream to completely transform....'

Maan began smiling, and lost the thread of what Rasheed was saying. For all Rasheed's knowledge about mahua trees and the finer points of the landscape, Maan felt that he was an impractical visionary. If he had been so exacting with Maan's meems, it would take a millennium for village life to attain the kind of perfection that would satisfy him. Rasheed was now walking very fast, and it was all Maan could do to keep up. Walking on the mud ridges dividing the fields was not easy, especially in rubber chappals. He slipped, and narrowly avoided a twisted ankle. His lota, however, fell, and the water in it splashed and trickled out.

Rasheed, noticing that his companion had fallen behind, turned around, and was alarmed to see him on the ground, rubbing his ankle.

'Why didn't you shout?' he asked. 'Are you all right?'

'Yes,' said Maan. Then, so as not to make a fuss, he added: 'But what were you saying about transforming all this?'

For a moment, Rasheed's rather lean-featured, lupine face carried a worried expression. Then he said: 'That pond, for instance. They could stock it with fish and use it. And there's a large pond, which is part of the common property of the village, like the common grazing ground. But it isn't used for anything. It's an economic waste. Even the water –' He paused, and looked at Maan's spilled lota.

'Here,' he said, about to pour half the water from his lota into Maan's. Then he stopped. 'On second thoughts,' he said, 'I'll pour it later, when we've reached our destination.'

'All right,' said Maan.

Rasheed, remembering that it was his duty to educate Maan and recalling how keen he had been to absorb information yesterday, now began telling him the names of various plants that they passed. But Maan was not in an educable mood this morning, and confined his responses to the occasional repetition of a word to show that his attention had not wandered.

'What's that?' he said suddenly.

They had reached the top of a gentle rise. About half a

mile away lay a beautiful blue pool of water with clearly
defined mud banks on each side, and a few white buildings
on the side farther away from them.

'That's the local school, the madrasa,' said Rasheed
matter-of-factly. 'It's actually in the neighbouring village,
but all the Muslim children from our village go to it as
well.'

'Do they teach mainly Islamic studies there?' asked
Maan, who had meant to ask about the pool but had been
diverted by Rasheed's reply.

'No – well, yes, some of course. But they begin by
taking in little children of five or so, and teach them a bit
of everything.' Rasheed paused to survey the landscape,
feeling momentarily happy to be back again. He liked
Brahmpur because life was less narrow and frustrating
there than in the rigid and – in his view – reactionary
village, but while in the city he was always rushing around
studying or teaching and there was far too much noise
everywhere.

He looked for a few seconds at the madrasa where he
had been such a difficult pupil that his teachers, at a loss
to control him themselves, had regularly reported him to
his father – and his grandfather. Then he added: 'It's got a
good standard of teaching. Even Vilayat Sahib began his
studies here before this fish-pond became too small for
him. Now that he's such a big name in archaeology, he
contributes books to the school library that none of the
children can understand. Several of them have been written
by himself. He's visiting for the week, but he's very reclu-
sive. Maybe we'll meet him. Well, here we are. Give me
your lota.'

They had reached a high field-divider near a small
copse of trees. Rasheed shared his water with Maan.
Then he squatted down and said: 'Anywhere around here
is a good place. Take your time. No one will disturb
us.'

Maan was embarrassed, but acted as casually as he
could. 'I'll go over there,' he said, and wandered off.

I suppose this is the shape of things to come for the next

month, he thought disconsolately. I may as well get used to it. I hope there are no snakes or other unpleasant things around. There isn't very much water either. What if I want to go later in the day? Will I have to walk out here and back in the heat? Better not think about it. And since he was good at avoiding unpleasant thoughts, he turned to other matters.

He began to think how good it would be to swim in the blue pool near the local school. Maan loved swimming, not for the exercise but for the luxury, the tactility of it. In Brahmpur in earlier days, he would go to the lake called Windermere not far from the High Court, and swim in the cordoned-off area reserved for swimmers. He wondered why in the last month he hadn't swum there – or even thought of doing so.

On the way back to the village he said to himself: I must write to Saeeda Bai. Rasheed has got to help me with my letter.

Aloud he said: 'Well, I'm ready for my first Urdu lesson under the neem tree when we get back. If you're not doing anything else, that is.'

'No, I'm not,' said Rasheed, pleased. 'I was afraid that I would have to bring up the subject.'

8.5

WHILE Maan was engaged in his Urdu lesson a crowd of small children gathered around him.

'They find you very interesting,' said Rasheed.

'I can see that,' said Maan. 'Why aren't they at school?'

'Term begins in two weeks' time,' said Rasheed. 'Now go away,' he told them. 'Can't you see that I'm giving a lesson?'

The children could indeed see that he was giving a lesson, and they were fascinated. They were particularly fascinated by an adult who was having a hard time with the alphabet.

They began to imitate Maan under their breath. 'Alif-be-pe-te ... laam-meem-noon,' they chanted, gathering courage as Maan tried to ignore them.

Maan didn't mind them at all. He suddenly turned on them and roared as fiercely as an angry lion, and they scattered, terrified. Some of them began giggling from a safe distance, and started to approach again, with tentative steps.

'Do you think we should go inside?' said Maan.

Rasheed looked embarrassed. 'Actually, the fact is that we maintain purdah at home. All your bags are inside, of course, for safe custody.'

'Oh!' said Maan, 'Of course.' After a while he said, 'Your father must have thought it very odd of me last night to say I'd sleep on the roof.'

'It's not your fault,' said Rasheed. 'I should have warned you. But I take everything about my own home for granted.'

'The Nawab Sahib has purdah in his house in Brahmpur, so I shouldn't have assumed it would be different here,' said Maan.

'It is, though,' said Rasheed. 'The Muslim women of the lower castes need to work in the fields, so they can't maintain purdah. But we Shaikhs and Sayyeds try to. It's simply a matter of honour, of being the big people in the village.'

Just as Maan was about to ask Rasheed if his village was mainly or exclusively Muslim, Rasheed's grandfather came along to look at what they were doing. The old man was still wearing his green lungi, but had added a white vest. With his white beard and somewhat failing eyes, he looked more frail than he did when he had loured over Maan in the morning.

'What are you teaching him, Rasheed?'

'Urdu, Baba.'

'Yes? Good, good.'

To Maan he said:

'How old are you, Kapoor Sahib?'

'Twenty-five.'

'Are you married?'

'No.'

'Why not?'

'Well,' said Maan, 'it hasn't happened yet.'

'There's nothing wrong with you, is there?'

'Oh, no!' said Maan. 'Nothing.'

'Then you should get married. This is the time, when you are young. Then you won't be an old man when your children are growing up. Look at me. I'm old now, but I wasn't once.'

Maan was tempted to exchange a glance with Rasheed, but sensed that it wasn't the right thing to do.

The old man picked up the exercise book that Maan had been writing on and held it away from his eyes. The whole page was covered with the same two letters. 'Seen, sheen,' said the old man. 'Seen, sheen, seen, sheen, seen, sheen. Enough of this! Teach him something more, Rasheed – this is all very well for children. He'll get bored.'

Rasheed nodded his head but said nothing.

The old man turned back to Maan and said: 'Are you bored yet?'

'Oh no,' said Maan, quickly. 'I've been learning to read. This is just the calligraphy part.'

'That's good,' said Rasheed's grandfather. 'That's very good. Carry on, carry on. I will go over there' – he pointed across the way to a charpoy lying in front of another house – 'and read.'

He cleared his throat and spat onto the ground, then walked slowly away. In a few minutes Maan saw him seated cross-legged on the charpoy with his spectacles on, swaying backwards and forwards, reciting from a large book placed in front of him that Maan assumed was the Quran. Since he was only about twenty steps away, the murmur of his recitation merged with the sounds of the children, who were now daring each other to go and touch Maan – 'the lion'.

Maan said to Rasheed, 'I've been thinking of writing a letter. Do you think you could write it for me and, well, help me compose it? I can still barely string two words together in this script.'

'Of course,' said Rasheed.

'You really don't mind?' said Maan.

'No, of course not. Why should I?' said Rasheed.

'Actually, it's to Saeeda Bai.'

'I see,' said Rasheed.

'Maybe after dinner?' said Maan. 'I'm not in the mood now with all these kids running around.' He was afraid that they might start chanting 'Saeeda Bai! Saeeda Bai!' at the top of their lungs.

Rasheed didn't say anything for a few moments, then waved away a fly and said: 'The only reason why I'm getting you to write these two letters again and again is that the way you draw the curve is too shallow. It should be more rounded. Like this –' And he drew the letter 'sheen' very slowly.

Maan could sense that Rasheed was not happy, that he in fact disapproved, but he did not know what to do about it. He could not bear to think that he would not hear from Saeeda Bai, and he feared that she might not write to him unless he wrote to her. In fact he wasn't even sure that she had his postal address. Of course 'c/o Abdur Rasheed, village Debaria, tehsil Salimpur, Distt Rudhia, P.P.' would get to him, but Maan was not certain that Saeeda Bai was certain that it would.

Since she could read nothing but Urdu, he would have to get an Urdu scribe to write his letter for him until he himself learned the script sufficiently well to be able to do so. And who other than Rasheed could or would help him by writing it, and – unless Saeeda Bai's hand was exceptionally clear and careful – by reading out her reply to him when it came?

Maan was staring down at the ground in his perplexity when he noticed that a huge crowd of flies had gathered around the spot where Baba had spat. They were ignoring the sherbet that Maan and Rasheed were drinking.

How strange, he thought, and frowned.

'What are you thinking of?' said Rasheed, quite brusquely. 'Once you can read and write the language you'll be free. So do pay attention, Kapoor Sahib.'

'Look at that,' said Maan.

'That's odd. You're not diabetic, are you?' said Rasheed, no longer with sharpness but concern in his voice.

'No,' said Maan, surprised. 'Why? That's where Baba spat just now.'

'Oh, yes, I see,' said Rasheed. 'He is. And the flies gather around his spittle because it's sweet.'

Maan looked over towards the old man, who was shaking his finger at one of the brats.

'But he insists he's in very good general health,' said Rasheed, 'and against all our advice, he still fasts every day during Ramazan. Last year it was in June, and he didn't have a morsel of food or a drop of water from sunrise to sunset. And this year it'll be at almost the same time of year. Long hot days. No one expects it of a man his age. But he won't listen.'

The heat had suddenly begun to get to Maan, but he didn't know what to do about it. He was sitting under the neem tree, which was the coolest place out of doors. If he had been at home, he would have turned on the fan, collapsed onto his bed and stared at the ceiling as the blades went round and round. Here there was nothing to do but suffer. The sweat trickled down his face, and he tried to be grateful that flies didn't settle upon it immediately.

'It's too hot!' said Maan. 'I don't want to live.'

'You should have a bath,' said Rasheed.

'Ah!' said Maan.

Rasheed went on: 'I'll go in and get some soap and tell the fellow to pump the water while you're under the tap. It would have been too cold after dark last night, but now's a good time. ... Use that tap.' He pointed to the pump directly in front of the house. 'But you should put on your lungi while bathing.'

There was a small, windowless room that jutted forward out of the house and Maan used this to change in. It was not part of the house proper but acted as a sort of shed. It contained spare parts for agricultural machinery and a few ploughs. Some spears and sticks stood in a corner. When

Maan entered it there was as much expectation among the children as if an actor had gone backstage to emerge in a brilliant new costume. When he came out they discussed him critically.

'Look at him, he looks so pale.'

'He looks even more bald now.'

'Lion, lion, without a tail!'

All of them became very excited. One odious child of about seven called 'Mr Biscuit' made use of the clamour to aim a stone at a girl. The stone went hurtling through the air and hit her on the back of the head. She started screaming in pain and shock. Baba, jolted out of his recitation, got up from his charpoy and appraised the situation in an instant. Everyone was staring at Mr Biscuit, who was trying to appear nonchalant. Baba caught hold of Mr Biscuit's ear and twisted it.

'Haramzada – bastard – you dare to behave like the animal you are?' cried the old man.

Mr Biscuit began to blubber, and snot ran down from his nostrils. Baba dragged him by the ear to where he had been sitting, and slapped him so hard the boy almost went flying. Then, ignoring him, he sat down to his recitation again. But his concentration had been spoilt.

Mr Biscuit sat stunned on the ground for a few minutes, then got up to perpetrate what further mischief he could. Meanwhile his victim had been taken back home by Rasheed; she was bleeding copiously from the back of her head, and crying her eyes out.

Ignorant and brutal at the age of seven! This, thought Rasheed, is what the village does to you. Anger against his surroundings welled up within him.

Maan had his bath under the scrutiny of the village children. The cool water poured generously out of the spout, pumped by a very vigorous middle-aged man with a friendly, square, deeply furrowed and wrinkled face. He showed no signs of tiring and appeared to enjoy being of service, continuing to pump water even after Maan had finished.

Maan at last was cool and, therefore, at a truce with the world.

MAAN did not eat much at lunch but praised the food a great deal, hoping that some of his praise would get through to the unseen woman or women of the house who had prepared it.

A little after lunch, after they had washed their hands and were resting on the charpoys outside, a couple of visitors arrived at the house. One was Rasheed's maternal uncle.

This man was the elder brother of Rasheed's late mother. He was a huge, kind bear of a man, with a pepper-and-salt stubble. He lived about ten miles away, and Rasheed had once run off and lived with him for a month after he had been beaten at home for half-throttling a schoolmate.

Rasheed got up from the charpoy the instant he saw him. Then he said to Maan – the others were still out of earshot – 'The big man is my Mamu. The round one is known as the "guppi" in my mother's village – he blathers on and on and tells ridiculous stories. We're stuck.'

By now the visitors had reached the cattle-shed.

'Ah, Mamu, I didn't know you were coming. How are you?' said Rasheed in warm welcome. And he nodded at the guppi civilly.

'Ah,' said the Bear, and sat down heavily on the charpoy. He was a man of few words.

The man of many words, his friend and travelling companion, also sat down and asked for a glass of water. Rasheed promptly went inside and got some sherbet.

The guppi asked Maan a number of questions and ascertained quickly who, why, what and how he was. He then described to Maan a number of incidents that had occurred on their ten-mile journey. They had seen a snake, 'as thick as my arm' (Rasheed's Mamu frowned in concentration, but did not contradict him); they had almost been blown off their feet by a sudden whirlwind; and the police had shot at them three times at the check-post just outside Salimpur.

Rasheed's Mamu merely mopped his brow and gasped gamely in the heat. Maan leaned forward, amazed by these unlikely adventures.

Rasheed returned, bearing glasses of sherbet. He told them that his father was sleeping. The Bear nodded benevolently.

The talkative one was asking Maan about his love-life, and Maan was attempting weakly to fend off the questions.

'People's love-lives are not very interesting,' said Maan, sounding unconvincing even to himself.

'How can you say that?' said the guppi. 'Every man's love-life is interesting. If he doesn't have one, that's interesting. If he has one, that's interesting. And if he has two, that's twice as interesting.' He laughed delightedly at his sally. Rasheed looked abashed. Baba had gone inside his house already.

Encouraged by the fact that he had not been immediately stifled, as he often was in his own village, the guppi went on:

'But what would you know of love – of true love? You young men have not seen much. You may think that because you live in Brahmpur you have seen the world – or more of the world than we poor yokels see. But some of us yokels have also seen the world – and not just the world of Brahmpur, but of Bombay.'

He paused, impressed by his own words, especially the entrancing word 'Bombay', and looked at his audience with pleasure. Several children had appeared in the last couple of minutes, drawn by the guppi's magic. Whenever the guppi appeared they could be sure of a good story, and probably one that their parents would not want them to hear – involving ghosts or deadly violence or passionate love.

A goat too had appeared, and was standing at the upper end of a cart, trying to graze on the leaves of a branch just overhead. With its crafty yellow eyes it stared at the leaves and strained its neck upwards.

'When I was in Bombay,' the round and reverberant

guppi went on, 'long before my fate changed and I had to return to this blessed countryside, I worked in a big shop, a very famous shop run by a mullah, and we would sell carpets to big people, all the very big people of Bombay. They would have so much money, they would take it in wads out of their bags and throw it down on the counter.'

His eyes lit up as if at the memory. The children sat enthralled – or most of them anyway. Mr Biscuit, the seven-year-old horror, was occupied with the goat. Whenever it got near its goal, the leafy branch, Mr Biscuit would tilt the cart downwards, and the poor goat would now try to clamber up to the other end. So far it had not succeeded in eating a single leaf.

'It's a love story, I'm warning you in advance, so if you don't want to listen to it, you can tell me to stop now,' said the guppi in a formulary way. 'Because once I've begun, I can't stop it any more than one can stop the act of love itself.'

Rasheed would have got up and left if he hadn't been so conscious of his duty as a host. But Maan wanted to stay and hear the story.

'Go on, go on,' he said.

Rasheed looked at Maan, as if to say: 'This man needs no encouragement. If you show any interest at all he'll go on twice as long.'

Aloud he said to the guppi: 'Of course, this is an eye-witness account as usual.'

The guppi shot him a glance, at first suspicious, then placatory. He had just been about to say that he had seen the events he was about to recount with his very own eyes.

'I saw these events with my very own eyes,' he said.

The goat started bleating piteously. The guppi shouted at the distracting Mr Biscuit: 'Sit down, or I'll feed you to that goat, your eyes first.'

Mr Biscuit, horrified by such a graphic description of his fate, thought that the guppi must mean business, and sat down on the ground like any ordinary child.

The guppi went on: 'So we'd sell carpets to all the big people, and there were such beautiful women who would come to our shop that our eyes would water with emotion. The mullah in particular had a weakness for beauty, and whenever he saw a beautiful woman walking past our shop or about to enter it he would say: "Oh God! Why have you made such angels? Farishtas have come to earth to haunt us mortals." We would all start laughing. He would get very cross and scold us: "When you're tired of saying Bismillah on your knees you should praise the angels of God."'

The guppi paused for effect.

'Well, one day – this happened before my very eyes – a beautiful woman called Vimla tried to start her car, which was parked near our shop. It wouldn't start, so she got out. She started walking towards our shop. She was beautiful, so beautiful – that we were all entranced. One of us said: "The ground is shaking." The mullah said: "She is so beautiful that if she looks at you, boils will break out all over your body." But then – suddenly –'

The guppi's voice started trembling with the recollection.

'Suddenly – from the other direction – and on the other side of the street – came a young Pathan, so tall and handsome that the mullah started praising God as excitedly as before: "As the Moon leaves the skies, the Sun approaches," and so on.

'They approached each other. Then the young Pathan boy crossed the road towards her – saying "Please, please –" in an importunate voice and holding out a card that he had whipped out of his pocket. He showed it to her three times. She was reluctant to read it, but finally she took it and bent her head to read it. No sooner had she done this than the young Pathan embraced her like a bear and bit her cheek so hard that the blood streamed down. She screamed!'

The guppi covered his face with his hands to ward off the awful image. Then he rallied and continued:

'The mullah cried, "Quick, quick, lie down, no one has seen anything – no one must get mixed up in this." But a man who was in his underwear on the roof of a nearby hotel saw it and cried, "Toba, toba!" He didn't come down to help but he called the police. Within minutes the streets were sealed off, and there was no way out, no escape at all. Five jeeps rushed towards the Pathan from all directions. The Superintendent of Police was merciless and the policemen used all the force they could, but the Pathan was clinging to the girl so tightly that they could not separate his arms, which were locked around her waist. He had shouldered aside three men before they finally succeeded in knocking him out with the butt of a pistol and separating his hands with a crowbar.'

The guppi paused for further effect before continuing. His audience was spellbound.

'The whole of Bombay was outraged at this gunda-gardi, this hooliganism, and a case was quickly registered against him. Everyone said: "Be strict – or all the girls in Bombay will have their cheeks bitten, and then what will happen?" There was a huge court case. He was put in a cage in court. He rattled the bars with such fury that the courtroom shook. But he was found guilty, and a death sentence was passed. Then the judge said: "Do you want to see anyone before you are hanging breathlessly from the gallows? Do you want one last glimpse of your mother?" The boy said: "No – I've seen enough of her. I've been fed by her breasts and have urinated in her arms when I was a baby – why should I want to see her again?" Everyone was shocked. "Anyone else?" said the judge.

'"Yes," said the doomed man. "Yes. One person, and one person alone: that person, a single sight of whom made me give up all hope of life on earth and made me willing to die – that person who has given me a taste of the world to come, for she has sent me to paradise. I have two things to say to her. She can stand outside the bars, I inside – I will not even touch her –"

'All the big people of Bombay, all the businessmen and ballishtahs stood up in court, turned to stone with the shock of his request. The girl's family started to scream. "Never!" they screamed – "Our daughter will never speak to him." The judge said: "I have said she can – and she must." So she went into the courtroom, and everyone was hissing: "Behayaa – besharam – how shameless can you get in the very face of your own death." But he only held the bars and laughed. It said in the papers also: He laughed.'

The guppi drained his glass of sherbet and held it out to be refilled. Resurrecting the past accurately was a thirsty job. The children stared impatiently as his Adam's apple moved up and down gulp after gulp. With a sigh he continued:

'The young man held the bars of his cage and looked deeply into Vimla's eyes. By God, it was as if he wanted to drink her soul out of her body. But she looked at him with contempt, holding her head up proudly, her once-beautiful cheek scarred and defiled. Finally he found his voice, and said: "I only want to say two things to you. First, no one will marry you now except an old and poor man ... you have been marked as the one bitten by the Pathan. Second" – and here the young man's voice broke and the tears started streaming down his face – "second, by God I didn't know what happened to me when I did that to you. I lost my senses when I saw you, I never knew what I was doing – forgive me, forgive me! I have had hundreds of offers of marriage. I have refused them all – the most beautiful women. Till I saw you I never knew I had a companion of the soul.

'"I will treat your scar as a mark of beauty and bathe it with my tears and shower kisses on it. I am London-returned and I have thirty-five thousand people in factories working for me and crores of rupees in wealth and I want to give it all to you. God is a witness between us – I never knew what I was doing – but now I am willing to die."

'Hearing this, the girl, who a minute ago could have killed him with her own hands, began to gasp as if she was ill with love, and threw herself towards the judge, begging him to spare the man, saying: "Spare him, spare him – I knew him for a long time, I begged him to bite me –" But the judge had given his sentence and said: "Impossible. Do not lie, or I will put you away." Then in despair she took a knife out of her bag and put it to her throat and said to the whole court – the High Court judge and all the high ballishtahs and sollishtahs and all – "If he is killed, I die. I will write here that I committed suicide because of the sentence you passed."

'So they had to undo the sentence – what could they do? Then she begged that the marriage should take place at the boy's place. The girl was a Punjabi, and there was such enmity towards the Pathan and his family that her parents would have killed her as well as the boy for revenge.'

The guppi paused.

'This is true love,' he said, deeply moved by his narration, and leaned back on the charpoy, spent.

Maan, despite himself, was enthralled. Rasheed looked at him, then at the enraptured children, and closed his eyes in mild contempt for all that had gone on. His large, taciturn Mamu, who hardly appeared to have been listening, patted his friend on the back and said:

'Now Radio Jhutistan takes leave of its listeners.' Then he switched off an imaginary knob near the guppi's ear and clapped his hand over his mouth.

8.7

MAAN and Rasheed were walking through the village. It was not very different in appearance from a thousand other villages in Rudhia District: mud walls within which people lived (often together with their cattle), thatched roofs, narrow lanes with no windows facing onto them (the conservative heritage of centuries of conquest and brigandage), the very occasional whitewashed one-storey brick house belonging to a 'big person' in the village. Cows and dogs meandered down the lanes, neem trees raised their heads from inner courtyards or near a village well, the low minarets of a small white mosque stood near the centre of the village close to the five brahmin houses and the bania's shop. Only two families had their own hand-pump: Rasheed's and one other. The rest of the population – about four hundred families in all – obtained their water from one of three wells: the Muslim well, which stood in an open space near a neem tree, the caste-Hindu well, which stood in an open space near a pipal tree, and the outcaste or untouchable well, which stood at the very edge of the village among a dense cluster of mud huts, not far from a tanning pit.

They had almost reached their destination, the grain-parcher's house, when they met Rasheed's younger uncle, who was about to set out for Salimpur. Maan got a better look at him by daylight than he had the previous night. He was a young man of medium height and fairly good looks: dark skin, even features, slightly curly black hair, a moustache. He evidently took care of himself. There was a bit of a swagger to his gait. Though younger than Rasheed, he was very conscious of the fact that he was the uncle and Rasheed the nephew.

'What are you doing walking around in the heat of the afternoon?' he said to Rasheed. 'And why are you dragging your friend around with you? It's hot. He should be resting.'

'He wanted to come,' said Rasheed. 'But what are you doing here yourself?'

'I'm off to Salimpur. There's a dinner there. I thought I'd go early and sort some things out at the Congress Party office there.'

This young man was very energetic and ambitious and had his finger in several pies, including local politics. It was because of these qualities of self-interested leadership that he was called Netaji by most people. Eventually his family had taken to calling him Netaji as well. He didn't like it.

Rasheed was careful not to do so. 'I don't see your motorcycle anywhere,' he said.

'It won't start,' said Netaji plaintively. His second-hand Harley Davidson (war stock originally sold off by the army, it had passed through several hands already) was the pride of his heart.

'That's a pity. So why don't you get your rickshaw to take you there?'

'I've hired it out for the day. Really, this motorcycle is more trouble than it's worth. Since I've got it I've spent more time worrying about it than using it. The village boys, and especially that bastard Moazzam, are always doing things to it. I wouldn't be surprised if they've put water in the fuel tank.'

Like a genie conjured up by his name, Moazzam appeared out of nowhere. He was a boy of about twelve or so, quite strong and compact, and one of the chief trouble-makers of the village. He had a very friendly face with hair that bristled up like a porcupine's. Sometimes his face would become dark with some unexpressed thought. He seemed to be beyond anyone's control, especially his parents'. People put him down as eccentric, and hoped that he would sort himself out in a few years. Whereas no one liked Mr Biscuit, Moazzam had his admirers.

'You bastard!' said Netaji as soon as he saw Moazzam. 'What have you done to my motorcycle?'

Moazzam, taken aback by this sudden attack, retreated into a dark expression. Maan looked at him with interest, and Moazzam appeared to wink at him in a fleeting expression of conspiracy.

'Can't you hear me?' said Netaji, advancing towards him.

Moazzam said, in a surly tone: 'I can hear you. I've done nothing to your motorcycle. Why should I care about your wretched motorcycle?'

'I saw you hanging around it this morning with two of your friends.'

'So?'

'Don't ever go near it again. Understand? If I ever see you near it again, I'll run you over.'

Moazzam gave a short laugh.

Netaji wanted to slap Moazzam, but thought better of it. 'Let's leave the swine,' he said dismissively to the others. 'By rights he should have his brain shown to a doctor, but his father is too much of a miser to do so. I must be on my way.'

Moazzam now performed a little dance of rage, and cried to Netaji: 'Swine! Swine yourself! You are the swine. And the miser. You lend money on interest, and you buy rickshaws and won't let anyone use them free. Look at our great leader, the Netaji of the village! I don't have time for you. Migrate to Salimpur with your motorcycle, I don't care.'

When Netaji, muttering black threats under his breath, had left, Moazzam decided to attach himself to Rasheed and Maan.... Now he asked to see Maan's watch.

Maan promptly took it off, and showed it to Moazzam, who, after examining it, put it in his pocket. Rasheed said quite sharply to Moazzam:

'Give the watch to me. Is this the way to behave with guests?'

Moazzam looked puzzled at first, then disgorged the watch. He handed it to Rasheed, who gave it back to Maan.

'Thank you, I'm very grateful,' said Maan to Moazzam.

'Don't be polite to him,' said Rasheed to Maan, as if Moazzam wasn't present, 'or he'll take advantage of you. Keep your things close by you if he's around. He's well-known for making things disappear by sleight of hand.'

'All right,' said Maan, smiling.

'He's not bad at heart,' Rasheed went on.

'Not bad at heart,' repeated Moazzam absently. His attention, though, was elsewhere. An old man with a stick was walking down the narrow lane towards him. There was an amulet around his wrinkled neck which attracted Moazzam's attention. As they passed each other, he reached out for it.

'Give it to me,' he said.

The old man leaned on his stick and said in a slow and exhausted voice: 'Young man, I have no strength.'

This appeared to please Moazzam, who promptly released the amulet.

A girl of about ten was walking towards them with a

goat. Moazzam, who was in an acquisitive mood, made as if to grab for the rope, and said: 'Give it to me!' in the voice of a fierce dacoit.

The girl began to cry.

Rasheed said to Moazzam: 'Do you want to feel the back of this hand? Is this the impression you want to give outsiders?'

Moazzam turned suddenly to Maan and said: 'I'll get you married off. Do you want a Hindu or a Muslim bride?'

'Both,' said Maan with a straight face.

Moazzam took this seriously at first. 'How can you have both?' he said. Then it dawned on him that Maan might be making fun of him, and a hurt look came over his face.

But his high spirits reasserted themselves when a couple of village dogs, seeing Maan, started barking loudly.

Moazzam also started barking with delight − at the dogs. They got more and more agitated and barked louder and louder as he passed.

By now the three were in a small open space in the middle of the village, and they could see a group of about ten people gathered around the grain-parcher's house. Most of them were getting wheat parched, but one or two had brought some rice or gram along.

Maan said to Moazzam: 'Do you want some parched maize?'

Moazzam looked at him in astonishment, then nodded vigorously.

Maan patted his head. His bristly black hair was springy, like the pile of a carpet.

'Good!' he said.

Rasheed introduced Maan to the men at the grain-parcher's. They looked at him suspiciously but were not overtly unfriendly. Most were from this village, one or two from the neighbouring village of Sagal, just beyond the school. After Maan joined them, they confined their conversation mainly to instructions to the parcher-woman. Soon it was Rasheed's turn.

The old parcher-woman divided the maize Rasheed gave

her into five equal portions, put one aside for herself as payment, and proceeded to parch the remainder. She heated the grain and a quantity of sand separately – the grain gently, the sand fiercely. Then she poured the sand into the shallow pan containing the warm grain, and stirred it for a couple of minutes. Moazzam looked at the process intently, though he must have seen it a hundred times before.

'Do you want it roasted or popped?' she asked.

'Just roasted,' said Rasheed.

Finally the woman sieved out the sand and returned the parched grain. Moazzam took more than the others, but less than he wanted to.

He ate some on the spot, and stuffed a few handfuls into the deep pockets of his kurta. Then he disappeared as suddenly as he had appeared.

8.8

IT was late, and they had reached the far end of the village. Clouds were gathering, and the red sky appeared to be on fire. The evening call to prayer had come faintly to their ears, but Rasheed had decided to complete his round of the village rather than interrupt it with a visit to the mosque.

The inflamed sky loured over the thatched huts, the fields, the spreading green mango and dry, brown-leaved shisham trees in the wasteland to the north of the village. One of the two threshing-grounds of the village was located here, and the tired bullocks were still at work on the spring harvest. Round and round they went on the threshing-floor, round and round. They would continue to do so till late at night.

A light evening breeze blew gently from the north towards the cramped huts of the various untouchables – the washermen, the chamars and the sweepers – that lay on the far outskirts of the village – a breeze that would be stifled by the mud walls and constricted lanes of the village and die before it reached its heart. A few ragged children with brown, sun-bleached, filthy, matted hair played in the dust outside their houses – one dragged a piece of blackened wood, another played with a chipped marble. They were hungry, and they looked thin and ill.

Rasheed visited a few chamar households. One family had continued in its ancestral profession of skinning dead animals and preparing the hides for sale. Most, however, were agricultural labourers, one or two with a bit of land of their own as well. In one house Maan recognized the man with the deeply furrowed face who had pumped water for him with so much willingness while he was having a bath. 'He has worked for our family since he was ten years old,' said Rasheed. 'His name is Kachheru.'

The old man and his wife lived by themselves in a single thatched room which they shared at night with their cow and a large number of insects.

Despite Rasheed's politeness, they treated him with extreme, even fearful, deference. It was only when he agreed to have a cup of tea with them in their hut – agreeing thus on Maan's behalf as well – that they seemed to be a little more at ease.

'What happened to Dharampal's son – your nephew?' asked Rasheed.

'He died a month ago,' said Kachheru shortly.

'All those doctors?'

'No use, except to eat money. Now my brother's in debt with the bania – and my sister-in-law, well, you wouldn't recognize her any more. She's just gone to her father's village. She'll stay there for a month or so – until the rains begin.'

'Why didn't he come to us if he needed money?' said Rasheed, distressed.

'You should ask your father that,' said Kachheru. 'He went to him, I believe, a couple of times. But after that your father became annoyed and told him not to fling good money after bad. But he helped with the funeral.'

'I see. I see. What can one do? God disposes –' Rasheed mumbled a few consolatory words.

After they left, Maan could see that Rasheed was very upset. Neither said anything for a while. Then Rasheed said:

'We are tied to earth by such fine threads. And there is so much injustice – so much – it drives me mad. And if you think this village is bad, it's because you don't know Sagal. There is a poor man there who – God forgive them – has been destroyed and left to die by his own family. And look at that old man and woman,' said Rasheed, pointing out a couple who were sitting outside their hut in rags, begging. 'They have been turned out by their children, all of whom are doing tolerably well.'

Maan looked at them. They were starving and filthy, in a pitiable state. Maan gave them a few annas. They stared at the money.

'They are destitute. They don't have enough to eat, but their children will not help them,' Rasheed went on. 'Each claims it is the other's responsibility, or the responsibility of no one at all.'

'Whom do the children work for?' asked Maan.

'For us,' said Rasheed. 'For us. The great and good of the village.'

'Why don't you tell them that this can't go on?' said Maan. 'That they can't treat their parents this way? Surely you can tell them that they must put their house in order if they want to work for you?'

'Ah, now that is a good question,' said Rasheed. 'But it is a question for my esteemed father and grandfather, not for me,' he added bitterly.

8.9

MAAN lay down on his string-bed and stared upwards into what, in contrast with the previous night, was a cloudy sky. No solution appeared to him from either cloud or constellation as to how to get his letter written. Once again he thought of his father with annoyance.

Nearby footsteps made him lean on one elbow and look

towards the source of the sound. Rasheed's huge bear-like uncle and his companion the guppi were approaching.

'Salaam aleikum.'

'Wa aleikum salaam,' replied Maan.

'Everything going fine?'

'Thanks to your prayers,' replied Maan. 'And you? Where are you coming from?'

'I went to meet my friends in the other village,' said Rasheed's uncle. 'And my friend came along. Now I am going inside the house, but I will have to leave my friend here with you. You don't mind?'

'Of course not,' lied Maan, who wanted no company, least of all the guppi's. But since he didn't have a room, he didn't have a door.

Rasheed's uncle, noticing a number of charpoys scattered in the outer courtyard, picked up one under each huge arm and put them on their sides along the verandah wall. 'It looks like rain,' he explained. 'And anyway, if they're on their sides, the hens won't come and make a mess of them. Where is Rasheed, by the way?'

'Inside,' said Maan.

Rasheed's uncle belched, stroked his bristly beard of stubble, then went on in a friendly manner: 'You know, he ran away from home and stayed with me a couple of times. He was always very sharp at school, very quarrelsome. It was the same when he went to Banaras for further studies. Religious studies! But since he's been at Brahmpur, there's been a change and he's become a good deal more sober. Or perhaps it began in Banaras.' He thought about the matter for a second. 'It often happens this way,' he said. 'But he doesn't see eye to eye with his people. And there'll be trouble. He sees injustice everywhere; he doesn't pause to understand things in their surroundings. You're his friend – you should talk to him. Well, I'll be going in.'

Left with the guppi, Maan did not know what to say, but he was not faced with the problem for long. The guppi, settling himself comfortably on the other charpoy, said:

'What beauty are you dreaming of?'

Maan was both startled and slightly annoyed.

'You know, I'll show you Bombay,' said the guppi. 'You should come with me.' At the word 'Bombay' excitement once again crept into his voice.

'There are enough beauties there to satisfy all the love-sick young gentlemen of the universe. Tobacco?'

Maan shook his head.

'I have a first-class house there,' continued the guppi. 'It has a fan. A view. There's no heat like this. I'll show you the Irani tea-shops. I'll show you Chowpatty Beach. For four annas of roasted peanuts you can see the world. Munch on them as you walk along and admire the view: the waves, the nymphs, the farishtas, all the beautiful women swimming so shamelessly in the ocean. You can join them. . . .'

Maan shut his eyes but could not shut his ears.

'Actually, it was near Bombay that I saw an amazing event which I will never forget. I'll share it with you if you want,' the guppi continued. He paused for a second and, encountering no resistance, continued with a story which was entirely irrelevant to what had gone before.

'Some Marathi dacoits got onto this train,' said the guppi, beginning calmly enough, but becoming increasingly excited as the tale continued. 'They said nothing, they just got on at a station. The train started to move, and then they stood up – all six of them, bloodthirsty villains – and threatened the people with knives. All the passengers were terrified, and handed their money and jewellery over. The six of them went through the entire compartment, and robbed everyone. Eventually they came to a Pathan.'

'Pathan', like 'Bombay', appeared to act as yeast to the guppi's imagination. He breathed reverently and went on:

'The Pathan – a broad, strong fellow – was travelling with his wife and children, and he had a trunk containing his possessions. Three of the villains were standing around him. "Well –" said one of them. "What are you waiting for?"

' "Waiting?" said the Pathan, as if he did not understand what they were saying.

'"Give me your money," cried one of the Marathi dacoits.

'"I won't," growled the Pathan.

'"What?" yelled the bandit, unable to believe what he was hearing.

'"You've robbed everyone," said the Pathan, remaining seated while the gundas loured over him. "Why rob me as well?"

'"No!" said the dacoits. "Give us your money. Quick."

'The Pathan saw that he couldn't do anything immediately. He played for time. He started fumbling with his key and the lock of his trunk. He bent down as if to open it, judged distances – and suddenly – with one kick here – dharaaam! – he knocked one of them out – then – dhoooosh! – he bashed the other two bandits' heads together, and flung them out of the train; one he actually lifted up by the neck and the crotch and flung out like a sack of wheat. The villain bounced on the next bogey before falling onto the ground.'

The guppi wiped his plump face, which was sweating with excitement and the effort of recall.

'Then the ringleader – who was still in the compartment – pulled out his pistol, and fired. Dhaaaaaaam! ... The shot went through the Pathan's arm and lodged in the compartment wall. There was blood everywhere. He raised the pistol again to fire. Everyone in the compartment was frozen with fear. Then the Pathan spoke in the voice of a tiger to the passengers: "Bastards! I, one man alone, beat up three of them, and no one raised a hand to help me. I'm saving your money and your wealth for you. Isn't there any one among you who can hold his hand to stop him from firing again?"

'Then they all came to their senses. They grabbed the bandit's hand and stopped him from killing the Pathan – and they beat him up – dharaaaash! dharaaaash! – till he cried for mercy and wept in pain – and then they thrashed him even more. "Do it properly," said the Pathan, and they did – until he was a mass of blood. And they threw him onto the platform of the next station, a broken pulp. Like a discarded, rotting mango!

'Then the women were all over the Pathan: bandaging his hand, etcetera, etcetera. They treated him as if there was only one man in the whole train. Beautiful women, all filled with admiration.'

The guppi, seeking approval, looked over towards Maan, who was feeling mildly sick.

'Are you feeling all right?' asked the guppi, after a long silence.

'Mmmmh.' said Maan. There was a pause, and he continued: 'Tell me, why do you tell such outrageous stories?'

'But they are all true,' said the guppi. 'Basically true.'

Maan was silent.

'Look at it this way,' continued the guppi. 'If I merely said, "Hello" and you said "Hello. Where have you come from?" and I said, "From the direction of Baitar. By train" – well, how would the day pass? How would we get through these boiling afternoons and hot nights? So I tell stories – some to keep you cool, some to make you hotter!' The guppi laughed.

But Maan was not listening any longer. He had sat up at the word 'Baitar', as galvanized by it as the guppi had been by 'Bombay'. A wonderful idea had struck him.

He would write to Firoz, that was it. He would write to Firoz and enclose a letter to Saeeda Bai. Firoz wrote excellent Urdu and had none of Rasheed's puritanism. Firoz would translate Maan's letter and send it on to Saeeda Bai. She would be astonished to get his letter: astonished and delighted! And she would write back to him by the next post.

Maan got up from the charpoy and began pacing up and down, composing the letter in his head, adding here and there a couplet or two from Ghalib or Mir – or Dagh – for ornamentation or emphasis. Rasheed could have no objection to mailing a letter to the son of the Nawab of Baitar; Maan would simply hand him the closed envelope.

The guppi, puzzled by Maan's erratic behaviour and disappointed that he had lost his audience, wandered off into the darkness.

Maan sat down once again, leaned against the edge of the verandah, and listened to the hiss of the lantern and the other sounds of the night. Somewhere a baby cried. Somewhere a dog barked, and other dogs joined in. Then all was quiet for a while, except for the drift of a voice or two from the roof, where Rasheed's father spent his summer nights. Sometimes the voices seemed to be raised in argument, sometimes subdued; but Maan could make out nothing of what was being said.

It was a cloudy night, and the papiha or brainfever bird called from time to time from a distant tree, its series of triple notes growing tauter and higher and more intense until it reached a climax and dropped into sudden silence. Maan did not think of the romantic associations of the sound ('pee-kahan? pee-kahan?' Where is my love? Where is my love?). He wanted the bird to be quiet so that he could concentrate on the voice of his own heart.

8.10

THAT night there was a violent storm. It was a sudden summer thunderstorm of the kind that builds up when the heat is most unbearable. It lashed through the trees and fields, whipped away thatch and even a few tiles from the houses in the village, and drenched the dusty ground. Those who had looked up at the clouds – so often bringers of nothing but the occasional gust of wind – and had decided to sleep outside anyway to avoid the heat, had picked up their charpoys and rushed inside when, without more warning than a heavy drop or two, the clouds had burst over their heads. Then they had gone out again to bring in the cattle tethered outside. Now they all steamed together in the darkness of the huts where most of the villagers lived, the cattle lowing plaintively in the front rooms, the humans talking together in the back.

Kachheru, the chamar who had worked for Rasheed's family since childhood, and whose hut consisted of only a single room, had judged the arrival of the storm to the hour. His buffalo was inside, and safe from the lashing rain. She snorted and urinated from time to time, but these were reassuring sounds.

A little rain came through the roof and fell on Kachheru and his wife, who were lying on the ground. There were many roofs that were flimsier than his, and some that would be blown away in this kind of storm, but Kachheru said sharply:

'Old woman – what use are you if you cannot even save us from the rain?'

His wife said nothing for a while. Then she said: 'We should see how the beggar and his wife are doing. Their hut is on low ground.'

'That is none of our business,' retorted Kachheru.

'On nights like these I think of the night when Tirru was born. I wonder how he's doing in Calcutta. He never writes.'

'Go to sleep, go to sleep,' said Kachheru wearily. He knew the work that lay ahead of him the next morning, and he did not want to waste his hours of sleep in idle and disturbing chatter.

But for a while he lay awake with his own thoughts. The wind howled and ceased and howled again, and water continued to leak in. In the end he got up to improvise some temporary repair to his wife's inefficient thatching.

Outside, the solid world of huts and trees, walls and wells, was now a shapeless, threatening roar of wind, water, moonlight, lightning, clouds and thunder. The land on which the untouchable castes lived was on the northern outskirts of the village. Kachheru was lucky; his own hut, though small, was not on the lowest land; it was in fact on the edge of a low escarpment of earth. But further below him he could see the rain-blurred outlines of huts that would be awash with water and filth by morning.

When he woke up, it was not yet light. He put on his dirty dhoti, and made his way through the slush of the village lanes to Rasheed's father's house. The rain had stopped, but the neem trees were still sprinkling droplets of water on him – and on the sweeper-women who were moving silently from house to house removing the garbage left outside at night by the women of the house. A few pigs grunted their way through the lanes, gobbling up whatever scraps or excrement they could find. All the dogs were silent, though a cock crowed occasionally in the waning darkness.

Gradually it became lighter. By now Kachheru, who had been walking slowly but in a deliberate manner along the slightly drier edges of the slushy lanes, was no longer near the scene of the worst damage, damage that sometimes distressed him as much as it did his wife, but which he had learned to ignore.

Kachheru looked around when he got to Rasheed's father's house. He could not see anyone, but he assumed that Baba at least was awake; he was a stickler for the pre-dawn prayer. A couple of people were sleeping on charpoys on the covered verandah; they must have been sleeping in the courtyard and had probably been caught in the sudden rain. Kachheru passed his hand over his wrinkled face and allowed himself to smile.

Suddenly there was a desperate mixture of quacks and clucks. A duck, king of the courtyard, with its head craned forward aggressively, but with an incongruously pacific expression on its face, was chasing (by turns) a cock, a couple of hens, and a few large chicks across the brick and mud – towards and then away from the cattle-shed, around the neem tree, and across the lane to the house where Baba and his younger son lived.

Kachheru rested on his haunches for a while. Then he went to the water-pump and splashed some water over his bare and muddy feet. A small black goat was butting its head against the shaft of the water-pump. Kachheru scratched its head. Its cynical yellow eyes looked back at him, and it bleated in complaint when he stopped.

Kachheru climbed the four steps to the door of the room where the ploughs were stored. Rasheed's father had three ploughs, two local or desi ones with pointed wooden shares and one mishtan plough with a curved metallic share which Kachheru ignored. He left open the door to the room, and pulled the desi ploughs into the light of the entrance. Then he sat down on his haunches once again and examined the two ploughs. Eventually he placed one on his shoulder and walked across the courtyard to the cattle-shed. The cattle turned their heads at his approach, and he, pleased to see them, said 'Aaaah! aaaaah!' in a low and comforting tone.

First, he fed all the cattle, mixing a little more grain than usual into the mush of hay and straw and water that was their fare in the hot weather. Even the black water-buffaloes – usually sent out to forage for themselves under the supervision of a herdboy – were fed, since it was difficult for them to find enough to graze on in this season. Then he adjusted muzzles and ropes to the necks and noses of the pair of intelligent white bullocks he most liked to work with. He picked up a long stick that was leaning against the wall of the cattle-shed and drove them out gently. Aloud, but so that no one would hear him, he said:

'If it weren't for me, you'd be finished.'

As he was about to yoke the bullocks together he suddenly remembered something. Telling them sternly to remain exactly where they were he went back across the courtyard to the room opposite. He got out a spade and carried it across. The bullocks had not strayed. He praised them, then yoked them, and placed the plough upside-down on the yoke, letting them drag it along while he shouldered his spade.

It was expected of Kachheru that whenever there was rain during the dry summer months he would go for the next day or two into his master's fields and plough them while there was still water in the soil. He was to go from field to field, and plough from morning till evening in order to take full advantage of this temporary moisture. It was exhausting labour, and it was not paid for.

Kachheru was one of Rasheed's father's chamars, and was on call at any time he wanted, not just for farming tasks but for any odd jobs – whether it was pumping water for a bath or taking a message to the other end of the village or hauling arhar stalks onto the roof of the house to dry for cooking fuel. Unlike other strangers he was granted the special and very occasional dispensation of entrance into the sanctum of the house, especially if something needed to be lugged onto the roof. After the death of Rasheed's elder brother, it had become necessary to have help in the house for the heavier tasks. But whenever Kachheru was called in, any women at home locked themselves in one of the rooms or slipped out into the vegetable garden at the back, staying as close to the wall of the house as possible.

In return for his services, he was taken care of by the family. This meant that he was given a certain amount of grain at harvest time: not enough, however, to provide for even a basic diet for himself and his wife. He had also been allowed a small plot of land to farm on his own, whenever his time was not required by his master. His master also lent him the use of his plough and bullocks if he felt he could spare them, as well as spades, hoes, and other tools, none of which Kachheru possessed or felt it worthwhile indebting himself to buy in order to till his small plot.

He was overworked, but it was not so much his mind as the exhaustion of his body that told him this. As the years had passed and he had never raised his head in rebellion or rudeness, he was now treated more politely by the family he had served for forty years, ever since he was a boy. They told him what he had to do, but did not shout at him in the voice of insulting command appropriate for the subservient caste to which he belonged. Rasheed's father sometimes called him 'my old one', which pleased Kachheru. He was given a kind of pre-eminence among his chamars, and was asked to supervise them from time to time during the busiest farming seasons.

Yet when his only son Tirru had said that he wanted to get out of Debaria and its caste-ridden, poverty-stricken, unrelievedly back-breaking, hopeless life, Kachheru had not objected. Kachheru's wife had pleaded with her son not to go, but her husband's unspoken support had weighed heavily on the other side.

What future lay for their son in the village? He had no

land, he had no money, and it was only at great sacrifice to the family – which had had to forgo the income that the boy would have brought in by herding cattle – that he had been educated to the sixth class at the government primary school a few miles away. Was this in order that he should kill himself working in the burning heat of the fields? Whatever Kachheru thought of his own life, he did not wish it upon his son. Let the boy go to Brahmpur or Calcutta or Bombay or wherever he chose and find work there: any kind of work, whether as a domestic servant or as a factory- or mill-hand.

At first Tirru had sent back money, and had written affectionate letters home in Hindi which Kachheru begged the postman or the bania at the shop – when they had the time – to read out for him. Sometimes he asked them to read them out several times, until they were irritated and puzzled. Then he would dictate replies which he would beg them to transcribe on a postcard. The boy had returned for the wedding of his two younger sisters, and had even helped with their dowries. But for the last year there had been no letters from Calcutta at all, and several of Kachheru's letters were returned to sender. Not all, though; and so he continued to write a monthly letter to their son's old address. But where he was, what had happened to him, and why he had stopped writing he could not imagine – and feared to. It was as if their son had half-ceased to exist. His wife was distraught. Sometimes she wept to herself in the dark, sometimes she prayed at a small orange-stained niche in a pipal tree where the village deity was said to live and where she had taken her son to be blessed before his departure. Every day she reminded Kachheru of how she had foreseen it all.

Finally one day he suggested to his wife that he would seek his master's permission and financial support (though he knew this meant falling into a bottomless pit of debt) to go to Calcutta to search for their son. But she had fallen weeping on the ground, full of nameless terrors. Kachheru had rarely even been to Salimpur, and never to the district town of Rudhia. Brahmpur, let alone Calcutta, was entirely outside his imagination. She, for her part, had only known two villages, the village into which she had been born and the village into which she had married.

8.11

IT was cool, and there was a morning breeze. From the pigeon-house came the sound of unfrantic, heavy cooing. Then a few pigeons began to fly around: some grey ones with black bands, some brownish ones, one or two white ones. Kachheru hummed a bhajan to himself as he walked the bullocks out of the village.

A few poor women and children, mostly of his own caste, had come out with baskets to glean the fields that had been harvested yesterday. Ordinarily by coming out as early as this they would have stolen a march on the birds and small animals that picked the fields bare. But now the gleaners were looking for grains of food in a morass of mud.

It was not unpleasant to be ploughing at this time of day. It was cool, and walking ankle-deep in cool water and mud behind a pair of well-trained and obedient bullocks (Kachheru had trained this pair himself) felt fine. He rarely needed to use his stick; unlike many peasants, he did not enjoy using it at all. The pair responded to his repertory of calls, moving anti-clockwise in intersecting circuits around the field, as close to the edge as possible, drawing the plough slowly behind them. Kachheru continued to sing to himself, interrupting his bhajan with 'wo! wo!' or 'taka taka' or other commands, and then picked up the tune not from where he had left off but from where he would have been had he never stopped singing. After the whole of the first field was covered with furrows – a field twice as large as the one he farmed for himself – he was sweating with exertion. The sun had now risen about fifteen degrees in the sky, and it was becoming warm. He let the bullocks rest, and went around the untouched corners of the field, digging up the earth with his spade.

As the morning progressed he stopped singing. A couple of times he lost patience with the bullocks, and gave them a stroke or two with the stick – especially the outer one, who had decided to halt when his fellow did, instead of continuing to wheel around as he had been ordered to.

Kachheru was now working at a steady pace, using with care his finite energy and that of his cattle. It had grown unbearably hot, and the sweat poured down from his forehead into his eyebrows and trickled down from there into his eyes. He wiped it from time to time with the back of his right hand, keeping steady his hold on the plough with the left. By midday he was exhausted. He led the cattle to a ditch, but the water there, though they drank it, was warm. He himself drank from the leather bag that he had filled at the water-pump before setting out.

His wife came out into the fields when the sun was at its height, bringing him rotis, salt, a few chillies, and some lassi to drink. She watched him eat in silence, asked him if he wanted her to do anything else, and returned.

A little later Rasheed's father turned up with an umbrella that he used as a parasol. He squatted on a low ridge of mud that divided one field from another, and said a word or two of encouragement to Kachheru. 'It's true what they say,' he said. 'There's no work as hard as farming.' Kachheru did not answer, but nodded respectfully. He was beginning to feel ill. When Rasheed's father left, the fact of his presence was marked by the red-stained earth where he had spat out his paan-juice.

By now the water in the fields was uncomfortably hot underfoot, and a hot breeze had begun to blow. 'I will have to rest for a while,' he told himself. But he realized the importance of ploughing while the fugitive water was still on the ground, and he did not wish it to be said that he had not done what he knew needed doing.

By the time it was late afternoon his dark face was flushed red. His feet, callused and cracked though they were, felt as if they had been boiled. After a short day's work he usually shouldered the plough himself as he drove the cattle back from the fields. But he had no energy to do so today and gave it to the spent cattle to haul. Hardly a coherent thought formed itself in his mind. The metal of his spade, when it touched his shoulder accidentally, made him wince.

He passed by his own unploughed field with its two mulberry trees and hardly noticed it. Even that small field was not really his own, but it did not strike him to say so – or even think so. His only intention was to place one foot after the other on the path that led back to Debaria. The village lay three-quarters of a mile ahead of him, and it seemed to him that he was walking there through fire.

8.12

RASHEED'S father's whitewashed house, while fairly imposing from the outside by the standards of Debaria, contained very few rooms. It basically consisted of a square colonnaded quadrangle open to the sky in the middle. On one side of this quadrangle three quite airless rooms had been constructed by the simple expedient of bricking in the space between the columns. These rooms were occupied by members of the family. There were no other rooms in the house. Cooking was done in a corner of the open colonnade. This saved the women of the household from the smoke of a chimney-less hearth in a closed kitchen – exposure to which in the course of time would have ruined their eyes and lungs.

Other sections of the colonnade contained storage-bins and shelves. In the central square was an open space with a lemon tree and a pomegranate tree. Behind the back wall of the quadrangle was a privy for the women and a small vegetable garden. A set of stairs led up to the roof where Rasheed's father held court and ate paan – as he was doing at this moment.

No man could enter the house who was not a close member of the family. Rasheed's maternal or paternal uncles had free access. This was true of the bear-like uncle even after his sister, Rasheed's mother, had died and

Rasheed's father had taken a second – and much younger – wife. Since the patriarch, Baba, despite his age and diabetes, didn't mind climbing the stairs, roof conferences were a regular phenomenon. A roof conference was always convened, for instance, when anyone returned from a long absence, in order to sort out family matters.

This evening's was in honour of Rasheed, but before the other men had assembled it had turned quite quickly into an argument – or a series of arguments – between Rasheed and his father. His father had raised his voice on a number of occasions. Rasheed had defended himself, but it would have been almost unthinkable for him to raise his voice in uncontrolled anger. Sometimes he remained silent.

When Rasheed had left Maan outside and entered the courtyard, he had been in an unquiet frame of mind. Maan had not mentioned the letter today, which was good. Rasheed had not liked the thought of disappointing his friend in the matter, but it would have been impossible for him to write the kinds of things that Maan would almost certainly want to dictate. Rasheed did not care for what he saw as the baser human instincts. They made him uncomfortable, even at times angry. In matters such as these, he preferred to keep his eyes closed. If he suspected that there was anything between Maan and Saeeda Bai – and considering the circumstances of their meetings it was hard to imagine how he could not have known it – he did not wish to dwell on it.

As he walked upstairs to meet his father, he thought about his mother, who had lived in that house until her death two years before. It had seemed unimaginable to him then, as it seemed unimaginable to him now, that after her death his father could have married anyone else. At the age of fifty-five, surely one's appetites became still; and surely the memory of a woman who had devoted her entire life to his service and to the service of his two sons would have stood like a wall between his father and the thought of taking a second wife. But here she was, his stepmother: a pretty woman, not ten years older than himself. And it was she who slept with his father on the roof whenever he decided she should, and who bustled around the house, apparently undaunted by the ghost of the woman who had planted the trees whose fruit she unthinkingly plucked.

What did his father do, Rasheed wondered, other than give in to his appetites? He sat at home and ordered people about, and he ate paan continuously from morning till night, like a chain-smoker. He had ruined his teeth and tongue and throat. His mouth was a mere red slash interrupted by the occasional black tooth. Yet this man with his black, curly, balding hair and thick-set, belligerent face was forever provoking and lecturing him – and had done so from Rasheed's infancy to his adulthood.

Rasheed could not remember a time when he had not been lectured to by his father. In school, when he was a small or even adolescent ruffian, he had no doubt deserved it. But later, as he had settled down, and done well in college, he had continued to be a target for his father's dissatisfaction. And everything had got worse since he had lost his elder and favourite son, Rasheed's beloved brother, in a train accident, just a year before the loss of his wife.

'Your place is here, on the land,' his father had told him afterwards. 'I need your help. I am no longer so young. If you want to remain at Brahmpur University, you yourself will have to find the means to do so.' His father was hardly poor, Rasheed thought bitterly. He was apparently young enough to take a young wife. And – Rasheed's mind rebelled at the thought – he was even young enough to want her to give him another child. Late fatherhood was something of a tradition in the family. Baba, after all, had been in his fifties when Netaji was born.

Whenever he thought of his mother, tears came to Rasheed's eyes. She had loved him and his brother almost to excess, and she had been adored in return. His brother had delighted in the pomegranate tree and he in the lemon. Now as he looked around the courtyard, freshened and washed by the rain, he seemed to see everywhere the tangible marks of her love.

The death of her elder son had certainly hastened her own. And before dying she had made Rasheed, heartbroken as he was by his brother's death and her own impending one, promise her something that he had wanted desperately to refuse but did not have the heart or will to: a promise that was no doubt good in itself, but that had tied his life down even before he had begun to taste freedom.

8.13

RASHEED sighed as he walked up the stairs. His father was sitting on a charpoy on the roof, and his stepmother was pressing his feet.

'Adaab arz, Abba-jaan. Adaab arz, Khala,' said Rasheed. He called his stepmother Aunt.

'You have taken your time coming,' said his father curtly.

Rasheed said nothing. His young stepmother looked at him for a second, then turned away. Rasheed had never been impolite to her, but in his presence she always felt conscious of the woman whom she had supplanted, and she felt hurt that he made no attempt to reassure her or show her any affection.

'How is your friend?'

'Fine, Abba. I've left him downstairs – writing a letter, I think.'

'I don't mind him coming, but I would like to have been warned.'

'Yes, Abba. I'll try to do so next time. This came up quite suddenly.'

Rasheed's stepmother got up and said: 'I'll go and make some tea.'

When she had gone, Rasheed said quietly: 'Abba, if you can, please spare me this.'

'Spare you what?' said his father in a sudden fit of temper. He understood just what Rasheed meant, but was unwilling to admit it.

Rasheed at first decided he would say nothing, then reconsidered it. If I don't speak my mind, he thought, will I have to continue to bear the intolerable? 'What I mean,

Abba,' he said in a low voice, 'is being criticized in front of her.'

'I will say what I like to you when and where I like,' said his father, chewing his paan and looking out over the edge of the roof. 'Where are the others? Oh, yes – and you can be sure that it is not only I who criticize you and your way of life.'

'My way of life?' said Rasheed, some slight sharpness escaping into his tone of voice. He felt that it hardly suited his father to criticize his way of life.

'On your first evening in the village, you missed both the evening and the night prayer. Today when I went into the fields I wanted you to accompany me – but you were nowhere to be seen. I had something important to show you and discuss with you. Some land. What kind of influence will people think you are under? And you spend your day going around from the house of the washerman to the house of the sweeper, asking about this one's son and that one's nephew, but spending no time with your own family. It is no secret that many people here think that you are a communist.'

Rasheed reflected that this probably meant only that he loathed the poverty and injustice endemic to the village, and that he made no particular secret of it. Visiting poor families was hardly cause for reproach.

'I hope you don't think that what I am doing is wrong,' said Rasheed in a mutedly sarcastic manner.

His father said nothing for a second, then remarked with great asperity: 'Your education in Brahmpur and so on has done a lot for your confidence. You should take advice where you can get it.'

'And what advice would that be?' said Rasheed. 'The advice of the elders of this village that I should make as much money as I can as quickly as I can? Everyone here, as far as I can see, lives entirely for their appetites: for women or drink or food –'

'Enough! You've said enough!' said his father, shouting at him, but losing several of his consonants in the process.

Rasheed did not add '– or paan', as he had been about

to do. Instead he kept quiet, resolved not to say anything to his father that he might later regret, no matter how much he was provoked. In the end what Rasheed said was couched in general terms: 'Abba, I feel that one is responsible for others, not only for oneself and one's family.'

'But first of all for one's family.'

'Whatever you say, Abba,' said Rasheed, wondering why he ever returned to Debaria. 'Do you think my marriage, for instance, shows that I don't care for my family? That I didn't care for my mother or my elder brother? I feel I would have been happier – and you as well – if I had been the one who died.'

His father was silent for a minute. He was thinking of his happy-go-lucky elder son who had been content to live in Debaria and help manage the family land, who had been as strong as a lion, who had taken pride in his place as the son of a local zamindar, and who, rather than seeing everything as a problem, had spread a kind of unconcerned goodwill wherever he had gone. Then he thought of his wife – Rasheed's mother – and he drew in a slow breath.

To Rasheed he said in a gentler voice than before: 'Why do you not leave these schemes of yours – all these educational schemes, historical schemes, socialist schemes, all these schemes of improvement and redistribution, all this, this'– he waved his hand around – 'and live here and help us. Do you know what will happen to this land in a year or so when zamindari is abolished? They want to take it away from us. And then all your imaginary poultry farms and high-yielding fish-ponds and improved dairy farms with which you intend to benefit the mass of mankind will have to be built in the air, because if all that comes to pass, there certainly won't be enough land to support them. Not in our family, anyway.'

His father might have intended to speak gently, but what had come out of his utterance was inescapable scorn.

'What can I do to prevent it, Abba?' said Rasheed. 'If the land is to be justly taken over it will be taken over.'

'You could do a lot,' his father began hotly. 'For one thing, you could stop using the word "justly" for what is nothing but theft. And for another, you could talk to your friend –'

Rasheed's face became tense. He could not bear the thought of demeaning himself in this way. But he chose an argument that he thought would be more suited to his father's view of the world.

'It would not work,' he said. 'The Revenue Minister is completely unbending. He won't make individual exceptions. In fact he has let it be known that those people who try to use their influence with him or anyone else in the Revenue Department will be the first to be notified under the act.'

'Is that so?' said Rasheed's father thoughtfully. 'Well, we have not been idle ourselves ... the tehsildar knows us; and the Sub-Divisional Officer is an honest fellow, but lazy ... let's see.'

'Well, what has been happening, Abba?' asked Rasheed.

'That is what I wanted to speak to you about.... I wanted to point out certain fields.... We have to make things clear to everyone. ... As the Minister says, there cannot be exceptions....'

Rasheed frowned. He could not understand what his father was getting at.

'The idea is to move the tenants around,' said his father, cracking a betel-nut with a small brass nutcracker. 'Keep them running – this year this field, next year, that....'

'But Kachheru?' said Rasheed, thinking of the small field with the two mulberry trees – Kachheru had not planted a mango tree for fear that such presumption might tempt providence.

'What about Kachheru?' said his father, displaying an anger that he hoped would seal the lid on this uncomfortable subject. 'He will get whatever field I desire to give him. Make an exception for one chamar, and I'll have twenty rebellions. The family is agreed on this.'

'But his trees –?'

'*His* trees?' said Rasheed's father dangerously. 'The trouble is these communist ideas you drink like mother's

58

milk at the university. Let him take one under each arm and clear off if he wants to.'

A sort of sickness gripped Rasheed's heart as he looked at his father. He said softly that he was not feeling well, and asked to be excused. At first his father looked at him intently, then suddenly said, 'Go. And find out what's happening about the tea. Ah, here comes your Mamu.' His brother-in-law's large stubble-bearded face had appeared at the top of the stairs.

'I was telling Rasheed what I thought about his grand idiocies,' said Rasheed's father with a laugh just before Rasheed walked downstairs and out of sight.

'Oh, yes?' said the Bear mildly. He thought highly of his nephew and did not care for his brother-in-law's attitude towards him.

The Bear knew that Rasheed liked him too, and sometimes wondered at it. After all, he was not an educated man. But what Rasheed admired about him was that he was a man who had attained tolerance and calm without losing his zest. Nor could he ever forget that at his uncle's home he had found a refuge when he had fled from his own.

The Bear's main concern about Rasheed was that he was not looking well. He was too thin, too dark, and too gaunt; and more white had appeared in his hair than should by rights appear in the hair of any young man.

'Rasheed is good,' he said.

He received a grunt in response to this absolute statement.

'The only problem with Rasheed,' added the Bear, 'is that he worries too much about everyone, including you.'

'Oh?' said Rasheed's father, parting his lips and opening his red mouth.

'Not only you, of course,' continued his brother-in-law calmly and with great and expansive definitiveness. 'About his wife. About his children. About the village. About the country. About true religion and false religion. Also about other matters: some important, some less so. Like how one should behave towards one's fellow-man. Like how the world can be fed. Like where the mud goes when you hammer a peg into the ground. And of course the greatest question of all. . . .' The Bear paused and belched.

'What is that?' his brother-in-law could not resist asking.

'Why a goat eats green and shits black,' said the Bear.

8.14

HIS father's words burning in his ears, Rasheed walked downstairs. He forgot to enquire about the tea. He did not at first know what he should think, let alone do. He felt, above all, ashamed. Kachheru, whom he had known since he was a child, who had carried him on his back, who had stood patiently by the hand-pump while he bathed, who had served the family trustingly and unflaggingly for so many years, ploughing and weeding and fetching and carrying: it was unimaginable that his father should so indifferently have suggested shifting him about from field to field in his old age. He was no longer young; he had aged in their service. A man of settled habits, he had become deeply attached to the small plot that he had tilled for fifteen years. He had made improvements to the field, connecting it by a series of small channels to a larger ditch; he had maintained the raised paths that bordered it; he had planted the mulberry trees for shade and occasional fruit. Strictly speaking, these too may have been the land-lord's under the old dispensation, but to speak strictly here was to speak inhumanly. And under the new dispensation that was doubtless soon to come, Kachheru had rights which could not be denied. Everyone knew that he was the tiller of that field. Under the impending zamindari legislation five years of continuous tenancy was enough to establish his right to the land.

That night Rasheed could hardly sleep. He did not want to talk to anyone, not even to Maan. During the night prayer – which he did not avoid – he mouthed the words through habit but his heart remained grounded. When he lay down he felt a painful pressure in his head. After a few hours of restlessness he got up at last and walked through the lanes towards the wastelands at the far northern end of the village. Everything was still. The bullocks had ceased their work on the threshing-ground. The dogs were unperturbed by his presence. The night was starlit and warm. In their cramped thatched huts the poorest of the village slept. They cannot do it, said Rasheed to himself. They cannot do it.

To make sure of this, however, he went the next morning after breakfast to visit the village patwari, the petty government functionary who acted as record-keeper and accountant of the village and who each year painstakingly updated the land records, noting down in detail the ownership and use of every plot. Rasheed estimated that a good third of the land in the village was let out by the landlords; in his own family's case, almost two-thirds of it was. He was confident that in the patwari's thick, cloth-bound ledgers would lie irrefutable proof of Kachheru's continuous tenancy.

The lean old patwari greeted Rasheed politely, with a tired smile. He had heard of Rasheed's social rounds of the village, and felt pleased to have merited a separate visit. Shading his eyes against the sun with his hand, he asked him how his studies were going and how long he planned to stay in the village. And he offered Rasheed some sherbet. It was some time before the patwari realized that the visit was not entirely social, but this did not displease him. His government salary was low, and it was widely accepted that he needed to augment it informally. He expected that Rasheed wished to see how his family's holdings stood. He had no doubt been sent by his grandfather to check the status of their lands. And he was going to be pleased by what he saw.

The patwari went inside to bring out three ledgers, a few field-books, and two large cloth maps, about three feet by five, which covered all the land in the village. He lovingly unrolled one of them upon the wooden seating platform in his small courtyard. He stroked a corner of it gently with the side of his hand. He also fetched his spectacles, which he now placed carefully on his nose.

'Well, Khan Sahib,' he said to Rasheed, 'in a year or two these books, which I have tended as carefully as a garden, will pass into other hands. If the government has its way it will rotate us from village to village every three years. Our lives will not be worth living. And how can some outsider understand the life of the village, its history, the reality of things? Just settling down will take him at least three years.'

Rasheed made sympathetic sounds. He had put down his glass of sherbet and was trying to locate Kachheru's field on the map, which was of fine silk, slightly yellowed.

'And the people of this village have always been very good to this sinful man,' continued the patwari, with a slightly more energetic laugh. 'Ghee, grain, milk, wood ... even a few rupees now and then – the Khan Sahib's family has been particularly munificent. ... What are you looking for?'

'Our chamar Kachheru's field.'

The patwari's finger went unerringly to the spot, and came to rest in the air half an inch above it.

'But don't worry, Khan Sahib, it has all been taken care of,' he said.

Rasheed looked at him questioningly.

The patwari was a little surprised that his competence or industry was being called into doubt. He wordlessly rolled up the silken map and unfurled the map of cruder cloth. This, his working map, which he took with him on his recording rounds, was slightly mud-stained, and displayed a denser patchwork of fields, covered with names and numbers and notations of various kinds in black and in red, all in Urdu. For a while he gazed at it, then went to the ledgers and the cracked and battered field-books, opened a few of them to the appropriate pages, consulted them alternately a few times, and with a serious and slightly injured look, nodded at Rasheed. 'See for yourself,' he said.

Rasheed looked at the columns and entries and measurements, landholding numbers and plot numbers and serial numbers, records of land type and land condition and land use; but, as the patwari well suspected, he could make nothing out of the esoteric jumble.

'But –'

'Khan Sahib,' said the mollified patwari, turning his palms upwards in a gesture of openness. 'It would appear from my records that the person who has been cultivating that field and those around it for the last several years has been yourself.'

'What?' cried Rasheed, staring first at the patwari's smiling face, and then at the entry at which his finger was now pointing; again it rested a little above the surface of the page, like the body of a water-insect.

'Name of cultivator as given in khatauni register: Abdur Rasheed Khan,' read out the patwari.

'How long has this been the case?' asked Rasheed with difficulty, his mind racing almost too fast for his tongue. He looked painfully agitated and distressed.

Even now the patwari, who was not by any means a stupid man, suspected nothing. He said simply: 'Ever since the land reform legislation became a possible threat, and your esteemed grandfather and father expressed their concern about eventualities, your servant has been diligently safeguarding your family's interests. The lands of the family have been nominally subdivided among the various members, and all of you are down in my records as owner-cultivators. It is the safest way. Large individual landholdings look too suspicious. Of course, you have been away in Brahmpur studying, and these small matters are not of interest to a scholar of history –'

'They are,' said Rasheed grimly. 'How much of our land is let out to tenants?' he asked.

'None,' said the patwari, indicating his ledgers with a casual gesture.

'None?' said Rasheed. 'But everyone knows we have both sharecroppers and rent-paying tenants –'

'Hired employees,' corrected the patwari. 'And in the future they will very wisely be rotated from field to field.'

'But Kachheru, for example' – burst out Rasheed – 'everyone knows that he's had that field for years. You yourself understood immediately what I meant by Kachheru's field.'

'It's a manner of speaking,' said the patwari, amused by Rasheed's attempt to play the devil's advocate. 'If I were to refer to Khan Sahib's university, it would not mean that Brahmpur University belonged to you – or that you had been there for five years.' He gave a short laugh, inviting participation; but when Rasheed did not respond, he continued: 'From my records it appears that, yes, Kachheru, son of Mangalu chamar, did sharecrop the field on occasion, but never for a period of five years without a break. There has always been an interruption –'

'You say the field is now nominally mine?' said Rasheed.

'Yes.'

'I want you to register a change of ownership to Kachheru.'

It was the patwari's turn to look shocked. He looked at Rasheed as if he had taken leave of his senses. He was about to say that the Khan Sahib was, of course, joking, when he realized with a start that he was not.

'Don't worry,' said Rasheed. 'I'll pay you your standard – what should I say? – your standard fee.'

The patwari licked his lips with anxiety.

'But your family? Are they all –'

'Are you questioning my credentials in this matter?'

'Oh no, Khan Sahib, heaven forbid –'

'Our family has discussed this matter at length,' said Rasheed carefully. 'And that is why I am here.' He paused. 'If the mutation of ownership cannot be performed quickly or involves other legal documents, it would be good if the tenancy records for this plot were made to reflect, well, the reality of things. Yes, that is a better method and will cause less disturbance. Make it clear, please, that the chamar has been a continuous tenant.'

The patwari nodded obediently. 'As Huzoor commands,' he said quietly.

Rasheed tried to hide his contempt as he took out some money.

'Here is a little something in advance to express my appreciation. As a student of history, I have been most impressed by the meticulousness of these records. And, as a landlord, I must agree with you that the government's policy of rotating patwaris is a great pity.'

'Some more sherbet, Khan Sahib? Or may I offer you something a little more substantial? Life in the city has worn you down ... you are looking very thin. ...'

'No thank you,' said Rasheed. 'I must go. But I will call again in a couple of weeks. That should be sufficient time, shouldn't it?'

'It should,' agreed the patwari.

'Good, then. Khuda haafiz.'

'Khuda haafiz, Khan Sahib,' said the patwari softly. And indeed God would have to protect Rasheed from the trouble he had just plunged himself – and not just himself – into.

Part Nine

'YOU'RE looking very thin, darling,' said Mrs Rupa Mehra to Kalpana Gaur – who was large-boned and and vivacious, but less substantial than usual. Mrs Rupa Mehra had just arrived in Delhi in search of a prospective husband for Lata. Since her sons had proven hopeless, she would get Kalpana Gaur, who was 'like a daughter' to her, to deliver the goods.

'Yes, the silly girl has been ill,' said her father, who was impatient with illness. 'God knows how at such a young age she manages to contract all these illnesses. It is some kind of 'flu this time: 'flu at the height of summer – very silly. No one goes for walks nowadays. My niece never walked; too lazy. She got appendicitis, had to be operated on, and, naturally, took a long time to recover. When I was in Lahore we would get up every morning at five, and all of us – from my father down to my six-year-old brother – would go walking for an hour. That was how we kept up our health.'

Kalpana Gaur turned to Mrs Rupa Mehra: 'Now you will need tea and rest.' Snuffling a bit, she got busy with the servants and the luggage, and paid off the tonga-wallah. Mrs Rupa Mehra protested, then submitted. 'You must stay with us for a month,' continued Kalpana. 'How can you go travelling in this heat? How is Savita? When is the baby due exactly? And Lata? Arun? Varun? I haven't heard from you in months. We keep reading about the floods in Calcutta, but in Delhi there isn't a cloud in the sky. Everyone is praying that the monsoons will come on time. Let me just tell the servants to get things ready, then you must tell us all your news. Fried tomatoes as usual for breakfast tomorrow? Daddy hasn't been too well, you know. Heart.' She looked indulgently at her father, who frowned back.

'I have been perfectly well,' said the old man dismissively. 'Raghubir was five years younger than me and I'm still going strong. Now you sit down. You must be tired. And give us everyone's news. There's nothing of interest in this.' He indicated the newspaper. 'Just the usual war-mongering with Pakistan, flood havoc in Assam, leaders leaving the Congress Party, gas workers on strike in Calcutta ... and as a result they can't even hold the chemistry practical exams in the university! Oh, but you've just come from Calcutta, so you know all that. And so on and so on. Do you know, if I ran a newspaper with nothing but good news – so-and-so gave birth to a healthy baby, such-and-such a country remained at peace with its neighbour, this river behaved well and that crop refused to be eaten by locusts – I believe people would buy it just to put themselves in good spirits.'

'No, Daddy, they wouldn't.' Kalpana turned her full but pretty face towards Mrs Rupa Mehra. 'Now why didn't you tell us you were coming? We would have come to fetch you from the station.'

'But I did. I sent a telegram.'

'Oh – it'll probably come today. Things have got so bad with the postal service even though they've just put up the rates.'

'It'll take time. They have a reasonable Minister in charge,' said her father. 'The young are always so impatient.'

'Anyway, why didn't you send us a letter?' asked Kalpana.

'I decided to come suddenly. It's Lata,' said Mrs Rupa Mehra in a rush. 'I want you to find her a boy at once. A suitable boy. She is getting involved with unsuitable boys, and I cannot have that.'

Kalpana reflected on her own attachments to unsuitable boys: on an engagement that had broken up because her friend had suddenly changed his mind; on her father's opposition to another. She was still unmarried, which made her rather sad whenever she thought about it. She said: 'Khatri, of course? One or two?'

Mrs Rupa Mehra gave Kalpana a worried smile. 'Two, please. I will stir it myself. Actually, I should have this saccharine but after a journey one can always make an exception. Of course khatri would be best. I think that one's own community creates a sense of comfort. But proper khatris: Seth, Khanna, Kapoor, Mehra – no, not Mehra preferably –'

Kalpana was virtually but not quite out of marriageable range herself; it was perhaps a measure of Mrs Rupa Mehra's desperation that she had decided to entrust such an enterprise to her. Her decision, however, was not un-based on reason. Kalpana knew young people, and Mrs Rupa Mehra knew no one else in Delhi who did. Kalpana was very fond of Lata, who was several years younger than her. And since it was only the khatri community that was to be dredged for prospective candidates, it was not likely that Kalpana herself, heaven forbid, should perceive a conflict of interest – especially since she was not a khatri but a brahmin.

'Don't worry, Ma, I don't know any Mehras except you,' said Kalpana Gaur. She beamed broadly and continued:

'I do know some Khannas and Kapoors in Delhi, though. I'll introduce them to you. Once they see you, they'll know that your daughter's bound to be good-looking.'

'I was much more good-looking before the car accident,' said Mrs Rupa Mehra, stirring her tea and looking through the window – towards a gardenia bush, dry with summer dust.

'Do you have a photograph of Lata? A recent one?'

'Of course.' There was very little that Mrs Rupa Mehra's black bag did not contain. She had a very simple black-and-white photograph of Lata with no jewellery or make-up; there were some flowers – a few phlox – in her hair. There was even a photograph of Lata as a baby, though it was unlikely that this would have impressed the family of a potential groom. 'But first you must get well, darling,' she said to Kalpana. 'I came with no warning at all. You asked me to come at Divali or Christmas but time and tide wait for no man.'

'I'm perfectly well,' said Kalpana Gaur, blowing her nose. 'And this problem will make me better.'

'She's quite right,' said her father. 'Half her illness is

laziness. If she isn't careful, she'll die young, like her mother.'

Mrs Rupa Mehra smiled weakly.

'Or your husband,' added Mr Gaur. 'He was a foolish man if ever there was one. Climbing the mountains of Bhutan with a weak heart – and overworking – for whom? For the British and their railways.' He sounded resentful, as he missed his old friend.

Mrs Rupa Mehra reflected that they were everyone's railways, and that what the late Raghubir Mehra was keen on was the work as such and not who his paymasters were. Everyone who was a government servant could be said to have served the British.

'He worked hard, but for the action, not for the fruits of the action. He was a true karma-yogi,' said Mrs Rupa Mehra sadly. The late Raghubir Mehra, though he did work excessively hard, would have been amused at this elevated description of himself.

'Go in and see to the guest room,' said Mr Gaur. 'And make sure that there are flowers in it.'

The days passed pleasantly. When Mr Gaur returned from his general store, they talked of old times. At night, with the jackals howling behind the house, and the scent of gardenias in her room, Mrs Rupa Mehra would think back anxiously on the day's events. She could not summon Lata to Delhi and out of harm's way without having something tangible in hand. So far, for all Kalpana's efforts, she had found no one suitable. She often thought of her husband, who would have allayed her fears – either by getting angry with her or by teasing her and then making up. Before she went to sleep she looked at the photograph of him she kept in her bag, and that night she dreamed of him playing rummy with the children in their saloon car.

In the morning Mrs Rupa Mehra woke up even before the Gaurs to chant in a soft voice her verses from the Bhagavad Gita:

'You grieve for those beyond grief,
and you speak words of insight;

but learned men do not grieve
for the dead or the living.

Never have I not existed
nor you, nor these kings;
and never in the future
shall we cease to exist.

Just as the embodied self
enters childhood, youth, and old age,
so does it enter another body;
this does not confound a steadfast man.

Contacts with matter make us feel
heat and cold, pleasure and pain.
Arjuna, you must learn to endure
fleeting things – they come and go!

When these cannot torment a man,
when suffering and joy are equal
for him and he has courage,
he is fit for immortality.

Nothing of nonbeing comes to be,
nor does being cease to exist;
the boundary between these two
is seen by men who see reality.

Indestructible is this presence
that pervades all this;
no one can destroy
this unchanging reality....'

But it was not the all-pervading essence of reality that
clutched at Mrs Rupa Mehra's consciousness but the loved
particularities that she had lost or that were losable. What
body was her husband in now? If he was born again in
human form – would she even recognize him if he passed
by her in the street? What did it mean when they said of

the sacrament of marriage that they would be bound together for seven lives? If they had no memory of who they had been, what use was such knowledge? For all she knew, this last marriage might have been her seventh one. Emotion made her literal; she longed for tangible assurance. The soothing Sanskrit of the small, green, cloth-bound volume passed through her lips, but, while it gave her peace – tears rarely came to her eyes while she was reciting the Gita – it answered none of her questions. And while ancient wisdom so often proved unconsoling, photography, that cruel modern art, helped to ensure that even the image of her husband's face would not grow dim with time.

9.2

MEANWHILE, Kalpana tried her best to ferret out likely prospects for Lata. In all she found seven, which was not bad at such short notice. Three were friends or acquaintances, three were friends or acquaintances of friends or acquaintances, and one was the friend of a friend of a friend.

The first, a lively and friendly young man, had been with her at university, and had acted with her in plays. He was rejected by Mrs Rupa Mehra as being too rich. 'You know our circumstances, Kalpana,' said Mrs Rupa Mehra.

'But he is sure not to want a dowry. He's very flush,' said Kalpana.

'They are far too well-to-do,' said Mrs Rupa Mehra with decision. 'There's no point talking about it. Even their normal expectations for the wedding will be too high. We'll have to feed a thousand people. Of those, probably seven hundred will be guests from their side. And we'll have to put them up, and give all the women saris.'

'But he's a good boy,' persisted Kalpana; 'at least look at him.'

Her 'flu had improved, and she was as energetic as ever.

Mrs Rupa Mehra shook her head. 'If I liked him it

would only upset me. He may be good, but he lives with his whole family. Lata will always be compared with the other daughters-in-law – she'll be the poor relation. I won't have it. She won't be happy.'

And so the first prospect was excluded.

The second, whom they went to see, spoke good English and seemed a sober fellow. But he was too tall. He would tower over Lata. He would not do. 'If at first you don't succeed, try, try again,' said Mrs Rupa Mehra to Kalpana, though she herself had begun to feel disheartened.

The third boy was also problematic.

'Too dark, too dark,' said Mrs Rupa Mehra.

'But Meenakshi –' began Kalpana Gaur.

'Don't talk to me about Meenakshi,' said Mrs Rupa Mehra in a tone that brooked no argument.

'Ma, let Lata decide what she thinks of him.'

'I will not have black grandchildren,' said Mrs Rupa Mehra.

'You said exactly that when Arun got married – and see how fond you are of Aparna. And she isn't even dark –'

Mrs Rupa Mehra said: 'Aparna is different.' After a pause she thought of something else. 'The exception proves the rule,' she added.

Kalpana Gaur said: 'Lata isn't all that fair herself.'

'All the more reason,' said Mrs Rupa Mehra. What this meant was unclear; what was clear was that her mind had been made up.

The fourth prospect was the son of a jeweller who had a prosperous shop in Connaught Circus. Within five minutes of their meeting his parents mentioned a dowry of two lakh rupees. Mrs Rupa Mehra stared at Kalpana in astonishment.

When they got out of the house, Kalpana said: 'Honestly, Ma, I didn't know they were like that. I don't even know the boy myself. A friend simply told me that they had a son for whom they were seeking a bride. I'd never have put you through all that if I'd known.'

'If my husband was alive,' said Mrs Rupa Mehra, still smarting, 'he might have been Chairman of the Railway

Board, and we'd never have to lower out heads before anyone, certainly not people like these.'

The fifth candidate, though decent enough, could not speak English properly. Try, try again.

The sixth was wanting – harmless, quite pleasant, but slightly deficient. He smiled innocently throughout the interview which Mrs Rupa Mehra conducted with his parents.

Mrs Rupa Mehra, thinking of Robert Bruce and the spider, was convinced that the seventh man would be the one for her daughter.

The seventh, however, had whisky on his breath and his uncertain laugh reminded her uncomfortably of Varun.

Mrs Rupa Mehra was deeply discouraged and, having exhausted her contacts in Delhi, decided that Kanpur, Lucknow, and Banaras (in each of which she or her late husband had relatives) would have to be dredged before she returned to try her luck in Brahmpur (where, however, lurked the undesirable Kabir). But what if Kanpur, Lucknow, and Banaras proved equally fruitless?

By now Kalpana had suffered a relapse and fallen quite seriously ill (though the doctors were puzzled about the diagnosis; she had stopped sneezing, but seemed to be weak and sleepy all the time). Mrs Rupa Mehra decided to spend a few days nursing her before she left Delhi for the rest of her slightly premature Annual Trans-India Rail Pilgrimage.

9.3

ONE evening, a rather short but energetic young man appeared at the door and was greeted by Mr Gaur.

'Good evening, Mr Gaur – I wonder if you remember me. I'm Haresh Khanna.'

'Oh, yes?' said Mr Gaur.

'I knew Kalpana at St Stephen's. We studied English together.'

'Weren't you the one who went to England to study physics or something? I don't think I've seen you in years.'

'Shoes.'

'Oh. Shoes. I see.'

'Is Kalpana in?'

'Well, yes – but she isn't very well.' Mr Gaur pointed his stick at the tonga, which had a suitcase on it together with a briefcase and a bedding roll. 'Were you thinking of staying here?' he asked, rather alarmed.

'No – no – not at all. My father lives near Neel Darvaza. I've come straight from the station. I work in Cawnpore. I thought I'd drop by and see Kalpana before I went to Baoji's house. But if she isn't well.... What is the matter? Nothing serious, I hope?' Haresh smiled, and his eyes disappeared.

Mr Gaur frowned at him for a few seconds, then spoke.

'The doctors can't agree. But she keeps yawning. Health is the most precious possession, young man.' (He had forgotten Haresh's name.) 'Don't forget that.' He paused. 'Well, come in.'

Even though her father had been surprised by his sudden, unannounced arrival, Kalpana, when she entered the drawing room, could not have been more happy than to see Haresh. They had corresponded off and on for a year or so after they left college, but time and distance had taken their toll, and the crush she had had on him had slowly faded. Then had come her unhappy affair and broken engagement. Haresh had heard of this through friends, and he told himself that the next time he was in Delhi he would go over and say hello.

'You!' said Kalpana Gaur, reviving.

'Me!' said Haresh, pleased with his restorative powers.

'You're every bit as good-looking as when I used to admire you during Dr Mathai's lectures on Byron.'

'And you're just as charming as when all of us were laying ourselves and our cloaks under your feet.'

A slight tinge of sadness entered the smile on Kalpana Gaur's face. Since she had been one of the very few girls at St Stephen's, she had been in natural demand. She was quite pretty too in those days; indeed, perhaps she still was. But for some reason none of her boyfriends remained boyfriends for long. She had a very decided personality and fairly soon took to telling them what they should do with their lives and studies and work. She began to mother them or perhaps brother them (since she was something of a tomboy) – and this sooner or later took the edge off their romantic excitement. They even began to find her vivacity overpowering, and sooner or later edged away from her – with guilt on their side and pain on hers. This was a great pity, for Kalpana Gaur was a lively, affectionate, and intelligent woman, and deserved some recompense for the help and happiness she gave others.

In Haresh's case, she had never really stood a chance. He was very fond of her at college, but his heart was then – as it was now – with Simran, a Sikh girl, the sweetheart of his adolescence whose family was determined that she should not marry him because he was not a Sikh.

Mutual compliments having been exchanged, Haresh and Kalpana started talking about the old days even before catching up on what had happened to them since they had last written to each other two years ago. Mr Gaur had gone inside; young people, he found, had remarkably little of interest to say.

Suddenly Kalpana Gaur got up. 'Do you remember my good-looking aunt?' She sometimes referred to Mrs Rupa Mehra as her aunt although, strictly speaking, she was nothing of the kind.

'No,' said Haresh. 'I don't think I've ever met her. But I remember you used to talk about her.'

'Well, she's staying with us at the moment.'

'I'd like to meet her,' said Haresh.

Kalpana went to fetch Mrs Rupa Mehra, who had been writing letters in her room.

She was dressed in a brown-and-white cotton sari, slightly crushed – she had been resting half an hour before – and Haresh thought her very fine-looking. His eyes crinkled into a smile as he stood up; Kalpana introduced them.

'Khanna?' said Mrs Rupa Mehra, wheels whirring.

The young man, she noted, was well dressed, in a cream-coloured silk shirt and a pair of fawn trousers. He had a pleasant, squarish face. And he was fairly fair.

Mrs Rupa Mehra for once didn't say much during the ensuing conversation. Although Haresh had been to Brahmpur just a few months ago, it didn't come up, and nor did any common names, so there was no obvious point of entry for her. Anyway, Kalpana Gaur had steered the conversation towards Haresh's recent history, and Mrs Rupa Mehra listened with growing interest. Haresh, for his part, was happy to regale Kalpana with some of his recent achievements and exploits. He was an energetic man, with a great deal of optimism and self-confidence, and was not hindered by too delicate a sense of modesty.

Haresh found his work at the Cawnpore Leather & Footwear Company fascinating, and assumed that everyone else would too. 'I've only been at CLFC a year, but I'm establishing a whole new department – and I've got them orders that they didn't have the know-how or the initiative to get themselves. But there's no future in it, that's the trouble. Ghosh is the top man, and it's all family owned, and I can't aspire to anything really. All of them are Bengalis.'

'Bengali entrepreneurs?' said Kalpana Gaur.

'Sounds odd, doesn't it?' agreed Haresh. 'Ghosh is an impressive man, though. Tall, self-made. He has a construction business that he runs from Bombay. This is only one of his interests.'

Mrs Rupa Mehra nodded in approval. She liked the idea of self-made people.

'Anyway, I'm not a political fellow,' continued Haresh, 'and there's far too much politics among the officers at CLFC. Far too much office politics and not enough work. And three hundred and fifty a month is not much for the kind of work I'm doing. It's just that I had to find the first job I could when I came back from England. I was broke, so I had no choice.' The memory did not appear to disturb him.

Mrs Rupa Mehra looked at Haresh anxiously.

He smiled. His eyes now crinkled up almost completely. He had once been promised ten rupees by his college friends to keep his eyes open when he smiled, and he had not been able to earn it.

Mrs Rupa Mehra couldn't help smiling back.

'So I've come to Delhi not just on work but also to look around.' Haresh passed his hand across his forehead. 'I've brought all my certificates and testimonials and so on, and I have an interview with a firm here. Of course Baoji thinks I should stick with a sure thing, and Uncle Umesh doesn't think much of anything I do, but I'm determined to give it a try. So, Kalpana, do you know of any jobs available in my line? Anyone whom I should see in Delhi? I'll be staying at Neel Darvaza with the family as usual.'

'I don't, but if I hear of anything that might suit you –' began Kalpana. Then, in a sudden flash of inspiration, she said: 'Listen, do you really have your testimonials and so on here?'

'They're in the tonga outside. I came straight from the station.'

'You did?' Kalpana beamed at Haresh.

Haresh threw up his hands in a gesture that could have meant that Kalpana's charm was an irresistible beacon to the weary traveller, or merely that he had decided to get long-deferred social business over with before he got caught up with the family and the world.

'Well, then, let's see them; fetch them.'

'Fetch them?'

'Yes, of course, Haresh. We want to see them even if you don't want to show them.' Kalpana gestured towards Mrs Rupa Mehra, who nodded quite vigorously.

But Haresh was only too willing to show off his certificates. He got his briefcase from the tonga, and brought out all his diplomas from the Midlands College of Technology together with a couple of glowing testimonials, one of them from the Principal himself. Kalpana Gaur read out several of these, and Mrs Rupa Mehra listened with close attention. From time to time Haresh mentioned a relevant fact or two, for example that he had topped the list in the examination for pattern-cutting or had won some medal or other. He was not at all bashful about his achievements.

At the end of it, Mrs Rupa Mehra said to Haresh: 'You should be very proud.'

She would have liked to talk with them further, but she had to go out that evening for dinner and had not yet changed out of her crushed sari. Excusing herself, she got up. As she was about to leave the room, Haresh said: 'Mrs Mehra, it's been a great pleasure to meet you. But are you sure we haven't met before?'

Mrs Rupa Mehra said: 'I never forget a face. I am sure I would have remembered if we had met.' She left the room, looking pleased but slightly preoccupied.

Haresh rubbed his forehead. He felt convinced that he had seen her before, but he couldn't remember where.

9.4

WHEN Mrs Rupa Mehra returned from dinner, she said to Kalpana Gaur:

'Of all the boys we have met, Kalpana, I like that young man the most. Why didn't you introduce me to him before? Was there some, well, particular reason?'

'Well, no, Ma, I didn't even think of him. He just happened to arrive from Kanpur.'

'Oh, yes, Kanpur. Of course.'

'Incidentally, he was much taken by you. He thinks you're very attractive. He said you were "strikingly good-looking".'

'You are a very naughty girl to call me your good-looking aunt.'

'But very truthful.'

'What does your father think of him?'

'My father only met him for a minute. But you really liked him?' continued Kalpana, with a speculative expression.

Mrs Rupa Mehra had indeed liked Haresh. She had

liked the fact that he was energetic, that he was independent of his family (though affectionate towards them), and that he clearly took great care with his appearance. Nowadays, many boys looked so scruffy. And one crucial point in Haresh's favour was his name. Being a Khanna, he was bound to be a khatri.

'We must fix up a meeting,' she said. 'Is he – you know –'

'Available?'

'Yes.'

'Well, he was in love with a Sikh girl once,' said Kalpana Gaur quietly. 'I don't know what came of it.'

'Oh. Why didn't you ask him about it when I left? You talked like old friends.'

'I wasn't sure at the time that you were so interested in him,' said Kalpana Gaur, her face reddening a little.

'I am. He might be just the boy for Lata, don't you think? I'll telegram her to come to Delhi immediately. Immediately.' Mrs Rupa Mehra furrowed her forehead. 'Do you know Meenakshi's brother?'

'No. I only met Meenakshi at the wedding –'

'He's causing no end of worry to me.' Mrs Rupa Mehra clicked her tongue.

'Isn't he the poet, Amit Chatterji?' asked Kalpana. 'He's quite famous, you know, Ma.'

'Famous! All he does is sit in his father's house and stare out of the upstairs window. A young man should do a job and earn his living.' Mrs Rupa Mehra enjoyed the poetry of Patience Strong, Wilhelmina Stitch, and various other writers, but that the creation of it involved any activity – or necessary inactivity – she found incomprehensible. 'Lata has been seeing far too much of him.'

'You're not saying that there's a chance –' laughed Kalpana, looking at Mrs Rupa Mehra's expression. 'Well, Ma, at least let him write a couple of poems to Lata.'

'I am not saying anything and I am not speculating,' said Mrs Rupa Mehra, upset by the thought of the developments in Calcutta. 'I am tired now. Why must I run from city to city? I think I must have eaten too much, and I have forgotten to take my homoeopathic medicine.' She got up, turned to speak again, thought better of it, and picked up her big black bag.

'Goodnight, Ma,' said Kalpana. 'I've put a jug of water by your bed. If there's anything you want, please tell me – Ovaltine or Horlicks or anything. And I'll get in touch with Haresh tomorrow.'

'No, darling, you must rest now. It's very late, and you are not very well.'

'Actually, Ma, I'm feeling a lot better than I felt earlier today. Haresh and Lata – Lata and Haresh. Well, no harm trying.'

But the next morning, Kalpana Gaur was not feeling at all well, and spent the day listless and yawning. And the day after, when she sent a message to Neel Darvaza, she found that Haresh Khanna had already returned to Kanpur.

9.5

IN the train from Calcutta to Kanpur Lata had plenty of time to wonder about her sudden summons. The telegram from Mrs Rupa Mehra had been cryptic, as the best telegrams are, and had required her to come to Kanpur in two days' time.

It was a day journey, though a long one. Arun had got up early to drop her at Howrah Station. Howrah Bridge was uncrowded. When they got to the station with its familiar smell of smoke, urine and fish, Arun made sure she was well-settled in her ladies' compartment.

'What'll you read on the way?'

'*Emma*.'

'Not like our saloons, is it?'

'No,' said Lata with a smile.

'I've telegrammed Brahmpur, so Pran ought to be at the station. Maybe Savita too. Look out for them.'

'All right, Arun Bhai.'

'Now, be good. It won't be the same without you at home. Aparna will be much more difficult.'

'I'll write ... and, Arun Bhai, when you reply, please type.'

Arun laughed, then yawned.

The train departed on time.

Lata was happy once again to see the green and moist countryside of Bengal, which she loved – with its palms and banana-trees, emerald fields of rice and village ponds. After a while, however, the landscape changed into a dry and hilly tract with small ravines over which the train clanked in a different voice.

The land became drier still as they moved westwards into the plains. Dusty fields and poor villages passed by between the telegraph poles and furlong markers. The heat was intense, and Lata's mind began to wander. She would have been happy to stay in Calcutta for the rest of her holidays, but her mother sometimes took it into her head to insist on companionship for her Rail-Pilgrimages – usually when she felt ill or lonely somewhere along the route. She wondered which it was this time.

The other women in her compartment were shy with each other at first, and only talked to those they were travelling with, but as time passed, through the catalysis of a rather charming baby, they established a web of conversation. Young men from their families stopped by to enquire whether everything was all right when the train halted at a station, brought cups of tea in earthenware cups, and replenished the earthenware pitchers with water, for the day was getting even hotter, and the fans functioned only about half the time.

A woman in a burqa, having established which direction was west, rolled out a small prayer-rug and began to pray.

Lata thought of Kabir, and she felt both miserable and – in a curious way that she could not understand – happy. She loved him still – it was pointless to pretend otherwise. Had Calcutta had any effect at all in diminishing what she felt for him? Certainly, his letter had not given her any great hope of the strength of his feelings for her. Was there anything at all to be said for loving and not being loved equally in return? She didn't think so. Why, then, did she smile when she thought of him?

Lata read her *Emma*, and was grateful to be able to. If she had been travelling with her mother, they would have formed the central node in the conversational web, and everyone in the compartment would by now have heard about Bentsen Pryce, Lata's brilliance in her studies, the details of Mrs Rupa Mehra's rheumatism, her false teeth and former beauty, the saloon-sheltered glory of her late husband's inspection tours, the harshness of fate, and the wisdom of acceptance and resignation.

Sootily, fitfully, the train made its way along the great, burning plain of the Ganga.

At Patna a swarm of locusts, a mile long, darkened the sky.

Dust and flies and soot somehow succeeded in entering the compartment even when the glass panes were pulled down.

The Brahmpur telegram could not have arrived, because neither Savita nor Pran was at the platform to meet her. Lata had been looking forward to seeing them, if only for the fifteen minutes that the train stopped at Brahmpur. As the train pulled out of Brahmpur Junction she felt a disproportionate sadness.

As the whistle of the train suddenly wailed out, she caught in the distance a glimpse of the roofs of the university.

> Always I am weeping, weeping.
> In your heart my image keeping.

If, for example, he had appeared at the station – say, in the casual clothes he had worn when he had been with her on the boat, smiling with his old friendliness, arguing with a porter about the rate he was charging – suppose he too had been going to Kanpur – or at least as far as Banaras or Allahabad – Lata felt that her heart would have leapt with happiness at the sound of his voice and the sight of his face

– and any misunderstanding between them would have vanished in a single puff of steam, a single turn of the wheels.

Lata looked down at her book.

'My poor dear Isabella,' said he, fondly taking her hand, and interrupting, for a few moments, her busy labours for some one of her five children – 'How long it is, how terribly long since you were here! And how tired you must be after your journey! You must go to bed early, my dear – and I recommend a little gruel to you before you go. – You and I will have a nice basin of gruel together. My dear Emma, suppose we all have a little gruel.'

An egret flew over a field towards a ditch.

A sickly smell of molasses rose from a sugar-cane factory.

The train stopped for an hour at a tiny station for no particular reason.

Beggars begged at the barred windows of the compartment.

When the train crossed the Ganga at Banaras, she threw a two-anna coin for luck out of the barred window. It hit a girder, then spun downwards into the river.

At Allahabad the train crossed over to the right bank again, and Lata threw another coin out.

> Ganga darshan is so nice.
> I have now completed twice.

She told herself that she was in danger of becoming an honorary Chatterji.

She began to hum Raag Sarang, then later drifted into Multani.

She rejected her sandwiches and bought some samosas and tea at the next station.

She hoped her mother was well. She yawned. She put *Emma* aside. She thought once again of Kabir.

She drowsed off for an hour. When she woke she found she had been leaning against the shoulder of an old woman in a white sari, who smiled at her. She had been keeping the flies off Lata's face.

A troop of monkeys were raiding a dusty mango tree in an orchard at dusk, while three men stood below, trying to shoo them off with stones and lathis.

Soon it was night. It was still warm.

In a while the train slowed down once more, and the word *Cawnpore* greeted her in black on a large yellow sign on the platform. Her mother was there, and her uncle Mr Kakkar, both smiling; but there was a look of strain on her mother's face.

9.6

THEY went home by car. Kakkar Phupha (as Lata called her father's sister's husband) was a successful accountant with a cheery manner.

When they were alone, Mrs Rupa Mehra told Lata about Haresh: 'a very suitable prospect'.

Lata was speechless for a moment. Then in a tone of disbelief she said: 'You treat me like a child.'

Mrs Rupa Mehra wavered for a few seconds between suppression and placation, then murmured: 'What is the harm, darling? I am not forcing anything on you. And day-after we will be leaving for Lucknow anyway and then back to Brahmpur the day after that.'

Lata looked at her mother, amazed that she should defend herself.

'And it was for this – not because you were unwell or needed my help – that I was summoned from Calcutta.' The tone of Lata's voice was so unloving that Mrs Rupa Mehra's nose reddened. But she pulled herself together and said:

'Darling, I do need your help. Getting you married is not easy. And the boy is of our community.'

'I don't care what community he belongs to. I am not going to see him. I should never have left Calcutta.'

'But he is a khatri – from U.P. originally,' protested her mother.

This cast-iron argument had no effect on Lata. She said:

'Ma, please. I know all your prejudices and I share none of them. You bring me up one way and you act in another.'

To this righteous attack her mother merely murmured: 'You know, Lata, I have nothing against – against Mohammedans as such. It is only your future I am concerned about.' Mrs Rupa Mehra had been expecting an outburst of sorts, and, with an effort, remained emollient.

Lata was silent. O, Kabir, Kabir, she thought.

'Why aren't you eating anything, dear? It's been such a long journey.'

'I'm not hungry.'

'Yes, you are,' insisted Mrs Rupa Mehra.

'Ma, you have brought me here under false pretences,' said Lata, unpacking her suitcase and not looking at her mother. 'You must have known that if you had given your reasons on the telegram I would never have come.'

'Darling, it isn't sensible to add words to a telegram. Telegrams have become terribly expensive these days. Unless of course you send a stock phrase like "Best wishes on a safe and pleasant journey" or "Heartiest Bijoya greetings" or some such thing. And he is such a nice boy. You'll see.'

Lata was so exasperated that a couple of tears squeezed their way into her eyes. She shook her head, even angrier now with herself, her mother, and the unknown Haresh.

'Ma, I hope I am not like you when I am your age,' she said passionately.

Mrs Rupa Mehra's nose immediately reddened again.

'If you don't believe me, at least believe Kalpana. I met him at her house. The boy is Kalpana's friend. He has studied in England and has excellent results. He is good-looking, and he is interested in meeting you. If you are not interested in meeting him, how can I show my face to Kalpana who went through all the trouble of arranging this? Even Mr Gaur approves of him. If you don't believe me, read this letter from her. It's for you.'

'I don't need to read it,' said Lata. 'You can tell me what's in it.'

'How do you know I've read it?' said Mrs Rupa Mehra indignantly. 'Don't you trust your own mother?'

Lata stood the empty suitcase in a corner. 'Ma, there is guilt written all over your face,' she said. 'But I'll read it all the same.'

Kalpana's letter was brief and affectionate. Just as she had told Haresh that Lata was like a sister to her, she now told Lata that Haresh was like a brother to her. Kalpana, it seemed, had written to Haresh. Haresh had written back, saying that he couldn't return to Delhi because he was required at the factory and had taken leave only recently, but that he would be very happy to meet Lata and Mrs Rupa Mehra in Kanpur. He had added that despite his affection for Simran, he had now come to realize that there was no hope for him there. As a result, he was not averse to meeting other girls. At the moment his life consisted of little but work; India was not England, where it was easy to get to know girls on their own.

As for a dowry [continued Kalpana in her curvaceously looped script], he isn't the kind of man to ask for it, and there is no one to ask for it on his behalf. He is very attached to his father – his foster-father, actually, though he calls him Baoji – but (unlike his foster-brothers) he has established his independence early enough. He ran away from home once when he was fifteen, but you should not hold that against him. If the two of you like each other, you will not have to live with your in-laws. The joint family lives in Neel Darvaza in Delhi, and though I have been there once and like most of them, I know that that environment would not suit you, given the way you have been brought up.

I can tell you honestly, Lata, that I have always liked Haresh. At one time I even had a slight crush on him –

we were in the same class at St Stephen's. When my father read his recent letter, he said: 'Well, it is a straightforward reply. At least he makes no bones about his earlier affections.' And certainly, Ma seems set on him. She has been getting more and more worried lately. Perhaps this is the answer to her dreams as well as yours. At any rate, Lata, whatever you do or don't do finally, do meet him, and don't be annoyed with your mother, who has been going frantic trying to ensure your happiness (as she sees it).

Ma will have told you about my health. If I were not myself I would be amused by my own symptoms, which range from yawning to spells of dizziness to hot spots on the soles of my feet. These hot spots are particularly puzzling. Your mother swears by some Doctor Nuruddin in Calcutta, but he sounds like a quack. And anyway, I can't travel. Why don't you visit me after Kanpur and we'll play Monopoly, just as we used to as children? It has been so long since I last saw you. My love to you and to Ma. Do pay some attention to her advice; I think that you are very lucky to be her daughter. Please report to me the moment you have something to report. Lying in bed all I can listen to is this painful classical music on the radio, which I know you don't think is painful, and the gupshup of empty-headed friends. A visit from you would do me good....

Something in the tone of the letter made Lata think of the time at Sophia Convent when, as a schoolgirl, overcome by a sudden impulse, a strange, trance-like state, she had wanted to become a Christian and a nun. She had wanted to convert immediately and Arun had been summoned to Mussourie to talk some sense into her head. He had promptly declared that it was all 'summer moonshine'. It was the first time that Lata had heard the phrase. Though she had been struck by it, she had refused to believe that these religious impulses were moonshine of any kind. She had been determined to go ahead with her resolve. It was in fact a nun at Sophia Convent who had finally sat her down on a bench and talked to her – a green bench some distance away from the school buildings. It had had a view of a slope covered with a well-kept lawn and beautiful flowers; at the foot of the slope was a cemetery in which nuns of the order, many of whom had taught at the school, lay buried. She had said: 'Give yourself a few months, Lata. Wait at least till you leave school. You can always decide a little later. Don't make an immediate commitment. Remember, it will be very hard on your mother, who is a young widow.'

Lata sat on the bed for a while with Kalpana's letter in her hand, trying to avoid looking at her mother's face. Mrs Rupa Mehra arranged her saris in a drawer, deliberately silent. After a minute Lata said:

'All right, Ma. I'll see him.' She did not say anything further. She was angry still, but saw no point in expressing it. When some of the lines of anxiety on her mother's forehead relaxed, she was glad she had left it at that.

9.7

FOR some time now, Haresh had kept a diary of sorts. These days he usually wrote it at night at a heavy writing-desk in the rooms he rented at Elm Villa. He was browsing through it, glancing from time to time at the photograph standing in a silver frame on his desk.

Brahmpur
Lasting here is good, as is the general standard of workmanship. Am having pair of brogues done in Ravi-daspur on design of shoes I had brought for Sunil. If my idea works, Brahmpur could become a good source of finished footwear. But quality is the key. Unless an infrastructure of good labour is built up the trade will not advance.

Purchasing of micro-sheets is not a problem: over-supply because of strike. Kedarnath Tandon took me around the market (troubles with labour and suppliers at the moment over local demands) and had lunch with his family. Bhaskar his son is very bright, and his wife is an attractive lady. Veena I think.

Praha people are very difficult to talk to, and are not impressed with my qualifications. The problem, as always, is one of ingress. If I can talk to the top, there is a possibility, otherwise none. They have not even answered my letters seriously.

Sunil in fine form as usual.

Letter to Baoji, Simran, M. and Mme. Poudevigne.

Cawnpore

Hot days, and working in the factory is hard. At least in the evening I can rest under the fan at Elm Villa.

I think of Simran all the time, but I know there is little hope. Now her mother has threatened to commit suicide if she marries someone outside her faith. It may be human nature, but I do not want to be at the receiving end of human nature. It is even harder for Simran. No doubt they are trying to get her married off to someone suitable, poor girl.

At work, as usual, supplies are holding things up. I am too short-tempered and impatient. Had row with Rao from the other department. He is a good for nothing man who only knows how to play labour off against each other. He has favourites and is unobjective, and it is to the detriment of the whole organisation. Sometimes he simply takes away one or two people who I need, and then I am short-staffed. Thin lean fellow like Uriah, with a sharp nose. Elsewhere they believe in 'Grow and make the business grow.' In India we believe that the way to rise is to do someone else down.

Today the problem I faced was not nails or soles or stitching thread but sheepskin again. There were quite a few uppers cut which needed lining, also the recent order required sheepskin. After setting the men to work I took Rs. 600/- in suspense a/c and went to the market myself. Buying material is always a training in itself. Maybe I should treat my experience at CLFC as a paid apprenticeship. I felt tired after the day's work. Came home, read a few pages of *The Mayor of Casterbridge* and slept early. No letters.

Watch strap Rs. 12/- (Crocodile skin).

Cawnpore

Very interesting day.

Reached factory in time. It rained. Went about work as usual, there seems no system in the work, one person has to handle so many things.

Saw a shop in market run by a Chinaman, Lee. He has a small shop, I saw a few shoes with striking designs, so entered on impulse, and talked to him. He speaks English – and also Hindi in a strange way. Makes shoes himself. I asked him who designed them, and he said he designed them himself as well. I was impressed. His technology of designing is not scientific, but he has a fairly good grasp of proportions and colour-schemes, even though I am colour-blind I could see that. The toe and tongue not lopsided, the type of sole and heel in balance, the total visual impact good. By seeing the quantity of business he did and through the conversation I found out without making him nervous how much he would be likely to make after rent and material and other costs. Lee cannot make much because Praha, Cooper Allen etc. flood the market with cheap shoes of a certain quality and Cawnpore is not a discriminating place for specially designed shoes. I think I could improve his prospects and also help my new department if I could convince Mukherji to take him on for Rs. 250 a month. Of course he will have to speak to Ghosh in Bombay, and that is the rub. If I were in business for myself I would take him on immediately. He would surely not be averse to have a designer's job without all the other troubles he must have.

Got ticket for Delhi and will be leaving tomorrow. A

private party is thinking of hiring me, so I should be well prepared. And CLFC wants to get into the Delhi market also. They should first set their own house in order.

Too sleepy to write more.

Delhi

Mukherji agrees about Lee, now it is up to Ghosh.

Was tired, so rested on the train, even though it was a day journey. Freshened up in waiting room, then went to Kalpana. Had a good talk about the old times. She is not well, and has had a sad life, but cheers up everyone around her. Did not talk about S though it was on both our minds. Met her father and her good-looking aunt Mrs Mehra.

Baoji still set upon farming plans. I tried to dissuade him because he has no experience. But once he decides on something, his mind is difficult to change. I was glad to avoid meeting Umesh Uncle.

Cawnpore

Woke late, reached the factory half an hour late. There was quite a mess and much had to be done. Telegram from Praha, which was not very encouraging, in fact insulting: they offer me Rs. 28 a week – do they think I am a fool? A letter from Simran, one from Jean, and one from Kalpana. Kalpana's letter was rather strange, suggesting engagement with Mrs Mehra's daughter Lata. Jean's letter the usual. Deferred dealing with labour till Monday in order to ascertain the exact position. At least labour knows I am not trying to play anyone off against anyone else. No one else talks to them properly: typical babu attitude. In the evening came home and slept quietly.

There is no place here to spread my wings. What is to be done?

cycle oil Re. 1/4
rent and board etc to Mrs Mason Rs. 185/-
stamps Re. 1/-

BEFORE dropping off to sleep, he re-read Kalpana's letter, which he looked around for before remembering that he had tucked it in at the back of the diary.

My dear Haresh,

I do not know what sort of reception this letter will get from you. I am writing to you after a very long time, even though we have just met once again. It was so good to see you, and to feel that you have not forgotten me and that my bonds in thee are not entirely determinate. I was not at my best, and I was not prepared for your arrival. But when you left I felt invigorated once again, and in fact mentioned that to my good-looking aunt.

In fact it is at her behest that I am writing this letter – but not only at her behest. I shall be businesslike and precise in whatever I have to say, and I shall expect you to be equally frank in your reply.

The point is that Mrs Mehra has a young daughter Lata – and she was so impressed by you that she wanted to know if there was any possibility of anything being arranged between Lata and you by way of matrimony. Don't be surprised at my writing all this, but I think Lata's marriage is also our responsibility. Her late father and my father were very close friends and thought of each other almost like brothers, so it was natural for my aunt to turn to us for help when she wanted to find a suitable match for her daughters. (The elder one is now happily married.) I showed my aunt all my eligible khatri friends, but because I had lost contact with you and also because you were not in Delhi I did not think of you as a possibility. There may also have been other reservations. But she saw you that evening and was extremely impressed. She thinks it would be a boy of your type who would have made Lata's late father happy.

As for Lata – she is nineteen years old, brilliant at her studies, came first in her Senior Cambridge exams from

Sophia Convent, did her Intermediate Arts from Brahmpur University, and has just finished (with excellent marks) her first year B.A. exams in English, also from Brahmpur University. Once she finishes her B.A. next year she is keen to find some work. Her elder brother is working at Bentsen Pryce in Calcutta, her second brother has just finished at Calcutta University and is studying for the IAS. Her elder sister is, as I mentioned, married. Their father died in 1942, and was working with the Railways. He would certainly have been on the Railway Board by now if he had been alive.

She is 5ft. 5 in. tall, not very fair, but attractive and smart in an Indian sort of way. She looks forward, I think, to a quiet, sober life in the future. I have played with her as a child – she is like my own little sister, and has gone so far as to say: 'If Kalpana thinks well of someone I'm pretty sure I will too.'

I have given you all the particulars. As Byron says, 'Though women are angels, yet wedlock's the devil.' You may hold that view. All I can say is, even if you do not, you are not bound to say 'yes' just because I am saying it. Think it over; if you are interested, just let me know. Of course you must see her and she must see you – and then your reactions and her reactions will count. If you (1) are thinking of getting married (2) have no previous commitments, and (3) are interested in this particular individual, you can come over to Delhi. (I tried to get in touch with you before you left Delhi but was unsuccessful.) If you are not comfortable about staying with your family at Neel Darvaza you can stay with us if you like; your family need not know the purpose of your visit or even that you are here. Lata's mother will be in Delhi for several more days, and tells me that Lata is planning to join her soon. She is a decent girl (if you are interested) and deserves a steady, honest and sincere type like her late father was.

So: the business being over, I should tell you that I am not at all well. I have been confined to bed since yesterday and the doctor does not know what is wrong. I yawn all the time and feel hot spots on the soles of my feet! I'm not allowed to move or talk very much. I'm writing this from bed, hence this terrible writing. I hope I get well soon, especially since Father's leg is also giving him trouble. He is much troubled by the heat as well. He hates ill health and June with an equal passion. All of us are praying that the monsoon is not delayed.

Lastly – if you think I've done anything wrong in writing so frankly to you, you must forgive me. I have presumed upon our friendship in writing to you in this way. If I ought not to have, let's just drop the matter and forget all about it.

I hope to hear from you soon or to see you. A telegram or letter – either would be fine.

Best wishes and everything,
Kalpana

Haresh's eyes closed once or twice as he read through the letter. It would be interesting to meet this girl, he thought. If the mother was anything to go by, she ought to be attractive too. But before he could give the matter his complete consideration, he yawned, and yawned again, and all thoughts whatsoever were displaced by exhaustion. He was asleep in five minutes; it was a pleasant and dreamless sleep.

9.9

'A call for you, Mr Khanna.'

'Just coming, Mrs Mason.'

'It's a lady's voice,' added Mrs Mason helpfully.

'Thank you, Mrs Mason.' Haresh went to the drawing room that her three lodgers used in common. No one else was down, but Mrs Mason was engaged in looking from various angles at a flower vase filled with orange cosmos. She was an Anglo-Indian woman of seventy-five, a widow who lived with her middle-aged, unmarried daughter. She liked to keep tabs on her lodgers.

'Hello. Haresh Khanna.'

'Hello, Haresh, this is Mrs Mehra, you remember, we met at Kalpana's in Delhi – Kalpana Gaur's – and –'

'Yes,' said Haresh with a glance at Mrs Mason, who was standing by the vase in a meditative manner, a finger on her lower lip.

'Do you – er, has Kalpana –'

'Yes, indeed, welcome to Cawnpore. Kalpana telegrammed. I was expecting you. Both of you –'

Mrs Mason cocked her head to one side.

Haresh passed his hand over his forehead.

'I cannot talk right now,' said Haresh. 'I'm a little late for work. When may I come over? I have the address. I'm so sorry I couldn't come to the station to meet you, but I didn't know which train you'd be on.'

'We were on different trains,' said Mrs Rupa Mehra. 'Can you come at eleven o'clock? I am very much looking forward to seeing you again. And so is Lata.'

'So am I,' said Haresh. 'The time suits me very well. I have to buy some sheep – and then I'll come over.' Mrs Mason shifted the vase to another table, then decided that the first one was better.

'Goodbye, Haresh. So we'll see you soon?'

'Yes. Goodbye.'

At the other end of the line Mrs Rupa Mehra turned to Lata and said: 'He sounded very brusque. He didn't even address me by name. And Kalpana says he called me Mrs Mehrotra in his letter to her.' She paused. 'And he wants to buy some sheep. I'm not sure I heard him right.' She paused again. 'But, believe me, he is a very nice boy.'

Haresh kept his bicycle, like his shoes and his comb and his clothes, in excellent condition, but he could not very well cycle down to meet Mrs and Miss Mehra at Mr Kakkar's house. He stopped by the factory and persuaded the factory manager, Mr Mukherji, to lend him one of the two factory cars. There was a big limousine with a grand and impressive driver and a small, rather rickety car with a driver who talked to all his passengers. He liked Haresh because he had no hierarchical airs, and always chatted to him in a friendly way.

Haresh tried for the beauty but ended up with the beast. 'Well, it's a car anyway,' he said to himself.

He bought the sheepskin for the lining, and asked the supplier to ensure that it got to the factory. Then he stopped for a paan, which was something he always enjoyed. He combed his hair once again in the mirror of the car. And he gave the driver strict instructions that he was not to speak to anyone travelling in the car that day (including Haresh) unless he was spoken to.

Mrs Rupa Mehra was waiting for him with increasing nervousness. She had persuaded Mr Kakkar to join them in order to relieve the awkwardness of a first meeting. Mr Kakkar, both as a man and as an accountant, had been held in great respect by the late Raghubir Mehra, and it reassured Mrs Rupa Mehra that he, not she, would be playing nominal host.

She greeted Haresh warmly. Haresh was wearing almost the same clothes as when she had first met him at Kalpana's house in Delhi: a silk shirt and fawn cotton gaberdine trousers. He also had on a pair of brown-and-white co-respondent shoes, which he considered exceptionally smart.

He smiled when he saw Lata seated on the sofa. A nice, quiet girl, he thought.

Lata was wearing a pale pink cotton sari with chikan embroidery from Lucknow. Her hair was in a bun. She wore no jewellery except a pair of plain pearl ear-tops. The first thing Haresh said to her was:

'We've met before, Miss Mehra, haven't we?'

Lata frowned. Her first impression of him was that he was shorter than she had expected. The next – when he opened his mouth to speak – was that he had been chewing paan. This was far from appealing. Perhaps, if he had been wearing kurta-pyjamas, a red-stained mouth would have been appropriate – if not acceptable. Paan did not go at all well with fawn gaberdine and a silk shirt. In fact paan did not go at all well with her idea of a husband. His whole mode of dressing struck her as being flashy. And flashiest of all were the co-respondent shoes. Whom was he trying to impress?

'I don't believe we have, Mr Khanna,' she replied politely. 'But I'm glad we've got the chance to meet.'

Lata had made an immediately favourable impression on Haresh by the simplicity and good taste of her dress. She didn't have any make-up on, yet looked attractive and self-possessed, and her accent was not a heavy Indian accent, he was pleased to note, but light, almost British, because of her convent-school background.

Haresh, on the other hand, had surprised Lata by his accent, which bore traces both of Hindi and of the local Midlands dialect which he had been exposed to in England. Why, both her brothers spoke English better than he did. She could imagine what fun Kakoli and Meenakshi Chatterji might have mocking Haresh's manner of speaking.

Haresh passed his hand over his forehead. Surely he couldn't be mistaken. The same large, beautiful eyes, the same oval face – the eyebrows, the nose, the lips, the same expression of intensity. Well, perhaps he had dreamed it, after all.

Mr Kakkar, a little nervous because of his undefined position as a host, asked him to sit down and offered him tea. For a while no one knew what to talk about, especially since it was quite obvious what the purpose of their meeting was. Politics? No. The weather? No. The morning's news? Haresh had not had time to glance at the papers.

'Did you have a comfortable journey?' he asked.

Mrs Rupa Mehra looked at Lata, and Lata at Mrs Rupa Mehra. Each deferred to the other. Then Mrs Rupa Mehra said:

'Well, go on, Lata, answer the question.'

'I thought Mr Khanna was talking to you, Ma. Yes, thank you, I had a comfortable journey. Perhaps it was a little tiring.'

'Where were you travelling from?'

'From Calcutta.'

'But you must be very tired then. The train arrives very early in the morning'

'No, I came by the day train, so I've slept in a proper bed and woken up at a reasonable hour,' said Lata. 'Is your tea all right?'

'Yes, thank you, Miss Mehra,' said Haresh, his eyes disappearing in a smile.

The smile was so warm and friendly that despite herself Lata could not help smiling too.

'You should call each other Lata and Haresh,' prompted Mrs Rupa Mehra.

'Perhaps we should leave the young people to talk by themselves,' suggested Mr Kakkar, who had an appointment.

'No, I don't think so,' said Mrs Rupa Mehra firmly. 'They will be very happy to have our company. It is not often that one gets the chance to meet such a fine boy as Haresh.'

Lata winced inwardly at this remark, but Haresh did not seem at all uncomfortable to be thus described.

'Have you ever been to Cawnpore, Miss Mehra?' he asked.

'Lata,' corrected Mrs Rupa Mehra.

'Lata.'

'Just once. Usually I meet Kakkar Phupha when he comes to Brahmpur or Calcutta on work.'

There was a long pause. Much tea was stirred, much tea was sipped.

'How is Kalpana?' asked Haresh finally. 'She didn't seem in the best of health when I saw her, and her letters talk about strange symptoms. I hope the poor girl is all right. She's been through such a lot these last few years.'

It was the right subject to choose. Mrs Rupa Mehra was off and running now. She described Kalpana's symptoms in detail, both from what she had seen, and from what she had read in the letter to Lata. She also talked about the unsuitable boy whom Kalpana had once got herself involved with. He had turned out not to be sincere. She wanted Kalpana to meet a sincere man, a sincere man with good prospects. She valued sincerity as a quality in men. And in women too of course. Didn't Haresh agree?

Haresh agreed. Being a frank and open-hearted fellow, he was about to talk about Simran, but stopped himself.

'Do you have those wonderful certificates with you?' asked Mrs Rupa Mehra suddenly.

'No,' said Haresh, surprised.

'It would be so nice if Lata could read them. Don't you think so, Lata?'

'Yes, Ma,' said Lata, thinking the opposite.

'Tell me, why did you run away from home at fifteen?' said Mrs Rupa Mehra, dropping an extra tablet of saccharine in her tea.

Haresh was startled that Kalpana had mentioned this fact. At his meeting with Lata's mother in Delhi, Kalpana, it seemed to him, had gone out of her way to show him in as favourable a light as possible.

'Mrs Mehra,' said Haresh, 'I believe that a time can come when a young man may have to part company even with those who love him and whom he loves.'

Mrs Rupa Mehra looked rather doubtful, but Lata a little interested. She nodded by way of encouragement, and Haresh continued.

'In this case an engagement was being forced upon me against my will by my father – well, my foster-father – and I could not accept it. I ran away. I had no money. In Mussourie I got a job cleaning a Praha shoe shop – it was my first experience of the shoe business, and not a pleasant one. Eventually I graduated to shop-boy. I starved and I froze but I was determined not to go back.'

'Didn't you even write a letter home?' asked Lata.

'No, Miss Mehra, I did not. I was very stubborn.'

Mrs Rupa Mehra frowned at his retreat into the surname.

'What happened in the end?' Lata asked.

'One of my foster-brothers from Neel Darvaza, the one whom I loved most of all, came to Mussourie for a holiday. He saw me in the shop. I pretended I was a customer, but the manager asked me quite sharply why I was gossiping when there was work to do. When my foster-brother realized the truth of the matter, he refused to go back home unless I came with him. You see, his mother had nursed me when my own mother died.'

This last sentence was not exactly an explanation of anything, but made sense to everyone.

'But now I am neither starving nor freezing,' continued Haresh proudly. 'In fact, could I invite you all to my place for lunch, perhaps?' He turned to Mrs Rupa Mehra: 'Kalpana mentioned in her telegram that you are vegetarian.'

Mr Kakkar asked to be excused, but Mrs Rupa Mehra accepted with alacrity on behalf of Lata and herself.

9.10

ON the way to Elm Villa, the driver was unusually quiet. The rickety car too behaved well.

'How do you enjoy your job?' asked Mrs Rupa Mehra.

'I enjoy it,' said Haresh. 'You know the department I was telling you about in Delhi? Well, the machinery has all been moved in, and I should begin next week with the new order that I've managed to procure. I'll take you around this afternoon. It's very well organized now that I've taken things in hand.'

'So you plan to live in Kanpur?' said Mrs Rupa Mehra.

'I don't know,' said Haresh. 'I can't advance to the top in CLFC, and I don't want to spend my life in a company where I can't get to the top. I've been trying Bata and James Hawley and Praha and Flex and Cooper Allen and even a job or two in government enterprises. Let's see what happens. I need a godfather to help me get a foot in the door. After that I can stand on my own abilities.'

'My son too thinks the same,' said Mrs Rupa Mehra. 'My elder son, Arun. He is with Bentsen Pryce – and well, Bentsen Pryce is Bentsen Pryce! Sooner or later he is bound to become a director. Maybe even the first Indian director.' She savoured the vision for a few moments. 'His late father would have been so proud of him,' she added. 'He, of course, would have been on the Railway Board by now. Possibly even the Chairman. We would always travel in saloons when he was alive.'

Lata was looking slightly disgusted.

'Here we are. Elm Villa!' said Haresh, rather as if he were announcing the Viceregal Lodge. They got down and went to the drawing room. Mrs Mason was out shopping, and they were alone except for a liveried bearer.

The drawing room was large and light, the liveried bearer extremely deferential. He bowed low and spoke softly. Haresh offered them nimbu pani, and the bearer brought the glasses on a plate, with doilies on the top: finely netted in white, with little glass beads hanging down from the edges. Two coloured prints of Yorkshire (which was where Mrs Mason traced her ancestry to) hung on the wall. The orange cosmos arranged in the vase added an additional touch of brightness to the flower-patterned sofa; it was one of the few flowers of the season that were not white. Haresh had told the cook the previous evening that he might be having guests for lunch, so there had been no need to make any last minute arrangements.

Mrs Rupa Mehra was impressed by the establishment at Elm Villa. She deferred drinking the nimbu pani for a few minutes after taking her homoeopathic powder. But when she did, she found it satisfactory.

Though the purpose of their meeting was continuously on all three minds, the conversation was easier than before. Haresh talked about England and his teachers, about his plans for improving his position, above all about his work. The order he had procured was much on his mind, and he assumed that Mrs Rupa Mehra and Lata too must be anxiously awaiting the outcome of that project. He talked about his life abroad – without, however, mentioning any of the English girls whom he had had affairs with. On the other hand he could not refrain from mentioning Simran once or twice, and could not entirely conceal his emotion when he did so. Lata did not mind; she was almost indifferent to the proceedings. From time to time her eye would fall on his co-respondent shoes, and she invented a Kakoli-couplet to amuse herself.

Lunch was presided over by Miss Mason, a desperately ugly and lifeless woman of forty-five. Her mother was still out; and the two other lodgers were lunching out as well. In contrast to the drawing room, the dining room was dingy and flowerless (except for a dark still life, which, though it contained roses, did not please Mrs Rupa Mehra). It was full of heavy furniture – two sideboards, an almirah and a huge, heavy table – and at the far end of the room, opposite the still life, hung an oil painting of an English country scene containing cows. Mrs Rupa Mehra immediately thought of their edibility, and was upset. But the meal itself was innocuous, and served on flower-patterned plates with wavy edges.

First there was tomato soup. Then fried fish for everyone except Mrs Rupa Mehra, who had vegetable cutlets. Then there was chicken curry and rice with fried brinjal and mango chutney. (Mrs Rupa Mehra had a vegetable curry.) And finally there was caramel custard. The imperial deference of the liveried servant and the lifelessness of Miss Mason succeeded in freezing most of the conversation.

After lunch Haresh offered to show Mrs Rupa Mehra and Lata his rooms. Mrs Rupa Mehra agreed eagerly. One could learn much from a room. They went upstairs. There was a bedroom, an ante-room, a verandah and a bathroom. Everything was neat, tidy, smart – to Lata it appeared to be in extreme, almost disturbing, order. Even the volumes of Hardy on the small bookshelf were arranged alphabetically. The shoes standing on a shoe-rack in a corner of the room were polished to a glacial shine. Lata looked out from the verandah at the garden of Elm Villa, which included a bed of orange cosmos.

Mrs Rupa Mehra, on the other hand – while Haresh was in the bathroom – looked around the room and drew in her breath sharply. A photograph of a smiling, long-haired young woman stood in a silver frame on Haresh's writing-table. There were no other photographs in the room, none even of Haresh's family. The girl was fair –

Mrs Rupa Mehra could make that out even from the black-and-white picture – and her features were classically beautiful.

She felt that Haresh, before inviting them to Elm Villa, could at least have put the photograph away.

Such a thought, however, would not even have occurred to Haresh. And had Mrs Rupa Mehra by any chance thought fit to talk slightingly about this omission, that would have been the end of matters as far as Haresh went. He would have forgotten about the Mehras' visit in a week.

When Haresh returned after washing his hands, Mrs Rupa Mehra said to him, frowning slightly:

'Let me ask you a question, Haresh. Is there someone else in your life still?'

'Mrs Mehra,' said Haresh, 'I told Kalpana and I am sure she has told you that Simran was and still is very dear to me. But I know that that door is closed to me. I cannot tear her away from her family, and for her family the fact that I am not a Sikh is all that matters. I am now looking for someone with whom I can live a happy married life. You need have no fears on that score. I am very glad that Lata and I have had the chance to get to know each other a little.'

Lata had come back in from the verandah during this exchange. She had overheard his forthright remarks and, without thinking, said to him: 'Haresh, what part will your family play in all this? You have talked very little about them. If – if – you intend to marry someone, will they have any say in the matter?' Her lips were trembling slightly. The thought of talking about such matters in such direct terms embarrassed her painfully. But something about the manner in which Haresh had said, 'I know that that door is closed to me,' had moved her, and so she had spoken.

Haresh, noticing her embarrassment, liked her for it, and smiled; as usual his eyes disappeared. 'No. I will ask for Baoji's blessing, naturally, but not for his consent. He knows that I feel strongly about my engagements.'

After a few moments of silence, Lata said:

'I see you like Hardy.'

'Yes,' said Haresh. 'But not *The Well Beloved*.' Then he looked at his watch and said: 'I have enjoyed this so much that I've lost track of the time. I have to do a bit of work at the factory, but I wonder if you'd like to come and see where I work? I don't want to hide anything from you; the atmosphere there is a little different from Elm Villa. Today I have managed to get the use of the car, so I could either take you there or have you dropped at Mr Kakkar's place. But perhaps you'll want to rest a little. It's a hot day and you must be tired.'

This time it was Lata who said, 'I would like to see the factory. But could I first –?'

Haresh indicated the bathroom.

Before she emerged she looked at the dressing-table. Here too everything was neatly and methodically laid out: the Kent combs, the badger-hair shaving-brush, the solidified stick of Pinaud deodorant that lent a cool fragrance to the warm day. Lata rubbed a little on the inside of her left wrist, and came out smiling. It was not that she didn't like Haresh. But the thought of their getting married was ridiculous.

9.11

SHE was no longer smiling a little later in the stench of the tannery. Haresh had to take the new employee Lee around CLFC's own tannery to show him the various kinds of leather (other than sheep, which they bought on the open market) that were available for making shoes. Lee's designs would depend partly on the leather available; and in his turn he could influence the choice of colours that the tannery would supply in future. Haresh's nose, after a year at CLFC, was somewhat used to its distinctive smell, but Mrs Rupa Mehra felt almost faint, and Lata sniffed her left wrist from time to time, amazed that Lee and Haresh could treat the foul stench almost as if it didn't exist.

Haresh was quick to explain to Lata's mother that the hides were from 'fallen animals', in other words cows that had died a natural death and had not, as in other countries, been slaughtered. He said that they did not accept hides from Muslim slaughter-houses. Mr Lee gave her a reassuring smile, and she looked a little less miserable if not much more enthusiastic.

After a quick visit to the temporary storage godowns where the hides lay piled in salt, they went to the soaking pits. Men with orange rubber gloves were pulling the swollen hides out with grappling-hooks and transferring them to the liming drums where the hair and fat would be removed. As Haresh explained the various processes – dehairing, de-liming, pickling, chrome tanning, and so on – in a voice of enthusiasm, Lata felt a sudden revulsion for his work, and a sense of disquiet about someone who could enjoy this sort of thing. Haresh meanwhile was continuing confidently: 'But once you have it at the wet-blue stage, it's easy enough to see what comes next: fat liquoring, samming, splitting, shaving, dyeing, setting, drying, and then there we are! The leather that we actually think of as leather! All the other processes – glazing, boarding, ironing and so on – are optional, of course.'

Lata looked at the lean, exhausted, bearded man who was squeezing the water out of the wet-blue leather with the help of a roller press, then at Mr Lee, who had gone over to have a word with him.

Mr Lee's Hindi was unusual, and Lata, the rebellion of her nose and eyes notwithstanding, could not help listening to him with interest. He appeared to be knowledgeable not only about shoe design and manufacture but about tanning as well. Soon Haresh had joined them, and they were talking about the reduced volume of hides that went through the tannery during the monsoon weeks, when air-drying was difficult and tunnel-drying had to be resorted to.

Suddenly remembering something, Haresh said, 'Mr Lee, I recall some Chinese tanners from Calcutta telling me that in Chinese there is a word, a special word for ten thousand. Is that so?'

'Oh yes, in proper Peking Chinese it is called "wan".'

'And a wan of wans?'

Mr Lee looked at Haresh in surprise, and, scribbling with the index finger of his right hand on the palm of his left he drew an imaginary character and said something like 'ee' – to rhyme with his own name.

'Ee?' said Haresh.

Mr Lee repeated the word.

'Why do you have such words?' asked Haresh.

Mr Lee smiled sweetly. 'I do not know,' he said. 'Why don't you?'

By now Mrs Rupa Mehra was feeling so weak that she had to ask Haresh to take her out of the tannery.

'Do you want to go to the factory then, where I work?'

'No, Haresh, thank you, that's very sweet of you, but we should go home now. Mr Kakkar will be waiting for us.'

'It will just take twenty minutes, and you can meet Mr Mukherji, my boss. Really, we are doing wonderful work there. And I'll show you the set-up for the new department.'

'Some other time. Actually, I am feeling the heat a little –'

Haresh turned to Lata. Though she was putting on a brave front, her nose was crinkling upwards.

Haresh, suddenly realizing what the matter was, said: 'The smell – the smell. Oh – but you should have told me. I'm sorry – you see, I hardly give it a thought.'

'No, no,' said Lata, a bit ashamed of herself. Somewhere within her had risen an atavistic revulsion against the whole polluting business of hides and carrion and everything associated with leather.

But Haresh was very apologetic. While taking them back to the car he explained that this was a comparatively odourless tannery! Not far away, there was a whole locality with tanneries on both sides of the road, whose wastes and effluents were left in the open to dry or stagnate. At one time there had been a drain that took the stuff to the river, the holy Ganga, itself, but there had been objections, and now there was no outlet at all. And people were very funny, said Haresh – they accepted what they had seen since childhood – shavings of leather and other offal strewn all around – they took it all for granted. (Haresh waved his arms to support his contention.) Sometimes he saw cart-loads of hides coming in from villages or marketplaces being pulled by buffaloes who were almost dead themselves. 'And of course in a week or two, when the monsoons come, it won't be worth drying these shavings, so they'll just let them lie and rot. And with the heat and the rain – well, you can imagine what the smell is like. It's as bad as the tanning pits on the way to Ravidaspur – in your own city of Brahmpur. There even I had to hold my nose.'

The allusion was lost on Lata and Mrs Rupa Mehra, who would no more have dreamed of going to Ravidaspur than to Orion.

Mrs Rupa Mehra was about to ask Haresh when he had been to Brahmpur when the stench once more overpowered her.

'I'm going to take you back at once,' said Haresh decisively.

He sent a message that he would be back a little late at the factory and summoned the car. On the way back to Mr Kakkar's house he said, a little humbly: 'Well, someone has to make shoes.'

Mrs Rupa Mehra said: 'But you don't work in the tannery, do you, Haresh?'

'Oh, no!' said Haresh. 'Normally I only visit it about once a week. I work in the main factory.'

'Once a week?' said Lata.

Haresh could sense the apprehension behind her words. He was sitting in the front with the driver. Now he turned around and said, in a slightly troubled voice: 'I am proud of the shoes I make. I don't like sitting in an office giving orders and expecting miracles. If this means that I have to stand in a pit and soak a buffalo's hide myself, I'll do it. People who work in managing agencies, for instance, are perfectly happy to deal in commodities but don't like smudging their fingers with anything except ink. If that. And they care less for quality than for profits.'

After a few seconds, in which no one spoke, he added:

'If you have to do something, you should do it without making a fuss. An uncle of mine in Delhi thinks that I have become polluted, that I have lost caste by working with leather. Caste! I think he is a fool, and he thinks that I'm one. I've come close to telling him what I think of him. But I'm sure he knows. People can always tell if you like or dislike them.'

There was another pause. Then Haresh, thrown off a little by his own unexpected profession of faith, said, 'I would like to invite you to dinner. We have very little time to get to know each other. I hope that Mr Kakkar won't mind.'

He had simply assumed that for their part the Mehras wouldn't. Mother and daughter looked at each other in the back seat of the car, neither able to anticipate the other. After five seconds or so, Haresh took their silence for consent.

'Good,' he said. 'I'll come to fetch you at seven-thirty. And I will be smelling as sweet as a violet.'

'A violet?' cried Mrs Rupa Mehra in sudden alarm. 'Why a violet?'

'I don't know,' said Haresh. 'A rose, if you like, Mrs Mehra. At any rate, better than wet-blue.'

9.12

DINNER was at the railway restaurant, which provided an excellent five-course meal. Lata was dressed in a pale green chanderi sari with little white flowers and a white border. She wore the same pearl ear-tops as before; they were virtually her only item of jewellery, and since she had not known she was going to be on display she had not bothered to borrow anything from Meenakshi. Mr Kakkar had taken a champa out of a vase and put it in her hair. It was a warm night, and she looked lively and fresh in green and white.

Haresh was wearing an off-white Irish linen suit and a cream tie with brown polka-dots. Lata disliked these expensive, over-smart clothes and wondered what Arun would have thought of them. Calcutta tastes were quieter. As for a silk shirt, sure enough, it was there too. Haresh even brought his shirts into the conversation: they were made of the finest silk, the only silk he deigned to have made into shirts – not the silk poplin that was so popular these days, but the kind that had the brand-mark of two horses at the base of the bale. All this meant no more to Lata than did wet-blue, samming and splitting. Luckily Haresh's co-respondent shoes were hidden beneath the table.

The meal was excellent; none of them drank anything alcoholic. The conversation ranged from politics (Haresh thought that Nehru was ruining the country with all his socialist waffle) to English literature (where, with a few misquotations, Haresh asserted that Shakespeare had been written by Shakespeare) to the cinema (Haresh, it seemed, had seen about four films a week while in England).

Lata wondered how he had found the time and energy to do so well in his course and earn a living simultaneously. His accent continued to put her off. She recalled that, by way of over-compensation, he had called daal 'doll' at lunch. And Kanpur 'Cawnpore'. But when she compared his company with that of the polished and covenanted Bishwanath Bhaduri that evening at Firpos not so long ago, she realized how very much she preferred it. He was lively (even if he repeated himself) and optimistic (even if over-confident of his own abilities), and he appeared to like her.

She reflected that Haresh was not westernized in the proper sense: she sensed that in his manners and style he was a bit half-baked (at least by Calcutta standards), and that consequently he sometimes put on airs. But though he wished to be liked by her, he did not ingratiate himself by attempting to anticipate her opinions before putting forward his own. If anything, he was too certain about the correctness of his views. Nor did he lay on the odious, insincere charm that she had got used to with Arun's young Calcutta friends. Amit, of course, was different; but he was Meenakshi's brother rather than Arun's friend.

Haresh found Mrs Rupa Mehra affectionate as well as good-looking. He had tried to maintain a respectful distance by calling her Mrs Mehra throughout, but she had eventually insisted on him calling her Ma. 'Everyone else does so after five minutes, so you must as well,' she told Haresh. She waxed voluble about her late husband and her coming grandson. She had already forgotten her afternoon's trauma and had appended her future son-in-law to the family.

Over ice-cream, Lata decided she liked his eyes. They were lovely, she thought, and surprisingly so; they were small and lively, did not spoil his good looks, and when he was amused they disappeared completely! It was fascinating. Then, for no accountable reason, she began to dread the thought that after dinner, while driving her back, he would offer to stop for paan – unconscious of how horribly it would jar with the spirit of the evening, the linen, the silverware, the china, how it would undo the threads of her goodwill with the blind torque of distaste, how it would sandwich the entire day with the image of a red mouth stained with betel-juice.

Haresh's thoughts were not complicated. He said to himself: This girl is intelligent without arrogance, and attractive without vanity. She does not reveal her thoughts easily, but I like that. And then he thought of Simran, and the old, not entirely appeasable pain came over his heart.

But sometimes, for a few minutes at a time, Haresh forgot about Simran. And, for a few minutes at a time, Lata forgot about Kabir. And sometimes both of them forgot that what they were undergoing amid the clink of cutlery and crockery was a mutual interview that might decide whether or not they would own a common set of those items some time in the whimsical future.

THE car (with Haresh and driver) picked up Mrs Rupa Mehra and Lata and took them to the railway station early the next morning. They arrived, they thought, just in time. The timing of the Kanpur-Lucknow train, however, had been changed, and they missed it. The bus they attempted to take was full. There was nothing for it but to wait for the 9.42 train. Meanwhile they returned to Elm Villa.

Mrs Rupa Mehra said that nothing like this would have happened in her husband's time. Then the trains ran like clockwork, and changes in train timings were like changes in dynasties: momentous and rare. Now everything was being changed at random: road names, train schedules, prices, mores. Cawnpore and Cashmere were yielding to unfamiliar spellings. It would be Dilli and Kolkata and Mumbai next. And now, shockingly, they were threatening to go metric with the currency – and even with weights and measures.

'Don't worry, Ma,' said Haresh with a smile. 'We've tried to introduce the kilogram since 1870, and it probably won't be brought in for another hundred years.'

'Do you think so?' said Mrs Rupa Mehra, pleased. Seers meant something exact to her, pounds something vague, and kilograms nothing at all.

'Yes,' said Haresh. 'We have no sense of order or logic or discipline. No wonder we let the British rule us. What do you think, Lata?' he added in an artless attempt to draw her in.

But Lata had no opinion handy. She was thinking of other matters. What was foremost on her mind was Haresh's panama hat, which (though he had doffed it) she thought exceptionally stupid. This morning too he had on his Irish linen suit.

They got to the station a little early and sat in the railway café. Lata and Mrs Rupa Mehra bought first-class tickets to Lucknow – the journey was a short one and tickets did not need to be reserved in advance. Haresh pressed a cup of Pheasant's cold chocolate – a Dutch concoction – on them. It was delicious, and Lata's face expressed her pleasure. Haresh was so delighted at her innocent enjoyment that he suddenly said, 'May I accompany you to Lucknow? I could stay there with Simran's sister, and come back tomorrow after seeing you off on the train to Brahmpur.' What he had almost said was: I would like to spend a few more hours with you today, even if it means that someone else has to purchase the sheepskin.

Mrs Rupa Mehra did not succeed in dissuading Haresh; he bought a ticket to Lucknow for himself. He made sure that their luggage was loaded safely on and below the berths, that the porter did not swindle them, that they were comfortably seated, that each of them was provided with a magazine, that all was well with them in every way. Throughout the two-hour journey he hardly said a word. He was thinking that contentment consisted of just such moments as these.

Lata on the other hand was thinking that it was very odd that he should have mentioned – as part of his reason for accompanying them to Lucknow – that he planned to stay with Simran's sister. For all the method to his books and brushes, he was an unaccountable man.

When the train steamed into Lucknow Station, Haresh said: 'I would very much like to be of some help to you tomorrow.'

'No, no,' said Mrs Rupa Mehra, almost in a panic. 'The tickets have been reserved already. We don't need any help. They have been reserved by my son – my son in Bentsen Pryce. We'll be travelling very comfortably. You must not come to the station.'

Haresh looked at Lata for a while and was about to ask her something. Then he turned to her mother instead and said: 'May I write to Lata, Mrs Mehra?'

Mrs Mehra was about to agree with enthusiasm, then, checking herself, she turned to Lata, and Lata nodded, rather gravely. It would have been too cruel to say no.

'Yes, you may write, of course,' said Mrs Rupa Mehra. 'And you really must call me Ma.'

'Now I'd like to make sure that you get to Mr Sahgal's place safely,' said Haresh. 'I'll get a tonga.'

It was pleasant to be taken care of, and the two women allowed Haresh to fuss competently over them.

In fifteen minutes they had arrived at the Sahgals'. Mrs Sahgal was Mrs Rupa Mehra's first cousin. She was a weak-brained, sweet-natured woman of about forty-five, married to a well-known Lucknow lawyer. 'Who is this gentleman?' she asked of Haresh.

'This is a young man who knew Kalpana Gaur at St Stephen's,' said Mrs Rupa Mehra by way of non-explanatory explanation.

'But he must come in and have tea with us,' said Mrs Sahgal. 'Sahgal Sahib will be so angry if he doesn't.'

Mrs Sahgal's saccharine, foolish life revolved around her husband. No sentence was complete for her without a reference to Mr Sahgal. Some people thought her a saint, some a fool. Mrs Rupa Mehra recalled that her own late husband, usually a good-natured and tolerant man, had thought Mrs Sahgal a doting idiot. He had said this angrily rather than amusedly. The Sahgals' son, who was about seventeen, was mentally deficient. Their daughter, who was Lata's age, was highly intelligent and highly neurotic.

Mr Sahgal was very pleased to see Lata and her mother. He was a sober, wise-looking man with a short-trimmed grey-and-white beard. If an expressionless portrait had been made of him, he would have looked like a judge. Rather than welcoming Haresh, however, he gave him a strange, conspiratorial smirk. Haresh took an instant dislike to him.

'Are you quite sure I can't be of any help to you tomorrow?' he asked.

'Quite sure, Haresh, God bless you,' said Mrs Rupa Mehra.

'Lata?' said Haresh, smiling, but with a trace of uncertainty; perhaps, for once, he was not entirely sure whether he was liked or disliked. Certainly the signals he was receiving were perplexingly mixed. 'You're sure I may write?'

'Yes, that would be nice,' said Lata, as if someone had offered her a piece of toast.

This sounded so lukewarm, even to her, that she added:

'It would really be very nice. It's a good way to get to know each other.'

Haresh was about to say something more, but decided against it.

'Au revoir, then,' he said, smiling. He had taken a few French lessons in England.

'Au revoir,' replied Lata with a laugh.

'Why are you laughing?' asked Haresh. 'Were you laughing at me?'

'Yes,' said Lata honestly. 'I was. Thank you.'

'For what?' asked Haresh.

'For a very enjoyable day.' She glanced once more at his co-respondent shoes. 'I won't forget it.'

'Neither will I,' said Haresh. Then he thought of several things to say but rejected each one.

'You must learn to say shorter goodbyes,' said Lata.

'Do you have any other advice for me?' asked Haresh.

Yes, thought Lata; at least seven pieces. Aloud she said: 'Yes, I do. Keep to the left.'

Grateful for the affectionate banality, Haresh nodded; and his tonga plodded off towards Simran's sister's house.

9.14

BOTH Lata and Mrs Rupa Mehra were so tired after their Kanpur visit that they went off to sleep soon after lunch. Each had her own room, and Lata welcomed these rare hours of privacy. She knew that the moment they were alone together her mother would begin asking her about what she thought of Haresh.

Before she dropped off to sleep her mother came to her room. The bedrooms were arranged in rows on both sides of a long corridor – as if in a hotel. It was a hot afternoon. Mrs Rupa Mehra had with her her bottle of 4711 eau-de-

Cologne, one of the objects that had a permanent home in her bag. With this she soaked a corner of one of her rose-embroidered handkerchiefs and dabbed Lata's head affectionately.

'I thought I would say a word to my darling daughter before she fell off to sleep.'

Lata waited for the question.

'Well, Lata?'

'Well, Ma?' Lata smiled. Now that it was a reality rather than an anticipation, the question was not so formidable.

'Don't you think he's suitable?' Mrs Rupa Mehra's voice made it clear that any rejection of Haresh would hurt her to the quick.

'Ma, I've only met him for twenty-four hours!'

'Twenty-six.'

'What do I really know of him, Ma?' said Lata. 'Let's say – it's not negative: he's all right. I've got to know him better.'

This last sentence being ambiguous, Mrs Rupa Mehra wanted an immediate clarification. Lata, smiling to herself, said:

'Let me put it like this. He's not rejected. He says he wants to write to me. Let's see what he has to say for himself.'

'You are a very fussy and ungrateful girl,' said her mother. 'You are always thinking of the wrong people.'

Lata said:

'Yes, Ma, you're quite right. I am very fussy and very ungrateful, but at the moment I am also very sleepy.'

'Here. You keep this handkerchief.' And her mother left her to herself.

Lata fell off to sleep almost immediately. The Sunny Park household in Calcutta, the long journey to Kanpur in the heat, the strain of being on display before a marriage-able man, the tannery, the tension between her liking and distaste for Haresh, the journey from Kanpur to Lucknow, and her repeated and unbidden thoughts of Kabir, all had exhausted her. She slept well. When she woke up it was four o'clock and tea-time. She washed her face, changed, and went to the drawing room.

Her mother, Mr Sahgal, Mrs Sahgal, and their two children were sitting there having tea and samosas. Mrs Rupa Mehra was catching up as usual on her enormous network of acquaintances. Though Mrs Sahgal was, strictly speaking, her cousin, they actually thought of each other as sisters: they had spent a great deal of their childhood together after Rupa's mother's death in the great influenza epidemic.

Mrs Sahgal's wish to please her husband was comic, or perhaps pathetic. Her eyes were constantly following his. 'Shall I bring that newspaper?' 'Will you have another cup?' 'Do you want me to bring the photograph album?' His eyes had only to rest on some object in the room for her to anticipate his wishes and scurry to fulfil them. He did not treat her with contempt, however; he praised her in measured tones. Sometimes he would stroke his short grey-and-white beard and say: 'You see my luck? With Maya as a wife I have to do nothing! I worship her as a goddess.' His wife would preen with pleasure.

And indeed, there were several photographs of his wife on the wall or in small frames here and there. She was a physically attractive woman (as was her daughter) and Mr Sahgal was something of an amateur photographer. He pointed out one or two to Lata; Lata couldn't help thinking that the poses were a little – she tried to think of a word – 'film-starrish'. There were also a couple of pictures of Kiran, the daughter, who was about Lata's age and was studying at Lucknow University. Kiran was tall and pale and quite attractive; but she was abrupt in her movements, and had agitated eyes.

'And now you will be embarking on the journey of life,' said Mr Sahgal to Lata. He leaned forward slightly, and spilt a little tea. His wife rushed to mop it up.

'Mausaji, I don't want to embark on any journey without checking the ticket first,' said Lata, trying to make light of his remark, but annoyed that her mother had presumed to talk about such matters to them.

Mrs Rupa Mehra did not consider her mention of Haresh

to be an act of presumption, but, on the contrary, of consideration. Mr and Mrs Sahgal were simply being told that they would not have to trawl their nets through the khatri community of Lucknow for Lata's sake – which they would otherwise certainly have been required to do.

At this point the feeble-minded son, Pushkar, who was a couple of years younger than Lata, began to sing to himself and rock slightly to and fro.

'What is the matter, son?' asked his father gently.

'I want to marry Lata Didi,' said Pushkar.

Mr Sahgal shrugged apologetically towards Mrs Rupa Mehra. 'He is like this sometimes,' he said. 'Come, Pushkar – let us go and make something with your Meccano set.' They left the room.

Lata suddenly felt a peculiar sense of unease, which seemed to reach back to the memory of an earlier visit to Lucknow. But it was so unspecific that she could not recall what had caused it. She felt she needed to be by herself, to get out of the house, to go for a walk.

'I'll take a walk to the old British Residency,' she said. 'It's cooler now, and it's only a few minutes away.'

'But you haven't eaten even one samosa yet,' said Mrs Rupa Mehra.

'Ma, I'm not hungry. But I do want to go for a walk.'

'You can't go by yourself,' said her mother firmly. 'This isn't Brahmpur. Wait till Mausaji comes back, maybe he'll go with you.'

'I'll go with Lata,' said Kiran quickly.

'That's very sweet of you, Kiran,' said Mrs Rupa Mehra. 'But don't dawdle. When girls get together they talk for hours without noticing the time go by.'

'We'll be back by dark,' said Kiran. 'Don't worry, Rupa Masi.'

9.15

THERE were a few clouds in the eastern sky, greyish, but not rain-bearing. The road to the Residency past the fine red-brick building of the Lucknow Chief Court – now the Lucknow Bench of the Allahabad High Court – was uncrowded. This was where Mr Sahgal practised. Kiran and Lata hardly talked at all, and this suited Lata.

Though Lata had been to Lucknow twice before – once when she was nine, when her father was alive, once when she was about fourteen, after his death – and had stayed each time with the Sahgals, she had never visited the ruined Residency. It was in fact a mere fifteen minutes' walk from the Sahgals' house near Kaiserbagh. What she remembered about her two previous stays were not the historical monuments of Lucknow but the fresh, home-made white butter Mrs Sahgal served; and for some reason she recalled being given a whole bunch of grapes for breakfast. She also remembered how friendly Kiran had been on her first trip, and how unfriendly – even resentful – she had been on the second. By then it was clear that all was not well with her brother, and perhaps she had envied Lata her two brothers, noisy, affectionate, and normal. But you have your father, Lata had thought, and I have lost mine. Why do you dislike me? Lata was glad that Kiran was at last trying to restore the friendship; she only wished that she herself were better placed today to reciprocate.

For today she had no wish at all to talk to Kiran or anyone – least of all to Mrs Rupa Mehra. She wanted to be by herself – to think about her life, and what was happening to it, to her. Or perhaps not even to think about it – to be distracted, rather, by something so far and past and grand that it would limit the scope of her own elations and distresses. She had felt something of that spirit in the Park Street Cemetery that day in the pouring rain. It was that spirit of distance that she was trying to recapture.

The great, shattered, bullet-mottled remains of the Residency rose above them on a hill. The grass at the foot of the hill was brown for lack of rain but green above, where it had been watered. All around, among the broken buildings, were trees and bushes – pipal, jamun, neem, mango, and here and there at least four huge banyan trees. Mynas cried from the rough-barked and smooth-barked palms, a spray of magenta bougainvillaea fell in a massive shower on a lawn. Chameleons and squirrels wandered around among the ruins and obelisks and cannons. Wherever the plaster of the thick walls had crumbled, the thin hard bricks of which it was built were exposed. Plaques and gravestones lay scattered through the sad acres. In the centre of it all, in the main surviving building, was a museum.

'Shall we go to the Museum first?' asked Lata. 'That might close early.'

The question threw Kiran into abrupt anxiety. 'I don't know – I – I don't know. We can do anything now,' she said. 'There's no one to say anything.'

'Let's do that then,' said Lata. They went in.

Kiran was so nervous that she bit – not her nails, but the flesh at the base of her thumb. Lata looked at her in astonishment.

'Are you all right, Kiran?' she asked. 'Shall we go back?'

'No – no,' cried Kiran. 'Don't read that –' she said.

Lata promptly read the plaque that Kiran was pointing at.

SUSANNA PALMER
killed in this room
by a cannon ball on the
1st July 1857
in her nineteenth year

Lata laughed. 'Really, Kiran!' she said.

'Where was her father?' said Kiran. 'Where was he? Why couldn't he protect her?'

Lata sighed. She now wished she had come here alone, but there had been no getting around her mother's insistence that she go nowhere in a strange town unaccompanied.

Since her sympathy appeared to disturb Kiran, Lata tried to ignore her, interesting herself instead in a minutely detailed model of the Residency and the surrounding area during the siege of Lucknow. On one wall hung sepia pictures of battle, of the storming of the batteries, of the billiard room, of an English spy disguising himself to get through the native lines.

There was even a poem by Tennyson, one of Lata's favourite poets. She had, however, never read this particular poem, 'The Relief of Lucknow'. It had seven stanzas, and she read them at first with interest, then with increasing disgust. She wondered what Amit would have thought of them. Each stanza ended with the line:

And ever upon the topmost roof our banner of England
blew!

Occasionally the 'and' was replaced by 'but' or 'that'. Lata could scarcely believe that this was the poet of 'Maud' and 'The Lotos Eaters'. It was hardly possible, she thought, to be more racially smug than this:

Handful of men as we were, we were English in heart
and in limb,
Strong with the strength of the race to command, to
obey, to endure....
Now let it speak, and you fire, and the dark pioneer is
no more....
Blessing the wholesome white faces of Havelock's good
fusiliers....

And so on and so forth.

She did not consider the fact that if the conquest had taken place the other way around, there would have been equally unspeakable poems, probably in Persian, possibly in Sanskrit, dotting England's green and pleasant land. She felt a great burst of pride for Savita's father-in-law who had played his part in throwing the English out of this country, and she momentarily forgot all about Sophia Convent and *Emma*.

In her indignation she had even forgotten about Kiran, whom she now found staring at the plaque commemorating poor Susanna Palmer. Kiran's body was shaking with sobs, and people were looking at her. Lata put her arm around her shoulder, but did not know what else to do. She drew her out of the building and sat her down on a bench. It was getting dark, and they would have to go home soon.

Kiran resembled her mother in her looks, though there was nothing stupid about her. Tears were now streaming down her face, but she was speechless. Lata tried fumblingly to find out what had upset her. The death of a girl her age almost a century before? The entire atmosphere of the Residency, haunted as it was by desperation? Was there something the matter at home? Near them a boy was standing on the grass, flying an orange and purple kite. Sometimes he stared at them.

Twice it seemed to Lata that Kiran was on the verge of a confidence or at least an apology. But since nothing was forthcoming, Lata suggested:

'We should go home now, it's getting late.'

Kiran sighed, got up, and walked down the hill with Lata. Lata started humming a little in Raag Marwa, a raag she loved with a passion. By the time they had got home, Kiran appeared to have recovered. As they got to the house she asked Lata:

'You're going by the evening train tomorrow, aren't you?'

'Yes.'

'I wish I could visit you in Brahmpur. But Savita's house, I hear, is so small, not like my father's luxury hotel.' She spoke the last words bitterly.

'You must come, Kiran. You can easily stay with us for a week – or more. Your term starts fifteen days after ours. And we'll get to know each other better.'

Again Kiran's silence grew almost guilty. She did not even respond aloud to what Lata had said.

Lata was relieved to see her mother again. Mrs Rupa Mehra ticked them off for taking such a long time to return. To Lata's ears the familiar reprimands were like music.

'You must tell me –' Mrs Rupa Mehra began.

'Ma, first we went along the road past the Chief Court,

and then we got to the Residency. At the foot of the Residency was an obelisk which commemorated the officers and sepoys who had remained loyal to the British. Three squirrels sat at the base of –'

'Lata!'

'Yes, Ma?'

'You are behaving very badly. All I wanted to know was –'

'Everything.'

Mrs Rupa Mehra frowned, then turned to her cousin.

'Do you have the same trouble with Kiran?' she asked.

'Oh, no,' said Mrs Sahgal. 'Kiran is a very good girl. It is all due to Sahgal Sahib. Sahgal Sahib is always talking to her and giving her advice. There could be no father like him. Even when clients are waiting. ... But Lata is a good girl too.'

'No,' said Lata, laughing. 'Unfortunately I am a bad girl. Ma, what will you do if I do get married and move away? Whom will you be able to tick off?'

'I will tick you off just the same,' said Mrs Rupa Mehra.

Mr Sahgal had entered meanwhile, and, having heard the last part of the conversation, said in a calm, avuncular voice: 'Lata, you are not a bad girl, I know. I have heard all about your results and we are very proud of you. Sometime soon we must have a long talk about the future.'

Kiran stood up. 'I am going to talk to Pushkar,' she said.

'Sit down,' said Mr Sahgal, in the same calm voice.

Kiran, white-faced, sat down.

Mr Sahgal's eyes wandered around the room.

'Shall I put on the gramophone?' asked his wife.

'Do you have any hobbies?' said Mr Sahgal to Lata.

'Oh, yes,' said Mrs Rupa Mehra. 'She has begun to sing classical music very beautifully. And she is a real bookworm.'

'I enjoy photography,' said Mr Sahgal. 'When I was in England studying law, I began to take an interest in it.'

'The albums?' asked Mrs Sahgal, breathless with the possibility of being of service to him.

'Yes.'

She laid them on the table before him. Mr Sahgal started showing them photographs of his English landladies and their daughters, other girls he had known there, then a few Indian photographs, followed by pages and pages of his wife and daughter, sometimes in poses that Lata found distasteful. In one, Mrs Sahgal had bent forward, and one of her breasts was almost spilling out of her blouse. Mr Sahgal carried on an explanation, gentle and measured, of the art of photography, about composition and exposure, grain and gloss, contrast and depth of field.

Lata glanced at her mother. Mrs Rupa Mehra was looking at the photographs with puzzled interest. Mrs Sahgal's face was flushed with pride. Kiran was sitting rigid, as if she had been taken ill. Again she was biting the base of her thumb in that unusual and disturbing gesture. When she noticed Lata's gaze on her, she looked at her with a mixture of shame and hatred.

After dinner Lata went straight to her room. She felt an acute sense of unease, and was glad they were leaving Lucknow the next day. Her mother, on the other hand, was thinking of postponing their departure, since both Mr and Mrs Sahgal were very keen that they stay on for a few days.

'What is this?' Mrs Sahgal had said at dinner. 'You come for one day, and then you disappear for a year. Is this the way a sister should behave?'

'I want to stay, Maya,' said Mrs Rupa Mehra. 'But Lata's term begins so soon. Otherwise we would have been very happy to stay with you and Sahgal Sahib. Next time we will stay longer.'

Pushkar had held his peace throughout dinner. He could just about feed himself with help from his father. Mr Sahgal had looked very tired by the end of the meal. He had then put Pushkar to bed.

Returning to the drawing room, he had wished everyone goodnight and gone immediately to his room at the near end of the long corridor. His wife's room was opposite his. Then came the guest rooms, and finally, at the far end of the corridor, Pushkar's and Kiran's rooms. Since Pushkar was fond of a huge grandfather clock – a family heirloom – Mr Sahgal had installed it just outside his room. Sometimes Pushkar would sing out the chimes. He had even learned to wind it up himself.

9.16

LATA lay awake for a while. It was the height of summer, so there was only a sheet by way of covering. The fan was on, but there was no need yet for a mosquito net. The chimes on the quarter-hour were soft, but when the clock struck eleven, then midnight, it resounded along the corridor. Lata read a little by the weak light at her bedside, but the events of the last two days swam between her and the pages. Finally she put out the light and closed her eyes, and dreamed, half-awake, of Kabir.

Slow footsteps padded down the carpeted corridor. When they stopped outside her door, she sat up, startled. They were not her mother's footsteps. The door opened, and she saw the silhouette of a man against the dim light in the corridor. It was Mr Sahgal.

Lata turned on the light. Mr Sahgal stood blinking mildly, shaking his head, protecting his eyes with his hand even from the weak light of the bedside lamp. He was dressed in a brown dressing-gown tied with a brown rope with tassels. He looked very tired.

Lata looked at him in dismay and astonishment. 'Are you all right, Mausaji?' she asked. 'Are you ill?'

'No, not ill. But I have been working late. That is why – and I saw your light was on. But then you put it off. You are an intelligent girl – a great reader.'

He looked around the room, stroking his short-trimmed beard. He was quite a large man. In a thoughtful voice he said: 'There is no chair here. I must speak to Maya about it.' He sat himself down at the edge of the bed. 'Is everything all right?' he asked Lata. 'Everything is all right, isn't it? The pillows and everything? I remember when you were a little girl you used to like grapes. You were very young. And it is the season for them now. Pushkar also likes grapes. Poor boy.'

Lata tried to pull the sheet closer to cover herself better, but Mr Sahgal was sitting on one corner of it.

'You are very good to Pushkar, Mausaji,' she said, wondering what she could do or what conversation she could make. She could hear and feel her heart beating.

'You see,' said Mr Sahgal in a calm voice, his hands clutching the tassels of the band of his dressing-gown, 'Living here there is no hope for him. In England they have special schools, special. ...' He paused, looking at Lata's face and neck. 'That boy, Haresh – he was in England? Maybe he also has photos of his landladies?'

'I don't know,' said Lata, thinking of Mr Sahgal's suggestive photographs and trying to check her rising fear. 'Mausaji, I am very sleepy, I have to go tomorrow –'

'But you are leaving in the evening. We must have our talk now. You see there is no one to talk to in Lucknow. Now in Calcutta – or even Delhi – but I cannot leave Lucknow. My practice, you see.'

'Yes,' said Lata.

'It would also not be good for Kiran. She already sees bad boys, reads bad books. I have to stop these habits. My wife is a saint, she does not see these things.' He was explaining things gently to Lata, and Lata was nodding mechanically.

'My wife is a saint,' he repeated. 'Every morning she does puja for an hour. She will do anything for me. Whatever food I want, she cooks with her own hands. She is like Sita – a perfect wife. If I want her to dance naked for me she will dance. She wants nothing for herself. She only wants Kiran to get married. But I feel that Kiran should complete her education – till then what is wrong with living at home? Once, a boy came to the house – actually to the house. I told him to get out – to get out!' Mr Sahgal no longer looked tired but livid, though his voice was still low. Then he calmed down, and continued in a tone of explanation: 'But who will marry Kiran when sometimes, you know, Pushkar makes such frightening noises. Sometimes I sense his rage. You don't mind my confiding like this in you? Kiran is a good friend of yours, I know. You must also tell me about yourself, your plans. ...' He sniffed in an appraising way. 'That is the eau-de-Cologne your mother uses. Kiran never uses eau-de-Cologne. Natural things are best.'

Lata stared at him. Her mouth had become completely dry.

'But I buy saris for her whenever I go to Delhi,' continued Mr Sahgal. 'During the War, society ladies used to wear saris with broad borders; even brocades and tissues. Before she became a widow I once saw your mother wearing her wedding tissue sari. But now all that has gone. Embroidery is considered so vulgar.'

As an afterthought he added:

'Shall I buy you a sari?'

'No – no –' said Lata.

'Georgette drapes better than chiffon, don't you think?'

Lata gave no answer.

'Recently Ajanta pallus have become the craze. The motifs are so – so – imaginative – I saw one with a paisley design, another with a lotus –' Mr Sahgal smiled. 'And now with these short cholis the women show their bare waists at the back as well. Do you think you are a bad girl?'

'A bad girl?' repeated Lata.

'At dinner you said you were a bad girl,' explained her uncle in a kindly, measured way. 'I don't think you are. I think you are a lipstick girl. Are you a lipstick girl?'

With sick horror Lata remembered that he had asked her the same question when they were sitting together in his car five years ago. She had completely buried the memory. She had been fourteen or so at the time, and he had asked her calmly, almost considerately: 'Are you a lipstick girl?'

'A lipstick girl?' Lata had asked, puzzled. At that time she had believed that women who wore lipstick, like those who smoked, were bold and modern and probably beyond the pale. 'I don't think so,' she had said.

'Do you know what a lipstick girl is?' Mr Sahgal had asked with a slow smirk on his face.

'Someone who uses lipstick?' Lata had said.

'On her lips?' asked her uncle slowly.

'Yes, on her lips.'

'No, not on her lips, not on her lips – that is what is known as a lipstick girl.' Mr Sahgal shook his head gently from side to side and smiled, as if enjoying a joke, while looking straight into her bewildered eyes.

Kiran had returned to the car – she had gone to buy something – and they had driven on. But Lata had felt almost ill. Later, she had blamed herself for misunderstanding what her uncle had said. She had never mentioned the incident to her mother or to anyone, and had forgotten it. Now it came back to her and she stared at him.

'I know you are a lipstick girl. Do you want some lipstick?' said Mr Sahgal, moving forward along the bed.

'No –' cried Lata. 'I don't – Mausaji – please stop this –'

'It is so hot – I must take off this dressing-gown.'

'No!' Lata wanted to shout, but found she couldn't. 'Don't, please, Mausaji. I – I'll shout – my mother is a light sleeper – go away – go away – Ma – Ma –'

The clock chimed one.

Mr Sahgal's mouth opened. He said nothing for a moment. Then he sighed. He looked very tired again. 'I thought you were an intelligent girl,' he said in a disappointed voice. 'What are you thinking of? If you had a father to bring you up properly, you would not behave in this way.' He got up. 'I must get a chair for this room, every deluxe hotel should have a chair in every room.' He was about to touch Lata's hair, but perhaps he could sense that she was tense with terror. Instead, in a forgiving voice, he said: 'I know that deep down you are a good girl. Sleep well, God bless you.'

'No!' Lata almost shouted.

When he left, his footsteps padding gently back towards his room, Lata began to tremble. 'Sleep well, God bless you,' is what she remembered her father used to say to her, his 'little monkey'. She switched off the light, then immediately switched it on again. She went to the door, and found that there was no way to lock it. Finally she dragged her suitcase and placed it against the door. There was water in a jug by the bedside lamp, and she drank a glass. Her throat was parched, and her hands trembling. She buried her face in her mother's handkerchief.

She thought of her father. During the school holidays, whenever he came back from work, he would ask her to make tea for him. She adored him, and she adored his memory. He was a jolly man and liked to have his family around him in the evenings. When he had died in Calcutta after a long cardiac illness, she had been at Sophia Convent in Mussourie. The nuns had been very kind. It was not just that she had been excused the test that had been set that day. They had given her an anthology of poetry that was still among the most valued of her possessions. And one nun had said, 'We are so sorry – he was very young to die.' 'Oh no,' Lata had replied. 'He was very old – he was forty-seven years old.' Even then, it had not seemed believable. The term would end in a few months, and she would go home as usual. She had found it difficult to cry.

A month later her mother had come up to Mussourie. Mrs Rupa Mehra had been almost prostrate with grief and had not been able to come up earlier, even to see her daughter. She was dressed in white, and there was no tika on her forehead. That was what had brought things home to Lata, and she had wept.

'He was very old.' Again she heard her uncle's voice saying: 'You were very young.' Lata put off her light once more, and lay in the darkness.

She could not speak to anyone about what had happened. Mrs Sahgal doted on her husband; could she even be aware of what he was like? They had separate rooms: Mr Sahgal often worked late. Mrs Rupa Mehra would hardly have believed Lata. If she had, she would have imagined – or wanted to imagine – that Lata had placed a dramatic construction on innocent events. And even if she had believed Lata entirely, what could she have done?

Denounced Maya's husband and destroyed her stupid happiness?

Lata recalled that neither her mother nor Savita had told her even about menstruation before it had suddenly happened to her with no warning while they were on a train. Lata had been twelve. Her father was dead. They were no longer travelling in saloons, but in the intermediate class between second and third. It was the heat of late summer – as now, the monsoons had not yet broken. For some reason she and her mother were travelling alone. She had gone to the toilet when she felt the onset of something uncomfortable – and there, when she saw what it was, she had thought she was bleeding to death. Terrified, she had rushed back to her compartment. Her mother had given her a handkerchief to absorb the flow, but had been very embarrassed. She had told Lata that she must not talk to anybody about it, especially men. Sita and Savitri didn't talk about such things. Lata wondered what she had done to deserve it. Finally, Mrs Rupa Mehra had told her not to get alarmed – that it happened to all women – that it was what made women very special and precious – and that it would happen every month.

'Do you have it?' Lata had asked.

'Yes,' said Mrs Rupa Mehra. 'Previously I used to use soft cloth, but now I use padded napkins, and you must keep a few with you. I have some at the bottom of the suitcase.'

It had been sticky and uncomfortable in the strong heat, but it had to be borne. Nor did it improve over the years. The mess, the backaches, its irregular arrival before exams – Lata felt there was nothing very special or precious about it. When she asked Savita why she hadn't told her about it, Savita said: 'But I thought you knew. I did, before it happened to me.'

The clock down the corridor struck three, and Lata was still awake. Then, once again, she caught her breath with fear. The padded footsteps were coming down the carpeted corridor. She knew they were going to pause at her door. Oh, Ma, Ma – thought Lata.

But the footsteps padded on, softly down the corridor towards the far end, towards Pushkar's and Kiran's rooms. Perhaps Mr Sahgal was going to see that his son was all right. Lata waited for his footsteps to return any minute. She could not sleep. But it was two hours later, a little before five in the morning, that they passed by her room gently, after a momentary pause by her door.

9.17

AT breakfast the next morning, Mr Sahgal was absent.

'Sahgal Sahib is not feeling very well. He is tired from working so hard,' said Mrs Sahgal.

Mrs Rupa Mehra shook her head: 'Maya, you must tell him to take it easy. It was overwork that killed my husband. And for what final aim? One must work hard, but enough is really enough. Lata, why aren't you eating your toast? It will get cold. And see, Maya Masi has made that lovely white butter you like so much.'

Mrs Sahgal smiled sweetly at Lata. 'She looks so tired and worried, poor girl. I think she is already in love with H. Now she is spending sleepless nights.' She sighed happily.

Lata buttered her toast in silence.

Without his father to help him, Pushkar was having a hard time with his toast. Kiran, who was looking as sleepy as Lata, went over to give him a hand.

'What does he do when he needs to shave?' asked Mrs Rupa Mehra in a low voice.

'Oh, Sahgal Sahib helps him,' said Mrs Sahgal. 'Or one of the servants does – but Pushkar prefers us to help him. Oh Rupa, I wish you could stay for a few more days. We have so much to talk about. And the girls can get to know each other also.'

'No!' The word was out before Lata could think of what she was saying. She looked frightened and disgusted.

Kiran dropped the knife on Pushkar's plate. Then she rushed out of the room.

'Lata, you must say sorry at once,' said Mrs Rupa Mehra. 'What do you mean by this? Have you no decency?'

Lata was about to tell her mother that all she had meant was that she did not want to stay in the house any longer, and had not meant to hurt Kiran. That, however, would merely exchange one offence for another. So she kept her mouth shut and her head bowed.

'Did you hear me?' Mrs Rupa Mehra's high voice held an edge of anger.

'Yes.'

'Yes what?'

'Yes, Ma, I heard you. I heard you. I heard you.'

Lata got up and went to her room. Mrs Rupa Mehra could hardly believe her eyes.

Pushkar began singing to himself and stuffing the small squares of toast that his sister had cut and buttered for him into his mouth. Mrs Sahgal looked distressed.

'I wish Sahgal Sahib was here. He knows how to deal with the children.'

Mrs Rupa Mehra said: 'Lata is a thoughtless girl sometimes. I am going to have a word with her.' Then she thought that perhaps she was being too harsh. 'Of course, Kanpur was a strain on her. It was on me, too, of course. She does not appreciate the efforts I have made for her. Only He appreciated me.'

'Finish your tea, first, Rupa mine,' said Mrs Sahgal.

A few minutes later, when Mrs Rupa Mehra entered Lata's room, she found her asleep. So soundly was she sleeping that she had to be woken for lunch a few hours later.

At lunch, Mr Sahgal smiled at Lata and said, 'See what I have got for you.' It was a small, flat, square packet wrapped in red paper. The wrapping paper was decorated with holly, bells and other Christmas paraphernalia.

'How lovely!' said Mrs Rupa Mehra, without knowing what it was.

Lata's ears burned with embarrassment and anger.

'I don't want it.'

Mrs Rupa Mehra was too shocked to speak.

'And then we can go to the cinema. There will be time before your train leaves.'

Lata stared at him.

Mrs Rupa Mehra, who had been brought up never to open gifts when they were given but to wait till she was alone, quite forgot herself.

'Open it,' she ordered Lata.

'I don't want it,' said Lata. 'You open it.' She pushed the packet across. Something jangled inside.

'Savita would never behave like this,' began her mother. 'And Mausaji has taken the afternoon off just for you – just so that Maya and I can have the time to talk. You don't know how much of an interest he takes in you. He is always saying you are so intelligent, but I am beginning to doubt it. Say thank you.'

'Thank you,' said Lata, feeling dirtied and humiliated.

'And you must tell me all about the film when you come back.'

'I will not go to the film.'

'What?'

'I will not go to the film.'

'Mausaji will be with you, Lata – what are you worried about?' said her mother uncomprehendingly.

Kiran looked at Lata with a bitter glance of jealousy. Mr Sahgal said, 'She is like my own daughter. I will see that she doesn't eat too many ice-creams and other unhealthy things.'

'I will not go!' Lata's voice rose in defiance and panic.

Mrs Rupa Mehra was struggling with the packet. At this cry of rank rebellion, her fingers lost control of themselves. Normally she unpacked every gift with infinite care in order to be able to re-use the paper later. But now the paper ripped open.

'See what you've made me do,' she said to Lata. But then, looking at the contents, she turned to Mr Sahgal, perplexed.

The present was a puzzle, a pink plastic maze with a transparent top. Seven little silver balls were to be jiggled around the square maze so that, with luck, they would eventually come to rest in the central cell.

'She is such a clever girl, I thought I would give her a puzzle. Normally she would be able to do it in five minutes. But on the train everything shakes so much that it will take her an hour,' Mr Sahgal explained in a gentle voice. 'Time passes so slowly sometimes.'

'How thoughtful,' murmured Mrs Rupa Mehra, frowning a little.

Lata lied that she had a headache, and returned to her room. But she did, indeed, feel ill – sick to the pit of her stomach.

9.18

MR SAHGAL'S car took them to the station late in the afternoon. He was working, and did not come. Kiran stayed behind with Pushkar. Mrs Sahgal came with them and chattered sweetly and vacuously throughout.

Lata did not say a word.

They were immersed in the crowds on the platform. Suddenly Haresh appeared.

'Hello, Mrs Mehra. Hello, Lata.'

'Haresh? I said you were not to come,' said Mrs Rupa Mehra. 'And I told you to call me Ma,' she added mechanically.

Haresh smiled, pleased to have surprised them.

'My own train back to Cawnpore leaves in fifteen minutes so I thought I would give you a hand. Now where is your coolie?'

He installed them in their compartment cheerfully and efficiently, and made sure that Mrs Rupa Mehra's black handbag was placed where it was both within reach and theft-proof.

Mrs Rupa Mehra looked mortified; it had been a hard decision for her to buy two first-class tickets from Kanpur to Lucknow, but she had felt she had to convey a certain impression to a potential son-in-law. Now he could clearly see that they usually travelled not even by second but by Inter class. And indeed, Haresh was puzzled, though he did not show it. After all this talk by Mrs Rupa Mehra about travelling in saloons and having a son in Bentsen Pryce, he had expected a different style from them.

But what does all that matter? he asked himself. I like the girl.

Lata, who had first seemed glad – relieved, he would have said – to see him, now appeared withdrawn, hardly aware of her own presence, or her mother's, or her aunt's, let alone his.

As the whistle blew, a scene came to Haresh's mind. It was set at about this time of day. It had been warm, so it could not have been many months ago. He had been standing at the platform of a busy station, about to catch a train himself, and his coolie had been about to disappear into the crowd ahead. A middle-aged woman, her back turned partly towards him, had been boarding another train together with a younger woman. This younger woman – he knew now that it had been Lata – had had on her face such a look of intensity and inwardness, perhaps even hurt or anger, that he had caught his breath. There had been a man with them, the young man whom he had met at Sunil Patwardhan's party – that English teacher whose name eluded him. Brahmpur, yes – that was where he had seen them before. He had known it; he had known it, and now it all came back to him. He had not been mistaken, after all. He smiled, his eyes disappearing.

'Brahmpur – a pale blue sari,' he said, almost to himself.

Lata turned to him through the window with a questioning look.

The train began to move.

Haresh shook his head, still smiling. Even if the train had been stationary, he would probably not have explained himself.

He waved as the train pulled out, but neither mother nor daughter waved back. However, being an optimist, Haresh put this down to their anglicized reticence.

A blue sari. That's what it was, he kept thinking to himself.

9.19

HARESH had spent his day in Lucknow at Simran's sister's house. He told her that he had met a woman just yesterday who – since he had no chance of succeeding with Simran – was someone he was thinking seriously about as wife material.

He did not put it exactly like that; but even if he had it would not have been intrinsically offensive. Most marriages he knew had been decided on that basis, and the deciders were usually not even the couple themselves but their elders: fathers or male heads of the concerned families – with the wished-for or unwished-for counsel of dozens of others thrown in. In the case of one of Haresh's distant rural cousins, the go-between had been the village barber; by virtue of his access to most of the houses in the village, this had been the fourth marriage he had been instrumental in arranging that year.

Simran's sister sympathized with Haresh. She knew how long and faithfully Haresh had loved her sister, and she felt that his heart still belonged to her.

Haresh himself would not have thought of this as casually metaphorical. He and his heart did belong to her. She could do with it and with him what she pleased, and he would still love her. The pleasure in Simran's eyes whenever they met – the sadness underlying that pleasure – the increasing certainty that her parents would not yield, that they would cut her off from themselves – that her mother, emotional woman that she was, might very well even carry out the threat against herself that she now spoke of in every letter to her and every day when she was home – all these had worn Simran out. Her correspondence, erratic even in England (partly because she herself would receive Haresh's letters erratically, whenever the friend to whose address they were sent visited her) became even more so.

Sometimes weeks would pass, and Haresh would not hear from her; then he would get three letters in as many days.

Simran's sister knew how hard it would be for Simran to hear the news that Haresh had decided he might live his life with someone else – or even consider doing so. Simran loved Haresh. Her sister loved him too – even if he was the son of a Lala, which among the Sikhs was something of a term of contempt for Hindus. Her brother too had been part of the conspiracy. When he and Haresh were both seventeen he had been paid to sing ghazals on his friend's behalf under his sister's window: Simran had been annoyed with Haresh for some reason, and Haresh had been trying to appease her. He had had to hire her brother because he himself had, together with a love of music and a belief in its power to move unyielding hearts, a singing voice that even his beloved Simran (who liked his speaking voice well enough) had declared to be tuneless.

'Haresh, have you made up your mind?' said Simran's sister in Punjabi. She was three years older than Simran, and her own marriage had been an arranged one – to a Sikh officer in the army.

'What choice do I have?' replied Haresh. 'I have to think of someone else sooner or later. Time is passing. I am twenty-eight. I'm thinking of her good too – she will refuse everyone whom your parents suggest until she knows that I'm married.'

Haresh's eyes grew moist. Simran's sister patted him on the shoulder.

'When did you make up your mind that this girl might suit you?'

'At Kanpur Station. She was drinking that chocolate drink – you know, Pheasant's.' Haresh, noticing the look on Simran's sister's face, realized she wished to be spared the exact details.

'Have you made any proposal?'

'No. We have agreed to write to each other. Her mother arranged the meeting. They are in Lucknow at the moment, but they didn't seem keen to see me here.'

'Have you written to your father?'

'I'll write to him tonight, when I get back to Kanpur.' Haresh had chosen a train that would enable him to meet Mrs Rupa Mehra and her daughter as if by chance at Lucknow Station.

'Don't write to Simran just yet.'

Haresh said in a hurt voice: 'But why? I'll have to say something sooner or later.'

'If nothing comes out of this you will have hurt her for nothing.'

'She'll wonder if she doesn't hear from me.'

'Write as you always write.'

'How can I do that?' Haresh baulked at the deception.

'Don't say anything that isn't true. Just don't touch on this.'

Haresh thought for a while. 'All right,' he said at last. But he felt that Simran knew him too well not to sense from his letters that something had begun to happen in his life, not just in hers, that could draw the two of them apart.

9.20

THE conversation turned after a while to Simran's sister herself. Her young son Monty (only three years old) wanted to join the navy, and her husband (who was crazy about the boy) was taking this decision extraordinarily badly. He treated it as a vote of no confidence in himself, and was, it seemed to her, sulking as a result. She herself attributed Monty's preference to the fact that he enjoyed playing with boats in his tub, and had not yet arrived at the model-soldier stage.

Monty, incidentally, had difficulty pronouncing certain words, and just the other day had said (talking in English instead of Punjabi) while splashing around in his favourite element after one brief pre-monsoon shower, that he wanted to go to 'the miggle of the puggle'. This Simran's sister took as being symptomatic of his intrinsic sweetness. She hoped that in years to come he would order his men 'into the heart of backle'. Monty sat through all this with a look of offended dignity. From time to time he tugged at his mother's fingers to get her to stop prattling.

Since he wasn't feeling hungry, Haresh decided to forgo lunch and went to see the twelve o'clock show of a film instead. *Hamlet* was playing at the local cinema-hall. He enjoyed it, but Hamlet's indecisiveness irritated him.

He then had a good haircut for a rupee. Finally, he had a paan and went off to the station in order to catch the train back to Kanpur – and, he hoped, to meet Lata and her mother, both of whom he had become quite fond of. That he was successful in this pleased him greatly; that they did not wave to him as the train moved out did not distress him unduly. The coincidence connecting Brahm-pur Station and Lucknow Station he took as a propitious sign.

On the two-hour train journey back to Kanpur, Haresh took out a blue writing pad from his portfolio ('H.C. Khanna' was embossed on the top of each page) and a cheap white scribbling pad as well. He looked from one to the other, then to a woman sitting opposite him, then out of the window. It was getting dark. Soon the train lights came on. Finally he decided that it would not do to write a serious letter in a jolting train. He put away the writing pad.

At the top of his scribbling pad, he wrote: 'To Do'. Then he crossed it out and wrote: 'Points to remember'. Then he crossed that out and wrote: 'Action Points'. It occurred to him that he was behaving as stupidly as Hamlet.

After he had listed his correspondence and various work-related items, his thoughts moved to more general matters, and he made a third list, under the heading, 'My Life':

1. Must catch up with news and world affairs.

Haresh felt he had not come off well on this account during his meetings with the Mehras. But his work kept him so busy that sometimes he hardly had time even to glance at the papers.

2. Exercise: at least 15 minutes each morning. How to find the time?
3. Make 1951 the deciding year of my life.
4. Pay off debts to Umesh Uncle in full.
5. Learn to control temper. Must learn to suffer fools, gladly or not.
6. Get brogue scheme with Kedarnath Tandon in Brahmpur working properly.

This he later crossed out and transferred to the work-related list.

7. Moustache?

This he crossed out, and then rewrote together with the question mark.

8. Learn from good people, like Babaram.
9. Finish reading major novels of T.H.
10. Try to keep my diary regularly as before.
11. Make notes of my five best and five worst qualities. Conserve latter and eradicate former.

Haresh read over this last sentence, looked surprised, and corrected it.

9.21

IT was late when he got back to Elm Villa. Mrs Mason, however, who sometimes complained when Haresh came late for meals (on the grounds that it would upset the staff), was very welcoming.

'Oh, you look so tired. My daughter has been telling me how busy you have been. And you didn't leave word that you would be gone for more than a day. We prepared lunch for you. And dinner. And lunch again today. But no matter. You're here, back at last, and that's the main thing. It's mutton. A good, hearty roast.'

Haresh was glad to hear it. Mrs Mason was bursting with curiosity, but refrained from asking questions while he ate his dinner. He had eaten nothing since morning.

After dinner Mrs Mason turned to Haresh to speak.

'How is Sophie?' interposed Haresh deftly. Sophie was the Masons' beloved Persian cat, an unfailing subject of animated discourse.

After five minutes of the Sophie saga, Haresh yawned and said, 'Well, goodnight, Mrs Mason. It was very kind of you to keep my dinner warm for me. I think I'll turn in.'

And before Mrs Mason could veer the conversation around to Simran or the two visitors, Haresh had gone to his room.

He was very tired, but he kept awake long enough to write three letters. The rest he was forced to leave unwritten till the next day.

He was about to write to Lata when, sensing Simran's eyes on him, he turned to a shorter and easier letter – a postcard in fact.

It was to Kedarnath Tandon's son Bhaskar.

Dear Bhaskar,

I hope all is well with you. The words you want, according to a Chinese colleague of mine, are wan (to rhyme with 'kaan') and ee (to rhyme with 'knee'). That will give you, in order of powers of ten: one, ten, hundred, thousand, wan, lakh, million, crore, ee, billion. A special word for ten to its own power you will have to invent for yourself. I suggest bhask.

Please give my regards to Dr Durrani, to your parents, and to your grandmother. Also, ask your father to send me the second sample of brogues that I was promised by the man in Ravidaspur. They should have arrived more than a week ago. Perhaps they are already on their way.

Affectionately,
Haresh Chacha.

Next he wrote a short letter of a page-and-a-half to his father, in which he enclosed the small snapshot of Lata he had got off the Mehras. He had wanted to take a photograph of them himself, but they had felt a bit embarrassed, and he had not pressed the matter.

To Lata he wrote a three page letter on his blue writing pad. Though he had almost been at the point of telling her (or, more strictly, them) over the cold chocolate that he knew that she was the right wife for him, something had held him back. Now he was glad of it. Haresh knew that despite his pragmatism he was highly impulsive. When he had decided to leave home at fifteen it had taken him a minute to decide and ten minutes to leave; it had been months before he had returned. In the market the other day he had almost hired Mr Lee, the designer, on the spot, though he had no real authority to do so; he knew that he was the right man to help design the new orders that he felt sure he could bring in.

So much for decisions that were (or would have been) if not laudable, at least admirable. The money that he once lent a friend of his in Patiala, however, was lent equally impulsively. It had been a good third of his assets, and he now knew that he would never get it back. But the decision that faced him at the present time dealt not with his assets but with himself. If he gave himself away he would not be able to retrieve himself.

He looked at Simran's photograph – nothing would induce him to turn it away even while writing his first letter to Lata. He wondered what she would have said, what advice she would have given him. Her kindness and purity of heart would have led him in the right direction, he knew. She wanted his good as much as he wanted hers.

'Look at it this way, Simran,' he said. 'I am twenty-eight. There is no possibility of anything between us. I will have to settle down one day. If I have to marry I may as well go ahead and do it. They like me. At least I'm confident the mother does; and that makes a change.'

Of the three pages of his letter to Lata, one-and-a-half were about the Praha Shoe Company, the Czech-founded establishment with Indian headquarters in Calcutta and a huge factory at Prahapore fifteen miles away. Haresh wanted his name and copies of his certificates brought to the attention of someone whom Mrs Rupa Mehra had known socially over a period of years and who himself knew someone fairly high up in the company. Haresh saw three advantages in a job with Praha. He would have a better chance of rising to the top in a company that was professionally managed. He would be near Calcutta, which could be considered to be the Mehra home base, and where Lata, he had ascertained, would be spending her Christmas holidays. And finally, he thought his income would surely be larger than the one he was at present living on. The insulting offer of a weekly wage that he had previously received from Praha he was prepared to discount as their badgered response to a persistent series of letters from a man writing to them without any prior introduction. What he needed to do, Haresh believed, was to get the attention of someone at the top.

This business being over [continued Haresh], let me hope in the usual way that you had a comfortable journey home and that you were missed by all who met you after such a long absence from Brahmpur.

I must thank you for your visit to Cawnpore and the nice time we spent together. There was none of that bashfulness or undue modesty and I am convinced that we can be very friendly if nothing else. I quite appreciate your frankness and the way of putting things. I must admit that I have met few English girls who could speak English quite as well as you do. These qualities coupled with your way of dressing and personality make you a person far above the average. I think Kalpana was right in her praise of you. These may all seem flattering remarks but I write as I feel.

I have just today sent your photograph to my foster-father along with my impressions of you formed during our brief hours together. I shall let you know what he has to say.

A couple of final paragraphs about generalities, and the letter was over. Haresh addressed the envelope. As he lay on his bed a few minutes later it struck him that the Mehras would certainly have seen Simran's silver-framed portrait on his writing-table. When he had invited them to Elm Villa he had not thought about the photograph at all. It was as much a part of the room as his bed. Between themselves, mother and daughter would doubtless have discussed it – and particularly the fact that he had let it remain there. He wondered what they must have thought, what they could have said. But he was asleep too soon to wonder long.

9.22

ONE morning, a few days later, Haresh arrived at the factory to find that Rao had assigned Lee to do some trivial work of his own.

'I need Lee,' said Haresh bluntly. 'It's for the HSH order.'

Rao looked at him with distaste down his sharp nose. 'You can have him when I've finished with him,' he said. 'He will be working with me this week.'

Lee, who had witnessed the scene, was very embarrassed. He owed his position to Haresh, and he respected him. He did not respect Rao, but Rao was nominally Haresh's senior in the company structure.

The weekly meeting later that morning in Mukherji's office produced a display of spectacular fireworks.

Mukherji congratulated Haresh heartily for his work in obtaining the HSH order, which had recently been confirmed. The factory would have been in severe difficulties without it.

'But the question of labour should be coordinated with Sen Gupta,' he added.

'Assuredly,' said Sen Gupta. He looked pleased. He was supposed to be in charge of labour and personnel, but there was nothing that this lazy man enjoyed more than chewing his paan and delaying any work that needed desperately to be done. Waiting for Sen Gupta to do anything except stare with his bloodshot eyes at a red-stained file was like waiting for a stupa to disintegrate. Sen Gupta had looked sour when Mukherji had praised Haresh.

'We will have to work a little harder all around, hn? Sen Gupta?' continued the factory manager. 'Now, Khanna,' he continued, turning to Haresh, 'Sen Gupta has been a bit unhappy of late about your interference in labour. Especially the construction job. He feels he could have hired better men more cheaply – and quicker.'

Actually Sen Gupta was hopping mad – and envious.

Quicker! Sen Gupta! was what Haresh was thinking.

'Talking of personnel,' he said aloud, deciding that this was the time to thrash matters out, 'I'd like to have Lee put back to work on the HSH order.' He looked at Rao.

'Back?' said Mukherji, looking from Haresh to Rao.

'Yes. Mr Rao decided to –'

Rao interrupted: 'You will have him back in a week. There is no need to bring it up in this meeting. Mr Mukherji has more important matters to deal with.'

'I need him now. If we fail in this order do you think they'll come back to us cap in hand begging us to make more shoes for them? Can't we get our priorities right? Lee cares about quality. I need him both for design and for the choice of leather.'

'I care for quality too,' said Rao with distaste.

'Tell me another,' said Haresh hotly. 'You steal my workers when I most need them – just two days ago two of my clickers disappeared into your department, because your men did not turn up for work. You can't keep discipline in your area, and you undermine it in mine. Quality is the last thing on your mind.' Haresh turned to Mukherji. 'Why do you let him get away with it? You are the factory manager.'

This was rather too direct, but Haresh's blood was up. 'I cannot work if my men and my designer are pinched,' he added.

'Your designer?' said Sen Gupta, staring redly at Haresh. 'Your designer? You had no authority to hold out a job to Lee. Who were you to hire him?'

'I did not. Mr Mukherji did, with a sanction from Mr Ghosh. I only found him. At least he's a professional.'

'And I am not? Before you were born I had learned how to shave,' said Mr Sen Gupta with hot irrelevance.

'Professional? Look at this place,' said Haresh with barely muted scorn. 'Compare it with Praha or James Hawley or Cooper Allen. How can we hope to keep our customers if we don't fulfil our orders in time? Or if our quality is below par? They make better brogues in the slums of Brahmpur. The way things are run here is just not professional. You need people who know about shoes, not politics. Who work, and don't just set up an adda wherever they are.'

'Unprofessional?' Sen Gupta seized on Haresh's remark and gave it a tiny twist. 'Mr Ghosh will hear of this! You call us unprofessional? You will see, you will see.'

Something about Sen Gupta's bluster and patent envy made Haresh say:

'Yes, it is unprofessional.'

'You heard? You heard?' Sen Gupta looked at Rao and Mukherji, then turned back to Haresh, his red tongue curled a little at the end, his mouth open. 'You are calling us unprofessional?' He pushed his chair not forwards but backwards with rage and puffed out his cheeks. 'You are getting too big for your boots, yes, for your boots.' His red eyes half popped out.

Haresh, having blundered in so far, blundered in a little further. 'Yes, Mr Sen Gupta, that is exactly what I am saying. You are forcing me to be blunt, but it is true, certainly of you. You are unprofessional in every sense – and one of the worst manipulators I have known, not excluding Rao.'

'Surely,' said Mukherji, who was trying to act as peacemaker, but who was wounded by the use of the word that Sen Gupta had inveigled out of Haresh, and which he took in a sense that Haresh had not, at least in the first instance, intended. 'Surely we must improve in any areas where we are deficient. But let us now talk calmly to one another.' He turned to Rao. 'You have been with the firm for many years, even before Mr Ghosh bought it and took it over. You are respected by everyone. Sen Gupta and I are comparative newcomers.' He then said to Haresh: 'And everyone admires the way you have obtained the HSH order.' Finally he said to Sen Gupta: 'Let us leave it at that.' And he added a pacifying word or two in Bengali.

But Sen Gupta turned towards Haresh, unpacifiable: 'You have one success,' he shouted, 'and you want to take over the whole place.' He was yelling and waving his hands about, and Haresh, incensed by this ludicrous display, cut in with disgust:

'I'd run it a good deal better than you, that's for certain. This thing is run like a Bengali fish-market.'

The words were spoken in the heat of the moment, but were unretractable. The unsavoury Rao was furious; and he was not even a Bengali. Sen Gupta was triumphantly indignant. And the simultaneous insult to Bengal and fish did not go down well with Mukherji either.

'You have been working too hard,' he said to Haresh.

That afternoon Haresh was told that Mr Mukherji wanted to see him in his office. Haresh thought it might be something to do with the HSH order, and he brought along a folder containing a week's work and plans to the office. There Mr Mukherji told him that the HSH order would be handled by Rao, not by him.

Haresh looked at him with a helpless sense of injustice. He shook his head as if to get rid of the last sentence he had heard.

'I slogged my guts out to get that order, Mr Mukherji, and you know it. It has changed the fortunes of this factory. You virtually promised it would be handled in my department and under my supervision. I've told my workmen. What will I tell them now?'

'I am sorry.' Mr Mukherji shook his head. 'It was felt that you had a lot on your plate. Let your new department start up slowly and iron out its problems; it will then be ready to undertake a big job like this. HSH will give us other orders. And I am impressed by the possibilities of this other scheme of yours as well. Everything in good time.'

'The new department has no problems,' said Haresh. 'None. It is already running better than the others. And I've been working on the details of fulfilment ever since last week. Look!' He opened the file. Mr Mukherji shook his head.

Haresh went on, anger building up under his voice: 'They won't give us another order if we mess this one up. Give it to Rao and he will butcher the job. I have even worked out how we can fulfil the order almost a fortnight before it is due.'

Mukherji sighed. 'Khanna, you must learn to be calm.'

'I shall go to Ghosh.'

'This instruction has come from Mr Ghosh.'

'It couldn't have,' said Haresh. 'There wouldn't have been time for that.'

Mukherji looked pained. Haresh looked perplexed before continuing: 'Unless Rao himself telephoned Ghosh in Bombay. He must have. Was this Ghosh's idea? I can't believe it came from you.'

'I can't discuss this, Khanna.'

'This won't be the end of the matter. I won't leave it at this.'

'I am sorry.' Mukherji liked Khanna.

Haresh went back to his room. It was a bitter blow. He had banked on the order. He wanted more than anything to get to grips with something substantial that he himself had brought in, to show what he and his new department could do – and, yes, to do something first-rate for the company of which he was an officer. For a while he felt as if his spirit was broken. He conjured up Rao's contempt, Sen Gupta's glee. He would have to break the news to his workers. It was intolerable. And he would not tolerate it.

Disheartened though he was, he refused to sit down and accept that these unfair dealings would form the future pattern of his working life. He had been ill-treated and used. It was true that Ghosh had given him his first job – and that too at short notice – and he was grateful for that. But such swift illogic and injustice shredded his sense of loyalty. It was as if he had rescued a child from a fire, and promptly been thrown into the fire himself as a reward. He would keep this job only as long as he needed to. If on a salary of three hundred and fifty rupees he had concerns about supporting a wife, with a salary of zero he could forget about it. He had heard nothing useful from anyone to whom he had applied for a job. But soon, he hoped very soon, something would come through. Something? – anything. He would take whatever came along.

He closed the door to his office, which he almost always left open, and sat down once more to think.

9.23

IT took Haresh ten minutes to decide on immediate action.

He had wanted for some time to explore the possibility of a job at James Hawley. He now decided that he would try to get a job there as soon as he possibly could. He admired the establishment; and it had its headquarters in Kanpur. The James Hawley plant was mechanized and fairly modern. The shoes they produced were of better quality than those that CLFC considered adequate. If Haresh had any god, it was Quality. He also felt in his bones that James Hawley would treat his abilities with more respect and less arbitrariness.

But, as always, ingress was the problem. How could he get a foot in at the door – or, to change metaphors, the ear of someone at the top. The Chairman of the Cromarty Group was Sir Neville Maclean; the Managing Director was Sir David Gower; and the manager of its subsidiary James Hawley with its large Kanpur factory (which produced as many as 30,000 pairs of shoes a day) was yet another Englishman. He could not simply march up to the headquarters of the establishment and ask to speak to someone there.

After thinking matters over, he decided he would go to the legendary Pyare Lal Bhalla, who was a fellow khatri, one of the first khatris to have entered the shoe business. How he entered this business and how he had risen to his present eminence was a story in itself.

Pyare Lal Bhalla came from Lahore. He had originally been a sales agent for hats and children's clothing from England, and had expanded into sportswear and paints and cloth. He was extremely good at what he did, and his business had expanded both through his own efforts and through the recommendation of satisfied principals. One could imagine someone from James Hawley, for instance, on his way out to India being told by a fellow clubman: 'Well, if you're in Lahore, and you're not happy with your chap in the Punjab, you could do worse than to look up Peary Loll Buller. I don't think he deals in footwear, but he's a first-rate agent, and it might very well be worth his while. And yours too of course. I'll drop him a line to say you might be coming to see him.'

Considering that he was a vegetarian (mushrooms were the closest he approached anything even faintly resembling meat), it was interesting that Pyare Lal Bhalla had quickly agreed to act as agent for the whole of the undivided Punjab for James Hawley & Company. Leather was polluting, and, certainly, many of the animals whose skins continued their post-mortem existence as an additional layer on human feet were not 'fallen'; they had been slaughtered. Bhalla said that he had nothing to do with the killing. He was a mere agent. The line of demarcation was clear. The English did what they did, he did what he did.

Still, he had been stricken with leucoderma, and many people thought that this was the disfiguring mark of the indignant gods, since he had tainted his soul, however indirectly, with the taking of animal life. Others, however, flocked around him, for he was enormously successful and enormously rich. From being sole agent in the Punjab he had become sole agent for the whole of India. He moved to Kanpur, the headquarters of the group of which James Hawley was a part. He dropped many of his other lines of business in order to concentrate on this particular lucrative account. In time he not only sold their shoes, but also told them what would sell best. He suggested that they reduce their output of Gorillas and increase their output of Champions. He virtually determined their product mix. James Hawley flourished because of his acumen, and he because they had grown dependent on him.

During the war, of course, the company had shifted its entire production to military boots. These did not go directly through Bhalla's hands, but James Hawley – out of a combination of fair-play and far-sighted interest – continued to pay Bhalla commission. Though this was a smaller percentage, it left him no worse off than before owing to the larger volumes of sales. After the War, again steered by the sales and marketing wizardry of Pyare Lal Bhalla, James Hawley had swung back into civilian lines of production. This too appealed to Haresh, since it was for this sort of production that he had been trained at the Midlands College of Technology.

Not more than an hour after he received the bitter news that the HSH order was to be taken away from him, Haresh bicycled up to the offices of Pyare Lal Bhalla. 'Offices' was perhaps too elevated a word for the warren of small rooms that constituted his residence, his place of business, his showroom and his guest-house, all of which occupied the first floor of a congested corner on Meston Road.

Haresh walked up the stairs. He waved a piece of paper at the guard, and muttered, 'James Hawley' and a few words in English. He entered an ante-room, another room with almirahs whose purpose he could not figure out, a store-room, a room with several clerks seated on the ground at their floor-desks and red ledgers, and finally the audience chamber – for that was its function – of Pyare Lal Bhalla himself. It was a small room, whitewashed rather than painted. The old man, energetic at the age of sixty-five, his face whitened with disease, sat on a great wooden platform covered with a spotless white sheet. He was leaning against a hard, cylindrical cotton bolster. Above him hung a garlanded photograph of his father. There were two benches along the walls contiguous to his platform. Here sat various people: hangers-on, favour-seekers, associates, employees. There were no clerks, no ledgers in this room; Pyare Lal Bhalla was himself the repository of whatever information, experience, and judgment he required for making decisions.

Haresh entered and, lowering his head, immediately put his hands forward as if to touch Pyare Lal Bhalla's knees. The old man raised his own hands over Haresh's head.

'Sit down, son,' said Pyare Lal Bhalla in Punjabi.

Haresh sat down on one of the benches.

'Stand up.'

Haresh stood up.

'Sit down.'

Haresh sat down once more.

Pyare Lal Bhalla looked at him with such intentness that he was almost mesmerized into submission to his orders. Of course, the greater one's need, the greater one's propensity to be mesmerized, and Haresh's need, as he himself saw it, was great.

Besides, Pyare Lal Bhalla expected deference as an elderly man and as a man of substance. Had not his daughter been married to the son – the eldest son – of a first-class gazetted officer – the executive engineer for the Punjab canals – in the finest wedding Lahore had known for years? It was not a question of the Services deigning to acknowledge the existence of Trade. It was an Alliance between them. It announced his arrival in a manner that the endowment of twenty temples would not have. In his usual off-hand manner he had said to the groom's father: 'I am, as you know, a poor man, but I've left word at Verma's and Rankin's, and they'll take measurements for whoever you think appropriate.' Sharkskin achkans, suits of the finest cashmere wool: the groom's father had thought nothing of having fifty sets of clothes made for his family – and the fulfilment of this carte blanche was a drop in the ocean of the wedding expenses that Pyare Lal Bhalla proudly and cannily bore.

'Get up. Show me your hand.'

It was Haresh's fourth tense encounter of the day. He breathed deeply, then put his right hand forward. Pyare Lal Bhalla pressed it in a few places, especially the side of the hand just below the little finger. Then, giving no indication of whether he was satisfied or not, he said:

'Sit down.'

Haresh obediently sat down.

Pyare Lal Bhalla turned his attention to someone else for the next ten minutes.

Reverting to Haresh he said, 'Get up.'

Haresh rose.

'Yes, son? Who are you?'

'I am Haresh Khanna, the son of Amarnath Khanna.'

'Which Amarnath Khanna? The Banaras-wallah? Or the Neel Darvaza-wallah?'

'Neel Darvaza.'

This established a connection of sorts, for Haresh's foster-father was very indirectly related to the executive engineer, Pyare Lal Bhalla's son-in-law.

'Hmm. Speak. What can I do for you?'

Haresh said: 'I'm working in the shoe line. I returned from Middlehampton last year. From the Midlands College of Technology.'

'Middlehampton. I see. I see.' Pyare Lal Bhalla was obviously somewhat intrigued.

'Go on,' he said after a while.

'I'm working at CLFC. But they make mainly ammunition boots, and my experience is mainly civilian. I have started a new department, though, for civilian –'

'Oh. Ghosh,' interrupted Pyare Lal Bhalla somewhat slightingly. 'He was here the other day. He wanted me to sell some of his lines for him. Yes, yes, he said something about this civilian idea.'

Considering that Ghosh ran one of the biggest construction companies in the country, Pyare Lal Bhalla's dismissive tone might have seemed a little incongruous. The fact, however, was that in the shoe line he was small fry compared to the plump carp of James Hawley.

'You know how things run there,' said Haresh. Having felt too often – but most painfully today – CLFC's inefficiency and arbitrariness, he did not feel that he was in any sense letting down his firm by speaking thus. He had worked his hardest for them. It was they who had let him down.

'Yes. I do. So you have come to me for a job.'

'You honour me, Bhalla Sahib. But actually I have come for a job with James Hawley – which is almost the same thing.'

For a minute or so, while Haresh remained standing, cogs clicked in Pyare Lal Bhalla's business brain. Then he summoned a clerk from the next room and said:

'Write him a letter for Gower and sign it for me.'

Pyare Lal Bhalla then put up his right hand towards Haresh in a combined gesture of assurance, blessing, commiseration and dismissal.

My foot's in the door, thought Haresh, elated.

He took this note and cycled off to the grand four-storey edifice of Cromarty House, the headquarters of the group of which James Hawley was a part. He planned to make an appointment with Sir David Gower, if possible this week or the coming week. It was five-thirty, the end of the working day. He entered the imposing portals. When he presented his note at the front office, he was asked to wait. Half an hour passed. Then he was told: 'Kindly continue to wait here, Mr Khanna. Sir David will see you in twenty minutes.'

Still sweaty from bicycling, dressed in nothing better than his silk shirt and fawn trousers – no jacket, not even a tie! – Haresh started at this sudden intimation. But he had no choice except to wait. He didn't even have his precious certificates with him. Luckily, and characteristically, he carried a comb in his pocket, and he used it when he went to the bathroom to freshen up. He passed through his mind what he needed to say to Sir David and the order in which it would be most effective to say it. But when he was escorted up the great, ornamented lift and into the vast office of the Managing Director of the Cromarty

Group he forgot his script entirely. Here was a durbar of an entirely different kind from the small whitewashed room in which he had been sitting (and standing) an hour earlier.

The cream-painted walls must have been twenty feet high, and the distance from the door to the massive mahogany table at the end at least forty. As Haresh walked across the deep red carpet towards the grand desk he was aware that behind that desk sat a well-built man – as tall as Ghosh and bulkier – who was looking at him through his spectacles. He sensed that, short as he was, he must look even shorter in these gigantic surroundings. Presumably any interviewee, anyone who was received in this office, was expected to quail with trepidation as he traversed the room under such intent inspection. Though Haresh had stood up and sat down for Pyare Lal Bhalla as unresistingly as a child would before his teacher, he refused to display any nervousness before Gower. Sir David had been kind enough to see him at such short notice; he would have to make allowances for his dress.

'Yes, young man, what can I do for you?' said Sir David Gower, neither getting up nor beckoning Haresh to a chair.

'Quite frankly, Sir David,' said Haresh, 'I am looking for a job. I believe I am qualified for it, and I hope you will give me one.'

Part Ten

10.1

A few days after the storm, there was something of an exodus from the village of Debaria. For a variety of reasons several people left within a few hours for the subdivisional town of Salimpur, the closest railway station for the branch line.

Rasheed left in order to catch the train to go to his wife's village; he planned to get his wife and two children back to Debaria, where they would remain until his studies called him back to Brahmpur.

Maan was to accompany Rasheed. He was not at all keen to do so. To visit the village where Rasheed's wife lived with her father, to travel back without being able to speak a word to her, to see her covered from head to foot in a black burqa, to spend his time imagining what she looked like, to sense Rasheed's discomfort as he attempted to keep two separate two-way conversations going, to exert himself in any way in this terrible heat, none of these struck Maan as being in the least enjoyable. Rasheed, however, had invited him; he had presumably felt that it would be inhospitable not to do so: Maan was, after all, his personal guest before he was his family's. Maan had found it difficult to refuse without a reasonable excuse, and there were none at hand. Besides, to remain in the village was driving him crazy. He was seized with frustration against his life in Debaria and all its discomforts and boredoms.

The Bear and his companion the guppi had completed whatever business they had in Debaria, and were headed somewhere else.

Netaji was going because he had 'some business in the subdivisional courts', but really because he wanted to hobnob with the local administrative functionaries and small-time politicians in Salimpur.

Finally, there was the eminent archaeologist, Vilayat Sahib, of whom Maan had not yet caught a glimpse. He was to return to Brahmpur on his way back to Delhi. Characteristically, he disappeared from Debaria on his own on a bullock-cart before anyone could make the friendly gesture of offering to share their rickshaw with him.

It's as if he didn't exist, thought Maan – as if he's in purdah. I've heard of him but I've never seen him – like the women of the family. I suppose they exist as well. Or perhaps they don't. Perhaps all women are just a rumour. He was beginning to feel immensely restless.

Netaji, very dashing and mustachioed, had insisted that Maan ride into Salimpur on the back of his Harley Davidson. 'Why would you want to ride for an hour in a ramshackle cycle-rickshaw in this heat?' he had asked. 'As a Brahmpur-wallah, you're accustomed to luxury, you couldn't be used to having your brains baked. Anyway, I want to talk to you.' Maan had acquiesced, and was now bouncing up and down along the pitted country road on the motorcycle, having his brains vibrated rather than baked.

Rasheed had warned Maan about Netaji and his attempt to extract personal advantage from every possible situation, so Maan was not surprised at the turn their conversation took.

'How are you enjoying yourself? Can you hear me?' asked Netaji.

'Oh, yes,' Maan replied.

'I said, how are you enjoying yourself?'

'Very much. Where did you get this motorcycle?'

'I meant, are you enjoying yourself in our village?'

'Why not?'

'Why not? That means you aren't.'

'No, no – I'm enjoying myself very much.'

'Well, what do you enjoy about it?'

'Er, there's a lot of fresh air in the country,' said Maan.

'Well, I hate it,' shouted Netaji.

'What was that?'

'I hate it. There's nothing to do here. There isn't even any proper politics. That's why if I don't leave the village and visit Salimpur at least twice a week, I fall ill.'

'Ill?' asked Maan.

'Yes, ill. Everyone in the village makes me ill. And the village louts are the worst. That Moazzam for instance, he has no respect for other people's property.... You aren't holding on tight. You'll fall off. Hold close to me for balance.'

'All right.'

'I can't even keep my motorcycle safe from them. I have to keep it in an open courtyard, and they damage it out of spite. Now Brahmpur, there's a city!'

'You've been to Brahmpur then?'

'Yes, of course,' said Netaji impatiently. 'You know what I like about Brahmpur?'

'What?' asked Maan.

'You can eat out in hotels.'

'In hotels?' Maan frowned.

'In small hotels.'

'Oh.'

'Now this is a bad patch. Hold on tight. I'll go slow. That way, if we slip, we'll be all right.'

'Fine.'

'Can you hear me?'

'Perfectly.'

'How about the flies?'

'No, you're my shield.'

After a pause, Netaji said, 'You must have a lot of contacts.'

'Contacts?'

'Yes, contacts, contacts, you know what I mean.'

'But –'

'You should use your contacts to help us,' said Netaji bluntly. 'I'm sure you could get me a kerosene dealer's licence. That should be easy enough for the Revenue Minister's son.'

'Actually, all that is under a different ministry,' said Maan, unoffended. 'Civil Supplies, I think.'

'Come on, come on, that doesn't matter. I know how it works.'

'I really can't,' said Maan. 'My father would kill me if I suggested it.'

'No harm in asking. Anyway, your father is very well-respected here.... Why doesn't he find you a comfortable job?'

'A job ... er, why do people respect my father here? After all, he'll take away your land, won't he?'

'Well ...' began Netaji, then stopped. He wondered whether he should confide in Maan that the village record-keeper had cooked the records to suit the family interests. Neither Netaji nor anyone else in the family had so far come to know of Rasheed's visit to the patwari. It was unimaginable that he could have asked him to uncook them on Kachheru's behalf.

'Was that your son who saw us off?' asked Maan.

'Yes. He's just over two, and he's in a bad mood these days.'

'Why?'

'Oh, he's returned from his grandmother's place, where he was spoilt. Now nothing we do pleases him, and he's acting as contrary as possible.'

'Maybe it's the heat.'

'Maybe,' Netaji agreed. 'Have you ever been in love?'

'What was that?'

'I said, have you ever been in love?'

'Oh yes,' said Maan. 'Tell me, what's that building we just passed?'

In a while they reached Salimpur. They had agreed to meet the others at a cloth and general merchandise shop. But the narrow, crowded streets of Salimpur were completely packed. It was the day of the weekly market. Hawkers, peddlers, vendors of every kind, snake-charmers with their torpid cobras, quacks, tinkers, fruit-sellers with baskets of mangoes and lichis on their heads, sweetsellers, their barfis and laddus and jalebis encrusted with flies, and a great part of the population not only of Salimpur but of many of the surrounding villages, had managed to squeeze into the centre of the town.

There was a tremendous din. Above the babble of the customers and the shouts of the hawkers came the conflicting sounds of two screeching loudspeakers, one blaring out the current broadcast from All India Radio Brahmpur, the other interspersing its medley of film songs with advertisements for Raahat-e-Rooh or Ease-for-the-Soul Hair Oil.

Electricity! thought Maan, with a sudden leap of joy. Maybe there'll even be a fan around somewhere.

Netaji, with impatient curses and prolonged beeps of his horn, was hardly able to move a hundred yards in fifteen minutes.

'They'll miss their train,' he said of the others, who were coming by rickshaw and were half an hour behind them. But since the train was already three hours late, this was in fact unlikely.

By the time Netaji got to his friend's shop (which, sadly, was not equipped with a fan) he had such a bad headache that, after introducing Maan, he immediately lay down on a bench and closed his eyes. The shopkeeper ordered a few cups of tea. Several other friends had gathered in the shop, which was a sort of den for political and other gossip. One of them was reading an Urdu newspaper, another – the goldsmith from next door – was picking his nose thoroughly and thoughtfully. Soon the Bear and guppi arrived.

Since it was in part a cloth shop, Maan was mildly interested to see how it was run. He noticed that there were no customers.

'Why is there so little business here today?' asked Maan.

'Market day – very little activity in any of the shops,' said the goldsmith. 'Just the occasional yokel from out of town. That's why I've deserted my own. Anyway, I can keep an eye on it from here.'

To the shopkeeper he remarked: 'What is the SDO from Rudhia subdivision doing here in Salimpur today?'

Netaji, who had been lying as still as a corpse, suddenly perked up when he heard 'SDO'. Salimpur had its own SDO, who was in effect administrative prince of this fief. A visit from a Sub-Divisional Officer of a different subdivision was news indeed.

'It must be the archives,' said the shopkeeper. 'I heard

someone saying that someone was being sent over from somewhere to look at them.'

'You donkey,' said Netaji, before falling back exhausted onto the bench, 'it's nothing to do with the archives. It has to do with coordinating the process of notification in the various subdivisions once the Zamindari Act comes into force.'

In fact Netaji had no idea why the SDO was in town. But he decided immediately to make it his business to meet him.

A spindly schoolteacher also dropped in for a few minutes, made the sarcastic comment that he did not have the whole day to spend in idle chatter like some people he knew, looked at the prone figure of Netaji with contempt, frowned slightly and quizzically at Maan, and left.

'Where's the guppi?' the Bear asked suddenly. No one knew. He had disappeared. He was found a few minutes later, staring in slack-jawed fascination at a display of bottles and pills that an aged quack doctor had arranged in a semicircle in the middle of the street. A crowd had gathered, and was listening to the quack's patter as he held up a bottle containing an opaque and viscous lime-green liquid:

'And this amazing medicine, truly a panacea, was given to me by Tajuddin, a great baba, and very close to God. He spent twelve years in the jungles of Nagpur, eating nothing – he just chewed leaves for their moisture, and kept a stone against his stomach for food. His muscles rotted, his blood dried, his flesh wasted away. He was mere bone and black skin. Then Allah said to two angels, "Go down and give him my salaams" –'

The guppi, who was staring open-mouthed and listening with absolute conviction to this nonsense, almost had to be dragged away from the scene and back into the shop by the Bear.

AS the tea, paan and newspaper went around, the conversation turned to politics at the state level, especially the recent communal troubles in Brahmpur. The prime object of hatred was the Home Minister, L.N. Agarwal, whose defence of the police firing on the Muslim mob near the Alamgiri Masjid had been widely reported in the newspapers – and who was known to be a strong supporter of the construction – or, as he would have had it, re-construction – of the Shiva Temple. Rhymed slogans such as the following, which were popular in Brahmpur among the Muslims, had found their way to Salimpur and were repeated with relish:

> Saanp ka zahar, insaan ki khaal:
> Yeh hai L.N. Agarwal!
>> The poison of a snake, the skin of a man:
>> This is L.N. Agarwal!

> Ghar ko loot kar kha gaya maal:
> Home Minister Agarwal!
>> He robbed our Home, and devoured our
>>> substance:
>> Home Minister Agarwal!

This might have been a reference to his 'cold steel' order, under which over-zealous policemen had confiscated not merely axes and spears but even household knives, or it might have referred to the fact that L.N. Agarwal, being a member of the Hindu shopkeeping community, was the most important collector of funds for the Congress Party of Purva Pradesh. His origins were also referred to slightingly in the following slogan:

> L.N. Agarwal, wapas jao,
> Baniye ki dukaan chalao!
>> L.N. Agarwal, go back,
>> Go and run your bania's shop!

The walls, however, might have echoed the uproarious laughter that greeted this final couplet at the expense of the laughers themselves. For it was taking place in a shop, and Maan, being a khatri, was no stranger to trade.

In sharp contrast to L.N. Agarwal, Mahesh Kapoor, though a Hindu, was well-known for his tolerance towards other religions – his wife would have said that the only religion he was intolerant towards was his own – and was liked and respected among knowledgeable Muslims. This was why, for example, when Maan and Rasheed first met, Rasheed had been well-disposed towards him. He now said to Maan:

'If it were not for people like Nehru at the national level, or your father at the state level, the situation of the Muslims would be even worse than it is.'

Maan, who was not feeling particularly well-disposed towards his father, shrugged.

Rasheed wondered why Maan was being so inexpressive. Perhaps, he thought, it was the way he had put it. He had used the words 'the situation of the Muslims' rather than 'our situation' not because he did not feel a part of his community, but because he examined even an issue as close to his heart as this through almost academically balanced categories. It was his constant habit to try to make objective sense of the world, but of late – especially since his rooftop discussion with his father – he felt more and more disgusted by it. He had hated his own deception – or perhaps prevarication – with the patwari, but knew that he had had no alternative. Had the patwari believed that Rasheed's family was not behind him, nothing would have protected Kachheru's right to his land.

'I'll tell you what I think,' said Netaji, sitting up and speaking in as leader-like a voice as his nickname required. 'We must get ourselves together. We have to work together for the good of things. We must get things off their feet. And if the old leaders are discredited, it requires young men – young men like – like we have all around us – who know how to get things done, of course. Doers, not impractical dreamers. Those who know the people, the top people of every subdivision. Now everyone respects my father, he may have known the people who mattered in his day, I don't deny that. But his day is, everyone will agree, now almost over. It is not enough to –'

But what it was not enough to do went unheard. The loudspeaker cart advertising Ease-for-the-Soul Hair Oil, which had been quiescent for a few minutes, now suddenly blared out its ear-splitting melodies from directly outside the shop. The din was so deafening – far worse than it had been in its earlier location – that they had to clap their hands to their ears. Poor Netaji went almost green and clutched his head in agony, and they all poured into the street to suppress the nuisance. But just at that moment Netaji noticed in the crowd a tall figure with an unfamiliar, rather weak-chinned young face under a pith helmet. The SDO from Rudhia – for Netaji with his unerring antennae knew instantly who this must be – looked disdainfully towards the source of the sound before being guided swiftly away by two policemen through the crowd and towards the railway station.

As the three heads (one turban on each side of the sola topi) bobbed through the crowd and disappeared, Netaji clutched at his moustache in panic at losing his quarry. 'To the station, to the station!' he screamed, forgetting his headache, and with such desperate urgency that even the loudspeaker could not stifle his cry. 'The train, the train, you will all miss your train. Grab your bags and run! Hurry! Hurry!'

All this was said with such conviction that no one questioned Netaji's authority or information. Pushing their way through the crowd, sweating and yelling, cursing and being cursed by turns, the convoy arrived at Salimpur Station in ten minutes. There they found that the train was not due for another hour.

The Bear turned with some annoyance towards Netaji. 'Why did you rush us like that?' he asked.

Netaji had been looking up and down the platform anxiously. Now suddenly his face broke into a smile.

The Bear frowned. Cocking his head gently to one side he looked at Netaji and said:

'Well, why?'

'What? What did you say?' asked Netaji. He had just noticed the sola topi at the far end of the platform, near the station master's office.

But the Bear, annoyed, and annoyed that he was annoyed, had turned away.

Netaji, his lust for a new contact aroused, now collared Maan and virtually frog-marched him towards the other end of the platform. Maan was so astonished that he didn't even protest.

With unembarrassed aplomb Netaji went straight up to the young SDO and said:

'SDO Sahib, I am so pleased to meet you. And so honoured. I say this from the bottom of my heart.'

The weak-chinned face under the sola topi looked at him in displeased puzzlement.

'Yes?' he said. 'What can I do for you?' The SDO's Hindi, though tolerable, had a Bengali intonation.

Netaji continued: 'But, SDO Sahib, how can you say that? The question is how I can be of service to you. You are our guest in Salimpur tehsil. I am the son of a zamindar of Debaria village. My name is Tahir Ahmed Khan. The name is known here: Tahir Ahmed Khan. I am a youth organizer for the Congress Party.'

'Good. Glad to meet you,' said the SDO in a voice that was utterly unglad.

Netaji's heart did not sink at this lack of enthusiasm. He now produced his trump card.

'And this is my good friend, Maan Kapoor,' he said with a flourish, nudging Maan forward. Maan looked rather sullen.

'Good,' said the SDO, as unenthusiastically as before. Then a slow frown crossed his face and he said, 'I think I have met you somewhere before.'

'Oh, but this is the son of Mahesh Kapoor, our Revenue Minister!' said Netaji with aggressive obsequiousness.

The SDO looked surprised. Then he frowned again in

concentration. 'Ah yes! We met very briefly, I believe, at your father's place about a year ago,' he said in a fairly amiable voice, speaking now in English and, as a result, unintentionally cutting Netaji out of the conversation. 'You have a place near Rudhia too, don't you? Near the town, that is.'

'Yes, my father has a farm there. In fact, coming to think of it, I should be visiting it one of these days,' said Maan, suddenly remembering his father's instructions.

'What are you doing here?' asked the SDO.

'Oh, nothing much, just visiting a friend,' said Maan. Then, after a pause, he added: 'A friend who is standing at the other end of the platform.'

The SDO smiled weakly. 'Well,' he said, 'I'm off to Rudhia later today, and if you want to go to your father's farm and don't mind a very bumpy ride in my jeep, you're most welcome to come with me. I have to do a bit of wolf-hunting myself: an activity, I should add, for which I am utterly untrained and unfit. But because I'm the SDO I have to be seen to be handling the menace myself.'

Maan's eyes lit up. 'Wolf-hunting?' he said. 'Do you really mean that?'

'Yes, indeed,' said the SDO. 'Tomorrow morning is when we go. Are you fond of hunting? Would you care to come along?'

'That would be wonderful,' said Maan with great enthusiasm. 'But I don't have anything except kurta-pyjamas to wear.'

'Oh, I should think we could get you togged up if necessary,' said the SDO. 'Anyway, it's nothing formal – just a beat to try to flush out a few man-eating wolves that have been bothering some villages in my subdivision.'

'Well, I'll speak to my friend,' said Maan. He realized that fortune had delivered him three gifts simultaneously: the chance to do something he loved, the release from a journey he did not wish to make, and a responsible excuse for effecting that release.

He looked at his unexpected benefactor in the friendliest

way and said: 'I'll just be back. But I don't think you mentioned your name.'

'I'm very sorry, you're quite right. I am Sandeep Lahiri,' said the SDO, shaking Maan's hand warmly and entirely ignoring the injured and fuming Netaji.

10.3

RASHEED was not unhappy that Maan could not come with him to his wife's village, and was glad to see how enthusiastic Maan was to go to his father's farm.

The SDO was pleased to have company. He and Maan agreed to meet in a couple of hours. After he had finished some work at Salimpur Station – involving a consignment of vaccines for an inoculation programme in the area – Sandeep Lahiri sat down in the station master's office and pulled *Howards End* out of his bag. He was still reading it when Maan found him there. They set out almost immediately.

The jeep ride southwards was as bumpy as Sandeep Lahiri had promised, and very dusty as well. The driver and a policeman sat in front, and Maan and the SDO at the back. They did not talk much.

'It really does work,' said Sandeep at one point, taking off his sola topi and looking at it with appreciation. 'I never believed it until I started work here. I always thought that it was part of the mindless uniform of the pukka sahib.'

At another point he told Maan a few demographic details about his subdivision: what percentage of Muslims, Hindus and so on there were. The details immediately slipped out of Maan's mind.

Sandeep Lahiri had a pleasant, rather tentative way of producing his occasional, well-rounded sentences, and Maan took a liking to him.

This liking increased when, at his bungalow that evening, he became more expansive. Although Maan was a Minister's son, Sandeep made no bones about his dislike of the politicians in his own subdivision and the way they inter-fered with his work. Since he was the judicial as well as the executive head of his subdivision – separation of powers had not yet been fully realized in Purva Pradesh – he had more work than a human being could be expected to handle. In addition, there were all kinds of emergencies that cropped up: like the wolves or an epidemic or the visit of a political bigwig who insisted on being shepherded around by the SDO himself. Strangely enough, it was not his local MLA who gave Sandeep Lahiri the most trouble but a member of the Legislative Council whose home was in this area and who treated it as his private domain.

This man, Maan learned over a nimbu pani laced with gin, saw the SDO as a competitor to his influence. If the SDO was compliant and consulted him on everything, he was content. If the SDO showed any independence, he tried quickly to bring him to heel.

'The problem is,' said Sandeep Lahiri with a rueful glance at his guest, 'that Jha is an important Congressman – the Chairman of the Legislative Council and a friend of the Chief Minister. Nor does he miss an opportunity to remind me of this. He also reminds me periodically that he is more than twice my age and embodies what he calls "the wisdom of the people". Oh well. In some respects he's quite right, of course. Within eighteen months of appointment we're put in charge of an area of half a million people – handling revenue work and criminal work, quite apart from keeping law and order and managing the general welfare of the subdivision and acting as father and mother of the population. No wonder he feels annoyed whenever he sees me, fresh from my training at Metcalfe House and my six months' field experience in some other district. Another?'

'Please.'

'This bill of your father's is going to make a vast amount of additional work for us, you know,' said Sandeep Lahiri a little later. 'But it's a good thing, I suppose.' He sounded unconvinced. 'Oh, it's almost time for the news.' He went over to his sideboard, on which rested a large radio in a handsome polished wooden cabinet. It had a great many white dials.

He turned it on. A big green valve-light slowly began to glow and the sound of a male voice singing an evening raag gradually filled the room. It was Ustad Majeed Khan. With a grimace of instinctive distaste Sandeep Lahiri turned the volume down.

'Well,' he said to Maan, 'I'm afraid there's no getting around this stuff. It's the price of the news, and I pay it for a minute or two every day. Why can't they put on something listenable, like Mozart or Beethoven?'

Maan, who had heard western classical music perhaps three times in his life, and had not enjoyed the experience, said:

'Oh, I don't know. Most people here wouldn't enjoy it.'

'Do you really think so?' said Sandeep. 'I feel they would. Good music is good music. It's just a question of exposure, I feel. Exposure, and a little bit of guidance.'

Maan looked doubtful.

'Anyway,' said Sandeep Lahiri, 'I'm sure they don't enjoy this awful stuff. What they really want is film songs, which All India Radio will never give them. As for me, if it weren't for the BBC, I don't know what I'd do out here.'

But as if in response to these remarks a series of pips now sounded and a distinctly Indian voice with a distinctly British veneer announced:

'This is All India Radio. ... The news, read by Mohit Bose.'

10.4

THE next morning they drove out for the hunt.

A few cattle were being herded along the road. When they saw the white jeep approach at high speed they scattered in alarm. As the jeep came closer, the driver leaned on the horn for a good twenty seconds, increasing their panic. When it passed them it raised a great cloud of dust. The herdboys coughed in admiration: they recognized the jeep as the SDO's. It was the only motor vehicle on the road, and the driver raced along as if he were absolute king of the highway. Not that the road was a highway exactly: it was a fairly solid dirt road, which might be more difficult to negotiate once the monsoon broke, but was fine for the present.

Sandeep had lent Maan a pair of khaki shorts, a khaki shirt, and a hat. Leaning against the door on Maan's side was the rifle that was kept at the SDO's bungalow. Sandeep had (with distaste) learned to fire it once but was not at all keen to fire it again. Maan could stand in for him.

Maan had gone hunting for nilgai and deer a number of times with friends from Banaras, had hunted wild boar too, and had once, without success, hunted for leopard. He had greatly enjoyed it. He had never hunted wolf before, and was not sure how exactly it would be managed. Presumably there would be beaters. Since Sandeep did not seem to be knowledgeable about matters of technique, Maan asked him about the background to the problem.

'Aren't wolves normally scared of the villagers?' he asked.

'That's what I thought too,' said Sandeep. 'We don't have so many wolves left anyway, and people don't have permission to go around shooting them unless they become a menace. But I've seen children who've been mauled by wolves, and even the remains of children killed and eaten by wolves. It's really terrible. The people of these villages are absolutely terrified. I suppose they are inclined to exaggerate, but the forest officers have confirmed from pug-marks and so on that it's wolves we're talking about, not leopards or hyenas or anything else.'

They were now driving through an area of undulating ground covered with scrub and rocky outcrops. It was getting warmer. The occasional village looked even more barren and destitute than those closer to the town. At one point they stopped and asked the villagers if they had seen the others in their party go past.

'Yes, Sahib,' said one villager, a middle-aged man with white hair, who was awestruck by the fact that the SDO had appeared in their midst. He told them that a jeep and a car had gone past earlier.

'Has there been any problem with wolves in this village?' asked Sandeep.

The villager shook his head from left to right. 'Yes, indeed, Sahib,' he said, his face taut with the memory. 'Bacchan Singh's son was sleeping outside with his mother and a wolf grabbed him and took him off. We chased him with lanterns and sticks, but it was too late. We found the boy's body the next day in a field. It was partly eaten. Sahib, please save us from this menace, you are our mother and father. These days we can neither sleep indoors for the heat nor outside for fear.'

'When did this happen?' asked the SDO sympathetically.

'Last month, Sahib, at the new moon.'

'One day after the new moon,' corrected another villager.

When they got back into the car, Sandeep said nothing more than: 'Very sad, very sad. Sad for the villagers, sad for the wolves.'

'Sad for the wolves?' said Maan, startled.

'Well, you know,' said Sandeep, taking off his sola topi and mopping his forehead, 'though this area looks very bare now, there used to be a lot of forest cover once – sal, mahua and so on – and it supported a lot of small wildlife that the wolves preyed on. But there has been so much logging, first in the War because it was needed, and then, illegally, after the War – often, I'm afraid, with the connivance of the forest officers themselves – and also of the villagers, who want more land for their fields. Anyway, the wolves have been crowded into smaller and smaller areas and have become more and more desperate. The summer's the worst time because everything is dry and there's nothing to eat – hardly any land-crabs or frogs or other small animals. That's when they are driven by hunger to attack the villagers' goats – and when they can't get at the goats, they attack the villagers' children.'

'Can you re-afforest any areas?'

'Well, they would have to be areas that aren't used for cultivation. Politically and, well, humanly, anything else isn't possible. I can imagine being flayed alive by the likes of Jha if I even suggested it. But anyway, that's a long term policy, and what the villagers need is that the terror stop now.'

Suddenly he tapped his driver on the shoulder. The startled man turned his neck around and looked at the SDO questioningly, while continuing to drive full speed ahead.

'Will you stop blaring that horn?' said the SDO in Hindi. Then, after a pause, he took up his conversation with Maan:

'The statistics, you know, are quite appalling. For the last seven years, each summer – from about February to June, when the monsoon breaks – there have been over a dozen kills and about the same number of mauls in an area of about thirty villages. For years officials have kept writing reports and referring and deferring and inferring and talking round and round in circles about what to do: paper solutions for the most part. Occasionally they've tied up a few goats outside the village of the latest victim in the hope that this will somehow solve things. But –' He shrugged his shoulders, frowned and sighed. Maan thought that his weak chin made him look rather grumpy.

'Anyway,' continued Sandeep, 'I felt that this year something practical just had to be done about it. Luckily my DM agreed and helped rope in the police at the district level and so on. They have a couple of good shots, not just with pistols but with rifles. A week ago we learned that a pack of man-eaters was operating in this area and – ah, there they are!' he said, pointing to a tree near an old and now deserted serai – a resting place for travellers – which stood by the side of the road a furlong or so ahead. A jeep and a car were parked underneath the tree, and a large number of people were moving around nearby, many of them local villagers. The SDO's jeep roared up and screeched to a halt, enveloping everyone in a haze of dust.

Although the SDO was the least expert among the

gathered officials and the least capable of organizing the task at hand, Maan noticed that everyone insisted on deferring to him, and sought his opinion even when he had none to give. Eventually, in polite exasperation, Sandeep said:

'I do not want to waste any more time in talk. The beaters and hired marksmen, you say, are at the site itself – near the ravine. That's good. However, you' – he indicated the two Forest Department officials, their five helpers, the Inspector, the two crack police shots and the policemen – 'have been here for an hour, waiting, and we have been here for half an hour, talking. We should have coordinated our arrival better, but never mind. Let us not waste further time. It is getting hotter by the minute. Mr Prashant, you say you have drawn up the plans with great care after examining the site for the beat three days ago. Well, please do not reiterate them and ask for my approval of every detail. I accept your plan. Now you tell us where to go, and we will obey you. Imagine that you are the DM himself.'

Mr Prashant, the Forest Officer, looked appalled at the thought, as if Sandeep had made a tasteless joke about God. 'Now, let's go ahead – and kill the killers,' continued Sandeep, almost managing to look fierce.

10.5

THE jeeps and car turned off the main road onto a dirt track, leaving the villagers behind. Another village went by, and then there was open countryside: the same scrub and outcrops as before, interspersed with pieces of arable land and the occasional large tree – a flame-of-the-forest, a mahua, or a banyan. The rocks had stored heat over the months, and the landscape began to shimmer in the morning sun. It was about eight-thirty, and it was already hot. Maan yawned and stretched as the jeep bounced on. He was happy.

The vehicles stopped near a great banyan tree on the

bank of a dried stream. There the beaters, armed with lathis and spears, two of them with rudimentary drums strapped across their bodies, sat and chewed tobacco, sang tunelessly, laughed, talked about the two rupees that they would be getting for their morning's work, and asked several times for a re-explanation of Mr Prashant's instructions. They were a mixed bunch in both shape and age, but all of them were eager to be of use and hopeful that they would flush out a man-eating wolf or two. Over the last week the suspected wolves had been sighted on a number of occasions – once as many as four of them together – and had sought escape in the long ravine into which the dry creek ran. This was where they would most likely be hiding. The beaters finally set out across the fields and ridges in the direction of the lower end of the ravine and disappeared into the distance as they trudged along. They would later move forward through the ravine and try to flush the quarry out at the other end.

The jeeps now headed dustily towards the upper end of the ravine. Yet at this upper end – as at the lower end – there were a number of outlets other than the main one, and each exit had to be guarded. The marksmen were distributed at these various exits. Beyond the exits lay rough open land for a couple of hundred yards, and beyond that a patchwork of dry fields and areas of woodland.

Mr Prashant tried to obey Sandeep Lahiri's order that he should forget that he was in the superior, heaven-blessed, twice-born presence of an IAS officer. He donned his cloth cap, nervously twisted it around, and finally mustered the courage to tell people where they should sit and what they should do. Sandeep and Maan were asked to sit at one of the smaller and steeper exits, which a wolf, Mr Prashant thought, would be unlikely to choose because it would too greatly reduce his speed. The police marksmen and hired professional hunters were assigned to different areas, where they sat in the skimpy and sweltering shade of a number of small trees. The long wait for the beat began. There was no stir in the air to provide the least relief.

Sandeep, who found the heat intolerably taxing, did not say much. Maan hummed a little; it was part of a ghazal that he had heard Saeeda Bai sing, but, oddly, it did not bring Saeeda Bai to his mind. He was not even conscious that he was humming. He was in a state of calm excitement, and from time to time he mopped his forehead or took a swig from his water-bottle or checked his ammunition. Not that I'll get more than half a dozen shots at most, he told himself. Then he moved his hand along the smooth wood of the rifle, and raised it to his shoulder a few times, aiming in anticipation at the bushes and thickets in the ravine from which a wolf would be most likely to emerge.

More than half an hour passed. The sweat dripped down their faces, and trickled down their bodies. But the air was dry, and it did evaporate; it did not torment them as it would have in the monsoon. A few flies buzzed around, occasionally settling on their faces or their bare arms and legs, and a cicada sitting on a small ber bush in a field chirped shrilly. The faint sound of the drums of the beaters, but not of their shouts, now came to their ears from the distance. Sandeep watched Maan with curiosity, curiosity not at his actions so much as at his expression. Maan had struck him as an easy-going, happy-go-lucky sort of man. But there was something intent and determined in his look now, something that seemed to say, with pleasurable anticipation: A wolf is going to come out there from that thicket, and I will follow it with my rifle until it gets to that spot along the path so that I can be sure of getting a good clear shot sideways on, and I will press the trigger, and the bullet will go true, and it will fall there – dead – and that will be that. A good morning's work.

This was not a bad approximation of Maan's actual thoughts. As for Sandeep's own independent thoughts, the heat had thinned and blurred them. He did not anticipate with any relish the killing of the wolves, but felt that this was the only immediate solution. He only hoped that the menace to the villagers could somehow be diminished or removed. Just last week he had visited the district hospital to see a seven-year-old boy who had been badly mauled by a wolf. The boy was sleeping on a cot in a general ward, and Sandeep had not wanted him woken. But he could not forget the look in the eyes of the boy's parents as they spoke to him – as if somehow he would be able to remove or ameliorate the tragedy that had struck their lives. Apart from severe injuries to his arms and upper body, the boy's neck had been injured, and the doctor had said that he would not be able to walk again.

Sandeep felt restless. He got up to stretch himself and looked down towards the unluxuriant summer vegetation below him in the ravine and the even sparser scrub outside. They could now hear the faint cries and shouts of the beaters in the distance. Maan too appeared lost in his own thoughts.

Suddenly, and far earlier than expected, a wolf, an adult grey wolf, larger than an alsatian and faster, broke through the main outlet of the gorge where many of the professional marksmen were stationed and bounded over the wasteland and dry fields. It rushed straight for the wood to its left, pursued by a few belated shots.

Maan and Sandeep were not in a position where they could see the wolf clearly, but the shouts and shots that followed it told them that something was going on. Maan caught a brief glimpse of it running across an unploughed, hard-baked field when it swung over to his side at a fair distance and disappeared among the trees, swift and desperate in the face of death.

It's got away! he thought angrily. But the next one won't.

There were shouts of dismay and recrimination for a minute or two, and then everything in the immediate area settled down to silence again. But a brainfever bird had taken up its obsessive triple-cry from somewhere in the wood, and the sound interlaced itself with the cries and drumbeats from the other direction: the beaters were coming swiftly up the ravine now, flushing out whatever was in it in the direction of the hunters. By now Maan could also hear the sounds they made as they whacked the bushes with their lathis and spears.

Suddenly another, smaller grey form bounded out in panic from the ravine, this time towards the steep outlet which Maan was guarding. With an instinctive reflex he swung his rifle towards it and was about to fire – earlier than he had planned to for a good sideways shot – when he muttered to himself, with a shock:

'But it's a fox!'

The fox, not knowing that it had just been spared, and out of its wits with fear, cut across the fields and streaked like lightning into the woods, its black-tipped grey tail stiff and horizontal to the ground. Maan laughed for a second.

But the laugh froze on his face. The beaters could not have been more than a hundred yards away when a huge wolf, grey and rugged, its ears drawn back, and with the hint of an irregularity in its swift bounds, broke cover and rushed up the slope towards the place where Maan and Sandeep were sitting. Maan swung the rifle around, but the wolf presented no large target. Rather, as it bounded towards them, its great grey face with its dark arched eyebrows seeming to stare at them with vengeful savagery, it was an object of gross terror.

All at once it sensed their presence. It swung away from them and leapt down to the path in the ravine where Maan had imagined a wolf might emerge in the first place. Giving himself no chance to think of his own relief, and paying not the least attention to the dazed Sandeep, he swung his rifle to follow the wolf to the point where he had earlier judged it would present the best target. It was now in his sights.

But just as he was about to fire, he suddenly saw two marksmen who had not been there before and who had no business to be there, sitting on the low ridge at the far side of the path, directly opposite him, their rifles trained on the wolf, and clearly about to fire as well.

This is mad! thought Maan.

'Don't shoot! Don't shoot!' he shouted.

One of the marksmen shot anyway but missed. The bullet pinged against a rock on the slope two feet away from Maan and ricocheted away.

'Don't shoot! Don't shoot! You crazy fools!' yelled Maan.

The great wolf, having changed its route once, did not do so again. With the same irregular heavy swiftness it charged out of the ravine and made for the woods, its paws raising a trail of dust until it disappeared for a second behind the low boundary of a rough-surfaced field. The moment they saw it in open countryside some of the marksmen positioned at other exits fired at its diminishing shape. But they had no real chance. The wolf, like the fox and his own earlier fellow, was in the woods in a matter of seconds, safe from this concerted human terror.

The beaters had reached the exit of the ravine, and the beat was over. Not disappointment but a fit of violent anger seized Maan. He unloaded his rifle with trembling hands, then went over to where the errant marksmen were standing and grabbed one of them by his shirt.

The man was taller and possibly stronger than Maan, but he looked apologetic and frightened. Maan released him, then stood before him, saying nothing, merely breathing swiftly and heavily with tension and aggression. Then he spoke. Instead of asking them whether they were hunting humans or wolves, as he had been about to do, he controlled himself somehow and simply said in a semi-feral growl:

'You were placed to guard that route. You were not intended to come over the ridge and hunt in some other place that you decided was more promising. One of us might have been killed. It might have been you.'

The man said nothing. He knew that what he and his companion had just done was inexcusable. He looked at his companion, who shrugged.

Suddenly, Maan felt a wave of disappointment wash over him. He turned away with a shake of the head, and walked back to where his rifle and water-bottle were standing. Sandeep and the others had gathered beneath a tree and were discussing the beat. Sandeep was using his sola topi to fan his face. He still looked shaken.

'The real problem,' said someone, 'is that wood there.

It's too close to the exit. Otherwise we could get about ten more marksmen and spread them in a very wide arc – there – and there, say –'

'Well, at any rate,' said someone else, 'they've had a bad shock. We'll flush this ravine out again next week. Only two wolves – I'd hoped that there'd be more of them here today.' He pulled a biscuit out of his pocket and munched it.

'Oh, so you think they'll be here next week awaiting your pleasure?'

'We set out too late,' said yet another. 'Early morning's the best time.'

Maan stood apart from them, struggling with a rush of overwhelming feelings – unbearably tense and unbearably slack at the same time.

He took a drink from his water-bottle and looked at the rifle from which he had not fired a single shot. He felt exhausted, frustrated, and betrayed by events. He would not join in their pointless post-mortem. And indeed a post-mortem was – in a literal sense – unjustified.

10.6

BUT later that afternoon Maan heard some good news. One of Sandeep's visitors mentioned that a reliable colleague of his had told him that the Nawab Sahib and his two sons had passed through Rudhia and gone to Baitar with the intention of staying at the Fort for a few days.

Maan's heart leaped up. The lustreless images of his father's farm vanished from his mind. They were replaced by thoughts both of a proper hunt (with horses) on the Baitar Estate and – even more delightfully – of news from Firoz about Saeeda Bai. Ah, thought Maan, the pleasures of the chase! He got his few things together, borrowed a couple of novels from Sandeep – to make his exile in Debaria more bearable – went off to the station, and caught the first possible train along the slow and halting branch line to Baitar.

I wonder if Firoz delivered it personally, he said to himself. He must have! And I shall find out what she said to him when she read his letter – my letter, rather – and discovered that Dagh Sahib, driven desperate by his absence from her and his own inability to communicate, had used the Nawabzada himself as translator, scribe and emissary. And what did she make of my reference to Dagh's lines:

> It is you who wrong me, and then you who ask:
> Dear Sir, please tell me, how do you fare today?

He got off at Baitar Station and hired a rickshaw to the Fort. Since he was dressed in crushed clothes (yet further crumpled from the hot and crowded train journey) and was unshaven, the rickshaw-wallah looked at him and his bag and asked:

'Meeting someone there?'

'Yes,' said Maan, who did not consider his question an impertinence. 'The Nawab Sahib.'

The rickshaw-wallah laughed at Maan's sense of humour. 'Very good, very good,' he said.

After a while he asked:

'What do you think of our town of Baitar?'

Maan said, hardly thinking of his words: 'It's a nice town. Looks like a nice town.'

The rickshaw-wallah said: 'It was a nice town – before the cinema-hall was built. Now what with the dancing girls and singing girls on the screen and all that loving and wiggling and so on' – he swerved to avoid a pot-hole in the road – 'it's become an even nicer town.'

The rickshaw-wallah went on: 'Nice from the point of view of decency, nice from the point of view of villainy. Baitar, Baitar, Baitar, Baitar.' He puffed out the words in rhythm to his pedal strokes. 'That – that building with the green signboard – is the hospital, as good as the district hospital in Rudhia. It was established by the present Nawab's father or grandfather. And that is Lal Kothi, which was used as a hunting lodge by the Nawab Sahib's great-grandfather – but is now surrounded by the town.

And that' – for, as they rounded a built-up corner of the road they all at once came within sight of a massive, pale yellow building towering on its small hill above a muddle of whitewashed houses – 'that is Baitar Fort itself.'

It was a vast and impressive building, and Maan looked at it admiringly.

'But Panditji wants to take it away and give it to the poor people,' said the rickshaw-wallah, 'once zamindari is abolished.'

Needless to say, Pandit Nehru – in distant Delhi, with a few other matters to think of – had no such plan. Nor did the Purva Pradesh Zamindari Abolition Bill – now only a presidential signature away from becoming an act – plan to take over forts or residences or even the self-managed land of the zamindars. But Maan let it go.

'What do you stand to gain from all this?' he asked the rickshaw-wallah.

'I? Nothing! Nothing at all, nothing at all. Not here, anyway. Now if I could get a room, that would be fine. If I could get two, that would be even better; I would rent one out to some other poor fool and live off the sweat of his efforts. Otherwise I will continue to pedal my rickshaw during the day and sleep on it at night.'

'But what do you do during the monsoon?' asked Maan.

'Oh, I find some shelter somewhere – Allah provides, Allah provides, and He will provide as He has always done.'

'Is the Nawab Sahib popular in these parts?' asked Maan.

'Popular? He's the sun and moon put together!' said the rickshaw-wallah. 'And so are the young Nawabzadas, especially Chhoté Sahib. Everyone likes his temperament. And what handsome figures of men. You should see them when they are together: truly a sight to behold. The old Nawab Sahib with one son on either hand. Like the Viceroy and his officers.'

'But if they are so well-liked, why do people want to take over their estates?'

'Why not?' said the rickshaw-wallah. 'People want to

get land wherever they can. In my village, where my wife and family live, we have worked our land for many years – since my father's uncle's time. But we still have to pay rent to the Nawab Sahib – to his bloodsucker of a munshi. Why should we pay rent? Tell me. We have watered it with our sweat for fifty years, it should be our land, we should own it.'

When they got to the huge, wooden, brass-studded gate in the wall of Baitar Fort, the rickshaw-wallah asked him for twice the normal fare. Maan argued for a minute, since the amount asked was clearly unreasonable; then, feeling bad for the rickshaw-wallah, he took out what he had asked for – plus another four annas – from his kurta pocket and gave it to him.

The rickshaw-wallah went off, well-satisfied with his judgment that Maan was slightly crazy. Perhaps he had really imagined he was going to meet the Nawab Sahib. Poor chap, poor chap.

10.7

THE porter at the gate took a similar view of things and told Maan to clear off. He had described Maan to the munshi, and the munshi had issued the instructions.

Maan, amazed, wrote a few words on a scrap of paper and said: 'I do not want to talk to any munshi. Now see that the Nawab Sahib or Burré Sahib or Chhoté Sahib gets this. Go and take it in.'

The porter, seeing Maan write something in English, this time asked Maan to follow him, though he did not offer to carry his bag. They entered the inner gate, and walked towards the main building of the Fort: a huge structure, four storeys high, with courtyards on two levels, and turrets at the top.

Maan was left in a courtyard flagged with grey stone; the porter climbed a flight of stairs and disappeared once again. It was late afternoon, and the heat was still intense in this paved and walled oven. Maan looked around him.

There was no sign of the porter or Firoz or Imtiaz or anyone. Then he detected a slight movement in one of the windows above. A rustic, middle-aged, well-fleshed face with a grey-and-white walrus moustache was examining him from the upper window.

A minute or two later, the porter returned.

'The munshi asks, what do you want?'

Maan said angrily: 'I told you to give that note to Chhoté Sahib, not the munshi.'

'But the Nawab Sahib and the Nawabzadas are not here.'

'What do you mean, not here? When did they leave?' asked Maan, dismayed.

'They have not been here for a week,' said the porter.

'Well, tell that oaf of a munshi that I am a friend of the Nawabzada's and will be spending the night here.' Maan had raised his voice, and it reverberated around the courtyard.

The munshi scurried down. Though it was hot, he was wearing a bundi over his kurta. He was irritated. It was the end of a long day and he had been looking forward to cycling back into Baitar town, where he lived. Now this unshaven and unfamiliar stranger was demanding to be received at the Fort. What was all this about?

'Yes?' said the munshi, placing his reading-glasses in his pocket. He looked Maan up and down and licked a corner of his walrus moustache. 'Of what service can I be to you?' he asked in polite Hindi. But behind his compliant tone and gentle demeanour Maan heard the rapid motion of the cogs of calculation.

'You can get me out of this baking courtyard for a start, and arrange for a room and some hot water for a shave and something to eat,' said Maan. 'I have had a hot and tiring morning hunting, and a hot and tiring train journey, and have been given the run-around for the last half-hour by you – and now this man tells me that Firoz has left – or rather, was never here. Well?' For the munshi had made no move to assist him.

'Would Sahib give me a letter of introduction from the

Nawab Sahib? Or one of the Nawabzadas?' the munshi said. 'I have not had the pleasure of Sahib's acquaintance, and in the absence of an introduction of some sort, I regret that –'

'You can regret what you like,' said Maan. 'I am Maan Kapoor, a friend of Firoz and Imtiaz. I want to use a bathroom immediately, and I am not going to wait for you to come to your senses.'

Maan's tone of command intimidated the munshi somewhat, but he made no move. He smiled to pacify Maan, but he saw his responsibility clearly. Anyone could come off the street, knowing that the Nawab Sahib and his sons were not there, claim to be a friend of one of them, and, by writing a bit of English and throwing his weight around, insinuate himself into the Fort.

'I am sorry –' he said unctuously. 'I am sorry, but –'

'Now listen,' said Maan. 'Firoz may not have talked about me to you, but he has certainly talked about you to me.' The munshi looked slightly alarmed: the Chhoté Sahib did not like him much. 'And I presume that the Nawab Sahib has mentioned my father's name to you. They are old friends.'

'And who might Sahib's father be?' asked the munshi with solicitous unconcern, expecting to hear at worst the name of some petty landowner.

'Mahesh Kapoor.'

'Mahesh Kapoor!' The munshi's tongue went rapidly to the other side of his moustache. He stared at Maan. It seemed impossible.

'The Minister of Revenue?' he asked, his voice quavering slightly.

'Yes. The Minister of Revenue,' confirmed Maan. 'Now, where is the bathroom?'

The munshi looked quickly from Maan to his bag to the porter and back to Maan. He got no confirmation of anything from anywhere. He thought of asking Maan to produce some proof, any proof, of his identity, not necessarily a letter of introduction – but he knew that this would anger him still further. It was an impossible quandary.

This man, judging from his voice and speech, was certainly educated, however sweaty and scruffy he looked. And if it was true that he was the son of the Minister of Revenue, the prime architect of the inexorable bill that was going to dispossess the house of Baitar – and indirectly himself – of its vast holdings of fields and forests and wasteland, he was a very, very important person indeed, and to have slighted him, to have been so unwelcoming to him – it did not bear thinking of. His head began to spin.

When it came to a stop, he bent down with folded hands in a gesture of servility and welcome and, instead of asking the guard or the porter to do so, picked up Maan's bag himself. He started laughing weakly, as if in amazement and embarrassment at his own foolishness. 'But, Huzoor, you should have said so from the beginning. I would have come out of the Fort to meet you. I would have been at the station, waiting with the jeep. Oh, Huzoor, you are welcome, welcome – welcome to the house of your friend. Anything you want, you just ask me. The son of Mahesh Kapoor – the son of Mahesh Kapoor – and I was so awed by Sahib's gracious presence that my senses took leave of me and I did not even offer you a glass of water.' He panted up the first flight of stairs, then handed the bag to the guard.

'Huzoor must stay in the Chhoté Sahib's own room,' continued the munshi with breathless and subservient enthusiasm. 'It is a wonderful room with a fine view of the countryside and the forest where Chhoté Sahib likes to hunt. Huzoor was pleased to mention, was he not, a minute ago, that he went out hunting this morning? I must organize a hunt for him tomorrow morning. Nilgai, deer, wild boar, perhaps even leopard. Is Huzoor amenable to that? There is no shortage of guns – and horses too, if Sahib wishes to ride. And the library is as good as the one in Brahmpur. The Nawab Sahib's father always ordered two of each book; money was no object. And Huzoor must see the town of Baitar: with Huzoor's permission, I will myself arrange a tour of Lal Kothi and the Hospital and the Monuments. Now what may Huzoor's poor munshi fetch him? Something to drink after his journey? I will at once get some almond sherbet with saffron in it. It will cool your head, and give you energy. And Sahib must give me all the clothes he needs washed. There are spare clothes in the guest-rooms, two sets of which I will immediately arrange to have brought up. And I will send Huzoor's personal manservant up in ten minutes with hot water for Huzoor's shave, and to receive the grace of any further commands from Huzoor.'

'Yes. Wonderful,' said Maan. 'Where is the bathroom?'

10.8

IN due course, after Maan had washed, shaved, and rested, the young manservant, Waris, who had been assigned to him, showed him around the Fort. This young fellow was an enormous contrast to the old servitor who had seen to Maan's needs in Baitar House in Brahmpur – and certainly to the munshi.

He was in his late twenties, tough, robust, handsome, very hospitable (as a servant trusted by his master has the self-confidence to be), and utterly loyal to the Nawab Sahib and his children, especially to Firoz. He pointed out a fading black-and-white photograph in a small silver frame on a side-table in Firoz's room. This showed the Nawab Sahib posing with his wife (not in purdah for the photograph, clearly), Zainab, Imtiaz and Firoz. Firoz and Imtiaz looked about five years old; Firoz was staring very intently at the camera with his head tilted sideways at an angle of forty-five degrees.

It was odd, thought Maan, that the very first time he was visiting the Fort, it was not Firoz but someone else who was taking him around.

The Fort seemed endless. The overwhelming impression was that of grandeur, the secondary impression that of neglect. They climbed level upon level by flights of steep stairs until they came to the roof with its ramparts and crenellations and its four square towers, each with an empty flagpost on top. It was almost dark. The countryside spread quietly around the Fort in all directions, and the fog of smoke from household fires cast a vagueness over the town of Baitar. Maan wanted to climb one of the towers, but Waris didn't have the keys. He mentioned that an owl lived in the closest tower and had been flying about hooting loudly for the last two nights – and had even made a foray in daylight, sweeping around towards the old zenana sections.

'I'll shoot the haramzada tonight if you want,' volunteered Waris generously. 'I don't want it to disturb your sleep.'

'Oh, no, no, that's not necessary,' said Maan. 'I sleep through anything.'

'That's the library below,' said Waris, pointing downwards through some thick, greenish glass. 'One of the best private libraries, they say, in India. It's two storeys high, and the daylight pours down through this glass. No one's in the Fort now, so we haven't lit it up. But whenever the Nawab Sahib comes here he spends most of his time in the library. He leaves all his estate work to that bastard of a munshi. Now be careful there – that's slippery; it's a depression where the rainwater runs off.'

Maan soon discovered that Waris used the word haramzada – bastard – fairly freely. In fact he used foul language in the friendliest way even when talking to the Nawab's sons. This was part of an easy rusticity which he curbed only when speaking to the Nawab Sahib himself. In his presence, awed, he spoke as little as possible, and kept severe control of his tongue when he did.

Waris usually felt either an instinctive wariness or an instinctive ease when he met new people, and he spoke and behaved with them accordingly. With Maan he felt no need for self-censorship.

'What's wrong with the munshi?' asked Maan, interested that Waris too did not like him.

'He's a thief,' said Waris bluntly. He could not bear the thought that the munshi was absorbing any of the Nawab Sahib's rightful revenues, and it was notorious that he did so all the time, undervaluing produce that he sold, overvaluing purchases that he made, claiming expenses where no work was done, and recording remissions in rent from the peasant tenants where no remissions were made.

'Besides that,' continued Waris, 'he oppresses the people. And besides that, he is a kayasth!'

'What's wrong with being a kayasth?' asked Maan. The kayasths, though Hindus, had been scribes and secretaries to the Muslim courts for centuries, and often wrote better Persian and Urdu than the Muslims themselves.

'Oh,' said Waris, suddenly recalling that Maan was a Hindu himself. 'I'm not against Hindus like you. It's only the kayasths. The munshi's father was the munshi here in the Nawab Sahib's father's time; and he tried to rob the old man blind; except that the old man was not blind.'

'But the present Nawab Sahib?' said Maan.

'He's too good at heart, too charitable, too religious. He never gets really angry with us — and with us the little anger he displays is enough. But when he rebukes the munshi, the munshi grovels for a few minutes and then carries on just as before.'

'How about you? Are you very religious?' said Maan.

'No,' said Waris, surprised. 'Politics is more my line. I keep things in order around these parts. I have a gun — and a gun licence, too. There is a man in this town — a base, pathetic man who was educated by the Nawab Sahib and has eaten his salt — who makes all kinds of trouble for the Nawab Sahib and the Nawabzadas — starting false cases, attempting to prove that the Fort is evacuee property, that the Nawab Sahib is a Pakistani — if this swine becomes MLA here we'll be in trouble. And he is a Congress-wallah and has made it known that he is in the running for the Congress ticket to contest from this constituency. I wish the Nawab Sahib would himself stand as an independent candidate — or let me stand for him! I'd wipe the ground clean with that bastard.'

Maan was delighted with Waris's sense of loyalty; he clearly felt that the honour and prosperity of the house of Baitar rested entirely on his shoulders.

Maan now descended to the dining room for dinner. What struck him there was not so much the rich carpet or long teak table or carved sideboard, but the oil portraits hanging on the walls: for there were four, two on each of the longer walls.

One was of the Nawab Sahib's dashing great-grand-father, complete with horse, sword and green plume, who had died fighting against the British at Salimpur. The other portrait on the same wall was of his son, who had been permitted his inheritance by the British and who had gone in for more scholarly and philanthropic pursuits. He was not on horseback, merely standing, though in full nawabi regalia. There was a sense of calm, even of withdrawal, in his eyes – as opposed to the attractive arrogance in his father's. On the opposite wall, the elder facing the elder and the younger the younger, hung portraits of Queen Victoria and King Edward VII. Victoria, seated, stared out of the painting with an air of glum plumpness that was emphasized by the tiny round crown on her head. She was wearing a long, dark blue gown and a cloak trimmed in ermine, and carrying a small sceptre. Her portly, rakish son stood crown-less but not sceptre-less against a dark background; he had on a red tunic with a dark grey sash, an ermine cloak and velvet gown, and he bristled with braid and tassels. He had a great deal more cheerfulness in his expression but none of his mother's assurance. Maan looked at each of the portraits in turn between courses during his over-spiced and solitary meal.

Later he returned to his room. For some reason the taps and flushes in his bathroom did not work, but there were buckets and brass pots of water sufficient for his needs. After a few days of going out into the fields, or the fairly rudimentary facilities of the SDO's bungalow, the marble-tiled bathroom of Firoz's room, even if he had to pour his own water, was for Maan an extreme luxury. Apart from a tub and shower and two sinks, there was a dusty-seated European-style toilet and an Indian one as well. The former was inscribed in a kind of quatrain as follows:

J B Norton & Sons Ld
Sanitary Engineers
Old Court House Corner
Calcutta

The latter said, more simply:

Norton's Patent
'The Hindu'
Combined Closet
Calcutta

Maan, as he used the latter, wondered whether anyone before him in this erstwhile stronghold of the Muslim League had meditated on this subversive inscription, rebelling perhaps at the thought that this item of their common cultural heritage should have been so arbitrarily ascribed by the British to those of the other and rival religion.

10.9

THE next morning Maan met the munshi as he was bicycling in; they exchanged a few words. The munshi was eager to know if everything had been to Maan's satisfaction: the food, the room, the behaviour of Waris. He apologized for Waris's crudity: 'But, Sir, what can we do, they are such yokels hereabouts.' Maan told him that he planned to be taken around town by the yokel, and the munshi licked his moustache in nervous displeasure.

Then he brightened up and informed Maan that he was going to arrange a hunt for him the next day.

Waris packed lunch, offered Maan a choice of hats, and showed him around the sights of the town, telling him all about the improvements that had taken place since the time of the Nawab Sahib's heroic great-grandfather. He shouted roughly at people who stared at the white-shirted, white-trousered sahib. By late afternoon they had returned to the Fort. At the gate the porter spoke sternly to Waris:

'Munshiji said you were to be back by three. There is a shortage of wood in the kitchen. He is very annoyed. He is sitting with the estate tehsildar in the big office room and he says you are to report to him immediately.'

Waris grimaced. He realized he was in some sort of minor trouble. The munshi was always irritable at this time of day; it was like a malarial cycle. Maan, however, said:

'Look, I'll come with you and explain things.'

'No, no, Maan Sahib, why bother? A hornet bites the haramzada's penis at four-thirty every day.'

'It's no trouble.'

'You are very good, Maan Sahib. You must not forget me when you go away.'

'Of course I won't. Now let's see what your munshi has to say.'

They entered the hot paved courtyard and walked up the stairs to the large office room. The munshi was sitting not at the big desk in the corner (reserved presumably for the Nawab Sahib) but cross-legged on the floor in front of a small, wooden, brass-inlaid writing desk with a sloping surface. The knuckles of his left hand were pressed into his grey-and-white moustache. He was looking disgustedly at an old woman, very poor by the look of her tattered sari, who was standing before him, her face streaked with tears.

The estate tehsildar was standing behind the munshi and was looking angry and fierce.

'Do you think you can enter the Fort like this under false pretences and then expect us to listen to you?' said the munshi testily. He did not notice Maan and Waris, who were standing just outside the door; they had paused when they heard the sound of his raised voice.

'I had no other way,' faltered the old woman. 'Allah knows I have tried to speak to you – please, Munshiji, listen to my prayers. Our family has served this house for generations –'

The munshi interrupted her: 'Were you serving this house when your son tried to get his tenancy onto the village records? What does he want to do? Take away the land that does not belong to him? If we have taught him a lesson, that is nothing strange.'

'But it is only the truth – the land has been farmed by him –'

'What? Have you come here to argue and to teach me about truth? I know how much truth there is in what you people say.' An abrasiveness now appeared beneath the smoothness of his voice. Nor did he bother to disguise his pleasure in exercising the power of crushing her under his heel.

The old woman started trembling. 'It was a mistake. He should not have done it. But apart from our land, what do we have, Munshiji? We will starve if you take our land away. Your men have beaten him up, he has learned his lesson. Forgive him – and forgive me, who have come to you with folded hands, for having given birth to the miserable boy.'

'Go,' said the munshi. 'I have heard enough. You have your hut. Go and parch grain. Or sell your withered body. And tell your son to plough someone else's fields.'

The woman started weeping helplessly.

'Go,' repeated the munshi. 'Are you deaf as well as stupid?'

'You have no humanity,' said the old woman between sobs. 'A day will come when your deeds will be weighed. On that day, when God says –'

'What?' The munshi had stood up. He stared into the woman's wrinkled face with its tearful and downcast eyes and its bitter mouth. 'What? What was that you said? I was thinking of being lenient, but now I know what it is my duty to do. We cannot have people like you creating trouble on the Nawab Sahib's land after having enjoyed his grace and hospitality for years.' He turned to the estate tehsildar. 'Get the old witch out of here – throw her out of the Fort and tell the men that I want her out of her house in the village by tonight. That will teach her and her ingrate of a son –'

He stopped in mid-sentence and stared, not in real or pretended anger but in unsimulated terror. His mouth closed and opened, he panted almost soundlessly, and his tongue moved towards his moustache.

For Maan, white-faced with rage, his mind a blank of fury, was walking towards him like an automaton, looking neither left nor right, and with murder in his eyes.

The tehsildar, the old woman, the manservant, the munshi himself – no one moved. Maan grabbed hold of the munshi's fat, rough-stubbled neck and started shaking him wordlessly and violently, hardly mindful of the terror in the man's eyes. His own teeth were bared, and he looked terrifying. The munshi gasped and choked – his hands flew up to his neck. The tehsildar stepped forward – but only a step. Suddenly Maan let the munshi go, and he crumpled downwards onto his desk.

No one said anything for a minute. The munshi gasped and coughed. Maan was stunned by what he had just done.

He could not understand why he had reacted in this disproportionate way. He should simply have yelled at the munshi and put the fear of God into him. He shook his head. Waris and the tehsildar each stepped forward now, one towards Maan, one towards the munshi. The old woman's mouth was open in horror, and she was repeating 'Ya Allah! Ya Allah!' softly to herself.

'Sahib! Sahib!' croaked the munshi, finding his voice at last. 'Huzoor knows it was only a joke – a way of – these people – I never intended – a good woman – nothing will happen – her son, his field back – Huzoor must not think – ' Tears were rolling down his cheeks.

'I am going,' said Maan, half to himself, half to Waris. 'Get me a rickshaw.' He was sure he had come within an inch of killing the man.

The resilient munshi suddenly leapt forward and almost lunged at Maan's feet, touching them with his hands and his head and lying gasping and prostrate before him. 'No, no, Huzoor – please – please – do not ruin me,' he wept, unmindful of his audience of underlings. 'It was a joke – a joke – a way of making a point – no one means such things, I swear by my father and mother.'

'Ruining you?' said Maan, dazed.

'But your hunt tomorrow –' the munshi gasped out. He realized well enough that he was in double jeopardy. Maan's father was Mahesh Kapoor, and such an incident would not increase his tenderness towards the Baitar Estate. And Maan was Firoz's friend; Firoz was volatile and his father was fond of him and sometimes listened to him; and the munshi feared to think what might happen if the Nawab Sahib, who liked to imagine that an estate could be run painlessly and benevolently, came to hear of the munshi's threats to an old woman.

'Hunt?' said Maan, staring at him.

'And your clothes are still in the wash –'

Maan turned away in disgust. He told Waris to follow him. He went to his room, dumped his belongings in his bag and walked out of the Fort. A rickshaw was summoned to take him to the station. Waris wanted to accompany him, but Maan did not let him come.

Waris's last words to him were: 'I sent a jungle fowl to the Nawab Sahib. Could you see if he got it? And give my best to that old fellow, Ghulam Rusool, who used to work here.'

10.10

'SO tell me,' said Rasheed to his four-year-old daughter Meher as they sat on a charpoy outside his father-in-law's house, 'what have you learned?'

Meher, who was sitting on her father's lap, rattled off her version of the Urdu alphabet as follows:

'Alif-be-te-se-he-che-dal-bari-ye!'

Rasheed was not pleased. 'That is a very abridged version of the alphabet,' he said. He reflected that during his absence in Brahmpur, Meher's education had very considerably regressed. 'Now, Meher, you must try harder than that. You are a bright girl.'

Though Meher was indeed a bright girl, she did not evince any further interest in the alphabet beyond adding two or three letters to her list.

She was pleased to see her father, but had been very shy with him when he had walked into the house the previous evening after an absence of several months. It had taken all her mother's persuasion and even the bribe of a cream biscuit to make her greet Rasheed. Finally, and very hesitantly, she had said, 'Adaab arz, Chacha-jaan.'

Very softly, her mother had said, 'Not Chacha-jaan. Abba-jaan.' This correction had brought on another attack of shyness. Now, however, Rasheed had re-established himself in her good graces, and she was chatting away with him as if the intervening months had not existed.

'What do they sell in the village shop?' asked Rasheed, hoping that Meher might give a better account of herself in practical affairs than she had with the alphabet.

'Sweets, savouries, soap, oil,' said Meher.

Rasheed was pleased. He bounced her up and down on his knee, and asked for a kiss, which he promptly got.

A short while later, Rasheed's father-in-law emerged from the house where he had been talking to his daughter. He was a tall, gentle man with a well-trimmed white beard, and was known in the village as Haji Sahib in recognition of the fact that he had performed the pilgrimage to Mecca some thirty years earlier.

Seeing his son-in-law and granddaughter still talking away outside the house and making no attempt at activity, he said:

'Abdur Rasheed, the sun is getting higher, and if you must go today, you had better make a move soon.' He paused. 'And be sure that you eat a large spoonful of ghee from that canister at every meal. I make certain that Meher does, and that's why her skin looks so healthy and her eyes shine as bright as diamonds.' Haji Sahib bent down to pick up his granddaughter and hugged her. Meher, who had figured out that she, her baby sister, and her mother would be going to Debaria with their father, clung to her Nana with great affection, and extracted a four-anna coin from his pocket.

'You come too, Nana-jaan,' she insisted.

'What have you found?' said Rasheed. 'Put it back. Bad habit, bad habit,' he said, shaking his head.

But Meher appealed to her Nana, who let her keep her doubtfully gotten gains. He was very sad to see them go, but he went inside to fetch his daughter and the baby.

Rasheed's wife emerged from the house. She was wearing a black burqa with a thin veil across her face, and was holding the baby in her arms. Meher went over to her mother, pulled at her burqa, and asked to hold the baby.

'Not now, Munia is asleep. In a little while,' her mother said in a soft voice.

'Have something to eat. Or at least a glass of sherbet before you go,' said Haji Sahib, who a few minutes earlier had been pressing them to make haste.

'Haji Sahib, we must go,' said Rasheed. 'We should spend a little time near the town.'

'Then I'll come with you to the railway station,' said Haji Sahib, nodding slowly.

'Please don't trouble yourself,' said Rasheed.

A sudden look of more than ordinary concern, even anxiety, crossed the sober features of the old man.

'Rasheed, I am worried that –' he began, then stopped.

Rasheed, who respected his father-in-law, had unburdened himself to him about his visit to the patwari, but he knew that that was not the source of the old man's concern.

'Please don't worry, Haji Sahib,' said Rasheed, his face also reflecting momentary pain. Then he busied himself with their bags and tins and canisters and they all set off for the road that led past the outskirts of the village. Here there was a small tea-stall where the bus to the town and the railway station stopped. A little crowd of passengers had gathered, together with a larger crowd of those who had come to see them off.

The bus clattered to a halt.

Haji Sahib was in tears as he embraced first his daughter, then his son-in-law. When he took Meher up in his arms, she followed one of his tears with her finger, frowning.

The baby slept through all this, even though she was passed from arm to arm.

With a great deal of bustle everyone got onto the bus except for two passengers; a young woman in an orange sari and a little girl of about eight, obviously her daughter.

The woman was embracing a middle-aged woman – presumably her mother, whom she had come to visit, or perhaps her sister – and weeping in a loud voice. They hugged and clutched each other with theatrical abandon, wailing and keening. The younger woman gasped with grief and cried:

'Do you remember the time when I fell down and hurt my knee. . . .'

The other woman wailed: 'You are my only one, my only one. . . .'

The little girl, who was dressed in mauve with one pink ribbon around her single plait, was looking profoundly bored.

'You fed me food – you gave me everything . . .' continued her mother.

'What will I do without you. . . . Oh God! Oh God!'

This went on for a few minutes despite the desperate honks of the driver's horn. But to drive off without them would have been unthinkable. The other passengers, though the spectacle had palled and they were now getting impatient, would never have allowed it.

'What is happening?' said Rasheed's wife in a low, troubled voice to Rasheed.

'Nothing, nothing. They are just Hindus.'

Finally, the young woman and her daughter came aboard. She leaned out of the window and continued to wail. With a sneeze and a growl the bus jolted forward. Within seconds, the woman stopped wailing and turned her attention to eating a laddu, which she took out of a packet, broke into two equal hemispheres and shared with her daughter.

THE bus was so ill that it kept collapsing every few minutes. It belonged to a potter who had made a spectacular change of profession – so spectacular in fact that he had got himself ostracized by his local caste-brethren until they found his bus indispensable for getting to the station. The potter drove it and tended it, fed and watered it, diagnosed its sneezes and false death-rattles, and coaxed its carcass along the road. Clouds of grey-blue smoke rose from the engine, raw oil leaked from its sump, the smell of burning rubber seared the air whenever it braked, and it punctured or blew a tyre every hour or two. The road, made of vertically laid bricks and little else, was cratered with holes, and the wheels had lost all memory of their shock absorbers. Rasheed felt he was in danger of castration every few minutes. His knees kept knocking the man in front of him because the back boards of the seat were missing.

None of the regular passengers, however, thought that there was any cause for complaint. This was far better and more convenient than a journey of two hours in a bullock-cart. Whenever the bus stopped involuntarily somewhere, the conductor leaned out of the window and looked at the wheels. Another man then jumped out with a pair of pliers and climbed under the bus. Sometimes the bus stopped because the driver wanted to chat to a friend along the route – or simply because he felt like stopping. Nor did the driver have any compunctions about pressing his customers into service. Whenever he needed the bus push-started he would turn around and yell in the powerfully vocalic local dialect:

'Aré, du-char jané utari aauu. Dhakka lagaauu!'

And when the bus was about to move, he would summon them with a battlecry of:

'Aai jao bhaiyya, aai jao. Chalo ho!'

The driver took particular pride in the signs (in standard Hindi) displayed in the bus. Above his seat for instance, it said *Officer Seat* and *Don't talk to the driver when the bus is in motion.* Above the door it said: *Only disembark when the bus has come to a halt.* Along one wall of the bus, the following message was painted in a murderous scarlet: *Do not travel when drunk or with a loaded gun.* But it said nothing about goats, and there were several in the bus.

Halfway to the station, the bus stopped at another small tea-stall, and here a blind man got on. His face was covered with cauliflower-like swellings, and he had a small snub nose. He walked with the help of a stick, and felt his way onto the bus. He could tell which bus it was from a distance by its characteristic sounds. He could also recognize people instantly by their voices, and he liked talking to them. One of his trouser legs was rolled long and the other short. Looking upwards he now sang out in a carefree and untuneful voice:

> 'Oh You Who Give, don't give anyone poverty.
> Give me death, but do not give misfortune.'

He sang this and lyrics of a similar nature while going around the bus collecting small coins and upbraiding the miserly with a volley of relevant couplets. Rasheed, whenever he travelled on this bus, was one of his more generous benefactors, and the beggar recognized his voice immediately. 'What?' he cried, 'you've only spent two nights at your father-in-law's? Shame, shame! You should spend more time with your wife, a young man like you. Or is that baby who is crying your own – and is that your wife with you here? Oh, Wife of Abdur Rasheed, if you are here on this bus, forgive this unfortunate for his insolence and accept his blessing. May you have many more sons, and all with lungs as loud. Give – give – God rewards the generous. ...' And he moved on through the bus.

Meher's mother blushed furiously beneath her burqa, and then started giggling. After a while she stopped. Then she started sobbing, and Rasheed touched her shoulder gently.

The beggar got off at the last stop, the railway station.

'Peace to you all,' he said. 'And health and safety to all who travel on Indian Railways.'

Rasheed discovered that the train was only a little late, and was disappointed. He had hoped to take a rickshaw and visit his elder brother's grave which was half an hour away in a graveyard outside this small town. For it was at this station that his brother had met with his death by falling under a train three years ago. Before the news had come to his family, the people of the town had arranged for the burial of his crushed remains.

It was now about noon and extremely hot. They had been sitting on the platform for only a few minutes when Rasheed's wife started shivering. Rasheed held her hand and said nothing. Then he said in a low voice: 'I know, I know what you must be feeling. I wanted to visit him too. We'll do it next time we are here. There was no time today. Believe me, there was no time. And with all this luggage – how could we?'

The baby, resting in an improvised crib of a few bags, continued to sleep. Meher too was exhausted and had dozed off. Rasheed looked at them and closed his eyes as well.

His wife said nothing, but moaned softly. Her heart was palpitating swiftly, and she seemed dazed. 'You are thinking of Bhaiyya, aren't you?' he said. She started sobbing again, and trembling uncontrollably. Rasheed felt a sense of pressure building up at the back of his head. He looked at her face, beautiful even through the veil – beautiful perhaps because he knew it was beautiful. He spoke again, holding her hand in his and stroking her forehead:

'Don't cry – don't cry – Meher and the baby will wake up – we'll have left this inauspicious place soon. Why grieve, why grieve, when you can do nothing about it. . . . Look, it could also be the heat. Take your veil off – let the air play a little on your face. . . . We would have had to rush there, and we might have missed the train and have had to spend the night in this miserable town. Next time we'll make time. It is my fault, I should have left the house earlier. But perhaps I could not have borne the grief of it myself. The bus stopped again and again and we got delayed. And now, believe me, Bhabhi, there is no time at all.'

He had addressed her as he used to do in the old days, using the word for sister-in-law. For she had been his brother's wife, and Meher had been his brother's child. He had married her at his mother's dying behest; his mother could not bear that her infant granddaughter should remain fatherless or her daughter-in-law (whom she loved) a widow.

'Take care of her,' she had said to Rasheed. 'She is a good woman and will make you a good wife as well.' Rasheed had promised to do as she had asked, and had kept his difficult and binding promise.

10.12

MOST respected Maulana Abdur Rasheed Sahib,

I am taking up my pen to write with much hesitation, and without the knowledge of my sister and guardian. I thought you would want to know how my Arabic was faring in your absence. It is faring well. I am practising every day. At first my sister tried to appoint another teacher for me, an old man who mumbles and coughs and makes no attempt to correct me when I make mistakes. But I was so unhappy that Saeeda Apa discontinued him. You never used to let me get away with any mistakes, and I am afraid I was tearful at times when it seemed I could do nothing right. But you never let me get away with tears either, and did not let me turn to something easier after I had collected myself. I have now come to realize the value of your teaching method, and I miss having to make the effort that I had to when you were here.

Nowadays I spend my time mainly in housework of one kind or another. Apa is in a bad mood these days, I think because her new sarangi player has been playing indifferently. So I am afraid to ask her to let me do something of interest. You advised me not to read novels, but I have so much time on my hands that I find myself turning to them. But I do read the Quran Sharif every day, and copy out a few excerpts. I will now copy out one or two quotations from the surah I am reading, complete with all the special vowel-marks to show you how my Arabic calligraphy is progressing. But I fear it is not progressing at all. In your absence, it is at best standing still.

> Have they not regarded the birds above them
> spreading their wings, and closing them?
> Naught holds them but the All-Merciful. Surely
>   He sees everything.

> Say: 'What think you? If in the morning
> your water should have vanished into
> the earth, then who would bring you
>   running water?'

The parakeet, who was looking feeble the day before you left, has lately begun to say a few words. Saeeda Apa has taken a fancy to him, I am happy to say.

I hope you will return soon, as I miss seeing you and hearing your criticisms and corrections, and I hope that you are well and in good spirits. I am sending this letter through Bibbo. She will post it; she says this address should be sufficient. I pray that it reaches you.

With many good wishes and renewed respects,

Your student,
Tasneem

Rasheed read this letter slowly, twice, sitting by the side of the lake near the school. He had returned to Debaria to find that Maan had come back a little earlier than expected, and, after enquiries, he had followed him to the lake to make sure he was all right. He appeared to be fine, from the vigorous way he was swimming back from the far end.

Rasheed had been surprised to receive the letter. It had

been waiting for him at his father's house. He was interested to see the excerpts, which he recognized instantly from the chapter of the Quran called The Kingdom. How like Tasneem, he thought, to select the most gentle excerpts from a surah that contained terrible descriptions of hell-fire and perdition.

Her calligraphy had not deteriorated. If anything it had slightly improved. Her own appraisal of it was both modest and just. There was something in the letter – quite apart from the fact that it had been sent to him behind Saeeda Bai's back – that troubled him, and despite himself he found his thoughts turning to Meher's mother, who was sitting inside his father's house, probably fanning the baby. Poor woman, good-hearted and beautiful though she was, she could barely write her own name. And he once again thought: If I had had any choice, would it ever have been a woman like her whom I would have chosen as my partner and companion through this life?

10.13

MAAN laughed a little, then coughed. Rasheed looked at him. He sneezed.

'You should dry your hair,' said Rasheed. 'Don't blame me if you catch a cold. Swimming and then not drying your hair is an absolutely certain way of catching a cold. Summer colds are the worst. Your voice sounds bad too. And you look much darker, more burnt by the sun than when I saw you just a few days ago.'

Maan reflected that his voice must have been affected by the dust of the journey. He hadn't actually shouted at anyone, not even at the marksman or the munshi. On his return from Baitar, perhaps to relieve his feelings, he had made straight for the lake near the school, and had swum across and back a few times. When he got out, he saw Rasheed sitting on the bank, reading a letter. Next to him was a small box – of sweets, it appeared.

'It must be all this Urdu you've been teaching me,' Maan

said. 'All those guttural letters, ghaaf and khay and so on – my throat can't survive them.'

'You are making excuses,' said Rasheed. 'This is an excuse not to study. In fact you haven't studied more than four hours since you've been here.'

'What are you saying?' said Maan. 'All I do from morning to night is repeat the alphabet forwards and backwards and practise writing Urdu letters in the air. Why, even when I was swimming just now I kept imagining letters: when I swam breaststroke, I was writing qaaf, when I swam backstroke I was writing noon –'

'Do you want to go up there?' asked Rasheed, with some impatience.

'What do you mean?' said Maan.

'I mean, is there even the slightest truth in what you have been saying?'

'Not the slightest!' laughed Maan.

'So when you go up there, what will you say to God?'

'Oh, well,' said Maan. 'I have topsy-turvy views about all that. Up is down to me, and down is up. In fact, I believe that if there is paradise anywhere, it is here, here on earth. What do you think?'

Rasheed did not much care for flippancy on serious subjects. He did not think paradise was on earth: certainly not in Brahmpur, certainly not here in Debaria, nor in his wife's virtually illiterate village.

'You look worried,' said Maan. 'I hope it isn't anything I said.'

Rasheed thought for a few seconds before answering. 'Actually,' he said, 'it wasn't your answer exactly. I was wondering about Meher's education.'

'Your daughter?' asked Maan.

'Yes. My elder daughter. She's a bright girl – you'll meet her in the evening. But there are no schools like this' – he waved an arm towards the nearby madrasa – 'in her mother's village – and she will grow up ignorant unless I do something about it. I try to teach her whenever I'm here, but then I go to Brahmpur for a few months, and the illiterate environment takes over.'

It never struck Rasheed as odd that he loved Meher every bit as much as his own daughter. Perhaps one element of this bond was precisely that Meher had at first been for him purely an object of love, not of responsibility. Even when, a year or so ago, she stopped calling him Chacha and started calling him Abba, some of that sense of the uncle – who would come home and spoil her with presents and affection – remained. With a start, Rasheed recalled that the baby was about as old as Meher had been when her father had died. Perhaps this too had been in her mother's mind when she had lost control of her emotions and broken down at the station.

Rasheed thought of his wife with tenderness, but not with passion, and he felt that she too felt no passion for him, merely a sense of comfort when he was with her. She lived for her children and the memory of her first husband.

This is my life, the only life I will live, thought Rasheed. If only things had been different, we might each have been happy.

At first the very thought of sharing a room with her for an hour had troubled him. Then he grew used to the brief visits he paid to her in the middle of the night when the other men were asleep in the courtyard. But even when fulfilling his obligations as a husband he wondered what she was thinking. Sometimes he imagined that she was close to tears. Had she begun to love him more after the baby had been born? Perhaps. But the women of the zenana in her father's village – her elder brothers' wives – were often quite cruel even when they teased each other, and she would not have been able to express her affection for him openly, even if there had been much to express.

Once more Rasheed began to unfold the letter he had received, then stopped and said to Maan:

'So – how is your father's farm?'

'My father's farm?'

'Yes.'

'Well,' said Maan. 'It should be all right. Not much going on at this time of the year.'

'But haven't you just visited the farm?'

'No. Not exactly.'

'Not exactly?'

'I mean, no. No, I meant to, but – I got caught up in things.'

'So what have you been doing?'

'Losing my temper mainly,' said Maan. 'And trying to kill wolves.'

Rasheed frowned, but did not follow up these interesting possibilities. 'You are being flippant as usual,' he said.

'What are those flowers?' asked Maan, to change the subject.

Rasheed looked across the tank to the far shore.

'The purple ones?'

'Yes. What are they called?'

'Sadabahar – or evergreen,' said Rasheed, 'because it's always spring for them. They never seem to die, and no one can get rid of them. I think they're beautiful – though they often grow in foul places....' He paused. 'Some people call them "behayaa" – or "shameless".' He was lost in meditation for a long while, one thought leading to another.

'Well,' said Maan, 'what were you thinking of?'

'My mother,' said Rasheed. After a pause he continued in a quiet voice: 'I loved her, God protect her spirit. She was an upright woman, and well-educated as women go. She loved my brother and me, and only regretted that she never had a daughter. Perhaps that's why – well, anyway, she was the only one who appreciated my wish to educate myself, to make something of myself and do something for this place.' Rasheed said 'this place' with such bitterness that it sounded almost as if he detested it. 'But my love for her has tied my life up in knots. And as for my father – what does he understand of anything outside property and money? I have to be discreet even in what I say at home. I'm always looking up towards the roof and lowering my voice. Baba, for all his piety, understands things – things one might not expect him to. But my father has contempt for everything I revere. And it has become worse lately with the changes in the house.' Maan guessed that Rasheed meant his father's second wife.

But Rasheed was continuing with great bitterness. 'Look all around you,' he said. 'Or look at history. It's always been the same. The old men cling to their power and their beliefs, which admit all their worst vices but exclude the least fault and strangle the smallest innovation of the young. Then, thank God, they die, and can do no more harm. But by then we, the young, are old, and strive to do what little mischief they left undone. This village is the worst,' continued Rasheed, pointing behind the school to the low buildings of Debaria's twin village of Sagal. 'Worse even than ours, and also, of course, more pious. I'll show you one good man in this village – I was on my way to see him when I saw you tempting fate by swimming alone. You'll see the state to which he has been driven by the others – and, I suppose, by the just or unjust anger of God.'

Maan was astonished to hear Rasheed talk in this vein. Rasheed's education before Brahmpur University had been a traditionally religious one, and Maan knew how firmly he believed in God and his Prophet and the Book, the transmitted word of God – even to the extent of refusing to abridge Tasneem's lesson from the Quran when summoned by Saeeda Bai. But Rasheed was not contented with the world that God had made, nor did he understand why it had been arranged in the pathetic way it had. As for the old man, Maan recalled that Rasheed had referred to him briefly during their long walk around the village, but he did not feel particularly eager to be shown assorted samples of village misery.

'Were you always so serious about the state of things?' asked Maan.

'Far from it,' said Rasheed, with a rather twisted smile at the corner of his mouth. 'Far from it. When I was younger, well, I was concerned only with myself and my fists. I've told you about this before, haven't I? I would look around and notice certain things. My grandfather was treated by everyone around him with great respect. People would come from far away to ask him to solve disputes. Sometimes he'd do this with great severity, beating the offenders. This I considered proof of the fact that beating people was a cause of his being honoured. I beat people up too.'

Rasheed paused to look up the slope towards the madrasa, then continued:

'At school I was always hitting the kids. I'd find one by himself, and I'd beat him up. Sometimes I'd come across a boy in the fields or along the road and I'd slap him hard across the face.'

Maan laughed. 'Yes, I remember you telling me that,' he said.

'It's no laughing matter really,' said Rasheed. 'And certainly my parents didn't think so. My mother would beat me very rarely, if at all; well, she did once or twice. But my father – he would beat me regularly.

'Baba, however, who was the real authority in the village, treated me with great love, and his presence would often save me. I was his favourite. He was very regular about his prayers. So I too would always say my prayers even though I did very badly at school. But every so often I would thrash a boy, and his father would report it to Baba. Once Baba told me to sit down and stand up one hundred times while holding my ears as a punishment. Some of my friends were standing around, and I refused to do any such thing. Perhaps I would have got away with it. But my father happened to be passing, and he was so shocked by my insolence towards his father that he hit me across the face very hard. I began crying from shame and pain, and I decided to run away. I ran quite far – till the mango trees beyond the threshing ground to the north – before they sent someone after me and brought me back.'

Maan was as rapt as if he had been listening to a story by the guppi.

'Was that before the time you ran away to stay with the Bear?' he prompted.

'Yes,' said Rasheed, a bit vexed that Maan appeared to know his story so well.

'Anyway, later,' he continued, 'I began to understand things. I think it happened at the religious training college I went to. It's in Banaras, I'm sure you must have heard of it, it's quite famous, and it has a high academic reputation – though it is a terrible place. Anyway, at first they wouldn't let me in because of my poor school marks from here; but within a year I had come third in my class of sixty boys. I even left off beating people up! And, because of the conditions we had to live in, I became interested in practical politics, and started organizing the boys to protest against the worst abuses at the college! That's probably where I got a taste for reform, though I wasn't a socialist yet. My former associates at school were amazed at me – and probably appalled by the righteous turn I had taken. One of them has become a dacoit. And now when I talk about village improvement and so on, they all think I'm mad. God knows these villages need improvement – and can be improved. But I doubt that God will find time to do it no matter how often people do their namaaz. As for legislation –' Rasheed got up. 'Come. It's getting late, and I have to go for this visit. If I'm not back in Debaria by sunset I'll have to do my namaaz with the elders of this village – hypocrites to a man.' Rasheed clearly viewed Sagal as a sink of iniquity.

'All right,' said Maan, beginning to be curious. 'I suppose it's all right for me to tag along.'

10.14

WHEN they were not far from the old man's place, Rasheed told Maan a little about his background:

'He is about sixty years old and comes from a very wealthy family of many brothers. He himself had many children, but they are all dead now except for the two daughters who take care of him alternately. He's a good man who never did anything wrong in his life – and while his crooked brothers are flourishing with wealth and children, he is in a pitiable condition.' Rasheed paused, then speculated: 'Some say a jinn did this to him. Though they are evil themselves, they often seek the company of good people. Anyway –' Rasheed stopped suddenly. A tall, venerable-looking man passed by him in the narrow lane, and they exchanged greetings, sullen on Rasheed's side.

'That is one of his brothers,' he said to Maan a few moments later, 'one of the brothers who has robbed him of his share of the family's wealth. He is one of the leaders of the community, and when the Imam of the mosque is absent he often leads the congregation in prayer. Even greeting him makes me uncomfortable.'

They now entered a courtyard and came across a strange scene.

Two thin bullocks were tethered to a peg near a feeding trough. A small goat was lying on a charpoy next to a sleeping child, a boy around whose beautiful face a few flies were buzzing. Grass was growing on the wall of the small courtyard; a broom made of twigs was leaning against it in a corner. A pretty eight-year-old girl dressed in red was looking at them. She was holding up the slack wing of a dead crow that stared at them with one opaque grey eye. A bucket, a broken clay drinking pot, a stone board and roller for crushing spices, a few other odds and ends – all these lay scattered around the courtyard as if no one knew what they were for and no one cared.

On the porch of the ramshackle two-room thatched house was a sagging charpoy, and on this lay an old man. Gaunt-featured, with peppery stubble and sunken eyes, he was lying on his side on a dirty, checked-green covering. His body was entirely emaciated and rib-ridden; his hands were like twisted claws, and his spindly legs too were twisted inwards. He looked as if he was ninety years old and near death. But his voice was clear and, when he saw them approach, he said, since he could see their forms only vaguely:

'Who? Who is that?'

'Rasheed,' said Rasheed loudly, knowing that the man was hard of hearing.

'Who?'

'Rasheed.'

'Oh, when did you come?'

'I've just come back from my wife's village.' Rasheed did not wish to say that he had been in Debaria for longer but had not visited until now.

The old man digested this, then said: 'Who is that with you?'

'This is a Babu from Brahmpur,' said Rasheed. 'He comes from a good family.'

Maan did not know what to think of this succinct biography, but reflected that 'Babu' was probably a term of respect in these parts.

The old man leaned forward slightly, then sank back with a sigh.

'How are things in Brahmpur?' he asked.

Rasheed nodded towards Maan.

'Very hot still,' said Maan, not knowing what was expected of him.

'Just turn towards that wall for a moment,' said Rasheed to Maan quietly.

Maan did so without asking why. He turned back, however, before he was told to do so, and caught a brief glimpse of the pretty and fair face of a woman dressed in a yellow sari who hurriedly disappeared behind a square pillar on the porch. In her arms was the child who had been sleeping on the charpoy. Later she joined the conversation from this improvised form of purdah. The little girl in red had dropped her dead crow somewhere and had gone to play with her mother and brother behind the pillar.

'That was his younger daughter,' said Rasheed to Maan.

'Very pretty,' said Maan. Rasheed silenced him with a sharp glance.

'Why don't you sit on the charpoy? Shoo the goat away,' said the woman hospitably.

'All right,' said Rasheed.

From where they were now sitting it was more difficult for Maan to avoid casting a furtive look at her every so often. He did so whenever he was sure Rasheed was not looking. Poor Maan, he had been deprived so long of female company that he felt his heart leap and thud every time he caught the slightest glimpse of her face.

'How is he?' Rasheed asked the woman.

'You can see. The worst is to come. The doctors refuse to treat him. My husband says we should make him comfortable, try to give him what he asks for, that's the extent of it.' She had a happy voice and a lively manner of speech.

They discussed him for a while as if he weren't present.

Then the old man suddenly roused himself to speak. 'Babu!' he said in a loud voice.

Rasheed nodded at Maan again.

'Yes?' said Maan, probably too softly for the man to hear.

'What can I tell you, Babu – I've been ill for twenty-two years – and bedridden for twelve. I am so crippled I can't even sit up. I wish God would take me. I had six children and six daughters too' – Maan was struck by his manner of describing his twelve children – 'and only two are left. My wife died three years ago. Never get ill, Babu. It is the worst fate. I eat here, I sleep here, I wash here, I talk here, I pray here, I weep here, I shit and piss here. Why did God do this to me?'

Maan looked at Rasheed. He looked stricken.

'Rasheed!' cried the old man.

'Yes, Phupha-jaan.'

'Her mother' – the old man indicated his daughter with his head – 'took care of your father when he was ill. Now he doesn't even visit. It's since your stepmother came. Previously, every time I went past their house – ah, twelve years ago – they insisted that I had to have tea. They visited when I fell ill. Now only you do. I hear Vilayat Sahib was here too. He didn't visit.'

'Vilayat Sahib never visits anyone, Phupha-jaan.'

'What's that you say?'

'Vilayat Sahib never visits anyone.'

'Yes. But your father? Don't take it badly. I'm not criticizing.'

'No, no,' said Rasheed. 'I know. It's not right. I don't say it's right.' He shook his head slowly and looked down. Then he went on: 'I don't take it badly. It's best to say what one thinks. I'm sorry that this is so. But I must listen to it. It's only right.'

'You must visit again before you go back.... How do you manage in Brahmpur?'

'I manage very well,' said Rasheed, reassuringly if not accurately. 'I give tuitions, and that covers things comfortably. I am in good shape. I've brought a small gift for you – some sweets.'

'Sweets?'

'Yes. I'll give them to her.'

To the woman Rasheed said: 'They are easy to digest, but don't give him more than one or two at a time.' To the old man he said: 'I must go now, Phupha-jaan.'

'You are a good man.'

'It's easy to earn that title in Sagal,' said Rasheed.

The old man chuckled a little. 'Yes,' he said, finally.

Rasheed got up to go, and Maan followed.

The old man's daughter, with a tender formality in her voice, said: 'What you have done restores our faith in people.'

But as they left the courtyard, Maan heard Rasheed say to himself:

'And what the good people have done to you makes me doubt my faith in God.'

10.15

ON the way out of the village of Sagal, they passed a small open area in front of the mosque. Here, standing and talking, was a group of about ten village elders, most of them bearded, including the man who had passed them outside the old man's house. Rasheed recognized two more of the invalid's brothers among the group, but could not see their expressions in the late twilight. They appeared, however, to be looking at him, and their stance was hostile. As he drew nearer, he saw that their expression was no less so. For a few seconds they looked him up and down. Maan, still in his white shirt and trousers, also came under their scrutiny.

'So you've come,' said one in a slightly mocking tone.

'Yes,' said Rasheed, without any warmth, and not even using the customary title of the man who spoke.

'You've taken your time.'

'Well,' said Rasheed, 'some things take time.'

'So you sat talking and exchanging the time of day until it became too late to say the namaaz,' said another, the man who had passed by him a little while ago.

This was indeed true; so involved had Rasheed been that he had not even noticed the evening call to prayer.

'Yes,' he responded angrily. 'That's precisely right.'

He was enraged that he was being baited in this open gathering, not out of any attempt to improve his attendance at prayer but out of sheer mockery and ill-will. They're jealous, he thought, because I'm young and have made progress. And they're threatened by my beliefs – they've decided that I'm a communist. And what they hate most of all is my association with that man whose life makes their own a source of shame.

A tall, thick-set man glowered at Rasheed. 'And who is this?' he asked, indicating Maan. 'Are you not going to do us the favour of an introduction? Then we will be able to judge what company the Maulana Sahib keeps and benefit from it too.' The orange kurta that Maan had been wearing when he first arrived had given rise to the rumour that he was a Hindu holy man.

'I don't think that is necessary,' said Rasheed. 'He is my friend, that is all. Like should be introduced to like.'

Maan ventured to come forward to stand with Rasheed, but Rasheed with a gesture kept him out of the main line of fire.

'Do you propose to attend the dawn prayer at the mosque at Debaria tomorrow, Maulana Sahib? We understand that you are a late riser and it may involve some sacrifice,' said the thick-set man to Rasheed.

'I will attend what prayers I choose to,' said Rasheed hotly.

'So, Maulana Sahib, this is your style,' said someone else.

'Look –' said Rasheed, almost beside himself with anger, 'if any of you want to talk about my style, come any time to my house and we'll talk about it, and we'll see whose style bests the other's. As for whose life is more decent and whose religious beliefs are deeper – society knows and can say. Why society? Even children know about the disreputable lives of many of the punctually pious.' He gestured towards the semicircle of bearded figures. 'If there was any justice, even the courts would ensure –'

'It is not for society or children or courts, but for Him to say,' cried one old man, shaking his finger in Rasheed's face.

'Well, that's a matter for opinion and argument,' retorted Rasheed.

'Iblis knew how to argue before his fall!'

'So did the good angels,' said Rasheed furiously. 'So do others.'

'Are you calling yourself an angel, Maulana Sahib?' sneered the man.

'Are you calling me Iblis?' cried Rasheed.

He suddenly realized that matters had gone far enough, had in fact gone too far. These were his elders, however insulting, reactionary, hypocritical, jealous. He also thought of Maan and how bad a scene like this would look to him – how unfavourable an impression it would convey of his religion.

Once again a pulsing pressure had begun building inside his head. He moved forward – his path had in effect been blocked – and a couple of men moved aside.

'It has become late,' said Rasheed. 'Excuse me. We must go. So, we'll meet again – and then we'll see.' He moved through the broken arc, and Maan followed.

'Perhaps you should say "Khuda haafiz,"' said a final sarcastic voice.

'Yes, khuda haafiz, God protect you too,' said Rasheed angrily, walking on without turning back.

10.16

THOUGH Debaria and Sagal were separate villages about a mile apart geographically, they could have been a single village for the purposes of rumour. For whatever was said in one was repeated in the other. Whether it was someone from Sagal coming to Debaria to bring some grain to be parched, or someone from Debaria dropping by at the post office at Sagal or the schoolchildren going to study in the common madrasa, or someone visiting someone in the other village or happening to meet him in an adjoining field, the two villages were so indissolubly interlinked through networks of friendship and enmity, ancient ancestry and recent marriage, information and disinformation as to form one single intersecting web of gossip.

Sagal had almost no upper-caste Hindus. Debaria had a few brahmin families, and they too formed a part of this web, for their relations with the better Muslim families like Rasheed's were good, and they would drop by sometimes at each other's houses. They took pride in the fact that feuds within each of the two communities dominated any friction between the communities. This was not the case in some of the surrounding villages, especially where there were memories of violence against Muslims at the time of Partition.

The Football, as one of the brahmin landowners was popularly called, was in fact just on his way to pay a morning visit to Rasheed's father.

Maan was sitting on a charpoy outside the house, playing with Meher. Moazzam was hanging around; he was delighted with Meher, and from time to time passed his hand wonderingly over her head. Mr Biscuit hovered around hungrily.

Rasheed and his father were sitting on another charpoy,

talking. A report of Rasheed's altercation with the elders of Sagal had reached his father.

'So you don't think namaaz is important?' he observed.

'It is, it is,' replied Rasheed. 'What can I say? I haven't observed it strictly these last few days – I've had unavoidable responsibilities and duties. And you can't roll out a prayer-mat on a bus. Part of it is my own laziness. But if someone had wanted to correct me and explain things to me with sympathy, he would have taken me aside – or spoken to you, Abba – not damaged my honour in a full and open gathering.' He paused, then added with fervour: 'And I believe one's life is more important than any namaaz.'

'What do you mean by that?' said his father sharply. He noticed Kachheru passing by. 'Ei, Kachheru, go to the bania's shop and get me some supari – I've run out of it for my paan. Yes, yes – I want the usual amount. ... Ah, the Football is waddling along to pay us a visit; he's probably come because of your Hindu friend. Yes, people's lives are important, but that is no excuse – anyway, no excuse for speaking in that way to the big people of a village. Have you considered my honour when you behave like that? Or your own position in the village?'

Rasheed's eye followed Kachheru for a while. 'All right,' he said, 'please forgive me – the mistake is all mine.'

But ignoring his insincere apology, his father was now greeting his guest with a broad smile, his red mouth wide open: 'Welcome, welcome, Tiwariji.'

'Hello, hello,' said the Football. 'What were father and son discussing so heatedly?'

'Nothing,' said both father and son simultaneously.

'Oh, well. Two or three of us have been thinking of visiting you for some time now, but what with the harvest and so on we couldn't find the time. And then we heard that your guest had gone away for a few days, so we decided to wait till his return.'

'So you've really come to see Kapoor Sahib, not us,' said his host.

The Football shook his head vehemently: 'What are you

saying, what are you saying, Khan Sahib? Our friendship goes back for decades. And one gets so little chance to talk to Rasheed either, now that he is improving his mind in Brahmpur most of the year.'

'Anyway,' continued Rasheed's father rather mischievously, 'why don't you have a cup of tea now that you've made such an effort to come? I'll summon Rasheed's friend, and we will talk. Who else is coming, by the way? Rasheed, ask for tea for all of us.'

The Football became agitated. 'No, no –' he said, gesticulating as if he were brushing away a swarm of wasps, 'no tea, no tea.'

'But we will all be having it together, Tiwariji, it is not poisoned. Even Kapoor Sahib will join us.'

'He drinks tea with all of you?' said Tiwari.

'Indeed. He eats with us too.'

The Football was silent while he, so to speak, digested this. After a while he said:

'But I have just had tea, you know, with my breakfast – I've just had tea and also far too much to eat before I left my house. Look at me. I must be careful. Your hospitality knows no bounds. But –'

'You aren't saying, by any chance, Tiwariji, are you, that what we are offering falls below your expectations? Why don't you like to eat with us? Do you think we will pollute you?'

'Oh, no, no, no, it is just that an insect of the gutter like myself does not feel happy when offered the luxuries of a palace. Heh heh heh!' The Football wobbled a little at his witticism, and even Rasheed's father smiled. He decided not to press the point. All of the other brahmins were straightforward about their caste rules, which forbade eating with non-brahmins, but the Football was always evasive.

Mr Biscuit approached their charpoy, attracted by tea and biscuits:

'Clear off, or I'll fry you in ghee,' Moazzam said, his hedgehog-hair bristling. 'He's a glutton,' he explained to Maan.

Mr Biscuit stared at them with a blank gaze.

Meher offered him one of her two biscuits, and he came forward like a zombie to ingest it.

Rasheed was pleased at Meher's generosity, but not at all pleased with Mr Biscuit.

'He does nothing but eat and shit, eat and shit the whole day,' he told Maan. 'That's his entire business in life. He's seven years old, and can hardly read a word. What can one do? – it's the atmosphere of the village. People think he's funny and encourage him.'

As if to prove his other skills, Mr Biscuit, having absorbed the offering, now put his hands to his ears and called out, in a mockery of the muezzin's call to prayer:

'Aaaaaaye Lalla e lalla alala! Halla o halla!'

Moazzam shouted: 'You low creature!' and made as if to slap him, but Maan restrained him.

Moazzam, once again fascinated by Maan's watch, said: 'Look: the two hands are coming together now.'

'Don't give Moazzam your watch,' advised Rasheed. 'I've warned you already. Or your torch. He likes to find out what makes them work, but he doesn't operate very scientifically. I once found him bashing my watch with a brick. He had taken it out of my bag when I wasn't looking. Luckily, the basic machinery still worked. But the glass, needle, spring – all were smashed. It cost me twenty rupees to have it repaired.'

But Moazzam was now counting and tickling Meher's toes – to her great delight. 'Sometimes he says the most interesting and even sensitive things,' said Rasheed. 'He is very puzzling. The trouble is that his parents spoiled him, and did not discipline him at all. Now he just follows his own inclinations. Sometimes he steals money from them or others and goes off into Salimpur. What he does there no one knows. Then he resurfaces after a few days. He's very intelligent, even affectionate. But he'll come to a bad end.'

Moazzam, who had overheard this, laughed and said, a little resentfully: 'I won't. It's you who will come to a bad end. Eight, nine, ten; ten, nine, eight – keep still – seven, six. Give me that charm – you've played with it long enough.'

Noticing a couple of other visitors approaching in the distance, he handed Meher to her great-grandfather, who had emerged from the house, and wandered off to investigate and – if necessary – challenge them.

'Quite a mischievous kid,' said Maan.

'Mischievous?' said Baba. 'He's a rogue – a thief – at the age of twelve!'

Maan smiled.

'He broke the fan of that bicycle-operated winnowing machine there. He's not mischievous, he's a hooligan,' continued Baba, rocking Meher to and fro, very vigorously for an old man.

'Now he's so big,' continued Baba, throwing a dirty look in Moazzam's direction, 'that he has to have fancy food. So he steals – from people's pockets. Every day he steals rice, daal, whatever he can, from his own house and sells it at the bania's shop. Then he's off to Salimpur to eat grapes and pomegranates!'

Maan laughed.

Suddenly Baba thought of something. 'Rasheed!' he said.

'Yes, Baba?'

'Where's that other daughter of yours?'

'Inside, Baba, with her mother. I think she's feeding.'

'She's a weakling. Hardly seems to be a child of my stock. She should be given buffalo's milk to drink. When she smiles she looks like an old woman.'

'Many children do, Baba,' said Rasheed.

'Now this is a healthy child. See how her cheeks glow.'

Two men – also brahmins from the village – now approached the open courtyard, preceded by Moazzam and followed by Kachheru. Baba went forward to greet them, and Rasheed and Maan moved their own charpoy closer to the end of the courtyard where Rasheed's father was sitting with the Football. It was becoming a conference.

To add to the numbers, Netaji also appeared shortly

from the direction of Sagal. Qamar, the sardonic school-teacher who had made a very brief appearance at the shop in Salimpur, was with him. They had just been visiting the madrasa to talk with the teachers.

10.17

EVERYONE greeted everyone else, though with varying degrees of enthusiasm. Qamar was not delighted to see such an accumulation of brahmins, and greeted them in the most perfunctory manner – although the recent arrivals, Bajpai (complete with his sandalwood-paste caste-mark) and his son Kishor Babu, were very good people. They for their part were not happy to see their fellow-brahmin, the Football, who was a mischief-maker and liked nothing better than to set people off against each other.

Kishor Babu was a shy and gentle soul. He told Maan that he was very pleased to make his acquaintance at last, and took both his hands in his own. After that he tried to pick up Meher, who, however, would not let him and ran off to sit on her grandfather's lap while he examined the betel-nuts that Kachheru had brought. Netaji went across the way to fetch another charpoy.

Bajpai had caught hold of Maan's right hand and was examining it carefully. 'One wife. Some wealth,' he said. 'As for the line of wisdom. . . .'

'. . . it seems not to exist.' Maan finished the sentence for him and smiled.

'The line of life is not very favourable,' said Bajpai encouragingly.

Maan laughed.

Qamar meanwhile was looking disgusted at this whole exercise. Here was another example of the pitiful superstition of the Hindus.

Bajpai continued: 'You were four children, only three remain.'

Maan stopped laughing, and his hand tensed.

'Am I right?' said Bajpai.

'Yes,' said Maan.

'Which one passed away?' asked Bajpai, looking at Maan's face intently and kindly.

'No,' said Maan, 'that's what you have to tell me.'

'I believe it was the youngest.'

Maan was relieved. 'I am the youngest,' he said. 'It was the third who died when he was less than a year old.'

'All bogus, all bogus,' said Qamar, with a look of contempt. He was a man of principle and could not abide charlatanism.

'You should not say so, Master Sahib,' said Kishor Babu mildly. 'It is quite scientific. Palmistry – and astrology too. Otherwise why would the stars be where they are?'

'Everything is scientific for you,' said Qamar. 'Even the caste system. Even worshipping the linga and other disgusting things. And singing bhajans to that adulterer, that teaser of women, that thief Krishna.'

If Qamar was spoiling for a quarrel, he did not get what he wanted. Maan looked at him in surprise but did not interfere. He too was interested in what Bajpai and Kishor Babu would say. As for the Football, his small eyes darted swiftly from one side to another.

Kishor Babu now spoke in a slow and considered voice: 'You see, Qamar Bhai, it is like this. It is not these images that we worship. They are only points of concentration. Now tell me, why do you turn towards Mecca when you pray? No one would say that you are worshipping the stone. And with Lord Krishna, we do not think of him in those terms. For us he is the incarnation of Vishnu himself. Why, even I am named after Lord Krishna in a way.'

Qamar snorted. 'Don't tell me,' he said, 'that the ordinary Hindus of Salimpur who do their puja every morning before their four-armed goddesses and their elephant-headed gods are using them as points of concentration. They are worshipping those idols, plain and simple.'

Kishor Babu sighed. 'Ah, the common people!' he said, in a manner that implied that this explained everything. He was a firm believer in the caste system.

Rasheed felt it necessary to intervene on the side of the

Hindu minority. 'Anyway, people are good or bad according to what they do, not according to what they worship.'

'Really, Maulana Sahib?' said Qamar sourly. 'So it doesn't matter who or what you worship? What do you think about all this, Kapoor Sahib?' he continued provocatively.

Maan thought for a few seconds but said nothing. He looked over to where Meher and two of her friends were trying to put their arms around the corrugated bark of the neem tree.

'Or don't you have any views on the subject, Kapoor Sahib?' Qamar persisted. Being from outside the village, he could be as abrasive as he wished.

Kishor Babu was now looking quite distressed. Neither Baba nor his sons had so far participated in the theological skirmish. Kishor Babu felt that as his hosts they ought to have intervened to prevent it from getting out of hand. He sensed that Maan did not care at all for Qamar's method of questioning, and feared that he might react strongly.

In the event, Maan did not. Still looking for the most part towards the neem tree and only occasionally glancing at Qamar, Maan said:

'I don't think about these matters. Life is complicated enough without them. But it is clear, Master Sahib, that if you think that I am evading your question, you are not going to give me or anyone else any peace. So I see that you are going to force me to be serious.'

'That is no bad thing,' said Qamar curtly. He had appraised Maan's character quickly and had come to the conclusion that he was a man of very little account.

'What I think is this,' said Maan in the same unusually measured manner as before. 'It is entirely a matter of chance that Kishor Babu was born in a Hindu family and you, Master Sahib, in a Muslim one. I have no doubt that if you had been exchanged after birth, or before birth, or even before conception, you would have been praising Krishanji and he, the Prophet. As for me, Master Sahib, being so little worthy of praise, I don't feel very much like praising anyone – let alone worshipping them.'

'What?' said the Football, rolling belligerently into the conversation and gathering momentum as he spoke: 'Not even holy men like Ramjap Baba? Not even the Holy Ganga at the full moon of the great Pul Mela? Not even the Vedas? Not even God himself?'

'Ah, God,' said Maan. 'God is a big subject – too big for the likes of me. I am sure that He is too big to be concerned about what I think of Him.'

'But don't you ever have the sense of His presence?' asked Kishor Babu, leaning forward in a concerned manner. 'Don't you ever feel that you are in communion with Him?'

'Now that you mention it,' said Maan, 'I feel in direct communion with Him just now. And He is telling me to halt this futile argument and drink my tea before it gets cold.'

Apart from the Football, Qamar and Rasheed, everyone smiled. Rasheed didn't enjoy what he saw as Maan's endemic flippancy. Qamar felt out-manoeuvred by a cheap and irrelevant trick, while the Football was foiled in his attempt to foment trouble. But social harmony had been re-established, and the gathering broke up into smaller groups.

Rasheed's father, the Football, and Bajpai began to discuss what would happen if the zamindari law came into force. It had now received the President's assent but its constitutionality was under challenge in the High Court in Brahmpur. Rasheed, who at present was uncomfortable with that subject, began to talk to Qamar about changes in the curriculum of the madrasa. Kishor Babu, Maan, and Netaji formed a third group – but since Kishor Babu insisted on gently questioning Maan about his views on non-violence while Netaji was eager to ask him about the wolf-hunt, the conversation was a curiously spliced one. Baba went off to amuse himself with his favourite great-granddaughter, whom Moazzam was taking for a piggy-back ride from the cattle-shed to the pigeon-house and back.

Kachheru sat against the wall in the shade of the cattle-shed, thinking his own thoughts and looking indulgently at the children playing in the court-yard. He had not listened to any of the discussion. He was not interested. Though pleased to be of service, he was glad that he had not been asked to do anything by anyone for the time it had taken him to smoke two biris.

10.18

THE days passed one by one. The heat increased. There was no more rain. The huge sky remained painfully blue for days on end. Once or twice a few clouds did appear over the unending patchwork of plains, but they were small and white, and soon drifted away.

Maan slowly got used to his exile. At first he fretted. The heat tormented him, the vast, flat, low-lying world of the fields disoriented him, and he was bored limp. Godforsaken in this godforsaken place, he was not where he wanted to be at all. He could not imagine he would ever adjust to it. The need for comfort and stimulus, he felt, was an upward-clicking ratchet. And yet, as the days went by, and things moved or did not move according to the volition of the sky or the circulation of the calendar or the wills of other people, he fell in with life around him. The thought struck him that perhaps his father's acceptance of imprisonment had been something like this – except that Maan's days were defined not by morning roll-call and lights-out, but by the muezzin's call to prayer and the cow-dust hour when the cattle returned lowing through the lanes.

Even his initial outrage against his father had waned; it was too much of an effort being angry for long, and besides, during his stay in the countryside, he had begun to appreciate and even admire the scope of his father's efforts – not that it aroused in him any spirit of emulation.

Being a bit of a layabout, he lay about a bit. Like the lion that the village children had dubbed him when he first arrived, he spent very few hours in active labour, yawned a great deal, and even appeared to luxuriate in his dissatisfied dormancy, which he interrupted off and on by a roar or two and a mild bout of activity – perhaps a swim in the lake by the school, or a walk to a mango grove – for it was the mango season, and Maan was fond of mangoes. Sometimes he lay on his charpoy and read one of the thrillers lent to him by Sandeep Lahiri. Sometimes he looked over his Urdu books. Despite his not very energetic efforts, he was now able to read clearly printed Urdu; and one day Netaji lent him a slim selection of the most famous ghazals of Mir, which, since he knew large parts of them by heart, did not prove too difficult for Maan.

What did people do in the village, anyway? he asked himself. They waited; they sat and talked and cooked and ate and drank and slept. They woke up and went into the fields with their brass pots of water. Perhaps, thought Maan, everyone is essentially a Mr Biscuit. Sometimes they looked upwards at the rainless sky. The sun rose higher, reached its height, sank, and set. After dark, when life used to begin for him in Brahmpur, there was nothing to do. Someone visited; someone left. Things grew. People sat around and argued about this and that and waited for the monsoon.

Maan too sat around and talked, since people enjoyed talking to him. He sat on his charpoy and discussed people, problems, mahua trees, the state of the world, everything and anything. He never doubted that he would be liked or trusted; since he was not suspicious by nature, he did not imagine that others would be suspicious of him. But as an outsider, as a city dweller, as a Hindu, as the son of a politician – and the Minister of Revenue at that – he was open to all kinds of suspicions and rumours – not all of them as fantastic as the one triggered off by his orange kurta. Some people thought that he was staking out the constituency that his father had chosen to fight from in the coming elections, others that he had decided to settle permanently here, having found that city life was not for him, yet others that he was lying low to avoid creditors. But after a while they got used to Maan, saw no harm in his lack of evident purpose, found his opinions pleasantly and humorously unaggressive, and liked the fact that he liked them. As 'lion, lion, without a tail' bathing under the hand-pump, as Maan Chacha dandling a wailing baby, as the source of intriguing objects like a watch and a torch, as the absorbed and incompetent calligrapher who used the wrong Urdu 'Z' in his spelling of simple words, he was fairly quickly accepted and trusted by the children; and the trust and acceptance of their parents followed soon enough. If Maan regretted that he only ever saw the men, he had enough sense not to mention it. Meanwhile he kept out of village feuds and discussions of zamindari or religion. His handling of Qamar and the Football on the subject of God was soon common knowledge throughout the village. Almost everyone approved. Rasheed's family grew to enjoy his company. He even became something of an open-air confessional for them.

The days stretched by, hardly differentiated one from another. When the postman came to the house, he usually greeted Maan's expectant expression with a rueful one. Over the weeks he received two letters: one from Pran, one from his mother. He learned from Pran's letter that Savita was well, that his mother had not been too well, that Bhaskar sent his love and Veena her affectionate admonitions, that the Brahmpur Shoe Mart had woken up, that the English Department was still sound asleep, that Lata had gone to Calcutta, that Mrs Rupa Mehra had gone to Delhi. How distant those worlds appeared, he thought, like the occasional white clouds that fluffed themselves into existence and disappeared miles above him. His father, it seemed, was coming home as late as ever: he was now deep into consultations with the Advocate-General about the legal challenge to the Zamindari Act; he could not spare the time to write, or so his mother explained, but he had asked after Maan's health and about the farm. She insisted that she herself was in good health; occasional minor complaints that Pran might have unnecessarily mentioned she attributed to old age – Maan was not to worry about her. The late onset of the rains had affected the garden, but they were expected soon, and when everything was green again, Maan would be interested to notice two small innovations: a slight unevenness in the side-lawn, and a bed of zinnias planted below his window.

Firoz too must be deeply involved in the zamindari case, thought Maan, excusing his friend's silence. As for the one silence that pounded most deeply in his ears, it had hurt him most of all in the days immediately following his own letter, when he could scarcely breathe without thinking of it. Now it too was a dull pain, mediated by the heat and the elastic days. Yet when he lay on the charpoy in the early evening light reading the poems of Mir, especially the one that reminded him of that first evening when he saw her in Prem Nivas, the memory of Saeeda Bai came back to Maan and pierced him with longing and bewilderment.

He could not talk to anyone about this. Rasheed's mildly Cassius-like smile when he saw him lost in tender contemplation of Mir would have turned to patent scorn if he had known whom he wished he were gazing at instead. The one time Rasheed had discussed love in general terms with Maan he had been as intense and definitive and theoretical about it as he was about everything else. It was clear to Maan that he had never experienced it. Maan was often exhausted by Rasheed's earnestness; in this particular case he wished he had never opened the subject.

Rasheed for his part was glad that he had Maan to talk to about his ideas and feelings, but he could not understand Maan's monumental directionlessness. Having got as far as he himself had from a background where higher education had seemed as unattainable as the stars, he believed that will and effort could get him anywhere. He attempted bravely, fervently, and perhaps obsessively, to reconcile everything – family life, learning, calligraphy, personal honour, order, ritual, God, agriculture, history, politics; this world and all the other worlds, in short – into a comprehensible whole. Exacting with himself, he was exacting with others. And it seemed to Maan, who was somewhat in awe of his energy and sense of principle, that he was wearing himself out by feeling so deeply and taking on so insistently all the burdens and responsibilities of mankind.

'By doing nothing – or worse than nothing – I've managed to displease my father,' said Maan to Rasheed as they sat talking under the neem one day. 'And by doing something – or better than something – you've managed to displease yours.'

Rasheed had added in a troubled tone that his father would be much more than displeased if he knew just what he had succeeded in doing. Maan had asked him to explain what he meant, but he had shaken his head, and Maan, though uneasy about the remark, had not followed it up. He was by now used to Rasheed's alternation of secretiveness with sudden, even intimate, confidences. As a matter of fact, when Maan had told him about the munshi and the old woman at Baitar Fort, Rasheed had been on the verge of unburdening himself about his own visit to the patwari. But something had stopped his tongue. After all, no one in this village, not even Kachheru himself, knew about that act of attempted justice; and it was best left so. Besides, the patwari had not been in the village for the past week or two, and Rasheed had not yet received the expected confirmation of his instructions.

Instead Rasheed had said: 'Did you get the woman's name? How do you know the munshi won't want to take his spite out on her?' Maan, shocked by the possible consequences of his own impracticality, had shaken his head.

A couple of times Rasheed did succeed in getting the reluctant Maan to discuss zamindari, but Maan's opinions were characteristically and vexatiously nebulous. He had reacted instinctively, indeed, violently, to suffering and cruelty, but he did not have much of an opinion on the general rights and wrongs of the system. He did not want the legislation on which his father had worked for years to be thrown out by the courts, but neither did he want Firoz and Imtiaz to lose the larger part of their family estate. To Rasheed's specific argument that the larger landlords did not work (or did not have to work) for their living, it was not to be expected that Maan would respond with proletarian indignation.

Rasheed had no qualms about speaking harshly about his own family and their treatment of those who served them. About the Nawab Sahib, though, whom Rasheed had met only once, he spoke no ill to Maan. He had known quite early, as a result of their train journey from Brahmpur, that Maan was a friend of the young Nawabzadas; and he did not wish either to make Maan uncomfortable or to remind himself of past humiliation by describing the treatment he had received when he had gone to Baitar House in search of employment some months ago.

10.19

ONE evening, when Maan was working on some exercises that Rasheed had set him before going off to the mosque, Rasheed's father interrupted him. He was carrying Meher, who was asleep, in his arms.

Without any preliminaries he said to Maan: 'Now that you're by yourself can I ask you a question? I've been wondering about it for some time.'

'Of course,' Maan replied, setting down his pen.

Rasheed's father sat down.

'Now, let me see,' he began, 'how do I put this? Not being married is considered by my religion and yours to be....' He paused, searching for the word. He had sounded disapproving.

'Adharma? Against correct principles?' suggested Maan.

'Yes, call it adharma,' said Rasheed's father, relieved. 'Well, you're twenty-two, twenty-three....'

'Older.'

'Older? That's bad. You should have got married by now. I believe that a man between the ages of seventeen and thirty-five is in the prime of his life.'

'Ah,' said Maan, nodding in wary agreement. Rasheed's grandfather had brought up the subject at the very beginning of his stay. No doubt Rasheed would be plaguing him next.

'Not that I noticed any falling off in my strength even when I was forty-five,' continued Rasheed's father.

'That's good,' said Maan. 'I know some people who are old at that age.'

'But then, you see,' continued Rasheed's father, 'then came the death of my son, and the death of my wife – and I fell apart.'

Maan remained silent. Kachheru arrived with a lantern, and placed it a little distance away.

Rasheed's father, who had intended to advise Maan, gently swerved off into his own memories: 'My elder son was a wonderful boy. In a hundred villages there was no one like him. He was strong as a lion and over six feet tall – a wrestler and a weight-lifter – he did English exercises. He would lift two maunds of iron easily. And he had a wonderful fresh face; and was always so good-natured and smiling – he greeted people with such great friendliness that he would make their hearts happy. And when he wore the suit I got made for him, he looked so good that people said he should be a Superintendent of Police.'

Maan shook his head sadly. Rasheed's father was telling his story without tears, but not coldly – as if he were recounting with sympathy the story of someone other than himself.

'Well, anyway,' he went on, 'after his accident at the railway station, I don't know what happened to me. I didn't leave the house for months. My strength drained away. I was unconscious for days. He was so young. And then a little later his mother died.'

He looked up towards the house, half-turning away from Maan, and continued:

'This house was ghostly. I don't know what would have happened to me. I was so full of grief and weakness that I wanted to die. There was no one in the house even to offer me water.' He closed his eyes. 'Where is Rasheed?' he asked somewhat coldly, turning back to Maan.

'At the mosque, I think.'

'Ah, yes, well, finally, Baba took me in hand and said I should pull myself together. Our religion says that the izzat, the honour of an unmarried man is half that of a married man. Baba insisted that I should get a second wife.'

'Well, he was speaking from experience,' said Maan with a smile.

'Yes. Well, Rasheed has told you no doubt that Baba had three wives. We two brothers and our sister are all from different wives. He didn't have three wives at the same time, mind you, just one wife at a time. "Marté gae, karté gae." When one died he married another. There's a tradition of remarriage in this family: my grandfather had four wives, my father three and I two.'

'Why not?'

'Why not, indeed,' said Rasheed's father, smiling. 'That's just what I thought eventually – once I'd got over my grief.'

'And was it difficult to find a wife?' asked Maan, intrigued.

'Not really,' said Rasheed's father. 'By the standards of this place we are well-off. I was advised to get not a young woman but someone who had been married before – a widow or a woman who had been divorced. So I did get married again – it's been about a year now – to a woman who is fifteen years younger than me – that's not much. She's even related to my wife – of blessed memory – in a distant way. And she handles the house well. My health has improved again. I can walk unaided to my land two miles away. My eyesight is fine, except for seeing things up close. My heart is fine. My teeth, well, my teeth were past treatment anyway. One should be married. No question about it.'

A dog began to bark. Others joined in after a while. Maan tried to veer away from the subject by saying:

'Is she asleep? Can she sleep through all this?'

Rasheed's father looked lovingly down at his granddaughter: 'Yes, she's asleep. She's very fond of me.'

'I noticed that when you came from the fields with the umbrella today she ran after you in the heat.'

Rasheed's father nodded with pride.

'When I ask her if she wants to live in Debaria or Brahmpur she always says Debaria – "because you, Dada-Jaan, are here." And once when I went to her mother's village, she left her Nana and ran after me.'

Maan smiled to think of this passionate competitiveness between the two grandfathers. He said: 'Presumably, Rasheed was with you.'

'Well, he may have been. But even if he hadn't been, she would have run after me.'

'In that case she must love you very much,' said Maan, laughing.

'Indeed she does. She was born in this house – which people later began to call ill-fated and inauspicious. But in those dark days she was like a gift of God to me. It was I who pretty much brought her up. In the morning, tea – tea and biscuits! "Dada-jaan", she'd say, "I want tea and biscuits. Cream biscuits" – none of this dry stuff. She'd tell Bittan, a maidservant here, to go and fetch her cream biscuits from my special tin. Her mother would be making the tea in a corner. And she wouldn't eat from her mother's hands. I had to feed her.'

'Well, luckily now there's another child in the house,' said Maan. 'To keep her company.'

'Doubtless,' said Rasheed's father. 'But Meher has decided that I belong to her alone. When she's told that I'm her sister's Dada too, she refuses to believe it.'

Meher shifted in her sleep.

'There has been no child like this in the whole family,' said Rasheed's father definitively.

'She seems to operate on that assumption,' agreed Maan.

Rasheed's father laughed, then continued: 'She has a right to do so. Oh, I remember, there used to be an old man in this village. He had fallen out with his sons, and had come to live with his daughter and son-in-law. Well, he had a pomegranate tree, which for some reason used to bear much better fruit than ours.'

'You have a pomegranate tree?'

'Oh yes, of course, inside. I'll show you some day.'

'How?'

'What do you mean, how?' said Rasheed's father. 'It's my house. ... Oh, I see what you mean. I'll shunt the women around as you go through. You're a good boy,' he said suddenly. 'Tell me, what do you do?'

'What do I do?'

'Yes.'

'Not much of anything.'

'That's very bad.'

'My father thinks so too,' agreed Maan.

'He's right. He's quite right. No young men want to work these days. It's either studies or staring at the sky.'

'Actually I do have a cloth business in Banaras.'

'Then what are you doing here?' said Rasheed's father. 'You should be making money.'

'Do you think I shouldn't be here?' asked Maan.

'No, no – of course, you are welcome,' said Rasheed's father. 'We are glad you are here as our guest. Though you have chosen a hot and boring time to come. You should visit at the time of Bakr-Id. Then you'll see the village at its most festive. Yes, do that – remember to. ... Oh, yes, pomegranates. This old man was very lively, and he and Meher made a fine pair. She knew that whenever she went to his house she'd get something. So she was always forcing me to take her there. I remember the first time he gave her a pomegranate. It wasn't ripe. Still, we peeled it with great excitement, and she ate six or seven spoonfuls of the grains and we kept the rest for breakfast!'

An old man walked past. It was the Imam of the Debaria mosque.

'You will drop by tomorrow evening, won't you, Imam Sahib?' asked Rasheed's father in an anxious manner.

'At this time tomorrow – yes. After the prayer,' added the Imam in mild rebuke.

'I wonder where Rasheed is,' said Maan, looking at his unfinished exercises. 'He'll probably be returning any minute.'

'He is probably taking a walk around the village,' said his father in an outburst of quite virulent anger, 'talking to all the low people. That is his style. He should show more sense of discrimination. Tell me, has he taken you to the patwari with him?'

Maan was so taken aback by the tone that he hardly registered the question.

'The patwari. Have you visited the village patwari?' There was a touch of iron in the voice as the question was repeated.

'No,' said Maan, surprised. 'Is something the matter?'

'No,' said Rasheed's father. After a pause he said: 'Please don't mention that I asked you this.'

'If you like,' said Maan readily, but he was still puzzled.

'Well, I've done enough damage to your studies,' said Rasheed's father. 'I'd better not disturb you any further.' And he walked back to the house with Meher in his arms, frowning in the light of the lantern.

10.20

MAAN, quite concerned now, fetched the lantern and tried to get back to reading and copying the words that Rasheed had written out for him. But Rasheed's father was soon back, this time without Meher.

'What's a giggi?' he asked.

'A giggi?'

'You don't know what a giggi is?' The disappointment was palpable.

'No. What is it?' asked Maan.

'I don't know either,' said Rasheed's father in distress.

Maan looked at him, mystified.

'Why do you want to know?' he asked him.

'Oh,' said Rasheed's father. 'I need one – immediately.'

'If you don't know what it is, how do you know you need one?' said Maan.

'It's not for me but for Meher,' said Rasheed's father. 'She woke up and said, "Dada, I want a giggi. Give me a giggi." And now she's crying for it, and I can't find out from her what it is or what it looks like. I'll have to wait till – well, till Rasheed comes back. Maybe he knows. Sorry to have disturbed you again.'

'No, not at all,' said Maan, who hadn't minded this interruption. For a while he couldn't get back to his work. He tried to decide whether a giggi was to be eaten or to be played with or to be ridden on. Finally he picked up his pen again.

Baba, who had returned from the mosque, seeing him sitting by himself in the open courtyard, joined him a minute later. He greeted him, then coughed and spat on the ground.

'What is a young man like you doing wasting your eyes on a book?'

'Well, I'm learning to read and write Urdu.'

'Yes, yes. I remember: seen, sheen ... seen, sheen.... Why bother?' said Baba, and cleared his throat again.

'Why bother?'

'Yes – tell me what is there in Urdu apart from a few sinful poems?'

'Now I've begun it, I should carry it through,' said Maan.

It was the right thing to say. Baba approved of this sentiment, then added: 'Now Arabic, you should learn Arabic. That's the language to learn. Then you can read the Holy Book. You might stop being a kafir.'

'Do you think so?' said Maan cheerfully.

'Oh, most assuredly,' said Baba. He added: 'You aren't taking what I've said badly?'

Maan smiled.

'One of my best friends is a thakur who lives a few villages away,' continued Baba reminiscently. 'In the summer of '47 around the time of Partition, a crowd gathered on the road to Salimpur in order to attack this village because of us Muslims. And Sagal too. I sent an urgent message to my friend, and he and his men went out with lathis and guns, and told the mob that they'd have to reckon with them first. And a good thing too. Otherwise, I'd have died fighting, but I'd have died all right.'

It suddenly struck Maan that he had become a universal confidant.

'Rasheed said that you were the terror of the tehsil,' he told Baba.

Baba nodded his head in vigorous approval. He said emphatically: 'I was strict with people. I turned him' – he pointed in the direction of the roof – 'out of the house, naked in the fields, at the age of seven because he would not study.'

Maan tried to imagine what Rasheed's father might have been like as a boy, with a book instead of a paan-pouch in his hand. But Baba was continuing:

'In the time of the English, there was honesty. The government was firm. How can you govern unless you are firm? Now, when the police catch some criminal, the Ministers and MPs and MLAs say, "He's my friend: release him!" And they do.'

'That's too bad,' said Maan.

'The police used to take little bribes then, now they are big ones,' said Baba. 'And the day will come when they will take huge ones. There is no respect for law. The whole world is being destroyed. These people are selling the country. And now they are trying to take away the land that our forefathers earned with their sweat and blood. Well, no one is going to take away a single bigha of my land, I can tell you that.'

'But if it's the law –' said Maan, thinking of his father.

'Now, you're a sober young man,' said Baba. 'You don't drink or smoke and you are law-abiding and respect our customs. But tell me, if they made a law that you should not pray to Mecca but to Calcutta instead, would you obey it?'

Maan shook his head, trying not to smile at the thought of either eventuality.

'It's the same thing,' said Baba. 'Now Rasheed tells me that your father is a great friend of the Nawab Sahib, who is well-respected in this district. What does the Nawab Sahib think of this attempt to grab his land?'

'He does not like it,' said Maan. He had learned by now to state the obvious as blandly as he could.

'And nor would you. I can tell you that things will get worse and worse. As it is, things have begun to fall apart. There's a family of low people in this village who have turned their mother and father out to starve. They eat well enough, but they've turned them out. Independence has come – and now the politicians want to finish the zamindars off – and the country has collapsed. In the old days if someone had done this – dared to turn his mother into a beggar – a mother who had fed him, cleaned him, clothed him – we would have beaten him until his bones and brains were set right. It was our responsibility. Now if we beat people up they'll immediately start a court case, they'll try to lock us up in the police station.'

'Can't you talk to them, convince them?' asked Maan.

Baba shrugged impatiently. 'Of course – but bad characters are improved less by explanations than by the lathi.'

'You must have been a very severe disciplinarian,' said Maan, quite pleased at the traits he would have found intolerable in his own father.

'Oh yes,' agreed Rasheed's grandfather. 'Discipline is the key. You have to work hard at everything you do. You, for instance, should be studying, not wasting your time talking to an old man like me. . . . Tell me, did your father want you to come here?'

'Yes.'

'Why?'

'Well, to learn Urdu – and I suppose to gain some experience of the villages,' improvised Maan.

'Good . . . good. Well, tell him this is a good constituency. He has a good reputation among our community. . . . To study Urdu? Yes, we must protect it . . . it's our heritage. . . . You know, you would make a good politician yourself. You kicked the Football through the goalposts very smoothly. Of course, if you join politics from this place, Netaji would probably assassinate you. . . . Oh, well . . . well, carry on, carry on. . . .'

And he got up and started walking towards his house.

A thought struck Maan.

'You wouldn't happen to know what a giggi is, Baba?' he asked.

Baba stopped. 'A giggi?'

'Yes.'

'No. I've never heard of such a thing. Are you sure you're reading it right?' He walked back and picked up Maan's exercise book. 'I don't have my glasses.'

'Oh, it's Meher who's demanding a giggi,' said Maan.

'But what is it?' asked Baba.

'That's the problem,' said Maan. 'She woke up and wanted a giggi from her grandfather. It must have been part of a dream. No one in the house knows what it means.'

'Hmm,' said Baba, considering the crisis. 'Perhaps I'd better go and help.' He changed his direction and went towards his son's house. 'I am the only one who really understands her.'

10.21

MAAN'S next visitor was Netaji. It was now quite dark. Netaji, who had been away on mysterious business for some days, wanted to ask Maan about many things: the SDO, the Nawab Sahib's estate at Baitar, the wolf-hunt, and love. But he could see that Maan was quite busy with his Urdu, and decided on love. After all, he had lent Maan the ghazals of Mir.

'Is it all right to sit here?' he asked.

'Fine,' said Maan. He looked up. 'How are things?'

'Oh, all right,' said Netaji. He had by now almost entirely forgiven Maan for his humiliation at the railway station because a number of grander humiliations and successes had occurred since then, and on the whole he was making progress in his plans for world conquest.

'You don't mind me asking you a question?' said Netaji.

'No,' said Maan, 'any question except that one.'

Netaji smiled, and proceeded. 'Tell me, have you ever been in love?'

Maan pretended to be annoyed in order to avoid the question. 'What kind of question is that?' he asked.

Netaji was apologetic. 'You see – I thought life in Brahmpur – in a modern family –' he began.

'So that's what you think of us –' said Maan.

Netaji retreated quickly: 'No, no, I don't – and anyway, why should I mind what your answer is? I only asked out of curiosity.'

'Well, if you've asked such a question,' said Maan, 'you must be prepared to answer it yourself. Have *you* ever been in love?'

Netaji was not at all unwilling to answer. He had given the matter a lot of thought of late. 'Our marriages, you see, are all arranged,' he said to Maan. 'It's always been so. If I had it my way, I'd do it differently. But what's done is done. I'm sure I would have fallen in love otherwise. But now it would only confuse me. How about you?'

'Look, here comes Rasheed,' said Maan. 'Should we ask him to join our discussion?'

Netaji took his leave hurriedly. He had to preserve his nominal position of superiority as Rasheed's uncle. As Rasheed approached, he gave him a peculiar look, and disappeared.

'Who was that?' said Rasheed.

'Netaji. He wanted to talk to me about love.'

Rasheed made an impatient sound.

'Where were you?' said Maan to Rasheed.

'At the bania's shop, talking to a few people – trying to undo some of that ancient Sagal damage.'

'What is there to undo?' said Maan. 'You were very fiery. I was full of admiration. But it seems that for some reason your father is very annoyed with you.'

'There's a great deal to undo,' said Rasheed. 'The latest version of that incident is that I came to blows with the good elders and claimed that the Imam of the Sagal mosque was an incarnation of Satan. I also have a plan to set up a commune on the lands of the madrasa – once I have persuaded you to persuade your father to somehow take it over. But people – at least in Debaria – seem to doubt this part of the story.' Rasheed laughed shortly. 'You have made quite a good impression in the village. Everyone likes you; it amazes me.'

'Looks like you're in trouble, though,' said Maan.

'Perhaps. Perhaps not. How can one argue with ignorance? People know nothing and want to know nothing.'

'Tell me,' said Maan, 'do you know what a giggi is?'

'No,' said Rasheed, frowning.

'Then you're really in worse trouble than you imagine,' said Maan.

'I am?' asked Rasheed, and for a second he looked genuinely worried. 'By the way, how are your exercises going?'

'Tremendously well,' said Maan. 'I've been working on them ever since you left.'

No sooner had Rasheed gone indoors than the postman dropped by on his way home, and handed Maan a letter.

He exchanged a few words with Maan; Maan responded without knowing what he said. He was dazed.

The envelope, a very pale yellow, seemed to be as cool and gentle as moonlight. The Urdu script was fluid, even careless. The postmark said 'Pasand Bagh P.O., Brahmpur'. She had written to him after all.

Desire made him weak as he held the envelope to the light of the lantern. He had to get back to her – at once – no matter what his father – or anyone – said. Whether his exile was officially over made no difference at all.

When he was alone again, Maan opened the envelope. The faint fragrance of her familiar perfume mingled with the night air. He saw immediately that to read this letter – with its almost evasive cursiveness, its casually sprinkled diacritical marks, its compressions – would be far beyond his own rudimentary ability in Urdu. He pieced together the salutation to Dagh Sahib, made out from the physical appearance of the letter that it was laced with poetic couplets, but for the moment could get no further.

If there was no aloneness here in the village, Maan reflected with frustration, there was no privacy either. If Rasheed's father or grandfather were to pass by and his letter happened to be lying open, they would pick it up quite unselfconsciously and read it. And yet to comprehend even part of it, he himself would have to look at it for hours and try to piece it together glyph by glyph.

Maan did not want to have to pore over it for hours. He wanted to know immediately what Saeeda Bai had written to him. But whom should he ask for help? Rasheed? No. Netaji? No. Who would serve as his interpreter?

What had she written? In his mind's eye he saw her right hand with its brilliant ring move from right to left over the pale yellow page. As he did so, he heard a descending scale on the harmonium. He realized with a start that he had never seen her writing anything. The touch of her hands on his face – the touch of her hands on the keyboard – these needed so little conscious interpretation. But here her hands had moved across the page in a pattern of speed and grace, and he had no inkling what it meant of love or indifference, seriousness or playfulness, pleasure or anger, desire or calm.

10.22

RASHEED was indeed in worse trouble than he imagined, but it was the next evening that he found out about it.

When, after an almost sleepless night, Maan had asked him that morning for help with Saeeda Bai's letter, Rasheed had gazed thoughtfully at the envelope for a moment, looked uncomfortable (probably with embarrassment at the request, thought Maan), and, to his great surprise, agreed.

'After dinner,' he had suggested.

Though dinner seemed months away, Maan had nodded gratefully.

But the crisis broke immediately after the evening prayer. Rasheed was summoned to meet five men gathered upstairs on the roof: his grandfather; his father; Netaji; his mother's brother who had arrived that afternoon without his friend the guppi; and the Imam of the mosque.

They were all seated on a large rug in the middle of the roof. Rasheed made his adaabs.

'Sit down, Rasheed,' said his father. No one else said anything beyond responding to the salutations.

Only the Bear appeared to be genuinely welcoming, though he looked profoundly uncomfortable. 'Have a glass of this sherbet, Rasheed,' he said after a while, handing him a glass with a red liquid inside. 'It's made from rhododendrons,' he explained. 'Excellent stuff. When I visited the hills last month. . . .' He tapered off into silence.

'What is this about?' asked Rasheed, looking first at the awkward Bear, then at the Imam. The Imam of the Debaria mosque was a good man, the senior member of the other big landowning family in the village. He usually greeted Rasheed in a warm manner, but Rasheed had noticed a distance in the last couple of days. Perhaps the Sagal incident had upset him as well – or perhaps the rumours that were proliferating had confused one Imam with another. Anyway, whatever his own theological or social errors, it was humiliating to be required to answer charges of rudeness to what looked like an accusatorial committee. And why had the Bear been called to join them from a considerable distance away? Rasheed sipped his sherbet and looked at the others. His father seemed disgusted, his grandfather stern. Netaji was trying to look judicious; he succeeded in looking complacent.

It was Rasheed's father who spoke in his paan-rough voice.

'Abdur Rasheed, how dare you abuse your position as my son and as a member of this family? The patwari came here looking for you two days ago. When he could not find you, he spoke to me, thank God.'

Rasheed's face went white.

He could not speak a word. It was all too clear what had happened. The wretched patwari, who knew perfectly well that it was Rasheed who was supposed to visit him, had decided to find an excuse to talk directly to his family. Suspicious and worried about his instructions, and knowing where the ghee on his roti came from, he had decided to bypass Rasheed himself to seek confirmation. Doubtless he had come during afternoon prayers, when he could be fairly certain that Rasheed would be at the mosque, and completely certain that his father would not.

Rasheed clutched his glass. His lips felt dry. He took a sip of sherbet. This action appeared to infuriate his father further. He pointed his finger at Rasheed's head.

'Don't be impertinent. Answer me. Your hair looks wiser than the mulch it is growing on, but – and keep this well in mind, Rasheed – you are not a child any longer and cannot expect a child's indulgence.'

Baba added: 'Rasheed, this land is not yours to give or take. The patwari has been told to undo your disgraceful instructions. How could you do this? I have trusted you since you were a child. You were never obedient, but you were never underhanded.'

Rasheed's father said: 'In case you are inclined to create further mischief, you should know that your name is no longer attached to those lands. And what a patwari writes is difficult for the Supreme Court to undo. Your communist schemes will not work here. We are not so easily taken in by theories and visions as the brilliant students of Brahmpur.'

Rasheed's eyes flashed with anger and resistance. 'You cannot dispossess me like that,' he said. 'The law of our community is clear –' He turned to the Imam, appealing for confirmation.

'I see you have made good use of your years of religious study as well,' said his father bitingly. 'Well, I would advise you, Abdur Rasheed, since you are referring to the law of inheritance, to wait until the auspicious moment when my father and I are both resting in peace near the lake before you avail yourself of it.'

The Imam looked profoundly shocked, and decided to intervene. 'Rasheed,' he said quietly, 'what induced you to go behind your family's back? You know that good order depends on the decent families of the village acting properly.'

Properly! thought Rasheed – what a joke, what a hypocritical joke. It was proper, no doubt, to tear virtual serfs away from the plots they had tilled for years in order to safeguard one's own self-interest. It was becoming increasingly clear that the Imam was present only partly in his capacity as spiritual adviser.

And the Bear? What did he have to do with all this? Rasheed turned his eyes towards him, wordlessly pleading for his support. Surely the Bear must understand and sympathize with his intentions. But the Bear could not hold his gaze.

Rasheed's father read his thoughts. Baring the remnants of his teeth he said: 'Don't look towards your Mamu for encouragement. You cannot go running to him to find shelter any longer. We have discussed the matter thoroughly together – as a family – as a family, Abdur Rasheed. That is why he is here. And he has every right to be involved in this, and to be shocked by your – your behaviour. Some of our land was bought with his sister's dowry. Do you think we will give up so easily what we have worked to develop, to cultivate, to expand for generations? Do you think we don't have enough trouble with the late rains this season to wish a plague of locusts upon our heads as well? If you give one plot of land to one chamar –'

The baby started wailing downstairs. Rasheed's father got up, leaned over the parapet into the courtyard and called out:

'Meher's mother! Can't you stop that child of Rasheed's from making such a racket? Can men not talk together without being disturbed?'

He turned back to say: 'Remember this, Rasheed: our patience is not unending.'

Rasheed, suddenly furious, and hardly thinking of his words, burst out: 'And do you think mine is? Ever since I have come to the village, I have received nothing but taunts and envy. That destitute old man, who was good to you, Abba, in the old days, and whom you now ignore –'

'Don't try to stray from the subject,' said his father sharply. 'Keep your voice low.'

'I am not straying — it is his evil and grasping brothers who waylaid me at their mosque and are now spreading these vile rumours —'

'You see yourself in a very heroic light —'

'If there was justice, they would be dragged to the court in chains and made to expiate their crimes.'

'Courts, now, so you want to bring courts into this, Abdur Rasheed —'

'Yes, I do, if there is no other way. And it will eventually be the courts who will make you too disgorge what for generations you have —'

'Enough!' Baba's voice broke in like a whiplash.

But Rasheed hardly heard him.

'Courts, Abba —' he cried, 'you are complaining about the courts? What do you think this is? This panchayat, this inquisitorial committee of five where you feel you can insult me freely —'

'Enough!' said Baba. He had never before had to raise his voice with Rasheed a second time.

Rasheed was quiet and bowed his head.

Netaji said: 'Rasheed, you must not see us as a court. We are your seniors, your well-wishers, who have gathered together in the absence of strangers to advise you.'

Rasheed kept a tight rein on himself and managed not to say anything. From below the baby began to cry again.

Rasheed got up before his father could, and called towards the courtyard: 'Wife! Wife! See that the child is comfortable.'

'Have you considered them in this matter?' asked his father, indicating with his head towards the courtyard.

Rasheed stared wildly.

'And have you considered Kachheru himself?' added Baba grimly.

'Kachheru — ?' said Rasheed. 'He doesn't know about this, Baba. He doesn't know anything about this at all. He didn't ask me to do anything.' He held his hands to his head. Again an intolerable pressure had begun to pound at his temples.

Baba sighed, then, looking above Rasheed's head in the direction of the village, said: 'Well, this affair is bound to get out. That is the problem. There are five of us here. Six. We may all promise not to speak a word, but the word will get spoken somehow. Of course, we understand from our guest, your friend, that you have not involved him in all this, which is good –'

'Maan?' said Rasheed, disbelievingly. 'You've been talking to Maan?'

'– but there is also the patwari, who will hide or reveal whatever suits his convenience. He is a sly man.' Baba paused to consider his next words. 'It will get out, and plenty of people will believe Kachheru put you up to this. We have to set an example. I am afraid you have not made things easier for him.'

'Baba –' protested Rasheed.

But his father cut in, his voice thick with rage: 'You should have thought of all this before. What would have happened to him at worst? We would have rotated him from field to field. He would still have the support of our family, he would still be able to use our cattle and our tools – it is you, it is you who have harmed my old chamar.'

Rasheed covered his face with his hands. The Bear said:

'Well, nothing has yet been decided finally, of course.'

'No,' agreed Baba after a pause. Rasheed was sighing deeply, his chest moving up and down.

Rasheed's father said: 'Instead of being censorious about other people's behaviour, I hope this experience will make you examine your own. We have heard from you no word of apology so far, no admission of wrongdoing. Believe me, if it had not been for your Mamu and the Imam Sahib here, we would not have been so lenient with you. You can still continue to live here whenever you wish. Some land may still be restored to your name in time, depending on whether you show yourself to be worthy of it. But rest assured, if you close the door of trust on this house, the doors of this house will be closed to you. I am not afraid of losing a son. I have lost one already. Now go downstairs.

See to your wife and child – children. We have the matter of Kachheru to discuss.'

Rasheed looked around the circle of faces. He saw sympathy in some, but support in none.

He got up, said a low 'Khuda haafiz', and walked down the stairs into the courtyard. For a while he looked at the pomegranate tree, then he went inside. The baby and Meher were asleep. His wife looked deeply worried. He told her he would not be having supper. In a daze he walked out of the house.

Maan, when he saw Rasheed emerge, smiled with relief. 'I heard sounds of people talking, and thought you were never coming down,' he said. He brought out Saeeda Bai's letter from the pocket of his kurta.

For a second, Rasheed thought of unburdening himself to Maan, even of seeking his help. This was the son of the very author of the act that aimed to do justice. But then he turned abruptly away.

'But this –' said Maan, waving the envelope.

'Later, later,' said Rasheed dully, and began to walk away from the house in a northerly direction.

Part Eleven

11.1

AT the stroke of ten, from behind the dull scarlet velvet hangings to the right of Courtroom Number One of the High Court of Judicature at Brahmpur, the five white-turbaned, red-liveried, gold-braided ushers of the judges emerged. Everyone rose to his feet. The ushers stood behind the tall-backed chairs of their respective judges and, at a nod from the Chief Justice's usher – who looked even more magnificent than the others owing to the insignia of crossed maces on his chest – pulled them back to give the judges room.

All eyes in the packed courtroom had followed the ushers as they moved towards the bench in what was almost a procession. Normal cases required a single judge or a bench of two, and cases of great importance and complexity might be assigned to three judges. But five judges implied a case of exceptional moment, and here were the heralds of the five in all their resplendent regalia.

And now the judges followed in their black gowns, a sad anticlimax to their ushers. They wore no wigs, and a couple of them appeared to shuffle slightly. They entered in order of seniority: the Chief Justice first, followed by the puisne judges whom he had assigned to this case. The Chief, a small, dry man with almost no hair on his head, stood before the central chair; to his right stood the next seniormost judge, a large, stooping man who fidgeted continually with his right hand; to the Chief's left stood the next seniormost judge of this bench, an Englishman who had served with the judicial service of the ICS and had stayed on after Independence; he was the only Englishman among the nine judges in the High Court at Brahmpur. Finally, at the wings, stood the two juniormost judges.

The Chief Justice did not look at the crowded courtroom – at the famous litigants, the eminent lawyers, the chattering public and the sceptical but excited journalists. He surveyed the table in front of him and his colleagues – the pads of paper, the lace-covered glasses of water laid out on the green baize. He then glanced cautiously to right and left as if checking the traffic on a busy highway, and began a judicious shuffle forward towards the table. As he did so, the other judges followed suit, and the ushers pushed the heavy chairs in, as it were, under the seat of justice.

The Nawab Sahib of Baitar was pleasantly impressed by the grandeur of it all. He recalled the only two other occasions when he had been in the High Court. Once he had gone as a litigant, when his own presence had been indispensable. The case – a property matter – had been up before a single judge. The other occasion was when he had decided to see his son practise. He had known that Firoz would be on his feet before a division bench one afternoon. Just before the case had begun to be argued, the Nawab Sahib had entered the uncrowded courtroom without any of his retainers, and had sat down directly behind Firoz, so that he would not be noticed unless Firoz turned completely around. He had not wished to make him nervous by indicating his presence, and, indeed, Firoz had had no inkling that day that his father was sitting behind him. He had argued well and the Nawab Sahib had been satisfied.

Today, of course, Firoz knew that his father was sitting directly behind him, for it was the constitutional validity of the Zamindari Abolition Act that was under challenge before the bench. If the courts decided for it, it would stand. If not, it would be as if it had never existed.

Two dozen or so writ petitions were to be considered jointly with the main one; these covered roughly the same ground but had a few points of difference. Some petitions were submitted by religious endowments, some by landlords who had been granted lands directly by crown grants, and some by ex-rulers – like the Raja of Marh – who believed that they would be protected by the treaty provisions of the Constitution, even if the lesser fry were fried. Firoz was one of the counsel for two such subsidiary petitions.

'May it please your Lordships –'

The Nawab Sahib's attention – which had wandered somewhat while the Court Reader was reciting the number of the case, the numbers of the main and connected writ petitions, the names of the parties, and the names of counsel appearing in the case – was drawn sharply back to the court. The great G.N. Bannerji was on his feet at the table in the front row that was closest to the aisle. Leaning his long, aged frame against a lectern on the table – upon which were lying both his brief and a small, red cloth-bound notebook – he repeated the opening phrase, then continued with deliberation, glancing up from time to time at the bench, particularly at the Chief Justice:

'May it please your Lordships, I am appearing in this case for all the applicants jointly. Your Lordships, needless to say, will appreciate the gravity of this case. It is probable that no case of similar significance for the people of this state has been fought in this court before, either under the emblem of the Ashoka lion or under the lion and unicorn.' Here G.N. Bannerji glanced slightly to the left of centre of the bench before continuing. 'My Lords, the entire way of life of this state is sought to be altered by the executive of this state through legislation that runs in express and implied contradiction to the Constitution of the country. The act that seeks, in so striking and wholesale a manner, to alter the life of the citizenry of Purva Pradesh is the Purva Pradesh Zamindari Abolition and Land Reform Act of 1951, and it is my contention and that of other counsel for the applicants that this legislation, apart from being patently to the detriment of the people, is unconstitutional, and therefore null and void. Null and void.'

The Advocate-General of Purva Pradesh, the small, plump Mr Shastri, smiled nonchalantly to himself. He had appeared against G.N. Bannerji before. Bannerji liked to repeat significant phrases at the beginning and end of each paragraph of speech. Despite his commanding presence, he had rather a high voice – not unpleasant to listen to, however; more silvery than tinny – and these repetitions were like small shiny nails hammered in twice so that they would imbed themselves properly. This might have been a verbal quirk of his, not something he consciously attempted. But G.N. Bannerji did consciously believe in the value of repetition in general. He would take especial pains to phrase his propositions in three or four different ways which he would then introduce at different points of his argument so that, without insulting the intelligence of the judges, he could be assured that the seeds of his case would take root, even assuming that a few fell upon stony ground. 'It is all very well,' he told his juniors, who in this case included his bespectacled son and grandson – 'it is all very well to state something once for our benefit or for the benefit of the other side. We've been steeped in this case for weeks. And Shastri and I have been well briefed by others. But for the bench we must follow the prime rule of advocacy: repeat, repeat, and repeat again. It is a great mistake to overestimate the judges' knowledge of the case even when they have read the affidavits of both sides. And it may even be a mistake to assume they have any detailed knowledge of the law. The Constitution, after all, is barely a year old – and at least one of the judges in this case probably has very little knowledge of what a Constitution is.'

G.N. Bannerji was referring (fairly politely for him) to the juniormost judge on the full bench trying this case, Mr Justice Maheshwari, who had come up through the district judiciary, and who, as it happened, did not possess great intelligence to counter-balance his lack of constitutional experience. G.N. Bannerji did not suffer fools gladly, and he considered Mr Justice Maheshwari, who, at fifty-five, was fifteen years his junior, to be a fool.

Firoz (who had been present for the conference of za-mindars' lawyers in G.N. Bannerji's hotel room when the great lawyer had made this remark) had passed it on to the Nawab Sahib. It had not made the Nawab Sahib more optimistic about the result of the case. He had a sense very similar to that of his friend the Minister of Revenue on the other side: less hope of victory than dread of defeat. So much hung on this case that apprehension was the dominant emotion on both sides. The only ones who seemed to be fairly unconcerned – apart from the Raja of Marh, who could not believe in the violation of his inviolate lands – were the lawyers on both sides.

'Sixthly, my Lords,' continued G.N. Bannerji, 'the Zamindari Abolition Act cannot be said to have a public purpose in the strict, or should I say proper, sense of the word. This, my Lords, is a clear requirement of all acts that involve the public taking over of private property according to Article 31 clause 2 of the Constitution. I shall return to this proposition in due course after I have stated the other grounds under which the impugned act is bad in law.'

G.N. Bannerji continued, after a pause to sip some water, to state his objections to the law, but without adducing detailed reasons at this stage. He found the Zamindari Act unacceptable because it provided derisory compensation and was therefore 'a fraud on the Constitution'; because the compensation offered was, moreover, discriminatory between large and small landowners and thus offended against the provisions of Article 14, which provided for 'the equal protection of the laws'; because it contravened the provisions of Article 19(1)(f) which stated that all citizens had the right 'to acquire, hold and dispose of property'; because, by leaving to junior officers in the administration vast areas for the exercise of discretion in deciding the order of the actual taking over of estates, the legislature had illegitimately delegated its own powers to another authority; and so on and so forth. Having hovered in a hawk-like circuit over the domain of his case for more than an hour, Mr G.N. Bannerji now plunged down on the various weaknesses of the act, attacking them – repeatedly, of course – one by one.

11.2

HE had barely begun to do so when the English judge spoke:
'Is there any reason, Mr Bannerji, why you have chosen to deal with the delegation argument first?'
'My Lord?'
'Well, you contend that the impugned act contravenes

certain specific provisions of the Constitution. Why not tackle those direct grounds first? There is nothing in the Constitution against delegation. I presume the powers of the legislatures are plenary in their own spheres. They can delegate powers to whomever they choose as long as they do not step beyond the four corners of the Constitution.'

'My Lord, if I may argue the case in my own way –'

Judges retired at sixty, and there was therefore no one on the bench who was not at least ten years G. N. Bannerji's junior.

'Yes, yes, Mr Bannerji. By all means.' The judge mopped his forehead. It was appallingly hot in the courtroom.

'It is precisely my contention, precisely my contention, my Lord, that the authority that the legislature of Purva Pradesh has chosen to delegate to the executive is an abdication of its own powers, and contrary both to the clear intention of the Constitution and to our own statute and constitutional law as laid down in a number of cases, most recently Jatindra Nath Gupta's case. In that case it was decided that a state legislature cannot delegate its legislative functions to any other body or authority, and that case is binding upon us, since it was decided by the Federal Court, the predecessor of the Supreme Court.'

The Chief Justice now spoke, his head still to one side: 'Mr Bannerji, was that case not decided by three judges to two?'

'Nevertheless, my Lord, it was decided. It is, after all, certainly possible that a judgment in the same proportions will issue from this bench too – though I am sure that neither I nor my learned friend opposite would hope for such an eventuality.'

'Yes. Go on, Mr Bannerji,' said the Chief Justice, frowning. It was the last thing he wanted either.

A little while later, the Chief Justice intervened again.

'But The Queen versus Burah, Mr Bannerji? Or Hodge versus The Queen?'

'I was coming to those cases, my Lord, in my own plodding manner.'

What might have been a smile passed across the Chief Justice's face; he was silent.

Half an hour later G.N. Bannerji was in full flow once more:

'But ours, unlike the British but like the American, is a written Constitution expressly declaring the will of the people. And precisely, my Lords, because the same vesting of the different powers of the state among the legislature, the executive and the judiciary exists in the two Constitutions, it is to the rules that have been laid down by the Supreme Court in the United States of America that we must turn for guidance and interpretation.'

'Must, Mr Bannerji?' This was the English judge.

'Should, my Lord.'

'You are not implying that these decisions are binding on us? This question cannot admit of two answers.'

'That, as from your question I have no doubt your Lordship perceives, would be a foolhardy contention. But there are certainly two sides to every question. What I meant was that the American precedents and interpretations, though not binding on us in the strict sense, are our only safe guide through what are for us comparatively uncharted waters. And the rule that has been laid down in America forbidding the delegation of power by any of the separate organs of the state should also be the yardstick for us to apply.'

'Well.' His Lordship sounded unconvinced but susceptible to persuasion.

'The reasons, my Lords, that powers not be delegated, have been succinctly stated by Cooley in *Constitutional Limitations*, Vol I, page 224.'

The Chief Justice interrupted.

'Just a minute, Mr Bannerji. We do not have this book with us on the bench, and we would like to follow you on the page. This is one danger of crossing the Atlantic for your arguments.'

'Presumably your Lordship means the Pacific.'

There was laughter from both the bench and the courtroom.

'Perhaps I mean both. As you have observed, Mr Bannerji, there are two sides to every question.'

'My Lord, I have had carbon copies made of the relevant pages.'

But the Court Reader promptly produced the book from his table below the rostrum. It was clear that there was only one copy of the volume, however, not five, as there would have been with the Indian and English law reports and authorities.

The Chief Justice said: 'Mr Bannerji, speaking for myself, I prefer the feel of a book in my hands. I hope we have the same edition. Page 224. Yes, it appears we do. My colleagues, however, may avail themselves of the carbon copies you have provided.'

'As your Lordships please. Now, my Lords, Cooley addresses the question in the following words:

Where the sovereign power of the State has located the authority, there it must remain; and by the constitutional agency alone the laws must be made until the Constitution itself is changed.

The power to whose judgment, wisdom and patriotism this high prerogative has been entrusted cannot relieve itself of the responsibility by choosing other agencies upon which the power shall be devolved, nor can it substitute the judgment, wisdom and patriotism of any other body for those to which alone the people have seen fit to confide this sovereign trust.

It is this sovereign trust, this sovereign trust, my Lords, that the legislature of Purva Pradesh has delegated to the executive in the Zamindari Abolition Act. Its date of activation; the sequence of the taking over of the estates of the zamindars, these decisions (quite possibly arbitrary, whimsical, even malicious) to be taken in many cases by very junior officials of the administration; the terms of the bonds sought to be offered by way of compensation, and the mix of cash and bonds; and many other points not merely of detail but of substance. My Lords, this is no mere filling in of details, this is improper delegation of authority, and the act, even if there were no other grounds, would be invalid on these grounds alone.'

Small, cheerful Mr Shastri, the Advocate-General, rose smilingly to his feet. His stiff white collar had gone limp with sweat. 'Your Lordships please. A slight cor-rec-tion to my learned friend. Date of vesting is au-to-ma-tic with President's assent. So act is ac-ti-va-ted at once.' Although this was his first interruption, it was offered with undramatic and amiable courtesy. Mr Shastri's English was not elegant (he pronounced 'carte blanche', for instance, as 'ka-thee bi-lan-chee'), nor his manner of advocacy fluent. But he argued superbly if simply from first principles (or, as his irreverent juniors might say, prin-ci-ples), and there were few lawyers in the state, perhaps in the country, who were a match for him.

'I am obliged to my learned friend for his clarification,' said G.N. Bannerji, leaning forward on the lectern once more. 'I was referring, my Lords, not so much to the date of vesting, which, as my learned friend points out, is immediate, but to the dates of the taking over of the estates.'

'Surely, Mr Bannerji,' said the large judge to the right of the Chief Justice, rubbing his thumb and forefinger together, 'you cannot expect the government to take over all the estates simultaneously? That would be administratively unworkable.'

'My Lord,' said G.N. Bannerji, 'it is not a question of simultaneity but equity. That is what worries me, my Lord. Guidelines could have been laid down in several ways – on the basis of income, for instance, or geography. The present act, however, enables the administration to pick and choose. If, for instance, they decide tomorrow that they do not like some particular zamindar, say the Raja of Marh, because he is too vocal on some issue that goes against the policy or even the interests of the government, they may under the impugned act issue an immediate notification that his estates in Purva Pradesh will be taken over. This is a gateway to tyranny, my Lords, a gateway to nothing less than tyranny.'

The Raja of Marh, who, owing to both heat and sloth, had been drowsing off while leaning further and further forward in his chair, suddenly came back to life on hearing his name. He floundered around in confusion for some time, unable to place himself in his surroundings after his fleshly dreams.

He tugged the gown of a junior lawyer who was seated in front of him.

'What did he say? What is he saying about me?' he demanded.

The lawyer turned around, his hand raised slightly upwards in a gesture of placation. He whispered an explanation. The Raja of Marh stared blankly and uncomprehendingly at him, then, sensing that nothing had been said that harmed his interests, became somnolent once again.

Thus the argument progressed. Those outsiders who had come with the expectation of high or low drama were deeply disappointed. Many of the litigants themselves were mystified by what was going on. They did not know that Bannerji would be on his feet for five days on behalf of the applicants, that this would be followed by five days of Shastri for the state and two final days for Bannerji's rebuttal. They had expected skirmishes and fireworks, the clang of sword on shield. What they were getting instead was an ecumenical but soporific fricassee of Hodge v. The Queen, Jatindra Nath Gupta v. Province of Bihar, and Schechter Poultry Corp. v. United States.

But the lawyers – especially those at the back of the court, who were not involved in the case – loved every minute of it. This, for them, was indeed the clang of sword on shield. They were aware that G.N. Bannerji's manner of constitutional argument, very different in this case from the statute-and-precedent traditions of British and therefore Indian advocacy, had come to be of increasing importance ever since the Government of India Act of 1935 set the frame which the Constitution of India itself would follow fifteen years later. But they had never heard a case argued in such wide-ranging form before, and that too by so distinguished a barrister at such length.

When the court adjourned at one o'clock for lunch, these lawyers streamed out, gowns flapping like bats' wings, and joined the smaller streams of lawyers from other courtrooms. They moved towards the part of the High Court building which was occupied by the Advocates' Association, and headed straight for the urinals, which stank frighteningly in the heat. Then they wandered off in groups to their own chambers, or to the library of the Advocates' Association or to the coffee shop or canteen. Here they sat and discussed with avidity the merits of the case and the mannerisms of eminent senior counsel.

11.3

AT the adjournment, the Nawab Sahib walked over to talk to Mahesh Kapoor. Upon discovering that he did not mean to attend the afternoon sitting, he asked him to join him for lunch at Baitar House, and Mahesh Kapoor agreed. Firoz too went over to talk for a few minutes to his father's friend – or his friend's father – before returning to his law-books. This was the most important case he had been associated with in his life, and he was working day and night on the small part of it that he might have to argue – or at least brief his senior in.

The Nawab Sahib looked at him with pride and affection and told him that he would be taking the afternoon off.

'But Abba, G.N. Bannerji will begin his argument on Article 14 today.'

'Now remind me –'

Firoz smiled at his father, but forbore from explaining Article 14.

'But you will be here tomorrow?' he asked.

'Yes, yes, perhaps. In any case, I'll be here when your part comes up,' said the Nawab Sahib, stroking his beard with a look of affectionate amusement in his eyes.

'It's your part too, Abba – lands granted by crown grant.'

'Yes.' The Nawab Sahib sighed. 'Anyway, both I and

the man who wants to wrest them away from me have been wearied by all this brilliance, and we're going off for lunch. But tell me, Firoz, why don't they close the courts at this time of year? The heat is dreadful. Doesn't the Patna High Court take its vacation in May and June?'

'Well, I suppose we follow the Calcutta model,' said Firoz. 'But don't ask me why. Well, Abba, I'll be off.'

The two old friends wandered into the corridor, where the heat hit them like a blast, and from there to the Nawab Sahib's car. Mahesh Kapoor instructed his driver to follow them to Baitar House. In the car both studiously avoided discussing the case or its implications, which, in a sense, was a pity because it would have been interesting to know what they would have said. Mahesh Kapoor could not, however, refrain from saying:

'Tell me when Firoz is going to argue. I'll come and listen.'

'I'll do so. That's very friendly of you.' The Nawab Sahib smiled. Although he had not intended it, perhaps his remark would be interpreted as ironic. He was reassured when his friend continued:

'Why – he's like my nephew.' After a pause, Mahesh Kapoor added: 'But isn't Karlekar leading him in the case?'

'Yes, but his brother is very ill, and he may have to go back to Bombay. If that's the case, Firoz will have to argue in his place.'

'Ah.' There was a pause.

'What news of Maan?' asked the Nawab Sahib at last, as they got out at Baitar House. 'We'll eat in the library; we won't be disturbed there.'

Mahesh Kapoor's face darkened.

'If I know him, he's still infatuated with that wretched woman. I wish I'd never asked her to sing at Prem Nivas on Holi. It all came about because of that evening.'

The Nawab Sahib was silent, but he seemed to have stiffened at the words.

'Keep an eye on your son too,' said Mahesh Kapoor with a curt laugh. 'Firoz, I mean.'

The Nawab Sahib looked at his friend, but said nothing. His face had gone white.

'Are you all right?'

'Yes, yes, Kapoor Sahib, I am all right. What were you saying about Firoz?'

'He visits that house too, I've heard. No harm in it if it's a brief thing, it's not as if it's an obsession yet –'

'No!' There was such sharp and unaccountable pain, almost horror, in the Nawab Sahib's voice that Mahesh Kapoor was taken aback. He knew that his friend had turned religious, but he had not imagined he had become such a puritan.

He quickly changed the subject. He talked about a couple of new bills, about how the delimitation of constituencies throughout the country was expected any day now, about the endless troubles in the Congress Party – both at the state level between him and Agarwal, and at the Centre between Nehru and the right wing.

'Why, I, even I, am thinking that this party is no longer a home for me,' said the Minister of Revenue. 'An old teacher – a freedom fighter – came to me the other day and said a number of things that I've been thinking over. Perhaps I should leave the Congress. I believe that if Nehru could be persuaded to leave the party and fight the next elections on his own platform and with a new party, he would win. I would follow him, as would many others.'

But even this startling and momentous confidence provoked no response from the Nawab Sahib. He was equally abstracted at lunch. Indeed, he appeared to have difficulty not only in speaking much but in swallowing his food.

11.4

TWO evenings later, all the lawyers for the zamindars and a couple of the clients themselves met in G.N. Bannerji's hotel room. He held these conferences from about six to eight each evening in order to prepare for the next day's arguments. Today, however, there was a dual purpose to the conference. First, the other lawyers were present to help him prepare for the morning session, when he would wind up his opening of the case. Secondly, he too had been requested today to give them advice for their own arguments of the afternoon, when they would be pleading their own particular sections of the case before the bench. G.N. Bannerji was happy to help them, but even more keen to see them go at eight o'clock sharp so that he could enjoy his evening in his standard manner with the person whom the juniors gossiped about as his 'lady-love': a Mrs Chakravarti, whom he had installed in great style (and at the expense of his clients) in a railway saloon on a siding at Brahmpur Junction.

Everyone arrived promptly at six. The local seniors and juniors brought the law-books and a waiter brought cups of tea. G.N. Bannerji complained about the fans in the hotel and about the tea. He was looking forward later to a Scotch or three.

'Sir, I have been waiting to say how fine your argument on public purpose was this afternoon.' This was a local senior lawyer.

The great G.N. Bannerji smiled. 'Yes, you saw how the Chief Justice appreciated the point about the connection between public purpose and public benefit.'

'Justice Maheshwari did not seem to.' This was guaranteed to provoke a response.

'Maheshwari!' The junior member of the bench was dismissed in a single word.

'But, Sir, his comment about the Land Revenue Commission will have to be answered,' piped up one enthusiastic junior.

'What he says is not important. He sits still for two days, then asks two stupid questions, one after another.'

'Quite right, Sir,' said Firoz quietly. 'You addressed the second point at length in yesterday's argument.'

'He's read the whole Ramayana, and still doesn't know whose *father* Sita is!' This twist to the standard witticism provoked laughter, some of it slightly sycophantic.

'Anyway,' continued G. N. Bannerji, 'we should concentrate on the arguments of the Chief Justice and Mr Justice Bailey. They are the best brains on the bench and they will sway the judgment. Is there anything they said that we might deal with?'

Firoz said, a little hesitantly: 'Sir, if I may. It seems to me from Mr Justice Bailey's comments that he is not convinced by your imputation of motives to the state in separating the two payments. You made the point, Sir, that the state had by sleight of hand divided the payment into two parts – the compensation proper and a rehabilitation grant. And that their motive in doing so was to get around the conclusions of the judges of the Patna High Court in the Bihar zamindari case. But would it not in fact be to our advantage to accept the government's contention that the rehabilitation grant and compensation are separate?'

G. N. Bannerji said: 'No, why? Why should we accept their contention? Anyway, let's see what the Advocate-General has to say. I can reply to all that later.' He turned away.

Firoz ventured on, rather earnestly: 'I mean, Sir, if it could be proved that even an ex-gratia payment like a rehabilitation grant can be thrown out under Article 14.'

G. N. Bannerji's rather pompous grandson cut Firoz off: 'Article 14 was fully argued on the second day.' He was trying to protect his grandfather from what seemed to be a perverse point. To accept the government's contention on such an important point would surely be to throw away their own case.

But G. N. Bannerji silenced his grandson in Bengali with, 'Aachha, choop koré thako!' and turned to Firoz with his finger pointed upwards. 'Say that again,' he said. 'Say that again.'

Firoz repeated his comment, then elaborated it.

G. N. Bannerji considered the point, then wrote something in his red notebook. Turning to Firoz he said, 'Find me whatever American case-law you can on the point, and bring it here to me at eight tomorrow morning.'

Firoz said, 'Yes, Sir.' His eyes were shining with pleasure.

G. N. Bannerji said: 'This is a dangerous weapon to use. It could go badly wrong. I wonder if at this stage –' He went off into his thoughts. 'Bring me the cases anyway, and I will see. Let me see the mood of the court. All right, anything else on Article 14?'

No one spoke.

'Where is Karlekar?'

'Sir, his brother has died and he has had to leave for Bombay. He got the telegram just a few hours ago – while you were on your feet.'

'I see. And who is his junior for the crown grant writs?'

'I am, Sir,' said Firoz.

'You have a momentous day ahead of you, young man. I imagine you will handle it.' Firoz glowed at this unexpected praise, and it was hard for him not to grin.

'Sir, if you have any suggestions –' he said.

'Not really. Just argue that the crown grants conferred absolute rights in perpetuity, and the grantees are therefore not like other intermediaries. But all this is obvious. If I think of something else I'll tell you tomorrow morning when you come here. On second thoughts, come ten minutes earlier.'

'Thank you, Sir.'

The conference continued for an hour-and-a-half. But G. N. Bannerji was becoming restless, and everyone felt that the great lawyer should not be overtaxed when he still had to argue the next day. The questions had not dried up, however, when he took off his spectacles, pointed two fingers upwards and said the single word:

'Aachha.'

It was the signal for people to gather up their papers.

Outside, it was getting dark. On the way out, a couple of juniors, unconscious of the fact that they were still within earshot of G. N. Bannerji's son and grandson, were gossiping about the lawyer from Calcutta.

'Have you seen his lady-love?' asked one.

'Oh, no, no,' said the other.

'I hear she is a real firecracker.'

The other laughed. 'Over seventy, and he has a lady-love!'

'But think of Mrs Bannerji! What must she think? The whole world knows.'

The other shrugged, as if to imply that what a Mrs Bannerji might think was outside either his concern or his imagination.

The son and grandson of the great lawyer heard this exchange though they did not see the shrug. They frowned to themselves, but said nothing to each other, and tacitly allowed the subject to drift away on the evening air.

11.5

THE next day G.N. Bannerji wound up the opening for the petitioners, and several other counsel argued for short periods about their own specific points. Firoz too got his chance.

For a few moments before Firoz got to his feet, his mind plunged suddenly into an inexplicable blackness – an emptiness, almost. He could see all his arguments lucidly, but could see no point to anything at all – this case, his career, his father's lands, the scheme of things of which this court and this Constitution were a part, his own existence, even human life itself. The disproportionate strength of the feelings he was undergoing – and the irrelevance of these feelings to the business at hand – bewildered him.

He shuffled his papers for a while, and his mind cleared. But now he was so nervous, so puzzled by the untimely incursion of these thoughts, that at first he had to hide his hands behind the lectern.

He began with the formulary remark: 'My Lords, I adopt the arguments of Mr G.N. Bannerji on all the main points, but would like to add my own arguments with respect to the question of the lands covered by crown grants.' He then argued with great force of logic that these lands fell into a different category from the others, and were protected by contract and proclamation from ever being taken over. The bench listened to him appreciatively; and he defended his contention against their questions as well as he could. His curious uncertainty had disappeared as suddenly as it had arisen.

Mahesh Kapoor had taken time off from his heavy workload to come and hear Firoz. Though he listened with warmth and enjoyment to Firoz's arguments he felt that it would be a disaster if the court accepted them. A fair proportion of the rented land in Purva Pradesh fell under the category of grants given by the crown after the Mutiny in order to establish order once more through the intermediation of powerful local men. Some of these, like the Nawab Sahib's ancestor, had fought against the British; but it had been felt that they and their families could not with safety be antagonized further. The grants were therefore given subject to good behaviour – but to nothing else.

Mahesh Kapoor was also particularly interested in another writ petition, one brought forward by those who had actually ruled their own states under the British, who had signed instruments of accession to the Indian Union after Independence and been granted certain guarantees in the Constitution. One such was the bestial Raja of Marh, whom Mahesh Kapoor would have been only too happy to dispossess completely. Although the state of Marh proper fell in Madhya Pradesh, the Raja's ancestors had also been granted land in Purva Pradesh – or Protected Provinces as it was called at the time. His lands in P.P. fell into the category of crown grants, but it was one of the contentions of the Raja's lawyers that his privy purse from the government had been set lower than it otherwise would have been in view of the income that his estates in P.P. were expected to bring in perpetuity. These lands had been allowed to the Raja as personal, rather than State, property, and (they contended) were guaranteed by two articles of the Constitution. One unambiguously declared that the government would pay due regard to any assurances given under the covenants of merger with respect to the personal rights, privileges and dignities of the ex-rulers; and another stated that disputes arising out of such covenants and similar instruments were not justiciable in the courts.

The government lawyers, on the other hand, had insisted in their affidavits that 'personal rights, privileges and dignities' did not include personal property; with regard to personal property the ex-rulers had the status and guarantees of any other citizen. And they too contended that the matter – as they saw it – was not justiciable.

If Mahesh Kapoor had had his way, he would have taken over not only the Raja's personal lands in P.P. but whatever had been allowed to him as personal land in M.P. as well – and all his urban property in Brahmpur besides – including the site of the Shiva Temple, which was now under a new spurt of construction on account of the approaching festival of the Pul Mela. This was, alas, not possible; had it been, it would have curbed the Raja's wretched mischief. It would have been a very unwelcome thought to Mahesh Kapoor that this desire of his was in essence not very different from that of the Home Minister L.N. Agarwal when he attempted to take over Baitar House.

The Nawab of Baitar noticed Mahesh Kapoor as he came into court a little into the afternoon session; though they sat on different sides of the aisle, they acknowledged each other with an unspoken salutation.

The Nawab Sahib's heart was full. He had listened with enormous pride and happiness to his son's speech. He could not help thinking once more how Firoz had inherited so many of the finer features of his mother. And she too had sometimes been most nervous when she was most forceful. The attentiveness of the judges to the young man's arguments were savoured even more by his father than by himself, for he was too busy parrying their questions to allow himself the pleasure of enjoying them.

Even his senior could not have done better, thought the Nawab Sahib. He wondered what the next day's report in the *Brahmpur Chronicle* would carry of Firoz's arguments. He even somewhat whimsically imagined the great Cicero appearing in the Brahmpur High Court and commending his son's advocacy.

But will it do much good in the end? – this thought struck him again and again in the middle of his happiness. When a government is determined to get its way it usually does so by one means or another. And history is against our class. He looked over to where the Raja and Rajkumar of Marh were sitting. I suppose that if it were merely our class it would not matter, he continued to himself. But it is everyone else besides. He found his thoughts turning not only to his retainers and dependants but to the musicians he used to listen to in his own youth, the poets he used to patronize, and to Saeeda Bai.

And he looked at Firoz with renewed concern.

11.6

DAILY the crowds in court lessened until finally hardly anyone other than the press, the lawyers, and a few of the litigants could be seen.

Whether the Nawab Sahib and his class had or did not have history on their side, whether the Law propelled Society or Society the Law, whether the patronage of poetry counter-balanced the torments of the tenantry, such questions of great pitch and moment lay outside the immediate business of the five men in whose hands rested the fate of this case. Their concerns were concentrated on Articles 14, 31(2), and 31(4) of the Constitution of India, and they were grilling the amiable Mr Shastri about his view of these articles and of the statute under challenge.

The Chief Justice was looking through his copy of the Constitution, and scanning for the fourth time the words of Articles 14 and 31.

The other judges (Mr Justice Maheshwari excepted) had been asking some questions of the Advocate-General which the Chief Justice had been following with only half an ear. The Raja of Marh, who seemed to enjoy the atmosphere of the courtroom, was listening with no ear at all. He was present in court, but once more not conscious of the fact. His son, the Rajkumar, did not dare to nudge him awake when he slumped forward.

The questions from the bench spread over the entire field of the immediate argument.

'Mr Advocate-General, what is your response to the argument of Mr Bannerji that the purpose of the Zamindari Act is not a public purpose but the policy of the political party which for the time being is holding office in the state?'

'Could you attempt, Mr Advocate-General, to reconcile these various American authorities? I mean, on the question of public purpose rather than the equal protection of the laws.'

'Mr Advocate-General, are you seriously asking us to believe that "notwithstanding anything in this Constitution" are the controlling words of Article 31 clause 4 and that any act under the aegis of that article is therefore unchallengable under Article 14 or any other article of that Constitution? Surely it only protects the act from challenge on grounds contained in Article 31 clause 2.'

'Mr Advocate-General, what about Yick Wo versus Hopkins with respect to Article 14? Or the passage in Willis approved by Justice Fazl Ali in a recent Supreme Court decision as being a correct exposition of the principles underlying Article 14? – "The guarantee of the equal protection of the laws means the protection of equal laws." And so on. Learned counsel for the applicants made much of that, and I do not see how you can counter their contention.'

Several reporters and even lawyers in the courtroom had the strong sense that the case was beginning to go against the government.

The Advocate-General appeared unconscious of this. He continued, unexcitedly, to weigh his words, even his syllables, with such care that he emitted them at only about a third of the rate of G.N. Bannerji.

His answer to the first question was: 'Di-rec-tive Prin-ci-ples, my Lords.' There was a long pause, and then he listed the relevant articles one by one. This was followed by a shorter pause, then the statement: 'Thus your Lordships see it is in Con-sti-tu-tion itself and not party policy merely.'

To the question about reconciling the various American authorities, he merely smiled and said: 'No, my Lords.' It was not for him to attempt to reconcile the irreconcilable, especially since it was not he who was leaning on the American cases for support. Indeed, had not even Dr Cooley said he was 'somewhat at sea' when attempting to determine the meaning of 'public purpose' in the light of conflicting judicial decisions? But why mention that? 'No, my Lords,' was enough.

Non-geographically speaking, the Chief Justice had been somewhat on the sidelines during the last few minutes. Now he too entered the fray. Having looked once more at the crucial articles and having doodled a fish on the pad in front of him, he cocked his head to one side and said:

'Now, Mr Advocate-General, I understand that the state contends that the two payments, the flat-scale compensation and the wealth-based, sliding-scale rehabilitation grant, are of an entirely different nature. One is compensation, the other not. Thus they cannot be lumped together, and it cannot be said that the compensation is on a graduated or sliding scale, and it cannot therefore be called discriminatory or unequal against large landlords.'

'Yes, my Lord.'

The Chief Justice waited in vain for elaboration. After a pause he continued:

'And it is further argued by the state that the two payments are different because, for example, different sections of the Zamindari Act relate to these two payments; because there are different officers in charge of their disbursement – Rehabilitation Grant Officers and Compensation Officers; and so on.'

'Yes, my Lord.'

'Mr Bannerji's contention for the applicants, on the other hand, was that this distinction is mere sleight of hand, especially since the compensation funds are only about a third of the rehabilitation funds.'

'No, my Lord.'

'No?'

'Not sleight of hand, my Lord.'

'And he says,' continued the Chief Justice, 'that since the distinction was not mentioned in the legislative debates until a late stage, it was introduced by the government after the adverse Patna High Court judgment as a way of fraudulently getting around the constitutional protections.'

'The act is act, my Lord. Debates are debates.'

'And what about the preamble to the act, Mr Advocate-General, which makes no mention of rehabilitation as an objective of the legislation?'

'O-ver-sight, my Lord. The act is act.'

The Chief Justice leaned his head on his other arm. 'Now suppose we were to accept your – that is, the state's – contention that the so-called compensation is all there is by way of real compensation under Article 31 clause 2, how would you then describe the so-called rehabilitation grant?'

'Ex-gratia payment, my Lord, which state may freely make to anyone in any way it chooses.'

The Chief Justice now leaned his head on both his hands, and examined his prey.

'Would the protection from judicial challenge that Article 32 clause 4 provides to compensation extend to ex-gratia payments as well? Could the unequal terms – the sliding scale – of this ex-gratia payment not still be challenged under Article 14, which provides for the protection of equal laws?'

Firoz, who had been listening to the argument with the utmost attentiveness, looked at G.N. Bannerji. This was precisely the point he had been veering towards in the conference that evening. The distinguished lawyer had taken off his spectacles and was polishing them very slowly. Finally, he stopped polishing them altogether, and stood completely still, looking – like everyone else in court – at the Advocate-General.

There was silence for a good fifteen seconds.

'Challenge to ex-gratia payment, my Lord?' said Mr Shastri, appearing genially shocked.

'Well,' continued the Chief Justice, frowning, 'it works on a sliding scale to the detriment of the larger zamindars. The smallest ones get ten times the computation based on rent and the largest ones get only one-and-a-half times the computation. Different multiples, ergo unequal treatment, ergo unfair discrimination.'

'My Lords,' protested Mr Shastri, 'ex-gratia payment confers no legal rights. It is pri-vi-lege conferred by the state. Therefore, it is not open to question on ground of un-fair dis-cri-mi-na-tion.' But the Advocate-General was not smiling quite as broadly. This had become almost a one-to-one cross-examination. The other judges did not interpose any questions.

'Now, Mr Advocate-General, in America it has been held by their Supreme Court that their fourteenth amendment – to which our Article 14 happens to correspond in language and spirit – applies not only to liabilities imposed but to privileges conferred as well. So would that not apply to ex-gratia payments?'

'My Lords, American Constitution is short, so gaps are filled by in-ter-pre-ta-tion. Ours is long, so the need is less here.'

The Chief Justice smiled. He looked rather wily now: an old, wise, bald tortoise. The Advocate-General paused. But this time he knew he would have to put forth a less unconvincing and general argument. The two fourteens were too alike. He said:

'My Lords, in India Article 31 clause 4 protects the act from any challenge whatsoever under the Constitution.'

'Mr Advocate-General, I heard your answer to the query of Mr Justice Bailey on that point. But if this bench does not find that argument convincing and at the same time comes to the conclusion that ex-gratia payments must satisfy the guarantees of Article 14, where does the state stand?'

The Advocate-General said nothing for a while. If self-defeating candour were enjoined on lawyers, his answer would have had to be: 'State does not stand, my Lord, it falls.' Instead he said: 'State would have to consider its position, my Lord.'

'I think the state would do well to consider its position in the light of this line of possible reasoning.'

The tension in court had become so palpable that some of it must have communicated itself into the dreams of the Raja of Marh. He woke up violently. He was in the grip of a paroxysm of anxiety. He stood up and stepped forward into the aisle. He had behaved well during the argument of his own writ petition. Now, when things seemed to be going dangerously for the state on a point that did not refer specifically to him but would have covered him safely as well, he grew desperately agitated.

'It is not right,' he said.

The Chief Justice leaned forwards.

'It is not right. We too love our country. Who are they? Who are they? The land –' he expostulated.

The courtroom reacted with shock and amazement. The Rajkumar stood up and took a tentative step towards his father. His father shoved him aside.

The Chief Justice said, rather slowly: 'Your Highness, I cannot hear you.'

The Raja of Marh did not believe this for one instant. 'I will speak louder, Sir,' he announced.

The Chief Justice repeated: 'I cannot hear you, Your Highness. If you have something to say, kindly say it through your counsel. And please be seated in the third row. The first two rows are reserved for the Bar.'

'No, Sir! My land is at stake! My life is at stake!' He glared belligerently upwards, as if he were about to charge the bench.

The Chief Justice looked at his colleagues to either side of him and said to the Court Reader and the ushers in Hindi:

'Remove that man.'

The ushers looked stunned. They had not imagined they would ever have to lay hands on Majesty.

In English, the Chief Justice said to the Reader: 'Call the watch and ward staff.' To the counsel of the Raja of Marh, he said: 'Control your client. Tell him not to test the forbearance of this court. If your client does not leave the court immediately I will commit him for contempt.'

The five magnificent ushers, the Court Reader, and several counsel for the applicants apologetically but bodily moved the Raja of Marh, still spluttering, from Courtroom Number One before he could do further damage to himself, his case, or the dignity of the court. The Rajkumar of Marh, red with shame, followed slowly. He turned around at the door. Every eye in court was following the spasmodic progress of his father. Firoz too was looking at him in contemptuous disbelief. The Rajkumar lowered his eyes and followed his father into the corridor.

11.7

A few days after he had suffered this indignity, the Raja of Marh, feather-turbaned and diamond-buttoned, together with a glittering retinue of retainers, performed a progress to the Pul Mela.

His Highness started out in the morning from the site of the Shiva Temple at Chowk (where he offered obeisance), advanced through the old town of Brahmpur, and arrived at the top of the great earthen ramp which led gently down from the mud cliffs to the sands on the south bank of the Ganga. Every few steps a crier announced the Raja's presence, and rose-petals were flung into the air to his greater glory. It was idiotic.

However, it was of a piece with the Raja's conception of himself and his place in the world. He was cross with the world, and especially with the *Brahmpur Chronicle*, which had dwelt lovingly on his ejaculations in and his ejection from the Chief Justice's court. The case had continued for four or five more days before being closed (the judgment was reserved for a later date), and on each day the *Brahm-*

pur Chronicle had found some occasion to hearken back to the Raja of Marh's unseemly exit.

The procession halted at the top of the ramp under the shade of the great pipal tree, and the Raja looked down. Below him, as far as the eye could see, lay an ocean of tents – khaki, haze-enveloped – spread out along the sands. Instead of the single pontoon bridge across the Ganga there were at present five bridges of boats, effectively cutting off all down-river traffic. But large flotillas of little boats were still plying across the river in order to ferry pilgrims to particularly auspicious bathing-spots along sand-spits on either side – or simply to provide a swifter and more enjoyable means of crossing the river than facing the crush of people on the improvised and grossly overcrowded bridges.

The grand ramp too was crowded with pilgrims from all over India, many of whom had just arrived by special trains that had been laid on for the Pul Mela traffic. For a few minutes, however, the Raja's retainers forced the crowd back sufficiently to give their master a regal and leisurely view of the scene.

The Raja gazed with reverence at the great brown river, the beautiful and placid Ganga. Its level was still low, and the sands broad. It was mid-June. The monsoons had not yet broken in Brahmpur, and the snow-melt had not yet swollen the river much. In two days it would be the grand bathing day of Ganga Dussehra (when, by popular tradition, the Ganga rose one step along the bathing ghats of Banaras), and four days after that would come the second grand bathing day of the full moon. It was thanks to the grace of Lord Shiva, who had broken the river's fall from heaven by allowing it to flow through his hair that the Ganga had not flooded the earth. It was to Lord Shiva that the Raja was raising the Chandrachur Temple. Tears came to the Raja's eyes as he looked at the holy river and contemplated the virtue of his actions.

The Raja was bound for a specific encampment down below: the tents of the holy man known as Sanaki Baba. This cheerful, middle-aged man was a devotee of Krishna, and spent his time in his praise and in meditation. He was surrounded by attractive disciples and had a great reputation as a source of peaceful energy. The Raja was determined to visit him even before he visited the encampments of the Shaivite holy men. The Raja's anti-Muslim feelings had resolved themselves in pan-Hindu aspirations and ceremonies: he had started his procession from a Shiva temple, it had wound its way through the city named after Brahma, and it would conclude with a visit to a devotee of Krishna, Vishnu's great avatar. The entire Hindu trinity would thus be appeased. Then he would take a dip in the Ganga (immersing one bejewelled toe would be sufficient), and he would have washed away the sins of seven generations, including his own. It was a useful morning's work. The Raja glanced back towards Chowk and stared for a few seconds at the minarets of the mosque. The trident on top of my temple will outsoar you soon enough, he thought, and the martial blood of his ancestors began to boil within him.

But thinking of his ancestors made him think of his descendants, and he looked with perplexed impatience at his son, the Rajkumar, who was trailing in a reluctant way after his father. What a useless fellow he is! thought the Raja. I should get him married off at once. I don't care how many boys he sleeps with as long as he gives me a grandson as well. A few days ago the Raja had taken him to Saeeda Bai's to make a man of him. The Rajkumar had almost run out in terror! The Raja did not know that his son was not unfamiliar with the brothels of the old town, which his university friends sometimes visited. But to be given intimate tutelage by his crass father had been too much for him.

The Raja had instructions from his formidable mother, the Dowager Rani of Marh, to pay more attention to her grandson. Recently he had been doing his best to comply. He had dragged himself and his son to the High Court in order to introduce him to Responsibility, Law and Property. The result had been a fiasco. Procreation and the Life of a Man of the World had not gone much better. Today's

lesson was Religion and the Martial Spirit. Even here the
Rajkumar had been a wash-out. While the Raja had bel-
lowed 'Har har Mahadeva!' with even greater zest whenever they passed by a mosque, the Rajkumar had lowered
his head and mumbled the words even more unwillingly.
Finally, there was Ritual and Education. The Raja was
determined to fling his son into the Ganga. Since the
Rajkumar had only a year to go before finishing his
university studies, he should partake – even if a trifle
prematurely – of the proper Hindu ritual of graduation –
the bath or snaan – in order to become a proper graduate
or snaatak. And what better place to become a snaatak
than in the Holy Ganga during the sexennial Pul Mela,
which was always grander than usual? He would fling him
in to the cheers of his retainers. And if the milksop couldn't
swim, and had to be dragged spluttering and gasping back
to land, that would be hilarious.

'Hurry up, hurry up!' shouted the Raja, as he stumbled
down the long ramp to the sands. 'Where is this Sanaki
Baba's camp? Where do all these sister-fucking pilgrims
come from? Isn't there any organization? Get me my car!'

'Your Highness, the authorities have forbidden all cars
except for police and VIPs. We could not get permission,'
murmured someone.

'Am I not a VIP?' The Raja's breast swelled with
indignation.

'Yes, your Highness. But –'

Finally, among the miles of tents and camps, after they
had walked for almost half an hour along makeshift roads
of metal plates laid out by army engineers on the sands,
they arrived within sight of Sanaki Baba's encampment,
and the Raja's retinue moved towards it gratefully. They
were only about a hundred yards away.

'At last!' cried the Raja of Marh. The heat was telling
on him. He was sweating like a swine. 'Tell the Baba to
come out. I want to see him. And I want some sherbet.'

'Your Highness –'

But hardly had the man run ahead with the message
than from the other side a police jeep screeched to a halt

before the camp, and several people got down and made their way in.

The Raja's eyes popped.

'We were here first. Stop them! I must see the Baba at once,' he cried in an outburst of outrage.

But the jeep people had gone in already.

11.8

WHEN the jeep had first descended to the sands below the Fort, Dipankar Chatterji, who was one of its passengers, had been truly astonished.

The roads on the Pul Mela sands among the tents and encampments were packed with people. Many were carrying rolls of bedding and other possessions with them, including pots and pans for cooking, food supplies, and perhaps a child or two tucked under an arm or clinging onto their back. They carried cloth bags, pails and buckets, sticks, flags, pennants, and garlands of marigolds. Some were panting with heat and exhaustion, others were chatting as if they were on a picnic outing, or singing bhajans and other holy songs because their enthusiasm at finally getting a glimpse of Mother Ganga had removed in an instant the weariness of the journey. Men, women and children, old and young, dark and fair, rich and poor, brahmins and outcastes, Tamils and Kashmiris, saffron-clad sadhus and naked nagas, all jostled together on the roads along the sands. The smells of incense and marijuana and sweat and noonday cooking, the sounds of children crying and loud-speakers blaring and women chanting kirtans and policemen yelling, the sight of the sun glittering on the Ganga and the sand swirling in little eddies wherever the roads were not packed with people, all combined to give Dipankar an overwhelming sense of elation. Here, he felt, he would find something of what he was looking for, or the Something that he was looking for. This was the universe in microcosm; somewhere in its turmoil lay peace.

The jeep struggled, honking, along the sandy, metal-plated routes. At one point the driver appeared to be lost. They came to a crossroads where a young policeman was attempting with difficulty to direct the traffic. The jeep was the only vehicle as such, but great crowds swirled around the policeman, who shouted and flailed his baton in the air to little effect. Mr Maitra, Dipankar's elderly host in Brahmpur, an ex-officer of the Indian Police who had in effect requisitioned the jeep, now took matters into his own hands.

'Stop!' he told the driver in Hindi.

The driver stopped the jeep.

The lone policeman, seeing the jeep, approached it.

'Where is the tent of Sanaki Baba?' asked Mr Maitra in a voice of command.

'There, Sir – two furlongs in that direction – on the left-hand side.'

'Good,' said Mr Maitra. A sudden thought struck him. 'Do you know who Maitra was?'

'Maitra?' said the young policeman.

'R.K. Maitra.'

'Yes,' said the policeman, but it sounded as if he was just saying so to satisfy the whim of his strange questioner.

'Who was he?' demanded Mr Maitra.

'He was our first Indian SP,' replied the policeman.

'I am he!' said Mr Maitra.

The policeman saluted with tremendous smartness. Mr Maitra's face registered delight.

'Let's go!' he said, and they were off again.

Shortly they arrived at Sanaki Baba's camp. As they were about to go in, Dipankar noticed that a flower-flinging procession of some kind was approaching from the other side. He did not pay it much attention, however, and they entered the first tent of the encampment – a large one that acted as a kind of public audience hall.

Rough red and blue rugs were spread on the floor in the tent, and everyone was seated on the ground: men on the left, women on the right. At one end was a long platform covered with white cloth. On this sat a young, thin, bearded man in a white robe; he was giving a sermon in a slow and hoarse voice. Behind him was a photograph of Sanaki Baba, a plump man, fairly bald, very cheerful, naked to the waist with a great deal of curly hair on his chest. A pair of baggy shorts was all he wore. A river – probably the Ganga, but possibly, since he was a devotee of Krishna, the Yamuna – was flowing behind him.

The young man was in mid-sermon when Dipankar and Mr Maitra entered. The policemen accompanying them stayed outside. Mr Maitra was smiling to himself in anticipation of meeting his favourite holy man. He paid no attention to the young man's sermon.

'Listen,' continued the young preacher hoarsely:

'You may have noticed that when it rains it is the useless plants, the grass and weeds and shrubs that flourish.

'They flourish without effort.

'But if you want to grow a worthwhile plant: a rose, a fruit-tree, a vine of paan, then you need effort.

'You must water, apply manure, weed it, prune it.

'It is not simple.

'So it is with the world. We are coloured by its colour. We are coloured by its colour without effort. As the world is, so we become.

'We go blindly through the world, as is our nature. It is easy.

'But for knowledge of God, for knowledge of truth, we have to make an effort....'

It was at this point that the Raja of Marh and his retinue entered. The Raja had sent a man a couple of minutes ahead, but he had not been so bold as to interrupt the sermon. The Raja, however, was not a man to be awed by a Chief Justice or a Subsidiary Baba. He caught the young preacher's eye. The young man did namasté, glanced at his watch, and directed a man in a grey khadi kurta to see what the Raja wanted. Mr Maitra thought this an excellent opportunity to get his own arrival announced to Sanaki Baba, who was known to be quite casual about times and places – and sometimes people – and might well not appear for hours. The man in the grey kurta left the tent and went to another, smaller tent deeper in the encampment. Mr Maitra looked impatient, the Raja impatient and highly agitated. Dipankar looked neither impatient nor agitated. He had all the time in the world, and he concentrated again on the sermon. He had come to find an Answer or Answers at the Pul Mela, and a Quest could not be rushed.

The young baba continued in his hoarse, earnest voice:

'What is envy? It is so common. We look at the outside, and we long for things. . . .'

The Raja of Marh was stamping his feet. He was used to giving audiences, not waiting for them. And what had happened to the glass of sherbet he had ordered?

'A flame goes up. Why? Because it yearns for its greater form, which is the sun.

'A clod of mud falls down. Why? Because it yearns for its greater form, the earth.

'The air in a balloon escapes if it can. Why? To join its greater form, the outer air.

'So also the soul in our bodies longs to join the greater world-soul.

'Now we must take God's name:

Haré Rama, haré Rama, Rama Rama, haré haré.
Haré Krishna, haré Krishna, Krishna Krishna, haré haré.'

He began chanting slowly and softly. A few of the women joined in, then some more women and some of the men, and soon almost everyone:

'Haré Rama, haré Rama, Rama Rama, haré haré.
Haré Krishna, haré Krishna, Krishna Krishna, haré haré.'

Soon the repetitions had built up to such an extent that the audience, still seated, was swaying from side to side. Small cymbals were clashed, high notes of ecstasy sounded on some of the words. The effect on the singers was hypnotic. Dipankar, feeling he ought to join in, did so out of politeness, but remained unhypnotized. The Raja of Marh glowered. Suddenly the kirtan stopped, and a hymn – a bhajan – began.

'Gopala, Gopala, make me yours –
I am the sinner, you are the merciful one –'

But hardly had this begun than Sanaki Baba, clad only in his shorts, entered the tent, still engaged in conversation with the man in the grey kurta. 'Yes, yes,' Sanaki Baba was saying, his small eyes twinkling, 'you had better go and make arrangements: some pumpkins, some onions, some potatoes. Where will you get carrots in this season? ... No, no, spread this there.... Yes, tell Maitra Sahib ... and the Professor.'

He disappeared as suddenly as he had come. He had not even noticed the Raja of Marh.

The man in the grey kurta approached Mr Maitra and told him that Sanaki Baba would see them in his tent. Another man, about sixty years old, presumably the Professor, was also asked to join them. The Raja of Marh almost exploded in wrath.

'And what about me?'

'Babaji will see you soon, Raja Sahib. He will make special time for you.'

'I must see him now! I don't care for his special time.'

The man, apparently realizing that the Raja would make mischief unless contained, beckoned to one of Sanaki Baba's closest disciples, a young woman called Pushpa. She was, Dipankar noted with appreciation, very beautiful and serious. He immediately thought of his Search for the Ideal. Surely it could run concurrently with his Quest for an Answer. He noticed Pushpa speak to the Raja and bewitch him into compliance.

Meanwhile the favoured ones entered Sanaki Baba's small tent. Mr Maitra introduced Dipankar to Sanaki Baba.

'His father is a judge of the Calcutta High Court,' said Mr Maitra. 'And he is searching for the Truth.'

Dipankar said nothing but looked at Sanaki Baba's radiant face. A sense of calm had come upon him.

Sanaki Baba appeared impressed. 'Very good, very good,' he said, smiling cheerfully. He turned to the Professor and said: 'And how is your bride?'

The Baba intended this as a compliment to his wife of many years, a woman who usually visited him when her husband came. 'Oh, she's visiting her son-in-law in Bareilly,' said the Professor. 'She's sorry she could not come.'

'These arrangements for my camp are all right,' said Sanaki Baba. 'Only this water problem persists. There is the Ganga, and here – no water!'

The Professor, who appeared to be on the advisory administrative board of the Mela, replied half-unctuously, half-confidently: 'It is all through your kindness and grace, Babaji, that things are basically running so smoothly. I will immediately go and see what can be done in this case.' However, he made no immediate move, and sat staring with adoration at Sanaki Baba.

11.9

NOW Sanaki Baba turned to Dipankar and asked:

'Where will you stay during the week of the Pul Mela?'

'He is staying with me here in Brahmpur,' said Mr Maitra.

'And coming such a long distance each day?' said Sanaki Baba. 'No, no, you must stay here in this camp, and go for a bath in the Ganga three times every day. You just follow me!' He laughed. 'You see, I am wearing swimming clothes. It is because I am the swimming champion of the Mela. What a Mela this is. Each year it gets bigger. And every six years it explodes. There are thousands of babas. There is a Ramjap Baba, a Tota Baba, even an Engine-Driver Baba. Who knows the truth? Does anyone? I can see you are searching.' He looked at Dipankar and continued kindly: 'You will find it, but who knows when.' To Mr Maitra he said: 'You can leave him here. He will be good. What did you say your name is – Divyakar?'

'Dipankar, Babaji.'

'Dipankar.' He said the word very lovingly, and Dipankar felt suddenly happy. 'Dipankar, you must speak to me in English, because I must learn it. I speak only a little. Some foreign people have come to listen to my sermons, so I am learning how to preach and meditate in English too.'

Mr Maitra had been containing himself longer than he could bear. Now he burst out: 'Baba, I can get no peace. What shall I do? Tell me a way.'

Sanaki Baba looked at him, smiling, and said: 'I will tell you an unfailing way.'

Mr Maitra said: 'Tell me now.'

Sanaki Baba said: 'It is simple. You will get peace.' He passed his hand backwards – his fingertips scraping the skin – over Mr Maitra's forehead, and asked: 'How does it feel?'

Mr Maitra smiled and said, 'Good.' Then he went on, pettishly: 'I take the name of Rama and tell my beads as you advise. Then I feel calm, but afterwards, thoughts come crowding in.' His heart was on his sleeve and he hardly cared that the Professor was listening. 'My son – he does not want to live in Brahmpur. He took a three-year extension in his job, and I accepted that, but I did not know that he was building a house in Calcutta. He will live there when he retires, not here. Can I live like a pigeon cooped up in Calcutta? He is not the same boy. I am hurt.'

Sanaki Baba looked pleased. 'Did I not tell you that none of your sons would come back? You did not believe me.'

'Yes. What shall I do?'

'What do you need them for? This is the stage of sannyaas, of renunciation.'

'But I get no peace.'

'Sannyaas itself is peace.'

But this did not satisfy Mr Maitra. 'Tell me some method,' he pleaded.

Sanaki Baba soothed him. 'I will, I will,' he said. 'When you come next time.'

'Why not today?'

Sanaki Baba looked around. 'Some other day. Whenever you want to come, come.'

'Will you be here?'

'I will be here until the 20th.'

'How about the 17th? the 18th?'

'It will be very crowded because of the full moon bathing day,' said Sanaki Baba, smiling. 'Come on the morning of the 19th.'

'Morning. What time?'

'19th morning ... eleven o'clock.'

Mr Maitra beamed with pleasure, having succeeded in getting an exact time for Peace. 'I will come,' he said delightedly.

'Now where will you be going?' asked Sanaki Baba. 'You can leave Divyakar here.'

'I am going to visit Ramjap Baba on the northern shore. I have a jeep, so we'll cross Pontoon Bridge Number Four. Two years ago I visited him and he remembered me – he remembered me from twenty years before. He had a platform in the Ganga then, and you had to wade out to see him.'

'Hiss mammary berry shurp,' said Sanaki Baba to Dipankar in English. 'Old, old, old man. Like a stick.'

'So now, I'll go and visit Sanaki Baba,' said Mr Maitra, getting up.

Sanaki Baba looked nonplussed.

Mr Maitra frowned, and explained again: 'On the other side of the Ganga.'

'But I am Sanaki Baba,' said Sanaki Baba.

'Oh yes,' said Mr Maitra, 'I meant – what's his name?'

'Ramjap Baba.'

'Yes, Ramjap Baba.'

So Mr Maitra left, and after a while the pretty Pushpa showed Dipankar to some straw lying on the sandy ground in one of the tents: this was to be his bed for the next week. The nights were hot, so a single sheet would do.

Pushpa went off to escort the Raja of Marh to Sanaki Baba's tent.

Dipankar sat down and began to read from Sri Aurobindo. But after an hour or so he became restless and decided to follow Sanaki Baba around.

Sanaki Baba appeared to be very practical and caring – happy, bustling, and un-dictatorial. Dipankar looked at him carefully from time to time. His little eyebrows were sometimes knit in thought. He had the neck of a bull, dark curly hairs on his barrel-chest, and a compact paunch. His hair grew only in a forehead tuft and on the sides. His brown oval pate gleamed in the June sunlight. And sometimes, when he listened, his mouth opened in concentration. Whenever he saw Dipankar looking at him, he smiled back.

Dipankar was also very taken with Pushpa and found himself blinking furiously whenever he spoke to her. But whenever she spoke to him it was in a very serious voice, and with a serious frown.

From time to time the Raja of Marh would appear in Sanaki Baba's encampment and roar with rage if Sanaki Baba was not in. Someone had told him of Dipankar's special status, and occasionally during the sermons he would glare at him murderously.

Dipankar felt that the Raja of Marh wanted to be loved, but found it hard to be lovable.

11.10

DIPANKAR sat in a boat on the Ganga.

An old man, a brahmin, with a caste-mark on his forehead, kept up a loud commentary to the splash of the oars. He compared Brahmpur to Banaras, to the great confluence at Allahabad, to Hardwar, and to Sagar Island where the Ganga met the sea.

'In Allahabad, the meeting of the blue waters of the Yamuna and the brown waters of the Ganga is like the meeting of Rama and Bharat,' said the old man piously.

'But what about the third river of the Triveni which meets them there?' asked Dipankar. 'What would you compare the river Saraswati to?'

The old man looked at Dipankar, annoyed. 'Where are you from?' he asked.

'From Calcutta,' said Dipankar. He had asked the question innocently, and was sorry he had annoyed the man.

'Hmmmh!' snorted the old man.

'And where are you from?' asked Dipankar.

'From Salimpur.'

'Where is that?' asked Dipankar.

'It is in Rudhia District,' said the old man. He was now bending down and examining his disfigured toe-nails.

'And where is that?' persisted Dipankar.

The old man looked at Dipankar incredulously.

'How far is it from here?' asked Dipankar, seeing that the old man was not going to reply without further prompting.

'It is seven rupees away,' said the old man.

'All right,' yelled the boatman, 'here we are. Now, good people, bathe your fill and pray for the good of all men, including myself.'

But the old man would have none of it. 'This is not the right spot,' he shouted. 'I have been here every year for twenty years and you cannot fool me. It is there.' He pointed to a spot in the middle of the line of boats.

'A policeman without a uniform,' said the boatman in disgust. Reluctantly, he pulled on the oars a few more times, and took the boat to the indicated spot. Here there were quite a number of bathers already. The water was shallow, and it was possible to stand. The splashing and chanting of the bathers merged with the sound of a temple bell. Marigolds and rose-petals floated in the muddy water, together with bits of soggy pamphlets, pieces of straw, the indigo-coloured wrapping of matchboxes, and empty packets made of stitched leaves.

The old man stripped down to his lungi, revealing the holy thread that stretched from his left shoulder to his right hip. In an even louder voice than before he exhorted the pilgrims to bathe. 'Hana lo, hana lo,' he shouted, spoonerizing the syllables in his excitement. Dipankar stripped to his underwear and plunged in.

The water did not look clean, but he stood around splashing himself for a minute or two. For some reason, this holiest of all spots did not attract him as much as the spot where the boatman had halted. There he had had the impulse to jump in. The old man, however, was transported with happy excitement. He squatted, ducking himself completely in the water, he cupped it in his hands and drank it, he pronounced 'Hari Om' as deeply and as often as he could. The other pilgrims were equally ecstatic. Men and women alike, they were delighting in the touch of the Ganga as babies delight in the touch of their mothers, and were shouting: 'Ganga Mata ki jai!'

'O Ganga! O Yamuna,' cried the old man, cupping his hands towards the sun and reciting in Sanskrit –

> 'O Ganga! O Yamuna!
> Godavari, Saraswati!
> Narmada, Indus, Kaveri,
> Be manifest in these waters.'

On the way back, he said to Dipankar:

'So you have had your first dip in the Ganga since you've come to Brahmpur!'

'Yes,' said Dipankar, wondering how he could have known that.

'I bathe here every day – five, six times a day,' continued the old man rather boastfully. 'This was only a short dip. I bathe day and night – sometimes for two hours at a time. Mother Ganga washes all your sins away.'

'You must sin a lot,' said Dipankar, some of his Chatterji acerbity rising to the surface.

The old man looked shocked at this sacrilegious humour.

'Don't you all bathe at home?' he asked Dipankar in scathing reproof.

'Yes,' laughed Dipankar. 'But not for two hours at a time.' He thought of Kuku's tub and began smiling. 'And not in the river.'

'Don't say "river",' said the old man sharply. 'Say "Ganga" or "Ganga Mata". It is not just a river.'

Dipankar nodded. He was amazed to notice tears in the old man's eyes.

'From the ice cave of Gaumukh in the glacier to the ocean surrounding Sagar Island, I have travelled along Ganga Mata,' said the old man. 'I could close my eyes and know where I was.'

'Because of the different languages they speak along the route?' asked Dipankar humbly.

'No! Because of the air in my nostrils. The thin piercing air of the glacier, the piny breeze of the gorges, the scent of Hardwar, the stench of Kanpur, the distinct fragrances of Prayag and Banaras ... and so on down to the humid, salty air of the Sundarbans and Sagar.'

He had closed his eyes and was summoning up his memories. His nostrils opened wider and a look of peace came over his irritable face.

'Next year I will make the return journey,' he said, 'from Sagar in the delta up to the snows of the Himalaya and the great Gaumukh glacier and the open mouth of the ice cave once again, under the great peak of Shiva-linga ... then I will have made a complete circuit, a complete parikrama of the Ganga ... from ice to salt, from salt to ice. Next year, next year, through ice and salt my spirit will surely be preserved.'

11.11

THE following day Dipankar noticed that there were a few perplexed-looking young foreigners in the audience – and wondered what they were making of all this. They probably couldn't understand a word of the sermon or the bhajans. But the beautiful, slightly snub-nosed Pushpa soon came to their rescue.

'Now,' she said in English, 'the idea is simply this: all we are gatting is surrendered to lotus feet of Lord.'

The foreigners nodded vigorously and smiled.

'Now I must mantion there will be maditation in English by Baba himself,' announced Pushpa.

But Sanaki Baba was in no mood for meditation that day. He was chatting away on whatever took his fancy to the Professor and the young preacher, both of whom he had brought up onto the white-sheeted platform. Pushpa looked displeased.

Perhaps sensing this, Sanaki Baba relented, and a very abbreviated meditation session began. He closed his eyes for a couple of minutes and told his audience to do the same. Then he said a long 'Om'. Finally, in a confident, warm and peaceful voice, in atrociously accented English, pausing long between each phrase, he murmured:

'The river of love, the river of bliss, the liver of right. . . .

'Take in environment and supreme being through nostrils. . . .

'Now you will feel anand and alok – blissness and lightness. Feel, do not think. . . .'

Suddenly he got up and began to sing. Someone struck up the rhythm on the tabla, someone else began clashing small cymbals together. Then he began to dance. Seeing Dipankar he said: 'Get up, Divyakar, get up and dance. And you, ladies, get up. Mataji, get up, get up,' he said, dragging a reluctant old woman of sixty to her feet. Soon she was dancing away by herself. Other women began dancing. The foreigners began dancing, and danced with great gusto. Everyone was dancing, each by himself and all together – and smiling with joy and contentment. Even Dipankar, who hated dancing, was dancing to the sound of the cymbals and the tabla and the obsessively chanted name of Krishna, Krishna, Radha's beloved, Krishna.

The cymbals, tabla, and chanting stopped, and the dancing was over as suddenly as it had begun.

Sanaki Baba was smiling benignantly all around and sweating.

Pushpa had some announcements to make, but before

she did so, she surveyed the audience and frowned with concentration. For a few seconds she gathered her thoughts. Then she told them rather reprovingly in English: 'You have now dancing and sermon and sankirtan and maditation. And the love. But when you are in offices and factories, then what? Then Babaji is not with you in physical form. Then Babaji is with you, but not in physical form. So you must not become attached to the dancing and the practice. If you get attached, it is no use. You must have the saakshi bhaava, the feeling of witnessing, or else what is the use?'

Clearly Pushpa was not entirely happy. She then announced the time of dinner and mentioned that Sanaki Baba would be speaking to a huge congregation at noon the next day. She provided clear instructions on how to get there.

Dinner was simple but good: curds, vegetables, rice – and rasmalai for dessert. Dipankar managed to sit next to Pushpa. Everything she said seemed to him to be utterly charming and utterly true.

'I used to be in teaching,' she said to him in Hindi. 'I was tied to so many things. But then this came, and Baba said to me, manage it all, and I felt as free as a bird. Young people are not stupid,' she added seriously. 'Most religious sadhus have destroyed religion. They like big funds, big followings, complete control. I am left free by Babaji. I have no boss. Even IAS officers, even Ministers have a boss. Even the Prime Minister has a boss. He must answer to the people.'

Dipankar nodded his head in vigorous assent.

All of a sudden he felt like renouncing everything – Sri Aurobindo, the Chatterji mansion, the possibility of a job in a bank, his hut under the laburnum tree, all the Chatterjis including Cuddles – and being free – free and boss-less as a bird.

'How true,' he said, looking at her wonderingly.

11.12

Postcard 1

Dear Amit Da,

I am writing to you from a tent near the Ganga, lying on a bed of straw. It's hot here, and noisy, because you can always hear loudspeakers with bhajans and kirtans and other announcements and the whistles of the frequent trains, but I am at peace. I have found my Ideal, Amit Da. I had a sense on the train coming here that it would be in Brahmpur that I would discover who I truly was and the direction of my individual existence, and I even hoped that I might find my Ideal. But since the only girl I knew in Brahmpur was Lata, I was worried lest it was she who should turn out to be my Ideal. That is partly why I have so far avoided visiting her family, and have deferred meeting Savita and her husband till after the Pul Mela is over. But now I need not worry.

Her name is Pushpa, and she is indeed a flower. But she is a serious person, so our pushpa-lila will consist of throwing ideas and feelings at each other, though I would like to sprinkle her with roses and jasmines. As Robi Babu says:

> ... for me alone your love has been waiting
> Through worlds and ages awake and wandering,
>   Is this true?
> That my voice, eyes, lips have brought you relief,
> In a trice, from the cycle of life after life,
>   Is this true?
> That you read on my soft forehead infinite Truth,
>   My ever-loving friend,
>   Is this true?

Just looking at her, listening to her is enough for me, though. I think I have gone beyond mere physical attraction. It is the Female Principle that I adore in her.

Postcard 2

A mouse is playing at my feet, and last night I was kept awake by it – and, of course, by my thoughts. But this is all the lila, the play of the Universe, and I have plunged into it with great happiness. I am afraid the first postcard disappeared quickly, so I'm continuing on another one of the two dozen self-addressed postcards that Ma insisted on my taking with me.

Also, you must forgive my handwriting, which is bad. Pushpa has wonderful handwriting. I saw her write my name in the entry book in English, and she put a mystical full moon of a dot above my 'i'.

How are Ma and Baba and Meenakshi and Kuku and Tapan and Cuddles and yourself? I do not miss any of you as yet, and when I think of you, I try to think of you with a disinterested love. I do not even miss my thatched hut where I meditate – or 'maditate', as Pushpa, with her delightful accent and warm smile, puts it. She says we should be free – free as birds – and I have decided to travel after the Mela wherever my spirit takes me in order that I can truly discover the Entirety of

Postcard 3

my own soul and the Being of India. Just wandering around at the Pul Mela has helped me to realize that the Spiritual Source of India is not the Zero or Unity or Duality or even the Trinity, but Infinity itself. If I felt that she might agree, I would ask her to travel with me, but she is a devotee of Sanaki Baba, and has decided to devote her whole life to him.

But I realize I haven't told you who he is. He is the holy man, the baba in whose compound I am staying down here on the sands of the Ganga. Mr Maitra brought me to see him, and Sanaki Baba decided I should stay here. He is a man of great wisdom and sweetness and humour. Mr Maitra told him how unhappy and peace-less he felt, and Sanaki Baba provided him with some relief and told him that he would later explain to him how to meditate. When he left, Babaji turned to me and said: 'Divyakar' – he likes to call me Divyakar sometimes for some reason – 'I crash into a table in the darkness, yet it is not the table that has hurt me but the lack of light. So, with old age, all these small things hurt, because the light of meditation is absent.' 'But meditation, Baba,' I said, 'is not easy. You make it sound as if it were easy.' 'Is sleep easy?' he asked. 'Yes,' I replied. 'But not for an insomniac,' he said. 'And meditation is easy, but you must gain that ease again.'

So I have decided to find that ease, and I have also decided that the bank of the Ganga is the place where I will find it.

Yesterday I met an old man in a boat who said that he had gone all

Postcard 4

the way along the Ganga from Gaumukh to Sagar, and it set up a yearning in my heart to do the same. Maybe I will even grow my hair long, renounce everything and take sannyaas. Sanaki Baba was quite interested in the fact that Baba (how confusing all these 'Babas' are) is a High Court Judge, but he said on another occasion during a sermon that even those who live in great mansions turn to dust in the end, in which even donkeys roll. It brought things home to me in every sense. Tapan will take care of Cuddles in my absence, and if not him, someone else will. I remember one of our school songs at Jheel School: Robi Babu's 'Akla Cholo Ré', which sounded absurd to me even then when it was shouted out by 400 voices. But now that I have decided to 'travel alone' myself, it has become a beacon to me, and I hum it all the time (though sometimes Pushpa tells me to stop).

Everything is so much at peace here, there is none of the acrimony that religion sometimes causes, well, such as we saw that evening of the lecture at the Ramakrishna Mission. I have been thinking lately of showing Pushpa my scribblings on various spiritual subjects. If you should meet Hemangini, please tell her to type out my jottings on the Void in triplicate; carbon copies stain one's fingers when one is reading them, and my handwriting is too much to ask Pushpa to read.

Postcard 5

One learns so much here every day, the horizons here are Infinite, and every day they expand. Over the whole of the Mela sands I can imagine the 'Pul' of pipal leaves, like a green rainbow spanning the Ganga from the ramp to the northern sands, carrying souls to the other side, and regenerating our polluted earth with its greenery. And when I bathe in the Ganga, which I do several times a day (don't tell Ila Kaki, she'll have a fit), then I feel a blessing flowing through my bones. Everyone chants, 'Gange cha, Yamune cha aiva', the mantra that Mrs Ganguly taught us to Ma's annoyance, and I too chant it with the best of them!

I remember, Amit Da, you once told me that the Ganga was a model for your novel, with its tributaries and distributaries and so on, but it now strikes me that the analogy is even more apt than you thought it at the time. For even if you now have to take on the additional burden of handling the family finances – since I won't be able to help you at all – and even if it takes you a few more years to complete your novel, you can still think of the new flow of your life as a Brahmaputra, travelling apparently in a different direction, but which will, by strange courses yet unseen to us, surely merge with the broad Ganga of your imagination. At least I hope so, Dada. Of course I know how much your writing means to you, but what is a novel after all compared to the Quest for the Source?

Postcard 6

Now I have filled up a whole stack of postcards, and I can't decide how to send them. Because if I post them separately at the post office here – they even have a Pul Mela post office! the administrative arrangements are quite amazing – they will arrive in random order, and I am afraid that will cause confusion. As it is, they look confusing with their mixture of Bengali and English, and my handwriting is worse than usual because I have nothing to rest the postcards on except my Sri Aurob- indo.

And I am afraid of causing you disquiet by the direc- tion I have decided to take, or, rather, have decided I cannot take. Please try to understand, Dada. Perhaps you can take over for a year or two at home, and then maybe I will come back and relieve you. But of course this may not be my final answer because I am learning new things every day. As Sanaki Baba says, 'Divyakar, this is a watershed in your life.' And you have no idea how charming Pushpa is when she says: 'The Vibrations of the true feelings will always reach the Point of Focus.' So perhaps, having written all this, I don't need to send it after all. Anyway, I'll decide about all this later in the day – or maybe it will be decided for me.

Peace and Love to all, and blessings from the Baba. Please reassure Ma that I am well.

Keep smiling!
Dipankar

11.13

DARKNESS had come over the sands. The city of tents shone with thousands of lights and cooking fires. Dipankar tried to persuade Pushpa to show him a little of the Mela.

'What do I know of all that world?' she insisted. 'This camp of Baba is my world. You go, Dipankar,' she said, almost tenderly. 'Go to the world – to the lights that attract and fascinate.'

This was a dramatic way of putting it, thought Dipankar. Anyway, it was his second night at the Pul Mela, and he wanted to see what it was like. He walked along, pushed here or there by the crowds, or pulled here or there by his curiosity or instinct. He passed a row of stalls – just about to close for the night – where handloom cloth, bangles, trinkets, vermilion powder, flossy candy, sweets, rations, and holy books were being sold. He passed groups of pilgrims lying down on their blankets and clothes or cooking their evening meal before smoky, improvised fires embedded in the sand. He saw a procession of five naked ash-smeared sadhus – carrying their tridents – wandering down to the Ganga to bathe. He joined a large crowd that was watching a religious play about the life of Krishna in a tent close to the handloom stalls. A lively white puppy rushed out at him from nowhere, and snapped playfully at his pyjamas; it wagged its tail and tried to bite his heel. While not vicious like Cuddles, it appeared to be equally persistent. The more Dipankar whirled around to avoid it, the more the puppy seemed to enjoy the game. Finally two sadhus, noticing what was going on, threw clods of sand at the puppy and it ran off.

The night was warm. The moon was a little over half full. Dipankar walked along, not quite knowing where he was going. He did not cross the Ganga, but wandered along the south bank for a long time.

Large areas of the Pul Mela sands were demarcated for various sects or orders of sadhus. Some of these large groups, known as akharas, were famous for their tightly knit, militant organization. It was sadhus from these akharas who formed the most striking part of the traditional procession that took place each year at the Pul Mela on the grand bathing day after the full moon. The various akharas vied with each other for proximity to the Ganga, for precedence in the procession, and in the splendour of their display. They sometimes became violent.

Dipankar chanced to wander through an open gate into the huge covered area that marked one such akhara. He felt a palpable sense of tension. But other people, clearly not sadhus themselves, were wandering in and out, and he decided to remain.

This was the akhara of a Shaivite order. The sadhus sat in groups at dull fires that stretched in a line deep into the smoky recesses of the akhara. Tridents were stuck into the ground beside them, sometimes wound around with garlands of marigolds, sometimes crowned with the small drum associated with Lord Shiva. The sadhus were smoking from clay pipes which they passed around from hand to hand, and the smell of marijuana was thick in the air. As Dipankar wandered deeper and deeper through the akhara, he suddenly stopped short. At the far end of the akhara, in a pall of the thickest smoke, several hundred young men, wearing nothing but short white loincloths, their heads shaven, sat around huge iron pots like bees around a row of hives. Dipankar did not know what was going on, but a sense of fear and awe seized him – as if he had come upon a rite of initiation, to view which meant danger to the curious outsider.

And indeed, before he could back away, a naked sadhu, his trident pointed straight at Dipankar's heart, said to him in a low voice:

'Go.'

'But I just –'

'Go.' The naked man pointed the trident towards the part of the akhara from which Dipankar had come.

Dipankar turned and almost ran. His legs seemed to have lost all their strength. Finally, he arrived near the entrance of the akhara. He was coughing – the smoke had caught at his throat. He bent over, and pressed his hands to his stomach.

Suddenly he was pushed to the ground by the thrust of a silver mace. A procession was going past, and he was an obstacle. He looked up to see a dazzling flash of silks and brocades and embroidered shoes. And it was gone.

He was not hurt so much as winded and bewildered. He looked around, still sitting on the rough matting that covered the sandy ground of the akhara. He became aware after a while of a group of five or six sadhus a few feet away. They were sitting around a small ashy fire and smoking ganja. From time to time they looked at him and laughed in high-pitched voices.

'I must go, I must go,' said Dipankar to himself in Bengali, getting up.

'No, no,' said the sadhus in Hindi.

'Yes,' said Dipankar. 'I must go. Om Namah Shivaya,' he added hurriedly.

'Put your right hand forward,' one of them ordered him.

Dipankar, tremblingly, did so.

The sadhu smeared a little ash on his forehead, and placed some in his palm. 'Now eat it,' he commanded.

Dipankar drew back.

'Eat it. Why are you blinking? If I were a tantrik, I would give you the flesh of dead man to eat. Or worse.'

The other sadhus giggled.

'Eat it,' commanded the sadhu, looking compellingly into his eyes. 'It is the prasad – the grace-offering – of Lord Shiva. It is his vibhuti.'

Dipankar swallowed the horrible powder and made a wry face. The sadhus thought this hilarious, and began to giggle once more.

One asked Dipankar: 'If it rained twelve months each year, why would the streams be dry?'

Another asked: 'If there were a ladder from heaven to earth, why would the earth be populated?'

A third asked: 'If there was a telephone from Gokul to Dwaraka, why would Radha be constantly fretting about Krishna?'

At this they all burst out laughing. Dipankar did not know what to say.

The fourth asked: 'If the Ganga is still flowing from the top-knot of Lord Shiva, what are we doing here in Brahmpur?'

This question made them forget about Dipankar, and he made his way out of the akhara, disturbed and perplexed.

Perhaps, he thought, it is a Question I am looking for, not an Answer.

But outside, the Mela was continuing just as it had been before. The crowds were pouring towards or back from the Ganga, the loudspeakers were announcing the lost and found, the sound of bhajans and shouts was interspersed with the whistles of trains arriving at the Pul Mela Railway Station, and the half moon was only a few degrees higher in the sky.

11.14

WHAT is so special about Ganga Dussehra?' asked Pran as they walked towards the pontoon bridge along the sand.

Old Mrs Tandon turned to Mrs Mahesh Kapoor. 'Does he really not know?' she asked.

Mrs Mahesh Kapoor said: 'I'm sure I told him once, but all this Angreziyat – this Englishness – has driven everything else out of his mind.'

'Even Bhaskar knows,' said old Mrs Tandon.

'That is because you tell him stories,' said Mrs Mahesh Kapoor.

'And because he listens,' said old Mrs Tandon. 'Most children take no interest.'

'Well?' said Pran with a smile, 'Is anyone going to enlighten me? Or is this another case of chicanery disguised as science?'

'Such words,' said his mother, hurt. 'Veena, don't walk so far ahead.'

Veena and Kedarnath stopped and waited for the others to catch up.

'It was the sage Jahnu, child,' said old Mrs Tandon mildly, turning towards him. 'When the Ganga came out of Jahnu's ear and fell to the ground, that day was Ganga Dussehra, and that is why it has been celebrated ever since.'

'But everyone says that it came out of Shiva's hair,' protested Pran.

'That was earlier,' explained old Mrs Tandon. 'Then it flooded Jahnu's sacrificial ground, and he drank it up in his anger. Finally he let it escape through his ear and it came to earth. That is why the Ganga is also called the

Jaahnavi, born of Jahnu.' Old Mrs Tandon smiled, imagining both the sage's anger and the eventual happy result.

'And,' she continued, a happy glow on her face, 'three or four days later, on the full-moon night of the month of Jeth, another sage who had been separated from his ashram went across on the pipal-pul, the bridge of pipal leaves. That is why that is the holiest bathing day of the Pul Mela.'

Mrs Mahesh Kapoor begged to differ. This Pul Mela legend, she believed, was pure fiction. Where in the Puranas or the Epics or the Vedas was any such thing mentioned?

'Everyone knows it is true,' said old Mrs Tandon.

They had reached the crowded pontoon bridge, and it was an effort to move, so dense were the crowds.

'But where is it written?' asked Mrs Mahesh Kapoor, gasping a little, but managing to remain emphatic. 'How can we tell that it is a fact? I don't believe it. That is why I never join the superstitious crowds who bathe on Jeth Purnima. It can only bring bad luck.'

Mrs Mahesh Kapoor had very definite views on festivals. She did not even believe in Rakhi, insisting that the festival that truly sanctified the bond between brother and sister was Bhai-Duj.

Old Mrs Tandon did not want to quarrel with her samdhin, especially in front of the family, and especially as they were crossing the Ganga, and she left it at that.

11.15

NORTH of the Ganga, across the crowded pontoon bridges, the crowds were sparser. There were fewer tents, and here and there the five of them walked across tracts of unsettled sand. The wind struck up and sand blew towards them as they struggled westward in the direction of the platform of Ramjap Baba.

They were part of a long line of other pilgrims who were bound for the same spot. Veena and the older women covered their faces with the pallus of their saris. Pran and

Kedarnath covered their mouths and noses with handkerchiefs. Luckily Pran's asthma did not cause him any immediate trouble, though there could have been no worse conditions imaginable. Finally the long trek took the company to the place where Ramjap Baba's thatched platform, raised high on stilts of wood and bamboo, ornamented with leaves and marigold garlands, and surrounded by a great throng of pilgrims, stood on the gently sloping northern sands about fifty yards from the present bank of the river. Here he would stay even when, in a few weeks, the platform would effectively become an island in the Ganga. He would spend his days doing nothing but reciting the name of God: 'Rama, Rama, Rama, Rama,' almost uninterruptedly throughout his waking hours, and often even in his sleep. This was the source of his popular name.

Because of his austerities and because of what people saw as his basic goodness, he had acquired great merit and power. People walked for miles in the sand, faith written in their eyes, to get a sight of him. They rowed out to him from July to September when the Ganga lapped at the stilts. They had done so for thirty years. Ramjap Baba always came to Brahmpur at the time of the Pul Mela, waited for the water to surround him, and left when it retreated beyond his platform about four months later. It was his own quadrimester or chatur-maas, even though it did not coincide in any strict sense with the traditional four-month sleep of the gods.

What people got from him was difficult to say. Sometimes he spoke to them, sometimes not, sometimes he blessed them, sometimes not. This thin man, as withered as a scarecrow, burned to the colour of dark tanned leather by the sun and the wind, gaunt, exhausted, squatted on his platform, his knees near his ears, his long head faintly visible over the ledge of the parapet. He had a white beard, matted black hair, and sunken eyes that stared almost sightlessly across the sea of people, as if they were so many grains of sand or drops of water.

The crowds of pilgrims – many of whom were clutching copies of the Shri Bhagvad Charit, a yellow-covered edition of which was on sale here – were held back by young volunteers, who were in turn controlled by the gestures of an older man. This man, who in some sense appeared to officiate over the proceedings, had thick spectacles, and looked like an academic. He had in fact been in government service for many years, but had left it in order to serve Ramjap Baba.

One scraggly arm of Ramjap Baba's frail frame rested on the parapet, and with it he blessed the people who were brought forward to receive his blessing. He whispered words to them in a weak voice. Sometimes he just stared ahead. The volunteers were holding the crowds back with difficulty. They were almost hoarse with shouting:

'Get back – get back – please only bring one copy of the book to be touched by Babaji –'

The old holy man touched it exhaustedly with the middle finger of his right hand.

'In order, please – in order – yes, I know you are a student of Brahmpur University with twenty-five companions – please wait your turn – sit down, sit down – get back, Mataji, please get back, don't make things difficult for us –'

Hands outstretched, tears in their eyes, the crowd surged forward. Some wanted to be blessed, some just to have closer darshan of Ramjap Baba, some to give offerings to him: bowls, bags, books, paper, grain, sweets, fruits, money.

'Put the prasad in this shallow basket – put the prasad in this basket,' said the volunteers. What the people had given would be blessed, and having been made sacred would be distributed among them again.

'Why is he so famous?' Pran asked a man standing next to him. He hoped he had not been overheard by his companions.

'I don't know,' said the man. 'But in his place and time he has done many things. He just is.' Then he tried to push himself forward once more.

'They say he takes Rama's name all day. Why does he do so?'

'Wood burns when rubbed and rubbed till it gives you the light you desire.'

While Pran pondered this answer, the thickly bespectacled man who was in charge of things came up to Mrs Mahesh Kapoor and did a very deep namasté.

'You have brought your presence here?' he said in surprise and with deep respect. 'And your husband?' Having been in government service, he knew Mrs Mahesh Kapoor by sight.

'He – well, he was detained by work. May we –?' asked Mrs Mahesh Kapoor shyly.

The man went to the platform, said a few words, and returned.

'Babaji said, it is kind of you to come.'

'But may we go forward?'

'I will ask.'

After a while he returned with three guavas and four bananas, which he gave Mrs Mahesh Kapoor.

'We want to be blessed,' she said.

'Oh, yes, yes, I'll see.'

Eventually they got to the front. They were introduced in turn to the holy man.

'Thank you, thank you –' whispered the haggard face through thin lips.

'Mrs Tandon –'

'Thank you, thank you –'

'Kedarnath Tandon and his wife Veena –'

'Aah?'

'Kedarnath Tandon and his wife.'

'Aah, thank you, thank you, Rama, Rama, Rama, Rama....'

'Babaji, this is Pran Kapoor, son of the Minister for Revenue, Mahesh Kapoor. And this is the Minister's wife.'

The Baba peered at Pran, and repeated tiredly:

'Thank you, thank you.'

He leaned a finger out and touched Pran on the forehead.

But before she could be hurried along, Mrs Mahesh Kapoor, in a beseeching voice, said:

'Baba, the boy is very ill – he has had asthma since he was a child. Now that you have touched him –'

'Thank you, thank you,' said the old wraith. 'Thank you, thank you.'

'Baba, will he be cured?'

The Baba pointed upwards to the sky with the finger that he had used to bless Pran with.

'And Baba, what about his work? I am so worried –'

The Baba leaned forward. The escort tried to plead with Mrs Mahesh Kapoor to give way.

'Work?' The voice was very soft. 'God's work?'

'No, Baba, he is looking for a position. Will he get it?'

'It will depend. Death will make all the difference.' It was almost as if the lips were opening and some other spirit speaking through the skeletal chest.

'A death? Whose, Baba, whose?' asked Mrs Mahesh Kapoor in sudden fear.

'The Lord – your Lord – the Lord of us all – he was – he thought he was –'

The strange, ambiguous words chilled her blood. If it should be her husband! In a panic-stricken voice, Mrs Mahesh Kapoor implored: 'Tell me, Baba, I pray you – will it be a death close to me?'

The Baba seemed to register the terror in the woman's voice; something that may have been compassion passed over the skin-stretched mask of his face. 'Even if so, it would not make a difference to you. ...' he said. The words appeared to cost him immense effort.

He was talking of her own death. That was what he must mean. She felt it in her bones. Her trembling lips could barely form the next question:

'Are you talking of my death?'

'No....'

Ramjap Baba closed his eyes. Relief and agitation struggled in Mrs Mahesh Kapoor's heart, and she moved forward. Behind her she could hear the voice whispering, 'Thank you, thank you.'

'Thank you, thank you,' it continued to whisper more and more faintly as she, her son, his sister, her husband,

and his mother – a chain of love and, consequently, of fear – moved slowly out of the crush onto the open sands.

11.16

SANAKI BABA, his eyes closed, was speaking.

'Om. Om. Om.

'Lord is ocean of the bliss, and I am his drop.

'Lord is ocean of love, and I am part and parcel of it.

'I am part and parcel of Lord.

'Inhale the bivrations through the nostrils.

'Inhale and exhale.

'Om alokam, Om anandam.

'The Lord is in you and you are part of Lord.

'Inhale the environment and divine master.

'Exhale the bad feelings.

'Feel, do not think.

'Do not feel or think.

'This body is not yours ... this mind is not yours ... this intellect is not yours.

'Christ, Muhammad, Buddha, Rama, Krishna, Shiva: mantra is anjapa jaap, the Lord is no any name.

'Music is unheard bivrations. Let music open the centres like lovely lotus flower.

'You must not swim, you must flow.

'Or float like lotus flower.

'OK.'

It was over. Sanaki Baba closed his mouth and opened his eyes. Slowly and reluctantly the meditators returned to the world they had left. Outside, the rain poured down. For twenty minutes they had found peace and oneness in a world far from strife and striving. Dipankar felt that everyone who had shared in the meditation must feel a warmth, an affection for all the others. He was all the more shocked by what followed.

The session was barely over when the Professor said: 'Can I ask a question?'

'Why not?' said Sanaki Baba dreamily.

The Professor cleared his throat. 'This question is addressed to Madam,' he said, stressing the word 'Madam' in a manner that implied an open challenge. 'In the inhalation and exhalation that you talked about, is the effect due to oxidation or meditation?'

Someone at the back said: 'Speak in Hindi.' The Professor repeated his question in Hindi.

But it was a curious question, which was either unamenable to any answer – or which could only be answered by a bewildered, 'Both.' For there was no either/or, no necessary contradiction in the two possibilities of oxidation and meditation, whatever they might mean. Clearly the Professor believed that the woman who had usurped too much power and closeness to Babaji needed to be put in her place, and that a question like this would show up both her ignorance and her pretensions.

Pushpa went and stood to the right of Sanaki Baba. He had closed his eyes again, and was smiling beatifically. Indeed, he continued to smile beatifically through the entire exchange that followed.

Everyone's eyes other than Baba's were on Pushpa. She reverted to English and spoke with spirit, and with cold anger:

'Let me make it quite clear that quastions here are not addrassed to "Madam" or anyone else but to the Master. If we give teachings here it is in his voice, and we translate or speak because of his vibrations speaking through us. The "Madam" knows nothing. So quastions should be addrassed to the Master. That is all.'

Dipankar was transfixed by the severity of her response. He looked at the Baba to see what he would say. The Baba's eyes were still closed in a smile, and he did not alter his stance of meditation. Now he opened his eyes and said:

'It is as Pushpa says, and I ask her to speak with my bivrations.'

At the word 'bivrations' there was a flash of lightning outside, followed by a clap of thunder.

The master had forced Pushpa to answer the question. She covered her face with a cloth from distress and embarrassment.

Then she spoke with anger and sincerity and embattled defensiveness.

Looking straight at the Professor, she said:

'One thing is a must to say, and that is that we are all sadhikas, we are all learning, no matter how aged, and we must only ask the quastion which is ralevant, not any quastion for sake of quastion only, or to hold an examination of "Madam" or Master or anyone. If you are truly troubled by a quastion then you can ask it – if otherwise, then you will not get grace from the guru. So I should make that clear, and now I will answer the quastion. Because I can tell that we will have more quastion and answer sassion, and I must make all that clear from the beginning –'

Here the Professor attempted to interrupt, but she shot him down.

'Let me speak and finish. I am answering Professor Sahib's quastion, whatever spirit it is asked in, then why should the Professor Sahib interrupt? Now I am not a scientist of oxidation ... oxidation is natural, but it is always there. But what is happening? You may be seeing or hearing, but word or picture as such: what is that? What is effect? It can be different. If you see obscene picture, that will have one effect on you, a strong effact' – she screwed up her nose and closed her eyes in distaste – 'and a beautiful picture, different. So, music also. Bhajan music is music, film music also is music, but in one you have certain effact; in other, other. In smell also. It may be burning, but incense burning has wonderful smell, and shoes burning has tarrible smell. Or take prosassions of akharas tomorrow: some are in good spirit, some are fighting. It depends what. And sankirtan also, like this evening: you can have sankirtan with good people, or with bad people.' This was said very pointedly. 'That is why Saint Chaitanya only had sankirtans with good people.

'So let me tell the Professor Sahib, it is not a quastion "Is it maditation? Is it oxidation?" The real quastion is: "What is your dastination? Where do you want to go?"'

Now Sanaki Baba opened his eyes and began to speak. The rain was loud, and his voice was soft, but it was not difficult to hear him. The guru's words were calm and soothing, even as they sought to make distinctions and point out errors. But Pushpa shook her head from left to right as her Master spoke, gleefully smiling as he made his telling points, points which she took to be directed against the 'defeated' Professor. It was all so unloving, possessive and defensive that Dipankar could hardly stand it. The violent revulsion of feeling he was undergoing made him see this beautiful woman in a completely different light. She was gloating over her rival's discomfiture in a way that almost made him sick.

11.17

THE wind' was now whistling down the alleys of Old Brahmpur and shaking the pipal tree on the ramp with all its force. The pilgrims who were making their way down were wet through by the time they reached the foot of the Fort. Rain was running down the steps of the ghats, merging with the surface of the Ganga, and gouging out channels in the Pul Mela sands. The face of the moon was almost hidden. Above, clouds scurried confusedly across the sky. Below, men and women scurried confusedly around on the ground – trying to protect their belongings; hammering their tent-pegs more firmly into the sand; and tottering through the lashing rain and howling sand-laden wind towards the Ganga to bathe, for the most auspicious bathing-time – which would last fifteen hours, until about three the next afternoon – had just begun.

The storm was violent enough to blow a few tents away on the Pul Mela sands, and – in the old town above – to flood a few alleys, shake tiles off some roofs, and even uproot a small pipal tree that stood more than a hundred yards away from the ramp that led down to the sands. But these events were soon magnified by darkness and fear.

'The great pipal tree has come down,' cried someone in dismay. And though it was not true, the rumour spread like the erratic wind itself through the crowds of awe-struck pilgrims. They looked at each other and wondered what it all could mean. For if the great pipal tree that stood by the ramp had indeed fallen, what would become of the bridge of leaves, of the Pul Mela itself, or indeed of the very order of things?

11.18

HALFWAY through the night the storm ceased. The clouds disappeared, the full moon reappeared. The pilgrims bathed in their hundreds of thousands through the night and into the next day.

In the morning the processions of the great akharas began. The sadhus of each order in turn paraded down the main road of the Mela, which ran parallel to the river but a couple of hundred yards up the sands. The display was magnificent: floats, bands, men on horseback, mahants carried on palanquins, banners, flags, drums, whisks, naked nagas bearing fire-tongs or tridents, a huge, barbaric man who yelled holy verses as he brandished a great sword from side to side. Great crowds gathered to gaze at the spectacle and cheer the sadhus on. Hawkers sold flutes, false hair, holy thread, bangles, earrings, balloons, and snacks – peanuts and chana-jor-garam and rapidly melting ice-cream. Policemen on foot – or mounted on horses and in one case on a camel – maintained order. The processions were staggered to avoid confusion – or conflict between one sect of sadhus and another. Since the sadhus were as militant as they were arrogant and competitive, the authori-ties of the Pul Mela had taken pains to ensure that at least fifteen minutes elapsed between one procession and the next. At the end of their march, the sadhus of each procession took a sharp left turn and made straight for the Ganga, where – to shouts of 'Jai Ganga!' and 'Ganga Maiya ki Jai!' – they took an enthusiastic and rowdy communal dip. Then they returned by another, narrower parallel road to their camps, satisfied that no akhara could be more magnificent or pious than theirs.

The great pipal tree above the broad earthen ramp was, as anyone could now see, intact, and would probably continue to flourish for a few hundred years more. It had not, unlike some lesser trees, been uprooted by the storm. The pilgrims continued to arrive in droves at the Pul Mela Railway Station; they passed by the tree, folded their hands in respect and prayer, and began to make the journey down the ramp to the sands and the Ganga. But today, from time to time, whenever a procession passed along the main Mela route by the foot of the ramp, there was a slight obstruction to the cross-traffic and some congestion on the ramp itself. However, it was all taken in good spirit, especially since the ramp provided to many who stood on it a general view of the processions below – and for those pilgrims who had just arrived on this auspicious day, a first view of the whole tent-covered expanse and the holy river beyond.

Veena Tandon and her friend Priya Goyal, together with a few members of their immediate families, were among the crowds looking downwards from the ramp. Old Mrs Tandon was there, and so was her grandson Bhaskar, who was very eager to see and count and estimate and calculate and enjoy everything. Priya had managed to escape specifically for this holy purpose from her virtual confinement in the joint family home in Old Brahmpur. Her sisters-in-law and mother-in-law had made a fuss, but her husband, in his mild way, had convinced them on religious grounds; in fact, when her friend Veena had come to fetch her, she had persuaded him to come along as well. As for the men of Veena's own family, none of them were present: Kedarnath was out of town on work, Maan was still in Rudhia, Pran had refused to subject himself to ignorance and superstition yet again, and Mahesh Kapoor had snorted in his most dismissive manner when his daughter brought up the suggestion that he accompany them. Today, in fact, even Mrs Mahesh Kapoor was not with them. She could not bring herself to believe in the scripturally unsanctioned myth of the pipal bridge which was supposed to have spanned the Ganga on this particular day. Jahnu's ear was one thing, the pipal bridge another.

Veena and Priya chatted away like schoolgirls. They discussed their schooldays, their old friends, their families sotto voce whenever Priya's husband appeared not to be listening (including him and his tendency to be more vocal asleep than awake), the sights of the Mela, the most recent antics of the monkeys of Shahi Darvaza. They were dressed up as gaudily as taste permitted, Veena in red and Priya in green. Although Priya planned, like everyone else, to bathe in the Ganga, she wore a thick gold necklace with a design of little buds – for if a daughter-in-law of the Rai Bahadur's house had to be seen out of doors, she could not be seen in unbejewelled nakedness. Her husband, Prem Vilas Goyal, carried Bhaskar on his back to give him a better view. Whenever Bhaskar had any questions, he asked his grandmother to explain things to him, and old Mrs Tandon, though she could not see too well – owing to both her height and her sight – was only too happy to do so. All of them, and everyone around them, was in high spirits. They were surrounded mainly by townspeople and peasants, though here and there a policeman could be seen, or even a sadhu who was not involved in the processions.

It was about ten in the morning, and, despite the previous night's storm, very hot. Some of the pilgrims carried umbrellas to protect themselves from the sun – or possible rain. For the same reason – and because it was a symbol of authority – the more important among the sadhus in the various processions were protected with parasols by their devotees.

The blaring announcements on the loudspeaker continued endlessly, as did the sound of drums and trumpets, and the alternating murmur and roar of the crowd. The processions continued, wave on wave: yellow-clad priests with orange turbans, announced by tubas and conches; a palanquin carrying a sleepy old man who looked like a stuffed partridge, preceded by a red velvet banner announcing that he was *Sri 108 Swami Prabhananda Ji Maharaj, Vedantacharya*, M.A.; semi-nude nagas, with a string tied around their waists and a small white pouch for their genitals; long-haired men carrying silver maces; bands of all kinds, one with black tunics and epaulettes of gold braid blaring tunelessly on clarinets, another (the *Diwana 786* band – obviously Muslim from the lucky number that it had adopted – but why had they been hired for this procession?) with red tunics and piercing oboes. One horse-drawn chariot had a fierce, toothless man on it, who shouted 'Har, har ...' at the crowd, to evoke the roared response '... Mahadeva!' Another mahant, fat and dark and with breasts as plump as a woman's, seated benignly on a man-drawn cart, was flinging marigold flowers at the pilgrims, who scrambled for them where they fell on the moist sand.

By now Veena and her party had got halfway down the broad ramp, which was crowded with pilgrims, almost fifty abreast. They were all being pushed forward continuously by the pressure of the pilgrims behind them who were coming from the town or countryside around, or continuing to arrive on the special Pul Mela shuttle-trains. Since there were deep ditches to either side of the ramp, there was nowhere to go but forward. Unfortunately, the current procession of sadhus that blocked their path was advancing more sluggishly than before, probably owing to some obstruction ahead – or possibly in order to prolong their own enjoyment of their popularity with the spectators. People began to get alarmed. Old Mrs Tandon suggested that they try to go back, but this was clearly impossible. Finally the procession moved on, a welcome gap appeared before the next procession, and the crowds on the ramp surged and stumbled forward across the main route into the mass of spectators who lined the other side of the route. The police managed to restore order, and in a few minutes Bhaskar, from Ram Vilas's shoulders, was able to watch the next procession: several hundred naga ascetics, completely nude, led by six and followed by six huge gold-caparisoned elephants.

Bhaskar and his family were still on the ramp, though now only about twenty feet from its base. They had a closer view of things, and with the release of the people in front of them the crush had eased a little. Bhaskar viewed with absolute astonishment the ash-smeared naked men, decrepit or sturdy, their hair matted, marigold flowers hanging from their ears or around their necks. Their grey penises, flaccid or semi-flaccid, hung down and swung to and fro as they marched past, four to a row, tridents or spears held high in their right hands. He was too astonished to ask his grandmother what all this was about. But a great cheer, almost a roar, rose from the crowd, and several women, young and middle-aged, rushed forward to touch the feet of the nagas, and to gather the dust on which they had trod.

The nagas, however, would not have their formation disturbed. They turned on them fiercely, brandishing their tridents. The police tried to reason with the women, but to no effect. This went on for a while, some women managing to elude the few policemen posted at the foot of the ramp and succeeding in prostrating themselves for an instant before the holy men. Then, suddenly, the procession stopped.

No one knew why. Everyone expected it to start up again in a minute or two. But it did not. The nagas began to get impatient. Once more the pressure on the ramp began to build, as the arriving crowds were pushed forward, and pushed forward others in their turn. The people who were at the base of the ramp now found themselves crushed by the weight of numbers behind them. A man pressed himself into Veena and, indignant, she tried to turn around. But there was no room. It was becoming difficult to breathe. People all around her were beginning to shout. Some yelled at the police to let them through, others shouted up the ramp to find out what was going on. But though the view was wider, the situation was not much clearer to people higher up on the ramp. They could see that the elephants that led the nagas had stopped because the procession in front of them had halted. But why that earlier procession had stopped was impossible to tell. At that distance, processions and spectators merged into one, and nothing was clear. Replies were shouted down the ramp, but in the shouts of the crowd, the sounds of the drums, and the continuous announcements on the loudspeakers, even these were lost.

Completely bewildered, the crowd on the lower reaches of the ramp began to panic. And when in a few minutes those above them saw that the next procession of sadhus had arrived and now formed a continuous barrier below the ramp, with no gap to come, they began to panic as well. The heat, terrible before, was now stifling. The police themselves got swallowed up in the crowd that they were trying to control. And still the tired, heat-battered, but enthusiastic pilgrims kept arriving at the station, and – ignorant of what was happening below – pushed eagerly forward towards the pipal tree and the ramp in order to get to the holy Ganga.

Veena saw Priya clutch the necklace round her neck. Her mouth was open and she was gasping. Bhaskar looked at his mother and grandmother. He could not grasp what was happening, but he was terribly frightened. Ram Vilas, seeing that Priya was being crushed, tried to move towards her, and Bhaskar toppled off his back. Veena managed to get hold of the boy. But old Mrs Tandon was nowhere to be seen – the crowd had swallowed her up in its helpless and irresistible movement. People were screaming now, clutching at each other and stepping on each other, trying to find their husbands and wives, their parents and children, or flailing around for their own survival, desperate to breathe and to avoid being crushed. Some pressed forward into the nagas, who, fearing to be crushed between them and the spectators on the other side, laid into them with their tridents, roaring with anger. People fell, blood pouring from their wounds, onto the ground. At the sight of blood, the crowd reacted with terror, and tried to turn back. But there was nowhere to go.

Some people at the edges of the ramp tried to slip through the bamboo barricades and scramble down to the ditches on either side. But last night's storm had made these steep slopes slippery, and the ditches themselves were filled with water. About a hundred beggars were sheltering by the side of one of the ditches. Many of them were cripples, some were blind. The injured pilgrims, gasping for breath and clawing for a foothold on the slope, now came tumbling down onto them. Some of the beggars were crushed to death, and some tried to flee into the water, which soon turned to a bloodied slush as more of those who were trapped on the ramp sought this, their only route of escape, and fell or slid onto the screaming people below.

At the foot of the ramp, where Veena and her family were trapped, people were maimed or dying. Many of the old and infirm fell to the ground. Some of them, exhausted by the long journey, had little strength to withstand the shock or the pressure of the crowd. A student, unable to move, watched helplessly nearby as his mother was trampled to death and his father's ribs crushed. Many people were literally squeezed to death against each other. Some were suffocated, some succumbed to injuries. Veena saw one old woman, blood pouring out of her mouth, suddenly collapse near her.

There was complete and dreadful chaos.

'Bhaskar – Bhaskar – don't let go of my hand,' cried Veena, clutching him tightly. She had to gasp out every word. But they were thrust to and fro by the great terrified injured mass all around them, and she could feel the weight of someone's body force itself between her hand and his.

'No – no –' she screamed, sobbing with dread. But she felt the small hand slip, palm first, and then digit by digit, out of her own.

WITHIN fifteen minutes more than a thousand people were dead.

Finally the police managed to communicate with the railway authorities and stop the trains. They set up barriers on the approach routes to the ramp, and cleared the area below and around the ramp. The loudspeakers started telling people to go back, not to enter the Mela grounds, not to watch the processions. They announced that the remaining processions themselves had been cancelled.

It was still not clear what had happened.

Dipankar had been among the spectators on the other side of the main route. He watched with horror the carnage that was taking place less than fifty feet away but – with the nagas between him and the ramp – there was nothing he could do. Anyway, there was nothing he could have done except get killed or injured. He did not recognize anyone on the ramp, so tightly packed was the crowd. It was a hellish scene, like humanity gone mad, each element indistinguishable from the other, all bent on a kind of collective suicide.

He saw one of the younger nagas stab furiously at a man, an old man who had in his terror tried to force his way to safety on the other side of the procession. The man fell, then rose again. Blood was streaming from wounds on his shoulder and back. With horror, Dipankar recognized him as the man whom he had met in the boat, the hardy old pilgrim from Salimpur who had been so insistent upon the correct spot for bathing. The man tried to struggle back, but was flung down by the crowd as it surged forward again. His back and his head were crushed by the trampling feet. When the crowd next surged back at the point of the tridents, the mangled body of the old man remained, like a piece of debris washed up by the tide.

11.20

MEANWHILE, a number of VIPs and army officers, who had been watching the great spectacle of the processions from the ramparts of the Brahmpur Fort looked down in disbelief at the scene far below them. The panic began so suddenly, and the whole thing was over so quickly, that the number of motionless bodies lying on the ground when the terrified mob had finally been able to ooze away was unbelievable. What had happened? What arrangements had gone wrong? Who was to blame?

The Fort Commander, without waiting for a formal request, immediately sent troops down to help the police and the Mela officers. They began to clear bodies away, to take the injured to the first aid centres and the corpses to the Pul Mela Police Station. He also suggested immediately setting up a central control room to deal with the aftermath of the disaster. The temporary telephone exchange that had been set up for the Mela was taken over for this purpose.

Those VIPs who had wanted to bathe on this auspicious day were on a launch in the middle of the Ganga when the captain came up to them in great agitation. The Chief Minister and Home Minister were standing side by side. The captain, holding out a pair of binoculars, said to the Chief Minister: 'Sir – I fear there is some trouble on the ingress ramp. You might wish to take a look for yourself.' S.S. Sharma took the binoculars wordlessly and refocused them. What had looked like a slight perturbation from a distance suddenly came alive to him in all its horrifying actuality. His mouth opened, he closed his eyes in distress, and opened them again to scan the upper reaches of the ramp, then the ditches on either side, the nagas, the embattled police. He handed the binoculars to L.N. Agarwal with the single word: 'Agarwal!'

The Home Minister's first thought was that in the ultimate analysis he might be held responsible for this calamity. Perhaps it is unjust to consider this thought atypically unworthy. Even in the worst calamities of others, some part of our mind, often the one that is quickest to respond, tries to brace itself for the vibration that will reach us from the epicentre. 'But the arrangements were perfect – I went over them with the Mela officer myself –' the Home Minister was about to say, but a second thought stopped him in his tracks.

Priya. Where was Priya? She had planned to go to the Mela today with Mahesh Kapoor's daughter – to watch the procession, to bathe. Surely she was all right. Surely nothing could have happened to her. Torn between love for her and fear of what might have happened, he could not say a word. He handed the binoculars back to the Chief Minister. The Chief Minister was saying something to him, but he could not understand what he was saying. He could not follow the words. He hid his head in his hands.

After a while, the fog in his mind thinned out, and he told himself that there were millions of people at the Mela today, and that the chances, the real chances, of her being one of the unfortunate people caught in the stampede, were very small. But he was still sick with worry for his only child. May nothing have happened to her, he said to himself. O God, may nothing have happened to her.

The Chief Minister continued to look grim, and speak grimly to him. But apart from the sharp tone, the Home Minister caught nothing, understood nothing. After a while he looked at the Ganga. A few rose-petals and a coconut were floating on the water near the launch. Pressing his hands together he began to pray to the holy river.

11.21

BECAUSE the launch needed a deeper draught than a regular boat, it was difficult to land it on the shallow bank of the Ganga. The captain finally resorted to the expedient of mooring it to a chain of boats, which he in effect commandeered. By the time the launch was moored, more than three-quarters of an hour had passed. The crowds at the main bathing areas on the Brahmpur side had thinned to almost nothing. The news of the disaster had spread swiftly. The bathing posts with their colourful signs – parrot, peacock, bear, scissors, mountain, trident and so on – were almost deserted. A few people, in a restrained, almost fearful way, were still dipping themselves in the river and hurrying away.

The Chief Minister, limping slightly, and the Home Minister, almost trembling with anxiety, accompanied by the few officials who had been with them on the boat, got to the area at the foot of the ramp. The scene was an eerie one. A large stretch of sand was entirely empty of people. There was nothing there: no people, not even bodies – just shoes, slippers, umbrellas, food, pieces of paper, clothes torn to shreds, bags, utensils, belongings of all kinds. Crows were pecking at the food. Here and there one could see patches where the damp sand had been stained darker, but there was nothing to indicate the terrible extent of the calamity.

The Fort Commander presented his compliments. So did the Mela Officer, an ICS man. The press had been fended off after a fashion.

'Where are the dead?' said the Chief Minister. 'You have shifted them rather quickly.'

'At the police station.'

'Which one?'

'The Pul Mela Police Station, Sir.'

The Chief Minister's head was shaking slightly – as it sometimes did when he was tired, but not for that reason now.

'We will go there immediately. Agarwal, this –' The Chief Minister pointed at the scene, then shook his head, and did not continue.

L.N. Agarwal, who could think of nothing but Priya, pulled himself together with an effort. He thought of his great hero, Sardar Vallabhbhai Patel, who had died less than a year ago. It was said that Patel had been in court, at a crucial stage in his defence of a client against a charge of murder, when the news of his wife's death had been brought to him. He had controlled his sorrow and continued with his argument. Only when the court rose did he allow himself to mourn the already dead without risk to the still living. This was a man who knew the meaning of duty, and its precedence over private grief.

> Wherever his faltering mind
> unsteadily wanders,
> he should restrain it
> and bring it under self-control.

The words of Krishna in the Bhagavad Gita came to L.N. Agarwal's mind. But they were followed immediately by Arjuna's more human cry:

> Krishna, the mind is faltering,
> violent, strong, and stubborn;
> I find it as difficult
> to hold as the wind.

On the way to the police station, the Home Minister apprised himself of the situation as well as he could.

'What about the injured?' he asked.

'They have been taken to the first aid centres, Sir.'

'How many injured are there?'

'I do not know, Sir, but judging from the number of the dead –'

'The facilities are inadequate. The seriously injured must be taken to hospital.'

'Sir.' But the officer knew it was impossible. He decided to risk the Minister's wrath. 'But how, Sir, can we do that when the exit ramp is full of departing pilgrims? We are trying to encourage everyone to leave as soon as possible.'

L.N. Agarwal turned on him caustically. So far he had not uttered one word of recrimination to the officer who had been in charge of the arrangements. He had wanted to ascertain where responsibility lay before he relieved his spleen. But now he said:

'Do you people ever use your brains? I am not thinking of the exit ramp. The ingress ramp is deserted, cordoned off. Use it to get vehicles in and out. It is broad enough. Use the area of the road at the base of the ramp as a car-park. And requisition every vehicle within the radius of a mile from the pipal tree.'

'Sir, requisition – ?'

'Yes. You heard me. I'll put it in writing in due course. Now give orders so that this is done immediately. And warn the hospitals of what to expect.'

'Yes, Sir.'

'Also get in touch with the university and the law college and the medical college. We will need all the volunteers we can get for the next few days.'

'But they are on vacation, Sir.' Then, catching L.N. Agarwal's look: 'Yes, Sir, I shall see what I can do.' The Mela Officer was about to leave.

'And while you are doing so,' added the Chief Minister, in a milder tone than his colleague, 'get the IG of Police and the Chief Secretary.'

The police station presented a painful sight.

The dead were laid out in rows for identification. There was nowhere to keep them but in the sun. Many of the bodies were horribly distorted, many of the faces crushed. Some of the dead looked merely asleep, but did not brush away the swarms of flies that settled thickly and filthily on their faces and their wounds. The heat was terrible. Sobbing men and women were moving from body to body, looking for their loved ones among the long lines of corpses. Two men were embracing tearfully nearby. They were brothers who had been separated in the crush, and each had come here fearing that the other might be dead. Another man was embracing the body of his dead wife and shaking both her hands almost in anger as if he hoped that this would somehow rouse her to life again.

'WHERE is the phone?' said L.N. Agarwal.

'Sir, I will bring it to you,' said a police officer.

'I'll make the call inside,' said L.N. Agarwal.

'But, Sir, here it is already,' said the obliging officer; a telephone on a long lead had been brought out.

The Home Minister called his son-in-law's house. At the news that his daughter and son-in-law had both gone to the Mela – and that they had not been heard from since – he said:

'And the children?'

'They are both at home.'

'Thank God. If you hear from them, you must call me at once at the police station. I will get the message wherever I am. Tell the Rai Bahadur not to worry. No, on second thoughts, if the Rai Bahadur doesn't know what has happened, don't tell him anything at all.' But L.N. Agarwal, who knew how news travelled, was sure that all Brahmpur – indeed, half of India – had probably heard the news of the disaster already.

The Chief Minister nodded at the Home Minister, a note of sympathy entering his voice: 'Ah, Agarwal, I didn't realize –'

L.N. Agarwal's eyes filled with tears, but he said nothing.

After a while he said: 'Has the press been here?'

'Not here, Sir. They were taking photographs of the dead at the site itself.'

'Get them here. Ask them to be cooperative. And get any photographers on the government payrolls here as well. Where are the police photographers? I want all these bodies photographed carefully. Each one of them.'

'But, Sir!'

'These bodies have begun to stink. Soon they will become a source of disease. Let relatives claim their own dead and take them away. The rest must be cremated tomorrow. Arrange a site for cremation on the bank of the Ganga with the help of the Mela authorities. We must have photographs of all the dead who have not yet been identified either by their relatives or by other means of identification.'

The Home Minister walked up and down the lines of the dead, fearing the worst. At the end he said: 'Are there any more dead?'

'Sir, they are still coming in. Mainly from the first aid centres.'

'And where are the first aid centres?' L.N. Agarwal still could not control the agitation in his heart.

'Sir, there are several, some quite far away. But the camp for lost and injured children is just over there.'

The Home Minister knew his own grandchildren were safe. He wanted above all to scour the first aid centres, where the injured were lying, before they began to be dispersed – by his own instructions – through the hospitals of the city. But something struggled in his heart, and he sighed and said: 'Yes, I'll go there first.'

The Chief Minister, S.S. Sharma, had begun to suffer from the heat, and was forced to return. The Home Minister went on to the compound where the children were being temporarily housed. It was chiefly their names that were being announced in the raucous and melancholy messages that the loudspeakers were now broadcasting continuously over the sands. 'Ram Ratan Yadav of Village Makarganj in District Ballia in Uttar Pradesh, a child of about six years old, is waiting for his parents in the lost children compound near the police station. Kindly come to collect him there.' But many children – and the ones here ranged from three months to ten years in age – did not know their names or the names of their villages; and the parents of some of the children, who were whimpering or weeping or just sleeping from shock and exhaustion, were themselves lying stilled in death in the nearby police enclosure.

Women volunteers were feeding the children and giving them what comfort they could. They had compiled lists of those who had been found – incomplete as such lists necessarily were – and transmitted them to the central control room, so that they could be matched with a state-wise list of the missing that was being compiled there. But it was clear to the Home Minister that the foundling children would, like the dead, have to be photographed if they were not claimed soon.

'Take a message to the police station —' he began. And then his heart almost stopped for joy and relief as he heard his daughter's voice say: 'Papa.'

'Priya.' The name, which meant 'beloved' was never truer than now. He looked at her, and began to weep. Then he embraced her and asked, noticing her sad face:

'Where is Vakil Sahib? Is he all right?'

'Yes, Papa, he's over there.' She pointed to the far end of the compound. 'But we can't find Veena's child. That's why we're here.'

'Have you checked at the police station? I didn't look at the children there.'

'Yes, Papa.'

'And?'

'No.'

After a pause she said:

'Do you want to talk to Veena? She and her mother-in-law are frantic with worry. Veena's husband is not even in town.'

'No. No.' L.N. Agarwal, after fearing he had lost his child, could not bear to face someone else in the same anguish.

'Papa —'

'All right. Give me a minute or two.'

In the end he went over to Mahesh Kapoor's daughter, and said what words of comfort and practicality he could. If Bhaskar had not been found so far at the police station the chances were good, etc. ... But even as he spoke he heard how hollow his words must sound to the mother and the grandmother. He told them that he would go around to the first aid centres and phone up Bhaskar's grandfather at Prem Nivas if there was any news, either good or bad; they too should phone in periodically to check.

But at none of the first aid centres was there any sign of the little frog, and as hour followed hour, Veena and old Mrs Tandon, and soon Mr and Mrs Mahesh Kapoor, and Pran and Savita, and of course Priya and Ram Vilas Goyal (who even began to feel themselves responsible for what had happened), sank into a deeper and deeper sense of hopelessness and desperation.

11.23

MAHESH KAPOOR, while sympathizing with Priya and reassuring her that she should not be so foolish as to hold herself responsible for what was beyond anyone's control, did not tell her where he placed the responsiblity: squarely on her father's shoulders. He was the Home Minister. It had been his duty to ensure that the arrangements were not susceptible to this horrendous eventuality. At least once before, in the firing at Chowk, L.N. Agarwal had shown either lack of personal foresight or unwise confidence in delegating authority to others who lacked it. Mahesh Kapoor, although he usually had very little time for his family, loved his only grandchild greatly, and was distressed beyond measure for his wife and his daughter.

Everyone stayed over at Prem Nivas that night. Kedarnath could not be contacted; he was out of town. Trunk calls were difficult to make, and he was not in Kanpur, where they had thought he might be on business. Maan, who was so fond of Bhaskar, was in Debaria still. Veena and old Mrs Tandon first went home in the flickering hope that Bhaskar might have gone back there. But no one in their neighbourhood had seen Bhaskar. They themselves had no telephone, and to spend the night alone at home would be unbearable. Their rooftop neighbour of the red sari reassured them that she would get in touch with the Minister Sahib's house if they had any news. And so they made their way back to Prem Nivas, Veena in her heart bitterly upbraiding Kedarnath for being, as he so often was, out of Brahmpur.

Like my father when I was born, she thought.

By then Pran and Savita were at Prem Nivas as well. Pran knew he would have to be with his parents and sister, but he was afraid of distressing his wife unduly in her present condition. If her mother or sister had returned from their travels, he would have felt no qualms about leaving her in their care and staying over at Prem Nivas himself. But Mrs Rupa Mehra's last letter had been from Delhi, and she was at this moment either in Kanpur or in Lucknow, far from where she could be of use.

That night the family discussed what could be done. No one could sleep. Mrs Mahesh Kapoor prayed. There was very little that had not already been attempted. All the hospitals of Brahmpur had been searched for Bhaskar, following the conjecture that he had been injured and taken there directly by some helpful person. So had all the police stations – but to no avail.

They were all certain that Bhaskar, intelligent and (usually) self-possessed as he was, would have either gone back home or contacted his grandparents if he had been able to. Had his body been misidentified and taken away for cremation by others? Had he been kidnapped in the confusion? As all the plausible possibilities disappeared one by one in the face of the facts, unlikely imaginings took on a credibility of their own.

No one could sleep that night. As disturbing as their own grief and anxiety was the sound of revelry that echoed through the darkness. For it was the month of Ramazan, the Muslim month of fasting. Because of the purely lunar Muslim calendar, the month of Ramazan had staggered its way back to summer over the last few years. The days were long and hot, and the deprivation great – since strict Muslims were enjoined even from drinking water during the daylight hours. After sunset, the relief therefore was the greater – and the nights were given over to feasting and celebration.

The Nawab Sahib, strict observant though he himself was, had, upon hearing of the calamity at the Pul Mela, forbidden any celebration in his own household. He was even more distressed when he heard that his friend's grandson could not be traced. But such fellow-feeling was not general, or at least not universal, and the sound of Muslim celebration in a town where the news of the disaster had spread like fire, and must be known to everyone, was embittering even to a man like Mahesh Kapoor.

The phone rang from time to time, exciting their hope and fear. But they were messages of sympathy – or intimations from one official source or another that nothing had come up – or else calls that had nothing to do with Bhaskar at all.

11.24

THE afternoon before, on the instructions of the Home Minister, a number of cars had been requisitioned in order to ferry the wounded to hospital. One of these cars was the Buick of Dr Kishen Chand Seth.

Dr Seth had decided to see a movie that afternoon, and his car was parked outside a cinema-hall, the Rialto. When he emerged, sobbing with sentiment, supported by his hardboiled young wife Parvati, he found two policemen leaning on his car.

Dr Kishen Chand Seth immediately flew into a rage. He raised his cane threateningly, and if Parvati had not restrained him, he would certainly have used it. The policemen, who knew Dr Seth's reputation, were very apologetic.

'We have orders to requisition this car, Sir,' they said.

'You – what?' spluttered Dr Seth. 'Get out, get out, get out of my sight before I –' He was at a loss for words. Nothing seemed severe enough retribution for their gall.

'Because of the Pul Mela –'

'All superstition, all superstition!' said Dr Kishen Chand Seth. 'Let me go at once.' He took out his key.

The Sub-Inspector apologetically took it from his hand in an unexpected and skilful movement. Dr Kishen Chand Seth almost had a heart attack.

'You – you dare –' he gasped. 'Teutonic frightfulness –' he added in English. This was worse than bayoneting babies.

'Sir, there has been a disaster at the Pul Mela, and we –'

'What nonsense! Had there been any such thing, I would certainly have heard of it. I am a doctor – a radiologist. You can't requisition a doctor's car. Let me see your written orders.'

'– we have orders to requisition any vehicle within a mile of the pipal tree.'

'I am just here to see a film, this car is not actually here,' said Dr Kishen Chand Seth, pointing to his Buick. 'Give me my keys back.' He reached out for them.

'Kishy, don't shout, darling,' said Parvati. 'Perhaps there really has been some disaster. We've been seeing a film for the last three hours.'

'I assure you, Sir, there has been,' said the policeman. 'There have been a great many deaths and injuries. I am requisitioning this car on the express instructions of the Home Minister of Purva Pradesh. Only cars of active – non-retired – doctors are exempt. We will take good care of it.'

This last remark was just a soothing formula. Dr Kishen Chand Seth realized immediately that his car would be virtually disabled through misuse and overuse. If what this idiot was saying was true, there would be sand in the engine and blood on the calfskin upholstery by the time he got it back. But had there really been such a disaster? Or was this just another example of post-Independence rot? People were shockingly high-handed these days.

'You!' he shouted at a passer-by.

Taken aback, not accustomed to being addressed in this manner, the man, a respectable clerk in a government department, stopped in his tracks and turned a face of polite, perplexed inquiry towards Dr Kishen Chand Seth.

'Me?'

'Yes, you. Has there been a disaster at the Pul Mela? Hundreds dead?' The last query was pronounced with scornful disbelief.

'Yes, Sahib, there has been,' said the man. 'I heard the rumour, then heard it on the radio. It is certainly true. Even the official estimate is in the hundreds.'

'All right – take it,' said Dr Kishen Chand Seth. 'But mind – no blood on the seats – no blood on the seats. I won't have it. Do you hear me?'

'Yes, Sir. Rest assured that we will return it to you within a week. Your address, Sir?'

'Everyone knows my address,' said Dr Kishen Chand Seth airily. And he stepped out onto the street, waving his cane. He was going to requisition a taxi – or some other car – to take him home.

11.25

L.N. AGARWAL was not popular with the students of Brahmpur. He was disliked both for his authoritarian ways and for his manipulativeness on the Executive Council of Brahmpur University. And the pronouncements of most of the political parties on the university campus were virulently anti-Agarwal in tone.

The Home Minister knew this, and his request for student volunteers to help with the aftermath of the disaster was therefore phrased as a request from the Chief Minister. Most of the students were not in Brahmpur, since it was the vacation. But many of those who were there responded. They would almost certainly have responded even if the request had been signed by the Home Minister.

Kabir, being the son of a faculty member, and therefore living close to the university, was one of the first to hear of the appeal. He and his younger brother Hashim went to the central control room that had been set up in the Fort. The sun was about to set over the city of tents. Apart from the lights and cooking fires there were a number of larger fires here and there, where bodies were being cremated. The loudspeakers continued their endless litany of names, and would continue to do so throughout the night.

They were allocated to different first aid centres. The

other volunteers were exhausted, and glad to be relieved. They could get some food and a couple of hours' sleep before they were called back to duty again.

Despite everyone's efforts – the lists, the centres, the stations, the control room – there was more confusion than order. No one knew what to do with the lost women – mostly aged and infirm, penniless and hungry – until the Congress women's committee, impatient with the indecisiveness of the authorities, took them in hand. Few knew where to take the lost or dead or injured in general, few knew where to find them. Unhappy people ran from one end of the hot sands to the other only to be told that the meeting place for pilgrims of their particular state was somewhere else. Injured or dead children were sometimes taken to the compound for lost children, sometimes to the first aid centres, sometimes to the police enclosure. The instructions on the loudspeaker appeared to change with the person who was temporarily manning it.

After a long night of assisting at the first aid centre, Kabir was staring blankly ahead of him when he saw Bhaskar being brought in.

He was carried in very tenderly by a fat, melancholy, middle-aged man. Bhaskar appeared to be asleep. Kabir frowned when he saw him and immediately got up. He recognized the boy as his father's mathematical companion.

'I found him on the sand just after the stampede,' explained the man, setting the boy down on the ground where there was a little space. 'He was lying not far from the ramp, so he's lucky not to have got crushed. I took him to our camp, thinking he would wake up soon enough and I could take him home. I'm fond of children, you know. My wife and I don't have any. ...' He drifted off, then returned to the subject at hand. 'Anyway, he woke up once, but didn't respond to any of my questions. He doesn't even know his name. And then he went off to sleep again, and hasn't woken up since. I haven't been able to feed him anything. I've shaken him, but he doesn't react.

He hasn't drunk anything either, you know. But, through the grace of my guru, his pulse is still beating.'

'It's good you brought him here,' said Kabir. 'I think I can trace his parents.'

'Well, you know, I was going to take him to a hospital, but then I happened to be paying attention to that horrible loudspeaker for a minute or two – and it said that those lost children who had been taken under protection by individuals should keep them in the Mela area, otherwise tracing them would be impossible. And so I brought him here.'

'Good. Good,' sighed Kabir.

'Now if there is anything I can do – I am afraid I will be leaving tomorrow morning.' The man passed his hand over Bhaskar's forehead. 'He doesn't have any identification on him so I don't really see how you'll trace him. But stranger things have happened in my life. You are looking for a person, not even knowing who they are, and then you suddenly find them. Well, goodbye.'

'Thank you,' said Kabir, yawning. 'You have done a great deal. Well, yes, you can do one thing more. Would you take this note to an address in the university area?'

'Certainly.'

It had struck Kabir that he might not be able to get through to his father by phone, and that a note to him would be useful. He wrote a few lines – his handwriting was something of a scrawl because of his tiredness – folded it in four, wrote the address on top, and handed it over to the fat man.

'The sooner the better,' he said.

The man nodded and left, humming mournfully to himself.

After he had done his rounds, Kabir picked up the telephone and asked the operator for Dr Durrani's number. The lines were congested, and he was asked to try a little later. Ten minutes later he got through, and his father happened to be at home. Kabir informed him of the situation and asked him to ignore the note he would be getting.

'I know he's your friend, the mini-Gauss, and that his name's Bhaskar. But where does he live?'

His father was at his absent-minded worst.

'Oh, hmm, er –' began Dr Durrani. 'It's very, er, difficult to say. Now what is his last, er, name?'

'I thought that you might know,' said Kabir. He could imagine his father scrunching up his eyes in concentration.

'Now, er, I'm not exactly sure, you see, er, he comes and goes, various people, well, leave him here, and then we talk, and then, er, they come and pick him up. He was here last week –'

'I know –'

'And we were discussing Fermat's conjecture about –'

'Father –'

'Oh, yes, and an, er, interesting variant of the Pergolesi Lemma. Something along the, er, lines of what my young colleague, er, I have an idea – why don't we, er, er, ask him?'

'Ask whom?'

'Yes, Sunil Patwardhan, er, wouldn't he know about the boy? It was his party, I believe. Poor Bhaskar. His, er, parents must be perplexed.'

Whatever this meant, Kabir realized that he would probably get more sense out of this new lead than out of his father. He got in touch with Sunil Patwardhan, who recalled that Bhaskar was Kedarnath Tandon's son and Mahesh Kapoor's grandson. Kabir phoned up Prem Nivas.

Mahesh Kapoor picked up the phone at the second ring.

'Ji?'

'May I speak to the Minister Sahib?' said Kabir in Hindi.

'You are speaking to him.'

'Minister Sahib, I am speaking from the first aid centre just below the eastern end of the Fort.'

'Yes.' The voice was like a taut spring.

'We have your grandson, Bhaskar here –'

'Alive?'

'Yes. We have just –'

'Then bring him to Prem Nivas immediately. What are you waiting for?' Mahesh Kapoor's voice cut in.

'Minister Sahib, I apologize, but I am on duty here. You will have to come down yourself.'

'Yes, yes, of course, of course –'

'And I should mention –'

'Yes, yes, go on, go on –'

'It may not be advisable to move him at present. Well, I shall expect you soon.'

'Good. What is your name.'

'Kabir Durrani.'

'Durrani?' Mahesh Kapoor's voice expressed surprise before he told himself that disaster knows no religion. 'Like the mathematician?'

'Yes. I am his elder son.'

'I apologize for my sharpness. We have all been very tense. I will come down immediately. How is he? Why can't he be moved?'

'I think it is best if you see for yourself,' said Kabir. Then, realizing how terrifying these words might sound, he added: 'He does not appear to have any external injury.'

'The eastern end?'

'The eastern end.'

Mahesh Kapoor put down the phone and turned to the family, which had been following every word at his end.

In fifteen minutes Veena had Bhaskar in her arms again. She held him so tight that they seemed to be a single being. The boy was still unconscious, although his face was calm. She touched her forehead to his and whispered his name again and again.

When her father introduced the tired young man at the first aid centre as Dr Durrani's son, she stretched her hands towards his head and blessed him.

DIPANKAR, who had been thinking of death and almost nothing but death since the meaningless disaster of the stampede, said: 'Does it matter, Baba?'

'Yes.' The kind face looked down at the two rosaries, and the small eyes blinked, as if in amusement.

Dipankar had bought these rosaries, one for himself and one – for some reason that he could not explain even to himself – for Amit. He had asked Sanaki Baba to bless them before he left the Mela.

Sanaki Baba had taken them in his cupped hands, and had said: 'What form, what power are you most attracted to? Rama? or Krishna? or Shiva? or Shakti? or Om itself?'

At first, Dipankar had hardly been able to register the question. His mind had reverted to the horror of what he had seen – experienced more than seen. Once more he saw the broken body of the old man a few feet away – the nagas stabbing at him, the crowd crushing him underfoot – the confusion and the madness. Was this what human life was about? Was this why he was here? How pathetic now appeared his hope to understand anything. He was more dismayed and horrified and bewildered than he had ever been.

Sanaki Baba placed his hand on his shoulder. Although he did not repeat his question, his touch brought Dipankar back to the present, back to the triviality, perhaps, of great concepts and great gods.

Now Sanaki Baba was waiting for his answer.

Dipankar thought to himself: Om is too abstract for me; Shakti too mysterious, and I get enough of it in Calcutta; Shiva is too fierce; and Rama too righteous. Krishna is the one for me.

'Krishna,' he said.

The answer seemed to please Sanaki Baba, but he merely repeated the name.

Then he said, taking both Dipankar's hands in his own: 'Now say after me: O God, today –'

'O God, today –'

'– on the bank of the Ganga at Brahmpur –'

'– on the bank of the Ganga at Brahmpur –'

'– on the auspicious occasion of the Pul Mela –'

'– on the occasion of the Pul Mela,' amended Dipankar.

'– on the auspicious occasion of the Pul Mela,' insisted Sanaki Baba.

'– on the auspicious occasion of the Pul Mela –'

'– at the hands of my guru –'

'But are you my guru?' asked Dipankar, suddenly sceptical.

Sanaki Baba laughed. 'At the hands of Sanaki Baba, then,' he said.

'– at the hands of Sanaki Baba –'

'– I take this, the symbol of all your names –'

'– I take this, the symbol of all your names –'

'– by which may all my sorrows be removed.'

'– by which may all my sorrows be removed.'

'Om Krishna, Om Krishna, Om Krishna.' Sanaki Baba began to cough. 'It's the incense,' he said. 'Let's go outside.'

'Now, Divyakar,' said Sanaki Baba, 'I am going to explain how to use this. Om is the seed, the sound. It is shapeless and without form. But if you want a tree, you must have a sprout, and that is why people choose Krishna or Rama. Now you hold the rosary thus –' and he gave one to Dipankar, who imitated his gestures. 'Don't use the second and fifth fingers. Hold it between your thumb and ring finger, and move it bead by bead with your middle finger while you say "Om Krishna". Yes, that's the way. There are 108 beads. When you get to the knot, don't cross it, return and circle the other way. Like waves in the ocean, forwards and backwards.

'Say "Om Krishna" on waking, on putting on your clothes, whenever you think of it. ... Now I have a question for you.'

'Babaji, I have one for you as well,' said Dipankar, blinking a little.

'My question, however is a shallow one, and yours a

deep one,' said the guru. 'So I will ask mine first. Why did you choose Krishna?'

'I chose him because I admire Rama but I find –'

'Yes, he was after worldly glory too much,' said Sanaki Baba, completing his thought.

'And his treatment of Sita –'

'She was crushed,' said Sanaki Baba. 'He had to choose kingship or Sita and he chose kingship. He had a sad life.'

'Also, his life was one from beginning to end – at least in his character,' said Dipankar. 'But Krishna had so many different stages. And at the end, defeated, when he was in Dwaraka –'

Sanaki Baba was still coughing from the incense.

'Everyone has tragedy,' he said. 'But Krishna had joy. The secret of life is to accept. Accept happiness, accept sorrow; accept success, accept failure; accept fame, accept disgrace; accept doubt, even accept the impression of certainty. Now, when are you leaving?'

'Today.'

'And what was your question?' Sanaki Baba said with gentle seriousness.

'Baba, how do you explain all this?' Dipankar pointed to the distant smoke from a huge funeral pyre, where hundreds of unidentified bodies were being burned. 'Is it all the lila of the universe, the play of God? Are they fortunate because they died on this auspicious spot at this auspicious festival?'

'Mr Maitra is coming tomorrow, isn't he?'

'I think so.'

'When he asked me to give him peace, I told him to return at a later date.'

'I see.' Dipankar could not disguise the disappointment in his voice.

Once again he thought of the old man, crushed to death, who had talked of ice and salt, of completing his journey back to the source of the Ganga the following year. Where would he himself be next year, he wondered. Where would anyone be?

'I did not, however, refuse him an answer,' said Sanaki Baba.

'No, you did not,' sighed Dipankar.

'But do you want an interim answer?'

'Yes,' said Dipankar.

'I think there was a flaw in the administrative arrangements,' replied the guru blandly.

11.27

THE newspapers, which had been consistently lauding the 'commendably high standard of the administrative arrangements' came down heavily on both the administration and the police. There were a great many explanations of what had happened. One theory was that a car which supported a float in the procession had overheated and stalled, and that this had started a chain reaction.

Another was that this car belonged not to a procession but to a VIP, and should never have been allowed on the Pul Mela sands in the first place, certainly not on the day of Jeth Purnima. The police, it was alleged, had no interest in pilgrims, only in high dignitaries. And high dignitaries had no interest in the people, only in the appurtenances of office. The Chief Minister had, it was true, made a moving statement to the press in response to the tragedy; but a banquet due to be held that same evening in Government House had not been cancelled. The Governor should at least have made up in discretion what he lacked in compassion.

A third said that the police should have cleared the path far ahead of the processions, and had failed to do so. Because of this lack of foresight the crowd at the bathing spots had been so dense that the sadhus had not been able to move forward. There had been bad coordination, poor communication, and under-staffing. The police had been manned by dictatorial but ineffectual junior officers in charge of groups of policemen from a large number of districts, a motley collection of men whom they did not know well and who were unresponsive to their orders. There had been less than a hundred constables and only two gazetted officers on duty on the bank, and only seven at the crucial juncture at the base of the ramp. The Superintendent of Police of the district had been nowhere in the vicinity of the Pul Mela at all.

A fourth account blamed the slippery condition of the ground after the previous night's storm for the large number of deaths, especially those that had taken place in the ditch on the edge of the ramp.

A fifth said that the administration should – when organizing the Mela in the first place – have used far more of the comparatively empty area on the northern shore of the Ganga for the various camps in order to relieve the predictably dangerous pressure on the southern shore.

A sixth blamed the nagas, and insisted that the criminally violent akharas should be disbanded forthwith or at any rate disallowed from all future Pul Melas.

A seventh blamed the 'faulty and haphazard' training of the volunteers, whose loss of nerve and lack of experience precipitated the stampede.

An eighth blamed the national character.

Wherever the truth lay, if anywhere, everyone insisted on an Inquiry. The *Brahmpur Chronicle* demanded 'the appointment of a committee of experts chaired by a High Court Judge in order to investigate the causes of the ghastly tragedy and to prevent its recurrence'. The Advocates' Association and the District Bar Association criticized the government, in particular the Home Minister, and, in a strongly worded joint resolution, pronounced: 'Speed is of the essence. Let the axe fall where it will.'

A few days later it was announced in a *Gazette Extraordinary* that a Committee of Inquiry with broad terms of reference had been constituted, and that it had been requested to pursue its investigations with all due promptitude.

11.28

THE five judges in the zamindari case maintained strict secrecy about their consultations. From the moment that the case was closed and judgment reserved, their taciturnity exceeded even the regular bounds of judicial discretion. They moved around in the same social world as many of those whose lives and properties were bound up in this case, and they were conscious of the weight that even their casual comments were certain to carry. The last thing they wanted was to be in the eye of a storm of speculation.

Even so, speculation was widespread, active, and furiously inconsistent. One of the judges, Mr Justice Maheshwari, unconscious of the low esteem in which he was held by G.N. Bannerji, had greatly praised the eminent lawyer's advocacy to a lady at a tea-party. He had made some extremely telling points, the judge confided. The news had spread, and the zamindars began to feel optimistic again. But on the other hand it was the Chief Justice, and not Mr Justice Maheshwari, who would almost certainly write the first draft of the judgment.

And yet it had been the Chief Justice who had given the Advocate-General such a grilling. Shastri had rallied, reconsidered his arguments, and accepted that if he maintained the line that had been so successful in the Bihar case, he might jeopardize his chances in the Purva Pradesh case. Here the judges seemed inclined to make different distinctions. But whether his attempt to double back had been successful was anyone's guess. G.N. Bannerji had, in his final two days of rebuttal, flayed what he called the 'opportunistic drift of my learned friend's rudderless raft, which looks to the current stirring about the bench and changes its course accordingly'. It was the general opinion of those present in court on the final two days that he had destroyed the government's case.

But the Raja of Marh, some of whose lands had been ravaged suddenly one day by a swarm of locusts, saw this as the warning of an unfavourable judgment. Others took note, with more substantial grounds for gloom, of the First Amendment Bill to the Constitution. This bill, which in mid-June received the assent of the President of India Dr Rajendra Prasad (whose father, interestingly, had been the munshi of a zamindar) sought further to protect land reform legislation from challenges under certain articles of the Constitution. Some zamindars believed this to be the final nail in their coffin. Yet others, however, believed that this amendment itself could be challenged – and that the land reform bills it sought to protect could in any case be declared unconstitutional since they infringed other, unprotected, articles – and indeed the spirit of the Constitution itself.

While the zamindars on the one hand and the framers of the act on the other, the tenantry on the one hand and the retainers of the landlords on the other, all underwent these swings of elation and depression, the judges continued to frame their judgment in secret. They assembled in the Chief Justice's chambers shortly after the arguments were over to discuss what shape and direction the judgment should take. There was considerable disagreement over the issues, the line to be taken in arriving at the judgment, and even over the judgment itself. The Chief Justice, however, persuaded the other judges to present a united front. 'Look at that Bihar judgment,' he said. 'Three judges, not essentially in disagreement, each insisting on having his own say, and at – I presume I will not be quoted – at such tedious length. How will the lawyers know what the judgment means? This isn't the House of Lords, and our judgments shouldn't be in the form of individual speeches.' He eventually brought his colleagues around to the idea of a single judgment unless there was strong dissent on a particular point. Rather than entrust any other judge with the first draft of the judgment, he decided to write it himself.

They worked with as much speed as care allowed. The draft judgment did the rounds of the judges in a single circular, gathering comments on separate sheets. 'In view of the argument on page 21 about the non-applicability of implicit concepts wherever specific provision covering a particular matter already exists in the wording of the Constitution, is not the rather lengthy discussion of eminent domain moot?' 'I suggest that on page 16 line 8, we delete the phrase "were tilling their own land" and substitute "were not in fact intermediaries between the agriculturists and the state".' 'I believe we should retain the eminent domain discussion as a second line of defence in case the Supreme Court overrules us on the non-applicability aspect.' And so on. None of the five were unconscious of the heavy burden of responsibility that lay on them in this decision: their judgment would be as momentous as any act of the legislature or executive and would alter the lives of millions.

The judgment – seventy-five pages long – was drawn up, amended, discussed, re-amended, examined, approved, finalized. A single copy was typed up by the private secretary of the Chief Justice. Gossip and leakage were as endemic in Brahmpur as in the rest of the country, but no one except these six people got to learn what the judgment – and, most crucially, its final operative paragraph – contained.

11.29

FOR the last week or so Mahesh Kapoor, like many other senior and junior state politicians, had been shuttling back and forth between Brahmpur and Patna, which was only a few hours away by road or rail. The political aftermath of the Pul Mela and the precarious state of his grandson's health kept him in Brahmpur. But he was pulled towards Patna every second day or so by the momentous events occurring there, events that were likely, in his view, to alter entirely the shape and configuration of the political forces of the country.

These matters came up in a discussion with his wife one morning.

The previous evening he had learned, upon his return from Patna (where several political parties, including the Congress Party, were holding sessions in the mad heat of June) news that would keep him in Brahmpur at least until that afternoon.

'Good,' said Mrs Mahesh Kapoor quietly. 'Then we can go together to visit Bhaskar in hospital.'

'Woman, I will not have time for that,' was Mahesh Kapoor's impatient reply. 'I can't be hanging around hospital wards all day.'

Mrs Mahesh Kapoor said nothing, but that she was upset was obvious to her husband. Bhaskar was no longer unconscious, but he was very far from normal. He had a high temperature, and he could remember nothing of what had happened during the day of the stampede. His memory, even of earlier events, was erratic.

When Kedarnath had returned, he had hardly been able to believe the news. Veena, who had reproached him in his absence, did not have the heart to do so now. They stayed by Bhaskar's bedside day and night. At first heartbreakingly vague even about the identity of his own parents, Bhaskar had slowly begun to identify himself and his surroundings. Numbers still mattered to him however; and he cheered up whenever Dr Durrani visited him. But Dr Durrani did not find these visits particularly interesting, since his nine-year-old colleague had lost some of the acuity of his mathematical insight. Kabir, however, for whom Bhaskar had previously been just an occasional face in his house, had become fond of him. It was in fact he who prodded his absent-minded father into visiting Bhaskar every two or three days.

'What is so important that you can't visit him?' asked Mrs Mahesh Kapoor after a while. Her husband had turned back to the newspaper.

'Yesterday's Cause List,' replied her husband laconically. But Mrs Mahesh Kapoor persisted, and the Minister for Revenue explained, as one would to an idiot, that the Cause List of the Brahmpur High Court contained a bench-by-bench list of the next day's agenda; and that the judgment in the zamindari case would be announced in the Chief Justice's court at ten o'clock that morning.

'And after that?'

'After that? After that – whatever the verdict is – I will have to decide what the next step must be. I'll be closeted with the Advocate-General and Abdus Salaam and God knows who else. And then, when I return to Patna, with the Chief Minister and – why am I explaining all this to you?' He returned pointedly to his newspaper.

'Can't you leave for Patna after seven o'clock? Evening visiting hours are from five to seven.'

Mahesh Kapoor put the newspaper down, and almost yelled: 'Can't a man have peace in his own house? Pran's mother, do you know what is happening in this country? The Congress is threatening to split down the middle, people are defecting left and right to this new party.' He stopped, then continued with increasing emotion: 'Everyone who is decent is leaving. P.C. Ghosh has gone, Prakasam has gone, both Kripalani and his wife have gone. They are accusing us, rightly enough, of "corruption, nepotism, and jobbery". Rafi Sahib, with his usual circus skills, is attending the meetings of both parties – and has got himself elected to the board of this new thing, this KMPP, this Peasants' and Workers' Peoples' Party! And Nehru himself is threatening to resign from the Congress. "We also are tired," he says.' Mahesh Kapoor gave an impatient snort before repeating the last phrase. 'And your own husband feels much the same,' he continued. 'This is not why I spent years of my life in prison. I am sick of the Congress Party, and I too am thinking of leaving it. I have to go to Patna, do you understand, and I have to go to Patna this afternoon. Every hour the shape of things is changing, at every meeting there's some new crisis or other. God knows what is being decided for this state in my absence. Agarwal is in Patna, yes, Agarwal, Agarwal, who should be clearing up the Pul Mela mess, he's in Patna, manoeuvring endlessly, giving as much support to Tandon and as much trouble to Nehru as he possibly can. And you ask me why I won't defer going back to Patna. Bhaskar won't notice my absence, poor boy, and you can explain my reasons to Veena – if you remember one-tenth of them. You take the car. I'll find my own way to the court. Now, enough –' And he held up his hand.

Mrs Mahesh Kapoor said nothing further. She would not change; he would not change; he knew that she would not change; she knew that he would not change; and each knew that the other knew this.

She took some fruit with her to the hospital, and he took some files with him to the court. Before departing to visit Bhaskar, she told a servant to prepare and pack some parathas for her husband so that he would have something to eat on the journey to Patna later in the day.

11.30

IT was a hot morning, and a scorching wind blew along the exposed corridors of the Brahmpur High Court. By nine-thirty, Courtroom Number One was packed solid. Inside the courtroom the physical atmosphere, though stuffy, was not unbearable. The long mats of khas recently suspended over a couple of the windows had been freshly sprinkled with water, converting the hot wind of June into a cooler breeze inside.

As for the emotional atmosphere, it was surcharged with suspense, excitement, and anxiety. Of those who had argued the case, only the local lawyers were present, but it seemed that the Brahmpur Bar, whether connected with the case or not, had decided en masse to attend this historic occasion. The press reporters too were present in force, and were already scribbling away. Swivelling and craning their necks in turn, they tried to catch sight of each famous litigant, each Raja or Nawab or great zamindar, whose fate hung in the balance. Or perhaps it would be more accurate to say that the balance had already tilted, but the curtain that hid the scales was still in place. A few minutes more, and it would be drawn aside.

Mahesh Kapoor entered, talking to the Advocate-General of Purva Pradesh. The reporter for the *Brahmpur Chronicle* could hear only a couple of sentences as they squeezed past him up the side-aisle. 'A trinity is sufficient to run the universe,' said the Advocate-General, his perennial smile a little broader than usual; 'but this case, it appears, needs two extra heads.'

Mahesh Kapoor said: 'There's that bastard Marh and his pederastic son – I'm surprised they have the brazenness to come to this court again. At least they look worried.' Then he shook his head, looking equally worried at the thought of an unfavourable outcome.

The court clock struck ten. The pageant of ushers began. The judges followed in sequence. They looked neither at the government lawyers nor at the advocates for the applicants. It was impossible to make out from their expressions what the judgment might be. The Chief Justice looked to left and right, and the chairs were moved forward. The Court Reader called out the numbers of the several conjoined writ petitions listed 'for pronouncement of judgment'. The Chief Justice looked down at the thick wad of typed pages in front of him, and riffled through them absently. Every eye in court rested on him. He removed the lace doily from the glass in front of him, and took a sip of water.

He turned to the last page of the seventy-five-page judgment, leaned his head to one side, and began reading the operative part of the judgment. He read for less than half a minute, clearly and quickly:

'The Purva Pradesh Zamindari Abolition and Land Reform Act does not contravene any provision of the Constitution and is not invalid. The main application, together with the connected applications, are dismissed. It is our view that parties should bear their own costs, and we order accordingly.'

He signed the judgment and handed it to the judge on his right, the senior puisne judge, who signed and handed it across the Chief Justice to the next-most-senior judge; thus the document ricocheted from side to side until it was handed down to the Court Reader, who stamped it with the seal of the court bearing the legend: 'High Court of Judicature, Brahmpur'. Then the judges rose, for that was the only item of business for which the full bench of five had been constituted. The chair shuffle was reversed, and the judges disappeared behind the dull scarlet curtain to the right, followed by the glittering ushers.

As was the custom of the Brahmpur High Court, all four puisne judges accompanied the Chief Justice to his chambers; then they walked to the chambers of the next-most-senior judge; and so on in order. Finally, Mr Justice Maheshwari walked back to his chambers alone. Having thrashed the issues out for weeks in person and on paper no one had been in the mood for further conversation; the black-gowned procession had been almost funereal. As for Mr Justice Maheshwari, he was still puzzled about the document to which he had just affixed his signature, but he was a little closer to understanding Sita's position in the Ramayana.

To say that there was pandemonium in court would be an understatement. As soon as the last judge disappeared from view, litigants and lawyers, press and public alike, began cheering and screaming, embracing each other or weeping. Firoz and his father hardly had the chance to look at each other when each was surrounded by a mixed group of lawyers and landlords and journalists – and all coherent speech became impossible. Firoz looked grim.

The Raja of Marh, like everyone else, had risen when the judges rose. But aren't they going to read the judgment? he thought. Have they postponed it? He could not grasp that so much significance could be contained in so few words. But the joy on the government side and the despair and consternation on his own brought home to him the full import of the baleful mantra. His legs gave way; he pitched forward onto the row of chairs in front of him and collapsed on the ground; and darkness came over his eyes.

11.31

TWO days later, the Advocate-General of Purva Pradesh, Mr Shastri, carefully perused the full text of the judgment which had been brought out by the High Court printing press. He was pleased that it was unanimous. It was tightly written and clear, and would, he believed, withstand the inevitable appeal to the Supreme Court, especially now that the additional, recently erected wall of the First Amendment stood around it.

The contentions based on delegation of legislation, lack of public purpose, and so on, had been dealt with and dismissed.

On the basic question – the one that could easily have gone either way in Mr Shastri's view – the judges had decided thus:

The 'rehabilitation grant' and 'compensation' both together formed the true recompense, the 'actual compensation' for the land taken over. This, according to the judges, put both items beyond constitutional challenge on the grounds either of inadequacy or of discrimination. Had the government's carefully planned contention that the two items were different been upheld, the rehabilitation grant would not have enjoyed the protection afforded under the Constitution to 'compensation', and would therefore have been struck down under its provision for the 'equal protection of the laws'.

As the Advocate-General saw it, the judges had given a violent blow to the government – and thereby moved it out of the path of an unseen but swiftly approaching train. He smiled to himself at the strangeness of it all.

As for the special cases – the Hindu charitable trusts, the waqfs, the crown grantees, the erstwhile rulers, and so on – none of their contentions had been upheld. Shastri had only one mild regret, and that had nothing to do with the judgment itself. It was that his rival, G.N. Bannerji, had not been in court to hear the judgment.

But G.N. Bannerji was away in Calcutta, arguing another vastly lucrative if less momentous case, and Mr Shastri reflected that he had probably merely shrugged and poured himself another Scotch when he had heard by telephone or telegram about the result of this one.

11.32

IN previous Pul Melas, although the crowds began to thin out after Jeth Purnima, large numbers of pilgrims still

remained eleven days later to bathe on the night of Eka-
dashi, or even fourteen days later at the next 'dark' moon
or amavas, which was sacred to Lord Jagannath. Not so
this time. The tragedy, apart from the dread it had aroused
among the pious, had resulted in a complete dislocation of
regular administration on the sands. The health staff,
overburdened by the emergency, was forced to neglect its
regular tasks. Hygiene suffered, and there were epidemics
of gastro-enteritis and diarrhoea, especially on the northern
bank. The food-stalls were dismantled in an attempt to
discourage the pilgrims from remaining, but those who
remained had to eat, and soon profiteering became rife: a
seer of puris cost five rupees, a seer of boiled potatoes cost
three rupees, and the price of paan trebled.

But soon the pilgrims did disperse entirely. The army
engineers removed the electricity poles and the steel plates
of the roads, and dismantled the pontoon bridges. River
traffic began to move downstream.

In time the Ganga rose with the monsoon rains and
covered the sands.

Ramjap Baba remained on his platform, surrounded
now on all sides by the Ganga, and continued to recite
unceasingly the eternal name of God.

Part Twelve

MRS RUPA MEHRA and Lata returned from Lucknow to Brahmpur about a week before the Monsoon Term of the university began. Pran was at the station to meet them. It was late at night, and though it was not cold, Pran was coughing.

Mrs Rupa Mehra scolded him for coming.

'Don't be silly, Ma,' said Pran. 'Do you think I'd have sent Mansoor instead?'

'How is Savita?' asked Mrs Rupa Mehra, just as Lata was about to ask the same question.

'Very well,' said Pran. 'But she's getting bigger by the minute –'

'No complications at all?'

'She's fine. She's waiting for you at home.'

'She should be asleep.'

'Well, that's what I told her. But she obviously cares more for her mother and sister than for her husband. She thought you might need a bite to eat when you got home. How was your trip? I hope there was someone to help you at Lucknow Station.'

Lata and her mother exchanged a quick glance.

'Yes,' said Mrs Rupa Mehra in a definitive manner. 'The very nice young man I wrote to you about from Delhi.'

'The shoemaker Haresh Khanna.'

'You shouldn't call him a shoemaker, Pran,' said Mrs Rupa Mehra. 'He will probably turn out to be my second son-in-law, God willing.'

Now it was Pran's turn to give Lata a quick glance. Lata was shaking her head gently from side to side. Pran did not know if she was disavowing the opinion or the certainty of it.

'Lata encouraged him to write to her. That can only mean one thing,' continued Mrs Rupa Mehra.

'On the contrary, Ma,' said Lata, who could hold back no longer. 'It can mean one of several things.' She did not add that she had not encouraged Haresh to write, merely consented to his doing so.

'Well, I agree, he's a good fellow,' said Pran. 'Here's the tonga.' And he got busy telling the coolies how to arrange the luggage.

Lata didn't quite catch Pran's remark, or she would have responded very much as her mother did, which was with great surprise.

'A good fellow? How do you know he is a good fellow?' asked Mrs Rupa Mehra, frowning.

'No mystery,' said Pran, enjoying Mrs Rupa Mehra's perplexity. 'I just happen to have met him, that's all.'

'You mean you know Haresh?' said his mother-in-law.

Pran was coughing and nodding simultaneously. Now both Mrs Rupa Mehra and Lata were looking at him in astonishment.

After his voice returned he said, 'Yes, yes, I know your cobbler.'

'I wish you wouldn't call him that,' said Mrs Rupa Mehra in exasperation. 'He has a degree from England. And I wish you would take care of your health. How can you take care of Savita if you don't?'

'I like him well enough,' said Pran. 'But I can't help thinking of him as a cobbler. When he came to Sunil Patwardhan's party he brought along a pair of brogues he'd made just that morning. Or that he wanted made. Or something like that –' he ended.

'What are you talking about, Pran?' cried Mrs Rupa Mehra. 'I wish you wouldn't speak in riddles. How can you bring along something that you want made? Who is this Sunil Patwardhan, and what brogues are these? And' – she added with a particular air of grievance – 'why didn't I know about all this?'

That Mrs Rupa Mehra, whose special business it was to know everyone else's, should not have known that Haresh had met Pran, in all likelihood before she had, irked her greatly.

'Now don't be annoyed with me, Ma, it's not my fault that I didn't tell you. I think things were a bit fraught here at home at the time – or perhaps it just slipped my mind. He was here on business a few months ago, and stayed

362

with a colleague and I happened to meet him. A short man, well-dressed, straightforward, and quite definite in his opinions. Haresh Khanna, yes. I particularly remembered his name because I thought he might be a suitable prospect for Lata.'

'You remember thinking –' began Mrs Rupa Mehra. 'And you did nothing about it?' Here was unbelievable dereliction of duty. Her sons were thoroughly irresponsible in this regard, but she had not believed it of her son-in-law.

'Well –' Pran paused for a while, considering his words, then said:

'Now I don't know how much or how little you know about him, Ma, and it's been a little while since the party, and I can't say that it all comes back to me exactly as I heard it, but it is my understanding from Sunil Patwardhan that there was some girl in his life, some Sikh girl, who –'

'Yes, yes, we know,' Mrs Rupa Mehra cut him off. 'We know perfectly well. But that will not stand in our way.' Mrs Rupa Mehra made it clear by her tone that an armoured corps of Sikh damsels could not come between her and her target.

Pran continued: 'Sunil had some perfectly idiotic couplet about him and this girl. I can't recall it right now. At any rate he gave me to understand that our cobbler was spoken for.'

Mrs Rupa Mehra let the appellation pass. 'Who is this Sunil?' she demanded.

'Don't you know him, Ma?' said Pran. 'Well, I suppose we haven't had him over when you've been here. Savita and I like him a lot. He's very lively, very good at imitations. He'd enjoy meeting you, and I think you'd enjoy meeting him. After a few minutes you'll imagine you're speaking to yourself.'

'But what does he do?' asked Mrs Rupa Mehra. 'What is his work?'

'Oh, sorry, Ma, I see what you mean. He's a lecturer in the Mathematics Department. He works in some of the same areas as Dr Durrani.'

Lata turned her head at the name. A look of tenderness and unhappiness passed over her face. She knew how difficult it would be to avoid Kabir on the campus, and she was uncertain now about whether she wanted to – or would be able to force herself to – avoid him. But after her long silence, what would his feelings towards her be? She feared that she had hurt him, as he had her, and neither thought gave her anything but pain.

'Now you must tell me all the other news about Brahmpur,' said Mrs Rupa Mehra quickly. 'Tell me about this terrible thing we've all been hearing about – at the Pul Mela. This stampede. No one we know was injured, I hope.'

'Well, Ma,' said Pran thoughtfully, unwilling to mention anything about Bhaskar tonight, 'let's talk about the news tomorrow morning. There's lots to tell – the Pul Mela disaster, the zamindari verdict, its effect on my father – oh yes, and on your father's car, the Buick' – here he began coughing – 'and, of course, my asthma's been cured by Ramjap Baba, except that the news doesn't seem to have reached my lungs yet. You're both tired, and I admit I feel a bit exhausted myself. Here we are. Ah, darling' – for Savita had come up to the gate – 'you really are foolish.' He kissed her forehead.

Savita and Lata kissed. Mrs Rupa Mehra hugged her elder daughter tearfully for a minute, then said: 'My father's car? –'

It was, however, not the time for talk. The tonga was unloaded, hot soup offered and declined, goodnights exchanged. Mrs Rupa Mehra yawned, got ready for bed, removed her false teeth, gave Lata a kiss, said a prayer, and went off to sleep.

Lata stayed awake longer, but – unlike in the tonga – she was thinking of neither Kabir nor Haresh. Even her mother's quiet and regular breathing failed to reassure her. The moment she lay down she remembered where she had spent the previous night. She thought at first that she would not be able to close her eyes. She kept imagining the sound of footsteps outside the door, and her imagination recreated for her the chimes of the grandfather clock that stood at the end of that long corridor, near Pushkar's and Kiran's rooms.

'I thought you were an intelligent girl,' the odious, disappointed, forgiving voice was saying.

But in a while her eyes closed of their own accord, and her mind yielded to a blessed exhaustion.

12.2

MRS RUPA MEHRA and her two daughters had just finished breakfast and had so far had no time to talk about anything of significance when two visitors from Prem Nivas arrived: Mrs Mahesh Kapoor and Veena.

Mrs Rupa Mehra's face lit up at the thought of their kindness and consideration. 'Come in, come in, come in,' she said in Hindi. 'I was just thinking about you, and here you are. You must have breakfast,' she continued, taking over her daughter's house in a manner that was impossible for her in Calcutta under the eye of the gorgon. 'No? Well, tea at least. How is everyone at Prem Nivas? And in Misri Mandi? Why has Kedarnath not come – or his mother? And where is Bhaskar? School hasn't begun yet – or has it? I suppose he is out flying kites with his friends and has forgotten all about his Rupa Nani. Minister Sahib of course is busy, I can imagine, so I don't blame him for not visiting us, but Kedarnath should certainly have come. He doesn't do much in the morning. But tell me all the news. Pran promised to, but far from being able to talk to him, I haven't even seen him this morning. He's gone to attend a meeting of some committee. You should tell him, Savita, not to over-exert. And' – turning to Pran's mother – 'you should also advise him not to be so active. Your words will carry a lot of weight. A mother's words always do.'

'Who listens to my words?' said Mrs Mahesh Kapoor in her quiet way. 'You know how it is.'

'Yes,' agreed Mrs Rupa Mehra, shaking her head in vehement agreement. 'I know exactly how it is. No one

listens to their parents these days. It's a sign of the times.'
Lata and Savita glanced at each other. Mrs Rupa Mehra
went on: 'Now with my father, no one dares to disobey
him. Or he slaps them. He slapped me once even after
Arun was born because he said I wasn't handling him
properly; Arun was being very difficult, crying for no
reason, and it disturbed my father. I began crying of course
when he slapped me. And Arun, who was only one at the
time, began crying even louder. My husband was on tour
at the time.' Her eyes misted over, then cleared up as she
remembered something.

'My father's car – the Buick – what has happened to it?'
she asked.

'It was requisitioned to help with the casualties at the
Pul Mela,' said Veena. 'I think it's been returned; it should
have been returned by now. But we haven't followed
things up these days, we've been so worried about
Bhaskar.'

'Worried? Whatever for?' said Mrs Rupa Mehra.

'What's happened to Bhaskar?' said Lata,
simultaneously.

Veena, her mother and Savita were all greatly surprised
that Mrs Rupa Mehra hadn't been informed fully by Pran
within minutes of her arrival the previous night of
Bhaskar's accident and its aftermath. Each filled in the
picture with eagerness and distress, and Mrs Rupa Mehra's
cries of alarm and sympathy added to the concern, excitement and noise.

If five of us can make the racket we're making, Birbal
really did see a miracle under that tree, said Lata to
herself, and her thoughts turned temporarily from Bhaskar
to Kabir at the very moment that the conversation itself
did the same.

Veena Tandon was saying: 'And, really, if it hadn't been
for that boy who recognized Bhaskar, God knows what we
would ever have done – or who would ever have found
him. He was still unconscious when we saw him – and
when he came to, he couldn't even remember his own
name.' She began to tremble at the thought that an even

worse disaster had been so close, so almost unavoidable. Even in her waking hours, even when holding her son's hand by his bedside, she often remembered with frightening distinctness the sense of his fingers slipping out of her grasp. And the return of that hand had depended on so tenuous a chance that there could be no possible explanation for it but the goodness and grace of God.

'Ah, the tea,' said Mrs Rupa Mehra in a rush of tenderness now that she had three young women to mother. 'You must have a cup immediately, Veena, no, you must, even if your hands are trembling. It will do you good instantly. No, Savita, you sit down, it isn't sensible for you in this condition to insist on acting as hostess. What is a mother for, don't you agree?' This last phrase was addressed to Mrs Mahesh Kapoor. 'Lata, darling, give this cup to Veena. Who was this boy who recognized Bhaskar? One of his friends?'

'Oh no,' said Veena, her voice a little steadier. 'He was a young man, a volunteer. We didn't know him, but he knew Bhaskar. He's Kabir Durrani, the son of Dr Durrani, who has been so good to Bhaskar –'

But Mrs Rupa Mehra's own hands, suddenly grown unsteady with shock, spilled the tea that she had just been pouring.

Lata had grown very still upon hearing the name.

What could Kabir have been doing down by the Pul Mela – and as a volunteer – at a Hindu festival?

Mrs Rupa Mehra put down the teapot and looked towards Lata, the original cause of her distress. She was about to say: 'Now look what you've made me do!' when some better instinct prevented her. After all, Veena and Mrs Mahesh Kapoor had no idea about Kabir's interest in Lata. (She preferred to think of it in that direction.)

Instead she said: 'But he's – well, he's – I mean, he must be from his name – what was he doing at the Pul Mela? Surely –'

'I think he was just a volunteer from the university,' said Veena. 'They sent an appeal for volunteers after the disaster, and he went to help. What a decent young man. He refused to leave his duty at the first aid centre even to oblige a Minister – you know how abrupt Baoji can be on the phone. We had to go down ourselves to see Bhaskar. That was good, because Bhaskar shouldn't have been moved. And though Durrani's son was tired, he spoke to us for quite a long time, reassuring us, telling us how Bhaskar had been brought in, how he did not appear to have any external injury. I was almost beside myself with worry. It makes you think there is God in all of us. He comes quite often to Prem Nivas these days. His father, who knows Bhaskar, often comes along as well. None of us have any idea what they talk about. It makes Bhaskar happy, though, so we just leave them alone with paper and pencil.'

'Prem Nivas?' said Mrs Rupa Mehra. 'Why not Misri Mandi?'

'Well, Rupaji,' said Mrs Mahesh Kapoor. 'I have insisted that Veena stay with us until Bhaskar has quite recovered. It's not good for him to move around too much, the doctor says.' Mrs Mahesh Kapoor had in fact taken the doctor aside and insisted that he say this. 'And for Veena too, it's exhausting enough to take care of Bhaskar without having to run a household. Kedarnath and his mother are staying with us too, naturally. They're both with Bhaskar now. Someone has to be.'

Mrs Mahesh Kapoor made no mention of any additional strain this arrangement imposed on her. Indeed, she did not consider the additional effort of putting four people up in her house to be anything out of the ordinary. The kind of household she ran – had always run – at Prem Nivas involved offering hospitality at all hours to all kinds of people – often strangers, political associates of her husband. If that was an effort she undertook willingly if not gladly, this was one which she undertook both gladly and willingly. She was happy that at a time of crisis like this one, she could be close enough to help. If there had been one silver lining to the dark cloud of Partition, it had been that it had brought her married daughter and her grandson back from Lahore to live in the same town as her. And now, by virtue of another trauma, they were back in Prem Nivas itself.

'He misses his friends, though,' said Veena. 'He wants to go back to our neighbourhood. And once school begins it'll be difficult to keep him away. And then there'll be the rehearsals for the Ramlila – and he insists he wants to be a monkey this time. He's too small to be Hanuman or Nal or Neel or any of the important ones, but certainly he can be part of the army.'

'There'll be plenty of time to catch up with studies,' said Mrs Mahesh Kapoor. 'And the Ramlila is far away. It doesn't take much practice to be a monkey. Health is the main thing. When Pran was ill as a child, he often had to skip his studies. But it hasn't done him any harm.'

Talking of Pran turned Mrs Mahesh Kapoor's thoughts to her younger son, but she had learned not to fret excessively about what it was pointless to fret about. She wished she could curb her anxieties completely. Mahesh Kapoor had insisted that Maan not be informed about the accident that had occurred, for fear that he would instantly return to Brahmpur in order to visit the little frog, and stay on in Brahmpur, entangled in the toils of 'that'. Mahesh Kapoor's spirits had been in turmoil since he had returned from the Congress session at Patna. It was hard enough to decide what he should do in the face of the disastrous turn taken by the affairs of the party and the country. He could do without the presence of Maan, an additional and equally ungovernable thorn in his side – and reputation.

Apropos of nothing that had gone before, Mrs Mahesh Kapoor said, with a slightly embarrassed laugh: 'I sometimes almost feel that Minister Sahib's conversation of late has grown as incomprehensible as Dr Durrani's.'

Everyone was surprised at such a remark, coming as it did from the mild-spirited Mrs Mahesh Kapoor. Veena in particular sensed that only great pressure and anxiety could have wrung such a statement from her. She reproached herself now; in her own anxieties about Bhaskar, she had been unconscious of what her mother must have been undergoing, worried as she must have been by Pran's asthma and Bhaskar's injury, quite apart from Maan's behaviour and her husband's increasing abruptness. She was not looking well herself, but this was probably the least of her worries.

Mrs Rupa Mehra's mind, meanwhile, had swerved onto quite another track as a result of the last comment. 'How did Dr Durrani get to hear of Bhaskar?' she asked.

Veena, whose mind had been far away, said, 'Dr Durrani?' in a puzzled sort of voice.

'Yes, yes, how did Bhaskar and Dr Durrani get together? This dutiful son of his, you say, recognized Bhaskar because of that connection.'

'Oh,' said Veena, 'It began when Kedarnath invited Haresh Khanna to lunch. He's a young man from Kanpur —'

Lata burst out laughing. Mrs Rupa Mehra's face went first white, then pink. This was completely intolerable. Everyone in Brahmpur knew of this Haresh, and she had been the last to hear of it. Why had Haresh not mentioned Kedarnath or Bhaskar or Dr Durrani in his conversation? Why was she, Mrs Rupa Mehra, the last to be informed on a subject closer to her than to anyone else in this room: the acquisition of a son-in-law?

Veena and Mrs Mahesh Kapoor looked astonished by the reactions of both Lata and her mother.

'How long has all this been going on?' demanded Mrs Rupa Mehra with accusation and even resentment in her voice. 'Why does everyone know about everything? Everyone knows this Haresh; everywhere I go it is Haresh, Haresh. And only I am left staring.'

'But you left for Calcutta so soon after he was here that there wasn't any chance to talk to you, Ma,' said Veena. 'Why is it so important?'

When it dawned on Veena and Mrs Mahesh Kapoor from the closeness of the interrogation to which they were being subjected that Haresh was considered to be a 'prospect', they pounced on Mrs Rupa Mehra with a volley of questions of their own, and upbraided her for keeping them in the dark.

Mrs Rupa Mehra, mollified, was soon as eager to divulge as to receive information. She had described Haresh's certificates and qualifications and clothes and looks and had moved onto Lata's reactions to Haresh and his to Lata, when, luckily for Lata's peace of mind, she was interrupted by the arrival of Malati Trivedi.

'Hello, hello,' beamed Malati Trivedi, almost bouncing in. 'I haven't seen you for months, Lata. Namasté, Mrs Mehra – Ma, I mean. And to both of you.' She nodded at Savita and the very visible bulge. 'Hello, Veenaji, how is the music going? How is Ustad Sahib? I turned on the radio the other night and I heard him singing Raag Bageshri. It was so lovely: the lake, the hills, and the raag – all of them merged into one. I felt like dying with pleasure.' With a final namasté to Mrs Mahesh Kapoor, whom she did not recognize, but whom she guessed to be Veena's mother, Malati completed the circle, and sat down. 'I've just come back from Nainital,' she announced happily. 'Where's Pran?'

12.3

LATA looked at Malati as if she were a knight-errant. 'Let's go!' she said to her. 'Let's go for a walk. At once! There are lots of things I want to talk about with you. I've been wanting to get out of the house all morning, but I've been too lazy to do so. And I thought of going to the women's hostel but I didn't know if you were back yet. We ourselves just got back last night.'

Malati obligingly got up again.

'Malati has just come in,' said Mrs Rupa Mehra. 'This is not very hospitable, Lata, or polite either. You must let her have some tea. Then you can go for your walk.'

'That's all right, Ma,' said Malati, smiling. 'I'm not really feeling like tea, and I'll be thirsty when I return. I'll have some then, and we'll catch up on things. Meanwhile Lata and I'll take a walk by the river.'

'Do be careful, Malati, that path down by the banyan

trees is very slippery in this weather,' warned Mrs Rupa Mehra.

After going to her room to fetch a couple of things, Lata made good her escape.

'Now what's all this about?' asked Malati as soon as they got out of the door. 'Why did you want to leave?'

Lata lowered her voice for no very good reason.

'They were discussing me and a man whom my mother made me meet in Kanpur just as if I wasn't there, and even Savita didn't object.'

'I'm not sure I would have objected either,' said Malati. 'What were they saying?'

'I'll tell you later,' said Lata. 'I've had enough of myself for a while, and I want to hear something different. What's your news?'

'What sort of news do you want?' asked Malati. 'Intellectual, physical, political, spiritual, or romantic?'

Lata considered the last two, then thought of Malati's comment about the lake, the hills, and a night raag. 'Romantic,' she said.

'That's a bad choice,' said Malati. 'You should get every idea of romance out of your head. But, well – I had a romantic encounter in Nainital. Except, well –' She paused.

'Except what?' asked Lata.

'Except, well, it wasn't really. Anyway, I'll tell you what happened and you decide for yourself.'

'All right.'

'You know my sister, my elder sister, the one who keeps kidnapping us?'

'Yes – I haven't met her, but the one who was married at fifteen to the young zamindar and lives near Bareilly.'

'That's right,' said Malati. 'Near Agra, actually. Anyway, they were having a holiday in Nainital, so I went along as well. And so did my three younger sisters and our cousins and so on. Everyone was given a rupee a day as pocket money, and this was quite enough to fill almost the whole day with one activity or another. I'd had a hard term, and I was eager to get Brahmpur out of my head.

Like you, I suppose.' She put her arm around Lata's shoulder.

'At any rate, I would ride in the morning – it's only four annas an hour to hire a horse – and I'd also row, and skate at the rink – I'd sometimes skate twice a day and forget to go home for lunch. The rest of the family were involved in their own activities. Now I bet you can't imagine what happened.'

'You had a fall, and some young gallant at the rink rescued you,' said Lata.

'No,' said Malati. 'I look too self-assured for any Galahads to come chasing after me.'

Lata reflected that this was quite likely. Men did fall for her friend at a rapid rate, it was true, but they would probably fear to pick her up if she fell. Malati's attitude towards most men was that they were beneath her attention.

Malati continued: 'As it happens, I did have a fall or two while skating, but I got up on my own. No, what happened was quite different. I began to notice that a middle-aged man was following me around. Every morning when I was out rowing, I'd see him looking at me from the shore. Sometimes he'd get a boat out himself. He'd even appear at the rink.'

'Horrible!' said Lata, her thoughts immediately turning to her uncle in Lucknow, Mr Sahgal.

'Well, no, not really, Lata, I wasn't disconcerted at first, just puzzled. He didn't come up to me or, well, approach me or anything. But after a while it began to trouble me. So I went up to him.'

'You went up to him?' asked Lata. This was asking for trouble, clearly. 'That was very adventurous.'

'Yes, and I said, "You've been following me around. Is something the matter? Would you like to say something to me?" He said, "Well, I'm on holiday, and I'm staying at such-and-such a hotel in room number so-and-so; would you come and have tea with me this afternoon?" I was surprised, but he looked pleasant and sounded decent, and so I agreed.'

Lata was looking astonished, even shocked. Malati noticed this with pleasure.

'Well,' continued Malati, 'at tea he told me that he had indeed been following me around, and for longer than I had realized. Don't look so thunderstruck, Lata, it's unsettling. Anyway, he told me he had seen me one day when he was out rowing, and, being on holiday with nothing better to do, he had followed me. Having rowed, I hired a horse and went for a ride. Later I skated. I did not seem to care, or so it seemed to him, about eating, about resting, about anything except the activity I was engaged in. He decided that he liked me very much. Don't look so disgusted, it's all true. He had five sons, he said, and he thought that I would make one of them a wonderful match. They lived in Allahabad. If I was ever passing that way, would I agree to meet them? Oh, incidentally, when we were making small talk, it turned out that he had known my family in Meerut many years ago, even before my father's death.'

'And you agreed?' said Lata.

'Yes, I agreed. At least to meet them. No harm in meeting them, Lata; five brothers – perhaps I'll marry them all. Or none. So that was it – that's why he was following me around.' She paused. 'That's my romantic story. At least, I think it's romantic. It's certainly not physical, intellectual, spiritual or political. Now what's been happening to you?'

'But would you marry someone under those circumstances?'

'Why not? I'm sure his sons are quite nice. But I have to have one more affair before I settle down. Five sons! How strange.'

'But you are five sisters, aren't you?'

'I suppose we are,' said Malati. 'Anyway, it seems less strange. I've spent most of my growing-up years among women, and it doesn't seem odd at all. Of course, it's not the same for you. Even though you lost your father, you had brothers. But I had a peculiar sort of feeling when I entered your sister's drawing room just now. As if I was back to an earlier life: six women and no men. But not like the feeling you get in a women's hostel. It was very comforting.'

'But now you're surrounded by men, aren't you Malati?' said Lata. 'Your subject –'

'Oh, yes,' said Malati, 'in class – but what does that matter? It was far worse in Intermediate Science. Sometimes I think that men should simply be lined up against a wall and shot. It's not that I hate them, of course. Now what about you? What has happened about Kabir? How have you dealt with him? And now that you're back, what do you plan to do – short of shooting him and halting an innings?'

12.4

LATA told her friend about what had happened since the painful phone call – it seemed years ago – in which Malati had told her about Kabir and had made it plain (in case Lata could not see this herself – but how could she not?) that the match was impossible. They were walking not far from the spot where Lata had suggested to Kabir that they go away by themselves and ignore the closed-minded closed-hearted world around them. 'Very melodramatic,' commented Lata about her actions that day.

Malati could tell how hurt Lata must have been.

'Very adventurous, rather,' she said reassuringly, thinking, however, that it would have been disastrous if Kabir had agreed to Lata's scheme. 'You're always telling me how bold I am, Lata, but you've outdone me.'

'Have I?' said Lata. 'Well, I haven't spoken or written a word to him since then. I can hardly bear to think of him, though. I thought that by not replying to his letter I could make myself forget him, but it hasn't worked.'

'His letter?' said Malati, surprised. 'Did he write to you in Calcutta?'

'Yes. And now that I've returned to Brahmpur I keep hearing his name. Just last night Pran mentioned his father, and this morning I heard that he himself had helped at the

Pul Mela after the stampede. Veena says he helped her recover her son, who was lost. And walking here with you, where we walked together –'

Lata trailed off into silence. 'What's your advice?' she said after a while.

'Well,' said Malati, 'when we go back, perhaps you'll let me read his letter. I need to understand the symptoms before I can make my diagnosis.'

'Here it is,' said Lata, producing the letter. 'I wouldn't let anyone except you read it.'

'Hmm,' said Malati. 'When did – oh, I see, when you went back to your room.' The letter looked well-read. Malati sat down on the root of the banyan tree. 'You're sure you don't mind?' she said when she was already half-way through.

After she had read it once, she read it again.

'What are frangrant waters?' she asked.

'Oh, that's a quotation from a guidebook.' Lata cheered up at the memory.

'You know, Lata,' said Malati, folding the letter and handing it back to her, 'I like it, and he seems quite open and good-hearted. But it reads like the letter of a teenage boy who'd rather be talking than writing to his girlfriend.'

Lata considered her friend's remark for a while. Something similar had struck her too, but had not reduced the letter's slow-working effect on her. She reflected that she herself might well be faulted for a lack of maturity. And Malati too. Who, for that matter, was mature? Her elder brother, Arun? Her younger brother, Varun? Her mother? Her eccentric grandfather with his sobs and his stick? And what was the point of being mature anyway? And she thought of her own unbalanced, unsent letter.

'But it's more than the letter, Malati,' she said. 'He's going to be mentioned by Pran's family all the time. And in a few months the cricket season will start and it'll be impossible to avoid reading about him. Or hearing about him. I'm sure I'll be able to pick out his name from fifty yards away.'

'Oh, do stop moaning, Lata, in that feeble way,' said Malati with as much impatience as affection.

'What?' exclaimed Lata, outraged out of her mournfulness. She glared at her friend.

'You need to do something,' said Malati decisively. 'Something outside your studies. Anyway, your final exams are almost a year away, and this is the term when people take things easy.'

'I do sing now, thanks to you.'

'Oh, no,' said Malati, 'that's not what I meant at all. If anything, you should stop singing raags and start singing film songs.'

Lata laughed, thinking of Varun and his gramophone.

'It's a pity this isn't Nainital,' continued Malati.

'You mean, so that I could ride and row and skate?' said Lata.

'Yes,' said Malati.

'The problem is,' said Lata, 'if I row I'll only think of the frangrant waters, and if I ride I'll think of him riding his bicycle. And anyway I can neither ride nor row.'

'Something that is active and takes you out of yourself,' continued Malati, partly to herself. 'Some society – how about a literary society?'

'No,' said Lata with a shake of her head and a smile. Mr Nowrojee's soirées or anything resembling them were too close for comfort.

'A play, then. They're putting on *Twelfth Night*. Get a part in the play. That'll make you laugh at love and life.'

'My mother wouldn't stand for my acting in a play,' said Lata.

'Don't be such a mouse, Lata,' said Malati. 'Of course she'll agree. After all, Pran produced *Julius Caesar* last year and there were a couple of women in it. Not many, not important parts perhaps, but real girl students, not boys dressed up as girls. He was engaged to Savita at the time. Did your mother object? No, she didn't. She didn't see the play, but she was delighted at its success. If she didn't object then, she can't now. Pran will be on your side. And the students in Patna University and in Delhi too have mixed casts now. This is a new age!'

Lata could only imagine what her mother might have to say about the new age.

'Yes!' said Malati with high enthusiasm. 'It's being put up by that philosophy teacher, what's his name – it will come back to me – and auditions are in a week. Female auditions one day, male auditions two days later. Very chaste. Perhaps they'll even rehearse separately. Nothing that a cautious parent could object to. And it's for Annual Day, so that lends it an additional stamp of respectability. You need something like that or you'll just wilt away. Activity – furious, unmeditative activity, in lots of company. Take my word for it, that's what you need. That's how I got over my musician.'

Lata, though she felt that Malati's heartbreaking affair with a married musician was hardly a matter to make light of, was grateful to her for trying to cheer her up. After the unsettling strength of her feelings for Kabir, she could understand better what she had not understood before: why Malati had allowed herself to get involved in something as complicated and hazardous as she had.

'But anyway,' Malati was saying, 'I'm bored with Kabir: I want to hear about all the other men you've met. Who is this Kanpur prospect? And what about Calcutta? And didn't your mother plan to take you to Delhi and Lucknow too? They should have been worth at least one man apiece.'

After Lata had rendered her a full account of her voyage, which turned out not to be a catalogue of men so much as a lively description of events, omitting only the indescribable episode in Lucknow, Malati said:

'It seems to me that the poet and the paan-eater are neck and neck in the matrimonial stakes.'

'The poet?' Lata was dumbfounded.

'Yes, I don't consider his brother Dipankar or the covenanted Bish to be in the running at all.'

'Nor do I,' said Lata, annoyed. 'But nor, I assure you, is Amit. He is a friend. Just as you are. He was the one person whom I felt I could really talk to in Calcutta.'

'Go on,' said Malati. 'This is very interesting. And did he give you a copy of his poems?'

'No, he did not,' said Lata crossly. After a while she reflected that Amit had in fact promised in a vague manner to give her a copy. But if he had really meant to, he could surely have sent one through Dipankar, who had been in Brahmpur and had met Pran and Savita. Lata felt, though, that she was not being quite honest with Malati, and now appended the remark: 'At least he hasn't yet.'

'Well, I'm sorry,' said Malati, uncontritely. 'This is a sensitive point with you.'

'It is not,' said Lata. 'It is not sensitive. It's just irritating. I find it reassuring to think of Amit as a friend, and very unreassuring to think of him in any other way. It's just because you saddled yourself with a musician that you want to saddle me with a poet.'

'Perhaps.'

'Malati, please believe me, you're barking up a nonexistent tree.'

'All right,' said Malati. 'Here's an experiment. Close your eyes, and think of Kabir.'

Lata wanted to refuse to go along. But curiosity is a curious thing, and after hesitating for a while she frowned and complied. 'Surely it isn't necessary to close my eyes,' she said.

'No, no, close your eyes,' insisted Malati. 'Now describe what he's wearing – and one or two physical features. Don't open your eyes while you're speaking.'

Lata said: 'He's wearing cricket clothes; a cap; he's smiling – and – this is ridiculous, Malati.'

'Go on.'

'Well, his cap's come off: he's got wavy hair, and broad shoulders, and nice even teeth. Rather a – what do they call it in silly romantic novels? – an aquiline nose. What is the purpose of all this?'

'All right, now think of Haresh.'

'I'm trying,' said Lata. 'All right, I have him in focus now. He's wearing a silk shirt – cream-coloured – and fawn trousers. Oh – and those horrible co-respondent shoes I told you about.'

'Features?'

'He's got small eyes, but they've crinkled up very nicely into a smile – they've almost disappeared.'

'Is he chewing paan?'

'No, thank God. He's drinking a cup of cold chocolate. Pheasant's, he said it was called.'

'And now Amit.'

'All right,' sighed Lata. She tried to picture him, but his features remained vague. After a while she said: 'He refuses to come into focus.'

'Oh,' said Malati, with something like disappointment in her voice. 'But what's he wearing?'

'I don't know,' said Lata. 'How odd. Am I allowed to think instead of imagine?'

'I suppose so,' said Malati.

But try as she might, Lata could not imagine what kind of shirts and trousers and shoes Amit wore.

'Where are you?' asked Malati. 'A house? A street? A park?'

'A cemetery,' said Lata.

'And what are you doing?' said Malati, laughing.

'Talking in the rain. Oh yes, he has an umbrella. Would that count as an item of clothing?'

'All right,' admitted Malati. 'I was wrong. But trees do grow, you know.'

Lata refused to follow up this unprofitable speculation. A little later, as they returned to the house for the promised tea, she said: 'There'll be no avoiding him, Malati. I'm bound to meet him. When he helped out after the disaster, that wasn't the mark of "just a teenage boy". He did that because he felt he had to, not because he meant me to hear about it.'

Malati said: 'What you have got to do is to build up your life without him, intolerable though that may appear at first. Accept the fact that your mother will never accept him. That is an absolute given. You're right, you're bound to bump into him sooner or later, and the one thing that you must make sure of is that you have very little idle time. Yes, a play's just the thing for you. You should act as Olivia.'

'You must think me a fool,' said Lata.

'Well, foolish,' said Malati.

'It's terrible, Malati,' Lata continued. 'I want to meet him more than anything. And I've told my Co-respondent to correspond. He asked at the station, and I couldn't bear to be mean to him when he'd been so helpful to Ma and me.'

'Oh, there's no harm in that,' said Malati. 'So long as you don't either dislike or love him, you can correspond with him. And didn't he make it clear that he was still half in love with someone else?'

'Yes,' said Lata, rather thoughtfully. 'Yes, he did.'

12.5

TWO days later Lata got a short note from Kabir asking her whether she was still annoyed with him. Couldn't they meet at the Brahmpur Literary Society on Friday? He would only go if there was a chance of meeting her.

At first Lata thought of asking Malati once again what she should do. Then, partly because Malati could hardly be expected to manage her love-life in every detail, and partly because Malati would probably have told her not to go and to ignore the letter, Lata decided to consult herself and the monkeys.

She took a walk, scattered some peanuts to the monkeys on the cliff, and was the centre of their approving attention for a while. During the Pul Mela the monkeys had been royally feasted, but now it was back to normal lean times; and very few people paused to consider their welfare.

Having performed a generous action, Lata felt she could think more clearly. Kabir had once before waited for her in vain at the Brahmpur Literary Society. He had even had to eat some of Mrs Nowrojee's cake. Lata felt she could not inflict such an experience on him again. She wrote him a short note:

Dear Kabir,
    I have got your note, but will not be going to the Nowrojees' this Friday. I got your letter too when I was in Calcutta. It made me think over and remember everything. I am not annoyed with you in any way; please do not think so. But I feel that there is no purpose at all in our writing or meeting. There would be a lot of pain and very little point.

Lata

After reading over her note three times, and wondering whether to rewrite it without the last sentence, Lata became impatient with herself and posted it as it was.

She did visit Prem Nivas that day, and was relieved to discover that Kabir was not visiting Bhaskar at the time.

A couple of days after the Monsoon Term began, Malati and Lata went to the auditions for *Twelfth Night*. A nervous young philosophy teacher with a lively interest in the theatre was directing the Annual Day play this year. The auditions – it was the day for female auditions – took place not in the university auditorium but in the staff room of the Philosophy Department. It was five o'clock in the afternoon. About fifteen girls were gathered there, chattering nervously in knots, or just looking at Mr Barua with fascinated anxiety. Lata recognized several girls from the English Department, a couple even from her year, but none whom she knew very well. Malati had come along with her in order to ensure that she didn't back out at the last moment. 'I'll audition as well, if you want.'

'But don't you have some of your practicals in the afternoon?' asked Lata. 'If you get a part and have to rehearse –'

'I won't get a part,' said Malati firmly.

Mr Barua made the girls stand up one by one and read various passages from the play. There were only three female parts and, besides, Mr Barua had not decided definitely that the part of Viola would go to a girl, so the competition was severe. Mr Barua read every role – male or female – other than the one that the auditioner was reading, and he read them so well, discarding entirely the nervousness of his ordinary manner, that many of the girls in the audience, and one or two who were auditioning, started giggling.

Mr Barua first made them read Viola's part beginning: 'Good madam, let me see your face.' Then, depending upon what they made of it, he asked them to read something else, either from Olivia's role or from Maria's, but only in Lata's case from both. Some girls read in a singsong voice or had some other irksome trait of speech; Mr Barua, reverting to his nervous manner, cut them off with: 'Good, thank you, thank you very much, that was good, very good, very good indeed, I have an excellent idea now, well, good, good –' until the girl who was reading got the idea, and (in a couple of cases, tearfully) returned to her chair.

After the auditions, Mr Barua said to Lata, within the hearing of a couple of other girls: 'That was well read, Miss Mehra, I'm surprised I haven't seen you on, well, on stage before.' Overcome by embarrassment he turned to gather his papers.

Lata was delighted with the nervous compliment. Malati told her that she had better prepare Mrs Rupa Mehra for the fact that she was bound to get a part.

'Oh, I'm not bound to get a part at all,' said Lata.

'Make sure that Pran's in the room when you bring up the subject,' said Malati.

Pran, Savita, Mrs Rupa Mehra, and Lata were sitting together after dinner that night when Lata said:

'Pran, what do you think of Mr Barua?'

Pran paused in his reading. 'The philosophy lecturer?'

'Yes – he's doing the Annual Day play this year, and I wanted to know whether you think he'll direct it well.'

'Mm, yes,' said Pran. 'I'd heard he was doing it. *Twelfth Night* or *As You Like It* or something. Makes a good contrast to *Julius Caesar*. He's very good – he's very good as an actor as well, you know,' continued Pran. 'But they say he's rather poor as a lecturer.'

After a moment's pause Lata said: 'It's *Twelfth Night*. I went to the auditions, and it's possible I might get a part in it, so I thought I'd better be forewarned about things.'

Pran, Savita, and Mrs Rupa Mehra all looked up. Mrs Rupa Mehra paused in her sewing and took in her breath sharply.

'Wonderful,' said Pran enthusiastically. 'Well done!'

'Which part?' asked Savita.

'No,' said Mrs Rupa Mehra vehemently, shaking her needle for emphasis. 'My daughter is not going to act in any play. No.' She glared at Lata over the top of her reading-glasses.

There was silence all around. After a while Mrs Rupa Mehra added: 'Not at all.'

After a further while, not encountering any response, she went on: 'Boys and girls together – acting!' It was obvious that such a tawdry, immoral thing could not be countenanced.

'Like in *Julius Caesar* last year,' ventured Lata.

'You be quiet,' snapped her mother. 'No one has asked you to speak. Have you ever heard of Savita wanting to act? To act on the stage with hundreds of people staring? And going to those nightly gatherings with boys –'

'Rehearsals,' prompted Pran.

'Yes, yes, rehearsals,' said Mrs Rupa Mehra impatiently. 'It was on the tip of my tongue. I won't have it. Think of the shame. What would your father have said?'

'Now, now, Ma,' said Savita. 'Don't get upset. It's just a play.'

Having invoked her late husband, Mrs Rupa Mehra had reached an emotional climax, and it was possible now to pacify her and even to reason with her. Pran pointed out that the rehearsals would take place during the day except in an emergency. Savita said that she'd read *Twelfth Night* at school, and it was a harmless play; there was nothing scandalous in it.

Savita had read the bowdlerized version that was approved as a school text, but it was very likely that Mr Barua would have to cut out certain passages anyway to avoid causing shock and distress to the parents who attended Annual Day. Mrs Rupa Mehra had not read the play; if she had, she would certainly have thought it unsuitable.

'It is Malati's influence, I know it,' she said.

'Well, Ma, it was Lata's decision to attend the auditions,' said Pran. 'Don't blame Malati for everything.'

'She is too bold, that girl,' said Mrs Rupa Mehra, who was continually struggling between her fondness for Malati and her disapproval of what she saw as her overly forward attitude to life.

'Malati said I needed something to distract me from other things,' said Lata.

It did not take long for her mother to see the justice and weight of this argument. But even while conceding the point, she said, 'If Malati says so, it must be so. Who am I to say anything? I'm just your mother. You'll only value my advice when I'm burning on my pyre. Then you'll know how much I cared for your welfare.' This thought cheered her up.

'Anyway, Ma, there's a good chance that I won't get the part,' said Lata. 'Let's ask the baby,' she added, placing her hand on Savita's stomach.

The litany, 'Olivia, Maria, Viola, nothing,' was recited slowly several times over, and the fourth time around the baby obliged with a sharp kick on the word 'nothing'.

12.6

TWO or three days later, however, Lata received a note assigning her the part of Olivia and asking her to attend the first rehearsal on Thursday afternoon at three-thirty. She rushed off in high excitement towards the women's hostel, only to meet Malati on the way. Malati had been given the part of Maria. Both of them were equally pleased and astonished.

The first rehearsal was to be merely a reading-through of the play. Again it was not necessary to book the auditorium; a classroom was sufficient. Lata and Malati decided to celebrate by having a preparatory ice-cream at the Blue Danube, and arrived at the classroom in high spirits, just five minutes before the reading was due to begin.

There were about a dozen boys, and only one girl, presumably Viola. She was sitting apart from them, contemplating the empty blackboard.

Also sitting apart from the main knot of actors, and not participating at all in the general air of masculine excitement when the two girls walked in, was Kabir.

At first Lata's heart leapt up when she saw him; then she told Malati to stay where she was. She was going over to talk to him.

His behaviour was too casual to be anything but deliberate. Clearly, he had been expecting her. This was intolerable.

'Who are you?' she said, anger below the low level of her voice.

He was taken aback, both by the tone and by the question. He looked rather guilty.

'Malvolio,' he said, then added: 'Madam.' But he remained seated.

'You never told me you had the least interest in amateur dramatics,' said Lata.

'Nor did you tell me,' was his reply.

'I was not interested until a few days ago, when Malati dragged me to the audition,' said Lata, shortly.

'And my interest dates to about the same time,' said Kabir with an attempt at a smile. 'I heard that you did very well at the auditions.'

Lata could see it all now. Somehow or other he had discovered that she had a good chance of getting a part, and he had decided to attend the auditions for male parts. It was precisely to get away from him that she had undertaken to act in the first place.

'I suppose you instituted the usual inquiries,' said Lata.

'No, I heard about it by chance. I haven't been following you around.'

'And so –'

'Why does there have to be a "so" to it?' said Kabir, innocently. 'I just happen to like the lines of the play. And he quoted with an easy and unselfconscious air:

> 'There is no woman's sides
> Can bide the beating of so strong a passion
> As love doth give my heart: no woman's heart
> So big to hold so much; they lack retention.
> Alas, their love may be called appetite, –
> No motion of the liver, but the palate, –
> That suffer surfeit, cloyment, and revolt;
> But mine is all as hungry as the sea,
> And can digest as much: make no compare
> Between that love a woman can bear me
> And that I owe Olivia.'

Lata felt her face burning. After a while she said: 'You're reciting someone else's lines, I'm afraid. Those weren't written for you.' She paused, then added: 'But you know them rather too well.'

'I learned them – and a good deal more besides – the night before the auditions,' said Kabir. 'I hardly slept! I was determined to get the part of the Duke. But I had to settle for Malvolio. I hope that doesn't mean anything by way of my fate. I got your note. I keep hoping we'll meet at Prem Nivas or somewhere –'

To her own surprise Lata found herself laughing. 'You're mad, absolutely mad,' she said.

She had turned away, but as she turned back towards him she noticed the last flicker of what was a look of real pain on his face.

'I was only joking,' said Lata.

'Well,' said Kabir, making light of it, 'some are born mad, some achieve madness, and some have madness thrust upon them.'

Lata was tempted to ask him which of the three categories he thought he belonged to. But instead she said: 'So you do know Malvolio's role as well.'

'Oh, those lines,' said Kabir. 'Everyone knows those lines. Just poor Malvolio playing the fool.'

'Why aren't you playing cricket or something else instead?' said Lata.

'What? In the Monsoon Term?'

But Mr Barua, who had arrived a few minutes ago, waved an imaginary baton towards the student who was to play the Duke, and said: 'All right, well, then, now, "If music be ...", all right? Good.' And the reading began.

As Lata listened, she got drawn into the other world. It was a while before her first entrance. And when she began reading, she lost herself in the language. Soon she became Olivia. She survived her first exchange with Malvolio. Later she laughed with the rest at Malati's rendering of Maria. The girl who played Viola too was excellent, and Lata enjoyed falling in love with her. There was even a slight resemblance between Viola and the boy who was to play her brother. Mr Barua had done his casting well.

From time to time, however, Lata, emerging from the play, remembered where she was. She avoided looking at Kabir as much as she could, and only once did she feel that his eyes were on her. She felt certain that he would wish to talk to her afterwards, and she was glad that Malati and she had both got parts. One passage caused her particular difficulty, and Mr Barua had to coax her through it.

Olivia: Why, how dost thou, man? What is the matter with thee?
Malvolio: Not black in my mind, though yellow in my legs. It did come to his hands, and commands shall be executed. I think we do know the sweet Roman hand.
Mr Barua [puzzled at the pause, and looking at Lata in expectation]: Yes, yes, good?
Olivia: Wilt –
Mr Barua: Wilt? Yes, wilt thou ... good, excellent, keep on going, Miss Mehra, you're doing very well.
Olivia: Wilt thou –

Mr Barua: Wilt thou? Yes, yes!

Olivia: Wilt thou go to bed, Malvolio?

Mr Barua [holding up one hand to still the guffaws, and waving at the dumbstruck Kabir with his imaginary baton]: How now, Malvolio?

Malvolio: To bed? ay, sweetheart; and I'll come to thee.

Everyone, other than the two actors and Mr Barua, joined in the laughter that followed. Even Malati. Et tu, thought Lata.

The clown recited, rather than sang, the song at the end of the play, and Lata, catching Malati's eye and avoiding Kabir's, left quickly afterwards. It was not yet dark. But she need not have feared that he would ask her out that evening. It was Thursday, and he had another obligation.

12.7

WHEN Kabir got to his uncle's house, it was dark. He parked his bicycle and knocked. His aunt opened the door. The house, single-storeyed and sprawling, was not well-lit. Kabir often remembered playing with his cousins in the large back garden in his childhood, but for the last several years the house had appeared to him almost to be haunted. It was on Thursday evenings that he usually visited it now.

'How is she today?' he asked his aunt.

His aunt, a thin, rather severe-looking but not unkind woman, frowned. 'For two or three days it was all right. Then again this thing began. Do you want me to be with you?'

'No – no, Mumani, I'd rather be with her alone.'

Kabir entered the room at the back of the house, which for the last five years had been his mother's bedroom. Like the rest of the house, the room was poorly lit, with just a couple of weak bulbs in heavy shades. She was sitting up in a hard-backed armchair, looking out of the window. She had always been a plump woman, but now she had grown fat. Her face was formed of a collection of pouches.

She continued to stare out of the window at the dark shapes of the guava trees at the end of the garden. Kabir came and stood by her. She did not appear to register his presence until she said:

'Close the door, it's cold.'

'I've closed it, Ammi-jaan.'

Kabir did not say that it was not cold at all, that it was July, and that he was sweating after his bicycle ride.

There was a pause. His mother had forgotten about him. He put his hand on her shoulder. She started for a second, then said:

'So it's Thursday night.'

She used the Urdu word for Thursday, 'jumeraat', literally Friday-night. Kabir remembered how, as a boy, he had considered it amusing that Friday-night could itself have a night. His mother used to explain such matters to him in an affectionate, light-hearted way, because his father was far too occupied, voyaging through strange seas of thought alone, to bother much with his children. It was only when they were of an age to talk to him properly that he began to take a fitful interest in them.

'Yes, Thursday night.'

'How is Hashim?' she asked. This was how she usually began.

'Very well, he's doing well in school. He had some very difficult homework, so he couldn't come.'

In fact, Hashim found it hard to bear such meetings, and when Kabir told him it was Thursday evening, he would usually find some reason not to go. Kabir, understanding his feelings only too well, would sometimes not remind him. That was the case this evening.

'And Samia?'

'Still in school in England.'

'She never writes.'

'Sometimes she does, Ammi – but rarely. We too miss her letters.'

It was impossible to tell his mother that her daughter was dead, dead of meningitis, buried a year ago. Surely, he thought, this year-long conspiracy of silence could not have worked. However disturbed people's minds may be, inklings, clues, suggestions, overheard fragments of conversation must work themselves into the mind and lodge themselves into a pattern indicating the truth. Once, indeed, a few months ago, his mother had said: 'Ah, Samia. I won't see her here, but in the other place.' But whatever this meant, it did not prevent her from asking about her daughter subsequently. Sometimes, within minutes of a conversation or a thought, it would be wiped clean from her mind.

'How is your father? Still asking if two plus two makes four?' For an instant Kabir noticed something of the old amused and amusing light in her eyes, then it was dead.

'Yes.'

'When I was married to him —'

'You still are, Ammi.'

'You're not listening to me. When I — you've made me forget —'

Kabir held her hand. There was no responsive pressure.

'Listen,' his mother said. 'Listen carefully to every word I say. We don't have much time. They want to get me married off to someone else. And they have guards around my room at night. There are several of them. My brother has posted them there.' Her hand became tense in his grasp.

Kabir did not dissuade her. He was thankful they were alone.

'Where?' he asked.

She jerked her head slightly in the direction of the trees.

'Behind the trees?' asked Kabir.

'Yes. Even the children know,' she said. 'They look at me, and they say, toba! toba! One day she will have another baby. The world —'

'Yes, Ammi.'

'The world is a terrible place and people like to be cruel. If this is humanity, I want no part in it. Why are you not paying attention? They play music to tempt me. But, Mashallah, I have my wits about me. It is not for nothing that I am the daughter of an army officer. What do you have there?'

'I brought a few sweets, Ammi. For you.'

'I asked for a brass ring, and you have brought me sweets?' Her voice rose in protest. She was, Kabir thought, much worse than usual. Usually the sweets pacified her and she stuffed them greedily into her mouth. This time, however, she would have none of them. She lost her breath, then continued:

'There is medicine in those sweets. The doctors have put them there. If God had wanted me to have medicine, He would have sent word. Hashim, you do not care –'

'Kabir, Ammi.'

'Kabir came last week, on Thursday.' The voice grew alarmed, wary, as if sensing that this too was part of a trap.

'I –' But now tears came to his eyes, and he could not speak.

His mother appeared to be irritated by this new development, and her hand slipped out of his own, like a dead creature.

'I am Kabir.'

She accepted it. It was irrelevant.

'They want to send me to a doctor, near the Barsaat Mahal. I know what they want.' She looked downwards. Then her head dropped onto her chest, and she was asleep.

Kabir stayed with her for another half-hour, but she did not wake up. Finally, he got up and went to the door.

His aunt, seeing his look of distress, said:

'Kabir, son, why don't you eat with us? It will do you good. And it will be good for us to get the chance to talk to you.'

But Kabir wanted to get away on his bicycle, as fast and as far as he could. This was not the mother he had loved and known, but someone stranger than a stranger.

There had been no history of such a condition in the family, nor any specific accident – a fall, a blow – that had caused it. She had been under some emotional strain for about a year after the death of her own mother, but then, that was a grief not unusual in the world. At first she was merely depressed, then she became anxious over trifles and incapable of handling the daily business of life. She had grown suspicious of people: the milkman, the gardener, her relatives, her husband. Dr Durrani, when he could not ignore the problem, sometimes hired people to help her, but her suspicions soon extended to them. Finally, she took it into her head that her husband was working out a detailed plot to harm her, and in order to foil it she tore up sheafs of his valuable and unfinished mathematical papers. It was at this stage that he asked her brother to take her away. The only other alternative was incarceration in an asylum. There was an asylum in Brahmpur, and it was located just beyond the Barsaat Mahal; perhaps it was this that she had been referring to earlier.

When they were children, Kabir, Hashim and Samia had always, and rather proudly, declared their father to be slightly mad. It was clearly his eccentricity – or something aligned with it – that made people respect him so much. But it was their affectionate, amusing and practical mother who had been afflicted with this strange visitation, so causelessly and so incurably. Samia at least, Kabir thought, has been spared the continuing torment of it all.

12.8

THE RAJKUMAR OF MARH was in trouble, and was up before Pran. Owing to problems with their landlord, the Rajkumar and his associates had been forced to seek housing in a students' hostel, but they had refused to adapt their style of life to its norms. Now he and two of his friends had been seen by one of the Proctor's assistants in Tarbuz ka Bazaar, just emerging from a brothel. When they were questioned, they had pushed him aside, and one of the boys had said:

'You sister-fucker, what's your business in all this? Are you a commission agent? What are you doing here

anyway? Or are you out pimping for your sister as well?'
One of them had struck him across the face.

They had refused to give their names, and denied that
they were students. 'We're not students, we're the grandfathers of students,' they had asserted.

In mitigation, or perhaps not in mitigation, it could be
said that they were drunk at the time.

On the way back, they had sung a popular film song, 'I
didn't sigh, I didn't complain –' at the top of their lungs
and had disturbed the peace of several neighbourhoods.
The Proctor's assistant had followed them at a safe distance. Being over-confident, they had returned to the hostel,
where a compliant watchman had let them enter, though it
was past midnight. They continued to sing for a while
until their fellow-students begged them to shut up.

The Rajkumar woke up the next morning with a bad
headache and a premonition of disaster, and disaster came.
The watchman, fearful now for his job, had been forced to
identify them, and they were hauled up before the warden
of the hostel. The warden asked them to leave the hostel
immediately and recommended their expulsion. The Proctor, for his part, was generally in favour of severe action.
Student rowdyism was getting to be a headache, and if
aspirin didn't cure it, decapitation would. He told Pran,
who was now on the student welfare committee, which
took care of discipline, to handle matters provisionally, as
he himself was going to be tied up with arrangements for
the students' union elections. Ensuring fair and calm elections was a recurrent problem: students from various
political parties (communists, socialists, and – under a
different name – the Hindu revivalist RSS) had already
started beating each other up with shoes and lathis as a
prelude to fighting for votes.

The onus of deciding the fate of others was exactly the
sort of thing that Pran fretted a great deal over, and Savita
could see how anxious this made him. He couldn't concentrate on his breakfast newspapers. He hadn't been feeling
at all well lately – and Savita could sense that the pressure
of having to dispense rough justice to these idiotic young

men was going to do him no good. He couldn't even work on his lectures on Shakespearian comedy, although he had set some time aside the previous evening.

'I don't see why you have to see them here,' Savita said. 'Ask them to go to the Proctor's office.'

'No, no, darling, that would only alarm them further. I just want to get their side of the story, and they'll be more forthcoming if they're less terrified – if they're sitting with me in a drawing room rather than standing and shuffling in front of a desk. I hope you and Ma don't mind. It'll take half an hour at the most.'

The culprits arrived at eleven o'clock, and Pran offered them tea.

The Rajkumar of Marh was thoroughly ashamed of himself and kept staring at his palms, but his friends, mistaking Pran's kindness for weakness, and knowing that he was popular with students, decided that they were in no danger, and smirked when Pran asked him what they had to say about the charges. They knew that Pran was Maan's brother, and took his sympathy for granted.

'We were minding our own business,' one of them said. 'He should have minded his.'

'He asked you for your names, and you said –' Pran looked down at the papers in his hand. 'Well, you know what you said. I don't need to repeat it. I don't need to quote the regulations of the university to you, either. You seem to know them well enough. According to this, as you approached the hostel you began to sing: "Any student who is seen in an undesirable place shall be liable to immediate expulsion."'

The two main culprits looked at each other with a smile of unbothered complicity.

The Rajkumar, fearing that if he was expelled, his infuriated father would castrate him or worse, mumbled: 'But I didn't even do anything.' It was just his luck that he had decided to go along to be sociable.

One of the other two said, rather contemptuously: 'Yes, that's true, we can vouch for that. He isn't interested in that kind of thing – unlike your brother, who –'

Pran cut the young man off sharply. 'That is not the point. Let us keep non-students out of this. You do not realize, it seems to me, that you will very likely be expelled. A fine is pointless, it will have no effect on you.' He looked from one face to the other, then went on: 'The facts are clear, and your attitude isn't helpful either. Your fathers are having a hard enough time already without being forced to add you to their worries.'

Pran noticed the first look of vulnerability – not of repentance so much as of fear – on their faces. With the impending abolition of zamindari, their fathers had indeed been increasingly impatient with their wastrel sons. Sooner or later their allowances might even be reduced. They had no idea of what to do with themselves other than to have a good time as students, and if this was taken away from them, there was nothing but darkness ahead. They looked at Pran, but he said nothing further for a while. He appeared to be reading the sheaf of papers in front of him.

It's difficult for them, thought Pran. It's sad, all this riotous high living; it's all they know, and it won't last long. They might even have to find work. It's not easy for students these days, whatever their class. Employment's hard to find, the country doesn't seem to be going in any direction, and the example of their elders is pathetic. Images of the Raja of Marh, of Professor Mishra, and of bickering politicians came to his mind. He looked up and said:

'I have to decide what to recommend to the Proctor. I tend to agree with the warden –'

'No, please, Sir –' said one of the students.

The other kept quiet, but gave Pran a beseeching look.

The Rajkumar was now wondering how he would face his grandmother, the Dowager Rani of Marh. Even his father's rage would be easier to bear than the look of disappointment in her eyes.

He began to sniffle.

'We didn't mean to do what we did,' he said. 'We were –'

'Stop,' said Pran. 'And think about what you are saying before you say it.'

'But we were drunk,' said the luckless Rajkumar. 'That's why we behaved like that.'

'So shamefully,' said one of the others in a low voice.

Pran closed his eyes.

All of them reassured him that they would never do anything like this again. They swore it on their fathers' honour, they pledged it in the names of several gods. They began to look repentant, and, indeed, they even began to feel repentant as a result of looking it.

After a while, Pran had had enough, and stood up.

'You'll hear in due course from the authorities,' he told them at the door. The bureaucratic, formulary words sounded strange to him even as he said them. They hesitated, wondering what else they could say in their own defence, then walked off forlornly.

12.9

AFTER telling Savita he would be back for lunch, Pran went to Prem Nivas. It was a warm day, though overcast. By the time he got there he was somewhat out of breath. His mother was in the garden, giving instructions to the mali.

She came forward to welcome him, then stopped. 'Pran, are you all right?' she asked. 'You don't look at all well to me.'

'Yes, Amma, I'm fine. Thanks to Ramjap Baba,' he couldn't resist adding.

'You should not make fun of that good man.'

'No, no,' said Pran. 'How is Bhaskar?'

'He's talking quite well, and even walking around. He insists on going back to Misri Mandi. But the air here is so much fresher.' She gestured towards the garden. 'And Savita?'

'She's annoyed that I spend so little time with her. I had to promise to return for lunch. I really don't like all this extra work on the committee, but if I don't do it, someone else will have to.' He paused. 'Other than that, she's very well. Ma fusses over her so much that she's going to want to have a baby every year.'

Mrs Mahesh Kapoor smiled to herself. Then an anxious look appeared on her face, and she said: 'Where has Maan got to, do you know? He isn't in the village, and he isn't on the farm, and no one in Banaras knows where he is. He's just disappeared. He hasn't written for two weeks. I'm very worried about him. All your father says is that he can be in the underworld for all he cares so long as he's not in Brahmpur.'

Pran frowned at this second reference to his brother that morning, then assured his mother that Maan disappearing for two weeks or even ten should not be cause for alarm. He may have decided to go hunting or for a trek in the foothills or for a holiday at Baitar Fort. Firoz might know his whereabouts; he'd be meeting Firoz this afternoon, and he would ask him if he'd heard from his friend.

His mother nodded unhappily. After a while she said:

'Why don't all of you come to Prem Nivas? It'll be good for Savita in the last few days.'

'No, Amma, she prefers to be where she's used to living. And now that Baoji's thinking of leaving the Congress Party the house will be full of politicians of every kind trying to persuade him or dissuade him. And you're looking tired too. You take care of everyone, and don't let anyone take care of you. You really look exhausted.'

'Ah, that's old age,' said his mother.

'Why don't you call the mali into the house, where it's cool, and give him his instructions there?'

'Oh no,' said Mrs Mahesh Kapoor. 'That wouldn't work at all. It would have a bad effect on the morale of the flowers.'

12.10

PRAN went home, and rested in lieu of lunch. He met Firoz a little later in the Chief Justice's courtroom at the

Brahmpur High Court. Firoz was appearing for a student who had a grievance against the university. The student had been one of the brightest chemistry students the university could remember, and was well-liked by his teachers. In the April examination, however, at the end of the academic year, he had done something so surprising that it was virtually inexplicable. He had gone to the bathroom in the middle of a paper, and then, seeing a couple of his friends standing just outside the exam hall, had stopped to talk to them for a minute. He claimed that they had talked about the fact that it was too hot to think; and there was no reason to assume that he was not telling the truth. His friends were both philosophy students, and could not possibly have helped him in his exam; in any case, he was by far the best chemistry student of his year.

But he was duly reported. It was clear that he had infringed the stringent rules for the examinations. On the grounds that an exception could not be made for him, his papers were cancelled and he was not allowed to appear for the remaining exams. In effect, he was to lose a year. He had appealed to the Vice-Chancellor to let him appear for the 'compartmental' exams; these exams, normally held in August for students who had failed in a single paper, would enable him to enter the next year if he took them as a set. His appeal had been turned down. In desperation he had turned to the possibility of a legal remedy. Firoz had agreed to be his lawyer.

Pran, being the junior member of the student welfare committee, which had been consulted in the original decision, had been asked by the Proctor to sit in on the hearings. He greeted Firoz with a nod in the courtroom, and said: 'Let's meet outside after this is over.' He was not used to seeing Firoz in a black gown with white bands round his neck, and he was pleasantly impressed even while he thought it looked rather silly.

Firoz had filed a writ petition on the student's behalf, claiming that his rights under the Constitution had been infringed. The Chief Justice made short work of his submission. He told him that hard cases made bad law; that the university could be trusted to act as its own overseeing authority unless the process of such oversight was blatantly unfair, as was not the case here; and that if the student insisted – unwisely, in his view – on recourse to the law, he should have been advised to file a suit with the local magistrate, not to come directly with a writ to the High Court. Writs to the High Court were a newfangled device that had come in under the recent Constitution, and the Chief Justice did not much care for them. He felt they were used far too often simply in order to jump the queue.

He cocked his head to one side, and said, looking down at Firoz: 'I see no reason for a writ at all, young man. Your client should have gone to a munsif magistrate. If he wasn't satisfied with his decision he could have gone to the District Judge on appeal, and then come here on further appeal. You should spend a little time choosing the appropriate forum rather than wasting the time of this court. Writs and suits are two quite different things, young man, two quite different things.'

Outside the court, Firoz was fuming. He had advised his client not to attend the hearing, and he had been glad he had. He himself had been shaken by the injustice of it all. And for the Chief Justice to have rebuked him, to have implied that he had not considered the proper forum – that too was intolerable. He had helped argue the zamindari case before this very judge in this very courtroom; the Chief Justice must know that he was not given to flippant arguments and unconsidered recourse. Nor did Firoz like being called 'young man' unless it was imbedded in an approving remark.

Pran, whose heart was on the student's side, sympathized with Firoz. He patted him on his shoulder.

'It's the correct recourse,' said Firoz, loosening the bands around his neck as if they were constraining the flow of blood to his head. 'In a few years writs will be the accepted method in such cases. Suits are just too slow. August would have come and gone by the time we got a hearing.' He paused, and added passionately: 'I hope they're flooded with writs soon.' Then, with a slight smile, he remarked: 'Of course, this old man will have retired by then. He and all his brethren.'

'Oh yes,' said Pran. 'I know what I meant to ask you. Where's Maan?'

'Is he back?' said Firoz with pleasure. 'Is he here?'

'No, I'm asking you. I haven't heard and I thought you might have.'

'Am I your brother's keeper?' said Firoz. 'Well, I suppose, after a fashion, I am,' he went on, gently. 'Or wouldn't mind being. But no, I haven't heard. I thought he might be here by now, what with his nephew and all that. But, as I said, I haven't heard from him. Nothing to worry about, I hope?'

'No, no, nothing. My mother's worried. You know how mothers are.'

Firoz smiled slightly ruefully, rather in the way his mother used to smile. He looked very handsome at that moment.

'Well,' said Pran, changing the subject. 'Are you your own brother's keeper? Why haven't I seen Imtiaz for so many days? Perhaps you can let him take a stroll outside his cage.'

'We hardly see him ourselves, you know. He's out all the time visiting some patient or other. The only way to get his attention is to fall ill.' And here Firoz quoted an Urdu couplet about how the beloved was both the illness and the medicine, not to mention the doctor whose visit made it all worthwhile. Had the Chief Justice been listening he could have been excused for saying, 'I fail to see the relevance of this particular submission.'

'Well, perhaps I'll do just that,' said Pran. 'I've been feeling oddly exhausted lately, with a sort of strain around the heart –'

Firoz laughed. 'One of the best things about genuine illness is that it's a licence for hypochondria.' Then, cocking his head to one side he added: 'The heart and the lungs are two quite different things, young man, two quite different things.'

THE next day Pran was lecturing when he suddenly felt weak and breathless. His mind too began to wander, a most unusual thing for him. His students were puzzled and began to look at one another. Pran continued to speak, leaning on the lectern and staring at the far wall of the classroom.

'Although these plays are permeated with images of the countryside, images of the chase, to the extent that the six words "Will you go hunt, my Lord?" lead you immediately –' Pran paused, then continued: 'lead you immediately to imagine that you are in the world of Shakespearian comedy, there is nevertheless no historical reason to believe that Shakespeare left Stratford for London because – because –' Pran rested his head on the lectern, then looked up. Why was everyone looking at everyone else? And now his eye fell on the first rows, where the girls sat. That was Malati Trivedi sitting there. What was she doing in his lecture? She had not asked for 'permission to attend' in the standard way. He passed his hand over his forehead. He hadn't noticed her when he was taking attendance. But then he never looked up from his ledger when taking attendance. Some of the boys were standing up. So was Malati. They were leading him back to the desk. Now they had sat him down. 'Sir, are you all right?' someone was saying. Malati was taking his pulse. And now there was someone at the door – Professor Mishra and a visitor passing by and looking in. Pran shook his head. As Professor Mishra retreated, Pran heard the words: '... fond of amateur dramatics ... yes, popular with students, but –'

'Please don't crowd around,' said Malati. 'Mr Kapoor needs air.'

The boys, startled at the authority in the voice of this strange girl, stood back a little.

'I'm all right,' said Pran.

'You'd better come with us, Sir,' said Malati.

'I'm all right, Malati,' said Pran impatiently.

But they escorted him to the staff room and sat him

down. A couple of his colleagues told the students that they would make sure that Mr Kapoor was all right. After a while things did return to normal for Pran, but he just couldn't understand it. He had not been coughing or breathless. Perhaps it was the heat and humidity, he thought unconvincedly. Perhaps it was just overwork, as Savita insisted.

Malati, meanwhile, had decided to go to Pran's house. When Mrs Rupa Mehra saw her at the door, her face lit up with pleasure. Then she remembered that it was probably Malati who had got Lata into the play, and she frowned. But Malati was looking worried, which was an unusual expression for her, and Mrs Rupa Mehra, in sympathetic concern, had hardly said, 'Is something wrong?' when Malati asked:

'Where's Savita?'

'Inside. Come in. Savita, Malati's here to see you.'

'Hello, Malati,' said Savita, smiling. Then, sensing that something was the matter, she said: 'Are you all right? Is Lata all right?'

Malati sat down, composed herself so as not to discompose Savita unduly, and said:

'I was just attending a lecture by Pran —'

'Why were you attending a lecture by Pran?' Mrs Rupa Mehra could not refrain from asking.

'It was on Shakespearian comedy, Ma,' said Malati. 'I thought it would help me to interpret my role in the play.' Mrs Rupa Mehra's mouth set, but she said nothing further, and Malati continued:

'Now, Savita, don't be alarmed, but he felt a bit faint while giving the lecture, and had to sit down. I had a word with some of the boys later and they said that a couple of days ago something similar had happened, but that it had only lasted a second, and he had insisted on continuing the lecture.'

Mrs Rupa Mehra, too anxious now to rebuke Malati even inwardly for talking so freely to boys, said: 'Where is he? Is he all right?'

Savita said, 'Was he coughing? Breathless?'

'No he wasn't coughing, but he did seem a little breathless. I think he should see a doctor. And perhaps, if he insists on lecturing, he should sit down and lecture.'

'But he's a young man, Malati,' said Savita, placing her hands on her stomach, almost as if to protect the baby from this conversation. 'He won't listen. He overworks, and I can't get him to take his duties less seriously.'

'If he listens to anyone, it'll be to you,' said Malati, getting up and putting her hand on Savita's shoulder. 'I think he's had a bit of a shock; now is probably the best time to talk to him. He has to think of you and the baby too, not only his duties. Now I'll just go back and see that he comes home immediately, and by rickshaw.'

Mrs Rupa Mehra would have marched into the English Department herself to rescue Pran if it hadn't meant leaving Savita behind. Savita for her part was wondering what she could tell her husband that might have greater success than her pleas had had so far. Pran had a stubborn streak and an absurd sense of duty, and might insist on continuing to stand on the strength of them.

12.12

HIS stubborn streak was being exercised at this very moment. Pran was alone in the staff room with Professor Mishra, who had discovered, though not much to his alarm, that the scene he had happened upon when passing the door of the classroom was not an enactment of Shakespeare, but, rather, real life. He liked to be well informed about things, and he asked the students a few questions. He settled the visitor he had been escorting in the office of the Head of Department, and went off to the staff room.

The bell had just rung, and Pran's colleagues were unsure whether or not to leave Pran to go to their own lectures, when Professor Mishra entered, smiled at them and at Pran, and said: 'Leave the patient to me. I shall cater to his every whim. How are you, dear boy? I have asked the peon to get you some tea.'

Pran nodded gratefully. 'Thank you, Professor Mishra. I don't know what came over me. I'm sure I could have continued to lecture, but my students, you know –'

Professor Mishra placed his vast, pallid arm on Pran's. 'But your students are so protective of you, so protective,' he said. 'That is one of the joys of teaching – contact with one's students. To inspire them in a lecture, to make them think, after forty-five minutes, that the world has changed for them, that it is somehow different from one bell to the next. To open out for them the heart of a poem – ah! Someone said to me the other day that they considered me to be one of those teachers whose lectures students would never forget – a great teacher like Deb or Dustoor or Khaliluddin Ahmed. I was, he said, a presence at the lectern. I was just a moment ago telling Professor Jaikumar of Madras University, whom I was escorting around our department, that it was a compliment I would never forget. Ah, but my dear fellow, I should be talking of your students, not my own. Many of them were intrigued by that charming and extremely competent girl who took charge a little while ago. Who was she? Had you ever seen her before?'

'Malati Trivedi,' said Pran.

'It's none of my business, I know,' continued Professor Mishra, 'but when she asked for permission to attend, what reason did she give? It's always gratifying when one's fame spreads beyond one's own department. I believe I've seen her somewhere before.'

'I can't imagine where,' said Pran. Then he suddenly remembered with a shock that it was probably at the dreadful submersion of Holi.

'I'm sorry, Professor Mishra, I didn't get your question,' said Pran, who was finding it hard to concentrate. The image of Professor Mishra floundering in a tub of pink water was getting the better of him.

'Oh, not to worry, not to worry. Time enough for all that later,' said Professor Mishra, puzzled by Pran's look of anxiety and – what almost appeared to be – amusement. 'Ah, here's the tea.' The subservient peon moved the tray backwards and forwards in deference to his imagined wishes, and Professor Mishra continued: 'But you know, I have been feeling for some time that these duties of yours really are rather onerous. It's difficult to shrug some of them off, of course. University duties, for example. I heard just this morning that the Raja of Marh's son had been to see you yesterday in connection with this unfortunate fracas he got into. Now of course, if anything were done to him, it would outrage the Raja himself, rather an excitable sort of man, wouldn't you say? One makes enemies on a committee such as the one you sit on. But then, the acceptance of power is never without its personal costs, and one must do one's duty. "Stern daughter of the voice of God!" Only, of course, it cannot fail to tell upon one's teaching.'

Pran nodded.

'Departmental duties, of course, are another matter entirely,' continued Professor Mishra. 'I have decided that if you wish to be released from the syllabus committee. . . .' Pran shook his head. Professor Mishra continued: 'Some of my colleagues on the Academic Council have told me frankly that they find your recommendations – our recommendations, I mean – quite untenable. Joyce, you know – a man of most peculiar habits.' He looked at Pran's face and saw that he was making no headway at all.

Pran stirred his tea, and took a sip.

'Professor Mishra,' he said, 'I've been meaning to ask you: has the selection committee been constituted yet?'

'Selection committee?' asked Professor Mishra innocently.

'To decide on the vacant readership.' Savita had been prodding Pran about the subject lately.

'Ah, well,' said Professor Mishra, 'things take time, things take time. The Registrar has been very busy of late. But we have advertised, as you know, and we hope to have all of the applications in soon. I've glanced at a few, and they are strong, very strong. Excellent qualifications, excellent teaching qualifications.'

He paused to give Pran a chance to say something, but Pran remained determinedly silent.

'Well,' said Professor Mishra. 'I don't want to discourage a young man like yourself, but I believe that in a year or two, when your health has settled, and everything else has stabilized –' He smiled sweetly at Pran.

Pran smiled back. After another sip of tea, he said, 'Professor, when do you think the committee will meet?'

'Ah, now, that's difficult to say, very difficult. We aren't like the Patna University, where the Department Head can just get a few people off the Bihar Public Service Commission to sit on the committee, though I must admit I can see advantages to that system. We have this needlessly elaborate system of selecting our committee members: two from a Panel of Experts – and the Chancellor's nominee – and so on. Professor Jaikumar of Madras, who saw your' – he was about to say 'performance' but checked himself – 'your distress just now, is on our Panel of Experts. But a time that's convenient for him to come to Brahmpur may not be convenient for someone else on the panel. And now, as you know, the Vice-Chancellor has himself been keeping such indifferent health that he has been talking of retirement. Poor man, he hardly finds time to chair selection committees. Everything takes time. Ah well, ah well, I'm sure you sympathize.' And Professor Mishra stared sadly at his large pale hands.

'With him, with you, or with myself?' asked Pran lightly.

'How acute!' said Professor Mishra. 'I hadn't thought of that. A fertile ambiguity. Well, with all of us, I hope. Sympathy does not run out by being generously bestowed. And yet, there is too little genuine sympathy in the world. People always tell others what they want to hear, not what they feel is truly in the interest of the other person. Now, if I were to advise you, for instance, to withdraw your application for the post of reader –'

'– I wouldn't do it,' completed Pran.

'Your health, my dear boy. I am only thinking of your own health. You are driving yourself too hard. All these articles you've been publishing –' He shook his head in gentle reproof.

'Professor Mishra, my mind is quite made up,' said Pran. 'I would like my name to go ahead. I'll take my chances with the committee. I know that you will be on my side.'

A look of bland ferocity passed over the Professor's face. But when he turned to Pran he was entirely soothing.

'Of course, of course,' he said. 'Some more tea?'

Fortunately, Professor Mishra had left Pran alone by the time Malati came to the door. She told him that Savita was expecting him at home and that he was to go home by the rickshaw that was standing outside.

'But it's just across the campus,' Pran protested. 'Really, Malati, I'm not crippled yet. I walked all the way to Prem Nivas yesterday.'

'Mrs Kapoor's orders, Sir,' said Malati. Pran shrugged, and complied.

When he got home, his mother-in-law was in the kitchen. He told Savita to keep sitting, and put his arms tenderly around her.

'Why are you so stubborn?' she said to him, his tenderness causing her anxiety to flare up again.

'We'll be all right,' whispered Pran. 'We'll all be all right.'

'I'm going to ask for a doctor,' said Savita.

'For yourself, not for me,' said Pran.

'Pran, I am going to insist. If you care for me, you'll take my advice now and then.'

'But my magical masseur is coming tomorrow. He cures both my body and my mind.' Seeing Savita continue to look worried, he said: 'I'll tell you what – if I don't feel fit after his kneading and pummelling, I'll see a doctor. How's that?'

'Better than nothing,' said Savita.

THIS skill is a gift of Lord Shiva – it came to me in a vision – in a dream – suddenly, not by degrees.'

The masseur, Maggu Gopal, a tough, stocky man, was rubbing Pran all over with oil. He was about sixty, had very short-cropped grey hair, and kept up a continuous patter which Pran found very soothing. Pran was lying flat on his stomach on a towel in the verandah, and was wearing only his underwear. The masseur had his sleeves rolled up and was tweaking Pran's rather scraggly neck muscles in a determined manner.

'Ai!' said Pran, wriggling a bit – 'that hurts.' He spoke in English, as Maggu Gopal's patter was entirely in English, except for quotations from Hindi. The magical masseur had been recommended to Pran by a friend, and had agreed to come twice a week. He was rather expensive as masseurs went, but he had massaged Pran half a dozen times, and Pran always felt better after his visits.

'If you always move, how you will improve?' asked Maggu Gopal, who was fond of rhyming couplets in his own way.

Pran obeyed and was still.

'I have been masseur in high circles – Chief Minister Sharma, some High Court Judges, two Home Secretaries also, and many Englishmen. And I have a handprint of all these dignitaries. It is all grace of Lord Shiva – you know, the Snake God' – he felt that Pran, as a teacher of English, needed such explanations – 'the God of Ganga and of the great Chandrachur Temple which is now ascending daily in Chowk.'

Some pummelling later, he said:

'This til oil is very good – it has the warming properties. I have rich clients also – many Marwaris of Calcutta know me. They are not taking care of bodies. But I say the body is like finest vintage car, of which there are no spare parts available in the market. Therefore it needs service and maintenance from competent engineer, namely' – and here he pointed to himself – 'Maggu Gopal. And you should not care about expense. Would you give your Swiss watch to the incompetent watchman because he charged cheaply? Some people sometimes call servants, like Ramu or Shamu, to do their massage. They think it is in the oil only.'

He paused, boxed Pran's calves in a businesslike manner, then said:

'Talking of oil, mustard oil is not good – and is internationally prohibited in massage. It stains also. The pores must breathe. Mr Pran, your feet are cold even in this weather. It is weak nervous system. You think too much.'

'Yes, I do,' admitted Pran.

'Too much education is not good,' said Maggu Gopal. 'Ninth standard, non-matric; somehow still I learn the trick.'

He twisted Pran's head violently and looked straight into his eyes.

'You see this boil here on your chin – it is a sign – I will not say a sign, an indication – of constipation – a tendency to constipation. All thinking people – that is, I mean, all those who are thinkers – have this tendency. So you must eat papaya twice a day and take a mild laxative tablet – and have tea without milk, with honey and lemon. And you are too dark – like Lord Shiva – but nothing to be done about it.'

Pran nodded in so far as this was possible. The magical masseur released his head, and went on.

'Thinkers, even if they eat boiled food and light food, will be constipated – their stomachs will not be soft. But your rickshaw-wallahs and servants, even if they eat fried food, will not get it – because they are doing physical labour. Always remember:

> Pair garam, pet naram, sir thanda.
> Doctor aaye to maro danda!

This saying I have translated for Englishmen:

> Cold head, soft tummy, warm feet.
> If doctor comes, you may him beat!'

Pran grinned. He was feeling better already. The magical masseur, reacting promptly to his change of mood, asked him why he had been sad.

'But I was not sad,' said Pran.

'No, no, you were sad.'

'Really, Mr Maggu Gopal.'

'Then you are worried.'

'No – no –'

'It is your work life?'

'No.'

'Your married life?'

'No.'

The magical masseur looked doubtful.

'I have had some health problems lately,' admitted Pran.

'Oh, health problems merely?' said the magical masseur. 'That you can leave all to me. Remember, honey is your god. You must substitute honey for sugar always.'

'Because honey has the warming qualities?' suggested Pran.

'Exactly!' said Maggu Gopal. 'Also, dry fruits should be taken in plenty, especially pistachio, which is very warming. But you can take assorted dry fruits also. Agreed?'

'Agreed!' said Pran.

'And take hot bath in tub, and also sun bath: sit in sun and face the sun. Recite the Gayatri Mantra.'

'Ah.'

'But it is also your work, I can see.' Maggu Gopal grabbed Pran's hand with the same painful vigour with which he had twisted his head. He examined it carefully. After a while he said in a solemn tone: 'Your hand is most remarkable. The sky is the limit of your success.'

'Really?' said Pran.

'Really. Consistency! That is the secret of success in any art. In order to obtain proficiency, you must have one goal – one track – consistency.'

'Yes, indeed,' said Pran, thinking, among many other things, of his baby, his wife, his brother, his nephew, his sister, his father, his mother, the department, the English language, the future of the country, the Indian cricket team, and his own health.

'There is a saying of Swami Vivekananda: "Rise! Awake! Stop not – until the goal is achieved!"' The magical masseur smiled assurance on Pran.

'Tell me, Mr Maggu Gopal,' Pran said, turning his head sideways, 'can you tell from my hand if I will have a daughter or a son?'

'Turn over please,' said Maggu Gopal. He examined Pran's right hand again. 'Yes,' he said to himself.

Turning over onto his back had made Pran start to cough, but Maggu Gopal ignored this, so intent was he on gazing at his hand.

'Now you see,' he said, 'you, or rather your missus, will have a daughter.'

'But my missus is sure she will have a son.'

'Mark my words,' said the magical masseur.

'All right,' said Pran, 'but my wife is almost always right.'

'You have a happy married life?' Maggu Gopal inquired.

'You tell me, Mr Maggu Gopal,' said Pran.

Maggu Gopal frowned. 'It is written in your hand that your married life will be a comedy.'

'Oh, good.'

'Yes, yes, you can see – your Mercury is very strong.'

'I suppose I can't escape from destiny,' said Pran.

This word had a magical effect on Maggu Gopal. He drew backward slightly and pointed his finger at Pran's chest. 'Destiny!' he said, and grinned at Pran. 'That is it.' After a pause he continued:

'Behind every successful man is a woman. Behind Mr Napoleon there was Josephine. Not that you have to be married. I do not believe it. In fact I predict that you have had auspicious women in your life before and will continue to after marriage.'

'Really?' said Pran, interested, but rather fearful. 'Will my wife like this? I fear my life may become a comedy of the wrong kind.'

'Oh, no, no,' said the magical masseur reassuringly. 'She will be very tolerant. But the women must be auspicious. If you drink tea made from dirty water you will fall ill. But if you drink tea made from deluxe water it will refresh you.'

Maggu Gopal stared at Pran with some fixity. Seeing that he had got the point he went on:

'Love is colourblind. Caste does not matter. It is karma – which means actions according to the vicious of God.'

'The vicious of God?' said Pran, bewildered, before he understood what Maggu Gopal was getting at.

'Yes, yes,' said the magical masseur, pulling Pran's toes one by one until they made clicking and cracking sounds: 'One should not get married just for bringing tea in the morning – or for sex or anything.'

'Ah,' said Pran, with a sudden sense of enlightenment, 'just for living day to day.'

'Today! Yes! Do not live for yesterday or tomorrow.'

'I meant from day to day,' explained Pran.

'Yes, yes, it is all the same. Family life with children is a comedy, both today, yesterday, and tomorrow.'

'And how many children will I have?' asked Pran. He had lately begun to wonder whether he should be bringing a child into the world at all, a terrible world of hatred, intrigue, poverty, and cold war – a world that was unlike even his own unsettled childhood in that the safety of the earth itself was now threatened.

'Ah, exact number is in wife's hand,' said the masseur regretfully. 'But once there is delight in your life through one child, it is like a tonic, a chyavanprash – and then the sky is the limit for offspring.'

'Two or three would be more than enough,' said Pran.

'But you must keep up the massage. To maintain the vital fluids.'

'Oh yes!' agreed Pran.

'It is most essential for all people.'

'But who massages the masseur?' asked Pran.

'I am sixty-three,' said Mr Maggu Gopal, rather affronted. 'I don't need it. Now turn around, please.'

WHEN Maan returned to Brahmpur, he made straight for
Baitar House. It was evening, and Firoz met him. He was
delighted to see Maan, but appeared a little awkward,
especially when he saw that Maan had brought his bags
with him.

'I thought I'd stay here,' said Maan, embracing his
friend.

'Not at home?' asked Firoz. 'God, how burnt and wild
you look.'

'What a welcome!' said Maan, not at all put out. 'No,
here's best – that is, if it's all right with you. Will you have
to ask your father? The reason is that I can't bear to deal
with my father and everything else at the same time.'

'Of course you're welcome,' said Firoz, smiling at the
'everything else'. 'Good. I'll get Ghulam Rusool to arrange
to put your bags in your room – the room you usually stay
in.'

'Thanks,' said Maan.

'I hope you'll stay for a while. I didn't mean to sound
unwelcoming. I just didn't expect you'd want to stay here
rather than at home. I'm glad you're here. Now come in,
wash up, and join me for dinner.'

But Maan begged off dinner.

'Oh, sorry,' said Firoz, 'I wasn't thinking. You haven't
been home yet.'

'Well,' said Maan. 'I wasn't thinking of going home.'

'Where then?' asked Firoz. 'Oh, I see.'

'Don't sound so disapproving. I can't wait. I'm all keyed
up!'

'I am disapproving,' said Firoz seriously. 'You should go
home first. Anyway, I made sure your letter got to her,' he
continued, with the air of one who does not wish to
continue a subject.

'I believe you're interested in Saeeda Bai yourself, and
are trying to keep me away,' said Maan, laughing at his
own joke.

'No – no –' said Firoz, rather unconvincingly. He didn't

want a long discussion about Tasneem, who had cast a light and delicate spell over him.

'Now what's the matter?' said Maan, seeing a complex cast of emotions pass over his friend's face. 'Oh, it's that girl.'

'No, no –' said Firoz, even more unconvincingly.

'Well, it's either the elder sister or the younger – unless it's the maid – Bibbo!' And at the thought of Firoz and Bibbo together Maan burst out laughing. Firoz put his arm around Maan's shoulder and drew him into the house.

'You're not very forthcoming with me,' complained Maan. 'I tell you everything that's in my heart.'

'You tell everyone everything,' said Firoz, smiling.

'Not everything,' said Maan, looking at Firoz.

Firoz coloured slightly. 'No, I suppose not. Anyway, most things. I'm not a very forthcoming person. I tell you as much as I tell anyone. And if I don't tell you more, it's a good thing. It might be disturbing.'

'To me?' said Maan.

'Yes – to you, to me, to us, to Brahmpur, to the universe,' said Firoz evasively. 'I presume you're going to have a bath after the journey?'

'Yes,' said Maan. 'But why are you so keen that I shouldn't go to Saeeda Bai's?'

'Oh,' said Firoz, 'I'm not keen that you shouldn't go there. I was just – what was it you said? – disapproving that you didn't visit your family first. Well, at least your mother. I met Pran the other day and he said that you'd just disappeared – hadn't been heard of or seen for ten days by anyone, not even in the village. And that your mother was very worried. And then I thought that with your nephew and all –'

'What?' said Maan, startled. 'Savita's baby's been born already?'

'No, no, your mathematical nephew – haven't you heard?'

From the expression on Firoz's face Maan could see that the news wasn't good. His mouth opened slightly. 'You mean the little frog?' asked Maan.

'What little frog?'

'Veena's child – Bhaskar.'

'Yes. Well, your only nephew. He was hurt in the stampede at the Pul Mela. You really haven't heard?' he said incredulously.

'But no one wrote to tell me!' said Maan, upset and annoyed. 'And then I went on this trek, and – how is he?'

'He's all right now. Don't look so worried. He really is. But apparently he was concussed, and had amnesia, and it took him some time to become coherent again. Perhaps it was as well that they didn't write. You're very fond of him, aren't you?'

'Yes,' said Maan, agitated with concern for Bhaskar. 'This must be my father's doing. He must have thought I'd come straight back to Brahmpur if I heard. Well, I would have –' he began vehemently, then stopped. 'Firoz, you should have written and told me.'

'I didn't think of it,' said Firoz. 'I'm really sorry. I assumed that your family would have told you. I couldn't have imagined that they wouldn't. It isn't as if it was a family secret. All of us knew.'

A sudden, irrelevant thought struck Maan again. 'You're not a secret admirer of Saeeda Bai's, are you?' he asked his friend.

'Oh no,' said Firoz, puzzled. 'Not that I don't admire her.'

'Good,' said Maan, relieved. 'I couldn't compete with a Nawabzada. Oh, er, bad luck about the zamindari case – I heard the news and thought of you. Hmm, will you lend me a walking-stick? I feel like twirling something this evening. Oh, and some cologne. And a clean kurta-pyjama. Civilization is hard on those who've reverted to savagery.'

'My clothes won't fit you. Your shoulders are too broad.'

'Imtiaz's would. They did at the Fort.'

'So they would,' said Firoz. 'I'll bring them up to your room. And a half-bottle of whisky.'

'Thanks,' said Maan, ruffling his friend's hair. 'Perhaps civilization isn't so hard after all.'

WHILE Maan was soaking himself in the delicious sensations of a hot bath, he kept imagining the even more delicious sensations that he was soon to feel in the arms of his beloved. He wrapped himself in the towelled robe that had been provided, and walked into the bedroom.

There, however, more sober thoughts presented themselves. He thought of his nephew, and how hurt he would be if he heard that his Maan Maama had been in town and had not come immediately to see him. Rather glumly Maan decided that he would have to visit Bhaskar first. He poured himself a whisky, drank it quickly, poured another, drank that equally quickly, and took the rest of the half-bottle with him in the pocket of Imtiaz's kurta.

Instead of hiring a tonga, he decided to walk to Prem Nivas, where Firoz had told him Bhaskar would be.

Walking in Pasand Bagh was a pleasure. Maan noticed for the first time in his life that there were even streetlamps on most streets. Just walking on solid roads after the mud and dirt of country tracks was a privilege. He tapped and twirled Firoz's walking-stick. After a while, however, he didn't feel much like it. He became rather depressed at the thought of having to face his father again. And his mother too in a way: she would act as a damper on the anticipated excitement of the evening. She would tell him to stay for dinner. She would ask him all about the villages and the state of his health. Maan's steps became slightly slower and more uncertain. Perhaps it was also the whisky taking effect. He had had very little to drink for weeks.

When he came to a fork in the road, not far from his destination, he looked up at the stars for a bit of guidance. Then he tapped his stick on the pavement, and turned first this way, then that. He looked very undecided. Finally, he took the right-hand fork to Saeeda Bai's rather than the road to Prem Nivas. This cheered him up immediately.

It's much better this way, he decided. If I go home, they'll insist I stay for dinner, and I just can't. And Bhaskar won't really mind. He only cares if I don't give him sums.

And how can I give him sums when my mind's distracted? Anyway, he's not well, he shouldn't stay up late, he's probably in bed already. No, it's much better this way. I'll visit him first thing tomorrow. He won't be angry with me.

After a while he said to himself: And besides, Saeeda Bai would never forgive me if she heard I was in Brahmpur and didn't come to see her before anyone else. I can imagine how hard it's been for her while I've been away. This will be a wonderful reunion – she'll be astonished to see me. And at the anticipation of their meeting he felt a pleasant weakness in his limbs.

Soon he was standing not far from the house, under a large neem tree, savouring in advance the delights to come. A thought occurred to him: I haven't brought a gift along with me.

But Maan, not being one to savour anticipations for long, decided after half a minute that he'd waited long enough to collect himself. I'm my own gift, as she is hers! he said cheerfully to himself, and, first tapping and then waving his cane, he walked the remaining distance to the gate.

'Phool Singh!' he greeted the watchman in a loud voice.

'Ah, Kapoor Sahib. It must be months –'

'No, it must be years –' said Maan, getting out a two-rupee note.

The watchman pocketed the note calmly, then said: 'You are in luck. Begum Sahiba has not instructed me about any particular guests this evening. So I think she expects to be alone.'

'Hmm.' Maan frowned. Then he brightened up. 'Well, good,' he said.

The watchman knocked at the door. The buxom Bibbo peered out. Catching a glimpse of Maan, she beamed. She had missed him. He was by far the pleasantest of her mistress's lovers, and the sprucest.

'Ah, Dagh Sahib, welcome, welcome,' she said from the door, loudly enough that he could hear her at the gate. 'Just a minute, I'll go up and enquire.'

'What is there to enquire about?' asked Maan. 'Aren't I welcome here? Do you think I'll bring the village soil of Mother India into the durbar of the Begum Sahiba?' He laughed and Bibbo giggled.

'Yes, yes, you're very welcome,' said Bibbo. 'Begum Sahiba will be delighted. But I should only speak for myself,' she added flirtatiously. 'I won't be a minute.'

She was as good as her word. Soon Maan was traversing the hall, walking up the stairs with the mirror halfway up on the landing (he halted to adjust his white embroidered cap), and then along the upstairs gallery that fringed the hall. Soon he was at the door of Saeeda Bai's room. But there was no sound of voices or of singing or even of the harmonium. When he entered, leaving his shoes outside the door, he noticed that Saeeda Bai was not in the room where she usually entertained. She must be in the bedroom, he thought with a rush of desire. He sat himself down on the sheeted floor, and leaned against a white bolster. Soon afterwards, Saeeda Bai came out from the bedroom. She looked tired but lovely, and enraptured by the sight of Maan.

Maan's heart leaped up when he saw her, and so did he. If she hadn't had a birdcage in her hand he would have embraced her.

But for now the look in her eyes would have to suffice. What an idiotic parakeet, thought Maan.

'Do sit down, Dagh Sahib. How I have pined for this moment.' An appropriate couplet followed.

She waited until Maan was seated before she set down the parakeet, who looked like a proper parrot now, not a ball of pale green fluff. Then she said to the bird:

'You have been very unresponsive, Miya Mitthu, and I can't say I am pleased with you.' To Maan she said, 'Rumour has it, Dagh Sahib, that you have been in town for some days now. Twirling, no doubt, that handsome ivory-headed cane. But the hyacinth that obtained favour yesterday appears withered today to the connoisseur.'

'Begum Sahiba –' protested Maan.

'Even if she has withered away only for lack of the

water of life,' continued Saeeda Bai, tilting her head a little to one side, and pulling her sari over her hair in that familiar adjustment that made Maan's heart pound ever since he had seen it that first evening in Prem Nivas.

'Begum Sahiba, I swear –'

'Ah,' said Saeeda Bai, addressing the parakeet: 'Why were you away for so long? Even one week was like agony. What are vows to one who is wilting in the desert under a scorching sun?' Suddenly tiring of her metaphor, she said: 'It has been rather hot these last few days. I shall ask for some sherbet for you.' Getting up, she went to the gallery outside the door and, leaning over the rail, clapped her hands: 'Bibbo!'

'Yes, Begum Sahiba?'

'Get us both some almond sherbet. And be sure to mix some saffron in Dagh Sahib's sherbet. He looks so worn out by his pilgrimage to Rudhia. And you have grown rather dark.'

'It was absence from you, Saeeda, that weakened me –' said Maan. 'And it was the laughing-cruel one who exiled me from herself who now blames me for this absence. Could anything be more unjust?'

'Yes –' said Saeeda Bai softly. 'If the heavens had kept us longer apart.'

Since Saeeda Bai's letter to Maan, full of endearments as it was, had urgently enjoined him to remain away from Brahmpur for even longer – for reasons she did not explain – her present answer was hardly fair.

But Maan found it satisfactory; no, more than satisfactory, delightful. Saeeda Bai had as good as confessed that she was longing to take him back in her arms. He made a slight gesture of his head towards the door of the bedroom. But Saeeda Bai had turned to the parakeet.

12.16

'THE sherbet first, then conversation, then music, and then we will see whether the saffron has taken effect,' said

Saeeda Bai teasingly. 'Or does he need the whisky that is peeping out of his pocket?'

The parakeet looked at Maan. It did not appear to be impressed. When Bibbo entered with the drinks, it cried out her name:

'Bibbo!'

It said this in rather a commanding, somewhat metallic, tone. Bibbo shot the bird a look of annoyance. Maan noticed this; he had been feeling equally irritated by the parakeet, and when he looked at Bibbo in amusement and sympathy, their eyes met for a second. Bibbo, who was a trouble-maker and a flirt, held his eyes for a second before turning away.

Saeeda Bai was not amused. 'Stop it, Bibbo, you mischievous girl,' she said.

'Stop what, Saeeda Begum?' asked Bibbo innocently.

'Don't be insolent. I saw you making eyes at Dagh Sahib,' said Saeeda Bai. 'Go to the kitchen at once, and stay there.'

'The accessory is hanged, the principal goes free,' said Bibbo and, having left the tray on the floor near Maan, turned to leave.

'Shameless,' said Saeeda Bai; then, thinking over Bibbo's remark, she turned to Maan with annoyance. 'Dagh Sahib, if the bee finds the bud of an inferior blossom more charming than the opened tulip –'

'Saeeda Begum, you deliberately misunderstand me,' said Maan, sulking a little. 'Every word I say, every look –'

Saeeda Bai did not want him to sulk. 'Drink your sherbet,' she advised him. 'It is not your brains that should be hot.'

Maan tasted his sherbet. It was delicious. Then he frowned, as if he had tasted something bitter.

'What is the matter?' asked Saeeda Bai with concern.

'Something's missing,' said Maan, as if in appraisal of his drink.

'What?' asked Saeeda Bai. 'That Bibbo – she must have forgotten to mix honey in your glass.'

Maan shook his head and frowned. 'I know exactly what's missing,' he said finally.

'Would Dagh Sahib vouchsafe us the solution?'

'Music.'

Saeeda Bai allowed herself a smile. 'All right. Fetch me the harmonium. I am so tired today that I feel that I am at the end of my four days' tenure in the world.'

Instead of asking Maan what he would like to hear, as she usually did, Saeeda Bai began to hum a ghazal to herself, and moved her fingers gently along the keys. After a while she began to sing. Then she stopped, distracted by her thoughts.

'Dagh Sahib, a woman by herself – what place can she find in an ungentle world?'

'That is why she must have someone to protect her,' asserted Maan stoutly.

'There are too many problems for mere admirers to handle. Admirers themselves are sometimes the problem.' She gave a sad laugh. 'House, tax, food, arrangements, this musician loses his hand, that landlord loses his land, this one has to go away for a family wedding, that one fears he can no longer afford his generosity, someone's education must be looked after, a dowry has to be arranged. And a suitable boy must be found. Endless. Endless.'

'You mean, for Tasneem?'

'Yes. Yes. Who would think that there would be people paying court to her? Here, in this house. Yes, it's true. It is for me, her sister, her guardian, to arrange these things. That Ishaq – he has now become Ustad Majeed Khan's disciple, so he moves with his head in the clouds even if his voice is very much of this earth – he visits here, supposedly to see me and pay his respects, but in fact to see her. I've taken to keeping the parakeet in my room. Yet still he contrives to find some excuse or another. And he is not a bad man; but he has no future. His hands are crippled, and his voice untrained. Miya Mitthu can sing better than him. Even my mother's wretched myna could.'

'Are there others?' asked Maan.

'You needn't act so innocent,' said Saeeda Bai, annoyed.

'Saeeda Bai – honestly –' said Maan.

'Not you, not you. Your friend the socialist, who has taken to organizing things in the university in order to be someone in the world.'

This description hardly fitted Firoz. Maan looked puzzled.

'Yes, our young maulvi, her Arabic teacher. Whose hospitality you have partaken of, whose instruction you have imbibed, whose company you have shared for weeks. Do not sell your wares here, Dagh Sahib. There is a market for injured innocence, and it is not to be found between these walls.'

But Maan must have looked completely perplexed. He could not imagine that Rasheed could possibly be paying court to Tasneem. Saeeda Bai continued: 'Yes, yes, it's true. This pious young student, who wouldn't come when summoned into my presence because he was involved with teaching her a passage from the Holy Book, has now taken it into his head that she is in love with him, that she is going mad for his love, and that he owes it to her to marry her. He is a sly and dangerous young wolf.'

'Honestly, Saeeda Begum, this is news to me. I have not seen him for two weeks,' said Maan. He noticed that her pale neck was flushed.

'That is hardly surprising. He returned here two weeks ago. If, as appeared from your protests, you have arrived recently –'

'Recently' exclaimed Maan. 'I have barely had time to wash my face and hands –'

'Do you mean he never breathed a word of this? That is very unlikely.'

'Indeed not, Saeeda Bai. He is a very earnest soul; he didn't even want to teach me ghazals. Yes, he talked once or twice about socialism and methods for improving the economic status of the village – but love! Why, he is a married man.'

Saeeda Bai smiled. 'Has Dagh Sahib forgotten that men have not forgotten to count to four in our community?' she asked.

'Oh, yes, of course,' said Maan. 'Of course. But – well, you are not pleased –'

'No,' said Saeeda Bai, with a flash of anger. 'I am not pleased.'

'Is Tasneem –'

'No, she is not, she is not, and I will not have her be in love with some village lout –' said Saeeda Begum. 'He wants to marry her for my possessions. Then he will spend them on digging a village ditch. Or planting trees. Trees!'

This did not at all accord with Maan's sense of Rasheed, but he thought better than to contradict Saeeda Bai, who had worked herself into a state of indignation.

'Well, how about a true-hearted admirer for Tasneem?' he suggested by way of diversion.

'It is not for admirers to choose her but to be chosen by me,' said Saeeda Bai Firozabadi.

'May not even a Nawabzada admire her, even if from afar?'

'Whom precisely are you referring to?' asked Saeeda Bai, her eyes flashing dangerously.

'Let me say, a friend,' said Maan, enjoying her unfeigned interest, and admiring the brilliance of her expression – like swordplay at sunset, he thought. How beautiful she looked – and what a wonderful night lay ahead.

But Saeeda Begum got up and went to the gallery. She was biting the inside of her cheek. She clapped her hands again. 'Bibbo!' she shouted. 'Bibbo! Bibbo! That stupid girl must have gone to the kitchen. Ah' – for Bibbo had come running up the stairs at the note of danger in her mistress's voice – 'Bibbo, you've decided to grace us with your presence at last? I have been shouting myself hoarse for the last half hour.'

Maan smiled to himself at the charming exaggeration.

'Dagh Sahib is tired, Bibbo. Kindly show him out.' Something caught in her voice.

Maan started. What on earth had got into Saeeda Begum?

He looked at her, but she had averted her face. She had sounded not merely angry but painfully upset.

It must be my fault, he thought. I have said or done something terribly wrong. But what on earth have I done or said? he asked himself. Why should the thought of a Nawabzada paying court to Tasneem worry Saeeda Begum so greatly? After all, Firoz is the very opposite of a village lout.

Saeeda Bai walked past him, picked up the birdcage, and went back to her bedroom, closing the door behind her. Maan was stunned. He looked at Bibbo. She was astonished too. It was her turn to look at him with sympathy.

'Sometimes this happens,' said Bibbo. But in fact it happened very rarely. 'What did you do?' she continued with immense curiosity. Her mistress was normally unshockable. Nothing even the Raja of Marh had done recently – and he had been in a foul mood because of the result of the Zamindari Abolition case – had had this effect.

'Nothing,' said Maan, staring at the closed door. After a minute he said softly, as if speaking to himself: 'But she can't really be serious.' And, he thought to himself, I, for my part, am not going to be brushed off like this. He went to the bedroom door.

'Oh, Dagh Sahib, please, please –' cried Bibbo, horrified. The bedroom, when Saeeda Bai entered it, was sacrosanct.

'Saeeda Begum,' said Maan in a tender and puzzled voice, 'what have I done? Please tell me. Why are you so angry with me? Was it Rasheed – or Firoz – or what?'

There was no answer from inside.

'Please, Kapoor Sahib –' said Bibbo, raising her voice and trying to sound firm.

'Bibbo!' came the parakeet's metallic and commanding voice from the bedroom. Bibbo started giggling.

Maan was now trying to open the door, but the handle wouldn't work. She must have locked it from the inside, he thought angrily. Aloud he said, 'This is an unjust way to treat me, Saeeda Begum – you promise me heaven one minute and you throw me the next minute into hell. I hardly had time to bathe and shave after arriving in

Brahmpur, and I came to see you. At least tell me why you are so upset.'

From inside the room came Saeeda Bai's voice: 'Just go away, please, Dagh Sahib, have pity on me. I can't see you today. I can't give you reasons for everything.'

'You didn't give me reasons for keeping me away in your letter, and now that I'm here –'

'Bibbo!' commanded the parakeet. 'Bibbo! Bibbo!'

Maan began to pound on the door. 'Let me in! Talk to me, please – and for God's sake shut that half-witted parakeet up. I know you're feeling bad. How do you think I feel? You've wound me up like a clock, and now –'

'If you ever want to see me again,' said Saeeda Bai from inside, her voice tearful, 'you'll go away now. Or I'll tell Bibbo to call the watchman. You caused me pain involuntarily. I accept it was involuntary. Now you should accept it was pain. Please go away. Come back some other time. Stop it, Dagh Sahib – for God's sake – if you wish to see me again.'

Maan, in the face of this threat, stopped pounding the door and walked into the gallery, pent up and utterly perplexed. He was so lost that he didn't even say he was going or wish her well. He couldn't understand it at all. This was like a hailstorm falling out of a clear sky. Still, it was clearly no mere coquettishness.

'But what did you do?' persisted Bibbo, a little frightened by her mistress's mood, but enjoying the drama. Poor Dagh Sahib! She had never heard anyone pound on Saeeda Bai's door before. What passion!

'Nothing at all,' said Maan, feeling frustrated and ill-used, and glad of someone's sympathy. 'Nothing at all.' Surely it was not for this that he had exiled himself in the countryside for weeks. She had just a few minutes earlier virtually promised him a night of tenderness and ecstasy, and now – for no reason at all – had decided not merely to default, but to impale him with emotional threats.

'Poor Dagh Sahib,' said Bibbo, looking at his bewildered but attractive face. 'You've forgotten your cane. Here it is.'

'Oh – you're right,' said Maan.

As they walked down the stairs, she contrived to brush, then press against him. She stood on tiptoe and turned her lips to his face. Maan could not refrain from kissing her. He was feeling so frustrated that he would have made immediate and frantically passionate love to anyone, even to Tahmina Bai.

What an understanding girl Bibbo is, thought Maan, as they stood there kissing and embracing for a minute. Intelligent, too. Yes, it isn't fair at all, it isn't fair, and she can see it.

But Bibbo was perhaps not intelligent enough. They were kissing on the landing, and the tall mirror carried their reflection to the gallery. Saeeda Bai's mercurial anger had been followed by mercurial regret at her treatment of Maan. She decided to reassure Maan of her affection for him by bidding him goodbye from the gallery as he walked across the hall. Now she glanced down the stairs to see what was keeping him. What she saw in the mirror made her bite her lower lip to the point where it almost bled.

She stood transfixed. After a bit, Maan came to his senses and disengaged himself. The pretty Bibbo, giggling a little, escorted him across the hall to the door.

When she returned, she crossed the hall and walked up the stairs to clear away the sherbet glasses from Saeeda Bai's outer room. The Begum Sahiba will probably lie on her bed for an hour, and come out only when she feels hungry, she thought. She giggled a little more at the memory of the kiss. She was still giggling to herself when she got to the gallery. There she saw Saeeda Bai. One look at Saeeda Bai's face, and the giggling stopped.

12.17

THE next day Maan visited Bhaskar.

Bhaskar had been bored for a few days. Then he had decided to train himself in the metric system, although it was not yet in use anywhere in India. The advantages of this system over the British one became immediately apparent to him when he started using volume measurements. All sorts of comparisons became obvious when he used the metric system. For instance, if he wanted to compare the volume of Brahmpur Fort with that of Savita's baby-to-be, he could do it instantly, without converting from cubic yards to cubic inches. It wasn't as if that conversion presented great difficulty to Bhaskar; it was just that it was inconvenient and inelegant.

Another delight of the metric system was that Bhaskar could roam with unfettered delight through his beloved powers of ten. But after a few days he had tired of the metric system and its joys. His friend Dr Durrani had not visited him for some time, though Kabir had. Bhaskar liked Kabir well enough, but it was Dr Durrani who always brought new mathematical insights in tow, and without him Bhaskar had had to fend for himself.

Again he was bored, and complained to Mrs Mahesh Kapoor. After a bit of grumbling – he wanted to go back to Misri Mandi, and his grandmother was very reluctant to let him go – he applied to his grandfather instead.

Mahesh Kapoor told Bhaskar with stern affection that he couldn't help him. All such decisions were in his wife's domain.

'But I'm terribly bored,' said Bhaskar. 'And I haven't had a headache in a week. Why must I spend half the day in bed? I want to go to school. I don't like it here in Prem Nivas.'

'What?' said his grandfather. 'Not even with your Nana and Nani here?'

'No,' stated Bhaskar. 'It's all right for a day or two. Besides, you're never actually here.'

'That's true. I have so much work to do – and so many decisions to make. Well, you'll be interested to know that I've decided to leave the Congress Party.'

'Oh,' said Bhaskar, doing his best to sound interested. 'And what does that mean? Will they lose?'

Mahesh Kapoor frowned. The effort and stress that the decision had cost him was not something a child could be expected to understand. Bhaskar, besides, apparently doubted even that two plus two always equalled four, and could not be expected to sympathize greatly when the certainties of his grandfather's life were shifting underfoot. And yet Bhaskar at other times was so certain of his facts and figures, though he may well have arrived at them by erratic frog-leaps of abstract thought. Mahesh Kapoor, who was not awed by anyone else in the family, was perhaps even a little afraid of Bhaskar. A strange boy! He must certainly, thought Mahesh Kapoor, be given every opportunity to develop his rather eerie powers.

'Well, for a start,' said Mahesh Kapoor, 'it means that I will have to decide what constituency I must fight from. The Congress Party is very strong in the city, but that's where my strength lies too. On the other hand, my old constituency in the city has been redrawn, and that will present me with certain problems.'

'What problems?'

'Nothing you would understand,' Mahesh Kapoor told Bhaskar. Then, seeing Bhaskar's intense, even hostile, frown, he continued: 'The caste composition is quite different now. I've been looking over many of the new constituencies that have been delineated by the Election Commissioner, and the population figures –'

'Figures,' breathed Bhaskar.

'Yes, arranged by religion and caste in the 1931 Census. Caste! Caste! You may think it's madness, but you can never ignore it.'

'Can I have a look at these statistics, Nanaji?' said Bhaskar. 'I'll tell you what to do. Just tell me what variables are in your favour –'

'Speak in clear Hindi, idiot, it's impossible to understand what you are saying,' said Mahesh Kapoor to his grandson, still affectionately, but rather irritated by Bhaskar's presumption.

Soon, however, Bhaskar had all the facts and figures he needed to keep him more than happy for at least three days, and he started poring over the constituencies.

WHEN Maan came to visit, he asked the servant to take him straight to Bhaskar's room. He discovered Bhaskar sitting up in bed. The bed was covered with paper.

'Hello, genius,' said Maan genially.

'Hello,' said Bhaskar, rather abstracted. 'Just a minute.' He stared at a chart for a minute, scribbled down a few numbers with a pencil, and turned towards his uncle.

Maan kissed him, and asked him how he had been.

'Fine, Maan Maama, but everyone makes such a fuss here.'

'How's the head?'

'Head?' said Bhaskar, surprised. 'My head is fine.'

'Well, then, do you want some sums?'

'Not just at the moment,' said Bhaskar. 'My head is full of them.'

Maan could hardly believe this response. It was as if Kumbhkaran had decided to wake up at dawn and go on a diet.

'What are you doing? It looks very serious,' he ventured.

'Very serious indeed,' said Mahesh Kapoor's voice. Maan turned around. His father, mother, and sister had come into the room. Veena hugged Maan tearfully, then sat down on the edge of Bhaskar's bed after moving away a few sheets of paper. Bhaskar didn't object.

'Bhaskar's been complaining that he's bored here. He wants to leave,' said Veena to Maan.

'Oh, I can stay for two or three days more,' said Bhaskar.

'Really?' said Veena, surprised. 'Perhaps I really should have your head examined twice a day.' Maan cheered up at his sister's response. If she could joke in this way, Bhaskar must be all right.

'What's he been up to?' he asked.

Mahesh Kapoor replied laconically: 'He's telling me which constituency I should fight from.'

'Why not from your old one?' asked Maan.

'They've redrawn it.'

'Oh.'

'Besides, I'm going to leave the Congress Party.'

'Oh!' Maan looked at his mother, but she did not say anything. She appeared rather unhappy, though. She was not in favour of her husband's decision, but did not feel she could stop him. He would have to resign as Minister of Revenue; he would have to move out of the party that was associated in the people's mind with the freedom movement, the party of which he and she had been lifelong members; he would have to find funds from somewhere to compete with the sizeable funds of the state Congress Party, so effectively garnered and dispensed by the Home Minister. Above all, he would have to struggle once again against hard odds, and he was not young.

'Maan, you've grown so thin,' said his mother.

'Thin? Me?' said Maan.

'Yes, and you're so much darker,' she said, sadly. 'Almost like Pran. This village life is not good for you. Now we must take care of you properly. You must tell me what you want at every meal –'

'Yes, well, it's good to see you back, and I hope that things have changed,' said Mahesh Kapoor, pleased but somewhat anxious to see his son.

'Why didn't anyone tell me about Bhaskar?' said Maan.

Both Veena and her mother glanced towards Mahesh Kapoor.

'Well,' said Mahesh Kapoor, 'you must trust us to decide certain things.'

'So if Savita's baby had been born –'

'You're here now, Maan, and that's the main thing,' said his father shortly. 'Where are your things? The servant can't find them. I'll have them sent up to your room. And before you leave for Banaras you must –'

'My things are at Firoz's house. I'm staying there.'

This remark was greeted with an amazed silence.

Mahesh Kapoor looked annoyed, and Maan was not too upset by this. But Mrs Mahesh Kapoor looked hurt, and he felt bad. He began to wonder if, after all, he had done the right thing.

'So this is not your home any more?' she said.

'Of course it is, of course it is, Ammaji, but with so many people staying here –'

'People – really, Maan,' Veena said.

'It's only temporary. I'll move back when I can. I have to talk things over with Firoz as well. My future, and so on –'

'Your future lies in Banaras, and no question about it,' said his father impatiently.

His mother, sensing possible trouble, said: 'Well, we will talk about all this after lunch. You can stay for lunch, can't you?' She looked at him tenderly.

'Of course I can, Ammaji,' said Maan, hurt.

'Good. We have alu paratha today.' This was one of Maan's favourite dishes. 'When did you come?'

'I just came. I thought I'd see Bhaskar before anyone else.'

'No, to Brahmpur.'

'Yesterday evening.'

'So why didn't you come and have dinner with us?' asked his mother.

'I was tired.'

'So you had dinner at Baitar House?' asked his father. 'How is the Nawab Sahib?'

Maan flushed but did not answer. This was intolerable. He was glad he was not going to live under the dominating eye of his father.

'So where did you have dinner?' repeated his father.

'I did not have dinner last night. I was not hungry. I nibbled throughout my journey, and by the time I arrived I was not hungry. Not hungry at all.'

'Did you eat well in Rudhia?' asked his mother.

'Yes, Ammaji, I ate well, I ate very well, all the time,' said Maan with a trace of irritation in his voice.

Veena had a good sense of her brother's moods. She remembered him following her all over the house when he was a small boy. He had always been good-humoured unless he was both baulked and perplexed. He had a bad temper, but he was seldom irritable.

Something must have happened to upset or frustrate him recently; she was sure of it. She was about to ask him about it – which would probably only have bothered him further – when Bhaskar, as if waking from a reverie, said: 'Rudhia?'

'What about Rudhia?' asked Maan.

'Which part of Rudhia were you in?' asked Bhaskar.

'The northern part – near Debaria.'

'That is definitely the most favourable constituency among the rural ones,' pronounced Bhaskar. 'Northern Rudhia. Nanaji said that a large proportion of Muslims and jatavs were factors in his favour.'

Mahesh Kapoor shook his head. 'Be quiet,' he told Bhaskar. 'You're nine years old. You don't understand anything about all this.'

'But, Nanaji, really, it's true, it's one of the best!' insisted Bhaskar. 'Why don't you fight from there – you said that the new party would give you any seat you wanted. If you want a rural seat, that's the one to choose. Salimpur-cum-Baitar in Northern Rudhia. I haven't sorted out the urban seats yet.'

'Idiot, you know nothing about politics,' said Mahesh Kapoor. 'I need those papers back.'

'Well, I'm returning to Rudhia at Bakr-Id,' said Maan, siding with Bhaskar. He had cheered up at his father's discomfiture. 'People insist I celebrate with them. I'm very popular! And you can come with me. I'll introduce you to everyone in your future constituency. All the Muslims, all the jatavs.'

Mahesh Kapoor said sharply: 'I know everyone, I don't need to be introduced to them. And it is not my future constituency, let me make that clear. And let me tell you that you are going back to Banaras to settle down, not to Rudhia to make merry at Id.'

12.19

MAHESH KAPOOR had not left the party to which he had dedicated his life without pain or regret, and he was still assailed by doubts about his decision. His fear and expectation were that the Congress would not lose. The party was too well-entrenched both in office and in the people's consciousness; unless it lost Nehru, how could it fail to win? Dissatisfied though he was with the way things were going, there were other excellent reasons why Mahesh Kapoor should have remained. His brain-child the Zamindari Abolition Act had still to be declared valid by the Supreme Court and to be implemented. And there was the obvious danger that L.N. Agarwal would accumulate yet further power into his hands in the absence of a strong ministerial rival.

Mahesh Kapoor had taken (or been persuaded to take) a calculated gamble to try to prod Nehru out of the Congress Party. Or perhaps it had been not a calculated but a whimsical gamble. Or perhaps not even whimsical but instinctive. For the real gambler behind the scenes was the Minister of Communications in Nehru's own Cabinet in Delhi, the adroit Rafi Ahmad Kidwai, who, leaning on his bed like a genial, white-capped, bespectacled Buddha, had told Mahesh Kapoor (who had come to pay him a friendly visit) that if he didn't jump out now from the drifting boat of the Congress Party, he would never be able to help pull it by its tow-rope back to shore.

It was a far-fetched image, made more dubious by the fact that Rafi Sahib, for all his immense agility of thought and love of fast cars, had never been addicted to swiftness of movement – or, indeed, exercise of any physical kind, let alone jumping, swimming, and tugging. But he was notoriously persuasive. Canny businessmen lost their canniness in his presence and divested themselves of thousands of rupees, which he promptly disbursed to harassed widows, poor students, party politicians and even his political rivals if they happened to be in need. His likeableness, generosity and astuteness had cast a spell over many a more hard-headed politician than Mahesh Kapoor.

Rafi Sahib had a taste for a great many things – fountain-pens, mangoes and watches among them – and he also had a taste for jokes; and Mahesh Kapoor, having finally taken the psychological plunge, wondered whether this might not be one of his more zany and disastrous ones. For Nehru had shown no effective sign of leaving the Congress yet, despite the fact that it was his ideological supporters who were bleeding away. Time would tell, however, and timing was the key. Rafi Sahib, who could sit silent and smiling while six conversations swirled all round him, would suddenly latch onto a single sentence of exceptional interest and insight like a chameleon catching a fly. He had a similar instinct for the shifting shoals and currents of politics: the sonar ability to distinguish dolphins from crocodiles even in these murky, silted waters, and an uncanny sense of when to act. Upon Mahesh Kapoor's departure, he had given him a watch – the spring of Mahesh Kapoor's own watch had snapped – and had said: 'I guarantee that Nehru, you and I will fight from the same platform, whatever that may be. At thirteen o'clock on the thirteenth day of the thirteenth month, look at this watch, Kapoor Sahib, and tell me if I was not right.'

12.20

AROUND the time of the elections to the Brahmpur University Students' Union there was a spurt of political activity both on and off campus. There was a great hodgepodge of issues: cinema concessions on the one hand, and a call for solidarity with primary schoolteachers in their wage bargaining on the other; demands for more employment opportunities together with support for Pandit Nehru's non-aligned foreign policy; amendments to the rigid code of conduct of the university – and insistence that Hindi be used for the civil service examinations. Some parties – or the leaders of some parties, for where parties ended and leaders began was itself a difficult business to fathom – believed that all India's ills would be cured by a return to ancient Hindu traditions. Others insisted that socialism, variously defined or felt, was the cure-all.

There was ferment and fighting. It was the beginning of

the academic year, and no one was concentrating on his studies; exams were nine months away. Students chattered in the coffee houses or the delegacy lodges or hostels, gathered in knots outside classes, led small marches, fasted, and beat each other up with sticks and stones. Sometimes they were helped in this by the local parties they were affiliated to, but this was not really necessary. Students had learned how to cause trouble under the British, and there was no reason why hard-earned corporate skills, passed on from batch to batch, should be wasted merely because of the change of dispensation in Delhi and Brahmpur. Besides, the Congress government, by its slow slide into complacency and its inability to solve the country's problems, was unpopular among the students, who by no means valued stability as an end in itself.

The Congress Party expected to win by default, as great, shapeless, centrist lumps often do. It expected to win even though its national leadership was riven by differences, even though Congressmen were leaving their party in droves ever since the meeting in Patna, even though the most prominent local Congressman's name was mud among the students – both as the Treasurer of the university with his manoeuvrings on the Executive Council, and as the lathi-happy Home Minister. The student Congress Party's theme was: 'Give us time. We are the party of Independence, of Jawaharlal Nehru, not really of L.N. Agarwal. Even though things have not improved, they will improve if you continue to place confidence in us. If you change horses now, they assuredly will not.'

But most students were not inclined to vote for the status quo; they had no spouses or children or jobs or income, possible injury to which might counterbalance the excitement of instability. Nor did they trust for the future those who had shown no signs of competence in the past. The country had to beg for food from abroad. The economy, under-planned and over-planned, lurched from crisis to crisis. There were few jobs waiting for the students themselves after graduation.

Their post-Independence romanticism and post-Independence disillusionment formed a volatile mixture. The Congress argument was rejected, and the Socialist Party won the election. Rasheed was on the party slate, and became an office-bearer.

Malati Trivedi, who considered herself an unlikely socialist, but joined in for the enjoyment of it all and because she liked the discussions, and because some friends of hers (including her musician) had been socialists, had no interest whatsoever in office. But she planned to join in the 'victory-cum-protest' march that was planned a week after the elections.

The 'protest' part of the title came from the fact that the Socialist Party – together with any other parties that cared to join in – was going to march in protest against the low pay of primary schoolteachers. There were over ten thousand primary schoolteachers, and it was a disgrace that their salaries were as low as they were, certainly not enough for a decent living, lower in fact than those of village patwaris. The teachers had gone on strike after a number of unsuccessful attempts to get themselves heard. A number of students' federations, including those of the medical and law colleges, had pledged their support to the cause. Education involved them, and it involved the future shape of the university, indeed, the calibre of the citizenry of the country itself. Besides, here was an excellent magnet to which they could attach anything else that came to mind. Some of these federations were interested in stirring up the whole of Brahmpur, not just the university; interestingly enough, one minor hotbed of radicalism was a group of Muslim girls who were still in purdah.

The Home Minister L.N. Agarwal had made it clear that a peaceful procession was one thing, a disorderly surge of rabble another. He would control it with whatever means were available. If a lathi charge was necessary, he would order it.

Since the Chief Minister was in Delhi for a few days, a delegation of ten students (Rasheed among them) went to see the Home Minister, who was in charge in S.S. Sharma's absence. They crowded into his office in the Secretariat.

They made brusque demands, as much to impress each other as to hope to persuade him. They did not pay him the respect that he believed was due to their elders, especially those who (unlike them) had suffered blows and ruin and years in jail in order to see their country free. He refused to concede their demands, saying that they should talk either to the Education Minister or to the Chief Minister himself upon his return. Nor did he budge from his stated stance that he would maintain order in the town at any cost.

'Does that mean you will shoot us if we get out of hand?' asked Rasheed with a malignant look.

'I would prefer not to,' said the Home Minister, as if the idea was not entirely unpleasant, 'but, needless to say, it will not come to that.' At any rate, he added to himself, the legislature is not presently in session to take me to task about it.

'This is like the days of the British,' continued Rasheed furiously, staring at the man who had justified the police firing in Chowk, and perhaps seeing embodied in him the image of other arbitrariness and authoritarianism. 'The British used lathis on us, they even shot at us, at us students, during the Quit India movement. Our blood was spilt by the British here in Brahmpur – in Chowk, in Captainganj –'

The rest of the delegation began to buzz rather angrily in response to his oratory.

'Yes, yes,' said the Home Minister, cutting him short. 'I know it. I lived through it. You must have been a boy of twelve then, watching anxiously in the mirror for the first signs of a man's hair. When you say "us students" you don't mean yourselves, it was your predecessors whose blood was spilt. And, I may mention, some of mine. It's easy enough to lubricate your way to office on others' blood. And as for Quit India, this is an Indian government now, and I hope you don't want us to quit India.' He laughed shortly. 'Now if you have anything useful to say, say it. Otherwise go. You may not have your books to read, but I have my files. I know exactly what this march is about. It isn't about the salaries of primary schoolteachers. It is a way of concertedly attacking the Congress government of the state and the country, and trying to spread disaffection and disorder in the town.' He made a dismissive gesture with the back of his hand. 'Stick to your books. That is my advice to you as your true friend – and as the Treasurer of the university – and as the Home Minister – and as the Acting Chief Minister; and it is the advice of your Vice-Chancellor too. And your teachers. And your parents.'

'And God,' added the President of the students' union, who was an atheist.

'Get out,' said the Home Minister in a calm voice.

12.21

BUT the evening before the day fixed for the march an incident occurred in town that brought the two sides temporarily together on the same side of an issue.

Manorma Talkies, the cinema-hall in Nabiganj that was showing *Deedar*, that had indeed been showing *Deedar* continuously to packed or almost packed houses for months, became the scene of what was almost a student riot.

The Brahmpur University ordinances forbade students from going to the second or late-night show, but this was an ordinance that hardly anyone paid any heed to. In particular, those students who lived outside the university hostels flouted it whenever they saw fit. *Deedar* was an immensely popular movie. Its songs were on everyone's lips, and it appealed to old and young alike; it may well have happened that on some evening Dr Kishen Chand Seth and the Rajkumar of Marh sobbed their hearts out to it simultaneously. People saw it several times over. It had an unusually tragic ending, but one which did not make one wish to tear the screen apart or set fire to the theatre.

What caused the trouble was that on this evening the management had given exceptionally strict instructions to the ticket office not to honour student concessions if they got enough ticket-buyers at the full price. It was the early evening show. Two students, one of whom had seen the film before, had been told that the house was full. From past experience they had learned to mistrust the management. When several others who came after them were sold tickets, they began to harangue first the people in the ticket queue – when one woman told them to shut up, they told her the ending of the film – and then began to yell at the employees at the box office. The employees went about their business unperturbed – until the students, one of whom had an umbrella, became desperate enough to smash the glass panes of the doors of the cinema-hall. Some of the patrons started shouting and threatening to call the police, but the management was not keen that the police be called. The employees got the projectionist and a few other people together, beat the students up, and threw them out. The mild mêlée was over in a few minutes, and did not disturb too deeply the subsequent mood of the audience.

By the time the first show ended, however, there was a crowd of about four hundred angry students demonstrating threateningly against the illegal actions of the management – and particularly the manhandling of their two fellows. They had driven away from the box office all those who were thinking of buying tickets for the second show or who, having bought their tickets in advance, were seeking to enter the lobby.

It had begun to drizzle, but the students refused to leave. They were angry, and yet they were elated, for here they were, displaying their might in front of the portals of the infamous Manorma Talkies which, because of the continuing success of *Deedar* in attracting customers at the full price, and also because of its hard-headed manager, who cared less for law than profits, had been discriminating against them for months. Refreshed by their vacation, excited by the recent student elections, and indignant at the attack on their pride and their pockets, the students shouted that they would show the management what stuff they were made of, that the cinema-hall must 'either learn or burn', and that sticks would teach the employees what passes couldn't. The sorrowful and subdued patrons of the first show began to come out. They were astonished to be faced by a belligerent crowd which condemned their acquiescence in the earlier violence. 'Shame! Shame!' shouted the students. The audience, among them old people and even children, looked perplexedly at them with tear-stained faces.

The scene began to grow ugly. There was no violence, but some of the patrons were not allowed to enter their cars, and hurried away, fearing that if they stayed, their own safety would be threatened. Finally the District Magistrate, the Deputy Superintendent of Police, and the Proctor of the university all arrived on the scene. They tried to ascertain the nature of the problem. All of them felt that the management was to blame but that the students should have taken their complaint through the proper channels. The Proctor even tried to make the point that the students had no right to demonstrate before the second show, but it was clear that when facing four hundred angry students on a rainy night, he could not immediately exercise his normally awesome authority. His voice was drowned out by the shouting. When he perceived that the students would not be pacified or persuaded about the adequacy of the proper channels except by office-bearers of their own union, he tried to seek them out. Two of them, though not Rasheed, happened to be in the crowd. But they made it clear that they would not act unless the Treasurer appeared on their behalf as a representative of the Executive Council in order to show that the Council in general acted to protect, not merely to impose its will on the student body. This was a way of demanding L.N. Agarwal's presence.

The manager, who had gone home just after the students had been thrashed and before the crowd had collected, came hurriedly to the scene when he heard that the police would protect his person from injury but that only he could protect Manorma Talkies. He was abject. He called the students 'my dear dear friends'. He wept when he saw the bruises on the arms and back of one of the students. He talked about his own student days. He offered them all a special showing of *Deedar*. It would not do. 'Our university Treasurer will represent us,' insisted the students' union. 'Only he knows how to restrain us.' As a matter of fact, they themselves were keen that the incident should not turn violent, because it would affect the next day's victory-cum-protest march, and they did not want it to be perceived by the public at large that students demonstrated only for their own trivial privileges and not for the good of society.

L.N. Agarwal, who had told the DSP that he should handle the matter on his own and that he should not ring up the Home Minister for every petty disturbance, was finally persuaded by a phone call from his colleague the Proctor to come to the scene. Most unwillingly, he did so. He found himself utterly out of sympathy with the unruly mob. Students did not realize how privileged they were in comparison to the rest of their countrymen. They chose deliberately to be ignorant of how little they themselves paid for their education, how two-thirds of it was subsidized by the government. They were a cosseted bunch, and he deplored the concessions that they received for what was, after all, mere entertainment. But since the concessions existed, he was forced to tell the manager that he would have to accede to the students' demands.

As a result, the offending employees were dismissed; the manager submitted a letter of apology to the Proctor expressing his regret over the incident and assuring the students of his 'best service at all times'; two hundred rupees was paid to each of the injured students; and the manager agreed to screen a slide of his letter of apology at all the cinema-halls of Brahmpur.

The students' union calmed the crowd down. The students melted away. The police retired. And L.N. Agarwal returned to his two rooms in the MLAs' hostel, furious at having had to act on behalf of the rowdy mob. Even when he had emerged from the manager's office, some of the students had jeered him. One went so far as to rhyme his surname with the Hindi word for pimp. For puerility, selfishness and ingratitude, thought the Home Minister, they were hard to beat. And tomorrow again, no doubt, their propensity for violence would come to the fore. Well, the police would be ready if they overstepped the line between propensity and action.

12.22

THE next day, L.N. Agarwal's fears or hopes were fulfilled. The march began peacefully when it set out from a primary school. The girls (Malati among them) marched in front so as to foil any police action, and the boys marched behind them. They shouted slogans against the government and in support of the primary schoolteachers, some of whom were marching with them. People looked out at the procession from the windows of their houses, or from the open fronts of their shops, or down from their roofs. Some of them encouraged the students, others complained about the disruption to their business. The primary schools had gone on another day's strike, and many children waved at teachers whom they recognized. The teachers sometimes waved back. It was a clear morning, and only a few puddles remained of the previous night's rain.

A couple of banners protested the action of the university that sought to make membership in the students' union voluntary. Yet others protested growing unemployment. But most of them protested the plight of the primary schoolteachers and expressed their solidarity with them.

When the crowd got to within a hundred yards of the Secretariat, they found their path blocked by a large contingent of policemen armed with lathis. The students stopped. The police advanced until they were within five yards of each other. On the instructions of the DSP an Inspector told the students to either disperse or return. They refused. They had been shouting slogans all the while, but these now became more and more insulting, and embraced not only the government but the police. The police, who were the lackeys of the British, had now become the lackeys of the Congress-wallahs; they should be wearing dhotis, not shorts; and so on.

The policemen became restive. They wanted to get at the loudest slogan-mongers in the crowd. But with a cordon of girls – some wearing burqas – surrounding the boys, it was difficult for them to do anything but brandish their lathis threateningly. The students, for their part, could see that for all L. N. Agarwal's threats, the police were carrying sticks, not firearms, and this made them bolder.

Some of them, recalling the Home Minister's devious behind-the-scenes style, started to bait him personally; apart from rhyming his name with 'dalal' as they had the previous night, they invented a number of new couplets, such as:

> 'Maananiya Mantri, kya hain aap?
> Aadha maanav, aadha saanp.'
>> Minister, what form do you take?
>> Half a human, half a snake.

Some challenged his manhood in more direct ways. Rasheed and another office-bearer of the students' union attempted to keep the students calm and their slogans to the purpose, but to little avail. For one thing, some of the protesters belonged to student federations over whom the newly-elected Socialist Party students' union had no real control. For another, a certain intoxication had seized hold of the assembly. The high-minded banners now contrasted pathetically with the low-minded mockery.

Finding that the protest that he had helped organize was getting completely out of hand, Rasheed now tried to persuade at least his immediate neighbours to calm down. They did, but others did not follow. Indeed, by then, loud jeers and insults had broken out in several other groups. He tried to shout that this was not what their march or their platform was all about, but found himself becoming a subsidiary butt of their indignation. One young man from the medical college, full of wit and zeal, told him:

'Just now you were All India Radio, now you're a little squirrel squeaking in Agarwal's pocket. First you try to whip us up, then you try to cool us down. We aren't clockwork toys.' And as if to prove his independence of the office-bearers, the boy now made his way through the protective cordon of girls and continued his pejorative peltings, retreating whenever the police advanced. His friends laughed, but Rasheed, frightened now as he looked at the faces of the police, and disgusted by what this principled march had degenerated into, turned away – and, despite the heckling of some other students, turned back. What the boy had said had had enough truth in it to make him feel sick at heart.

It was only small groups that concentrated on the worst kind of unwitty taunt. But these taunts began to antagonize most of the girls and some others in the crowd, including many teachers. They began to leave. L.N. Agarwal, who had been looking down from his office in the Secretariat, noticed with satisfaction that the protective cordon was becoming thinner, and sent a message down that the remaining students should be dispersed. 'Teach them that lessons can be taught outside the classroom as well as inside,' were his words to the DSP who came to him for instructions.

'Yes, Sir,' said the DSP, almost gratefully.

After the insults to the police, the DSP would fulfil his instructions with little regret.

He ordered the Inspectors, Sub-Inspectors and constables to teach the students a good lesson, and this they did with a vengeance. The lathi charge was savage and sudden. Several students were badly beaten. A certain amount of blood mixed with the previous night's rain in the puddles, and stained the surface of the road. Many of the blows were severe. Some young men suffered broken bones: ribs, or legs, or arms which they had lifted in order to protect their heads from injury. The policemen pulled them off the road, sometimes by the feet, their heads bouncing or dragging along the road surface, towards the police vans. They were too incensed to use stretchers.

One boy lay in a van at the point of death, with an

injury to the skull. He was the student from the medical college.

12.23

WHEN S.S. Sharma returned that afternoon he found a dangerous situation on his hands. What had begun as a protest march had now upset and unnerved the whole town. Regardless of their political affiliations, the students closed ranks against the brutality, some said criminality, of the police. A vigil began near the medical college, where (once the police realized how serious his injuries were) the student had been unloaded. Several thousand students sat outside the medical college, waiting for news of the boy's health. Needless to say, there were no classes anywhere in the university that day, nor would there be for a while.

The Home Minister, fearing the worst if the boy died, advised the Chief Minister to call out the army, and if necessary to impose martial law. He himself had already imposed a police curfew, which was due to take effect that evening.

S.S. Sharma listened in silence. Then he said: 'Agarwal, why is it that I cannot leave town for two days without you presenting me with some problem? If you are tired of your portfolio, I will give you something else.'

But L.N. Agarwal enjoyed the power that went along with being Home Minister, and he knew that it was not a portfolio that could be given to anyone else, especially now that it was an open secret that Mahesh Kapoor was about to announce his resignation from the Congress Party and the government. He said: 'I have done my best. One cannot run a state by kindness.'

'So you suggest calling out the army?'

'I do, Sharmaji.'

S.S. Sharma looked tired. He said, 'That will be good neither for the army nor for the people of Brahmpur. As for the students, it will inflame them as little else can.' His head began to shake slightly. 'I feel they are like my children. This is a wrong thing we have done.'

L.N. Agarwal smiled somewhat contemptuously at the Chief Minister's sentimentality. But he was relieved to notice the collective 'we'.

'I believe, Sharmaji, that no matter what we do, the students will be inflamed when that student dies.'

'*When*, you say, not *if*? There is no hope for him, then?'

'I don't believe so. But it is difficult to get at facts in this situation. It is true, people exaggerate. Still, it is best to be prepared.' L.N. Agarwal's tone was cold, and not defensive.

The Chief Minister sighed, then continued in his slightly nasal voice: 'Because of this curfew, whatever happens to the student, we will have a problem this evening. What if the students do not disperse? Do you suggest we start firing at them?'

The Home Minister remained silent.

'And when the boy dies, I tell you that the funeral will become uncontrollable. They will want to cremate him by the Ganga, probably near that other unfortunate pyre.'

The Home Minister refused to flinch at this needless reference. When one did one's duty properly, one could face reproof without being inwardly shaken. He had no doubt that the Pul Mela Inquiry Commission, which had begun its sittings a week ago, would absolve him.

'That will be impossible,' he said. 'They will have to do it at a ghat or somewhere else. The sands on this side of the river are already under water.'

S.S. Sharma was about to say something, then thought better of it. Pandit Jawaharlal Nehru, embattled though he was in his own party, had once again asked him to come to the centre to join his Cabinet. It was getting difficult to refuse. But now, with the imminent resignation of Mahesh Kapoor, Sharma's departure would almost certainly result in L.N. Agarwal becoming Chief Minister. And Sharma felt that he could not in conscience hand his state over to this shrewd and rigid man who, for all his intelligence, lacked any human touch. Sharma in his philosophical moments felt like a father towards those in his protection. Sometimes this led to unnecessary conciliation or avoidable compromise, but he believed these were preferable to Agarwal's alternative. Needless to say, a state could not be run on kindness alone. But he dreaded to think of one run on nothing but discipline and fear.

'Agarwal, I am taking over this problem from you. Kindly issue no further instructions in this matter,' said the Chief Minister. 'But do not undo any instructions you have already issued. Let the curfew stand.'

The Chief Minister then looked at his watch, and told his personal assistant to get the Superintendent of the medical college on the telephone. He picked up the day's newspaper, and ignored Agarwal. When the PA got through to the Superintendent, he said: 'The Chief Minister would like to speak to you, Sir,' and handed the phone to the Chief Minister.

'This is Sharma speaking,' said the Chief Minister. 'I wish to come to the medical college immediately.... No, no police, no police escort at all. Just one assistant.... Yes.... I am sorry to hear about the boy.... Yes, well, my safety is my concern. I will avoid the students on vigil.... What do you mean, impossible? Surely there must be a side gate or something. A private gate to your house? Yes, I'll use that. If you would kindly meet me there. ... Good, in fifteen minutes then. Do not mention this to anyone, or I will face the kind of reception committee I can do without. ... No, he won't be with me – no, definitely not.'

Not looking at L.N. Agarwal but at a glass paperweight on his desk, the Chief Minister said: 'I must go to the medical college and see what I can do. I think it best if you don't come with me. If you remain here in my office, I will be able to get in touch with you immediately if there are developments, and my staff will be at your service.'

L.N. Agarwal passed his hand restlessly through the horseshoe of hair around his head.

'I would prefer to come with you,' he said. 'Or at least to give you a police escort.'

'I do not think that would be for the best.'

'You need protection. Those students –'

'Agarwal, you are not Chief Minister yet,' said S.S. Sharma quietly, but with a rather unhappy smile. L.N. Agarwal frowned, but did not say another word.

12.24

WHEN he got to the room where the injured boy was lying, the Chief Minister, hardened though he had been by the deaths and injuries caused by British lathi charges and firings, shook his head for a minute in pity and disbelief. He glanced through the window at the students sitting on the lawn and the road and tried to imagine their feelings of shock and anger. It was as well that they did not know he was in the college. The Superintendent was saying something to him, something about the impossibility of resuming classes. The Chief Minister's attention, however, had wandered to an old man in typical Congress garb, who was sitting quietly in a corner and had not stood up to greet him. He appeared to be lost in his own world, as he himself was.

'And who are you?' asked the Chief Minister.

'I am the father of this unfortunate boy,' said the man.

The Chief Minister bowed his head.

'You must come with me,' he said. 'We can settle the issues later. But you and I have to sort out the immediate problem immediately. In a private room, not with so many people around.'

'I cannot leave this room. My son does not have long to live, I understand.'

The Chief Minister looked around the room and asked everyone to leave except for one doctor. Then he said to the old man:

'I am guilty of letting this happen. I accept the responsibility for it. But I need your help. You see how it is. Only you can save the situation. If you do not, there will be many more unfortunate boys and many more grief-stricken fathers.'

'What can I do?' The old man spoke calmly, as if nothing much mattered to him any more.

'The students are inflamed. When your son dies, they will want to take out a procession. It is bound to be an emotional event, and will get out of hand. If that occurs, and it is almost inevitable, who can answer for what will happen?'

'What do you want me to do?'

'Speak to the students. Tell them to condole with you, tell them to attend the funeral. It will take place wherever you wish it to; I will not allow any police to be present. But please advise them not to take out a procession. That will have an uncontainable effect.'

The old man began to weep. After a while he controlled himself and, looking at his son, whose head was covered almost entirely in bandages, he said in the same calm voice as before: 'I will do as you say.'

Then, to himself, he added: 'So he will have died for nothing?'

The Chief Minister caught the remark, though it was uttered in a low voice. He said: 'Indeed, I will make sure that he will not have. I will try to defuse the situation in my own way. But nothing I do can have the chastening effect of a few words from you. Your act will have prevented more grief than most people can prevent in their lives.'

The Chief Minister returned, as he had come, incognito. Once back in his office he asked L.N. Agarwal to cancel the curfew and to release all the students who had been arrested in the demonstration earlier. 'And send for the President of the students' union,' he added.

Over L.N. Agarwal's protest that it was a march instigated by the union that had been the genesis of this problem in the first place, the Chief Minister met the young man, who seemed less self-assured but more determined than before. He had wanted to bring Rasheed with him – one Hindu, one Muslim, to emphasize the secularism of the socialists – but Rasheed had looked so ill with distress and guilt that he had changed his mind. Now the young man was here alone, face to face with the Chief Minister and the Home Minister, and he was patently nervous.

The Chief Minister said: 'I agree to your terms, but I want the movement to be called off. Are you prepared to do that? Do you have the courage to avoid further bloodshed?'

'The question of membership of the students' unions?' said the young man.

'Yes,' said the Chief Minister. L.N. Agarwal stood tight-lipped nearby, and could not trust himself to utter a word. His silence, he knew, implied consent, and it was a difficult silence to maintain.

'The primary schoolteachers' salaries?'

'We will go into the question, and we will improve the salaries, but we do not know if the extent of the improvement will satisfy you completely. The resources of the state are limited. Still, we will try.'

Thus they went down the list of demands one by one.

'What I can offer,' said the young man, 'is a temporary withdrawal. I have your promise, and you have mine – assuming I can persuade the others. But if the demands are not in fact met, this understanding will no longer hold.'

L.N. Agarwal, disgusted with the proceedings, reflected that the young man thought nothing of the fact that he was parleying on equal terms with the chief executive of the state. And even S.S. Sharma, who normally loved the outward forms of respect and obeisance, had, it appeared, so far forgotten what was due to him as not to mind their absence.

'I understand and agree,' the Chief Minister was saying. L.N. Agarwal looked at S.S. Sharma and thought: You are getting old and weak. You have acceded to unreason in order to buy a temporary peace. But the precedent of this peace will remain to haunt us, your successors. And you may not have bought peace anyway. Still, we will know soon enough about that.

That night the injured student died. The grieving father spoke to those who were holding vigil outside. The next day the body was cremated at the cremation ghat on the Ganga. The students sat on the great steps leading down to the ghat. There was no procession. The dense crowd of mourners was quiet as the flames crackled around the body. The police had been instructed to keep away. There was no violence.

12.25

DR KISHEN CHAND SETH had booked two tables in the small bridge room of the Subzipore Club. Noticing his name on the roster for the day, none of the other members had booked either of the two remaining tables. The librarian, who usually made it a point to look at the roster himself (the bridge room was located next door to the library), sighed when he saw the name of the eminent radiologist. There would be little peace for him that afternoon; and, if they continued to play through the film, that evening either.

Dr Kishen Chand Seth was seated facing a tiger-skin that was hanging head downwards on the wall. The tiger had been there for as long as anyone could remember, though its connection with bridge was unclear. Prints of Oxford colleges – including one with a pelican perched on a pillar in the quad – hung on the remaining walls. The four green baize-covered bridge-tables were arranged squarely in the small square room. Apart from the sixteen hardbacked chairs there were no others. It was a fairly austere room, if one excepted the tiger. Its one large window looked out upon a gravel drive, and beyond that the lawn where members and their guests sat on white cane chairs in the shade of large trees and sipped long drinks; and far beyond that the Ganges.

The seven others constituting Dr Kishen Chand Seth's bridge party were: his wife Parvati, who was wearing an exceptionally tasteless sari with roses printed on it; his relation by marriage, the ex-Minister of Revenue, Mahesh Kapoor, whom Dr Seth seemed to recall he was currently on good terms with; Mr Shastri, the Advocate-General; the Nawab Sahib of Baitar; Professor and Mrs O.P. Mishra; and Dr Durrani. There were six men and two women, and the draw of cards had placed them in such a way that the two women were seated at the same table, though they were not partners. Mrs O.P. Mishra, a frightened but babbling sort of woman, was a good bridge player. Parvati Seth was not a good player, and irritated her husband a great deal by her hesitant and obtuse bidding whenever she happened to be his partner. He very rarely dared to rebuke her, however, and vented his spleen on anyone else who happened to be nearby.

Dr Kishen Chand Seth's idea of an ideal afternoon of bridge was furious, ruthless play combined with continuous conversation; and his idea of entertaining conversation was a series of small shocks and explosions.

When he was most delighted, he actually cackled. And it was a cackle that preceded the following remark:

'Two spades. Hm, hm, hmm, now, Minister – ex-Minister, I should say – you are taking as long to bid as it must have taken you to decide to resign.'

Mahesh Kapoor frowned in concentration. 'What? Pass.'

'Or as long as it took him to frame the Zamindari Act, wouldn't you say, Nawab Sahib? He was always a slow bidder; let's hope he takes his time gobbling up your estates. But there's no reason for you to bid so slowly.'

The Nawab Sahib, somewhat distracted, said, 'Three hearts.'

'But I forget,' said Dr Kishen Chand Seth, turning to the left. 'You won't be doing that any longer. Who will, I wonder. Agarwal? Could he handle both Revenue and Home?'

Mr Mahesh Kapoor sat up a little more stiffly, but said nothing. He held his cards in a slightly tighter grip. He thought for a moment of reminding his host that it had been L.N. Agarwal himself who had issued the order for requisitioning cars. But he held his tongue.

'No, er, no bid,' said Dr Durrani.

Dr Kishen Chand Seth, having seen three of his squibs fizzle out, sent up a fourth. 'It's a portfolio that requires someone responsible, and who else is there in the Cabinet as competent as Agarwal? Now, what shall I bid? What shall I bid? Three spades. Good. But I must say he did a good job teaching those students a lesson. In my day, medical students stuck to their Anatomy and did not make cadavers of themselves. Three spades. Yes, what's your bid, now, Kapoor Sahib?'

Mahesh Kapoor looked across at his partner, and thought of the student who had restored his grandson to him. Dr Durrani seemed to be going through a struggle with himself. 'Well, er, do you, well, consider that the lathi charge was, um, justified?' he asked, scrunching his eyes up. There was as much disapproval in his voice as it was ever capable of holding, which wasn't much. He had expressed only the mildest verbal disapproval when his wife had tried to destroy a large part of his life's work by tearing up his mathematical papers.

'Oh, but I do, I do –' cried Dr Kishen Chand Seth with relish. 'One must be cruel only to be kind. The surgeon's knife; we doctors learn that at an early age. But you are a doctor too, of course. A doctor of a kind. Not yet a professor, but no doubt that will come. You should ask Professor Mishra there what it takes to rise to such a height.'

By such means did Dr Kishen Chand Seth knit the two tables together into a web of distracting conversation. His own game thrived upon the stimulus that this turmoil provided. Most of the others were used to him through acquaintance, and tried not to get provoked. But anyone else who was present and attempting to play in the bridge room at that time would have been tempted to complain to the committee, had Dr Kishen Chand Seth himself not been a member of it. Since he was one of the oldest members of the Subzipore Club and since he believed in terrorizing everyone else before they could complain even mildly about him, his odd behaviour escaped its normal consequences.

When he saw the dummy's hand, Dr Kishen Chand Seth almost had a fit. After he had played the hand, he and the Nawab Sahib were one trick down, and Dr Seth turned roundly on his partner. 'Good heavens, Nawab Sahib, with such a poor hand, how did you go on to bid three hearts? We had no chance of making nine tricks.'

'You could have had hearts.'

Dr Kishen Chand Seth bristled with rage. 'If I had hearts, partner, I would have bid the suit earlier,' he almost shouted. 'If you didn't have spades, you should have shut up – the bidding. This is what happens when you turn your back on your religion and play cards with infidels.'

The Nawab Sahib told himself, as he often had before, that he would never respond to one of Dr Kishen Chand Seth's invitations in the future.

'Now, now, Kishy,' said Parvati mildly, glancing across from the other table.

'Sorry – sorry –' said Dr Kishen Chand Seth. 'I – well – well, whose turn is it to deal? Ah, yes, drinks. What will everyone have to drink?' And he clicked out the small wood and brass extension located immediately to his right in the table; it contained an ashtray and a coaster. 'First the ladies. Gin for the ladies?'

Mrs O.P. Mishra cast a terrified look at her husband. Parvati Seth, catching the look, said, 'Kishy!' rather sharply.

Kishy was brought to heel for the next few minutes. He alternated his concentration between his cards, the tiger, and (once the waiter had brought it in) his whisky. Normally he was restricted to tea and nimbu pani, but he threw such a tantrum if he was not allowed his whisky when playing bridge that Parvati thought it best to husband her strength for more winnable battles. The only problem was that the whisky had unpredictable effects. On some days it made him slightly mellow, on other days more belligerent. It never made him amorous. And rarely did it make him, as it makes some men, sentimental; only movies had that power.

Dr Kishen Chand Seth was looking forward to the movie which was to be screened in the club today: a Charlie Chaplin movie, he recalled. His granddaughter Savita had very much wanted to see it, and despite her husband's and mother's advice, had availed herself of his membership to do so. Pran and Mrs Rupa Mehra, reasonably enough, had insisted on coming along. But Dr Seth could not see them sitting anywhere on the lawn even after an hour had gone by and they were well into the second rubber and thirteenth argument.

'Er, well,' Dr Durrani was remonstrating, 'I can't entirely, you know, agree with you. A fine calculation of probabilities is an essential part –'

'Essential, nothing!' Dr Kishen Chand Seth cut him off. 'Most good bridge play is simply deduction, not a judgment of probabilities. Now I'll give you an example,' he went on. Dr Kishen Chand Seth liked arguing from examples. 'It happened to me just a week ago. A week ago, wasn't it, dear?'

'Yes, dear,' said Parvati. She remembered the game well, because her husband's triumph had spiced their evening conversations throughout the week.

'I was the declarer and I played clubs early in the game. I had five, my dummy had two, and the man on the right ruffed.'

'Woman, Kishy.'

'Yes, yes, woman!' said Dr Kishan Chand Seth, expostulating as much as he dared.

'That meant that the man on my left had to have had six clubs, or, rather, five after this round. Now later in the game it was clear that he could only have space in his hand for two hearts; since he had bid spades, I assumed he must have had at least four spades, and the residue of those had to take up the rest of the place in his hand.'

'Isn't that Rupa, dear?' asked Parvati suddenly, pointing towards the lawn. She had heard the story so often that she had entirely forgotten to treat it with reverence.

This cruel interruption threw her husband completely off his stride. 'Yes, yes, it is Rupa. Let it be Rupa – or anyone else,' he cried, dismissing his daughter from his mind. 'Now, you see, I had the ace, the king, and the jack of hearts. So I played the ace first and then the king. As I had deduced, the queen fell.' He paused to retaste the memory. 'Everyone said that I was a lucky player or that the probabilities were in my favour. But that was not the case at all. Luck – nothing! Probabilities – nothing! I had my eyes open, and, most of all, my brain open. To deduction,' he ended triumphantly. Then, since it sounded like a toast, he took a good gulp of whisky.

Dr Durrani looked unconvinced.

The next table, though often dragged by Dr Seth into the vortex of his own, was much calmer. Mr Shastri, the Advocate-General, was at his genial best, and did his best (in his syllabic manner) to draw out Mrs O.P. Mishra, who played a good game but seemed to be worried that she was doing so; she kept darting glances at her husband opposite. Bridge, where the bidding consisted almost entirely of monosyllabic words, was the ideal game for Mr Shastri. He was happy that he was not sitting at the other table, where he would have been forced by his host into an embarrassing conversation about the taking over of the estates and his estimation of the government's chances when the zamindari case went to the Supreme Court. He sympathized equally with the Nawab Sahib and Mahesh Kapoor. Mahesh Kapoor had exploded twice in the face of Dr Kishen Chand Seth's opinions, and appeared about to do so for the third time. The Nawab Sahib had subsided into icy etiquette; he now refused to contradict even the most outrageous of his host's comments, or to take visible offence at his repeated offers of whisky – indeed, even to repeat what Dr Kishen Chand Seth well knew, that he was a teetotaller. Only Dr Durrani was able to maintain an absent-minded and undisagreeable disagreement, and this exasperated Dr Kishen Chand Seth.

Meanwhile, Professor O.P. Mishra was holding forth for the benefit of Parvati and the Advocate-General:

'Politicians, you know, prefer to appoint mediocrities to important posts not merely because they themselves will look better in comparison or because they are afraid of competition, but also because, you see, a person appointed on merit feels that it is owed to him, while a mediocrity is only too conscious that it is not.'

'I see,' smiled Mr Shastri; 'and it is not so with your pro-fes-sion?'

'Well,' said Professor Mishra, 'there's always the odd case here or there, you know, but in general, in our department at least, one makes every attempt to ensure the pre-eminence of excellence. ... Simply because someone may, for instance, be the son of an illustrious person ought not, in our eyes –'

'What's that you're saying, Mishra?' cried Dr Seth from the next table. 'Do repeat that – I didn't quite hear you; nor did my friend Kapoor Sahib. . . .'

Dr Seth was never happier than when walking through an emotional minefield – unless it was when he was dragging seven other troops along with him.

Professor Mishra pursed his lips sweetly and said: 'My dear Dr Seth, I have quite forgotten what I was rambling on about – perhaps because I feel so relaxed in these delightful surroundings. Or perhaps it is your excellent whisky that has made my memory as limp as my limbs. But what an amazing mechanism the human body is: who could imagine that one could feed in, say, four arrowroot biscuits and one boiled egg and get an output, say, of three spades – and one trick down?'

Parvati quickly interjected: 'Professor Mishra, a young lecturer was telling us just a few days ago about the pleasures of teaching. What a noble profession it must be.'

'My dear lady,' said Professor Mishra, 'teaching is a thankless task, but one undertakes it because one feels one has a calling, as it were. A couple of years ago I had rather an interesting discussion on the radio about the concept of teaching as a vocation – with a lawyer by the name of Dilip Pandey, in which I said – or was it Deepak Pandey – anyway, I said –'

'Dilip,' said the Advocate-General. 'He is now dead, in fact.'

'Oh, is he? What a pity. Well, I made the point that there are three kinds of teachers: those who are forgotten, those who are remembered and hated, and the third, the lucky ones, and I hope I am one of them, those who are remembered and' – he paused – 'forgiven.'

He looked rather pleased with his formulation.

'Oh, you are, you are –' said his wife eagerly.

'What's that?' cried Dr Kishen Chand Seth. 'Speak louder, we can't hear you.' He banged his stick on the floor.

Towards the end of the second rubber, the librarian (having been requested to do so twice already by the users of the library) sent a note to the bridge room. If Parvati had not restrained him, Dr Kishen Chand Seth would have screamed in wrath upon receiving it. As it was, he could neither believe nor stomach the insubordination of the librarian in requesting that the volume of conversation in the bridge room be reduced. He would haul the fellow up before the committee. A useless fellow, who spent most of his time dozing in the stacks, who treated the job as a sinecure, who –

'Yes, dear,' said Parvati. 'Yes, dear, I know. Now we at our table have finished our second rubber, but we're talking quite quietly. Why don't you concentrate on finishing yours, and then we can all go out onto the lawn; the film will begin in about twenty minutes. It's a pity that in the monsoon they screen it indoors. Ah, yes, Pran and Savita are sitting there; eating chips, I suppose. She looks enormous. I think perhaps we'll go and join them immediately, and you can follow.'

'I am afraid we must now be going,' said Professor Mishra, getting up hastily. His wife stood up too.

'Must you go? Can't you join us?' asked Parvati.

'No – no – far too busy these days – there are guests in the house – and I have been saddled with a good deal of unnecessary curriculum revision,' explained Professor Mishra.

Mahesh Kapoor looked at him for a second, then returned to his cards.

'Thank you, thank you,' said the whale, and glided quickly out of sight, followed by his minnow.

'How peculiar,' said Parvati, turning back to the table. 'What do you make of it?' she asked Mr Shastri.

'Force-ful per-son-al-it-y,' was Mr Shastri's opinion. Though it was unrevealing, it was delivered with a smile and conveyed the sense that Mr Shastri had some knowledge of the world, and did not opine where opinion was unnecessary.

Parvati had begun to have second thoughts about letting her husband follow her. For one thing, he might still need to be managed. For another, she did not relish meeting Mrs Rupa Mehra without his support. The reaction of Kishy's daughter to her rose-spangled sari was unpredictable. So Parvati waited for a few more minutes to see if the rubber would end. It did. Her husband was on the winning side. With some glee he was totting up his points for the hand – including an overtrick and a hundred honours. She breathed more freely.

12.26

OUT on the lawn, everyone was introduced to everyone else. Savita found herself engaged in a slow and deliberate conversation with Mr Shastri. She found him very interesting. He was telling her about a woman lawyer at the Brahmpur High Court, who was very successful in criminal practice despite the fact that she had had to overcome the reservations of clients, colleagues and judges.

Pran was feeling a bit exhausted, but Savita had insisted on seeing Charlie Chaplin 'once more before I become a mother and see everything differently'; her grandfather's Buick, a little the worse for having been requisitioned, had been sent to fetch them. Lata had gone off to one of those evening rehearsals so dreaded by Mrs Rupa Mehra; the director had said that it was necessary to make up for the rehearsals lost because of the student agitation.

Savita was looking happy and energetic, and eating with

great appetite the club speciality: small goli kababs, each with a raisin in the middle. The more she talked to Mr Shastri, the more she thought that it would be very interesting to study law.

Pran walked towards the low wall that separated the Subzipore Club lawn from the sands and the river. He looked over it at the brown water and the few slow boats plying silently along. He was thinking that soon, like his father, he would be a father too, and he was doubtful that he would make a good one. I'll be too worried for my child's own good, he thought. But in a while he reflected that Kedarnath's perpetual air of anxiety had not had a damaging effect on Bhaskar. And, he reflected, thinking with a smile of Maan, one can be too carefree as well. Since he was feeling a little out of breath, he leaned against the wall and watched the others from a few yards away.

Mrs Rupa Mehra had started when she heard Dr Durrani's name. She could hardly believe that her father had known him so well as to invite him for bridge. After all, it had been Dr Kishen Chand Seth to whom she had gone for advice in extremis, and who had told her to get Lata out of Brahmpur as soon as possible in the face of the Durrani threat. Had he deliberately not told her of the acquaintance? Or was it of very recent standing?

Dr Durrani was sitting next to her now, leaning forward slightly in his cane chair, and she was compelled by both politeness and curiosity to swallow her astonishment and talk to him. In response to a question from her, he mentioned that he had two sons.

'Ah, yes,' said Mrs Rupa Mehra, 'one of them rescued Bhaskar at the Pul Mela. What a terrible business. How brave of him. Do have another chip.'

'Yes. Kabir. I fear, though, that the, er, acuity of his, um, um, insight –'

'Whose? Kabir's?'

Dr Durrani looked startled. 'No, er, Bhaskar's.'

'Has suffered?' asked Mrs Rupa Mehra anxiously.

'Er, quite.'

There was a silence; then Mrs Rupa Mehra asked, 'And where is he now?'

'In bed?' asked Dr Durrani, presenting a question in lieu of a reply.

'Isn't it rather early for him to go to bed?' said Mrs Rupa Mehra, puzzled.

'As I, er, understand, his mother and er, grandmother, are quite strict. They tuck him up at, er, seven or so these days. Doctor's orders.'

'Oh,' said Mrs Rupa Mehra. 'We have been talking at cross purposes. I meant, what is your son Kabir doing? Was he involved in these recent student activities?'

'Only after the, er, lamentable, er, injury to that boy. . . .' He shook his head and his eyelids squeezed themselves together. 'No, well, he has other interests. At the moment he is, er, rehearsing in a play . . . er, is something the matter? Dear Mrs Mehra?'

Mrs Rupa Mehra had nearly swallowed some nimbu pani the wrong way.

In order to cover her embarrassment, Dr Durrani tried to pretend that nothing was amiss. He kept on talking – hesitantly, of course – about this and that. When Mrs Rupa Mehra had partially recovered from the shock, she found him discussing the Pergolesi Lemma in a courtly and sympathetic manner.

'It was my paper on that, er, Lemma which my, um, wife nearly destroyed,' he was saying.

'Oh, why?' asked Mrs Rupa Mehra, seizing upon the first two sensible syllables on hand in order to show that she had been following him.

'Ah,' said Professor Durrani. 'Because my wife is, er, mad.'

'Mad?' whispered Mrs Rupa Mehra.

'Yes, er, quite mad. It seems that the film is, er, about to, er, er, commence. Shall we go in?' asked Dr Durrani.

THEY entered the dance-hall of the club, where, in the cold or rainy seasons, the weekly films were screened. It was much pleasanter in the open air, for the hall was inevitably crowded; but these days there was the risk of a sudden evening shower.

City Lights began, and laughter resounded all around. For Mrs Rupa Mehra, however, this was the laughter of mockery. Too clearly now she saw the deeply-laid plot, the scheme whereby Lata, with Malati's connivance, had contrived to act in the same play as Kabir. Lata had not mentioned him once since their return to Brahmpur. When his involvement in the Bhaskar episode had come up in conversation, she had pointedly ignored it. She could well afford to do so, thought Mrs Rupa Mehra indignantly, because she could get all the facts from the protagonist himself in their tête-à-têtes.

That Lata should have acted so furtively with her mother, her mother who loved her and had sacrificed every comfort for the education and happiness of her children, wounded Mrs Rupa Mehra deeply. So this was her reward for being tolerant and understanding. This was what happened if you were a widow, and all alone in the world, with no one to help you control your children for their own good. Her nose had reddened in the darkened hall; and when she thought of her late husband, she started sobbing.

'My wife is, er, mad.' The words started echoing in her head. Who had spoken them? Dr Durrani? A voice in the film? Her own husband Raghubir? Not content with being Muslim, this wretched boy was half-mad as well. Poor Lata, poor, poor Lata. And Mrs Rupa Mehra, out of pity for and anger at her daughter, began to weep noisily and unashamedly.

To her surprise, she saw that people to both left and right of her were sobbing as well. Dr Kishen Chand Seth, for instance, who was sitting next to her, was juddering with grief. When she realized what had brought this about, she glanced sharply up at the small screen. But concentration was impossible. She was not feeling well. She opened her black handbag to get out her eau-de-Cologne.

Someone else who was not feeling at all well was Pran. He could sense, in the crowded and enclosed atmosphere of the slightly musty hall, one of his frightening attacks coming on. He had been feeling a little breathless earlier, but this had improved when he had sat down. Now it was again becoming hard to breathe. He opened his mouth. It was difficult either to expel the stale air or to take in fresh air. He leaned forward, bent over, sat up straight. It was no good. He began to gasp for breath. His chest and neck moved, but to no effect. In a fog of desperation he heard the laughter of the audience, but he had closed his eyes, and could not see the screen.

Pran began to wheeze, and Savita, who had half-turned to him, thinking that his paroxysm was probably one brought on by laughter, and would subside, heard the characteristic danger signal. She held his hand. But Pran had only one thought: how to get oxygen into his lungs. The more he tried, the harder it seemed to be. His efforts became more frantic. He was forced to stand up and bend over. Now other people had turned around, and were beginning to look at the source of the disturbance. Savita spoke in a low voice to the other members of the family, and they all got up to leave. Mrs Rupa Mehra's sobbing for her daughter was converted into a new and more urgent concern for her son-in-law. But Dr Kishen Chand Seth, welded mentally as he was to the joys and woes of *City Lights*, was gnashing his teeth in frustration, and was only restrained from going up in smoke by a warning word from his wife.

Somehow they got to his car, and there Pran collapsed. His struggles to breathe were painful to observe; and Mrs Rupa Mehra tried to prevent her daughter from observing them. The baby was due in two weeks, and she had advised Savita against even the mild excitement of the movie.

Savita held Pran's hand tightly and said to Dr Kishen Chand Seth: 'This is a worse attack than usual, Nanaji. We should go to the hospital.' But Pran managed to gasp out the single word: 'Home.' He felt that once he was there the spasm would subside of its own accord.

They drove back to the house. Pran was put to bed. But the spasm continued. The veins in his neck and forehead stood out. His eyes, even when open, registered very little of the outside world. His chest continued to heave. His coughing, gasping, and wheezing filled the room, and there was a desperate darkness in his mind.

It was now almost an hour since it had begun. Dr Kishen Chand Seth phoned a colleague. Then, despite her mother's dissuasion on the grounds that she should be resting, not distressing herself like this, Savita walked carefully out of the bedroom, picked up the receiver, phoned Baitar House and asked for Imtiaz. By some miracle he was in, though in that vast house it took a little while to summon him to the phone.

'Imtiaz Bhai,' said Savita, 'Pran is having one of his asthma attacks, but it is much worse than usual. Could you come over, please? ... it's been an hour or more.... Yes, I'll remain calm – but please come over ... please. ... At the club during the movie. ... No, your father's still there, but my grandfather is with us, here at home.... Yes, yes, I will remain calm, but I'll be calmer once you're here.... I can't describe it. It's much worse than usual, and I've seen many of them.'

While she was talking, the young servant, Mansoor, concerned that in her situation she should be standing, had brought a chair for her. Now she sat down, looked at the phone, and sobbed.

After a while, having collected herself, she went back to the bedroom, where everyone was standing around, upset and agitated.

A sound was heard at the front door. 'I'll see who it is,' said Mrs Rupa Mehra.

It was Lata and Malati, back from the rehearsal of *Twelfth Night*.

'Whenever I act or sing,' said Malati, 'I feel I could eat a horse.'

'We're not serving horse today,' said Lata, as the door opened. 'It's one of Ma's fast days. Where is everyone?' she continued, noticing that, despite the car standing outside, the drawing room was empty. 'Ma? Now what are you crying for? I didn't mean to tease you. It was a stupid joke, anyway.... Is something the matter? Is anything wrong?'

Part Thirteen

13.1

MAAN, Firoz and Imtiaz were over very shortly. Maan tried to cheer Savita up a bit. Firoz said little. Like everyone else, he was distressed to see Pran in such a pitiable state, labouring and panting for breath.

Imtiaz, on the other hand, was not visibly upset by his friend's painful struggles and went about his task of diagnosis swiftly. Parvati Seth was a trained nurse and helped move Pran when necessary. Imtiaz knew that Pran was not in a position to answer questions except occasionally by nodding or shaking his head, so he addressed what questions he could about the background as well as the suddenness of this recent attack to Savita. Malati described fairly clinically the incident in the lecture room a few days earlier. Firoz had already told Imtiaz on the way to the house that Pran had been complaining of exhaustion when he had met him at the High Court a few days earlier – and, of all things, discomfort around his heart.

Mrs Rupa Mehra sat silently in a chair, and Lata stood behind her, an arm on her shoulder. Mrs Rupa Mehra did not say anything to Lata. Concern for Pran had pushed other matters to the side.

Savita looked sometimes at her husband, sometimes at Imtiaz's long, fair, appraising face. There was a small mole on his cheek which drew her attention in particular, though she could not have said why. At the moment Imtiaz was feeling Pran's liver – which seemed an unusual proceeding after an asthmatic attack.

To Dr Kishen Chand Seth he said: 'Status asthmaticus, of course. It should be self-limiting, but if it doesn't go away in a little while I'll administer some adrenaline subcutaneously. If I can, though, I'd prefer to avoid it. I wonder if you could arrange for the ECG machine to be brought in tomorrow?'

At the word 'ECG' not only Dr Seth but everyone else started.

'What do you need that for?' said Dr Seth sharply.

There was only one ECG machine in Brahmpur, and it was at the medical college hospital.

'Well, I'd like to take a reading. I would not like Pran to be moved at all, so I wonder if you could arrange for it to be brought here. If I ask for it, they'll just think I'm a young man with newfangled ideas who doesn't know how to treat asthma.'

That was exactly what Dr Kishen Chand Seth himself was thinking. Was Imtiaz implying that he, Dr Seth, had oldfangled ideas? But something in Imtiaz's confident manner of examining the patient had impressed him. He said he would make the necessary arrangements. He knew that institutions with ECG machines guarded them like gold.

Lucknow had a single such machine, and there were none in Banaras at the time. The medical college hospital at Brahmpur was extremely proud and possessive of its recent acquisition. But Dr Seth was a force to be reckoned with there, as elsewhere. The next day the ECG machine was brought in.

Pran, who had stabilized after another traumatic hour of wheezing, and had then collapsed into an exhausted sleep, woke up to find Imtiaz and the machine in his bedroom.

'Where's Savita?' he asked.

'She's resting on the sofa in the other room. Doctor's orders. She's fine.'

'What's that?' Pran asked.

'The ECG machine.'

'It's not very big,' said Pran, rather unimpressed.

'Nor are viruses,' said Imtiaz with a laugh. 'How did you sleep?'

'Fine.' Pran's voice was clear; there was no wheezing.

'How do you feel?'

'A little weak. Really, Imtiaz, what's the purpose of an ECG? That's for the heart, and my problem is my lungs.'

'Why don't you leave that for me to decide? You may well be right, but there's no harm in checking. I suspect that this time a cardiogram may help. I believe that it may not be a simple asthmatic attack.'

Imtiaz knew that he could not lull Pran to peace in a

soothing hammock of ignorance, and felt that he should take him into his confidence.

But 'Oh,' was all Pran said. He was still sleepy.

After a while, Imtiaz asked him for some other details of his medical history, and added, 'I'm going to ask you to move as little as possible.'

'But my lectures –'

'Out of the question,' said Imtiaz cheerfully.

'And my committees?'

Imtiaz laughed. 'Forget them. Firoz tells me you loathe them anyway.'

Pran lay back on the pillows. 'You always were a bully, Imtiaz,' he said. 'Anyway, it's clear what kind of friend you are. You pop up at Holi, get me into trouble, and then only come to visit me when I'm ill.'

Imtiaz yawned.

'I suppose your excuse is that you work too hard.'

'I do,' said Imtiaz. 'Dr Khan, despite his youth, or perhaps because of it, is one of the most sought-after doctors in Brahmpur. His devotion to his profession is exemplary. And he exacts obedience to his decrees from even the most rebellious of his patients.'

'All right, all right,' said Pran, and submitted to the reading. 'So, when do I expect you next?'

'In a day. Remember, you're not to move out of the house and, preferably, not out of bed.'

'Please, Sir, may I go to the bathroom?'

'Yes.'

'And may I accept visitors?'

'Yes.'

At Imtiaz's next visit, he looked grave. He had examined the ECG reading, and told Pran, without beating about the bush:

'Well, I was right, this time it was not asthma alone, but heart. You have what we like to call "severe right ventricular strain". I am recommending three weeks of complete rest, and I'm going to put you in hospital for a little while. Don't get alarmed. But lectures are out. And committee work and so on.'

'But the baby –'

'Oh, the baby? Are there problems there?'

'Do you mean the baby will be born when I'm in the hospital myself?'

'I suppose that's up to the baby. As far as I am concerned, you are to rest for three weeks, starting now. The baby is none of my concern,' said Imtiaz heartlessly. Then he added: 'You've done what you needed to in the creation of the baby. The rest is up to Savita. If you insist on endangering yourself further, it won't be good for her – or for the baby either.'

Pran accepted the justice of this argument. He closed his eyes, but the moment he did so a wave of nameless anxieties washed over him.

He quickly opened his eyes again, and said: 'Imtiaz, please tell me what this thing is – this ventricular strain you mentioned. Don't tell me I don't need to know. Have I had a heart attack or something?' He recalled Firoz's remark: 'The heart and the lungs are two quite different things, young man, two quite different things,' and, despite himself, began to smile.

Imtiaz looked at him with the same grave expression that seemed so atypical of him, and said: 'Well, I can see that the idea of a heart attack amuses you. It's good you've never had one, and – well – you aren't likely to, exactly. But since you've asked, let me explain things to you as clearly as I can.' He paused, thought a little about how to put it, then continued: 'There's an intimate connection between the heart and the lungs; they share the same cavity, and the right side of the heart supplies stale blood to the lungs for it to freshen, to oxygenate, as we say. So when the lungs don't do their job properly – for instance because of not getting enough air when the air-tubes to the lungs seize up asthmatically – the heart is affected. It tries to supply more blood to the lungs to make up for the bad oxygen exchange, and this causes its own supplying chamber to fill up with blood, to become congested and distended. Do you understand?'

'Yes. You explain things very well,' Pran said sadly.

'Now because of this congestion and distension, the heart loses its efficiency as a pump, and that is what we like to call "congestive cardiac failure". It's got nothing to do with what laymen understand by the term "heart failure". To them that means a heart attack. Well, as I said, you are not in danger of that.'

'Then why must I stay in bed for three weeks? It seems a terribly long time. What will happen to my work?'

'Well, you can do a bit of light work in bed,' said Imtiaz. 'And later, you can go for walks. But cricket is out for a while.'

'Out?'

'I'm afraid so. Now as for medicine. Here are two sets of white tablets. You are to take these three times a day, and these once a day for the first week. Then I'll probably cut down a bit on the digoxin, depending on your pulse rate. But you'll keep on with the aminophylline for a few months. If necessary I might have to give you an injection of penicillin.'

'You sound serious, doctor,' said Pran, attempting to add a touch of lightness to the conversation. This Imtiaz was very different from the one who had helped duck Professor Mishra in the tub.

'I am serious.'

'But if this isn't a heart attack, what danger am I in?'

'If you have congestive heart failure, you will have all the effects of pent-up blood in your system. Your liver will become enlarged, so will your feet, your neck veins will become prominent, you will cough, and you will get very breathless, especially on walking or exertion. And it is possible that your brain might become confused as well. I don't want to alarm you – this isn't life-threatening –'

'But you are alarming me,' said Pran, looking at Imtiaz's mole and finding it very irritating. 'What else are you doing? I can't take all this bed rest seriously. I know I'm all right. I'm a, well, I'm a young man. I feel fine. And it's always been the case that when my breathing spasms pass off, I'm as well as ever – as healthy as anyone – every bit as fit. I play cricket. I enjoy trekking –'

'I am afraid,' said Imtiaz, 'that the picture is different now. Formerly you were an asthmatic patient. Now, however, the main problem is with the right side of your heart. You will need rest. You would do well to take my advice seriously.'

Pran looked hurt at the formality with which his friend was addressing him, and did not protest any further. Imtiaz had said that the condition was not immediately life-threatening. Pran knew without asking – both from the seriousness of his friend's demeanour and from his list of possible complications – that it was almost certainly life-shortening in the long run.

When Imtiaz left, Pran tried to face the new fact. But today seemed to be very much like yesterday, and the sudden intrusion of the fact was something that Pran almost felt he could shrug off – like an irrelevant memory or a bad dream. But he was depressed, and found it difficult to conceal this and behave normally with Lata or his mother-in-law or, most of all, with Savita.

13.2

THAT afternoon Pran was moved to the medical college hospital. Savita had insisted on being able to visit him, so he was given one of the few rooms on the ground floor. About half an hour after he came in, it began to rain heavily, and did not let up for a few hours. Pran found that the rain was the best thing for him in these circumstances. It took him out of himself in a way that even reading would not have been able to do. Besides, Imtiaz had told him that on the first day he should not read or exert himself in any other way at all.

The rain came down. It was a continuing event, and yet it was not stimulating: just the combination that Pran needed. In a short while he found himself dozing off.

He woke up to a mosquito bite on his hand.

It was almost seven o'clock, the end of the visiting hour. He noticed, as he opened his eyes and reached for the spectacles on the night-stand, that apart from Savita there was no one else in the room.

'How are you feeling, darling?' said Savita.

'I've just been bitten by a mosquito,' said Pran.

'Poor darling. Bad mosquitoes.'

'That's the problem with a room on the ground floor.'

'What is?'

'The mosquitoes.'

'We'll close the windows.'

'Too late, they're already in.'

'I'll get them to spray the room with Flit.'

'That spray will knock me out as well; I can't leave the room while they're doing it.'

'That's true.'

'Savita, why don't we ever quarrel?'

'Don't we?'

'No, not really.'

'Well, why should we?' asked Savita.

'I don't know. I feel I'm missing out on something. Now look at Arun and Meenakshi. You tell me they're always having tiffs. Young couples always have tiffs.'

'Well, we can have tiffs about the baby's education.'

'That's too long to wait.'

'Well, about its feeding times. Do go back to sleep, Pran, you're being very tiresome.'

'Who's that card from?'

'Professor Mishra.'

Pran closed his eyes.

'And those flowers?'

'Your mother.'

'She was here – and no one woke me up?'

'No. Imtiaz said you were to rest – and we let you rest.'

'Who else came today? Do you know, I'm feeling rather hungry.'

'Not many people. Today we were supposed to leave you to yourself.'

'Oh.'

'Just to get over things.'

Pran sighed. There was a silence. 'Food?'

'Yes, we've brought some from the house. Imtiaz warned us that the hospital food is horrible.'

'Isn't this the hospital where that boy died – that medical student?'

'Why are you being so morbid, Pran?'

'What's morbid about dying?'

'Well, I wish you wouldn't talk about it.'

'Better to talk about it than to do it,' said Pran.

'Do you want me to have a miscarriage?'

'All right, all right. What's that you're reading?'

'A law-book. Firoz lent it to me.'

'A law-book?'

'Yes. It's interesting.'

'What's the subject?'

'Tort.'

'Are you thinking of studying law?'

'Yes, perhaps. You shouldn't talk so much, Pran, it's not good for you. Shall I read out a bit of the *Brahmpur Chronicle*? The political news?'

'No, no. Tort!' Pran began to laugh a little, then started coughing.

'You see?' said Savita, moving to the bed to prop him up.

'You shouldn't get so worried,' said Pran.

'Worried?' said Savita guiltily.

'I'm not going to die, you know. Why have you suddenly decided to take up a profession?'

'Really, Pran – you seem bent on having that tiff. If I take up law it'll be because Shastri got me interested in it. I want to meet that woman lawyer, Jaya Sood, who practises in the High Court. He told me about her.'

'You're about to have a baby; you shouldn't take up studies immediately,' said Pran. 'And think about what my father would say.'

Mahesh Kapoor, who believed in women's education, did not believe in women working, and made no bones about it.

Savita did not say anything. She folded the *Brahmpur Chronicle* and swatted a mosquito. 'Are you ready for dinner?' she asked Pran.

'I hope you're not here by yourself,' said Pran. 'I'm surprised your mother let you come here unaccompanied. What if you suddenly feel unwell?'

'Only one person is allowed to stay beyond visiting hours. And I threatened to kick up a fuss if it wasn't me. Emotional excitement is very bad for me in my delicate state,' said Savita.

'You are extremely stupid and stubborn,' said Pran tenderly.

'Yes,' said Savita. 'Extremely. But your father's car is waiting downstairs in case it's needed. Incidentally, what does your father think about Nehru's sister, who is a working woman if ever there was one?'

'Ah,' said Pran, preferring not to take up the last remark: 'Fried brinjal. Delicious. Yes, let's hear a bit of the *Brahmpur Chronicle*. No, read me a bit of the *University Regulations*, beginning where that bookmark is. That bit about leave.'

'What does that have to do with your committee?' asked Savita, resting the volume on her stomach.

'Nothing. But I'll have to take leave, you know, for at least three weeks, and I may as well find out what the rules are. I don't want to fall into one of Mishra's traps.'

Savita thought of suggesting that he should forget about the university for a day, but she knew that this was impossible. So she took up the volume and started reading:

'The following kinds of leave are permissible:
    (a)   Casual leave
    (b)   Compensation leave
    (c)   Deputation leave
    (d)   Duty leave
    (e)   Extraordinary leave
    (f)   Maternity leave
    (g)   Medical leave
    (h)   Privilege leave
    (i)   Quarantine leave
    (j)   Study leave.'

She paused. 'Shall I go on?' she asked, glancing briefly down the page.

'Yes.'

Savita continued: 'Except in urgent cases in which the Vice-Chancellor or the Pro Vice-Chancellor shall take decisions, the power to grant leave in general shall be vested in the Executive Council.'

'No problem there,' said Pran. 'This is an urgent case.'

'But with L. N. Agarwal on the Executive Council – and your father no longer a Minister –'

'What can he do?' said Pran calmly. 'Nothing much. All right – what's next?'

Savita frowned, and read on:

'When the day immediately preceding the day on which the leave begins or immediately following the day on which the leave expires is a holiday or a series of holidays or a vacation the person to whom the leave is granted or who is returning from leave may make over charge at the close of the day before or return to duty on the day following such holiday or series of holidays or the vacation provided such early departure or delay in return does not involve the University in extra expenditure. When leave is prefixed or suffixed to such holidays or vacation, the consequential arrangement shall begin or end as the case may be, from the date when the leave begins or expires.'

'What?' said Pran.

'Shall I read it again?' asked Savita, smiling.

'No, no, that's fine. I'm feeling a bit light-headed. Your statutes are going to be as bad as that – or worse, you know. Read something else. Something from the *Brahmpur Chronicle*. No politics – some human interest story – like a child eaten by a hyena. Oh, sorry! Sorry, darling. Like someone winning a lottery – or the 'Brahmpur Diary' – that's always soothing. How's the baby?'

'He's sleeping, I think,' said Savita, with a look of concentration.

'He?'

'According to my law-books, "he" includes "she".'

'Books, is it now?' said Pran. 'Oh, well.'

13.3

MRS RUPA MEHRA, torn between solicitude for Pran, concern for Savita, who was due to deliver any day now, and desperate anxiety on behalf of Lata, would have liked nothing better than to have an emotional breakdown. But the press of events would not allow it at present, and she therefore abstained.

When Savita was in the hospital, Mrs Rupa Mehra wanted to be with her. When Lata was at the university – especially when she was at one of her rehearsals – Mrs Rupa Mehra's heart started pounding at the mischief she could be up to. Yet Lata was so busy that her mother hardly got a moment alone with her, let alone the chance for a heart-to-heart talk. At night it was impossible, for when Savita came home to sleep, emotional excitement in the house was the last thing her mother wanted to inflict upon her.

Mrs Rupa Mehra did not know what to do, and neither the Gita nor invocations to her late husband helped her in this exigency. To withdraw Lata from the play at this stage might drive her to God knows what rash action – even outright defiance. She could not avail herself of either Savita's advice or Pran's, since the one was close to birth, and the other – so Mrs Rupa Mehra had convinced herself – to death. She still recited her two chapters from the Gita when she woke up, but the world was too much with her, and the verses were occasionally interrupted by silent starings into space.

Pran, however, had begun to enjoy his stay in hospital. The monsoon weather was too muggy for his liking, but at least the moisture in the air was not too bad for his bronchial tubes. He had managed to rid his room of mosquitoes. He had exchanged the *Brahmpur University*

Calendar and Regulations for Agatha Christie. Savita no longer complained that he spent no time with her. He felt like a calm captive, floating along on the currents of the universe. Occasionally the universe would fling someone up near him. If he was asleep, the visitor might wait for a while and then go away. If he was awake, they talked.

This afternoon a whispered and urgent conversation was taking place around him. Lata and Malati had come to visit him after a rehearsal. Finding him asleep, they decided to sit on the sofa and wait. Just a few minutes later, Mrs Rupa Mehra arrived with Savita.

Mrs Rupa Mehra saw the two of them and her eyes narrowed with exasperation.

'So!' she said.

Lata and Malati could not mistake the tone of her voice, but could not understand the cause of it.

'So!' said Mrs Rupa Mehra in a strong whisper, glancing at the sleeping Pran. 'You have come from the rehearsal, I imagine.'

If she thought that this oblique reference to the conspiracy would make the culprits collapse, she was mistaken.

'Yes, Ma,' said Lata.

'It was an excellent rehearsal, Ma – you should see how Lata has opened out,' said Malati. 'You'll really enjoy the play when you come for Annual Day.'

Mrs Rupa Mehra flushed red at the thought of Lata opening out. 'I will certainly see the play, but Lata will not be in it,' said Mrs Rupa Mehra.

'Ma!' said Lata and Malati simultaneously.

'Girls should not be in plays –'

'Ma, we thrashed all this out earlier,' began Lata, with a glance at Savita. 'Let's not wake Pran up.'

'Yes, Ma, that's true,' said Savita. 'You can't withdraw Lata now. You agreed to let her act. It'll be impossible for them to find someone else. She's learned her lines –'

Mrs Rupa Mehra sat down on a chair. 'So you know as well?' she said reproachfully to Savita. 'Children cause one nothing but pain,' she added.

Luckily, Savita did not relate this remark to her present condition. 'Know? Know what?' she said.

'That – that that boy, K' – Mrs Rupa Mehra could not bring herself to take his name – 'is acting in the play with Lata. I am ashamed of you, Malati,' she continued, her nose beginning to redden, 'I am ashamed of you. I trusted you. And you have been so devious.' Her voice rose, and Savita put a finger to her lips.

'Ma, please –'

'Yes, yes, it is all very well, when you become a mother you too will find out –' said Mrs Rupa Mehra. 'You will make sacrifices, and then they will break your heart.'

Malati could not help smiling. Mrs Rupa Mehra rounded on her, the prime architect of this plot.

'You may think you are very clever, but I always know what is going on,' said Mrs Rupa Mehra. She did not mention that only a chance conversation had enabled her to discover that Kabir was acting in *Twelfth Night*. 'Yes, you can smile and smile and smile, but it is I who will do the crying.'

'Ma, we had no idea that Kabir would be acting,' said Malati. 'I was trying to keep Lata out of his way.'

'Yes, yes, I know, I know, I know it all,' said Mrs Rupa Mehra in miserable disbelief. She reached into her bag for her embroidered handkerchief.

Pran stirred; Savita went over to stand by his side.

'Ma, let's talk about this later,' said Lata. 'It certainly isn't Malati's fault. And I can't back out now.'

Mrs Rupa Mehra quoted a line from one of her favourite didactic poets to show that nothing was impossible, then said: 'And you have had a letter from Haresh as well. Aren't you ashamed to be even seeing this other boy?'

'How do you know I have had a letter from Haresh?' whispered Lata indignantly.

'I am your mother, that's how I know,' said Mrs Rupa Mehra.

'Well, Ma,' whispered Lata hotly, 'you may trust me or not, but let me tell you that I did not know that Kabir would be in the play, and I am not meeting him afterwards, and there is no plot at all.'

None of this convinced Mrs Rupa Mehra, who – glancing at Savita for a second – had begun to think of the brood of misfits that this unimaginable match could create.

'He is half mad, do you even know that?' asked Mrs Rupa Mehra.

To her bafflement and shock, this only produced a smile from Lata.

'You are laughing at me?' she said, appalled.

'No, Ma, at him. He's achieving madness quite nicely,' said Lata. Kabir had taken to the part of Malvolio alarmingly well; his initial awkwardness had vanished.

'How can you laugh at this? How can you laugh at this?' said Mrs Rupa Mehra, rising from her chair. 'Two tight slaps will do you some good. Laughing at your own mother.'

'Ma, softly, please,' said Savita.

'I think I'd better go,' said Malati.

'No, you stay there,' said Mrs Rupa Mehra. 'You should hear this too, then you will advise Lata better. I met this boy's father at the Subzipore Club. He told me that his wife was fully mad. And the peculiar way he said it made me think that he was also partly mad.' Mrs Rupa Mehra could not entirely conceal from her voice the triumph of vindication.

'Poor Kabir!' said Lata, appalled.

Kabir's long-forgotten remark about his mother began to make a horrible kind of sense.

But before Mrs Rupa Mehra could reproach Lata further, Pran had woken up. Looking around him, he said: 'What's going on? Hello Ma, hello Lata. Ah, Malati, you've come too – I asked Savita what had happened to you. What's the matter? Something dramatic, I hope. Come on, tell me. I heard someone say someone was mad.'

'Oh, we were discussing the play,' said Lata. 'Malvolio, you know.' It cost her an effort to speak.

'Oh, yes. How's your part going?'

'Fine.'

'And yours, Malati?'

'Fine.'

'Good, good, good. Whether I'm allowed to or not, I'll come and see it. It must be just a month or so away. Wonderful play, *Twelfth Night* – just the thing for Annual Day. How's Barua running the rehearsals?'

'Very well,' said Malati, taking over; she could see that Lata was in no mood to speak. 'He's got real flair. One wouldn't think so, he's so mild-mannered. But from the very first line –'

'Pran is very tired,' said Mrs Rupa Mehra, interrupting this unpleasant description. She wanted to hear nothing positive about the play. In fact she wanted to hear nothing at all from that brazen girl, Malati. 'Pran, you have your dinner now.'

'Yes, excellent idea,' said Pran, rather eagerly for a patient. 'What have you brought for me? This lack of exercise makes me enormously hungry. I seem to live from meal to meal. What's for soup? Oh, vegetable soup,' he said, disappointed. 'Can't I have tomato soup once in a while?'

Once in a while? thought Savita. Pran had had his favourite tomato soup the previous day and the day before, and she had thought that this would make a change.

'Mad! Remember that!' said Mrs Rupa Mehra sotto voce to Lata. 'You remember that when you go gallivanting around having a gala time. Muslim and mad.'

13.4

WHEN Maan came in, he found Pran eating his supper quite happily.

'What's the matter with you now?' he asked.

'Nothing much. Just lungs, heart and liver,' said Pran.

'Yes, Imtiaz said something about your heart. But you don't look like a man with heart failure. Anyway, it doesn't happen to people your age.'

'Well,' said Pran. 'I don't have heart failure yet. At least I don't think I do. What I have is a severe strain.'

'Ventricular,' said Mrs Rupa Mehra.

'Oh. Ah, hello, Ma.' Maan said his hellos all around, and eyed Pran's food with intent. 'Jamuns? Delicious!' he exclaimed, and popped two into his mouth. He spat the seeds into the palm of his hand, placed them on the side of the plate, and took another two. 'You should try them,' he advised Pran.

'So what have you been up to, Maan?' said Savita. 'How's your Urdu?'

'Oh, good, very good. Well, at any rate, I've certainly made progress. I can write a note in Urdu now – and what's more, someone can read it at the other end. And that reminds me, I need to write a note today.' His good-natured face grew perplexed momentarily, then recovered its smile. 'And how are you? Two women in a cast of a dozen men. They must be slobbering all over you. How do you shake them off?'

Mrs Rupa Mehra looked daggers at him.

'We don't,' said Lata. 'We maintain a frigid distance.'

'Very frigid,' agreed Malati. 'We have our reputations to guard.'

'If we aren't careful,' said Lata severely, 'no one will marry us. Or even elope with us.'

Mrs Rupa Mehra had had enough. 'You can make fun,' she exclaimed in exasperation. 'You can make fun – but it's not a laughing matter.'

'You're quite right, Ma,' said Maan. 'Not a laughing matter at all. Why did you allow them – I mean Lata – to act in the first place?'

Mrs Rupa Mehra kept a black silence, and Maan at last realized that this was a sensitive subject.

'Anyway,' he said to Pran, 'I bring for you the affection-ate regards of the Nawab Sahib, the love of Firoz, and the concern of Zainab – by way of Firoz. Yes, and that's not all. Imtiaz wants to know if you are having your little white pills. He plans to see you tomorrow morning and count them. And someone else said something else, but I can't remember what it was. Are you really all right, Pran? It's quite upsetting to see you lying in the hospital like this. When's the baby expected? Maybe, if Savita clings to you all the time, the baby'll be born in the same hospital. Perhaps in the same room. How about that? Delicious jamuns.' And Maan popped another two into his mouth.

'You seem very well,' said Savita.

'Except I'm not,' said Maan. 'I fall upon the knives of life, I bleed.'

'Thorns,' said Pran with a grimace.

'Thorns?'

'Thorns.'

'Oh, well, then that's what I fall upon,' said Maan. 'At any rate, I'm miserable.'

'Your lungs are in good shape, though,' said Savita.

'Yes, but my heart isn't. Or my liver,' said Maan, plaintively including both seats of emotion according to the conventions of Urdu poetry. 'The huntress of my heart –'

'Now we must really be going,' said Mrs Rupa Mehra, gathering her daughters chick-like to her side. Malati also took her leave.

'Was it something I said?' asked Maan when he and his brother were left alone.

'Oh, don't worry about it,' said Pran. It had rained again this afternoon, quite heavily, and he had become very philosophical. 'Just sit down and be quiet. Thanks for visiting me.'

'I say, Pran, does she love me still?'

Pran shrugged his shoulders.

'She threw me out of the house the other day. Do you think that's a good sign?'

'Not on the face of it.'

'I suppose you're right,' said Maan. 'But I love her dreadfully. I can't live without her.'

'Like oxygen,' said Pran.

'Oxygen? Yes, I suppose so,' said Maan gloomily. 'Anyway, I'm going to send her a note today. I'm going to threaten to end it all.'

'End what all?' said Pran, not very alarmed. 'Your life?'

'Yes, probably,' said Maan in a doubtful voice. 'Do you think that'll win her back?'

'Well, do you plan to back your threat up with action? To fall upon the knives of life or shoot yourself with the guns of life?'

Maan started. This lapse into practicality was in poor taste. 'No, I don't think so,' he said.

'I don't think so either,' said Pran. 'Anyway, don't. I'll miss you. So will all the people who were in this room. So will all the people whose regards you've brought me. So will Baoji and Ammaji and Veena and Bhaskar. So will your creditors.'

'You're right!' said Maan in a determined manner. He polished off the last two jamuns. 'You're absolutely right. You're a pillar of strength, you know that, Pran? Even when you're lying down. Now I feel I can face everyone and everything. I feel as if I'm a lion.' He roared experimentally.

The door opened, and Mr and Mrs Mahesh Kapoor, Veena, Kedarnath and Bhaskar came in.

The lion subsided, and looked a little shamefaced. He hadn't visited home for two days, and though there was no reproach in his mother's eyes, he felt bad. While she said a few words to Pran, she arranged a fragrant bunch of bela from the garden in a vase that she had brought with her. And she asked Maan about the Nawab Sahib's family.

Maan hung his head. 'They are all very well, Ammaji,' he said. 'And how is the frog? Recovered enough to be hopping around like this?' He gave Bhaskar a hug, then exchanged a few words with Kedarnath. Veena went over to Pran, put her hand on his forehead, and asked not how he was but how Savita was taking his illness.

Pran shook his head. 'I couldn't have timed it worse,' he said.

'You must take care of yourself,' said Veena.

'Yes,' said Pran. 'Yes, of course.' After a pause he added, 'She wants to study law — in case she becomes a widow and the child an orphan – I mean, fatherless.'

'Don't say such things, Pran,' said his sister sharply.

'Law?' said Mr Mahesh Kapoor equally sharply.

'Oh, I only say them because I don't believe them,' said Pran. 'I'm protected by a mantra.'

Mrs Mahesh Kapoor turned to him and said, 'Pran – Ramjap Baba also said one other thing; he said your chances for a job would be affected by a death. Do not make fun of fate. It is never good. If any of my grown-up children were to die before me, I would want to die myself.'

'What's all this talk of dying?' said her husband, impatient with all this needless emotion. 'This room is full of mosquitoes. One just bit me. Tell Savita she should concentrate on her duties as a mother. All this law will do her no good.'

Mrs Mahesh Kapoor, surprisingly, demurred.

'Unh! What do you understand about anything?' said her husband. 'Women should have rights. I'm all for giving them property rights. But if they insist on working, they won't be able to spend time on their children, and they'll be brought up neglected. If you had been working, would you have had time to nurse Pran? Would he have been alive today?'

Mrs Mahesh Kapoor said nothing further on the subject. She looked back on Pran's childhood, and thought that what her husband had said was probably true.

'How's the garden, Ammaji?' asked Pran. The scent of the bela blossoms had filled the room.

'The zinnias under Maan's window are out,' said his mother. 'And the malis are laying down the new lawn. Since your father resigned, I've had a little time to spend on it, though we have to pay the malis ourselves now. And I've planted a few new rose bushes. The ground's soft. And the pond-herons have been visiting.'

Maan, who had so far been rather subdued and unleonine, could not resist quoting from Ghalib:

'The breeze of the garden of faithfulness has dispersed
from my heart,
And nothing remains to me except unfulfilled desire.'

He lapsed into atypical moroseness.

Veena smiled; Pran laughed; Bhaskar's expression did not change, for his mind was on other things.

But Kedarnath looked more perturbed than usual; Mrs Mahesh Kapoor scanned her younger son's face with fresh anxiety; and the ex-Minister of Revenue told him irritably to shut up.

13.5

MRS MAHESH KAPOOR walked around her garden slowly. It was early morning, cloudy, and comparatively cool. A tall jamun tree, though rooted in the pavement outside, spread its branches over a corner of the garden walk. The purple fruit had indelibly stained the stone path; the pits lay scattered around a corner of her lawn.

Mrs Mahesh Kapoor, like Maan, was very fond of jamuns, and felt that their arrival was more than adequate compensation for the departure of the mango season. The jamun-pickers, who had been given a contract by the horticultural section of the Public Works Department, walked along the street in the early morning, climbing each tree and shaking down with their long lathis the dark, olive-sized, sweetly acerbic fruit. Their women, standing below, collected them on large sheets to sell them in the busy market near Chowk. Every year there would be a tussle about the rights to the fruit that fell on Mrs Mahesh Kapoor's side, and every year it would be peacefully settled. The jamun-pickers would be allowed to enter her garden as long as they gave her a share of the fruit and an undertaking not to trample all over her lawn and flower-beds.

The jamun-pickers tried to be careful, but the lawn and flower-beds did suffer. Well, thought Mrs Mahesh Kapoor, at least it is the monsoon, and the beauty of the garden at this time of year doesn't really lie in its flowers but in its greenery. She had learned by now not to plant the few bright monsoon flowers – zinnias, balsam, orange cosmos

– in the beds that lay close to the jamun trees. And she liked the jamun-pickers, who were cheerful, and without whom she would probably not have benefited even from those branches that did stretch out over her lawn.

Now she walked slowly around the garden of Prem Nivas, thinking of many things, but mainly of Pran. She was dressed in an old sari: a short, nondescript woman who to a stranger might almost have looked like one of the servants. Her husband dressed very well – if, as a Congress MLA, he was compelled to wear homespun cotton it had nevertheless to be of the best quality – and he had often rebuked her for her dowdiness. But since this was only one of many rebukes, just or unjust, she felt that she had neither the energy nor the taste to act on it. It was like her lack of knowledge of English. What could she do about it? Nothing, she had long since decided. If she was stupid, she was stupid; it was God's doing.

The fact that year after year she carried away some of the best prizes in the Rose and Chrysanthemum Show in December as well as in the Annual Flower Show in February never ceased to amaze the more sophisticated inhabitants of Brahmpur. The committee of the Race Club marvelled that her roses displayed a compactness and freshness that theirs could never attain; and the wives of the executives of Burmah Shell or the Praha Shoe Company even deigned, in their anglicized Hindi, to ask her once or twice what it was she put into her lawn that made it so even and springy and green. Mrs Mahesh Kapoor would have been hard-pressed to answer even if she had fully understood their brand of Hindi. She simply stood with gratefully folded hands, accepting their compliments and looking rather foolish, until they gave up. Shaking their heads they decided that she was indeed foolish, but that she – or more probably her head gardener – 'had a gift'. Once or twice they had tried to bribe him to leave her by offering him twice his present salary; but the head mali, who was originally from Rudhia, was content to remain at Prem Nivas and see the trees he had planted grow tall and the roses he had pruned bloom brightly. His disagreement with her about the side-lawn had been amicably resolved. It had been left slightly uneven, and had become something of a sanctuary for her favourite bird.

The two under-gardeners were in government service, and had been allotted to Mahesh Kapoor in his capacity as Minister of Revenue. They loved the garden at Prem Nivas, and were unhappy that they were to be torn away from it. 'Why did Minister Sahib resign?' they asked sadly.

'You will have to ask Minister Sahib,' said Mrs Mahesh Kapoor, who herself was not happy about his decision, and thought it was an unwise one. Nehru, after all, despite his carping and complaining about his party, was still in Congress. Surely any precipitate action by his followers – such as resignation – was premature. The question was, would it help to force the Prime Minister's hand, and make him leave as well, thus giving birth to a new and possibly more vigorous party? Or would it merely weaken his position in his own party and make things worse than before?

'They will assign us some other house,' said the under-gardeners with tears in their eyes. 'Some other Minister and some other Memsahib. No one will treat us as well as you have.'

'I'm sure they will,' said Mrs Mahesh Kapoor. She was a gentle-hearted and soft-spoken woman, and never raised her voice at her employees. In consequence, and because she often asked about their families, and helped them out in small ways, they loved her.

'What will you do without us, Memsahib?' asked one.

'Can you work for me part-time at Prem Nivas?' she asked. 'That way you won't lose the garden you've worked so hard on.'

'Yes – for an hour or two each morning. The only thing is –'

'Of course, you'll be paid for your work,' said Mrs Mahesh Kapoor, anticipating their awkwardness and making a calculation of her household expenses. 'But I will have to employ someone else full-time. Do you know of anyone?'

'My brother would be a good man,' said one.

'I didn't know you had a brother,' said Mrs Mahesh Kapoor in surprise.

'Not my real brother – my uncle's son.'

'All right. I'll let him work for a month on probation, and Gajraj will tell me how good he is.'

'Thank you, Memsahib. This year we will see that you win First Prize for the best garden.'

This was one prize that had eluded Mrs Mahesh Kapoor, and she thought how pleasant it would be to win it. But, doubting her own abilities, she smiled at their ambition.

'That would be a great feat,' she said.

'And don't worry about Sahib not being a Minister. We'll get you plants from the government nursery at cheap rates. And from other places too.' Good gardeners were adept at filching plants from here and there, or coaxing their fellow-gardeners to part with some of their superfluous seedlings.

'Good,' said Mrs Mahesh Kapoor. 'Tell Gajraj to come here. I want to discuss the layout of things now that I have a bit of time. If Sahib becomes a Minister again, I'll be doing nothing except arranging for cups of tea.'

The malis were rather pleased at this small irreverence. The head mali was summoned, and Mrs Mahesh Kapoor talked to him for a while. The new front lawn was being planted in careful rows, shoot by shoot, and a corner of the lawn was already a mild emerald in colour. The rest was mud, except for the stone path on which they were walking.

Mrs Mahesh Kapoor told him what the others had said about the Flower Show. His opinion was that the reason why they won second and not first prize for the best garden overall was two-fold. First, that Mr Justice Bailey (who had won for three years in succession) was bullied by his wife into spending half his income on his garden. They hired a dozen gardeners. Secondly, every bush, shrub or flower in his garden was planted with a particular date in mid-February in mind, the date of the Flower Show. That was when everything was at its most brilliant. Gajraj could arrange something similar if Mrs Mahesh Kapoor desired. But it was clear from his expression that he was sure she did not desire it. And the unevenness of the side-lawn this year would not help either.

'No, no – that wouldn't be a garden at all,' said Mrs Mahesh Kapoor. 'Let's plan the winter garden just like we always do – with different flowers blooming at different times, so that it is always a pleasure to sit out. And where that neem tree stood, we should plant a Sita ashok. Now is a good time.' With great regret Mrs Mahesh Kapoor had agreed to have an old neem tree cut down two years ago because of her painful allergy to its blossom; the blankness of the spot had been a continual rebuke to her. But the one outside Maan's window that he used to climb as a boy she had not had the heart to cut down.

Gajraj folded his hands. He was a thin, short man, gaunt of feature, barefooted, and dressed in a plain white dhoti and kurta. He looked dignified, more like the priest of a garden than a gardener. 'Whatever you say, Memsahib,' he said. After a while he added: 'What do you think of the water-lilies this year?' He felt they deserved comment, and so far Mrs Mahesh Kapoor had said nothing about them. Her mind had probably been on other matters of late.

'Let's go over and have a look at them again,' she said.

Gajraj, quietly pleased, walked on the muddy lawn beside Mrs Mahesh Kapoor as she negotiated the path slowly, pausing for a second by the pomelo tree. They stopped by the lily-pond. The water was turbid, and filled with tadpoles. Mrs Mahesh Kapoor gazed for a minute at the round lily-pads and the half-open lilies: pink, red, blue, and white. Three or four bees were buzzing about them.

'No yellow ones this year?' she asked.

'No, Memsahib,' said Gajraj, rather crestfallen.

'They are very beautiful,' said Mrs Mahesh Kapoor, continuing to look at the lilies.

Gajraj's heart leaped up. 'They are better than ever this year,' he ventured. 'Except that the yellow ones have not come out, I don't know why.'

'It doesn't matter,' said Mrs Mahesh Kapoor. 'My children like the bright ones – red and blue. I think it is only you and I who care for the pale yellow lilies. But if they've died, can we get them from somewhere else next year?'

'Memsahib, I don't think you can get them in Brahmpur. It was your Calcutta friend who brought them two years ago.'

Gajraj was referring to a friend of Veena's in fact, a young woman from Shantiniketan who had stayed at Prem Nivas as a guest a couple of times. She had very much enjoyed the garden, and Mrs Mahesh Kapoor found her good company even if her ways were a little surprising. On her second visit, she had brought the yellow lilies with her on the train in a bucket of water.

'A pity,' said Mrs Mahesh Kapoor. 'Anyway, the blue ones are very striking.'

13.6

OUT on the muddy surface of the lawn, a few birds – babblers, red-wattled lapwings, and mynas – were walking around, pecking at whatever presented itself. This was the season for earthworms, and the lawn was full of their curled castings.

The sky had grown dark and the sound of distant thunder could be heard.

'Have you seen any snakes this year?' asked Mrs Mahesh Kapoor.

'No,' said Gajraj. 'But Bhaskar said he saw one. A cobra. He shouted for me, but by the time I came, it had disappeared.'

'What?' Mrs Mahesh Kapoor's heart beat more rapidly for a minute. 'When?'

'Just yesterday afternoon.'

'Where did he see this?'

'He was playing on that pile of bricks and rubble over there – standing on it and flying his kite – I told him to be careful, because it was a likely place for snakes, but –'

'Tell him to come out at once. And call Veena Baby as well.'

Veena, though now a mother, was still called Baby by the older servants at Prem Nivas.

'No,' continued Mrs Mahesh Kapoor. 'On second thoughts, I'll go back to the verandah for tea. It looks as if it's about to rain.'

'Veena,' she told her daughter when they came out, 'this boy is like you used to be – very wilful. He was playing on that pile of rubble yesterday, and it is full of snakes.'

'Yes!' said Bhaskar, enthusiastically. 'I saw one yesterday. A cobra.'

'Bhaskar!' said Veena, her blood running cold.

'It didn't threaten me or anything. It was too far away. And by the time I called for Gajraj it wasn't there any more.'

'Why didn't you tell me?' asked his mother.

'I forgot.'

'That's not the sort of thing one forgets,' said Veena. 'Were you intending to play there again today?'

'Well, when Kabir comes we were thinking of flying kites –'

'You are not to play there, do you understand? Neither there nor in any part of the back garden. Do you understand me? Or I won't let you out in the garden at all.'

'But, Mummy –'

'No "but Mummy" or "please Mummy" – you are not to play there. Now go back inside and have your milk.'

'I'm sick of milk,' said Bhaskar. 'I'm nine years old – almost ten. Why should I drink milk for ever?' He was not pleased to have been disciplined in front of his grandmother. He also felt that Gajraj, whom he had looked upon as a friend, had betrayed him.

'Milk is good for you. Many boys don't get any milk at all,' said Veena.

'They are lucky,' said Bhaskar. 'I hate the skin that forms on it as it cools. And the glasses here are one-sixth larger than those at home,' he added ungratefully.

'If you drink your milk quickly, nothing will form on it at all,' said his mother unsympathetically. It was very unlike Bhaskar to be so sullen, and she was determined not to encourage it. 'Now, if you disobey me again and behave as if you're six, I'm going to slap you – and Nani won't stop me either.'

There was a roll of thunder, and a few drops of rain pattered down.

Bhaskar withdrew into the house with some dignity. His mother and grandmother smiled at each other.

Neither of them needed to mention that Veena too used to make a great fuss about drinking her milk when she was a child, and that she often gave it to her younger brothers to dispose of.

After a while Mrs Mahesh Kapoor said:

'He looked in good spirits last night despite all that the doctors said. Didn't you think so?'

'Yes, Amma, I did.' There was a silence. 'It's a difficult time for them,' Veena continued. 'Why don't you ask Savita, Lata and Ma to stay here in Prem Nivas until the baby's born? We're going to be leaving in a day or two anyway.'

Her mother nodded. 'I asked once before, but Pran thought she wouldn't like it, that she'd feel happier in familiar surroundings.'

Mrs Mahesh Kapoor also reflected that Mrs Rupa Mehra, when she visited Prem Nivas, was liable to mention that she found the rooms exceedingly bare. And this was true. Mahesh Kapoor, though he was of no help in running the house, often exercised his veto on proposed furnishings. It was only on the puja-room and the kitchen that his wife had been able to exercise that loving care that she lavished on the garden.

'And Maan?' said Veena. 'This house feels odd without him. When he's in Brahmpur it is very bad that he isn't staying with his family. We hardly get a chance to meet as it is.'

'No,' said her mother. 'I felt hurt at first, but I think he's right, it's for the best that he stays with his friend. Minister

Sahib is going through a hard time, and they would find each other's company difficult, I think.'

This was a mild prediction. Mahesh Kapoor was short with everyone these days. It was not merely the fact that the house was suddenly less full of hangers-on and aspirants of various kinds, company he claimed to despise but in fact now fretted for; it was also the unpredictability of the future that ate at him and made him snap with less than usual cause at whoever happened to be around.

'But apart from his moods, I enjoy this relief,' said Mrs Mahesh Kapoor, completing the arc of her own thoughts aloud. 'In the evening there is time for some bhajans. And I can walk around the garden in the morning now, without feeling that I am ignoring some important political guest.'

By now the clouds had blotted out the sun completely. Gusts of wind were blowing across the garden and turning the silver undersides of the leaves on a nearby poplar tree so violently that it appeared not dark green but silver. But the verandah where they were sitting was protected by a low wall decorated with shallow urns of portulaca and was covered with a corrugated roof, and neither of them felt like moving indoors.

Veena hummed to herself the first few lines of a bhajan, one of her mother's favourites: 'Rise, traveller, the sky is bright'. It came from the anthology used at Gandhi's ashram, and reminded Mrs Mahesh Kapoor of how they would give themselves courage in the most hopeless days of the freedom struggle.

After a few seconds, she too began to hum along, and then to sing the words:

'Uth, jaag, musafir, bhor bhaee
Ab rayn kahan jo sowat hai....'

    Rise, traveller, the sky is bright.
    Why do you sleep? It is not night....

Then she laughed. 'Think of the Congress Party in those days. And look at it now.'

Veena smiled: 'But you still get up early,' she said. 'You don't need this bhajan.'

'Yes,' said her mother. 'Old habits die hard. And I need less sleep these days. But I still need the help of that bhajan several times a day.'

She sipped her tea for a while. 'How is your music?' she asked.

'My serious music?' asked Veena.

'Yes,' said her mother with a smile. 'Your serious music. Not bhajans, but what you learn from your Ustad.'

'My mind's not really on it,' said Veena. After a pause she continued: 'Kedarnath's mother has stopped objecting to it. And it's closer from Prem Nivas than from Misri Mandi. But I can't concentrate these days. I can't shut the world out. First it was Kedarnath, then Bhaskar, now Pran; and I hope it isn't Savita next. If only they would all have their troubles simultaneously, it would help: my hair might go white once, but I'd make some real progress the rest of the time.' She paused again. 'But Ustad Sahib is more patient with me than with his other disciples. Or perhaps it's just that he is more content these days, less bitter about life.'

After a while Veena went on: 'I wish I could do something about Priya.'

'Priya Goyal?'

'Yes.'

'What made you think of her?'

'I don't know. I just suddenly thought of her. What was her mother like when she was young?'

'Ah, she was a good woman,' said Mrs Mahesh Kapoor.

'I think,' said Veena, 'the state would be in better shape if you and she ran it rather than Baoji and L.N. Agarwal.'

Instead of ticking Veena off for this subversive remark, Mrs Mahesh Kapoor merely said: 'I don't think so, you know. Two illiterate women – we wouldn't even be able to read a file.'

'At least you would have been generous to each other. Not like men.'

'Oh no,' said her mother sadly. 'You know nothing of the pettiness of women. When brothers agree to split a joint family they sometimes divide lakhs of rupees' worth of property in a few minutes. But the tussle of their wives over the pots and pans in the common kitchen – that nearly causes bloodshed.'

'At any rate,' said Veena, 'Priya and I would run things well. And it would enable her to escape from that wretched house in Shahi Darvaza and from her husband's sister and sisters-in-law. Yes, you're right about women, perhaps. But do you think a woman would have ordered that lathi charge on the students?'

'No, maybe not,' said her mother. 'At any rate, it's pointless thinking about such things. Women will never be called upon to make such decisions.'

'Some day,' said Veena, 'this country will have a woman Prime Minister or a woman President.'

Veena's mother laughed at this forecast. 'Not in the next hundred years,' she said gently, and looked out at the lawn again.

A few plump brown partridges, some big, some small, ran awkwardly across the far end of the lawn and with an immense effort got themselves airborne for a few seconds. They landed on the broad swing that hung down from a branch of the tamarind tree. There the partridges sat while the rain suddenly pelted down.

The gardeners quickly took shelter at the back of the house near the kitchen.

The thunder made a growling noise, and squirrels ran up the tree in alarm. Lightning flashed in sheets all over the sky. The rain came down in torrents, and soon the mud of the lawn had become a thick paste. The partridges disappeared in the grey barrage; even the swing became indistinct. The sound of the storm on the corrugated roof made speech difficult, and an occasional violent gust of wind drove rain onto the verandah itself.

After a while the door to the house opened, and Bhaskar came out. He sat next to his mother, and the three of them stared at the wall of water.

For about five minutes they looked at the rain in silence, enchanted by the power and the noise of it, and the sight of great trees swaying and shuddering in the wind. Then the rain let up slightly, and speech became possible again.

'It'll be good for the farmers,' said Mrs Mahesh Kapoor. 'There hasn't been enough rain so far this year.'

'But not for the cobblers,' said Veena. Kedarnath had once told her that the small shoemakers, who stretched moistened shoe-uppers onto wooden lasts in order to shape them, sometimes had to wait for a week in this weather till they were dry and could be taken off. Since they lived from hand to mouth, and their capital was tied up in their materials and tools, this was a great hardship.

'Do you like the rain?' Mrs Mahesh Kapoor asked Bhaskar when there was another respite.

'I like flying kites after the rain,' said Bhaskar. 'The air currents are more interesting.'

The rain increased once more, and once again each was lost in private thought.

Bhaskar was thinking of his return in a couple of days to his own house, where there were many more kites in the sky than here, and where he could play once again with his friends. Life here in the 'colonies' was rather limited.

Mrs Mahesh Kapoor thought about her mother, who used to be terrified of storms, and whose final illness had taken a severe turn for the worse in just such a violent storm as this.

And Veena thought of her Bengali friend (she of the yellow water-lilies) who, when the monsoon rains first struck after the terrible months of heat, would walk out of the house dressed as she was, humming a Tagore song in welcome, and let the rain streak down her face and her hair, run down her body to her bare feet, and soak her blouse and her sari to the skin.

TIME hung very heavily on Maan's hands. But he realized that he had to make up with Saeeda Bai quickly or he would go crazy with boredom and desire. He therefore wrote his first note in Urdu to her, in which he entreated her to be kind to him, her faithful vassal, her enchanted moth, etc., etc. There were a number of spelling errors, and his script was somewhat unformed, but there was no mistaking the strength of his sentiment. He thought of getting Rasheed's help with some aspects of phrasing, then decided that since Rasheed was out of favour with Saeeda Bai this might merely cause complications. He gave it to the watchman to give her, but did not wait for her response immediately.

He went for a walk to the Barsaat Mahal and stared across the river in the moonlight. Apart from Firoz, no one appeared to be on his side in the world at all. Everyone wanted him to mould himself in one direction or another according to their opinion or will. And even Firoz these days was fairly busy in court, and had only once suggested that they go for polo practice. That too had had to be cancelled at the last moment because of a conference called by his senior in a case.

Something needed to happen soon, thought Maan. He was feeling uncontrollably restless. If Savita had her baby quickly, that would be a good thing. There would be some cheerful activity somewhere. Everyone was going around looking oppressed and careworn these days.

Or if he could persuade his father to explore the option of a rural constituency, they could go on a whirlwind tour of Rudhia District for a few days and perhaps he could forget Saeeda Bai for a bit. His father, being at a loose end himself, had lost a little of his moral authority vis-à-vis Maan, and his company might not be so intolerable; in any case, he had not for the last few days told Maan to settle down. But precisely because he had not come to terms with his own situation, Mahesh Kapoor was exceptionally irritable these days. Perhaps Rudhia was not such a good idea after all.

To add to Maan's woes, he needed money; he had almost none left. Firoz, whom he had approached for a small loan upon his return to Brahmpur, had simply handed over his wallet to Maan and told him to take what he wanted out of it. A few days later, after lunch, without being asked but perhaps in response to a certain hangdog look on Maan's face, he made the same generous gesture. This had helped Maan get by. But he couldn't keep borrowing from his friend. A number of people in Banaras owed him money, some for goods supplied, some because of hard luck stories which Maan had found difficult to withstand, and Maan felt that now that he was down on his own luck, they would be eager to help him out. He decided to visit Banaras for a couple of days to recoup his funds. It would be easy enough to keep out of the way of one or two of his rather irksome creditors. The problem was that his fiancée's people might well find out that he was in Banaras. Besides, he wasn't sure if this was the best time to visit Banaras at all. He wanted to be on hand to help Savita when the baby was born, since Pran was not able to do so himself in his present condition, and Maan feared that it would be just his luck if the baby was born when he was out of town.

He waited for two whole days for a reply from Saeeda Bai to his note. He had given his address as Baitar House. None came.

Tiring of his own iffing and butting, and being eager for action of some kind, Maan borrowed some more money from Firoz, sent a servant to get his ticket for the next morning's train to Banaras, and prepared to spend a despondent and eventless last evening.

First, he visited the hospital, and instructed Savita to hold off having her baby for at least two days. Savita laughed, and promised to do her best.

Then he had dinner with Firoz. Zainab's husband was present at dinner – he had come alone to Brahmpur for the meeting of some waqf committee or other – and Maan could sense that Firoz was no more than polite to him. Maan could not understand this. Zainab's husband appeared to be a fairly cultivated if rather tremulous man. He kept insisting that he was a peasant at heart, and backing up this assertion with Persian couplets. The Nawab Sahib dined on his own.

Finally, Maan penned another note in Urdu, and gave it to Saeeda Bai's watchman to deliver. Surely Saeeda Bai should tell him what his crime was – and if she couldn't bring herself to forgive him at least she could respond to his letters.

'Please give her this at once – and say that I am going away.' Maan, sensing the drama of this last phrase, sighed deeply.

The watchman knocked at the door, and Bibbo came out.

'Bibbo –' said Maan, gesturing with the ivory-topped cane.

But Bibbo appeared rather scared, and refused to look him in the face. What's the matter with her? thought Maan. She was happy enough to kiss me the last time I was here.

A few minutes later Bibbo came out and said: 'The Begum Sahiba instructs me to admit you.'

'Bibbo!' said Maan, both delighted by his admittance, and hurt by the formal, even lifeless, tone of its announcement. He was so pleased that he wanted to hug her, but by turning half away from him when they walked up the stairs, she made it clear that there was no question of that.

'You keep repeating my name, like that parakeet,' said Bibbo. 'All I get for my kindness to people is trouble.'

'But you got a kiss from me last time!' laughed Maan.

Bibbo clearly did not want to be reminded of that. She pouted, Maan thought charmingly.

Saeeda Bai was in a good mood. She, Motu Chand, and an older sarangi player, were sitting in her outer chamber, gossiping. Ustad Majeed Khan had recently performed in Banaras, and had been backed up by Ishaq Khan. Ishaq Khan had done well; at all events, he had not shamed his teacher.

'I'm going to Banaras myself,' announced Maan, who had heard the tail end of the conversation.

'And why must the huntsman take himself away from the tame gazelle that, rejoicing, offers itself to his sight?' asked Saeeda Bai, twirling her hand and blinding Maan with a sudden flash of gem-reflected light.

This was an unlikely description of Saeeda Bai, considering how she had avoided him for the last few days. Maan looked at her eyes, but could read nothing there but the most patent sincerity. Instantly he saw that he had misjudged her: she was as delightful as she had always been, and he was an unperceptive dolt.

Saeeda Bai was exceptionally good to him all evening; it almost appeared as if she were wooing him, not he her. She begged him to forgive her lack of courtesy, as she put it, on the earlier occasion. Many things had conspired to upset her that day. Dagh Sahib should excuse the ignorant saki who had, in her excessive nervousness, poured wine over his innocent hands.

She sang for him like one inspired. And then she sent the musicians away.

13.8

THE next morning, Maan got to the station just in time to catch the train to Banaras. He was almost puppy-like with happiness. Even the fact that each puff of steam and each circuit of the wheels was taking him further away from Brahmpur did not diminish his pleasure. He smiled to himself from time to time at the memory of the previous evening, with all its endearments and witticisms, all its suspense and fulfilment.

When he got to Banaras, Maan discovered that those who owed him money for goods already received were not delighted to see him. They swore that they had no money at present, that they were moving heaven and earth to pay off their debts, of which his was just one, that the market was moving slowly, that by winter – or next spring at the latest – they envisaged no problem of repayment at all.

Nor did those whose tales of misfortune had led Maan to open his purse, now open their purses to him. One young man looked well-dressed enough, and appeared to be flourishing. He invited Maan to eat with him in a good restaurant, so that he could explain matters to him at leisure. Maan ended up paying for the meal.

Another man was distantly related to his fiancée's family. He was eager to drag Maan off to meet them, but Maan pleaded that he had to return to Brahmpur by the early afternoon train. He explained that his brother, who was ill and in hospital, was due to become a father any day now. The man appeared surprised at Maan's new-found sense of family obligation, but said nothing further. But Maan, feeling on the defensive, could no longer bring himself to mention the subject of his outstanding loan.

One debtor implied in a circuitous and inoffensive way that now that Mahesh Kapoor had resigned as Minister of Revenue in the neighbouring state, Maan's outstanding loan had stopped preying so frequently or pressingly on his mind.

Maan managed to get back about an eighth of what he had lent, and borrowed about the same amount from various friends and acquaintances. This came to just over two thousand rupees. At first he felt disappointed and disillusioned. But with two thousand rupees in his pocket, and a train ticket back to bliss, he felt that life was pretty good after all.

13.9

TAHMINA BAI meanwhile visited Saeeda Bai.

Tahmina Bai's mother had been the madam of the establishment in Tarbuz ka Bazaar where Saeeda Bai and her mother Mohsina Bai had earlier lived.

'What shall we do? What shall we do?' cried Tahmina Bai in high excitement. 'Play chaupar and gossip? Or gossip and play chaupar? Tell your cook to make those delicious kababs, Saeeda. I've brought some biryani – I told Bibbo to take it to the kitchen – now tell me, tell me everything. I have so much to tell you –'

After they had played a few games of chaupar, and exchanged endless gossip, together with some more serious news of the world – such as the effect that the Zamindari Act would have on them, especially on Saeeda Bai, who had a better class of customer; and the education of Tasneem; and the health of Tahmina Bai's mother; and the rising rents and property values, even in Tarbuz ka Bazaar – they turned to the antics of their various clients.

'I'll be Marh,' said Saeeda Bai. 'You be me.'

'No, I'll be Marh,' said Tahmina Bai. 'You be me.' She was giggling away in high delight. She grabbed a flower vase, threw the flowers onto a table, and pretended to drink from it. Soon she was lurching from side to side and grunting. Then she made a lunge for Saeeda Bai, who whipped the pallu of her sari out of reach, ran, screaming 'toba! toba!' to the harmonium, and quickly played a descending scale through two octaves.

Tahmina Bai's eyes grew blurred. As the scale descended, so did she. Soon she was snoring on the carpet. After ten seconds, she heaved her body up, cried 'wah! wah!' and collapsed again, this time squealing and snorting with laughter. Then she leapt up again, upsetting a bowl of fruit, and flung herself on Saeeda Bai, who started moaning in ecstasy. With one hand Tahmina Bai reached for an apple and bit it. Then, at the moment of orgasm, she cried for whisky. And finally she rolled over, belched, and went off to sleep again.

They were almost choking with laughter. The parakeet was squawking in alarm.

'Oh, but his son is even better,' said Tahmina Bai.

'No, no,' said Saeeda Bai, helpless with laughter. 'I can't bear it. Stop, Tahmina, stop, stop –'

But Tahmina Bai had begun enacting the Rajkumar's behaviour on the occasion when he had failed to grace her with his poetry.

Bewildered and protesting, the traumatized Tahmina

pulled an imaginary but very drunk friend to his feet. 'No, no,' she cried in a terrified voice, 'no, please, Tahmina Begum – I've already, no, no, I'm not in the mood – come, Maan, let's go.'

Saeeda Bai said: 'What? Did you say Maan?'

Tahmina Bai was having a giggling fit.

'But that's my Dagh Sahib,' continued Saeeda Bai, amazed.

'You mean that that was the Minister's son?' said Tahmina Bai. 'The one whom everyone is gossiping about? Balding at the temples?'

'Yes.'

'He couldn't grace me either.'

'I'm glad to hear it,' said Saeeda Bai.

'Be careful, Saeeda,' said Tahmina Bai affectionately. 'Think of what your mother would say.'

'Oh, it's nothing,' said Saeeda Bai. 'I entertain them; he entertains me. It's like Miya Mitthu here; I'm not a fool.'

And she followed it up with quite a good imitation of Maan making desperate love.

13.10

THE first thing Maan did when he got back to Brahmpur was to phone Prem Nivas to find out about Savita. She had been as good as her word. The baby was still inside her, unexposed as yet to the joys and woes of Brahmpur.

It was too late for Maan to visit Pran in hospital; humming to himself, he wandered along to Saeeda Bai's. The watchman looked rather abstracted tonight; he knocked at the door, and held a consultation with Bibbo. Bibbo glanced at Maan, who was standing eagerly at the gate, then turned back to the watchman and shook her head.

But Maan, who had interpreted the negative signal correctly, had leaped over the fence in a flash, and was at the door before she could close it.

'What?' he said, his voice barely controlled. 'The Begum

Sahiba said that she would receive me this evening. What has happened?'

'She is indisposed,' said Bibbo, with great emphasis on 'indisposed'. It was clear that Saeeda Bai was nothing of the kind.

'Why are you annoyed with me, Bibbo?' said Maan, helplessly. 'What have I done that all of you should treat me this way?'

'Nothing. But the Begum Sahiba is not receiving anyone today.'

'Has she received anyone already?'

'Dagh Sahib –' said Bibbo, pretending to relent but throwing out a provocative hint instead, 'Dagh Sahib, someone whom I might call Ghalib Sahib is with her. Even among poets there is an order of precedence. This gentleman is a good friend, and she prefers his company to that of all others.'

This was too much for Maan. 'Who is he? Who is he?' he cried, almost beside himself.

Bibbo could simply have told Maan that it was Mr Bilgrami, Saeeda Bai's old admirer whom she found boring but soothing, but she was excited to have evoked such a dramatic response. Besides, she was angry with Maan and felt like giving him a spoonful or two of jealousy as punishment for her own misfortunes. Saeeda Bai had slapped Bibbo very hard several times after the kiss on the staircase, and had threatened to turn her out of the house for her shamelessness. In Bibbo's recollection it was Maan who had initiated the kiss that had got her into all this trouble.

'I can't tell you who he is,' she said, raising her eyebrows slightly. 'Your poetic intuition should tell you.'

Maan grabbed Bibbo by the shoulders and began to shake her. But before he could get her to speak and before the watchman could come to her rescue, she had escaped from his grip and slammed the door in his face.

'Come now, Kapoor Sahib –' said the watchman calmly.

'Who is he?' said Maan.

The watchman slowly shook his head. 'I have no

memory for faces,' he said. 'If someone asked me if you had visited this house, I would not remember.'

Stunned by the brazen manner in which the appointment had been broken, and burning with jealousy, Maan somehow made his way back to Baitar House.

Sitting on top of the great stone gate at the entrance to the drive was a monkey. Why it was awake so late was a mystery. It snarled at him as he approached. Maan glared at it.

The monkey leaped down from the gate and rushed at Maan. If Maan had not been away in Banaras over the previous two days, he would have read in the *Brahmpur Chronicle* of a vicious monkey that was loose in the Pasand Bagh area. This monkey had apparently lost her mind when some schoolchildren had stoned her baby to death. She had since been charging at and biting and generally terrifying the local residents. She had attacked seven people so far, usually biting off chunks of flesh from their legs, and Maan was to be the eighth.

She charged at him with fearless malignity. Even though he did not turn and flee, she did not slacken her pace, and when she was close enough, she made a final lunge at his leg. But she had not accounted for Maan's anger. Maan had his cane ready and gave her a blow that stopped her dead.

Into that blow went all his bodily strength and all the power of his jealousy and rage. He raised his stick again, but the monkey was lying on the road, not moving, either stunned or dead.

Maan leaned against the gate for a minute, trembling with anger and nervous shock. Then, feeling suddenly sick at himself, he walked slowly towards the house. Firoz was not in, nor Zainab's husband, and the Nawab Sahib had retired already. But Imtiaz was up reading.

'My dear fellow, you've had a shock. Is everything all right – at the hospital, I mean?'

'I've just killed a monkey, I think. It charged at me. It was sitting on the gate. I need a whisky.'

'Ah, you're a hero,' said Imtiaz, relieved. 'It's a good

thing you had that stick on you. I was worried it might be Pran or Savita. The police have been trying to catch her all day. She's bitten quite a few people already. Ice and water? Well, perhaps not such a hero if you've killed her. I'd better get her moved from near the house, or we'll have a religious disturbance on our hands. But did you do anything to upset her?'

'Upset her?' said Maan.

'Yes, you know, did you wave your stick at her or something? Throw a stone perhaps?'

'Nothing,' said Maan with great vehemence. 'She just took one look at me and charged. And I'd done nothing to upset her. Nothing. Nothing at all.'

13.11

EVERYONE had told Savita that the baby would be a boy; her way of walking, the size of the bulge, and other infallible indications all pointed to a boy.

'Think nice thoughts, read poems,' Mrs Rupa Mehra was continually exhorting her, and this Savita tried to do. She also read a book called *Learning the Law*. Mrs Rupa Mehra advised Savita to listen to music, but this, since she was not particularly musical, she did not do.

The baby kicked from time to time. But sometimes it seemed to sleep for days on end. Lately it had been very quiet.

Mrs Rupa Mehra, while telling Savita to think restful thoughts, often shared her own birth experiences and those of other mothers with her. Some stories were charming, some not. 'You were overdue, you know,' she told Savita fondly. 'And my mother-in-law insisted that I must try her own method of inducing labour. I had to drink a whole glass of castor oil. It's a laxative, you know, and it was supposed to begin my birth pangs. It tasted horrible, but I felt it was my duty, so I had to drink it; it was lying on the sideboard. It was winter, I remember, bitterly cold, the middle of December –'

'It couldn't have been December, Ma, my birthday's in November.'

Mrs Rupa Mehra frowned at this interruption of her reverie, but she quickly saw that the logic of it was irrefutable, and continued calmly:

'November, yes, winter, and I saw it lying on the sideboard, and I drank it in a sudden gulp on the way to lunch. I remember we had parathas for lunch, and so on. I normally didn't eat much, but that day I stuffed myself. But it had no effect. Then came dinner. Then your Daddy came with a pot full of my favourite sweet, rasagullas. I had one, and then I had a second, and the second one was just going down, when it suddenly felt like it had turned into a fist in my stomach! The birth pangs had begun, and I had to run.'

Savita said, 'Ma, I think –'

But Mrs Rupa Mehra continued: 'Our Indian remedies are the best. Now they say that in this season I should eat lots of jamuns, because they are good for diabetes.'

'Ma, I think I'd better finish this chapter,' said Savita.

'Arun was the most painful,' continued Mrs Rupa Mehra. 'You must be prepared, darling; with the first child the pain is so terrible that you want to die, and if I hadn't thought of your Daddy I would have surely died.'

'Ma –'

'Savita, darling, when I'm talking to you you shouldn't be reading that book. Reading about law is not very restful.'

'Ma, let's talk about something else.'

'I am trying to prepare you, darling. Otherwise what is a mother for? I had no mother living to prepare me, and my mother-in-law was not sympathetic. Afterwards she wanted me to be in confinement for more than a month, but my father said this was all superstition and put his foot down, being a doctor himself.'

'Is it really that painful?' said Savita, quite frightened now.

'Yes. Truly unbearable,' said Mrs Rupa Mehra, ignoring all her own admonitions about not scaring or upsetting

Savita. 'Worse than any pain I have ever had in my life, especially with Arun. But when the baby is born, it is such a joy to behold – if everything is all right, that is. But with some babies, it is very sad, like Kamini Bua's first child – still, such things happen,' ended Mrs Rupa Mehra philosophically.

'Ma, why don't you read me a poem?' said Savita, trying to get her mother off this latest subject. But when Mrs Rupa Mehra turned to one of her favourites, 'The Blind Boy' by Colley Cibber, Savita regretted her suggestion.

The tears already starting to her eyes, Mrs Rupa Mehra began to read in a tremulous voice:

> 'Oh say, what is that thing called Light,
> That I must ne'er enjoy?
> What are the blessings of the sight?
> Oh, tell your poor blind boy!'

'Ma,' said Savita, 'Daddy was very good to you, wasn't he? Very tender – very loving –'

'Oh, yes,' said Mrs Rupa Mehra, the tears flowing copiously now, 'he was a husband in a million. Now Pran's father would always disappear when Pran's mother gave birth. He couldn't stand childbirth – so when the baby was young and noisy and messy he would try to be away as much as he could. If he had been there, maybe Pran would not have half-drowned in that soapy tub as a baby, and then all this asthma would not have happened – and his heart would have been undamaged.' Mrs Rupa Mehra lowered her voice at the word 'heart'.

'Ma, I'm feeling tired. I think I'll turn in,' said Savita. She insisted on sleeping alone in her bedroom, though Mrs Rupa Mehra had offered to sleep with her in case her labour pains started and she would be too helpless to move or get help.

*

One night at about nine o'clock, while she was reading in

bed, Savita suddenly felt a severe pain, and called out aloud. Mrs Rupa Mehra, her ears preternaturally sensitive to Savita's voice these days, came rushing into the room. She had taken out her false teeth already and only had her bra and petticoat on. She asked Savita what the matter was, and whether the pains had begun.

Savita nodded, gripping her stomach, and said she thought so. Mrs Rupa Mehra promptly shook Lata awake, put on a house-coat, roused the servants, put in her false teeth, and telephoned Prem Nivas for the car to be sent. She could not get through to the obstetrician at his home number. She phoned Baitar House.

Imtiaz answered the phone. 'How often are the contractions taking place?' he asked. 'Who is your obstetrician? Butalia? Good. Have you called him yet? Oh, I see. Leave it to me; he may be at the hospital with another delivery. I'll make sure that they have a private room ready, and are prepared for everything.'

The pains were more frequent now, but irregular. Lata was holding Savita's hand, and sometimes kissing her or stroking her forehead. When the pains were on, Savita closed her eyes. Imtiaz was over in an hour or so. He had had a difficult time tracking down the obstetrician, who had happened to be at a party.

Once she was in the hospital – the medical college hospital – Savita looked around and asked where Pran was. 'Shall I get him?' asked Mrs Rupa Mehra.

'No, no, let him sleep – he shouldn't get out of bed,' said Savita.

'She's quite right,' said Imtiaz firmly. 'It would do him no good at all. There are enough of us here for support and company.'

A nurse informed them that the obstetrician would be coming very soon, and that there was nothing to be alarmed about. 'First births take a long time in general. Twelve hours is quite normal.' Savita's eyes opened wide.

Though she was in great pain, she did not cry out aloud. Dr Butalia, a short Sikh doctor with rather dreamy eyes, arrived, examined her briefly, and again assured her that things were fine.

'Excellent, excellent,' he said with a smile, his eyes fixed on his watch while Savita writhed on the bed. 'Ten minutes – well, good, good.' He then disappeared.

Maan turned up next. The nurse, noting that he was a Mr Kapoor, and that he looked quite dishevelled and concerned, decided that he must be the father, and addressed him in those terms for a few minutes before he corrected her.

'I'm afraid the father is another patient in this hospital,' said Maan. 'I am his brother.'

'Oh, but how awful,' said the nurse. 'Does he know –'

'Not yet.'

'Oh.'

'Yes, he's sleeping, and it's his doctor's orders – and his wife's – that he not move or suffer unnecessary excitement. I'm standing in for him.'

The nurse frowned. 'Now lie quietly,' she advised Savita. 'Lie quietly and think calm thoughts.'

'Yes,' said Savita, tears squeezing themselves out of her eyes.

The night was hot, and despite the fact that the room was on the second floor there were a number of mosquitoes. Mrs Rupa Mehra asked for another bed to be brought in so that she and Lata could take turns to rest. Imtiaz, having made sure that things were in good order, left. Maan sat on a chair in the corridor and went off to sleep.

Savita could not think calm thoughts. She felt as if her body had been taken out of her own control by some terrible, brutal force. She gasped when the pains came, but because her mother had told her that they would be unbearable, and she kept expecting them to get worse, she tried not to cry out aloud, and succeeded. Hour followed hour, and the sweat stood out on her forehead. Lata tried to keep the mosquitoes away from her face.

It was four o'clock, and still dark. In a couple of hours, Pran would be awake. But Imtiaz had made it quite clear that he would not be allowed out of his room. Now Savita began to cry softly to herself, not only because she would be deprived of the comfort of his support, but because she could imagine how anxious he would be for her.

Her mother, thinking she was crying because of the pain, said: 'Now, darling, be brave, it'll all be over soon.'

Savita groaned, and held her mother's hand tightly.

The pain was now very nearly unbearable. Suddenly, she felt the bed wet around her legs, and turned to Mrs Rupa Mehra, flushed with embarrassment and perplexity.

'Ma –'

'What is it, darling?'

'I think – I think the bed is wet.'

Mrs Rupa Mehra woke Maan and sent him to get the nurses on duty.

The bag of waters had broken, and the contractions began coming very fast now, every couple of minutes or so. The nurses took one look at the situation, and wheeled Savita into the labour room. One of them telephoned Dr Butalia.

'Where's my mother?' asked Savita.

'She's outside,' said one rather abrupt nurse.

'Please tell her to come in.'

'Mrs Kapoor, I'm so sorry, we can't do that,' said the other nurse, a large, kind, Anglo-Indian woman. 'The doctor will be here very soon. Hold on to the railing behind your bed if the pain is too bad.'

'I think I can feel the baby –' began Savita.

'Mrs Kapoor, please try to hold on till the doctor arrives.'

'I can't –'

Luckily the doctor appeared almost immediately, and the nurses now both exhorted her to push.

'Hold on to the spring and handle above you.'

'Push, push, push –'

'I can't bear it – I can't bear it –' said Savita, her lips drawn apart in agony.

'Just push –'

'No,' she wept. 'It's horrible. I can't bear it. Give me an anaesthetic. Doctor, please –'

'Push, Mrs Kapoor, you're doing very well,' said the doctor.

Out of a haze of pain, Savita heard one nurse say to the other: 'Is the baby's head coming out first?'

Savita felt a tearing sensation below, then a sudden warm gush. Then more stretching and such pain that she thought she would pass out.

'I can't bear it, oh Ma, I can't bear it any more,' she screamed. 'I never want to have another baby.'

'They all say that,' said the abrupt nurse, 'and they all come back next year. Keep pushing –'

'I won't. I'll never – never – never have another child,' said Savita, who felt herself being stretched beyond endurance, almost torn apart. 'Oh God.'

Suddenly the head slipped out, and she felt a sense of immediate relief.

When, after what seemed a long time, she heard the baby's cry, she opened her eyes, which were still hazy with tears, and looked at the red, wrinkled, black-haired, bawling baby, covered with blood and a sort of greasy film, that the doctor was holding up in his arms.

'It's a girl, Mrs Kapoor,' said the dreamy-eyed doctor. 'With a very powerful voice.'

'A girl?'

'Yes. Quite a large baby. Well done. It was a difficult birth, as such things go.'

Savita lay exhausted for a couple of minutes. The light in the labour room was too bright for her. A baby! she thought.

'Can I hold her?' she asked after a while.

'Just one minute more, and we'll have her cleaned up.'

But the baby was still quite slippery when it – she – came to rest on the cradle of Savita's slack stomach. Savita looked at the top of its head, adoringly and accusingly, then held it gently and closed her eyes with exhaustion once more.

13.12

PRAN woke to find himself a father.

'What?' he said in disbelief to Imtiaz.

But seeing his parents sitting there by his bedside, something that would not normally have occurred outside visiting hours, he shook his head and believed it.

'A girl,' added Imtiaz. 'They're upstairs. Maan's there too, quite happy to be mistaken for the father.'

'A girl?' Pran was surprised, perhaps even a little disappointed. 'How is Savita?'

'Fine. I've had a word with the obstetrician. He says the birth was a little difficult, but nothing unusual.'

'Well, let me go to see her and the baby. I suppose she can't move.'

'No, she can't. Not for a couple of days. She has a few stitches. And I'm sorry, Pran, you can't move either. Neither movement nor excitement will conduce to your recovery.' Imtiaz spoke with the slightly severe formality that he found worked best with patients when he wanted to ensure their compliance.

'This is ridiculous, Imtiaz. Be sensible. Please. I suppose you're going to tell me that I can only see photographs of my baby.'

'That's an idea now,' said Imtiaz unable to resist a smile, and rubbing the mole on his cheek. 'But the baby, unlike the mother, is a transportable item, and she can certainly be brought to you here. It's a good thing you aren't infectious, or even that wouldn't have been possible. Butalia guards his babies as if they were something of value.'

'But I must speak to Savita,' said Pran.

'She's doing well, Pran,' said his father reassuringly. 'When I was upstairs she was resting. She's a good girl,' he added irrelevantly.

'Why don't you write her a note?' suggested Imtiaz.

'A note?' said Pran with a short laugh. 'She's not in a different city.' But he asked his mother to give him the pad on the night-stand, and scribbled a few lines:

Darling,
    Imtiaz has forbidden me a sight of you; he claims that walking up a couple of flights of stairs and the excitement of seeing you will undo me. I know that you must

be looking as beautiful as ever. I hope you are all right, and I wish I were there to hold your hand and tell you how wonderful our baby is. Because I'm sure she must be wonderful.

I haven't seen her either yet, and this is to request you to relinquish her for a few minutes.

Incidentally, I am fine and, in case you were wondering, had a restful night!

All my love,
Pran

Imtiaz went off.

'Don't worry that it's a girl, Pran,' said his mother.

'I'm not worried at all,' said Pran. 'I'm just surprised. Everyone kept talking about a boy, so after a while I believed it.'

Mrs Mahesh Kapoor herself was not displeased that she had a granddaughter, since Bhaskar (though not in the male line) had fulfilled her wish for a grandson.

'Rupa couldn't be pleased, though,' she told her husband.

'Why?' said her husband.

'Two granddaughters and no grandsons.'

'Women should have their brains examined,' was his response, before he returned to the day's newspaper.

'But you always say –'

Mahesh Kapoor held up his hand, and continued reading.

In a short while Mrs Rupa Mehra appeared with the baby.

Pran's eyes filled suddenly with tears. 'Hello, Ma,' he said, reaching out for the baby.

The baby's eyes were open but because of the folds around them, she looked almost as if she was squinting. To Pran she looked extremely raw and wrinkled, but not unattractive. In an unfocused way she too appeared to register Pran.

He held her, not knowing what to do. How did one communicate with a baby? He hummed for a bit. Then he said to his mother-in-law: 'How is Savita? When will she be able to move around?'

'Oh, she's sent a customs note with the parcel,' said Mrs Rupa Mehra, handing Pran a piece of paper.

Pran looked at his mother-in-law, surprised by this sudden flippant touch of wit. He felt that if he had made a joke in the same vein she would have rebuked him.

'Really, Ma!' he said. But Mrs Rupa Mehra was laughing, and tickling the back of the baby's head in a doting manner. Pran rested the note against the baby, and read as follows:

Dearest P,

Herewith find enclosed one baby, size M, sex F, colour R, to be returned after inspection and approval.

I am very well, and longing to see you, and I have been told that in two or three days I can move around carefully. It's these stitches, which make certain things difficult for me.

The baby has a definite personality, and I feel she has taken a liking to me. I hope you are equally lucky. Her nose reminds me of Ma's, but nothing else reminds me of anything in either of our families. She was very slippery when she came out, but now she has been cleaned and talcumed for presentability.

Please don't worry about me, Pran. I am very well, and Ma will be sleeping in my room next to the baby's cot so that I'll be able to rest except for feeding times.

I hope you are all right, my darling, and congratulations. It's difficult to think of myself in my changed status. I know I've had a baby all right, but I can't believe I'm a mother.

Lots of love,
Savita

Pran rocked his daughter for a while. He smiled at the last sentence. Imtiaz had congratulated him on being a father rather than on having a baby, and he had no difficulty in accepting the fact of his fatherhood.

The baby was asleep in his arms. Pran was amazed at how perfect she was, all of her. Even though she was so small, each vein, each limb and lid and lip, each tiny finger was there – and functioning.

The baby's mouth was open in an unmeaning smile.

Pran saw what Savita meant about the nose. Even though it was very small, he could see that it had the potential of Mrs Rupa Mehra's rather hawk-like nose. He wondered if it would redden in the same way when she cried. At any rate, it couldn't be redder than it was now.

'Isn't she lovely?' asked Mrs Rupa Mehra. 'How proud He would have been to see his second granddaughter.'

Pran rocked the baby a bit more, and touched his nose to hers.

'What do you think of your daughter?' asked Mrs Rupa Mehra.

'She has a nice smile, considering that she's a baby,' said Pran.

As he had thought, Mrs Rupa Mehra did not approve of his flippancy. She told him that if he had given birth to the baby he would have appreciated her more.

'Quite right, Ma, quite right,' said Pran.

He wrote a short note back to Savita, informing her that the baby met with his approval, and reassuring her that slippery people were necessary in the scheme of things. When Mrs Rupa Mehra returned upstairs with the baby, Mr and Mrs Mahesh Kapoor followed, and Pran stared at the ceiling, lost in his thoughts, more happy about the present than worried about the future.

The baby was a little difficult to feed on the first day. At first she didn't want to acknowledge the breast, but once Savita brushed her finger against her cheek she turned around quite swiftly and opened her mouth. This was the opportunity for the nipple to be put to the baby's mouth. The baby's face registered an expression something like surprise. She also had a little difficulty in pulling properly. After that there was no trouble, except that she tended to go to sleep while feeding, and had to be woken up to complete her feed. Sometimes Savita tickled her behind the ears, sometimes on the soles of her feet. The baby was comfortable and contented to the extent that she required a great deal of persuasion to wake up at times.

Grandmother, mother and baby each had a bed in the private room. Lata had to go for classes in the morning, but usually managed to relieve her mother's watch for an hour or two around lunchtime. Sometimes Mrs Rupa Mehra, Savita, and the baby would all be sleeping, with only Lata watching, and an occasional nurse stopping by to ensure that everything was all right. It was a quiet time, and Lata used it to learn her lines. At other times she simply mused. If the baby woke, or needed its nappy changed, she took care of what needed to be done. The baby was content to be rocked by her.

Sometimes, sitting here, with the marked script of *Twelfth Night* open on her lap, Lata substituted the word 'happiness' for 'greatness' in the famous quotation. She wondered what one could do to be born happy, to achieve happiness, or to have it thrust on one. The baby, she thought, had arranged to be born happy; she was placid, and had as good a chance as anyone of happiness in this world, her father's poor health notwithstanding. Pran and Savita, different though their backgrounds were, were a happy couple. They recognized limits and possibilities; their yearnings did not stretch beyond their reach. They loved each other – or, rather, had come to do so. They both assumed, without ever needing to state it – or perhaps without even thinking explicitly about it – that marriage and children were a great good. If Savita was restless – and at the moment in the shaded noon light her sleeping face showed no restlessness but, rather, a peace and pleasure that Lata wondered at – if she was restless, it was because she feared the undoing by forces outside themselves of this great good. She wanted above all to ensure that no matter what happened to her husband, insecurity and unhappiness would not unavoidably thrust themselves on their child. The law-book resting on the table on one side of her bed balanced the baby resting in the cot on the other.

Nowadays, when Mrs Rupa Mehra fussed about Savita

or her as-yet-nameless granddaughter, or voiced to Lata her fears about Pran's health or Varun's shiftlessness, Lata was not so impatient as she had earlier been. Her mother appeared to her now as the guardian of the family; and with life and death so near each other here in the hospital, it seemed to Lata that all that provided continuity in the world or protection from it was the family. Calcutta, Delhi, Kanpur, Lucknow – the visits to endless relatives – the Annual Trans-India Rail-Pilgrimages that Arun mocked so relentlessly and the water-works that vexed him, the sending of cards to third cousins thrice removed on their birthdays, the family gossip at every ritual ceremony from birth to death, and the continual recollection of her husband – that absent but no doubt still benevolently supervising god – all these could be seen as part of the works of a corresponding domestic goddess, whose symbols (false teeth, black bag, scissors and thimble, gold and silver stars) would be remembered with tenderness long after she was gone – as she herself was over-fond of pointing out. She wanted Lata's happiness just as Savita wanted her baby's; and had tried to arrange for it in as determined a manner as she could. Lata no longer resented it.

Thrust so suddenly into the marriage market this year, forced to travel from city to city, Lata had begun to look at marriages (the Sahgals, the Chatterjis, Arun and Meenakshi, Mr and Mrs Mahesh Kapoor, Pran and Savita) with more than a disinterested eye. But whether it was owing to the hectoring of her mother or her overly copious love or the vision of these different families or Pran's illness or the birth of Savita's baby or all of them combined, Lata felt she had changed. The sleeping Savita was perhaps a more powerful adviser than the voluble Malati.

Lata looked back on her wish to elope with Kabir with a kind of amazement, even as she could not shake off her feelings for him. But where would these feelings lead? A gradual, stable attraction such as Savita's for Pran – was this not the best thing for her, and for the family, and for any children that she might have?

Each day at the rehearsal she feared and hoped that

Kabir would come up to her to say something or do something that would begin to unravel once again the unfamiliar, too-solid fabric that she had woven – or that had been woven – around her. But rehearsals passed, and visiting hours came, and matters remained as unspoken and unresolved as ever.

Plenty of people came in to look at the baby: Imtiaz, Firoz, Maan, Bhaskar, old Mrs Tandon, Kedarnath, Veena, the Nawab Sahib himself, Malati, Mr and Mrs Mahesh Kapoor, Mr Shastri (bearing a law-book he had promised Savita), Dr Kishen Chand Seth and Parvati, and many others, including a troop of Rudhia relatives whom Savita did not know. Clearly, the baby had been born not to a couple but to a clan. Dozens of people cooed above her (some acclaiming her looks, others deprecating her sex) and great exception was taken to any proprietary instincts displayed by the mother. Savita, imagining that she had certain special rights to the baby, attempted to protect her from the mist of appreciative droplets that formed a continuous haze around her head for two days. But she gave up at last, and accepted that the Kapoors of Rudhia and Brahmpur had the right to welcome in their own way this freshly-minted member of their tribe. She wondered what her brother Arun would have made of the Rudhia relatives. Lata had dispatched a telegram to Calcutta, but so far nothing had been heard from that branch of the Mehras.

13.13

'NO, really, Didi – I'm enjoying it. It's no bother at all. I like reading things I don't understand sometimes.'

'You're strange,' said Savita, smiling.

'Yes. Well, as long as I know they do actually make sense.'

'Would you hold her for a while?'

Lata put the book on tort down, went over to Savita, and took over the baby, who smiled at her for a while and then went off to sleep.

She rocked the baby, who appeared to be quite content in her arms.

'Now what's all this, baby?' said Lata. 'What's all this now? Wake up a little and speak to us, speak to your Lata Masi. When I'm awake you go off to sleep, when I'm asleep you wake up, let's do things straight for a change, shall we, this won't do at all, will it, will it now?'

She moved the baby from one arm to the other surprisingly skilfully, cradling her head all the while.

'What do you think about my studying law?' said Savita. 'Do you think I have the temperament for it? Savita Mehra, Government Counsel; Savita Mehra, Senior Advocate; good heavens, I forgot for a moment I'm a Kapoor. Savita Kapoor, Advocate-General; Mrs Justice Savita Kapoor. Will I be called "My Lord" or "My lady"?'

'Don't count your chickens before they're hatched,' said Lata, laughing.

'But they might never get hatched,' said Savita. 'I may as well count them now. Ma, you know, doesn't think law is such a bad idea. She feels that if she had had a profession it might have helped.'

'Oh, nothing's going to happen to Pran,' said Lata, smiling at the baby. 'Is it, now? Nothing's going to happen to Papa, nothing, nothing, nothing. He will play his silly, silly April fool jokes for many, many years to come. Do you know, you can actually feel her pulse through her head?'

'How amazing!' said Savita. 'It's going to be very difficult for me to get used to being slim again. When you're pregnant and bulge, you are popular with all the cats on the university campus, and people tell you intimate things about themselves.'

Lata crinkled her nose. 'But what if we don't want to hear intimate things?' she inquired of the baby. 'What if we are quite happy to paddle our own canoe in a pleasant little backwater – and are not interested in the Niagara Falls and the Barsaat Mahal?'

Savita was quiet for a few moments, then she said: 'OK,

I'll take her back now. And you can read to me a bit more. What's that book?'

'*Twelfth Night.*'

'No, the other one – the one with the green and white cover.'

'*Contemporary Verse*,' murmured Lata, blushing for some unaccountable reason.

'Oh, read me some of that,' said Savita. 'Ma thinks poetry is good for me. Soothing. Calming.

> It was a summer evening,
> Old Caspar's work was done.'

Lata took up the recitation:

> 'And he beside his cottage door
> Was sitting in the sun.

There's a skull in that poem somewhere, I remember. Oh yes, and Ma also loves that grisly "Casabianca" with the boy burning on the deck – and "Lord Ullin's Daughter". There has to be some death and heartbreak in it somewhere or it isn't real poetry. I don't know what she'd make of the poetry in this book. All right, what do you want to hear?'

'Open it at random,' suggested Savita. And the book opened to Auden's 'Law, Say the Gardeners'.

'Apt,' said Lata, and began to read. But as she turned the page to the last few lines, and read the poet's similitude between law and love, her face grew pale:

> 'Like love we don't know where or why
> Like love we can't compel or fly
> Like love we often weep
> Like love we seldom keep.'

She shut the book.

'Strange poem,' she said.

'Yes,' said Savita carefully. 'Let's go back to tort.'

MEENAKSHI MEHRA arrived in Brahmpur three days after
the birth of the baby. She came with her sister Kakoli but
without her daughter Aparna. She was tired of Calcutta
and needed a break, and the telegram provided her with an
excuse.

She was tired, for a start, of Arun, who was being very
boring and covenanted these days, and appeared to have
lost interest in anything but premiums on tea to Khorram-
shahr. She was exhausted with Aparna, who had begun to
get on her nerves with her 'Mummy this' and 'Mummy
that' and 'Mummy you aren't listening'. She was sick of
arguing with the Toothless Crone and Hanif and the part-
time mali. She felt she was going mad. Varun would slope
and slither guiltily in and out of the house, and every time
he went 'heh-heh-heh' in his furtive Shamshu way she
would feel like screaming. Even occasional afternoons with
Billy and canasta with the Shady Ladies seemed to have
lost their savour. It was too, too awful. Truly, Calcutta
was nothing but tinsel in the mouth.

And then came this telegram informing them that Arun's
sister had had a baby. Well, it was nothing less than a
godsend. Dipankar had filled postcard after postcard with
descriptions of what a beautiful place Brahmpur was, and
how nice Savita's in-laws were. They were bound to be
hospitable and she would be able to lie under a fan and
calm her fraught nerves. Meenakshi felt she needed a
holiday, and this was a wonderful opportunity to pounce
upon Brahmpur with the intention of helping out. She
could give her sister-in-law excellent advice on how to
take care of her daughter. She had successfully managed
Aparna, and this gave her the authority to manage her
niece.

Meenakshi was quite pleased to be an aunt, even if only
through her husband's sister. Her own brothers and sisters
had not provided her with a single nephew or niece. Amit
was the most culpable in this regard; he should have got
married at least three years ago. In fact, thought Meenak-

shi, he should make up for his error at once: by marrying Lata.

Here was another reason for going to Brahmpur; she would prepare the ground when she got there. Of course there was no question of mentioning her plan to Amit; he would have hit the roof in so far as he was capable of it. Sometimes she wished he would hit the roof. Surely poets should be more passionate than Amit was. But she could certainly imagine him saying acidly: 'Do your own wooing, Meenakshi darling, and let me do mine.' No, she had better not mention anything to Amit.

Kakoli, however, when she came to visit Sunny Park late one afternoon, was let into the plot, and was delighted. She considered Lata to be quiet but nice, with sudden surprising sparks here and there to leaven things. Amit appeared to like her, but he was incapable of doing anything determined for himself, being content simply to contemplate things and let the years roll on. Kakoli felt that Lata and Amit were well-matched but that each needed prodding. She rolled off a Kakoli couplet to consecrate their match:

> 'Luscious Lata, born to be
> Lady Lata Chatterji.'

She was rewarded by the tinkle of Meenakshi's laughter, and the return of her service:

> 'Luscious Lata, is it hard
> Being wife of famous bard?'

Kakoli, giggling, volleyed the ball low across the net:

> 'Oh, so hard it is in rhyme:
> Loving, doving, all the time.'

And Meenakshi continued the rally:

> 'Kissing, missing, every day,
> Cuddling, muddling all the way.'

Kakoli, suddenly remembering that she had left Cuddles tied up to her bed-post, told Meenakshi she had to go home immediately. 'But why don't both of us go to Brahmpur together?' she suggested. 'To the provinces,' she added airily.

'Why not?' said Meenakshi. 'We could chaperone each other. But wouldn't you miss Hans?'

'We need only go for a week. It'll be good for him to miss me. It'll be well worth the pain of my missing him.'

'And Cuddles? It really is very tiresome of Dipankar not to say when he's coming back. He's been gone for years, and now that he's run out of postcards, we'll never hear from him.'

'It's just typical of him. Well, Amit can be Cuddles' keeper.'

When Mrs Chatterji heard of the trip, she was more concerned with Kakoli missing classes than missing Hans.

'Oh, Ma,' wailed Kakoli, 'don't be such a bore. Weren't you ever young? Didn't you ever want to flee from the chains of life? I have excellent attendance at college, and a week won't make any difference. We can always get a doctor to certify that I've been ill. With a wasting sickness.' She quoted two snowy lines from *Winterreise* about the Inn that represented Death. 'Or malaria,' she continued. 'Look, there's a mosquito.'

'We will do no such thing,' said Mr Justice Chatterji, looking up from his book.

But Kakoli, while conceding this point, wore her parents down on the general question of the Brahmpur jaunt. 'Meenakshi needs me to accompany her. Arun's too busy with work. The family needs us,' she pleaded. 'Babies are so complicated. Every pair of hands helps. And Lata's such a nice girl, her company will improve me. Ask Amit if she isn't nice. And improving.'

'Oh shut up, Kuku, leave me to Keats,' said Amit.

'Kuku, Keats, Kuku, Keats,' said Kakoli, sitting down at the piano. 'What shall I play for you, Amit? La-La-Liebestraum?'

Amit fixed her with a Look.

But Kakoli rippled on:

> 'Amit lying on his bed,
> Dreams of Lata in his head.
> Weeping, weeping on his sheets,
> Cannot concentrate on Keats.'

'You are by far the stupidest girl I know,' said Amit. 'But why do you advertise your stupidity?'

'Perhaps because I am stupid!' said Kakoli, and giggled at her idiotic answer. 'But don't you like her — a teeeeny weeeeny bit? A soupçon? A little? A tittle?'

Amit got up to go to his room, but not before another Kakoli-couplet had been shot at him.

> 'Kuku-clock chimes out her name.
> Poet fleeing, red with shame.'

'Really, Kuku!' said her mother. 'There are limits.' She turned to her husband. 'You never say anything to her. You never set any limits. You never stop her from doing anything. You always give in. What is a father for?'

'To say no at first,' said Mr Justice Chatterji.

13.15

MOST of the Brahmpur news had already got through to Calcutta via the informative letters of Mrs Rupa Mehra. But her last letter had been overtaken by the telegram. So when Meenakshi and Kakoli got to Brahmpur with every intention of plonking themselves and their baggage down at Pran's doorstep, they were shocked to find that he wasn't there at all, but ill in hospital. With Savita in hospital herself, and Lata and her mother fussing about with Pran and Savita, it was clear that Meenakshi and Kuku could not be put up and fussed over in the style to which they were accustomed.

Meenakshi found it hard to believe that the Kapoors had timed their affairs so badly as to have husband and wife bedridden at the same time.

Kakoli was more sympathetic, accepting the fact that baby and bronchi could not confer in advance. 'Why don't we stay at Pran's father's place, what is it called, Prem Nivas?' she asked.

'That's impossible,' responded Meenakshi. 'The mother doesn't even speak English. And they won't have western-style toilets – just those dreadful holes in the ground.'

'Well, what are we to do?'

'Kuku, how about that old dodderer whose address Baba gave us?'

'But who wants to stay with someone who's full of senile reminiscences?'

'Well, where is it?'

'He gave it to you. It must be in your bag,' said Kakoli.

'No, Kuku, he gave it to you,' said Meenakshi.

'I'm quite sure he didn't,' said Kakoli. 'Do check.'

'Well – oh, yes, here it is. Maybe it's on that. Yes, it is: Mr and Mrs Maitra. Let's land on them.'

'Let's see the baby first.'

'What about our luggage?'

So Meenakshi and Kakoli freshened up, changed into a mauve and a red cotton sari respectively, ordered Mateen to provide them with a fortifying breakfast, and set off in a tonga for Civil Lines. Meenakshi was astonished that it was so difficult to hail a taxi in Brahmpur, and shuddered every time the horse farted.

Meenakshi and Kakoli quickly imposed themselves on Mr and Mrs Maitra and then rushed off, waving from the back of the tonga, towards the hospital.

'Well, they claim that they're Chatterji's daughters,' said the old policeman. 'His children seem to be very restless. What was the name of that other boy, their son?'

Mrs Maitra, who was scandalized by the fact that she could see almost four inches of their waists, shook her head and wondered what Calcutta had come to. Her own son's letters did not contain any mention of waistlines.

'When will they be back for lunch?'

'They didn't say.'

'Well, since they are our guests, we should wait for them. But I get so hungry by noon,' said old Mr Maitra. 'And then I have to tell my beads for two hours, and if I begin late, that puts everything out. We'd also better get some more fish.'

'We'll wait till one, and then eat,' said his wife. 'If they can't come, they'll telephone us.'

And so the two considerate old people accommodated themselves to the two young women, who had no intention of eating with them, and to whom the thought of a telephone call would certainly not occur.

*

Mrs Rupa Mehra was transporting the baby from Pran's room to Savita's when she saw the mauve Meenakshi and the crimson Kakoli bearing down upon her along the corridor. She all but dropped the baby.

Meenakshi was wearing those little gold horrors that never failed to upset Mrs Rupa Mehra. And what was Kakoli doing here during term-time? Really, thought Mrs Rupa Mehra, the Chatterjis impose no discipline upon their children. That is why they are all so peculiar.

Aloud she said: 'Oh, Meenakshi, Kakoli, what a lovely surprise. Have you seen the baby yet? No, of course you couldn't have. Just look at her, isn't she sweet? And everyone says she has my nose.'

'How adorable,' said Meenakshi, thinking that the baby looked rather like a red rat, not at all as beautiful as her Aparna had looked a few days after birth.

'And where is my sweetheart?' demanded Mrs Rupa Mehra.

For a second Meenakshi thought Mrs Rupa Mehra was referring to Arun. Then she realized that it was Aparna whom her mother-in-law was talking about.

'In Calcutta, of course.'

'You didn't bring her with you?' Mrs Rupa Mehra

could hardly conceal her amazement at this maternal callousness.

'Oh, Ma, one can't drag the whole world with one when one travels,' said Meenakshi coolly. 'Aparna does get on one's nerves sometimes, and I'd be much less help here if she was with me.'

'You've come to help?' Mrs Rupa Mehra could hardly keep the astonishment and displeasure out of her voice.

'Yes, Ma,' said Kakoli simply.

But Meenakshi elaborated: 'Yes, of course, Ma, darling. What a sweet little thing. Reminds me of a, of a – well, she's unique, she doesn't remind me of anything but herself.' Meenakshi laughed a tinkly laugh. 'Now where is Savita's room?'

'Savita is resting,' said Mrs Rupa Mehra.

'But she'll be so pleased to see us,' said Meenakshi. 'Let's go and see her. It must be feeding time. Six, ten, two, six, ten, as Dr Evans recommended with Aparna. And it's just about ten o'clock now.'

And they descended upon Savita, who was still fairly exhausted, and in quite a lot of pain because her stitches were pulling. She was sitting up in bed, though, and reading a women's magazine rather than a law-book.

Savita was astonished, but pleased to see them. Lata, who had been keeping her company, was very pleased. She enjoyed Meenakshi's attempts to beautify her; and Kuku's flightiness would, she hoped, lighten everyone's mood. Savita had met Kuku only twice since Arun's wedding.

'How did you get here outside visiting hours?' Savita asked, looking rather warrior-like now, with bright lipstick on both her cheeks.

'Oh, Kakoli and I were more than a match for the reception desk,' said Meenakshi. And indeed, the dumbfounded clerk had not known how to prevent these glamorous, waist-bare ladies from breezing past him.

Kakoli had blown him a kiss with casual hauteur. He was still recovering.

CALCUTTA and Brahmpur news was exchanged rapidly. Arun was extremely busy with work, Varun showed no signs of studying seriously for the IAS exams, and there were lots of rows between the brothers, with Arun threatening periodically to throw Varun out of the house. Aparna's vocabulary was increasing apace; a few days ago she had said: 'Daddy, I'm in the doldrums.' Meenakshi suddenly began to miss Aparna. Seeing the baby snuggling up to Savita's breast, she thought of Aparna's own babydom, the lovely feeling of closeness she had experienced when she was suckling her, the sense of 'myness' that she had had towards her before Aparna had grown into a clearly differentiated, and often contrary, individual.

'Why doesn't she have a name-tag?' she asked. 'Dr Evans always insisted on name-tags, in case babies got lost or exchanged by mistake.' Meenakshi's little earrings glinted as she shook her head at the frightful thought.

Mrs Rupa Mehra got irritated. 'I am here to ensure that nothing happens. Mothers should stay with their children. Who can steal the baby when her cot is in this room?'

'Of course, things are much better arranged in Calcutta,' continued Meenakshi. 'In the Irwin Nursing Home, where Aparna was delivered, there's a separate nursery where the babies are kept, and you can only view them through glass – to prevent infection, of course. Here everyone breathes and talks above the baby, and the air is full of germs. She could easily fall ill.'

'Savita is trying to rest,' said Mrs Rupa Mehra severely. 'These are not very restful thoughts, Meenakshi.'

'I agree,' said Kakoli. 'I think things are run splendidly here. In fact, I think it would be rather fun if babies got exchanged. Like in *The Prince and the Gipsy*.' This was a romantic pot-boiler that Kuku had recently read. 'In fact,' she continued, 'this particular baby looks rather too red and crinkled for my liking. I'd ask for a replacement.' She giggled.

'Kuku,' said Lata. 'How's your singing and piano going? And how is Hans?'

'I think I want to go to the bathroom, Ma – could you help me?' asked Savita.

'Let me help,' said Meenakshi and Kakoli simultaneously.

'Thanks, but Ma and I are used to things,' said Savita with calm authority. It was difficult for her to walk to the bathroom; the stitches made everything more painful. Once she closed the door, she told Mrs Rupa Mehra that she was rather tired, and that Meenakshi and Kakoli should be told to return in the evening at visiting time.

Meenakshi and Kakoli, meanwhile, had been talking to Lata, and had decided that they would come and see that afternoon's rehearsal of *Twelfth Night*.

'I wonder what it must have been like to be married to Shakespeare,' breathed Meenakshi, 'and have him say such wonderful poetic things to one all the time – about love and life –'

'He didn't say much to Anne Hathaway,' said Lata. 'He wasn't there most of the time. And according to Professor Mishra, his sonnets imply that he was interested in other people too – more than one.'

'But who isn't?' said Meenakshi, then suddenly stopped, recalling that Lata was, after all, Arun's sister. 'In any case, I'd forgive Shakespeare anything. It must be so wonderful to be married to a poet. To be his muse, to make him happy. I was just saying so to Amit the other day, but he's so modest, he only said: "I think my wife would have a hell of a time."'

'Which is nonsense, of course,' said Kakoli. 'Amit has a lovely nature. Why, Cuddles bites him less often than anyone else.'

Lata said nothing. Meenakshi and Kuku were being remarkably unsubtle, and their talk about Amit irritated her. She felt fairly sure that Amit could not have acquiesced in this mission. She looked at her watch, and realized that she was almost late for a class.

'See you at three o'clock at the auditorium,' she said. 'Don't you want to see Pran as well?'

'Pran? Oh, yes.'

'He's in room 56. On the ground floor. Where are you staying?'

'With Mr Maitra in Civil Lines. He's a sweet old man, but completely senile. Dipankar stayed with him as well. It's become the Chatterji hostel in Brahmpur.'

'I wish you were staying with us,' said Lata. 'But you see how difficult things are at present.'

'Now, don't worry about us, Lata,' said Kuku kindly. 'Just tell us how to occupy ourselves between now and three o'clock. I think we've had our fill of the baby for the moment.'

'Well, you could go to the Barsaat Mahal,' said Lata. 'I know it's hot at this time of day, but it's as beautiful as they say it is, and much more so than any of the photographs.'

'Oh, monuments! –' said Meenakshi, yawning.

'Isn't there something livelier in Brahmpur?' asked Kakoli.

'Well, there's the Blue Danube café on Nabiganj. And the Red Fox. And the movies, though the English ones are a couple of years out of date. And the bookstores –' Even as she spoke, Lata realized how dreary Brahmpur must seem to the ladies of Calcutta. 'I'm really sorry, I have to run now. My lecture.'

And Kuku was left wondering at Lata's enthusiasm for her studies.

13.17

WHAT with the activity surrounding Pran's illness and the baby's arrival, Lata's own reticence and Malati's protective presence at rehearsals, Lata and Kabir had merely exchanged Shakespeare's lines, and none of their own, for the last few days. Lata longed to tell him how much she sympathized with him about his mother, but did not know how to do so without eliciting an intensity of feeling on both sides that she feared would shake her – and probably him – too painfully. So she said nothing. But Mr Barua noticed that Olivia was kinder to Malvolio than he thought the script merited, and he tried to correct her.

'Now, Miss Mehra, do try that again. "O you are sick of self-love, Malvolio –"'

Lata cleared her throat for a second attempt. 'O you are sick of self-love, Malvolio, and taste with a distempered appetite –'

'No, no, Miss Mehra – like this: "O you are sick –" and so on. Slightly sharp, slightly tired. You are irritated by Malvolio. It is he who is mooning over you.'

Lata tried to think of how angry she had been when she saw Kabir at the first rehearsal. She began once more:

'O you are sick of self-love, Malvolio, and taste with a distempered appetite. To be generous, guiltless, and of free disposition, is to take those things for bird-bolts that you deem cannon-bullets –'

'Ah, yes, much better, much better. But you seem rather too annoyed. Tone it down, Miss Mehra, if you would, tone it down a little. That way, when he seems to be really mad later on, even offensive, you'll have an unused range of emotions that you can bring into play. Do you see what I mean?'

'Yes, yes I think I do, Mr Barua.'

Kakoli and Meenakshi had been chatting to Malati for a while, but she suddenly disappeared. 'My cue,' she explained, and bounced into the wings to come on as Maria.

'What do you think, Kuku?' said Meenakshi.

'I think she has a soft spot for that Malvolio chap.'

'Malati assured us she hadn't,' said Meenakshi. 'She even called him a cad. Seemed a strange word to use. A cad.'

I think he's delicious. He looks so broad-shouldered and soulful. I wish he'd shoot a cannon-bullet at me. Or his bird-bolt.'

'Really, Kuku, you have no decency at all,' said Meenakshi.

'Lata has certainly opened up since she was in Calcutta,'

said Kakoli thoughtfully. 'If Amit is to stand a chance, he can't continue to lie low –'

'The early worm catches the bird,' said Meenakshi.

Kakoli giggled.

Mr Barua turned around in annoyance.

'Er, would the two young ladies at the back –'

'But it's so amusing – the lines, I mean – under your direction,' said Kakoli with brazen sweetness. Some of the boys laughed, and Mr Barua turned around, blushing.

But after a few minutes of foolery by Sir Toby, both Kakoli and Meenakshi got bored, and left.

That evening, the two sisters went to the hospital. They spent a few seconds with Pran, whom they found unattractive and negligible – 'I knew it the minute I saw him at the wedding,' said Meenakshi – and most of their time upstairs in Savita's room. Meenakshi advised Savita about her feeding times. Savita listened carefully, thinking about other matters. Lots of other people came in, and the room became as crowded as a concert. Meenakshi and Kakoli, pheasants among the Brahmpur pigeons, looked around them with unfeigned contempt, especially at the Rudhia relatives and Mrs Mahesh Kapoor. Some of these people were incapable of speaking English. And the way they dressed!

Mrs Mahesh Kapoor for her part could not believe that these two shamelessly bare-waisted and bold-mouthed girls were the sisters of that nice boy Dipankar, who was so simple in his dress, amiable in his manners, and spiritual in his tastes. She was upset that Maan appeared to be hovering fascinatedly nearby. Kuku was looking at him with liquid eyes. Meenakshi's eyes held a look of come-hither disdain which was as challenging as Kuku's was appealing. Perhaps because she did not understand much English, Mrs Mahesh Kapoor was able more keenly to observe the unobvious undercurrents of hostility and attraction, contempt and admiration, tenderness and indifference that tied together the twenty or so people talking non-stop in this room.

Meenakshi was telling a story, punctuated by her bell-like laugh, about her own pregnancy. 'It had to be Dr

Evans, of course. Dr Matthew Evans. Really, if one has to have a baby in Calcutta, there's no other choice. Such a charming man. Absolutely the best gynaecologist in Calcutta. He has such a nice way with his patients.'

'Oh, Meenakshi, you're only saying that because he flirts with his patients shamelessly,' interrupted Kakoli. 'He pats them on their bottoms.'

'Well, he certainly cheers them up,' said Meenakshi. 'That's part of his bedside manner.'

Kakoli giggled. Mrs Rupa Mehra looked at Mr Mahesh Kapoor, who seemed to be going through a paroxysm of self-control.

'Of course he's terribly terribly expensive – his fee for Aparna was 750 rupees. But even Ma, who's so penny-pinching, agrees he was worth every paisa. Don't you, Ma?'

Mrs Rupa Mehra did not agree, but did not say so. When Dr Evans had heard that Meenakshi was in labour, he had merely said, as if sighting the Armada: 'Tell her to hold on. I'm finishing my game of golf.'

Meenakshi was continuing. 'The Irwin Nursing Home is spotless. And there's a nursery too. The mother isn't exhausted by having the baby with her all the time in a cot, yelling and needing its nappy changed. It's just brought to her at feeding times. And they're strict about the number of visitors there.' Meenakshi looked rather pointedly at the riffraff from Rudhia.

Mrs Rupa Mehra was too embarrassed by Meenakshi's behaviour to say anything.

Mr Mahesh Kapoor said: 'Mrs Mehra, this is very fascinating, but –'

'Do you think so?' said Meenakshi. 'I do think childbirth is so – so ennobling.'

'Ennobling?' said Kuku, astonished.

Savita was beginning to look pale.

'Well, don't you think one shouldn't miss out on the whole thing?' Meenakshi hadn't thought so when she had actually been pregnant.

'I don't know,' said Kakoli. 'I'm not pregnant – yet.'

Maan laughed, and Mr Mahesh Kapoor almost choked.

'Kakoli!' said Mrs Rupa Mehra in a warning voice.

'But not everyone knows when they're pregnant,' continued Kakoli. 'Remember Brigadier Guha's wife in Kashmir? She didn't go through the ennobling experience.'

Meenakshi laughed at the memory.

'What about her?' said Maan.

'Well –' began Meenakshi.

'She was –' began Kakoli simultaneously.

'You tell it,' said Meenakshi.

'No, you tell it,' said Kakoli.

'All right,' said Meenakshi. 'She was playing hockey in Kashmir, where she'd gone for a holiday to celebrate her fortieth birthday. She fell down, and got hurt, and had to return to Calcutta. When she got back, she began to feel shooting pains every few minutes. They called the doctor –'

'Dr Evans,' added Kakoli.

'No, Kuku, Dr Evans came later, this was another one. So she said, "Doctor, what is this?" And he said, "You're going to have a baby. We've got to get you to the nursing home at once."'

'It really caused shock-waves in Calcutta society,' said Kakoli to the assembled company. 'When they told her husband he said: "What baby? Bloody nonsense!" He was fifty-five years old.'

'You see,' continued Meenakshi, 'when she stopped having periods, she thought it was her menopause. She couldn't imagine she was going to have a baby.'

Maan, noticing his father's frozen face, began to laugh uncontrollably, and even Meenakshi graced him with a smile. The baby too appeared to be smiling, but it was probably just wind.

13.18

THE baby and mother got along very well over the next couple of days. What was most surprising to Savita about the baby was her softness. She was almost unbearably soft, especially the soles of her feet, the inside of her elbows, the back of her neck – here she was even more amazingly, heartbreakingly tender! Sometimes she laid the baby beside her on the bed and looked at her admiringly. The baby appeared satisfied with life; she was quite a hungry baby, but not a noisy one. When she had had her fill, she would look at her mother with half-opened eyes: a snug, smug expression. Savita found that, being right-handed, it was easier to feed her from the left breast. This fact had never struck her before.

She had even begun to consider herself a mother now.

Cushioned by her mother, daughter, and sister in a feminine and loving world, Savita felt the days pass placidly and happily. But from time to time a wave of deep depression swept over her. Once this happened when it was raining outside and a couple of pigeons were cooing on the window ledge. Sometimes she would think of the student who had died in this very hospital a few days ago, and wonder about the world into which she had brought her daughter. Once, when she heard how Maan had dispatched the crazed monkey, she burst into tears. The depth of her sudden sadnesses was unaccountable.

Or perhaps it was not as unaccountable as it seemed to her. With Pran's heart trouble hanging over the family, they would always live under a shadow of uncertainty. Savita began to feel more and more that she had to learn a profession, no matter what Pran's father might say.

Notes passed between Pran and Savita as usual, but most of them these days were about suitable names for the baby. Both agreed that she should be named soon; it was not necessary to wait for her character to develop in order to pick a suitable name.

Everyone made suggestions of one kind or another. Eventually, Pran and Savita decided by correspondence on Maya. Its two simple syllables meant, among other things: the goddess Lakshmi, illusion, fascination, art, the goddess Durga, kindness, and the name of the mother of the Buddha. It also meant: ignorance, delusion, fraud, guile, and hypocrisy; but no one who named their daughter Maya ever paid any attention to these pejorative possibilities.

When Savita announced the baby's name to the family, there was an appreciative murmur from the dozen or so people in the room. Then Mrs Rupa Mehra said:

'You cannot name her Maya, and that is that.'

'Why ever not, Ma?' said Meenakshi. 'It's a very Bengali name, a very nice name.'

'Because it is just impossible,' said Mrs Rupa Mehra. 'Ask Pran's mother,' she added in Hindi.

Veena too, who, like Meenakshi, had just become an aunt by virtue of this baby and felt that she had some rights in the matter, thought the name was a good one. She turned to her mother in surprise.

But Mrs Mahesh Kapoor agreed with Mrs Rupa Mehra.

'No, Rupaji, you are quite right, it won't do.'

'But why, Ammaji?' asked Veena. 'Do you think Maya is inauspicious?'

'It isn't that, Veena. It's just that – as Savita's mother is thinking – you must not name a child after a living relative.'

Savita's aunt in Lucknow was called Maya.

No amount of arguing by the younger generation could budge either of the grandmothers.

'But this is gross superstition,' said Maan.

'Superstition or not, it is our way. You know, Veena, when you were young, Minister Sahib's mother did not even allow me to call you by your name. One should never call the eldest child by her real name, she said, and I had to obey.'

'So what did you call me?' said Veena.

'Bitiya, or Munni, or – I can't remember all the names I called you to get around it. But it was very hard to keep it up. Anyway, I think that is all blind belief. And when my mother-in-law passed away, I dropped it.'

'Well, if you call that blind belief, what do you think this is?' said Veena.

'This has reason to it. How can you scold the child

without invoking your aunt? That is very bad. Even if you call her by some other name, it will still be Maya you are scolding in your heart.'

It was no use arguing. The parents were overruled, the name Maya had to be scratched, and the search for a new name began.

Pran, when Maan told him of the veto, took it philosophically.

'Well, I was never a Maya-vadi,' he said; 'I never believed that the whole universe was illusion. Certainly, my cough is real. Like Doctor Johnson, I could refute it thus. So what do the two grandmothers want her to be named?'

'I'm not sure,' said Maan. 'They only agreed on what was not acceptable.'

'This reminds me of my committee work,' said Pran. 'Well, Maan, you'd better rack your brains as well. And why not consult the magical masseur? He's never short of ideas.'

Maan promised to do so.

Sure enough, a few days later, when Savita was fit enough to go home with the baby, she received a card from Mr Maggu Gopal. The picture on the card was one of Lord Shiva complete with his family. In the card Maggu Gopal stated that he had known that Savita would have a daughter despite everyone's opinion to the contrary. He assured her that only the following three names were sufficiently auspicious, given what he had seen of her husband's hand: Parvati, Uma, and Lalita. And he asked whether Pran had replaced sugar with honey 'for all the daily necessaries'. He hoped for Pran's speedy recovery, and reassured him once more that his married life would be a comedy.

Other cards came in as well, and letters of congratulation, and telegrams, many of them with stock phrase number 6: 'Best congratulations on new arrival'.

A couple of weeks after the baby's birth, it was decided by consensus to name her Uma. Mrs Rupa Mehra sat down with scissors and paste to make a grand congratulatory card to celebrate the baby's arrival. It had taken her a little while to accept the fact that she did not yet have a grandson; and now that she was happy with her granddaughter, she decided to give tangible expression to her pleasure.

Roses, a small, rather malignant looking cherub, and a baby in a crib were pasted together, and a puppy and three golden stars completed the picture. Under the three stars the three letters of the baby's name were inscribed in red ink and green pencil.

The message inside was a rather prosaically formatted poem in Mrs Rupa Mehra's small and careful hand. She had read it about a year ago in an edifying volume, *The Fragrant Minute for Every Day* by a certain Wilhelmina Stitch – an appropriate name in view of Savita's present condition – and she had copied it out at that time into her small notebook. It was the poem for the 'Twelfth Day'. She was certain that it would draw from Savita's and Pran's eyes the same tears of gratitude and joy that it had drawn from her own. It read as follows:

THE LADY BABY

'A Lady Baby came to-day –' What words are quite so nice to say? They make one smile, they make one pray for Lady Baby's happiness. 'To-day a Lady Baby came.' We have not heard her winsome name, we can address her all the same, as Lady Baby-Come-to-Bless.

When Lady Baby came to earth, her home was filled with joy and mirth. There's not a jewel of half the worth of Lady Baby-to-Caress. We're glad that Lady Baby's here, for at this sunless time of year, there's nought that brings such warmth and cheer as Lady Baby's daintiness.

Hush! Lady Baby's fast asleep, the friendly fire-flames dance and leap and angels' wings above her sweep as on her eyes a kiss they press. 'A Lady Baby!' Lovely phrase, it means she'll have such gentle ways, and grow to goodness all her days – may God this Lady Baby bless!

SIR DAVID GOWER, the Managing Director of the Cromarty Group, looked through his gold-edged, half-moon spectacles at the short but confident young man standing in front of him. He had shown no sign of intimidation, which, in Sir David's experience was unusual, given the vastness and plushness of his office, the great distance from the door to the desk which he had had to walk under scrutiny, and his own intimidating bulk and glower.

'Do sit down,' he said eventually.

Haresh sat down in the middle chair of the three facing Sir David across his desk.

'I've read Peary Loll Buller's note, and he has had the kindness to call me up as well. I didn't expect you quite so soon, but, well, here you are. You say you want a job. What are your qualifications? And where have you been working?'

'Just across the road, Sir David.'

'You mean at CLFC?'

'Yes. And before that I was at Middlehampton – that's where I studied footwear technology.'

'And why do you want to work with us?'

'I see James Hawley as an excellently run organization, in which a man like myself has a future.'

'In other words, you want to join us to better your own prospects?'

'Put like that, yes.'

'Well, that's no bad thing,' said Sir David in a sort of growl.

He looked at Haresh for a while. Haresh wondered what he was thinking. His glance did not appear to take in his clothing – slightly sweaty for having bicycled over – or his hair, just smoothed and combed back. Nor did it appear to look into his soul. It appeared to concentrate on his forehead.

'And what do you have to offer us?' said the Managing Director after a while.

'Sir, my results in England speak for themselves. And I have, in a short space of time, helped turn around CLFC –in terms both of orders and a sense of direction.'

Sir David raised his eyebrows. 'That is quite a claim,' he said. 'I thought Mukherji was the General Manager. Well, I think you should see John Clayton, our own General Manager.' He picked up the telephone.

'John, ah, you're still here. Good. I'm sending a young man, a Mr' – he glanced down at a piece of paper – 'a Mr Khanna, to you.... Yes, the one old Peary Loll Buller phoned me about a few minutes ago when you were here.... Middlehampton.... Well, yes, if you think so.... No, I leave it to you.' He put down the phone, and wished Haresh good luck.

'Thank you very much, Sir David.'

'Well, whether we take you on or not depends on what Clayton thinks of you,' said Sir David Gower, and dismissed Haresh from his thoughts.

A letter arrived on Monday morning from James Hawley. It was signed by the General Manager John Clayton, and specified the terms they wished to offer Haresh, which were generous: Rs 325 as salary, and Rs 450 as 'dearness allowance' – an adjustment for inflation over the last few years. That the tail was bigger than the dog struck Haresh as odd but pleasant.

The injustice with which he had been treated by CLFC receded, the crawliness of Rao, the creepiness of Sen Gupta, the decent ineffectuality of Mukherji, the high-handedness of the distant boss Ghosh – and he began to think of his new future, which struck him as glowing. Perhaps some day he would sit on the other side of that huge mahogany desk. And with a job as good as this one, one that was not a cul-de-sac like his job at CLFC, he could embark on married life without any qualms.

Two letters in hand, he went to see Mukherji.

'Mr Mukherji,' he said, once they were both seated, 'I feel I should take you into confidence. I have applied for a job with James Hawley, and they have made me an offer. After last week's events you can imagine how I feel about continuing here. I would like your advice on what I should do.'

'Mr Khanna,' said Mr Mukherji quite unhappily, 'I am sorry to hear this. I assume that you must have applied some time ago.'

'I applied on Friday afternoon, and got the job within the hour.'

Mr Mukherji looked startled. If Haresh said so, however, it must be the truth.

'Here is the letter of appointment.'

The General Manager scanned it, and said, 'I see. Well, you have asked me for my advice. I can only say that I am sorry about the way that that order was taken out of your hands last week. It was not my doing. But I cannot accept your resignation myself – certainly not immediately. The matter will have to go to Bombay.'

'I am sure Mr Ghosh will agree.'

'I am sure he will,' agreed Mr Mukherji, who was his brother-in-law. 'But, well, it has to have his sanction before I can accept it.'

'At any rate,' said Haresh. 'I am tendering my resignation to you now.'

But when Mr Mukherji phoned him to tell him that Haresh was leaving, Mr Ghosh was livid. Haresh was important for the success of his Kanpur factory, and he was not willing to let him go. He was due to go to Delhi to procure a government order for army footwear, and he told Mr Mukherji to hold on to Haresh Khanna until he himself came to Kanpur immediately afterwards.

Upon his arrival he summoned Haresh and tore into him in the presence of Mukherji. His eyes were bulging, and he seemed almost berserk with anger, although he was far from incoherent.

'I gave you your very first job, Mr Khanna, when you arrived in India. And, if you recall, you gave me your assurance at the time that you would stay with us for two years, as long as we wanted you. Well, we do. Looking for another job is an underhand action on your part, and I refuse to let you go.'

Haresh coloured at Ghosh's words and manner. A word like 'underhand' was like a red rag to him. But Ghosh was an older man, and one whose business sense at least he admired. Besides, it was true that he had given him his first job. 'I do recall that conversation, Sir,' he said. 'But you might remember that you gave me certain assurances as well. You said, for one thing, that I should accept three hundred and fifty rupees at the time, because you would increase it once I had proved my worth to the organization. Well, I have certainly proved my worth to you, but you have not kept your side of the understanding.'

'If it is a question of money, there is no problem,' said Ghosh abruptly. 'We can accommodate you – we can match their offer.'

This was news to Haresh – and to Mukherji as well, who looked startled – but the word 'underhand' so rankled against him that he continued: 'I am afraid it is not merely money, Sir, it is the whole style of things.' He paused, then went on: 'James Hawley is a professional organization. I can make my way up that ladder in a way that I cannot in a family organization. I am hoping to get married, and I am sure you will see that I have to look to the future.'

'You are not leaving us,' said Ghosh. 'That is all I have to say.'

'We shall see about that,' said Haresh, very angry himself by Ghosh's high-handedness. 'I have a written offer, and you have my written resignation. I fail to see what you can do about it.' And he stood up, nodded wordlessly to his two superiors, and left.

The moment Haresh left the office, Ghosh phoned John Clayton, whom he had met a number of times in Delhi in a couple of ministries; both had been concerned with procuring government orders for their companies.

Ghosh told Clayton in no uncertain terms that he considered his action in 'pinching' his man to be unethical. He refused to countenance it, and he would not release Haresh. If necessary he would take the matter to court. This was an extremely unfair trade practice, and no way for a reputable British company to behave.

Mr Ghosh was related to various important civil servants and a politician or two – it was partly as a result of this that he had been able to get government orders for CLFC's shoes, which were not of the best quality. He was clearly a man who wielded a great deal of influence. At the moment he was also a very angry man, and he could create problems for James Hawley, indeed for the Cromarty Group as a whole, both in Kanpur and elsewhere.

A couple of days later Haresh got another letter from James Hawley. The crucial sentence read: 'You will have to get clearance from your present employers before we can confirm our offer.' There had been no question in the previous letter of the necessity of any confirmation, and it was clear that James Hawley had buckled under pressure. No doubt Ghosh now believed that Haresh would have no choice but to come to him cap in hand and beg for his old job again. But for Haresh one thing was certain: he would not work one day longer in CLFC. He would rather starve than cringe.

The next day he went to the factory to collect his things and unscrew his brass name-plate from his door. Mukherji happened to pass by as he was doing this, and murmured an offer of help for the future. Haresh shook his head. He spoke to Lee and apologized for the fact that he was leaving so soon after hiring him. He then spoke to the workmen in his department. They were upset and angry at the treatment meted out by Ghosh to a man they had grown to like and respect and whom they had even begun to see – in a curious way – as their champion; certainly they had got more work and more money since he had joined the company, even if he worked them, like himself, very hard. They even offered, astonishingly, to go on strike for him. Haresh could hardly believe this, and was touched almost to the point of tears, but told them that they should do nothing of the sort. 'I would have been leaving in any case,' he said, 'and whether the management behaves nicely or nastily to me makes no difference. I am only sorry that I have to leave you to the incompetence of someone like

Rao.' Rao was standing nearby when he said this, but Haresh was past caring.

To take his mind off things, he went to Lucknow for a day to visit Simran's sister. And three days later, seeing nothing further in Kanpur to keep him, and having very little money, he left for Delhi to stay with his family and to see what he might find there. He could not decide whether to write to Lata to tell her the news. He was deeply disheartened; he could see all his prospects of happiness receding into nothingness now that he was unemployed.

But this mood ceased to be continuous after a few days. Kalpana Gaur sympathized with him, his old St Stephen's friends took him up into their jovial company almost as soon as he got to Delhi. And, being basically an optimist – or at any rate having an abundance, perhaps a super-abundance, of self-confidence – he refused to believe, even in these hard times, that nothing at all would turn up.

13.20

HIS own foster-father was understanding, and told him not to be disheartened. But Umesh Uncle, a close friend of the family, who loved to dispense wisdom, told him he had made a big mistake to let pride get in the way of good sense.

'You think you can walk down the street and job offers will drop down on you like ripe mangoes,' he remarked.

Haresh did not say anything. Umesh Uncle always got his goat.

Besides, he thought that his uncle, although he had a Rai Bahadur in front of his name, and an O.B.E. behind it, was an idiot.

Rai Bahadur Umesh Chand Khatri, O.B.E., one of the six brothers of a Punjabi family, was a good-looking man: fair, with delicate features. He was married to the adopted daughter of a very rich and cultured man, who, having no sons, had decided to get a son-in-law to live in the house. Umesh Chand Khatri's only qualifications were his good looks. He managed his father-in-law's estate after a fashion, read perhaps one book a year out of his vast library, and gave him three grandchildren, including two boys.

He had never worked in his life, but felt compelled to tender advice to anyone within earshot. However, when the Second World War broke out, circumstances contrived to give him a fortune. He had access to the Adarsh Condiment Company, and he got government contracts for the manufacture of condiment powder, including curry powder, for the Indian troops. On the basis of this he minted money. He was created a Rai Bahadur 'in recognition of war efforts', became Chairman of the Adarsh Condiment Company, and continued to dispense advice even more insufferably to everyone except Haresh's foster-father, who (being his not very tolerant friend) would tell him periodically to shut up.

Umesh Chand Khatri's grouse against Haresh, whom he loved to needle, was the fact that Haresh was always smartly turned out. Umesh Chand believed that he and his own two sons should be the smartest and most elegant of all his acquaintances. Once, just before he left for England, Haresh had indulged himself by buying a silk handkerchief for thirteen rupees from the Army and Navy Stores in Connaught Place. Uncle Umesh had rebuked him publicly for extravagance.

Now that Haresh was down on his luck, Uncle Umesh said to him:

'So – you think you've done a clever thing – coming back to Delhi to loaf around?'

'I had no choice,' replied Haresh. 'There was no point to my remaining in Kanpur.'

Umesh Uncle laughed shortly. 'You young men are too cocksure, too happy to drop perfectly good jobs. We'll see what happens to all your bravado in two or three months.'

Haresh knew that his money would not last even as long as that. He got annoyed. 'I'll have a job – as good or better than the one I've given up – within a month,' he said – indeed, almost snapped.

'You're a fool,' said Umesh Uncle with genial contempt. 'Jobs are not easy to get.'

His tone and certainty got under Haresh's skin. That afternoon he wrote to several companies and filled in a number of applications, including one for a government job in Indore. He had already applied in vain a number of times to the great Praha Shoe Company. Now he applied once again. Praha, originally a Czech company, and still largely run by Czechs, was one of the biggest shoe manufacturers in the country, and prided itself on the quality of its products. If Haresh could get a decent job at the Praha Shoe factory either in Brahmpur or in Calcutta, he would have achieved two things at once: the re-attainment of his self-respect, and proximity to Lata. Umesh Uncle's taunts rang in his ears, as did Ghosh's accusations of underhandedness.

It was a meeting with Mr Mukherji that gave Haresh a contact in the Praha world. Someone told Haresh that his old boss was in town. Haresh went to see him. He had no grudge against Mukherji, who he felt was a decent man, if not a very courageous one. Despite his brother-in-law's obdurate attitude to Haresh, Mukherji felt bad about what had happened. He had previously mentioned to Haresh that Mr Khandelwal – the Chairman of the Praha Shoe Company, and, very remarkably, not a Czech but an Indian – was in town on business. Haresh, who knew no one in the Praha organization, felt that this was a heavensent opportunity to try his luck with them – or at least to get an answer to his many requests and letters. He told Mukherji that he would be grateful if he would introduce him to Mr Khandelwal.

Mukherji took Haresh along late one evening to the Imperial Hotel, where Mr Khandelwal always stayed when in Delhi. In fact, Mr Khandelwal always stayed in the Moghul Suite, the fanciest suite of all. He was a relaxed sort of man, of medium height, running both to fat and to the beginning of grey hair. He was dressed in kurta and dhoti. Apparently, he was even more fond of paan than Haresh; he chewed three at a time.

Haresh could not at first believe that this man sitting in a dhoti on the sofa was the legendary Mr Khandelwal. But when he saw how everyone scurried around him, some of them actually trembling while handing him papers which he quickly scanned and commented on, usually in a couple of words, Haresh got a sense both of his acuity and of his undoubted authority. One short, eager Czech, moving around in a most deferential manner, took down notes whenever Mr Khandelwal wanted something done or checked or reported on.

When Mr Khandelwal noticed Mr Mukherji he smiled and welcomed him in Bengali. Despite being a Marwari, Mr Khandelwal, having lived in Calcutta all his life, was fluent in Bengali; in fact he conducted meetings with trade union leaders from the Prahapore factory near Calcutta entirely in Bengali.

'What can I do for you, Mukherji Shaib?' he said, and took a gulp of whisky.

'This young man, who has been working for us, is now looking for a job. He wanted to see if Praha could give him one. He has excellent academic qualifications in foot-wear technology, and I can vouch for him in all other respects.'

Mr Khandelwal smiled benevolently and, looking now not at Mr Mukherji but at Haresh, exclaimed: 'Why are you being so generous as to give me such a good man?'

Mr Mukherji looked a little shamefaced. He said, quietly: 'He has been hard done by, and I do not have the courage to talk to my brother-in-law about it. I fear, anyway, that it would do no good; his mind is entirely made up.'

'What do you want me to do?' asked Mr Khandelwal of Haresh.

'Sir, I have applied for a job with Praha several times, and have sent several letters, but have not had any proper reply at all. If you were to see that my application is at least considered, I'm sure that my qualifications and work experience will get me a job with the firm.'

'Take his application,' said Mr Khandelwal, and the

dapper Czech took it and jotted something down on his pad.

'So –' said Mr Khandelwal, 'you will hear from Praha in less than a week.'

But Haresh, though he did indeed hear within a few days from Praha, was once again offered by the Personnel Office a job at Rs 28 a week: a pittance which succeeded in doing nothing but making him angry.

However, it reassured Umesh Uncle. 'I told you that you would not get a job if you left this one. But you never took my advice; you considered yourself so smart. Look at you now, sponging off others, rather than working, like a man should.'

Haresh controlled himself before replying: 'Thank you for your advice yet again, Umesh Uncle. It is as valuable as it has always been.'

Umesh Uncle, faced by Haresh's sudden meekness, felt that his spirit had been broken, and that he would be an easier recipient for his counsel from then on. 'It's good that you've seen sense at last,' he told him. 'A man should never have too high an opinion of himself.'

Haresh nodded, his thoughts anything but meek.

13.21

WHEN, some weeks previously, Lata had received Haresh's first letter – three pages written in his small, forward-slanting hand on his blue writing pad – she had replied to it in a friendly way. Half of Haresh's letter had been concerned with trying to get a contact at the Praha Shoe Company to present his application to. Mrs Rupa Mehra had mentioned when they had all met in Kanpur that she knew someone who knew someone who might be able to help. In fact, it had turned out to be more difficult than she had imagined, and nothing had come of it. Haresh could not have known at the time that a strange series of events and the sympathy of Mr Mukherji would have got him to meet Mr Khandelwal, the Chairman of Praha, himself.

The other half of the letter had been personal. Lata had read it over a number of times. Unlike Kabir's letter, it had made her smile:

This business being over [Haresh had written], let me hope in the usual way that you had a comfortable journey home and that you were missed by all who met you after such a long absence from Brahmpur.

I must thank you for your visit to Cawnpore and the nice time we spent together. There was none of that bashfulness or undue modesty and I am convinced that we can be very friendly if nothing else. I quite appreciate your frankness and the way of putting things. I must admit that I have met few English girls who could speak English quite as well as you do. These qualities coupled with your way of dressing and personality make you a person far above the average. I think Kalpana was right in her praise of you. These may all seem flattering remarks but I write as I feel.

I have just today sent your photograph to my foster-father along with my impressions of you formed during our brief hours together. I shall let you know what he has to say....

Lata tried to work out what exactly it was about this letter that she liked. Haresh's English was slightly odd. 'In the usual way' and 'the way of putting things', to take just two out of about ten examples in those three short paragraphs, jarred against her sense of the language. And yet the whole was not unpleasing. It was pleasant to be praised by someone who did not seem practised at praising – and who, for all his own abundant self-confidence, clearly admired her.

The more she read the letter, the more she liked it. But she waited a while before replying:

Dear Haresh,
    I was very glad to get your letter, as you had indicated

at the station that you wanted to write to me. I believe that this is a good way of getting to know each other.

We have not had much luck with the Praha Shoe Company, but the reason for that is that we are not at present in Calcutta and, apart from it being the Head Office of the company, Ma's acquaintance lives there. But Ma has written to him, and let's see what happens. She has also mentioned the matter to Arun, my brother, who lives in Calcutta, and he may be able to help. Let's keep our fingers crossed.

It would be good if you were in Prahapore, for then when I am in Calcutta over the New Year holidays, we could see much more of each other in the ordinary course of things. It was good to meet you in Kanpur. I am very glad I broke journey there. I must thank you again for the trouble you took at Lucknow Station to see us safely into a compartment and to install our luggage there. We had a very comfortable journey back, and Pran − my brother-in-law − was there to greet us at the other end.

I am glad to know that you have written to your foster-father. I shall be keen to know what he thinks and says.

I must admit that it was interesting going around the tannery. I liked your Chinese designer. The way he spoke Hindi was delightful.

I like to see men with ambition like you − you should make good. It is also refreshing to meet a man who doesn't smoke − I can assure you I admire it − because I think it requires a lot of character. I liked you because you were so frank and clear in all your statements − so different from the young men one generally meets in Calcutta, but not only in Calcutta − so polished, so charming, yet so insincere. Your sincerity is refreshing.

You did mention when we met that you had been in Brahmpur very briefly earlier this year, but we got onto other subjects and did not follow this one up. So Ma (and not only Ma, I should admit) was astonished to find that you already know at least two members of our family. Pran mentioned he had met you at a party. In case you don't remember him, he is a thin, tall lecturer in the English Department. It is his address that you have just written to. And then there is Kedarnath Tandon, who is Pran's jijaji – which makes him my jijaji's jijaji, but that is (in the Brahmpur context, and perhaps in your Delhi context too) a fairly close relation. His son Bhaskar has apparently just had a letter from you as well, even shorter than the one you sent me. You will be sorry to hear that he was slightly injured in the Pul Mela stampede, but now appears to be almost fully recovered. Veena mentioned how happy he was to get the postcard and the information it contained.

Brahmpur is unpleasantly hot these days and I am a little concerned for my sister Savita, who is expecting a baby very soon. But Ma is here to take care of things, and there could not be a better or more solicitous husband than Pran.

I have not quite settled back into my studies, but have decided, a little against my wishes but on the advice of a friend, to take a part in *Twelfth Night*, which is our Annual Day play this year. I have the part of Olivia, and am busy learning my lines, which takes up a lot of my time. My friend came to the audition to lend me moral support, but ended up with the part of Maria, which in a way serves her right. Ma, being of the old school, has very mixed feelings about my acting. What do you think?

I look forward to your next letter – do write about yourself. I shall be interested in whatever you have to say.

I'd better say goodbye, for already this letter has grown considerably and I presume you must be yawning by now.

Ma sends you her best wishes, and I wish you all the best,

Lata

There was no mention in Lata's letter of Haresh's opinionatedness, his pronunciation of Kanpur as 'Cawnpore', the stench of the tannery, paan, co-respondent shoes, or the photograph of Simran on his desk. It was not that Lata had forgotten them, but rather that the memory of some of them had grown dimmer, some of them no longer appeared to her in quite such a negative light, and one of them was not something she felt she would ever want to mention – unless it became necessary to do so.

But Haresh brought it up himself in his next letter. He mentioned that one of the things that he had most liked about Lata was her own directness, and that this emboldened him to speak freely, especially since she had asked him to tell her about himself. He talked at some length about how important Simran had been in his life, how he had despaired of finding anyone who could mean anything to him after he had realized that there was no hope for him there, and how she – Lata – had appeared at what was a crucial time for him. He now suggested that she write a note to Simran so that the two of them could get better acquainted. He had already written to Simran about his meeting with her, but because the only photograph that he had of her had been with his foster-father at the time, he was unable to enclose it in his letter to Simran. He wrote:

... I hope you will forgive me for talking about Simran so much but she is a wonderful girl and you two are likely to be good friends. If you should like to write to her, here is her address. You cannot write directly to her as her people might intercept the letter, so address the letter to Miss Pritam Kaura, at the address at the bottom of this letter. I should like you to know me well, specially my past life before you make up your mind, and Simran is part and parcel of it.

Sometimes it seems to me that meeting you is too good to be true. I was at a dead end, I knew not what to do and where to look for company. Poor Simran, she is so placed that she cannot express her feelings, her people are the conservative type – nothing like your mother, even if she has mixed feelings about plays. You came into my life like a brightening influence, like someone for whom I have the desire to become better.

You have used very many compliments with regard to my sincerity – given the circumstances I have lived in, one could not afford to be otherwise. Along with sincerity and frankness there is the worse side of it – just because one cannot hurt someone else one postpones a decision to remove someone's illusions – in the long run one has to suffer for it. When we know each other better and can forgive and forget I shall explain this statement fully. I will give you a hint – perhaps I had better not. Because there are some parts of my life that are far from perfect, and for which you might find it hard to forgive me. Perhaps I have said too much already.

Anyway, I have to thank Kalpana for our chance meeting. But for her we would never have known each other.

Please send me the impression of your foot, because I wish to design something for you – maybe the Chinese man, Mr Lee, can help! Would you like a low sandal for the summer or do you wear the usual High Heels?

Also, I hardly ever see the photograph you gave me because it does the postal rounds. Please do send me another photograph of yourself, recently taken. I will not send that one around. Today I tried to get a frame for your photograph but failed to get it. I am therefore waiting for your next photograph before I expend the money for a good frame. Do you mind if I keep your photograph on my table? It may tend to keep me more ambitious. As I look at your photograph, just back from my father, I find that smile on the brink very attractive. You certainly have a poise which makes you very attractive to me, but then you must, I am sure, be knowing it yourself – others will have told you all that before me.

My father appears to be in favour of a match.

Remember me to your mother and to Pran, Kedarnath

and his wife, and Bhaskar. I find it very hard to think of that boy being hurt in that stampede. I trust he is all right by now.

Affectionately,
Haresh

Lata was unsettled by this letter. Everything from the photograph to the foot impression worried her, and the hints about his past life troubled her too. She could not understand how he could expect her to write to Simran. But because she liked him, she replied as kindly as she could. With Pran's hospitalization, Savita's imminent baby, and the daily rehearsals with Kabir all weighing on her heart, she could manage no more than a couple of pages, and when she re-read the letter it appeared to her to be nothing but a linked chain of refusals. She did not encourage him to spill out whatever he was hinting at; indeed she did not mention it at all. She did say that she could not write to Simran until she felt more confident about her feelings (though she was pleased that he had trusted her enough to confide in her about so many things). She was shy about her feet, which she did not think looked very attractive. And as for the photograph:

To tell you the truth, it is real agony for me, being photographed in a studio or by people from a studio. I know it's very silly of me, but I feel dreadful. I think the last photograph that Ma got taken of me – before the one that I gave you – was taken about six years ago, and it wasn't at all good. The one you have was taken in Calcutta this year under compulsion. For the last three years I have been promising to send one in for my old school magazine; really I felt quite ashamed of myself when, just before coming to Kanpur, I met one of my old nuns and she confronted me again about it. At least now I have been able to send her one. But I can't go through that ordeal again. As for the 'smile on the brink' among other things – altogether, I think you flatter me. This is paradoxical, because I think of you as a very

sincere and frank sort of person, and surely sincerity and
flattery don't go together! Anyway, anything that's ever
told me, I have learned to take with a large pinch of salt.

There was a long pause between this letter and Haresh's
next one, and Lata felt that her triple refusal must have hurt
him too much. She discussed with Malati the question of
which of the three refusals had upset Haresh the most, and
their discussion of this helped her make light of the matter.

13.22

ONE day, when Kabir had acted particularly well, Lata
told Malati: 'I'm going to tell him afterwards how good I
thought his acting was. It's the only way to break the ice.'

Malati said: 'Lata, don't be foolish, it won't be breaking
the ice, it'll be releasing the steam. Just leave well enough
alone.'

But after the rehearsal was over, when the three of them,
among others, were milling around outside the auditorium,
Kabir came up to Lata and said: 'Could you give this to
Bhaskar? My father thought he might find it interesting.' It
was a kite with an unusual shape: a sort of lozenge with
streamers behind it.

'Yes, of course,' said Lata, a little uneasily. 'But you
know he's no longer at Prem Nivas. He's gone back to his
parents' house in Misri Mandi.'

'I hope it's not too much trouble –'

'No, it isn't, Kabir – it isn't at all – we can't thank you
enough for what you've done for him.'

Both of them were silent. Malati hung around for a
while, thinking that Lata might be grateful if she interposed
herself into any intense conversation that Kabir might
start. But after a glance or two at Lata, she judged that
Lata would be happier if she could talk to him by herself.
So she took her leave of both of them – though Kabir had
not, in fact, greeted her.

'Why have you been avoiding me?' said Kabir to Lata in
a low voice the moment Malati had gone.

Lata shook her head, unable to look at his face. But there was no avoiding a conversation that would not be in the least casual.

'What do you expect?' she said.

'Are you still angry with me – about that?'

'No – I'm getting used to it. Today you acted very well.'

'I don't mean the play,' said Kabir. 'I meant our last real meeting.'

'Oh, that –'

'Yes, that.' He was determined to have it out, it seemed.

'I don't know – so much has happened since then.'

'Nothing has happened except a vacation.'

'I meant, I've thought so much about things –'

'Do you think I haven't?' he said.

'Kabir, please – what I meant was that I've thought about us as well.'

'And no doubt you still think I was unreasonable.' Kabir sounded slightly amused.

Lata looked at his face, then turned away. She didn't say anything.

'Let's take a walk,' said Kabir. 'At least it'll give us something to do in our silences.'

'All right,' said Lata, shaking her head.

They walked along the path that led from the auditorium to the centre of the campus – towards the jacaranda grove, and beyond that, to the cricket nets.

'Do I deserve an answer?' asked Kabir.

'It was I who was unreasonable,' said Lata after a while.

This took the wind out of Kabir's sails. He looked at her in astonishment as she continued:

'You were quite right. I was being unfair and unreasonable and everything else you said. It's not possible – it never was – but not because of time and careers and studies and other practical things.'

'Why then?' said Kabir.

'Because of my family,' said Lata. 'However much they irritate me and constrain me, I can't give them up. I know that now. So much has happened. I can't give up my mother –'

Lata halted, thinking of what effect this last remark might have on Kabir, but decided that she had to explain herself now or never.

'I just see how much she cares about everything and how she would be affected by this,' she said.

'By this!' said Kabir. 'You mean, by you and me.'

'Kabir, do you know of any mixed marriages that have worked out?' said Lata. But even as she said it she thought that perhaps she had gone too far. Kabir had never explicitly mentioned marriage – he wanted to be with her, to be close to her – but marriage? Perhaps he had implied it when he had asked her to wait for a year or two – when he had mentioned his plans for future study, for the Foreign Service, for Cambridge. But now he didn't retreat from the word.

'Do you know of any that haven't?' he said.

'I don't know of any at all in our family,' said Lata.

'Unmixed marriages aren't always ideal either.'

'I know, Kabir; I've heard –' said Lata, miserably, and with such sympathy that Kabir understood that she was referring to his mother.

He stopped, and said:

'Does that also have something to do with it?'

'I can't say –' said Lata. 'I don't know – I'm sure my mother would be affected by that as well.'

'So what you are saying is that my heredity and my religion are insuperable factors – and it doesn't matter if you care for me or not.'

'Don't put it like that, Kabir,' cried Lata. 'That's not how I feel.'

'But it's the basis on which you're acting.'

Lata was unable to reply.

'Don't you care for me?' asked Kabir.

'I do, I do –'

'Then why didn't you write? Why don't you talk to me –'

'Just because of that –' she said, completely overcome.

'Will you always love me? Because I know I will –'

'Oh, please stop, Kabir – I can't take this –' she cried. What she might just as well have said was that she was trying to convince herself as much as him that their feelings were nothing but futile.

He would not allow her to do this, however.

'But why should we stop meeting?' he persisted.

'Meeting? Kabir, you don't see the point. Where would it lead to?'

'Does it have to lead to something?' he said. 'Can't we just spend time together?' After a pause: 'Do you "mistrust my intentions"?'

Lata remembered their kisses in a daze of unhappiness. So intense was the memory that she half mistrusted her own intentions. 'No,' she said, more quietly, 'but wouldn't it all just be miserable?'

She realized that his questions were leading to further questions on her own part and in her own mind, and that every one of these caused a further knot in the huge tangle. Her heart ached for him, but everything told her that it had to come to nothing. She had wanted to tell him that she was writing to someone else, but she could not bring herself to do so now because of the pain she knew it would cause him.

They were passing by the steps outside the examination hall. Kabir looked up at them and frowned. The light was low, and the trees and benches below were casting long shadows on the grass.

'So what do we do?' he said, his mouth set in an attempt at decisiveness.

'I don't know,' said Lata. 'We have to spend some time together now, in a way, at least on stage. At least for another month. We've trapped ourselves into it.'

'Can't you wait for another year?' he said with sudden desperation.

'What will change?' she said despondently, and walked off the path, away from him, towards a bench. She was almost too tired to think — emotionally exhausted, exhausted from watching over the baby, exhausted from the effort of acting — and she sat down on the bench, her head resting on her arms. She was too tired even for tears.

It was the same bench under the gul-mohur tree on

which she had sat after the exam. He didn't know what to make of this. Should he console her again? Was she even conscious of where she was sitting? She looked so forlorn that he wanted more than anything to put his arms around her. He could sense how close she was to tears.

Both had said what was inevitable, yet Kabir could not feel that they were adversaries. He felt that he had to try and understand her. The pressure of the family, the extended family that enforced a slow and strong acceptance on its members, was something that with his own father and mother he had never had to face. Lata had moved away from him in these last months, and was perhaps already out of reach. If he went up to her now and helped her overcome her unhappiness, could he retrieve some of what was lost? Or would he only burden her with a further and more painful vulnerability?

What was she thinking? He stood there in the late light, looking at her beyond his own long shadow. Her head had not moved from her hands. The strange kite was resting on the bench beside her. She looked weary and unreachable. After a minute or two he walked away sadly.

13.23

LATA sat still for about fifteen minutes, then got up, taking the kite with her. It was almost dark. She had found it hard to think. But now, through her own pain, she began to feel a sympathy for the difficulties of others. She thought of Pran and his anxieties. She reminded herself that it had been a long time since she had written to Varun.

She also thought, strangely enough, of her last letter to Haresh, and how curt she had been on the matter of Simran, which obviously had meant a great deal to him. Poor Haresh – he too had been pursuing an impossible relationship, and here too the difficulty was a similar one.

As for herself, there was another rehearsal tomorrow. Would she face that with more or less trepidation than before? How would it be for Kabir? At least they had talked; she would not be tensely anticipating the terrible moment. Anyway, perhaps it had been less terrible to suffer it than to await it. But how disheartening it had been. Or was it so disheartening after all in the scheme of things?

That evening was a quiet one: her mother, Pran, Savita, the baby, and herself. One of the topics of discussion was Haresh and why he hadn't written yet.

In general, Mrs Rupa Mehra wanted to read every letter that came from Haresh, but Lata only passed on his news and greetings, keeping his agreeable comments to herself, and finding herself unable to share with her mother the more troubling ones.

Haresh had in fact been a little disappointed by Lata's letter, but what had kept him from replying almost immediately was not this disappointment but his sudden status as a workless man. He was very worried about the effect that this news would have on Lata – and even more so on her mother, who, for all the goodwill she bore him, was – he judged – exacting and pragmatic in her criteria for a suitable boy for her daughter.

But when a week had passed, and James Hawley, despite his appeals, had not rectified their injustice, and Delhi too had borne no immediate fruit except Mr Mukherji's promise of a meeting with Mr Khandelwal, he felt he could keep up his silence no longer, and wrote to Lata.

As it happened, Mrs Rupa Mehra had received a letter from Kalpana Gaur the day before Haresh's letter finally arrived, and had come to know that he was out of a job. With Pran, Savita and the baby all back home, there was a great deal to be done, but this latest and somewhat shocking news occupied Mrs Rupa Mehra's mind more than anything else. She talked about it to everyone including Meenakshi and Kakoli, who had dropped by to baby-gaze. She could not understand how Haresh could have dropped his job 'just like that'; her husband had always believed in having two birds in the hand before leaving one in the bush. Mrs Rupa Mehra began to worry about Haresh in more ways than one; and she began to express her reservations to Lata.

'Oh, he's bound to write soon,' said Lata, rather too off-handedly for Mrs Rupa Mehra's taste.

She was proved to be correct the next day, sooner than she herself had expected.

When Mrs Rupa Mehra saw an envelope in Haresh's by now familiar handwriting in the mail, she insisted that Lata open it immediately and read out its contents to her. Lata refused. Kakoli and Meenakshi, delighted to be in on the scene, snatched the letter from the table and began to tease Lata. Lata snatched it back from Kakoli, rushed into her room, and locked the door. She did not emerge for more than an hour. She read the letter, and replied to it without consulting anyone. Mrs Rupa Mehra was extremely annoyed by her daughter's insubordination, and also at Meenakshi and Kakoli.

'Think of Pran,' she said. 'This excitement is not good for his heart.'

Kakoli sang out, so that the sound could be heard on the other side of the locked door:

> 'Sweetest Lata, have a heart!
> Come and kiss me. Don't be tart.'

When she heard no response to this crass creation, she continued:

> 'Let me kiss your hands, my queen:
> Softest pigskin I have seen.'

Mrs Rupa Mehra was about to shout at Kakoli, but the baby began yowling and distracted everyone on that side of the door. Lata continued to read in noisy peace.

Haresh's letter was as straightforward as usual. After mentioning the bad news, he went on to write:

It can be no easy time for you with Pran's illness and by now maybe his baby too, so I feel sorry to burden you with the news I have given above. But I had to write to you today under the very great stress of circumstances. So far I have heard nothing by way of reconsideration from Mr Clayton of James Hawley, and I am now not quite so hopeful that anything will happen in that direction. It was a fine job fetching Rs. 750/- per month all told, but I have not yet lost hopes entirely. I feel that they will realize the injustice of the whole thing. But perhaps with my resignation from CLFC I have indeed fallen between two stools. Mr Mukherji, the General Manager, is a fine man but Mr Ghosh, it seems, is dead set against me.

Yesterday I was with Kalpana for over two hours when you were the only topic of discussion. I do not know how much of my feelings I could hide, for the thought of you was exciting.

Excuse this scribbling pad. I have none other at my disposal at the moment. Kalpana says she has written to your mother about my news, and that I must write to you today – and I have been feeling the same myself.

I have an interview later in the month in Indore (with the State Public Service Commission) for a Small Scale Industry job. And it may be that the Praha matter will work out. At least if I can meet Mr Khandelwal through the good offices of Mr Mukherji, I am sure I will get a job interview in Calcutta. There are however a few things that you shall have to decide:

1. Whether you would like me to go to Calcutta via Brahmpur, given so many different factors including your brother-in-law's illness.

2. Whether in my unemployed position you think I am the same as before – i.e. whether you think you could be quite happy in considering me as someone you could care for.

I hope that your mother does not take this too seriously – there are other jobs in the offing I am sure, and it will not take too long to fix up.

Somehow I feel there is a lot of good in my present position – being unemployed gives one a better insight into human character and gives the right value to the right things. I hope Pran is better. Remember me to the family. I shall write again soon.

Yours,
Haresh

13.24

NOTHING could have brought out Lata's warmth and tenderness more effectively than this letter. She felt very bad for Haresh, particularly at the thought that there might be a great deal of anxiety behind his brave front. If she had problems, so had he, and far more pressing ones. Yet instead of allowing himself to get depressed by his misfortune, he claimed to see advantages in it. Lata felt a little ashamed of herself for not behaving in a more robust manner in the face of emotional adversity.

She wrote back:

My dear Haresh,

Your letter came today and I am replying immediately. Yesterday Ma got a letter from Kalpana. Ever since then I have been wanting to write to you, but I felt I couldn't till I had heard the news directly from you. You must believe that it doesn't make any difference to me. Affection doesn't depend on things like jobs. It is unfortunate that you should have missed such a good chance at James Hawley – it really is a very good firm – I should think almost the best. Anyway, don't worry. Everything happens for the best – and, as you say, there is still hope – nothing like going on trying. I feel sure something will emerge.

Here Lata paused and looked out of the bedroom window before continuing. But it was his problems she had to address, not her own, and she continued to write before thoughts could crowd too closely in on her:

Perhaps, Haresh, you didn't do a very wise thing in not letting your firm know that you were trying elsewhere. Perhaps you should have gone through them. Anyway, let's forget about it – it's all in the past now. The unkindness of people only hurts if we continue to remember it. Now that you are out of a job, perhaps you should try for the best rather than the first that comes your way. Maybe it's worthwhile waiting a little.

You ask if I want you to come to Brahmpur on your way to Calcutta. It would be good to talk to you again. I hope you have not lost your smile. It doesn't sound so from your letter, anyway. You have a very pleasant smile – when you are amused your eyes disappear altogether – and it would be a pity if you lost it.

Here Lata paused again. What on earth am I writing? she asked herself. Is this too much? Then she just shrugged, told herself she wouldn't correct it, and wrote on:

The only problem is that the house is in chaos at the moment, and even if you were to live in a hotel, you would see us at a very confused time. Also, my brother Arun's wife and sister-in-law are here, and though I like them very much, they will not give either of us a moment of peace. And then my afternoons are taken up with rehearsals, which put me in a very confused state. I don't know if I'm myself or one of Shakespeare's creatures. Ma also is in a peculiar mood. All in all, it is not a good time for us to see each other. I hope you do not think that I am trying to put you off.

I am glad that Mr Mukherji has been so kind and understanding. I hope he is successful in helping you.

Pran looks much better for his three weeks in hospital, and the constant presence of the baby – who has been named Uma by the whole family at a sort of board meeting – does him a world of good. He sends his regards to you, as does everyone else here. Ma was worried to get your news from Kalpana, but not exactly in the way you think. She was more worried because she thought I was worried, and she kept telling me not to worry, that everything would be all right. I was only worried because I thought you must be very upset – especially as you hadn't written for a while. So you see it was a sort of vicious circle. I am happy that you haven't lost any of your optimism and are not bitter. I hate people to wear martyred airs – just as I dislike self-pity. It is the cause of too much unhappiness.

Please keep me informed about everything that happens, and write soon. No one else has lost their faith in you, except your Umesh Uncle, who never had it anyway, so you mustn't lose it in yourself.

Affectionately,
Lata

13.25

LATA sent the letter off with Mansoor to be posted at the general post office on his way to the market.

Mrs Rupa Mehra was displeased that she had not been allowed to' read either the letter or the response.

'I'll let you read his letter, Ma, if you insist,' said Lata. 'But my reply's gone off, so there's no question of reading that.'

Haresh's letter had contained far less of a personal nature than usual, and was therefore showable. Under 'the very great stress of circumstances' – or possibly because of Lata's short response to the subject – Haresh had omitted to bring up the question of Simran again.

Meanwhile, Kakoli had got hold of Mrs Rupa Mehra's card to Pran and Savita, and was enjoying herself, mouthing 'winsome' and 'dainty' to the helpless Lady Baby, and reformulating the lines while kissing Uma on the forehead.

'Hush! Lady Baby's fast asleep, the friendly fire-flames dance and leap and burning her to ash they sweep across the Lady Baby's dress.'

'How horrible!' said Mrs Rupa Mehra.

'A Lady Baby burned today – Her dainty soul has flown

away – God's called her back to frisk and play – and that's one Lady Baby less.'

Kakoli giggled. 'Don't worry, Ma, we won't light a fire in Brahmpur in August. It's not a sunless time of year.'

'Meenakshi, you must control your sister.'

'No one can do that, Ma. She's hopeless.'

'You are always saying that with Aparna also.'

'Am I?' said Meenakshi absently. 'Oh, that reminds me, I think I'm pregnant.'

'What?' cried everyone (except the Lady Baby).

'Yes – I've missed my period – it's far too late to be merely delayed. So you may get your grandson after all, Ma.'

'Oh!' said Mrs Rupa Mehra, not knowing what to think. After a pause she added: 'Does Arun know?'

An abstracted look appeared on Meenakshi's face. 'No, not yet,' she said. 'I suppose I'll have to tell him. Should I send him a telegram? No, such things are best done in person. Anyway, I'm tired of Brahmpur. There's no Life here.' She had begun to pine once again for canasta, mahjongg, the Shady Ladies and the bright lights. About the only lively person in Brahmpur was Maan, and he appeared far too rarely. Mr and Mrs Maitra, her hosts, were too deadly for words. As for the Rudhia riffraff – words failed her. Besides, Lata appeared to be too immersed in this cobbler and his concerns to be vulnerable to hints about Amit.

'What do you say, Kuku?'

'Say?' said Kuku. 'I'm flabbergasted. When did you know?'

'I meant, about going back to Calcutta.'

'Oh, all right,' said Kakoli obligingly. It wasn't as if she wasn't enjoying herself here. But she missed Cuddles, and Hans, the telephone, the two cooks, the car, and even the family. 'I'm ready to leave whenever you want. But why are you looking so thoughtful?'

It was a look that Meenakshi was to wear off and on for quite a while.

When exactly had she managed to get pregnant?

And with whom?

HARESH was disappointed that he had not been encouraged to stop in Brahmpur on his way to Calcutta
or asked to visit Lata's brothers in Calcutta despite
the fact that they were surely going to be his future
brothers-in-law, but the tone of understanding in Lata's
letter gave him great consolation among his uncer-
tainties. The letter from the Praha Shoe Company reiter-
ating their offer to him of a job at Rs 28 a week was
such a pathetic response to his application that he
couldn't believe that Mr Khandelwal had had anything to do with it. It had probably been passed on to
the Personnel Department, they had been forced to respond, and they had done so in their standard, dismissive
manner.

Haresh decided that he would go to Calcutta anyway,
and he lost no time after his arrival in trying to get
Praha to change its corporate mind. He went to Prahapore by train, a journey of less than fifteen miles.
It was raining, so his first impression of the grand complex – one of the largest and most efficient in Bengal –
took place under gloomy conditions. The endless rows
of workers' houses; the offices and cinema; the green
palm trees lining the road and the intensely green playing fields; the great, walled factory – the wall itself
painted in neat segments advertising the latest lines of
Praha footwear; the officers' colony (almost exclusively
Czech) hidden behind even higher walls; all these were
seen by Haresh through the discomfort and greyness of a
hot, wet morning. He was wearing an off-white suit and
carrying an umbrella. But the weather and Bengal itself –
both of which he found dampening – had seeped a little
into his spirits. Memories of Mr Ghosh and Mr Sen
Gupta came flooding back as he got a rickshaw from
the train station to the Personnel Office. Well, at least
I'll have to deal with Czechs here, not Bengalis, thought
Haresh.

The Czechs for their part treated all Indians (with one exception) the same, whether they spoke Bengali or not: with contempt. Indians, they had decided from experience, were fond of talking, not working. The Czechs liked nothing better than to work: in order to increase production, quality, sales, profits, and the glory of the Praha Shoe Company. Talking usually put them at a disadvantage; by and large they did not speak or write good English, nor did they have a great deal of culture. It could be said of them that when anyone talked about culture they reached for their awl. People started out young in the Praha Shoe Company, whether in Czechoslovakia or in India; they began on the shop floor; there was no need for the niceties of a university education. The Czechs mistrusted on the one hand what they saw as an Indian glibness with words (union negotiators were the worst), and resented on the other the fact that the British commercial establishment in Calcutta did not treat them, although they were fellow-Europeans, as anything like their equals. The directors and heads of department and even covenanted assistants of the managing agency of Bentsen & Pryce, for example, would not dream of fraternizing with the Czechs of the Praha Shoe Company.

The Czechs had transformed the face of the Indian footwear industry by rolling up their sleeves and creating a great factory and township on what had been virtually a swamp, by following this up with four smaller factories including the one at Brahmpur, and by running a tight network of shops throughout the country, not by hobnobbing over Scotch at the Calcutta Club. The Czech officers, including their Managing Director, had not been born to white collars. For them the Praha Shoe Company was their life and the Praha creed virtually their religion. Their branches and factories and shops spread around the world; and though they had been taken over by the communists in their own homeland, those 'Prahamen' who were abroad at the time or had managed to escape had not been dispossessed of their employment. The Praha Shoe Company was owned and run by Mr Jan Tomin, the eldest and identically named son of its legendary founder, now referred to as 'Old Mr Tomin'. Mr Tomin had made sure that his flock, whether in Canada or England or Nigeria or India, were well taken care of, and they repaid his loyalty to them with a fierce gratitude that verged on feudal fealty. When he decided to retire, this vassalage had been transferred to his son. Whenever Young Mr Tomin visited India from his world headquarters in London (not, alas, Prague any longer), the entire Praha world would be abuzz with excitement. Telephones rang all over Prahapore and urgent messages went back and forth from the head office in Calcutta to announce his god-like progress: 'Mr Tomin has arrived at the airport,' the rumour would go around. 'He is now on the flyover near the Prahapore Station. Mrs Tomin is with him.' 'Mr Tomin is visiting the 416 Department. He praised Mr Bratinka's efforts and showed great interest in the Goodyear Welted shoe line.' 'Mr and Mrs Tomin will be playing tennis this afternoon.' 'Mr Tomin had a swim at the Officers' Club, but thought the water was too warm. The baby too was floated in a rubber tube.'

Mr Tomin's wife was English, with a lovely oval face to contrast with his straightforward, genial, square one. Two years ago, she had given birth to a son, and this son too had been christened Jan, like his father and grandfather before him. This son had been taken along on Mr Tomin's most recent tour of India so that he could survey with infant eyes what would one day all be his.

But the Chairman of the Indian branch of the Praha Shoe Company, who sat in the luxurious head office on Camac Street in Calcutta (far from the sirens and smoke of Prahapore) and who lived in the posh 'Praha Residency' on Theatre Road, a mere five minutes' purr of his Austin Sheerline away, was no stocky Husek or Husak but the cheerful, greying, paan-chewing, Scotch-drinking Marwari, Mr Hiralal Khandelwal, who knew almost nothing (and did not care much more) about the day-to-day manufacture of shoes. How this had come about was an interesting story.

This odd configuration had a history of more than twenty years. Mr Khandelwal had been the solicitor in the family firm of Khandelwal and Company who had handled the legal account of Praha. When one of the grand supremos of Praha had been sent out from Prague in the late twenties to establish the Indian company, Khandelwal had been recommended to him as a capable man. Khandelwal got the company registered and did all the necessary legal spade-work, tasks which the Czechs treated with incomprehension and distaste. They wanted to get down to making shoes as quickly and sturdily and excellently as possible.

Mr Khandelwal facilitated whatever needed to be facilitated: the purchase of land, the necessary permissions from the Government of British India, negotiations with labour leaders. But it was in 1939, when the Second World War broke out, that he really came into his own. Since the Germans had occupied Czechoslovakia, Praha's possessions in India were in grave danger of being declared enemy property and confiscated. With his good contacts in government (especially with a powerful group of rising Indian officers in the Indian Civil Service whom he used to wine and dine and to whom – over bridge – he would lose money), Mr Khandelwal was able to retrieve the position of Praha. The powers of the Raj did not declare Praha to be enemy property after all; instead, they gave it massive orders for the manufacture of army boots and other footwear. The Czechs were not merely bewildered but astonished. Mr Khandelwal was promptly taken onto the board of Praha (India), and soon afterwards was made Chairman.

And he was the most shrewd and powerful Chairman that Praha had. One of his great advantages was that labour would eat out of his hands. To them he was a living deity – Khandelwal devta! – the brown man who ruled over the white rulers of Praha. Jawaharlal Nehru had met him, and several Cabinet Ministers knew him, including the Minister for Labour. The previous year there had been a prolonged strike at Prahapore, and a petition against the management had been sent by the workmen to the Prime Minister. Nehru had said to them: 'If you have Hiralal Khandelwal there, why do you need me?' And once the workmen had got him to agree to look into their grievances, Khandelwal had acted as the sole arbitrator between the Czech management and the unions – and that too as the Chairman!

Apart from having met him, Haresh had heard a great deal about the Chairman of Praha from Mr Mukherji, including an interesting snippet or two about his private life. Khandelwal was fond of good living, which definitely included women; and he was married to an attractive singer and ex-courtesan from Bihar – a woman with a formidable temperament.

The fact that it was Khandelwal who had forwarded his application gave Haresh a little courage as he stepped into the outer office of Mr Novak, the head of Personnel at Prahapore. Haresh had on an Irish linen bespoke suit from the best tailors in Middlehampton. His shoes were Saxone, five pounds the pair. He had Trugel in his hair, and he radiated a mild fragrance of expensive soap. Nevertheless, he was told to sit outside in the queue.

Finally, after an hour, he was asked to come in. Novak wore an open shirt and fawn trousers. His coat was hanging across his chair. He was a well-proportioned man, about 5 feet 9 inches in height, and extremely soft-spoken. He was unsmiling and unbending and as hard as nails; it was usually he who dealt with the unions. His eyes were penetrating.

He had Haresh's application before him as he interviewed him. At the end of ten minutes he said:

'Well, I see no reason to change our offer. It is a good one.'

'At twenty-eight rupees a week?'

'Yes.'

'You cannot imagine I can accept an offer like that.'

'That is up to you.'

'My qualifications – my work experience –' said Haresh helplessly, waving a hand at his application.

Mr Novak did not deign to answer. He looked like an old, cold fox.

'Please reconsider your offer, Mr Novak.'

'No.' The voice was soft, and the eyes unsmiling and even – it seemed to Haresh – unflickering.

'I have come here all the way from Delhi. At least give me half a chance. I have been in management on a reasonable monthly salary, and you are asking me to take the weekly wage of a workman – not even a supervisor, a foreman. I am sure you see how unreasonable this offer is.'

'No.'

'The Chairman –'

Mr Novak's voice cut across like a quiet whip:

'The Chairman asked me to consider your application. I did that and sent you a letter. That should have been the end of the matter. You have come here from Delhi for no reason, and I see no reason to change my mind. Good morning, Mr Khanna.'

Haresh got up, fuming, and left. It was still pouring outside. In the train back to Calcutta, he considered what to do. He felt he had been treated like dirt by Novak, and it burned him up. He had hated to plead, and his pleading had not worked.

He was a proud man, but now he had other compulsions. He had to have a job if he was to court Lata. From what he knew of Mrs Rupa Mehra, she would never allow her to marry an unemployed man – and Haresh could anyway not be so irresponsible as to ask Lata to share a hand-to-mouth existence with him. And what would he tell Umesh Uncle when he went back to Delhi? It would be galling beyond endurance to have to put up with his taunts.

So he decided to take the bull by the horns. He stood in the rain that afternoon outside the Praha head office in Camac Street. The next day was sunny, and he did the same. As a result of this reconnaisance he worked out Mr Khandelwal's movements. It became clear that at one o'clock in the afternoon he left the office for lunch.

The third day at lunchtime, as the gates opened to let the Chairman's Austin Sheerline glide out, Haresh stopped

the car by standing in front of it. The watchmen ran
helter-skelter in confusion and dismay and did not know
whether to reason with him or drag him away. Mr Khandelwal, however, looked at him, recognized him, and opened
the window.

'Ah,' he said, trying to recall the name.

'Haresh Khanna, Sir –'

'Yes, yes, I remember, Mukherji brought you to see me
in Delhi. What happened?'

'Nothing.' Haresh spoke calmly, though he could not
bring himself to smile.

'Nothing?' Mr Khandelwal frowned.

'As against an offer of seven hundred and fifty a month
with James Hawley, I was offered twenty-eight rupees a
week by Mr Novak. It seems that Praha doesn't want
qualified people.'

Haresh did not mention that the James Hawley offer
had been effectively rescinded, and he was glad that that
aspect of the matter had not come up when he and
Mukherji had met Khandelwal in Delhi.

'Hmm,' said Mr Khandelwal, 'come and see me the day
after tomorrow.'

When Haresh went to see him two days later, Mr
Khandelwal had got his file before him. He was brief. He
nodded at Haresh and said: 'I have looked over this. Havel
will meet you tomorrow for an interview.' Havel was the
General Manager at Prahapore.

Mr Khandelwal appeared to have no further questions
for Haresh except an inquiry or two about how Mukherji
was. 'All right, let us see how things go,' was his parting
comment. He did not seem unduly concerned whether
Haresh sank or swam.

13.27

BUT Haresh was nevertheless very encouraged. An interview with Havel meant that the Chairman had forced the
Czechs to take his application seriously. The next day,

when he boarded the train for the forty-five minute trip to Prahapore, he was in a fairly confident mood.

The Indian personal assistant to the General Manager told him that Novak would not be attending the interview. Haresh was relieved.

In a few minutes Haresh was ushered into the office of the General Manager of Prahapore.

Pavel Havel – so named by playfully idiotic parents, who had no conception of how he would be teased at school – was a short man like Haresh, but almost as broad as he was tall.

'Sit, sit, sit –' he said to Haresh.

Haresh sat down.

'Show me your hands,' he said.

Haresh offered Mr Havel his hands, palms upwards.

'Bend your thumb.'

Haresh bent it as much as possible.

Mr Havel laughed in a not unfriendly but rather final way.

'You are not a shoemaker,' he said.

'I am,' said Haresh.

'No, no, no –' Mr Havel laughed. 'Some other line, some other job is best for you. Join some other company. What do you want to do in Praha?'

'I want to sit on the other side of this desk,' said Haresh.

Mr Havel stopped smiling.

'Oh,' he said. 'That high?'

'Eventually,' said Haresh.

'We all start on the shop floor,' explained Mr Havel, feeling sorry for this rather incapable but ambitious young man who would never make a shoemaker. It was perfectly obvious the moment he had tried to bend his thumb. The way shoes were made in Czechoslovakia required bending the thumb. This young man had no more future with Praha than a one-armed man in a wrestling pit. 'Myself, Mr Novak, Mr Janacek, Mr Kurilla, all of us, we all started on the shop floor. If you cannot make shoes,' he continued, 'what hope is there for you in this company?'

'None,' said Haresh.

'So you see –' said Pavel Havel.

'You have not even seen me trying to make a shoe,' said Haresh. 'How would you know what I can or can't do?'

Pavel Havel got slightly irked. He had a great deal of work to do today, and endless empty talk bothered him. Indians always talked big and performed miserably. He looked slightly weary. Gazing out of his window at the bright – too-bright – greenery outside, he wondered if the communists would ever leave Czechoslovakia, and if he and his family would ever get the chance in his lifetime to see his hometown of Bratislava again.

The young man was saying something about being able to make a shoe.

Pavel Havel stared at the lapel of his fancy suit and said rather brutally: 'You will never make a shoe.'

Haresh could not understand Havel's sudden change of tone, but he was not cowed by it. 'I think I can make a shoe right from the design pattern to the finished product,' he said.

'All right,' said Pavel Havel. You make a shoe. You make a shoe, and I will give you a foreman's job at eighty rupees a week.' No one had ever started as a foreman at Praha, but Pavel Havel was sure that this was a riskless bet. Paper qualifications were one thing, rigid thumbs and a flaccid national spirit another.

But Haresh was willing to try for something better. He said: 'I have a letter of appointment here from James Hawley offering me a job at seven hundred and fifty rupees. If I make a shoe to your satisfaction, not just an ordinary shoe, but the most difficult one on your production line, will you match their offer?'

Pavel Havel looked at the young man, disconcerted by his confidence, and put a finger to his lips, as if reconsidering his calculated likelihoods. 'No,' he said, slowly. 'That would put you in the managerial grade and cause a revolution at Praha. It is impossible. As it is, if you can make a pair of shoes – of a kind I will choose – if you can make it – you will become a foreman, and that in itself is half a revolution.' Pavel Havel, having suffered from one in Czechoslovakia, did not approve of revolutions.

He phoned Kurilla, the head of the Leather Footwear Division, and asked him to come to his office for a few minutes.

'What do you think, Kurilla?' he said. 'Khanna wants to make a shoe. What should we give him to make?'

'Goodyear Welted,' said Kurilla cruelly.

Pavel Havel smiled broadly. 'Yes, yes, yes,' he said. 'Go and make a pair of Goodyear Welted shoes according to our ready-made pattern.'

This was the most difficult type of shoe to make, and involved over a hundred different operations. Havel frowned, looked at his own thumbs, and dismissed Haresh.

13.28

NO poet ever worked harder or more inspiredly to craft a poem than Haresh worked for the next three days on his pair of shoes. He was supplied the materials, and told where the various machines were, and he set to work amid the heat and din of the factory.

He examined and selected fine pieces of upper and lining leather, measured them for thickness, cut, skived, cemented and folded the components, stamped the lining for size and style, fitted the upper and lining components together and carefully stitched them to each other.

He inserted and shaped the counter and toe-puff in the upper, and attached the insole to the last.

Then he mounted the upper to the wooden last and attached it to the insole by toe-lasting, heel-lasting and side-lasting, and checked with satisfaction that the upper was truly down to the last without a wrinkle, that it clung as tightly as a skin.

He stitched a welt all around. He trimmed the surplus material, and bottom-filled the gap with a mixture of cork and adhesive.

He hardly ate. On the way back to Calcutta each night he dreamed of the finished pair of shoes and how they would transform his life.

He cut the sole leather and split it to the correct thickness. He layed it, stitched it through, and attached the heel. Then he trimmed the heel and the sole. He paused for a few minutes before starting this difficult and delicate operation; trimming was like cutting hair – a mistake would be critical and irretrievable. A pair of shoes had to be completely symmetrical, left and right absolutely in proportion to each other. He paused for a few minutes afterwards as well. He knew from experience that after performing a difficult job well he was prone to the kind of relief and over-confidence that led to botching something simple.

After trimming, he fine-scoured the heel, and indented the welt to make it look good. When he had finished, he allowed himself to think that things were going well. He coloured the edges, and hot-waxed and ironed them to make them impermeable to water.

Mr Novak, the cold fox, came around at one stage to see how he was progressing. Haresh was taking his post-trimming breather. Mr Novak nodded but did not greet him, Haresh nodded but did not greet him, and Mr Novak went wordlessly away.

The shoes were now practically ready except that the soles, where stitched, looked a little crude. So Haresh fine-buffed the soles, waxed them and shone them. And lastly he fudged the bottom edges against a hot revolving wheel that hid the ugly stitches under a fine decorative pattern.

That, thought Haresh, carries a lesson for me. If James Hawley hadn't retracted their offer I would still be stuck in the same city. Now perhaps I'll get a job near Calcutta. And in terms of quality, Praha footwear is the best in India.

Appropriately enough, his next operation was to brand-stamp the sole with the name of Praha. He removed the wooden last. He attached the heel (which was attached only temporarily before) with nails. With gold foil he brand-stamped the inside sock with the Praha name and pasted it and cemented it inside the shoe. It was done!

He was halfway to Havel's office when he turned back, shaking his head and smiling at himself.

'What now?' said the man who had been designated to police him while he worked.

'A pair of laces,' said Haresh. 'I must be exhausted.'

The General Manager, the head of Leather, and the head of Personnel gathered together to look at Haresh's pair of shoes, to twist them and turn them, to prod them and peer at them. They spoke in Czech.

'Well,' said Kurilla, 'they're better than anything you or I could make.'

'I've promised him a foreman's job,' said Havel.

'You can't do that,' said Novak. 'Everyone starts on the floor.'

'I've promised him a foreman's job, and he will get one. I don't want to lose a man like this. What do you think Mr K will say?'

Though Khandelwal had appeared indifferent to Haresh's fate, he had in fact (as Haresh was later to learn) been very tough with the Czechs. After looking at Haresh's papers he had said to Havel: 'Show me any other applicants, Czech or Indian, who have the same qualifications.' Havel had not been able to. Even Kurilla, the head of Leather, though he had himself graduated from the Middlehampton College of Technology many years earlier, had not had the distinction, as Haresh had had, of standing first. Mr Khandelwal had then said: 'I forbid you to recruit any person below this man's qualifications until he is first offered a job.' Havel had tried to dissuade Khandelwal from this drastic veto, but had not succeeded. He had tried to persuade Haresh to withdraw, but had not succeeded. He had then set him a task that he had not remotely imagined he could succeed in. But Haresh's shoes were as good as anything he had seen. Pavel Havel, whatever he thought about Indians, would never again speak slightingly about people's thumbs.

The Goodyear Welted shoes were to lie in Havel's office

for over a year, and he was to point them out on various occasions to visitors whenever he wanted to discuss fine workmanship.

Haresh was called in.

'Sit, sit, sit,' said Havel.

Haresh sat down.

'Excellent, excellent!' said Havel.

Haresh knew how good his shoes were, but he could not help looking delighted. His eyes disappeared in his smile.

'So I keep my part of the bargain. You get the job. Eighty rupees a week. Starting on Monday. Yes, Kurilla?'

'Yes.'

'Novak?'

Novak nodded, unsmilingly. His right hand was moving over the edge of one of the shoes. 'A good pair,' he said quietly.

'Then good,' said Havel. 'You accept?'

'The salary is too low,' said Haresh. 'Compared both to what I was getting before and what I have been offered.'

'We will put you on probation for six months, and then reconsider the salary. You do not realize, Khanna, how far we go to accommodate you, to make you a Prahaman.'

Haresh said: 'I am grateful. I accept these terms, but there is one thing I will not compromise on. I must live inside the colony and be able to use the Officers' Club.'

He realized that, however momentous in terms of the Praha culture was his direct entry at the supervisory level, he would be fatally disadvantaged in social terms if he was not seen – by Lata and her mother and her much-vaunted Calcutta brother, for example – to be on easy terms with the managers of his company.

'No, no, no –' said Pavel Havel. He looked thoroughly worried.

'Impossible,' said Novak, his eyes boring into Haresh, willing him to give in.

Kurilla did not say anything. He looked at the pair of shoes. He knew that no supervisor – and only one Indian – had been allocated a place among the forty or so houses in the walled compound. But he was glad to see the excellence of the training of his old college vindicated by Haresh. Among his Praha colleagues, most of whom had learned their skills on the job, Kurilla's technical training was often treated as something of a joke.

Haresh too had found out from Havel's Indian assistant that only one Indian had so far gained admittance into the hallowed colony – a manager from the Accounts Department.

He sensed Kurilla's sympathy and Havel's hesitancy. Even the icy Novak had a little earlier – and most uncharacteristically for him – praised his work in three brief syllables. So there appeared to be hope.

'I want above everything else to work for Praha,' said Haresh with feeling. 'You can see how much I care for quality. That is what has drawn me to your company. I have been an officer at the Cawnpore Leather and Footwear Company, and I was offered a manager's, an officer's grade at James Hawley, so my living in the compound would not be so extraordinary. I cannot take the job otherwise. I am sorry. I want to work here so much that I am willing to compromise on salary and on status. Keep me as a foreman, a supervisor, if you wish, and pay me less than I was getting before. But please compromise on this small matter of accommodation.'

There was a confabulation in Czech. The Managing Director was out of the country and could not be consulted. More importantly, the Chairman, who sometimes treated the Czechs as brusquely as they treated Indians, would not be sympathetic to what he would see as their exclusivism. If Haresh refused the job after all this, there would be hell to pay.

Like a litigant listening to legal incomprehensibilities in court, incomprehensibilities that would decide his fortune, Haresh listened to the three men, sensing from their tones and gestures and the occasional word – 'colony', 'club', 'Khandelwal', 'Middlehampton', 'Jan Tomin' and so on – that Kurilla had persuaded Havel and that both were now bearing down on Novak. Novak's replies were brief, trenchant, entrenched, consisting only rarely of more than five or six syllables. Then, quite suddenly, Novak made an expressive gesture – he half shrugged, he half threw up his hands. He did not utter a word or even a nod of assent, but there was no further dissent from him either.

Pavel Havel turned to Haresh with a broad smile.

'Welcome – welcome to Praha!' he said, as if he were offering Haresh the keys to the kingdom of heaven.

Haresh beamed with pleasure, as if indeed he were.

And everyone civilly shook hands.

13.29

ARUN MEHRA and his friend Billy Irani were sitting on the verandah of the Calcutta Club overlooking the lawn. It was lunchtime. The waiter had not yet come around to take his order for a drink. Arun, however, did not wish to press the little brass bell at his white cane table. As a waiter walked past a few yards away, Arun got his attention by patting the back of his left hand with the palm of his right.

'Abdar!'

'Yes, Sir.'

'What'll you have, Billy?'

'A gimlet.'

'One gimlet and one Tom Collins.'

'Yes, Sir.'

The drinks came around in due course. Both of them ordered grilled fish for lunch.

They were still on their drinks when Arun, looking around, said: 'That's Khandelwal sitting there by himself – the Praha chap.'

Billy's comment was relaxed: 'These Marwaris – there was a time when membership in this club meant something.'

They had both on several occasions noted with distaste Khandelwal's drinking habits. Being limited at home by the powerful Mrs Khandelwal to one drink in the evening,

Khandelwal made it his business to get in as many as possible during the day.

But Arun today found nothing much to object to in Khandelwal's presence, particularly in the fact that he was sitting alone and drinking his fourth Scotch. Mrs Rupa Mehra had written to Arun, ordering him to acquaint himself with Haresh Khanna and to write to her telling her what he thought of him. Haresh apparently had got some job or other in Praha and lived and worked in Prahapore.

It would have been too demeaning for Arun to approach him directly, and he had been wondering how to go about it. But yes, he could certainly mention the matter to the Chairman of Praha and perhaps inveigle a common invitation to tea – on neutral grounds. Here was an excellent opportunity.

Billy was continuing: 'It's remarkable. He no sooner finishes one than another's at his elbow. He never knows when to stop.'

Arun laughed. Then another thought struck him. 'Oh, by the way – Meenakshi's expecting again.'

'Expecting?' Billy was looking slightly blank.

'Yes, you know, old fellow, preggers!'

'Ah, yes, yes, preggers!' Billy Irani nodded his head. Then suddenly a thought struck him, and he began to look bewildered.

'Are you feeling all right, old chap? Another? Abdar –'

The waiter came by. 'Yes, Sir.'

'Another gimlet. Though we were taking the usual precautions. Still, it shows you never can tell. Determined fellows –'

'Fellows?'

'Yes, you know, babies. They want to appear, so they do so without consulting their parents. Meenakshi's been looking worried – but I suppose it's all for the best. Aparna could do with a brother. Or sister, I suppose. I say, Billy, I might have to go over and have a few words with Khandelwal. It's about the new hiring policies of our firm. Praha's apparently have been taking on some Indians lately, and I might get a few ideas from him – well, I shouldn't be more than a few minutes. You don't mind, do you?'

'Oh, no, no – not at all.'

'You're looking rather poorly. Is it the sun? We can change tables.'

'No, no – just tired – working too hard, I suppose.'

'Well, take it easy. Doesn't Shireen tick you off? Act as a moderating influence and all that?' Arun smiled as he moved away.

'Shireen?' Billy's handsome face was pale. His mouth was open in rather a fish-like gape. 'Oh, yes, Shireen.'

Arun wondered for a second whether Billy's IQ had sunk to zero, but his mind was soon occupied with other thoughts. He winched up a smile as he approached Mr Khandelwal's table at the far end of the verandah.

'Ah, Mr Khandelwal. Good to see you.'

Mr Khandelwal looked up, half sozzled already, but very genially. This was Arun Mehra, one of a handful of young men in Calcutta who had been accepted into the British commercial establishment – and who with their wives were therefore the leaders of Indian society in Calcutta. Chairman of Praha though he was, he was flattered to be recognized by Arun, to whom he had once been introduced at the races. Khandelwal remembered that the young man had an exceedingly glamorous wife, but he had a bad memory for names, and groped around a bit before Arun, who could not believe that anyone could have forgotten him, said, 'Arun Mehra.'

'Yes, yes, of course – Bentsen Pryce.'

Arun was mollified.

'I wonder if I could have a few words with you, Mr Khandelwal,' he said.

Mr Khandelwal gestured towards a chair and Arun sat down.

'Will you have a drink?' offered Mr Khandelwal, his hand poised above the small brass bell.

'No, thank you, I've had one already.'

In Mr Khandelwal's view that was no good reason not to have another half-dozen. 'What is on your mind?' he asked the younger man.

'Well, as you know, Mr Khandelwal, our firm, and several others like ours, have been recruiting Indians – suitable Indians, of course – for management positions, on a gradual basis. And one hears that you, too, being a big organization, have been thinking of doing the same thing.'

Khandelwal nodded.

'Well,' said Arun. 'In some respects we are in the same predicament. It's rather difficult to get the sort of people we need.'

Khandelwal smiled.

'You may find it difficult,' he said slowly, 'but we find no problem getting qualified people. Only the other day we recruited a man with a good background.' He lapsed into Hindi. 'A good man – he has studied in England, has a fine technical background. They wanted to give him a lower position, but I insisted –' He gestured for another Scotch. 'I can't remember his name, oh yes, Haresh Khanna.'

'From Kanpur?' replied Arun, permitting himself two words in Hindi.

'I don't know,' said Mr Khandelwal. 'Oh yes, from Kanpur. He came to my attention through Mukherji of CLFC. Yes, have you heard of him?'

'It's very curious,' said Arun, to whom none of this was in the least curious. 'But now that you mention the name, Mr Khandelwal, I believe this must be the young man whom my mother talked about a little while ago as a – well, as a prospect for my sister. He's a khatri, and, as you know, so are we – though I'm not in the least a believer in caste and so on. But of course there's no arguing with my mother – she believes in all this khatri-patri business. How interesting; so he works for you?'

'Yes. A good boy. Good technical qualifications.'

Arun shuddered inwardly at the word 'technical'.

'Well, we wouldn't mind his coming over some day to our place,' Arun said. 'But perhaps it might be better if it were not quite so face-to-face, with just him and us. I wonder if perhaps you and Mrs Khandelwal might care to come over for tea one day. We live in Sunny Park, which, as you know, is in Ballygunge: not all that far away from you. I've been thinking of inviting you over for some time anyway; I understand you play an excellent game of bridge.'

Since Mr Khandelwal was a notoriously reckless player – his skill at bridge consisted largely of losing while playing for high stakes (though sometimes in the interests of a larger game) – Arun's remark was pure flattery. But it had its effect.

Mr Khandelwal, although not blind to Arun's charming manipulativeness, was pleased to be flattered. He was a hospitable man – and he had a mansion to display. So, as Arun had hoped and intended that he might when he had tendered his reverse invitation, the Chairman of Praha invited them over instead.

'No, no, you come and join us for tea at our place,' said Mr Khandelwal. 'I'll get this boy over – Khanna. And my wife will be very interested in meeting Mrs Mehra. Please bring her too.'

'That's very kind of you, Mr Khandelwal.'

'Not at all, not at all. Sure you won't have a drink?'

'No, thank you.'

'We can discuss recruiting procedures then.'

'Oh, yes, recruiting,' said Arun. 'Well, which day would suit you?'

'Come any time.' Mr Khandelwal left the matter up in the air. The Khandelwal household ran on very flexible principles. People dropped in and vast formal parties were given, often at the same time. Six large alsatians joined in the mêlée and terrified the guests. Mrs Khandelwal ruled over Mr Khandelwal with a whip, but he often went astray with drink or women.

'How about next Tuesday?'

'Yes, yes, next Tuesday, any day,' said Mr Khandelwal vaguely.

'At five?'

'Yes, yes, at five, any time.'

'Well, then, at five next Tuesday. I look forward to it,'

said Arun, wondering whether Mr Khandelwal would remember this conversation five minutes later.

'Yes, yes, Tuesday, at five,' said Mr Khandelwal, deep
in his cups. 'Yes. Abdar –'

13.30

EVERYONE punched in at the Praha factory gate before the
second siren went at eight in the morning; but there was a
separate gate for the supervisors and managers, from the
foremen upwards. Haresh was shown where he would sit.
It was at a table in the open hall next to the conveyor belt.
Here he would both supervise and do any office work that
was necessary. Only group foremen got cubicles. There
was nowhere for him to screw in the brass plate bearing
his name that he had removed from his office door at
CLFC not very long ago.

But perhaps he would not have been able to use that
brass plate anyway. Everything was uniform in Praha and
no doubt there was a standard lettering and size to brass
plates as to everything else. The Czechs, for example, had
brought the metric system with them, and refused to work
with anything else, regardless of what had prevailed in the
Raj or what now prevailed in Independent India. As for
the litany that every Indian schoolchild learned – 'three
pies to a paisa, four paisas to an anna, sixteen annas to a
rupee,' – the Czechs treated this as a joke. They had
decimalized the rupee for all internal Praha purposes by
fiat decades before the government came around to even
deciding to do so.

Haresh, who liked order, did not disapprove of this at
all. He was happy to be working in a well-organized, well-
lit, well-knit environment, and was determined to do his
best for the company.

Because he had been started off at the foreman level and
granted permission to live in the colony, a number of
rumours had begun to do the rounds among the workmen.
These were enhanced when he was invited to tea with Mr

Khandelwal. The first rumour was that the fair, compact, well-dressed Haresh Khanna was actually a Czech, who for purposes best known to himself had decided to pose as an Indian. The second was that he was Mr Khandelwal's brother-in-law. Haresh did nothing to dispel these rumours, as he found both of them helpful when he wanted to get things done.

Haresh took an hour's leave on the day that he had to go to Calcutta for tea with the Chairman. When he arrived at the huge house on Theatre Road – the 'Praha Residency' as it was popularly known – he was saluted smartly by the guards. The immaculate lawn, the five cars in the drive (including the Austin Sheerline that he had bodily halted a few days before), the palms lining the drive, the grand mansion itself, all impressed him greatly. The only thing that troubled him a little was that one palm tree was slightly out of line.

Mr Khandelwal greeted him in a friendly manner, in Hindi. 'So you have become a Prahaman. Very good.'

'It is because of your kindness –' began Haresh.

'You're quite right,' said Mr Khandelwal, instead of making some self-deprecating rejoinder. 'It was my kindness all right.' He laughed. 'Those crazy Czechs would have got rid of you if they could. Come in, come in. . . . But it was your qualifications that did it. I heard about that pair of shoes.' He laughed again.

Haresh was introduced to Mrs Khandelwal, a strikingly attractive woman in her late thirties, dressed in a gold and white sari. A diamond nose-stud and diamond earrings and a charming and lively smile added to the dazzling effect.

Within a few minutes she had sent him off to repair a tap that was not working in the bathroom. 'We must get it going before the other guests arrive,' she said in her most charming manner. 'I hear you are very good with your hands.'

Haresh, slightly puzzled, went to do as he was bid. It was not a test of any kind – either of the Pavel Havel kind or of his vulnerability to her smile. It was simply that when something needed to be done, Mrs Khandelwal expected everyone around her to do it. When she wanted a handyman, she seized upon any man who was handy. All Indian Prahamen had learned that they could be called upon at any time to do the Queen's bidding. Haresh didn't mind; he liked putting things right. He took off his jacket, and wandered through the huge house with a servant until he came to the erring tap. He wondered who these important guests were.

Meanwhile, the guests themselves were on their way. Meenakshi was quite looking forward to it all. After the yawn that was Brahmpur it was good to be back in Calcutta. Aparna had become a little more placid by spending a few days with her grandmother Mrs Chatterji (which is where she had been parked this evening as well); and even the shiftless Varun (who was also out this evening) was a welcome homecoming sight after the Brahmpur baby smells and the Rudhia relatives and the doddering Maitras.

This evening was to be a grand one: tea with the Khandelwals; two cocktail parties to follow (at at least one of which she was bound to meet Billy – what would he say, she wondered, when she laughingly told him her news?); then dinner and dancing. She was curious about the Khandelwals, with their grand house and six dogs and five cars, and she was very interested in meeting the upstart cobbler who had designs on Luts.

The lawns and flowers of the Praha Residency were more than impressive, even for a season when almost nothing bloomed. Mrs Khandelwal, who was an obsessive woman, would have thought nothing of transplanting Kew to Calcutta if it had suited her ends.

Haresh was back in his jacket by the time he was introduced to the tall young gentleman and his elegant wife, both of whom appeared to be appraising him from a height that was not merely literal. The moment he heard his host's words – 'Arun Mehra – from Bentsen Pryce' – he realized why. So this was Lata's Calcutta brother.

'Very pleased to meet you,' said Haresh, shaking Arun's

hand in perhaps too firm a grip. This was his first real meeting with a brown sahib. They had never been a part of his life. When he had lived for a while in Patiala he had often wondered why people made such a fuss about the young man from Imperial Tobacco or Shell or some other foreign firm who was based in the town or travelling through, not realizing that for a mere trader such a member of the comprador classes was a man important beyond his years; he could dispense and revoke agencies, he could make or break one's fortune. He invariably travelled around in a car with a chauffeur, and a car with a chauffeur in a small town was a great thing.

Arun for his part was thinking: short; a bit brash; something about his manner of dressing that's a bit flashy; has too good an opinion of himself.

But they all sat down to tea, and the opening moves of the conversation were made by the women. Meenakshi noticed that the Rosenthal service in white and gold too perfectly matched her hostess's sari. Typical of these people! she thought. They try too hard.

She looked around the room for something to praise. She couldn't very well praise the heavy furniture, most of which was in rather overdone taste, but there was a Japanese painting that she quite liked: two birds and a bit of calligraphy.

'That's a lovely painting, Mrs Khandelwal,' said Meenakshi. 'Where did you get it?'

'From Japan. Mr Khandelwal went on a trip there –'

'From Indonesia,' said Mr Khandelwal. It had been given to him by a Japanese businessman at a conference in Djakarta that he had attended on behalf of Praha India.

Mrs Khandelwal flashed her eyes at him, and he quailed.

'I know what you got and when,' said Mrs Khandelwal.

'Yes, yes –' said her husband in rather a worried tone.

'Nice furniture!' said Haresh, in the belief that this was the kind of small talk that needed to be made.

Meenakshi looked at him and forbore from comment.

But Mrs Khandelwal gazed at him with her sweetest, most charming expression. He had provided her with an opportunity to say what she had been waiting to say. 'Do you think so?' she asked Haresh. 'It has been done by Kamdar's – Kamdar's of Bombay. Half our rooms are decorated by them.'

Meenakshi looked at the heavy corner-settee – in dark, solid wood with dark blue upholstery. 'If you like this sort of thing, you can always get it in Calcutta,' she said. 'There's the Chowringhee Sales Bureau, for instance, for old-fashioned furniture. And if you want something more modern in style, there's always Mozoomdar. It's a little less' – she paused for a word – 'a little less ponderous. But it depends on your taste. These pakoras are delicious,' she added by way of compensation, helping herself to another one.

Her bright laugh tinkled across the china, though there was nothing very obviously humorous in her previous remarks.

'Oh, but I think,' said Mrs Khandelwal, oozing charm, 'I do think that the quality of workmanship and the quality of wood at Kamdar's is unbeatable.'

And the quality of distance, thought Meenakshi. If you lived in Bombay, you'd be importing your furniture from Calcutta. Aloud she said: 'Well, Kamdar's is Kamdar's, of course.'

'Do have some more tea, Mrs Mehra,' said Mrs Khandelwal, pouring it out herself.

She was exquisitely charming, and believed in winning people over – including women. Though she suffered from some insecurity because of her past background, she was never aggressive with them. It was only where sweetness didn't work that she gave vent to fury.

Mr Khandelwal appeared to be getting impatient. After a little while he excused himself to get a breath of fresh air. He came back a minute or two later, smelling of cardamoms and looking happier.

Mrs Khandelwal viewed him with suspicion when he returned, but he looked completely innocent.

Suddenly, without warning, three large alsatians bounded into the room, barking frenetically. Haresh was bewildered and almost spilled his tea. Arun jumped up. Khandelwal was perplexed; he wondered how they could have got in. Only the two women remained cool. Meenakshi was used to the vicious Cuddles and was fond of dogs. And Mrs Khandelwal turned on them in a low, commanding hiss:

'Sit down! Down, Cassius, down – down – Crystal – down, Jalebi!'

The three dogs sat down in a line, trembling and silent. Each of them knew that if they disobeyed, Mrs Khandelwal would have thought nothing of whipping them unmercifully there and then.

'See –' said Mrs Khandelwal, 'see how sweet he is, my Cassius, look at him, my little pet – how unhappy he looks. He didn't mean to disturb anyone.'

'Well,' said Arun, 'I'm afraid my wife is in rather a – a – well, a delicate state, and these sudden shocks –'

Mrs Khandelwal, horrified, turned on her husband. 'Mr Khandelwal,' she said in a tone of absolute authority, 'do you know what you have done? Do you have any idea?'

'No,' said Mr Khandelwal in fear and trembling.

'You have left the door open. That is how these three beasts have entered. Take them out at once and close the door.'

Having dispatched the dogs and her husband, she turned – dripping concern – towards Meenakshi.

'My poor Mrs Mehra, I cannot apologize enough. Have another pakora. Have two. You must build up your strength.'

'Excellent tea, Mrs Khandelwal,' said Haresh bravely.

'Do have another cup. We get our own blend directly from Darjeeling,' said Mrs Khandelwal.

13.31

THERE was a pause, and now Haresh decided to beard the lion.

'You must be Lata's brother,' he said to Arun. 'How is Lata?'

'Very well,' said Arun.

'And your mother?'

'Very well, thank you,' said Arun, with some hauteur.

'And the baby?'

'The baby?'

'Your niece.'

'Flourishing, no doubt.'

There was another pause.

'Do you have any children?' asked Haresh of Meenakshi.

'Yes,' said Meenakshi. 'A girl.'

This cobbler, she decided, would make a very poor rival to Amit.

Arun turned to Haresh and said: 'What is it you do exactly, Mr Khanna? I understand you've been taken on by Praha's in some sort of position. A managerial position, I presume.'

'Well, not managerial,' said Haresh. 'I am in a supervisory position at the moment, though my previous job was managerial. I decided to take this job because it has more of a future.'

'Supervisory?'

'I am a foreman.'

'Ah! A foreman.'

'Praha usually starts people on the shop floor, not even in supervisory jobs.'

'Hmm.' Arun took another sip of tea.

'James Hawley offered me a managerial job –' began Haresh.

'I could never understand why the Cromarty Group hasn't moved its head office to Calcutta,' said Arun in a distant manner. 'Puzzling that they should wish to remain a provincial concern. Ah well.'

Meenakshi felt that Arun was being too unfriendly. 'You're from Delhi originally, aren't you, Mr Khanna?' she asked.

'Yes, indeed,' said Haresh. 'And I went to St Stephen's College.'

'And then, I understand, you went to England for your education. Was that to Oxford or to Cambridge?'

'I went to the Middlehampton College of Technology.'

There was silence for a few seconds, only interrupted by Mr Khandelwal's return. He was looking even happier. He had an arrangement with the watchman to keep a bottle of whisky and a glass for him at the gate, and he had mastered the art of gulping down a peg in five seconds flat.

Arun continued his conversation with Haresh: 'What plays have you seen recently, Mr Khanna?' Arun named a few that were running in London.

'Plays?'

'Well, since you've come from England, I presume you would have taken the opportunity to visit the theatre.'

'I didn't have much of an occasion to see plays in the Midlands,' said Haresh. 'But I did see a large number of films.'

Arun received this information without comment. 'Well, I expect you visited Stratford; it's not far from Middlehampton.'

'I did,' said Haresh, relieved. This was worse than Novak, Havel and Kurilla put together.

Arun began to talk about the restoration of Anne Hathaway's cottage, and by slow degrees moved from the provinces to post-war reconstruction work in London.

Meenakshi talked about friends of hers who were doing up a mews off Baker Street.

From there the conversation moved to hotels. At the mention of Claridges, Mr Khandelwal, who always booked a suite there whenever he visited London, said:

'Oh, yes, Claridges. I have a good relation with Claridges. The manager always asks me, "Is everything to your satisfaction, Mr Khandelwal?" And I always say, "Yes, it is all to my satisfaction."' He smiled, as if at a private joke.

Mrs Khandelwal looked at him with suppressed anger. She suspected that his trips to London had a carnal as well as a business element to them, and she was right. Sometimes she would phone him up in the middle of the night to ensure that he was where he had said he would be. If he complained, which he rarely dared to do, she would tell him that she had mixed up her time zones.

'What do you like best about London – when you do happen to go there?' asked Arun, turning to Haresh.

'The pubs, of course,' said Haresh. 'No matter where you go you bump into a pub. One of my favourites is that wedge-shaped pub near Trafalgar Square – the Marquis of Anglesey – or is it the Marquis of Granby?'

Mr Khandelwal looked somewhat interested, but Arun, Meenakshi, and Mrs Khandelwal gave a collective shudder. Haresh was behaving like a real bull among the Rosenthal.

'Where do you buy toys for your daughter?' asked Mrs Khandelwal quickly. 'I am always telling Mr Khandelwal to buy toys from England. They make such good gifts. People are always being born in India and I don't know what to give them.'

Arun quickly, and with accuracy and aplomb, gave the names of three toy-shops in London, but ended with a hymn to Hamleys:

'I always believe, though, Mrs Khandelwal, that one should go for the tried and tested stores. And really, there still is nothing to compare with Hamleys. Toys from top to bottom – nothing but toys on every floor. And it's done up beautifully at Christmas. It's on Regent Street, not far from Jaeger's –'

'Jaeger's!' said Mr Khandelwal. 'That's where I bought a dozen sweaters last month.'

'When were you last in England, Mr Mehra?' asked Haresh, who was feeling left out of the conversation.

But something appeared to have got stuck in Arun's throat, because he took a handkerchief out of his pocket and began to cough, pointing with his left hand to his Adam's apple.

His hostess was all solicitude. She ordered a glass of water for him. The servant brought in a thick tumbler of water on a stainless steel thali. Seeing Meenakshi's horrified look, Mrs Khandelwal shouted at the servant.

'Is this how you have learned to bring water? I should

send you back to the village.' The steel platter contrasted dreadfully with the gold-and-white tea service. Meenakshi looked still more horrified at the public outburst of her hostess.

When Arun had recovered, and the drift of the conversation was about to change, Haresh, feeling that Arun might appreciate his interest in him, repeated his question:

'When was the last time you were in England?'

Arun went red, then collected himself. There was no escape for him. He had to answer the question.

'Well,' he said with as much dignity as he could muster, 'as it happens, it might surprise you to learn that I've never actually had the opportunity to go there – but of course we're going in a few months' time.'

Haresh was startled. He would never have dreamed of asking Arun *whether* he had ever been to England. He felt like laughing, but dared not do so. His eyes, however, disappeared in an expression of amusement. His host and hostess looked startled too.

Meenakshi began to talk quickly about bridge, and how they simply had to have the Khandelwals over some time. And after a few minutes of polite conversation the Mehras looked at their watches, exchanged glances, thanked their hosts, got up, and left.

13.32

MEENAKSHI was right. Billy Irani was at the second of the two cocktail parties they went to that evening. Shireen was with him, but Meenakshi managed with some light flirtatious banter to draw him aside in an amusingly public way.

'Do you know, Billy,' she said, softly and laughingly, in a voice that did not carry, and with an expression that indicated that they were making small talk, 'do you know that I'm expecting?'

Billy Irani looked nervous. 'Yes, Arun mentioned it to me.'

'Well?'

'Well – should I congratulate you?'

Meenakshi laughed tinklingly, her eyes cold.

'No, I don't think that's a good idea. You might be congratulating yourself in a few months.'

Poor Billy looked rather haunted.

'But we were careful.' (Except that once, he thought.)

'I've been careful with everyone,' countered Meenakshi.

'Everyone?' Billy looked shocked.

'I mean, with you, and with Arun. All right, let's change the subject, here he comes.'

But Arun, who had spied Patricia Cox and was determined to be gallant to her, walked past them with a nod. Meenakshi was saying:

'– and of course, I understand nothing about these handicaps and so on, but I do like the names, eagles and birdies and so on. They sound so – so – it's all right, he's gone. Now, Billy, when should we meet?'

'We can't meet. Not after this!' Billy sounded horrified. He was moreover, transfixed by Meenakshi's little pearlike earrings, which he found curiously disconcerting.

'I can't get pregnant twice,' said Meenakshi. 'It's perfectly safe now.'

Billy was looking ill. He glanced quickly across the room at Shireen.

'Really, Meenakshi!'

'Don't "really Meenakshi" me,' said Meenakshi with a sharp edge to her voice. 'We are going to continue as before, Billy, or I won't answer for the consequences.'

'You wouldn't tell him –' gasped Billy.

Meenakshi drew her elegant neck upward and smiled at Billy. She looked tired, perhaps even a little worried. She did not answer his question.

'And the – well – the baby?' said Billy.

'I'll have to think of what to do about that,' said Meenakshi. 'I'd go mad wondering about it otherwise. Not knowing. That's something I might need a little help with too. So, let's say Friday afternoon?'

Billy nodded his head helplessly.

'Friday afternoon, then, that's fixed,' said Meenakshi. 'It really is lovely to see you again. But you're looking a little under the weather, Billy. Eat a raw egg before you come.' And she moved away, blowing him a kiss when she was halfway across the room.

13.33

AFTER dinner and a little dancing ('Don't know how long you'll be able to do this, darling,' said Arun to her), they returned home. Meenakshi turned on the lights, and opened the fridge for a drink of cold water. Arun looked at the thick stack of gramophone records lying on the dining table and growled:

'This is the third time Varun's done this. If he wants to live in this house, he must learn that a house is not a sty. Where is he anyway?'

'He said he'd be out late, darling.'

Arun headed for the bedroom, undoing his tie as he went. He put on the light, and stopped dead.

The place had been ransacked. The long black iron trunk, usually covered with a mattress and a piece of brocade and used as a window-seat, was lying open, its lock broken. The sturdy leather attaché-case that lay inside the trunk was empty. Its nine-lever lock had been too hard to force, so the top of the thick hide had been slashed and hacked with a knife in a gaping, S-shaped curve. The jewellery boxes inside had been emptied of their contents and were lying scattered here and there on the floor. He looked quickly around the room. Nothing else had been touched, but everything in the attaché-case had gone: everything from the jewellery given by both sides of the family to his father's one remaining gold medal. Only the necklace that Meenakshi had worn the previous night and that she hadn't locked away but left on the dressing-table had been overlooked; and, of course, whatever she was wearing tonight. Much had been taken that was of great sentimental value. Worst of all – considering that he belonged to the insurance department at Bentsen Pryce and should perhaps have taken the coverage despite the expense of the premium – none of it was insured.

When Arun went back to the drawing room, he looked ashen.

'What's the matter, darling?' asked Meenakshi, moving towards the bedroom.

'Nothing, darling,' said Arun, barring her way. 'Nothing. Sit down. No, in the drawing room.' He could imagine what the scene might do to her, especially in her present state. He shook his head at the image of the hacked attaché-case.

'But something is terribly wrong, Arun,' said Meenakshi.

Slowly, and with his arm around her, he told her what had happened. 'Thank God Aparna's with your parents tonight. But where are the servants?'

'I let them off early.'

'We must see if Hanif is asleep in the quarters at the back.'

The bearer-cum-cook was horrified. He had been asleep. He had seen and heard nothing. And he was very afraid that suspicion would fall on him. Clearly there appeared to have been inside knowledge of where the jewellery was kept. Perhaps it was the sweeper, he suggested. He was terrified of what the police would do to him under interrogation.

Arun tried to phone the police, but there was no response on the line.

After a stream of six obscenities, he came to his senses. The last thing he wanted to do was to upset his wife.

'Darling, you wait here,' he said. 'I'll drive over to the police station and inform them.'

But Meenakshi did not want to remain alone in the house, and said that she would go along with Arun. She had begun to tremble slightly. In the car she put her hand on his shoulder while he drove.

'It's all right, darling,' said Arun. 'At least all of us are all right. Don't worry. Try not to think of it. It isn't good for you or the baby.'

13.34

MEENAKSHI was so upset by the robbery and the loss of her jewellery, which did not include the gold earrings that she had got made but did include her father-in-law's second gold medal, that she needed to recover at her parents' house for a week. Arun was as sympathetic as he could be, and though he knew he would miss her and Aparna, he felt that it would be good for her to be away from the house for a while. Varun returned the next morning after a night with his friends. He grew pale when he heard the news. When Arun told him that if he hadn't been 'drinking around town all night there would have been someone at home to prevent the robbery', his face grew red. Arun too, after all, had been out having a good time. But instead of provoking Arun, who appeared to be at the end of his tether, Varun kept quiet and slunk into his room.

Arun wrote to Mrs Rupa Mehra, telling her about the robbery. He assured her that Meenakshi was well, but was forced to mention that the other medal too had been lost. He could imagine how badly she would take this. He too had loved his father and was upset most particularly about the loss of this medal. But there was nothing to be done except hope that the police would trace the culprit or culprits. They were already interrogating the sweeper-boy: beating him up, to be precise. Arun, when he heard of this, tried to stop them.

'But how else can we find out what happened – how the thieves came to know where you kept the jewellery?' asked the station house officer.

'I don't care. I won't have this,' said Arun, and made sure that they didn't beat him up further. The worst of it was that Arun himself suspected that it was the sweeper-boy who had been in league with the criminals. It was unlikely that it was the Toothless Crone or Hanif. As for the part-time mali or the driver, they never entered the house.

Another matter about which Arun wrote to his mother was his meeting with Haresh. The loss of face he had suffered at the Khandelwals' still made him flush whenever he thought about it. He told Mrs Rupa Mehra precisely what he thought of his prospective brother-in-law: that he was a short, pushy, crass young man with too good an opinion of himself. He had a smattering of the grimy Midlands over a background of the malodorous alleys of Neel Darvaza. Neither St Stephen's nor the culture of London had had much effect on him. He dressed dressily; he lacked the social graces; and his English was oddly unidiomatic for one who had studied it at college and had lived two years in the country. As for mixing in Arun's kind of company (the Calcutta Club and the Tollygunge Race-course: the elite of Calcutta society, both Indian and European), Arun could not see how it would be possible. Khanna was a foreman – a foreman! – in that Czech shoemaking establishment. Mrs Rupa Mehra could not seriously believe that he was fit material to marry a Mehra of their class and background, or to drag her daughter down with him. Arun added that Meenakshi, by and large, agreed with him.

What he did not add, because he did not know it, was that Meenakshi had other plans for Lata. Now that she was staying with the Chatterjis, she began to work on Amit. Kakoli was a willing accomplice. Both of them liked Lata, and both of them thought that she would be just the right match for their elder brother. She would put up with his quirks, and appreciate his work. She was intelligent and literary; and though Amit could subsist on very little conversation in life (unlike his sisters, or even Dipankar), what conversation he did have could not be fatuous or vacuous – unless, of course, it was with his brothers or sisters, where he was comparatively unbuttoned.

At any rate, Kakoli – who had once told him that she reeeeeally pitied the woman who had to marry him – had decided that she needn't pity Lata, who would be capable both of understanding and of handling her eccentric brother.

Perhaps Meenakshi's plotting was a good thing. Amit, who had liked Lata a great deal, would not have been prodded into action had it not been for his energetic and conniving sisters.

Instead of employing the usual Kakoli-couplets, which had proven to be ineffectual, the two sisters were much more gentle with Amit this time. Meenakshi told him that there was a vague Other on the scene. At first she had thought it was a fellow called Akbar or something who was acting with Lata in *As You Like It*, but the main contender had turned out to be a bumptious cobbler, who was utterly unsuited to Lata; she thus implied that Amit would be rescuing Lata from an unhappy marriage by intervening. Kakoli simply told him that Lata liked him, and that she knew he liked Lata, and that she couldn't see what he was making such a fuss about. Why didn't he send her a love-letter and one of his books?

Neither Meenakshi nor Kakoli felt they had much chance of success unless they had appraised Amit's feelings for Lata correctly; but if they had, then they would act as the necessary spurs to action. They did not know much about his time at Oxford and what affairs, if any, he had had there, but they did know that in Calcutta he had rebuffed all the efforts of his female admirers or their mothers to get to know him better. He had remained faithful to Jane Austen. He appeared to be content to lead a life of contemplation. He had a strong, if not very patent, will, and never did anything he didn't want to. As for the law, in which he had earned his degree, in spite of Biswas Babu's exhortations and his father's annoyance, Amit had showed no signs of exerting himself in it at all.

His justification to himself for his idleness went something like this: I need not worry about money; I shall never be in real want. Why earn more than I need? If I take up practising law, apart from boring myself and being irritable to everyone around me, I will achieve nothing of permanent worth. I will be just one among thousands of lawyers. It is better to write one lasting sonnet than to win a hundred spectacular cases. I think I can write at least one lasting sonnet in my life – if I allow myself the scope and time to do so. The less I clog up my life with needless busy-ness, the better I find I write. Therefore I will do as little as possible. I will work on my novel whenever I can, and write a poem whenever inspiration seizes me, and leave it at that.

It was this scheme of his that had been threatened by his father's ultimatum and Dipankar's abscondence. What would happen to his novel if he was saddled with financial drudgery?

Unfortunately, doing as little as possible by way of breadwinning was accompanied in Amit's case by doing as little as possible in his social life as well. He had a few good friends, but they were all abroad – friends from his university days, to whom he wrote and from whom he received short letters, corresponding in style to the desultory conversations he used to have with them. They had been quite different from him in temperament and usually it was they who had befriended him. He was reserved, and found it difficult to make the first move, but was not slow to respond. In Calcutta, however, he had not responded much to anyone. The family had sufficed for society whenever he had needed it. It was because Lata was a member of the clan by marriage that he had felt obliged to make sure she was taken care of at the Chatterji party. Because she was quasi-family he had talked to her almost from the first in an easy and casual manner that normally came to him after months of acquaintance. Later he had grown to like her for herself. That he should have bothered to take her around Calcutta to show her the sights of the city had struck both his sisters and Dipankar as an unusual expenditure of energy. Perhaps Amit too had found his Ideal.

It had stopped there, however. After Lata left Calcutta, they did not correspond. Lata had found Amit kind and comforting; he had taken her out of her sadness into the world of poetry, into the history of the city, and – equally important – into the open air, whether of the cemetery or of College Street. Amit for his part had liked Lata a great deal, but had stopped short of declaring his fondness for her. Though he was a poet and had some insight into human emotion in general, he was far too reticent in his own life for his own happiness. When he was at Oxford, he had been wordlessly attracted to a woman, the sister of one of his friends, and as lively and explosive as a firecracker; only later did he learn that she had liked him too – and had finally in impatience given up on him and attached herself to someone else. 'Wordlessly' meant that he had not said what he had felt for her. He had, however, written a great many words, rhymed and somewhat reasoned, about his feelings, though he had crossed out most of them, published very few of those that were left, and sent or shown her none.

Meenakshi and Kakoli did not know of this affair (or non-affair), though everyone in the family believed that there had to be some explanation for all the unhappy love poems in his first, very successful, volume. Amit was, however, more than capable of fending off in his acid way any sisterly inquiries that approached too closely his sensitive, fertile, lazy core.

His second volume showed a kind of philosophical resignation unusual in a man who was not yet thirty – and who was fairly famous. What on earth, wondered one of his English friends in a letter, was he resigned about? He did not realize that Amit was probably, and perhaps even undiagnosed by himself, lonely. He had no friends – either men or women – in Calcutta; and the fact that this was the fault of his own lack of effort and sociability didn't mitigate his resultant mood: a sort of jocular weariness, and even at times plain if private despondency.

His novel, set in the period of the Bengal famine, took him outside himself into the lives of others. But even here Amit wondered from time to time if he hadn't chosen too black a canvas. The subject was complex and deep – man against man, man against nature, the city against the countryside, the desperate expediencies of war, a foreign government against an unorganized peasantry – perhaps he would have been better off writing social comedy. There was enough material for it in the family around him. And he had a taste for it; he often found himself escaping into light reading – detective stories, the ubiquitous Wodehouse, even comics – from his task of weighty prose.

When Biswas Babu had broached the question of marriage with Amit, he had stated, with his usual vibratory emphasis: 'An arranged marriage with a sober girl, that is the solution.' Amit had said that he would reserve judgment on the matter, though he had felt immediately that nothing would be more repugnant to him; he would rather live a bachelor all his days than under a canopy of feminine sobriety. But after his walk in the cemetery with Lata, when she had not been put off by his whimsical manner and the wild and whirling nature of his words, and had responded to them with surprising liveliness, he had begun to wonder if the fact that she was 'a sober girl' should count so greatly against her. She had shown no awe of him, though he was well-known, nor any defensive need to emphasize her own opinions. He remembered her unselfconscious gratitude and pleasure when he had given her a garland of flowers for her hair after the dreadful lecture at the Ramakrishna Mission. Perhaps, he thought, my sisters are right for once. But, well, Lata will be coming to Calcutta at Christmas, and I can show her the great banyan tree at the Botanical Gardens, and we'll see how things work out from there. He felt no sense of urgency about events, only a very mild foreboding about the cobbler, and no concern at all about this Akbar fellow.

13.35

MOURNFULLY, languishingly, Kuku was warbling to her own accompaniment on the piano:

> 'In this house I am so lonely.
> I am loved by Cuddles only.'

'Oh, do shut up, Kuku,' said Amit, putting down his book.

'Must we have this non-stop nonsense? I'm reading this unreadable Proust, and you're making it worse.'

But Kuku felt that it would be a dereliction of inspiration to stop. And a betrayal of Cuddles, who was leashed to the far leg of the piano.

> 'Chatterjis can go to hell,
> I will live in Grand Hotel.'

> What room number is or where,
> With my Cuddles – I don't care!'

Her left-hand accompaniment livened up, and the rather Schubertian melody gave way to jazz:

> 'I would like room 21:
> With my Cuddles: that is fun!

> I would like room 22:
> With my Cuddles: that will do.

> I would like room 23:
> With my Cuddles: just for me.

> I would like room 24:
> With my Cuddles:....'

She played a little, in an extemporaneous manner – trills, broken chords and fragments of uncertain melody – until Amit could bear the suspense no longer, and added: 'To be sure.'

They improvised the rest of the song together:

> 'I would like room 25:
> With my Cuddles: we will thrive.

> I would like room 26:
> With my Cuddles: please to fix.

I would like room 27:
With my Cuddles: that is heaven.

I would like room 28:
With my Cuddles: that is great.

I would like room 29:
With my Cuddles: that is fine.

I would like room number 30.
"Sorry, no, that room is dirty."'

Both of them laughed with pleasure, and told each other
how stupid they were. Cuddles barked hoarsely, but then
suddenly grew very excited. His ears pricked up and he
strained at the leash.

'Pillow?' said Amit.

'No, he looks pleased.'

The front door-bell rang, and Dipankar walked in.

'Dipankar!'

'Dipankar Da! Welcome back.'

'Hello, Kuku, Hello, Dada – Oh, Cuddles!'

'He knew you were back even before you rang the bell.
Put that bag down.'

'Clever dog. Clever, clever dog.'

'So!'

'So!'

'Look at you – black and gaunt – and why have you
shaved your head?' said Kuku, stroking the top of it. 'It
feels like a mole.'

'Have you ever stroked a mole, Kuku?' asked Amit.

'Oh, don't be pedantic, Amit Da, you were so nice a
moment ago. The prodigal returns, and – what does "prodigal" mean anyway?'

'What does it matter?' said Amit. 'It's like "lambent",
everyone uses it, no one knows what it means. Well, why
have you shaved your head? Ma's in for a shock.'

'Because it was so hot – didn't you get my postcards?'

'Oh, yes,' said Kuku, 'but you wrote in one of them that

you were going to grow your hair long and that we would never see you again. We loved your postcards, didn't we, Amit Da? All about the Quest for the Source and the whistles of the pregnant trains.'

'What pregnant trains?'

'That's what it looked like in your handwriting. Welcome back. You must be ravishingly hungry.'

'I am —'

'Bring out the fatted marrow!' said Amit.

'Tell us, have you found another Ideal?' demanded Kuku. Dipankar blinked.

'Do you worship the Female Principle in her? Or is there more to it than that?' asked Amit.

'Oh, Amit Da,' said Kuku reproachfully. 'How can you!' She became the Grande Dame of Culture, and pronounced with pontifical languor: 'In our India, like the stupa, the breast nourishes, inflates ... the breast is not an object of lust to our young men, it is a symbol of fecundity.'

'Well —' said Dipankar —

'We were just floating away on the wings of song, when you came in, Dipankar Da,' said Kuku:

> 'Auf Flügeln des Gesanges ...
> Fort nach den Fluren des Ganges

and now you can keep us firmly on earth —'

'Yes, we need you, Dipankar,' said Amit. 'All of us except you are helium balloons —'

Kuku broke in.

> 'Morning bathing in the Ganga,
> Guaranteed to make you younger,'

she sang. 'Was it really very filthy? Ila Kaki will be furious —'

'Do you mind not interrupting me, Kuku, once I've interrupted you?' said Amit. 'I was saying that you, Dipankar, are the only one who keeps this family sane. Calm down, Cuddles! Now have some lunch and a bath and a rest – Ma's out shopping, but she should be back in an hour.... Why didn't you tell us when you were coming? Where have you been? One of your postcards was from Rishikesh! What have you decided about the family business? Won't you handle all that and let me work on my wretched novel? How can I give it up or postpone it when all those characters are howling in my head? When I am pregnant and hungry and full of love and indignation?'

Dipankar smiled. 'I'll have to let my Experiences merge with my Being, Amit Da, before I can come to an Answer.'

Amit shook his head in exasperation.

'Don't bully him, Amit Da,' said Kuku. 'He's just come back.'

'I know I'm indecisive,' said Amit, midway between despair and mock-despair, 'but Dipankar really takes the cake. Or, rather, doesn't even know whether to.'

13.36

THE Chatterji parliament convened as usual at breakfast; apart from Tapan, who was back in boarding-school, everyone was there; Aparna was attended by her ayah; and even old Mr Chatterji had joined them, as he sometimes did after walking his cat.

'Where's Cuddles?' asked Kakoli, looking around.

'Upstairs, in my room,' said Dipankar. 'Because of Pillow.'

'Piddles and Cullow – like the Whalephant,' said Kakoli, referring to her favourite Bengali book, *Abol Tabol*.

'What's that about Pillow?' asked old Mr Chatterji.

'Nothing,' said Mrs Chatterji. 'Dipankar was only saying that Cuddles is afraid of him.'

'Oh, yes?' said the old man, nodding. 'Pillow can hold his own against any dog.'

'Doesn't Cuddles have to go to the vet today?' asked Kakoli.

'Yes,' said Dipankar. 'So I'll need the car.'

Kakoli made a long face. 'But I need it too,' she said. 'Hans's car is out of order.'

'Kuku, you always need the car,' said Dipankar. 'If you're willing to take Cuddles to the vet yourself, you can have it.'

'I can't do that, it's terribly boring, and he snaps at whoever's holding him.'

'Well, then, take a taxi to meet Hans,' said Amit, who always found this breakfast tussle over the car immensely irritating, and the worst way to begin the day. 'Do stop bickering about it. Pass me the marmalade, please, Kuku.'

'I'm afraid neither of you can have it,' said Mrs Chatterji. 'I am taking Meenakshi to see Dr Evans. She needs a check-up.'

'I don't really, Mago,' said Meenakshi. 'Stop fussing.'

'You've had a very unpleasant shock, darling, and I'm taking no chances,' said her mother.

'Yes, Meenakshi, no harm in having a check-up,' said her father, lowering the *Statesman*.

'Yes,' agreed Aparna, spooning her quarter-boiled egg into her mouth with a great deal of energy. 'No harm.'

'Eat your food, darling,' said Meenakshi to Aparna, a little annoyed.

'The marmalade, Kuku, not the gooseberry jam,' said Amit in a brittle voice. 'Not the gazpacho, not the anchovies, not the sandesh, not the soufflé; the marmalade.'

'What's got into you?' said Kakoli. 'You've been very short-tempered of late. Worse than Cuddles. It must be sexual frustration.'

'Something that you wouldn't know about,' said Amit.

'Kuku! Amit!' said Mrs Chatterji.

'But it's true,' said Kakoli. 'And he's taken to chewing ice-cubes, which I've read somewhere is an infallible sign of it.'

'Kuku, I will not have you talking this way at breakfast – with A sitting here.'

Aparna sat up with interest, setting her egg-coated spoon down on the embroidered tablecloth.

'Mago, A doesn't understand the first word we're saying,' said Kakoli.

'Anyway, I'm not,' said Amit.

'I think you must be dreaming about her.'

'Who?' said Mrs Chatterji.

'The heroine of your first book. The White Lady of your sonnets,' said Kakoli, looking at Amit.

'You should talk!' said Amit.

> 'Foreign woman is so shameless.
> Indian also is not blameless,'

murmured Kakoli.

She had tried to eschew couplets, but this one had simply presented itself and rolled off her tongue.

Amit said: 'Marmalade, please, Kuku, my toast is getting cold.'

> 'Foreign woman is a vulture.
> Goes against our ancient culture –'

blurted Kuku blindly. 'It's a good thing you made poetry out of that affair rather than little Chatterjis. Marry someone nice and Indian, Dada; don't follow my example. Have you sent Luts that book yet? She told me you'd promised her one.'

'Less wit. More marmalade,' requested Amit.

Kuku passed it to him at last and he spread it on his toast very carefully, covering every corner. 'She told you that, did she?' asked Amit.

'Oh, yes,' said Kakoli. 'Meenakshi will vouch for me.'

'Oh, yes,' said Meenakshi, looking intently at her tea. 'Everything Kakoli says is true. And we're concerned about you. You're almost thirty now –'

'Don't remind me,' said Amit with dramatic melancholy. 'Just pass me the sugar before I'm thirty-one. What else did she say?'

Rather than invent something entirely implausible and thus risk undoing the effect of her previous statement, Meenakshi wisely refrained.

'Nothing very specific,' she said. 'But with Lata, a small

comment goes a long way. And she mentioned you several times.'

'Quite wistfully, I thought,' said Kakoli.

'How is it,' said Amit, 'that Dipankar and I – and Tapan – have turned out to be so honest and decent, and you girls have learned to lie so brazenly? It's amazing that we belong to the same family.'

'How is it,' countered Kakoli, 'that Meenakshi and I, whatever our faults, can make important decisions and make them fast, when you refuse to make them and Dipankar can never decide which one to make?'

'Don't get annoyed, Dada,' said Dipankar, 'they're just trying to bait you.'

'Don't worry,' said Amit. 'They won't succeed. I'm in too good a mood.'

13.37

Late, I admit, but better late than not, /never
A gift to one who can appraise its worth, /need not spare its
This book got ever lot /got /rot /hot /shot /over-shot /sot
        comes to you from a word-drunk sot, flaws
A earth hackney bard and bachelor of laws laws.

Amit paused in his scribbling and doodling. He was attempting an inscription for Lata. Now that he had run out of inspiration he began to wonder which of his two books of poems he should send her. Or should he send her both? Perhaps the first one was not such a good idea. The White Lady of his sonnets might give Lata the wrong idea. Besides, the second, though it too contained some love-poems, had more of Calcutta in it, more of the places that reminded him of her, and might perhaps remind her of him.

Resolving this problem helped Amit get on with his poem, and by lunchtime he was ready to write his dédicace on the fly-leaf of *The Fever Bird*. His scrawled draft was legible only to himself, but what he wrote for Lata was easy enough to read. He wrote it out slowly, using the sterling silver fountain pen which his grandfather had given him on his twenty-first birthday, and he wrote in the comparatively handsome British edition of his poems, of which he had only three copies left.

> Late, I admit, but better late than not,
> A gift to one who need not spare its flaws,
> This book comes to you from a verbal sot,
> A babu bard and bachelor of laws.
>
> Lest you should think the man you meet here seems
> A lesser cynic than the one you knew,
> The truth is that apart from wine and dreams
> And children, truth inheres in poems too.
>
> Lies too lie here, and words I do not say
> Aloud for fear they savour of despair.
> Thus, passionless, I wing my even way
> And beat a soundless tattoo on the air.
>
> Love and remembrance, mystery and tears,
> A surfeit of pineapples or of bliss,
> The swerve of empires and the curve of years,
> Accept these in the hand that carves you this.

He signed his name at the bottom, wrote the date, re-read the poem while the ink dried, closed the dark blue and gold cover of the book, packed it, sealed it, and had it sent off by registered post to Brahmpur that same afternoon.

13.38

IT would have been too much to hope that Mrs Rupa Mehra would not have been at home when the post arrived two days later at Pran's house. She hardly ever went out these days, what with Savita and the baby. Even Dr Kishen Chand Seth, if he wanted to see her, had to come to the university.

When Amit's parcel arrived, Lata was at a rehearsal. Mrs Rupa Mehra signed for it. Since the mail from Calcutta carried nothing but disaster these days, and her curiosity about the contents was unassuageable (especially when she saw the sender's name), she almost opened the parcel herself. Only the fear of being condemned jointly by Lata, Savita and Pran restrained her.

When Lata returned, it was almost dark.

'Where have you been all this time? Why didn't you get back earlier? I've been going mad with anxiety,' said her mother.

'I've been at rehearsal, Ma, you know that. I'm not much later than usual. How's everyone? Baby's sleeping, by the sound of it.'

'This package arrived two hours ago – from Calcutta. Open it at once.' Mrs Rupa Mehra was about to burst.

Lata was going to protest, but then, noticing the anxiety on her mother's face and thinking of her volatility and tearfulness ever since she had received the news about the second medal, she decided that it was not worth asserting her right to privacy if it meant causing her mother further pain. She opened the package.

'It's Amit's book,' she said with pleasure: 'The Fever Bird by Amit Chatterji. Very handsome – what a beautiful cover.' Mrs Rupa Mehra, forgetting for a second the threat that Amit had once posed, picked up the book and was enchanted. The plain blue-and-gold cover, the paper, which appeared to be far superior to the stock they had seen during the war, the wide margins, the clear, spacious print, the luxury of it all delighted her. She had seen the smaller and shabbier Indian edition of the book in a bookstore once; the poems, which she had glanced through, had not seemed to her to be very edifying, and she had put it down. Mrs Rupa Mehra could not help wishing that the handsome book that she was now holding had been blank: it would have made a wonderful vehicle for the poems and thoughts that she often copied down.

'How lovely. In England they really make such beautiful things,' she said.

She opened the book and began to read the inscription. Her frown grew deeper as she reached the bottom.

'Lata, what does this poem mean?' she asked.

'How can I tell, Ma? You haven't given me a chance to read it myself. Let me have a look at it.'

'But what are all these pineapples doing here?'

'Oh, that's probably Rose Aylmer,' said Lata. 'She ate too many and died.'

'You mean, "A night of memories and sighs"? That Rose Aylmer?'

'Yes, Ma.'

'How painful it must have been!' Mrs Rupa Mehra's nose began to redden in sympathy. Then a sudden alarming thought struck her: 'Lata, this is not a love-poem, is it? I can't even understand it, it could be anything. What does he mean by Rose Aylmer? Those Chatterjis are very clever.'

Mrs Rupa Mehra had just had a renewed attack of resentment against the Chatterjis. She attributed the theft of the jewellery to Meenakshi's carelessness. She was always opening the trunk in the presence of the servants, and putting temptation in people's way. Not that Mrs Rupa Mehra wasn't worried about Meenakshi too (who must have been very upset after this shock) – and about her third grandchild, assuredly a grandson this time. In fact, if it hadn't been for Savita's baby, she might well have rushed off to Calcutta, to busy herself with help and commiseration. Besides, there were several things she wanted to check in Calcutta in the wake of Arun's letter, particularly how Haresh was faring – and what exactly it was he was doing. Haresh had said that he was working 'in a supervisory capacity, and living in the European colony at Prahapore'. He had not mentioned that he was a mere foreman.

'I doubt it's a love-poem, Ma,' said Lata.

'And he hasn't written "Love" or anything at the bottom, just his name,' said Mrs Rupa Mehra, reassuring herself.

'I like it, but I'll have to re-read it,' Lata mused aloud.

'It's too clever for my liking,' said Mrs Rupa Mehra. 'Tattoo and sot and what not. These modern poets are like this. And he hasn't even had the politeness to write your name,' she added, further reassured.

'Well, it's on the envelope, and I can't imagine he talks about pineapples to everyone,' said Lata. But she too thought it a little strange.

Later, lying on her bed, she read the poem again at her leisure. She was secretly very pleased to have a poem written for her, but much in it was not immediately clear. When he said that he winged his even and passionless way, did he mean that the temperature of his poems was cool? That he was speaking in the voice of the bird of the title but was not fevered? Or did it mean something private to his imagination? Or anything at all?

After a while, Lata began to read the book, partly for itself, partly as a clue to the inscription. The poems were, by and large, no more unclear than their complexity required; they made grammatical sense, and Lata was grateful for that. And some of them were poems of deep feeling, by no means passionless, though their diction was at times formal. There was an eight-line love-poem that she liked, and a longer one, a bit like an ode, about walking alone through the Park Street Cemetery. There was even a humorous one about buying books on College Street. Lata liked most of the poems that she read, and was moved by the fact that when she had been lonely and unoccupied in Calcutta Amit had taken her to places that had meant so much to him and that he was used to visiting alone.

For all their feeling, the tenor of the poems was muted – and sometimes self-deprecating. But the title poem was anything but muted, and the self that it presented appeared to be gripped almost by mania. Lata herself had often been kept awake on summer nights by the papiha, the brainfever bird, and the poem, partly for this reason, disturbed her profoundly.

The fever bird sang out last night.
I could not sleep, try as I might.

My brain was split, my spirit raw.
I looked into the garden, saw

The shadow of the amaltas
Shake slightly on the moonlit grass.

Unseen, the bird cried out its grief,
Its lunacy, without relief:

Three notes repeated closer, higher,
Soaring, then sinking down like fire

Only to breathe the night and soar,
As crazed, as desperate, as before.

I shivered in the midnight heat
And smelt the sweat that soaked my sheet.

And now tonight I hear again
The call that skewers through my brain,

The call, the brain-sick triple note –
A bone of pain stuck in its throat.

I am so tired I could weep.
Mad bird, for God's sake let me sleep.

Why do you cry like one possessed?
When will you rest? When will you rest?

Why wait each night till all but I
Lie sleeping in the house, then cry?

Why do you scream into my ear
What no one else but I can hear?

Her thoughts a whirl of images and questions, Lata read this poem through five or six times. It was far clearer than most of the poems in the book, clearer certainly than the inscription he had written for her, and yet it was far more mysterious and disturbing. She knew the yellow laburnum, the amaltas tree that stood above Dipankar's meditation hut in the garden at Ballygunge, and she could imagine Amit looking out at its branches at night. (Why, she wondered, had he used the Hindi word for the tree rather than the Bengali – was it just for the sake of the rhyme?) But the Amit she knew – kindly, cynical, cheerful – was even less the Amit of this poem than of the short love-poem that she had read and liked.

Did she even like this poem, she wondered? The thought of Amit sweating disturbed her – he was to her a disembodied and comforting spirit, and it was best that he remained that way. By now it had been dark for more than an hour, and Lata could imagine him lying on his bed, hearing the papiha sing its triple note, and tossing restlessly from side to side.

She looked at the personalized inscription again. She wondered why he had used the word 'carve' in the final line. Was it simply to chime – in a slightly overdone manner, she could not help feeling – with the 'swerve' and 'curve' of the previous line? A poem could hardly be carved. But this was probably just poetic licence, like the bird's wings beating a tattoo, or the claim that he was drunk on words.

Then, suddenly, and for no apparent reason at all, for she was not looking out for such a curious feature as this, she realized, with simultaneous delight and dismay, how carved, how personalized the inscription indeed was, and why, after all, he had not written her name above the poem. It went far beyond the reference to pineapples, to the moment in the cemetery that they had shared. She had only to look down the first letters of each of the four lines in each of the four quatrains to realize how inextricably bound she was not merely to the sentiment but to the very structure of Amit's poem.

Also available in paperback